Dead Witches Tell No Tales

Other Books by Kim Harrison

Dead Witch Walking
The Good, the Bad, and the Undead

Dead Witches Tell No Tales

Every Which Way But Dead
A Fistful of Charms

Kim Harrison

SFBC
FANTASY

First HarperTorch special printing: March 2005
First HarperTorch paperback printing: July 2005

First HarperTorch paperback printing: July 2006

Science Fiction Book Club omnibus edition: July 2006

Published by arrangement with
HarperTorch
an imprint of HarperCollins*Publishers*
10 East 53rd Street
New York, New York 10022-5299

ISBN: 978-0-7394-7083-1

Visit our website at www.sfbc.com
Visit the HarperCollins website at www.harpercollins.com

Printed in the United States of America

Dead Witches Tell No Tales

Contents

EVERY WHICH WAY BUT DEAD

To the guy who gave me my first pair of handcuffs.
Thanks for being there.

One

I took a deep breath to settle myself, jerking the cuff of my gloves up to cover the bare patch of skin at my wrist. My fingers were numb through the fleece as I moved my next-to-largest spell pot to sit beside a small chipped tombstone, being careful to not let the transfer media spill. It was cold, and my breath steamed in the light of the cheap white candle I had bought on sale last week.

Spilling a bit of wax, I stuck the taper to the top of the grave marker. My stomach knotted as I fixed my attention on the growing haze at the horizon, scarcely discernable from the surrounding city lights. The moon would be up soon, being just past full and waning. Not a good time to be summoning demons, but it would be coming anyway if I didn't call it. I'd rather meet Algaliarept on my own terms—before midnight.

I grimaced, glancing at the brightly lit church behind me where Ivy and I lived. Ivy was running errands, not even aware I had made a deal with a demon, much less that it was time to pay for its services. I suppose I could be doing this inside where it was warm, in my beautiful kitchen with my spelling supplies and all the modern comforts, but calling demons in the middle of a graveyard had a perverse rightness to it, even with the snow and cold.

And I wanted to meet it here so Ivy wouldn't have to spend tomorrow cleaning blood off the ceiling.

Whether it would be demon blood or my own was a question I hoped I wouldn't have to answer. I wouldn't allow myself to be pulled into the ever-after to be Algaliarept's familiar. I couldn't. I had cut it once and made it bleed. If it could bleed, it could die.

God, help me survive this. Help me find a way to make something good here.

The fabric of my coat rasped as I clutched my arms about myself and used my boot to awkwardly scrape a circle of six inches of crusty snow off the clay-red cement slab where I had seen a large circle etched out. The room-sized rectangular block of stone was a substantial marker as to where God's grace stopped and chaos took over. The previous clergy had laid it down over the adulterated spot of once hallowed ground, either to be sure no one else was put to rest there accidentally or to fix the elaborate, half-kneeling, battle-weary angel it encompassed into the ground. The name on the massive tombstone had been chiseled off, leaving only the dates. Whomever it was had died in 1852 at the age of twenty-four. I hoped it wasn't an omen.

Cementing someone into the ground to keep him or her from rising again sometimes worked—and sometimes it didn't—but in any case, the area wasn't sanctified anymore. And since it was surrounded by ground that was still consecrated, it made a good spot to summon a demon. If worse came to worst, I could always duck onto sanctified ground and be safe until the sun rose and Algaliarept was pulled back into the ever-after.

My fingers were shaking as I took from my coat pocket a white silk pouch of salt that I had scraped out of my twenty-five-pound bag. The amount was excessive, but I wanted a solid circle, and some of the salt would be diluted as it melted the snow. I glanced at the sky to estimate where north was, finding a mark on the etched circle right where I thought it should be. That someone had used this circle to summon demons before didn't instill me with any confidence. It wasn't illegal or immoral to summon demons, just really, really stupid.

I made a slow clockwise path from north, my footprints paralleling the outside track of the salt as I laid it down, enclosing the angel monolith along with most of the blasphemed ground. The circle would be a good fifteen feet across, a rather large enclosure which generally took at least three witches to make and hold, but I was good enough to channel that much ley line force alone. Which, now that I thought about it, might be why the demon was so interested in snagging me as its newest familiar.

Tonight I'd find out if my carefully worded verbal contract made three months ago would keep me alive and on the right side of the ley lines. I had agreed to be Algaliarept's familiar voluntarily if it testified against Piscary, the catch being that I got to keep my soul.

The trial had officially ended two hours after sunset tonight, sealing the demon's end of the bargain and making my end enforceable. That the undead vampire who controlled most of Cincinnati's underworld had been sentenced to five centuries for the murders of the city's best ley line witches hardly seemed important now. Especially when I was betting his lawyers would get him out in a measly one.

Right now the question on everyone's mind on both sides of the law was whether Kisten, his former scion, would be able to hold everything together until the undead vampire got out, because Ivy wasn't going to do it, scion or no. If I managed to get through this night alive and with my soul intact, I'd start worrying about me a little less and my roommate a little more, but first I had to settle up with the demon.

Shoulders so tight they hurt, I took the milky green tapers from my coat pocket and placed them on the circle to represent the points of a pentagram I wouldn't be drawing. I lit them from the white candle I used to make the transfer media. The tiny flames flickered, and I watched for a moment to be sure they weren't going to go out before I stuck the white candle back on the broken grave marker outside the circle.

The hushed sound of a car pulled my attention to the high walls dividing the graveyard from our neighbors. Steadying myself to tap the nearby ley line, I tugged my knit cap down, stomped the snow from the hem of my jeans, and made one last check that I had everything. But there was nothing left to procrastinate with.

Another slow breath, and I touched my will to the tiny ley line running through the church's graveyard. My breath hissed in through my nose and I stiffened, almost falling as my equilibrium shifted. The ley line seemed to have picked up the winter chill, slicing through me with an unusual coldness. Putting out a gloved hand, I steadied myself against the candlelit tombstone while the incoming energy continued to build.

Once the strengths equilibrated, the extra incoming force would flow back to the line. Until then I had to grit my teeth and bear it as tingling sensations backwashed at the theoretical extremities in my mind that mirrored my real fingers and toes. Each time it was worse. Each time it was faster. Each time it was more of an assault.

Though it seemed like forever, the force balanced in a heartbeat. My hands started to sweat and an uncomfortable sensation of being both hot and cold took me, like being in a fever. I took off my gloves and jammed them into a deep pocket. The charms on my bracelet jingled, clear in the winter-silenced air. They wouldn't help me. Not even the cross.

I wanted to set my circle quickly. Somehow Algaliarept knew when I tapped a line, and I had to summon it before it showed up on its own and robbed me of the thread of power I might claim as its summoner. The copper spell pot with the transfer media was cold when I picked it up and did something no witch ever did and lived to tell of it; I stepped forward, putting myself into the same circle I was going to call Algaliarept into.

Standing across from the person-sized monument cemented to the ground, I exhaled. The monolith was covered in a black smut from bacteria and city pollution, making it look like a fallen angel. That the figure was bowed weeping over a sword held horizontally in his hands as an offering only added to the creepy feeling. There was a bird's nest wedged into the fold of the wings as they curved around the body, and the face didn't look right. The arms, too, were too long to be human or Inderlander. Even Jenks didn't let his kids play around this one.

"Please let me be right," I whispered to the statue as I mentally moved the white rill of salt from this reality to that of the ever-after. I staggered as most of the energy pooling in my center was yanked out to force the shift. The media in the pot sloshed, and still not having found my balance, I set it down in the snow before it spilled. My eyes went to the green candles. They had turned eerily transparent, having been moved to the ever-after with the salt. The flames, though, existed in both worlds, adding their glow to the night.

The power from the line began to build again, the slow increase as uncomfortable as the first quick influx of tapping a line, but the ribbon of salt had been replaced with an equal amount of ever-after reality arching high to close over my head. Nothing more substantial than air could pass the shifting bands of reality, and because I set the circle, only I could break it—providing I had made it properly to begin with.

"Algaliarept, I summon you," I whispered, my heart pounding. Most people used all sorts of trappings to summon and contain a demon, but seeing as I already had an arrangement with it, simply saying its name and willing its presence would pull it across the lines. Lucky me.

My gut clenched when a small patch of snow melted between the warrior angel and me. The snow steamed, the cloud of reddish vapor billowing up to follow the confines of a body not yet taken shape. I waited, my tension growing. Algaliarept varied its shape, sifting through my mind without me even knowing to choose what scared me the most. Once it had been Ivy. Then Kisten—until I had pinned him in an elevator in a foolish moment of vampire-induced passion. It's hard to be scared of someone after you've French-kissed him. Nick, my boyfriend, always got a slavering dog the size of a pony.

This time, though, the mist was definitely a human shape, and I guessed it was going to show up either as Piscary—the vampire I had just put in prison—or perhaps its more typical vision of a young British gentleman in a green velveteen coat with tails.

"Neither scares you anymore," came a voice from the mist, jerking my head up.

It was my voice. "Aw, crap," I swore, picking up my spell pot and backing away until I almost broke my circle. It was going to show up as me. I hated that. "I'm not afraid of myself!" I shouted, even before it finished coalescing.

"Oh, yes you are."

It had the right sound, but the cadence and accent were wrong. I stared, riveted, as Algaliarept took on my outline, running its hands suggestively down itself, flattening its chest to my lame excuse of womanhood and giving me hips that were probably a little more curvaceous than I deserved. It dressed itself in black leather pants, a red halter top, and high-heeled black sandals that looked ridiculous out in the middle of a snowy graveyard.

Eyelids lightly closed and lips open, it shook its head to make my frizzy shoulder-length red curls take shape out of the lingering haze of ever-after. It gave me more freckles than I could possibly have, and my eyes weren't the red orbs it showed when it opened them, but green. Mine weren't slitted like a goat's either.

"You got the eyes wrong," I said, and I set my spell pot down at the edge of the circle. I gritted my teeth, hating that it heard my voice quaver.

Hip cocked, the demon put out a sandaled foot and snapped its fingers. A pair of black shades materialized in its grip, and it put them on, hiding its unnatural eyes. "Now they're right," it said, and I shuddered at how close it matched my voice.

"You don't look anything like me," I said, not realizing I had lost so much weight, and deciding I could go back to eating shakes and fries.

Algaliarept smiled. "Perhaps if I put my hair up?" it mocked coyly as it gathered the unruly mass and held it atop my, er, its head. Biting its lips to redden them, it moaned and shifted as if its hands were tied above it, looking like it was into bondage games. Falling back onto the sword the angel held, it posed like a whore.

I hunched deeper into my coat with the fake fur around the collar. From the distant street came the slow sound of a passing car. "Can we get on with this? My feet are getting cold."

It pulled its head up and smiled. "You are *such* the party pooper, Rachel Mariana Morgan," it said in my voice, but now with its customary highbrow British accent. "But a *very* good sport. Not making me drag you into the ever-after shows a *fine* strength of mind. I'm going to enjoy breaking you."

I jerked when a smear of ever-after energy cascaded over it. It was shifting forms again, but my shoulders eased when it turned itself into its usual vision of lace and green velvet. Dark hair styled long and round smoked glasses twisted into existence. Pale skin and a strong-featured face appeared, matching its trim, narrow-waisted figure in elegance. High-heeled boots and an exquisitely tailored coat finished the outfit, turning the demon into a charismatic young businessman of the eighteenth century, possessing wealth and poised for greatness.

My thoughts touched on the horrific crime scene I had contaminated last fall while trying to pin the murders of Cincinnati's best ley line witches on Trent Kalamack. Al had slaughtered them in Piscary's name. Each of them had died in pain for its enjoyment. Al was a sadist, no matter how good the demon looked.

"Yes, let's get on with it," it said as it took a tin of a black dust that smelled like Brimstone and inhaled a pinch deeply. It rubbed its nose and moved to poke at my circle with a boot, making me wince. "Nice and tight. But it's cold. Ceri likes it warm."

Ceri? I wondered as all the snow within the circle melted in a flash of condensation. The scent of wet pavement rose strong, then vanished as the cement dried to a pale red.

"Ceri," Algaliarept said, its voice shocking me in its soft tone, both coaxing and demanding. "Come."

I stared when a woman stepped from behind Algaliarept, seemingly from nowhere. She was thin, her heart-shaped face sallow and her cheekbones showing too strongly. Standing substantially shorter than I, she had a diminutive, almost childlike mien. Her head was down, and her pale translucent hair hung straight to her mid-back. She was dressed in a beautiful gown that dropped to her bare feet. It was exquisite—lush silk dyed in rich purples, greens, and golds—and it fitted her curvaceous form like it had been painted on. Though she was small, she was well-proportioned, if perhaps a shade fragile looking.

"Ceri," Algaliarept said, putting a white-gloved hand to tilt her head up. Her eyes were green, wide, and empty. "What did I tell you about going barefoot?"

A glimmer of annoyance crossed her face, far away and distant behind the numb state she was in. My attention dropped as a matching pair of embroidered slippers materialized about her feet.

"That's better." Algaliarept turned from her, and I was struck by the picture of the perfect couple they made in their finery. She was beautiful in her clothes, but her mind was as empty as she was lovely, insane from the raw magic the demon forced her to hold for it, filtering the ley line power through her mind to keep itself safe. Dread twisted in my gut.

"Don't kill her," I whispered, my mouth dry. "You're done with her. Let her live."

Algaliarept pulled its smoked glasses down to look over them, its red orbs fixing on me. "You like her?" it said. "She is pretty, isn't she? Over a thousand years old, and aged not a moment since the day I took her soul. If I were honest, she's the reason I was invited to most of the parties. She puts out without a fuss. Though, of course, for the first hundred years it was all tears and wailing. Fun in itself, but it does get old. You'll fight me, won't you?"

My jaw clenched. "Give her back her soul, now that you're done with her."

Algaliarept laughed. "Oh, you are a love!" it said, clapping its white-gloved hands once. "But I'm giving that back to her anyway. I've sullied it beyond redemption, leaving mine reasonably pure. And I will kill her before she has the chance to beg forgiveness from her god." Its thick lips split in a nasty grin. "It's all a lie, anyway, you know."

I went cold as the woman slumped into a small spot of purple, green, and gold at its feet, broken. I would die before letting it drag me into the ever-after to become . . . become this. "Bastard," I whispered.

Algaliarept gestured as if to say, "So what?" It turned to Ceri, finding her small hand in the mass of fabric and helping her rise. She was barefoot again. "Ceri," the demon coaxed, then glanced at me. "I should have replaced her forty years ago, but the Turn made everything difficult. She doesn't even hear anymore unless you say her name first." It turned back to the woman. "Ceri, be a love and fetch the transfer media you made this sundown."

My stomach hurt. "I made some," I said, and Ceri blinked, the first sign of comprehension crossing her. Big eyes solemn and blank, she looked at me as if seeing me for the first time. Her attention went to the spell pot at my feet and the milky green candles about us. Panic stirred in the back of her eyes as she stood before the angel monument. I think she had just realized what was going on.

"Marvelous," Algaliarept said. "You're trying to be useful already, but I want Ceri's." It looked at Ceri, her mouth open to show tiny white teeth. "Yes, love. Time for your retirement. Bring me my cauldron and the transfer media."

Tense and shirking, Ceri made a gesture and a child-sized cauldron made of copper thicker than my wrist appeared between us, already filled with amber liquid, the flecks of wild geranium suspended as if it were a gel.

The scent of ozone rose high as it grew warmer, and I unzipped my coat. Algaliarept was humming, clearly in a grand mood. It beckoned me closer, and I took a step, fingering the silver knife tucked in my sleeve. My pulse quickened, and I wondered if my contract would be enough to save me. A knife wasn't going to be much help.

The demon grinned to show me flat, even teeth as it gestured to Ceri. "My mirror," it prompted, and the delicate woman bent to retrieve a scrying mirror that hadn't been there a moment ago. She held it before Algaliarept like a table.

I swallowed, remembering the foul sensation of pushing my aura off of me and into my scrying mirror last fall. The demon took off its gloves, one by one, and placed its ruddy, thick-knuckled hands atop the glass, long fingers spread wide. It shuddered and closed its eyes while its aura precipitated out into the mirror, falling from its hands like ink to swirl and pool in its reflection. "Into the medium, Ceri, love. Hurry now."

She was almost panting as she carried the mirror holding Algaliarept's aura to the cauldron. It wasn't the weight of the glass; it was the weight of what was happening. I imagine she was reliving the night she had stood where I was now, watching her predecessor as I watched her. She must have known what was going to happen, but was so deadened inside that she could only do what was expected. And by her obvious, helpless panic, I knew that something was left in her worth saving.

"Free her," I said, hunched in my ugly coat as my attention

flicked from Ceri to the cauldron, and then to Algaliarept. "Free her first."

"Why?" It looked idly at its nails before putting the gloves back on.

"I'll kill you before I let you drag me into the ever-after, and I want her free first."

Algaliarept laughed at that, long and deep. Putting a hand against the angel, the demon bent almost double. A muted thump reverberated up through my feet, and the stone base cracked with the sound of a gunshot. Ceri stared, her pale lips slack and her eyes moving rapidly over me. Things seemed to be starting to work in her, memories and thoughts long suppressed.

"You *will* struggle," Algaliarept said, delighted. "Stupendous. I *so* hoped you would." Its eyes met mine, and it smirked, touching the rim of its glasses. *"Adsimulo calefacio."*

The knife in my sleeve burst into flame. Yelping, I shrugged out of my coat. It hit the edge of my bubble and slid down. The demon eyed me. "Rachel Mariana Morgan. Stop trying my patience. Get over here and recite the damned invocation."

I had no choice. If I didn't, it would call my deal breached, take my soul in forfeit, and drag me into the ever-after. My only chance was to play the agreement out. I glanced at Ceri, wishing she would move away from Algaliarept, but she was running her fingers over the dates engraved in the cracked tombstone, her sun-starved complexion now even paler.

"Do you remember the curse?" Algaliarept asked when I came even with the knee-high cauldron.

I snuck a glance in, not surprised to find the demon's aura was black. I nodded, feeling faint as my thoughts went back to having accidentally made Nick my familiar. Was it only three months ago? "I can say it in English," I whispered. *Nick. Oh God. I hadn't said good-bye.* He had been so distant lately that I hadn't found the courage to tell him. I hadn't told anyone.

"Good enough." Its glasses vanished and its damned, goat-slitted eyes fixed on me. My heart raced, but I had made this choice. I would live or die by it.

Deep and resonate, seeming to vibrate my very core, Algaliarept's voice slipped from between its lips. It was Latin, the words familiar, yet not, like a vision of a dream. *"Pars tibi, totum mihi. Vinctus vinculis, prece factis."*

"Some to you," I echoed in English, interpreting the words from memory, "but all to me. Bound by ties made so by plea."

The demon's smile widened, chilling me with its confidence. *"Luna servata, lux sanata. Chaos statutum, pejus minutum."*

I swallowed hard. "Moon made safe, ancient light made sane," I whispered. "Chaos decreed, taken tripped if bane."

Algaliarept's knuckles gripping the vat went white in anticipation. *"Mentem tegens, malum ferens. Semper servus dum duret mundus,"* it said, and Ceri sobbed, a small kitten sound, quickly stifled. "Go on," Algaliarept prompted, excitement making its outline blur. "Say it and put your hands in."

I hesitated, my eyes fixing on Ceri's crumpled form before the gravestone, her gown a small puddle of color. "Absolve me of one of my debts I owe you, first."

"You are a pushy bitch, Rachel Mariana Morgan."

"Do it!" I demanded. "You said you would. Take off one of your marks as agreed."

It leaned over the pot until I could see my reflection, wide-eyed and frightened, in its glasses. "It makes no difference. Finish the curse and be done with it."

"Are you saying you aren't going to hold to our bargain?" I goaded, and it laughed.

"No. Not at all, and if you were hoping to break our arrangement on that, then you're sadly the fool. I'll take off one of my marks, but you still owe me a favor." It licked its lips. "And as my familiar, you belong—to me."

A nauseating mix of dread and relief shook my knees, and I held my breath so I wouldn't get sick. But I had to fulfill my end of the bargain completely before I would see if my beliefs were right and I could slip the demon's snare by a small point called choice.

"Lee of mind," I said, trembling, "bearer of pain. Slave until the worlds are slain."

Algaliarept made a satisfied sound. Jaw gritted, I plunged my hands into the cauldron. Cold struck through me, burning them numb. I yanked my hands out. Horrified, I stared at them, seeing no change in my red-enameled fingertips.

And then Algaliarept's aura seeped farther into me, touching my chi.

My eyes seemed to bulge in agony. I took a huge breath to scream but couldn't let it out. I caught a glimpse of Ceri, her eyes pinched in memory. Across the cauldron, Algaliarept was grinning. Gagging, I struggled to breathe as the air seemed to turn to oil. I fell to my hands and knees, bruising them on the concrete.

Hair falling to hide my face, I tried to keep from retching. I couldn't breathe. I couldn't think!

The demon's aura was a wet blanket, dripping with acid, smothering me. It coated me, inside and out, and my strength was surrounded by its power. It squeezed my will to nothing. I heard my heart beat once, then again. I took a shuddering breath, swallowing back the sharp tang of vomit. I was going to live. Its aura alone couldn't kill me. I could do this. I could.

Shaking, I looked up while the shock lessened to something I could deal with. The cauldron was gone, and Ceri was huddled almost behind the huge grave marker beside Algaliarept. I took a breath, unable to taste the air through the demon's aura. I moved, unable to feel the rough concrete scraping my fingertips. Everything was numb. Everything was muted, as if through cotton.

Everything except the power of the nearby ley line. I could feel it humming thirty yards away as if it were a high-tension power line. Panting, I staggered to my feet, shocked to realize I could see it. I could see everything as if I was using my second sight—which I wasn't. My stomach roiled as I saw that my circle, once tinged with a shading of cheerful gold from my aura, was now coated in black.

I turned to the demon, seeing the thick black aura surrounding it and knowing a good portion of it coated mine. Then I looked at Ceri, hardly able to see her features, so strong was Algaliarept's aura on her. She didn't have an aura to combat the demon's, having lost her soul to it. And that was what I had pinned everything on.

If I retained my soul, I still had my aura, smothered as it was under Algaliarept's. And with my soul came free will. Unlike Ceri, I could say no. Slowly I was remembering how.

"Free her," I rasped. "I took your damned aura. Free her now."

"Oh, why not?" the demon chortled, rubbing its gloved hands together. "Killing her will be a banger of a way to get your apprenticeship started. Ceri?"

The slight woman scrambled up, her head high and her heart-shaped face showing panic.

"Ceridwen Merriam Dulciate," Algaliarept said. "I'm giving you your soul back *before* I kill you. You can thank Rachel for that."

I started. Rachel? I had always been Rachel Mariana Morgan before. Apparently as a familiar, I wasn't worth my full name anymore. That ticked me off.

She made a small sound, staggering. I watched with my new

vision as Algaliarept's bond fell from her. The barest, faintest glimmer of purest blue rimmed her—her returned soul already trying to bathe her in protection—then vanished under the thousand years of darkness the demon had fostered on her soul while it had been in his keeping. Her mouth worked, but she couldn't speak. Her eyes glazed as she panted, hyperventilating, and I leapt forward to catch her as she fell. Struggling, I dragged her back to my end of the circle.

Algaliarept reached after her. Adrenaline surged. I dropped Ceri. Straightening, I drew on the line. "Rhombus!" I shouted, the word of invocation I had been practicing for three months to set a circle without drawing it first.

With a force that sent me lurching, my new circle exploded into existence, sealing Ceri and me in a second, smaller circle inside the first. My circle had lacked a physical object to focus on, so the excess energy went everywhere instead of back in the ley line where it was supposed to. The demon swore, blown backward until it slammed against the inside of my original circle, still up and running. With a ping that reverberated through me, my first circle broke and Algaliarept hit the ground.

Breathing heavily, I hunched with my hands on my knees. Algaliarept blinked at me from the concrete, then a wicked smile came over it. "We're sharing an aura, love," it said. "Your circle can't stop me anymore." Its grin widened. "Surprise," it sang lightly, standing up and taking the time to meticulously brush its coat of crushed velvet.

Oh, God. If my first circle didn't hold it now, neither would my second. I had thought that might happen. "Ceri?" I whispered. "Get up. We have to move."

Algaliarept's eyes tracked behind me to the hallowed ground that surrounded us. My muscles tensed.

The demon leapt. Shrieking, I jerked Ceri and myself backward. The surge of ever-after flowing into me from breaking the circle was almost unnoticed. My breath was knocked from me as we hit the ground, Ceri on top of me. Still not breathing, I sent my heels scrabbling against the snow and pushed us farther away. The gold-colored trim on Ceri's ball gown was rough under my fingers, and I yanked her to me until I was sure we were both on holy ground.

"Damn you all to hell!" Algaliarept shouted from the edge of the cement, furious.

I got up, shaking. My breath caught, and I stared at the frustrated demon.

"Ceri!" the demon demanded, and the scent of burnt amber rose when it set its foot across the unseen barrier and jerked it back. "Push her at me! Or I'll blacken your soul so badly that your precious god won't let you in no matter how you beg it!"

Ceri moaned, clutching my leg as she huddled, hiding her face, trying to overcome a thousand years of conditioning. My face grew tight from anger. *This would have been me. This still could be me.* "I won't let it hurt you anymore," I said, one hand dropping to touch her shoulder. "If I can stop it from hurting you, I will."

Her grip on me shook, and I thought she seemed like a beaten child.

"You're my familiar!" the demon shouted, spittle flying from it. "Rachel, come here!"

I shook my head, colder than the snow warranted. "No," I said simply. "I'm not going into the ever-after. You can't make me."

Algaliarept choked in disbelief. "You will!" it thundered, and Ceri clutched my leg tighter. "I own you! You're my bloody familiar. I gave you my aura. Your will is mine!"

"No, it isn't," I said, shaking inside. *It was working. God save me, it was working.* My eyes warmed, and I realized I was almost crying from relief. It couldn't take me. I might be its familiar, but it didn't have my soul. I could say no.

"You're my familiar!" it raged, and Ceri and I both cried out as it tried to cross into holy ground and yanked itself back again.

"I'm your familiar!" I yelled back, frightened. "And I say no! I said I'd be your familiar and I am, but I'm not going into the ever-after with you, and you can't make me!"

Algaliarept's goat-slitted eyes narrowed. It stepped back, and I stiffened as its anger chilled. "You agreed to be my familiar," it said softly, smoke curling up from its shiny, buckled boots as they edged the circle of blasphemed ground. "Come here now, or I'll call our agreement breached and your soul will be mine by default."

Double jeopardy. I knew it would come to this. "I've got your stinking aura all over me," I said as Ceri quivered. "I'm your familiar. If you think there's been a breach in contract, then you get someone out here to judge what happened before the sun comes up. And take one of these damned demon marks off me!" I demanded, holding my wrist out.

My arm shook, and Algaliarept made an ugly noise, deep in its throat. The long exhalation set my insides to quiver, and Ceri ventured to peek at the demon. "I can't use you as a familiar if you're on the wrong side of the lines," it said, clearly thinking aloud. "The binding isn't strong enough—"

"That's not my problem," I interrupted, legs shaking.

"No," Algaliarept agreed. It laced its white-gloved hands behind its back, its gaze dropping to Ceri. The deep fury in its eyes scared the crap out of me. "But I'm making it your problem. You stole my familiar and left me with nothing. You tricked me into letting you slip payment for a service. If I can't drag you in, I'll find a way to use you through the lines. And I will never let you die. Ask her. Ask her of her never-ending hell. It's waiting for you, Rachel. And I'm not a patient demon. You can't hide on holy ground forever."

"Go away," I said, my voice trembling. "I called you here. Now I'm telling you to leave. Take one of these marks off me and leave. Now." I had summoned it, and therefore it was susceptible to the rules of summoning—even if I was its familiar.

It exhaled slowly, and I thought the ground moved. Its eyes went black. Black. Black, black, then blacker still. *Oh, shit.*

"I'll find the way to make a strong enough bond with you through the lines," it intoned. "And I'll pull you through, soul intact. You walk this side of the lines on borrowed time."

"I've been a dead witch walking before," I said. "And my name is Rachel Mariana Morgan. Use it. And take one of these marks off of me or you forfeit everything."

I'm going to get away with it. I outsmarted a demon. The knowledge was heady, but I was too frightened for it to mean much.

Algaliarept gave me a chilling look. Its gaze dropped to Ceri, then it vanished.

I cried out as my wrist flamed, but I welcomed the pain, hunched as I held my demon-marked wrist with my other hand. It hurt—it hurt as if the dogs of hell were chewing on it—but when my blurred vision cleared, there was one scared line crossing the welted circle, not two.

Panting through the last of the pain, I slumped, my entire body collapsing in on itself. I pulled my head up and took a clean breath, trying to unknot my stomach. It couldn't use me if we were on opposite sides of the ley lines. I was still myself, though I was coated with Algaliarept's aura. Slowly my second sight faded and the red smear of the ley line vanished. Algaliarept's aura was getting easier to bear, slipping almost into an unnoticed sensation now that the demon was gone.

Ceri let go of me. Reminded of her, I bent to offer her a hand up. She looked at it in wonder, watching herself as she put a thin pale hand in mine. Still at my feet, she kissed the top of it in a formal gesture of thanks.

"No, don't," I said, turning my hand to grip hers and pull her upright and out of the snow.

Ceri's eyes filled and spilled over as she silently wept for her freedom, the well-dressed, abused woman beautiful in her tearful, silent joy. I put my arm around her, giving her what comfort I could. Ceri hunched over and shook all the harder.

Leaving everything where it was and the candles to go out on their own, I stumbled to the church. My gaze was fixed to the snow, and as Ceri and I made two trails of footprints over the one leading out here, I wondered what on earth I was going to do with her.

Two

We were halfway to the church before I realized Ceri was walking barefoot in the snow. "Ceri," I said, appalled. "Where are your shoes?"

The crying woman made a rough hiccup. Wiping her eyes, she glanced down. A red blur of ever-after swirled about her toes, and a pair of burnt embroidered slippers appeared on her tiny feet. Surprise cascaded over her delicate features, clear in the porch light.

"They're burned," I said as she shook them off. Bits of char stuck to her, looking like black sores. "Maybe Big Al is having a tantrum and burning your things."

Ceri silently nodded, a hint of a smile quirking her blueing lips at the insulting nickname I used so I wouldn't say the demon's name before those who didn't already know it.

I pushed us back into motion. "Well, I've got a pair of slippers you can wear. And how about some coffee? I'm frozen through." *Coffee? We just escaped a demon, and I'm offering her coffee?*

She said nothing, her eyes going to the wooden porch that led to the living quarters at the back of the church. Her eyes traveled to the sanctuary behind it and the steeple with its belfry. "Priest?" she whispered, her voice matching the iced-over garden, crystalline and pure.

"No," I said as I tried not to slip on the steps. "I just live here. It's not a real church anymore." Ceri blinked, and I added, "It's kinda hard to explain. Come on in."

I opened the back door, going in first since Ceri dropped her head and wouldn't. The warmth of the living room was like a blessed wave on my cold cheeks. Ceri stopped dead in the threshold when a handful of pixy girls flew shrieking from the mantel above the empty fireplace, fleeing the cold. Two adolescent pixy boys gave Ceri a telling glance before following at a more sedate pace.

"Pixies?" I prompted, remembering she was over a thousand years old. If she wasn't an Inderlander, she wouldn't have ever seen them before, believing they were, ah, fairy tales. "You know about pixies?" I asked, stomping the snow from my boots.

She nodded, closing the door behind her, and I felt better. The adjustment to modern life would be easier if she didn't have to come to grips with witches, Weres, pixies, vampires, and the like being real on top of TVs and cell phones, but as her eyes ranged over Ivy's expensive electronic equipment with only a mild interest, I was willing to bet that things on the other side of the ley lines were as technologically advanced as they were here.

"Jenks!" I shouted to the front of the church where he and his family were living out the duration of the cold months. "Can I see you for a minute?"

There was the tight hum of dragonfly wings faint over the warm air. "Hey, Rache," the small pixy said as he buzzed in. "What's this my kids are saying about an angel?" He jerked to a hovering halt, his eyes wide and his short blond hair swinging as he looked behind me.

Angel, huh? I thought as I turned to Ceri to introduce her. "Oh God, no," I said, pulling her back upright. She had been picking up the snow I had knocked off my boots, holding it in her hand. The sight of her diminutive form dressed in that exquisite gown cleaning my mess was too much. "Please, Ceri," I said, taking the snow from her and dropping it on the carpet. "Don't."

A wash of self-annoyance crossed the small woman's smooth brow. Sighing, she made an apologetic face. I don't think she had even realized what she was doing until I stopped her.

I turned back to Jenks, seeing his wings had taken on a faint red tint as his circulation increased. "What the hell?" he muttered, gaze dropping to her feet. Pixy dust sifted from him in his surprise to make a glittering spot of sun on the gray carpet. He was dressed in his casual gardening clothes of tight-fitting green silk and looked like a miniature Peter Pan minus the hat.

"Jenks," I said as I put a hand on Ceri's shoulder and pulled her forward. "This is Ceri. She's going to be staying with us for a while. Ceri, this is Jenks, my partner."

Jenks zipped forward, then back in agitation. An amazed look came over Ceri, and she glanced from me to him. "Partner?" she said, her attention going to my left hand.

Understanding crashed over me and I warmed. "My business partner," I reiterated, realizing she thought we were married. *How on earth could you marry a pixy? Why on earth would you want to?* "We work together as runners." Taking my hat off, I tossed the red wool to the hearth where it could dry on the stone and fluffed the pressure marks from my hair. I had left my coat outside, but I wasn't going out to get it now.

She bit her lip in confusion. The warmth of the room had turned them red, and color was starting to come back into her cheeks.

In a dry clatter, Jenks flitted close so that my curls shifted in the breeze from his wings. "Not too bright, is she," he pointed out, and when I waved him away in bother, he put his hands on his hips. Hovering before Ceri, he said loudly and slowly as if she were hard of hearing, "We—are—good—guys. We—stop—bad—guys."

"Warriors," Ceri said, not looking at him as her eyes touched on Ivy's leather curtains, plush suede chairs, and sofa. The room was a salute to comfort, all of it from Ivy's pocketbook and not mine.

Jenks laughed, sounding like wind chimes. "Warriors," he said, grinning. "Yeah. We're warriors. I'll be right back. I gotta tell that one to Matalina."

He zipped out of the room at head height, and my shoulders eased. "Sorry about that," I apologized. "I asked Jenks to move his family in for the winter after he admitted he usually lost two children to hibernation sickness every spring. They're driving Ivy and me insane, but I'd rather have no privacy for four months than Jenks starting his spring with tiny coffins."

Ceri nodded. "Ivy," she said softly. "Is she your partner?"

"Yup. Just like Jenks," I said casually to make sure she really understood. Her shifting eyes were cataloging everything, and I slowly moved to the hallway. "Um, Ceri?" I said, hesitating until she started to follow. "Do you want me to call you Ceridwen instead?"

She peeked down the dark corridor to the dimly lit sanctuary, her gaze following the sounds of pixy children. They were supposed to stay in the front of the church, but they got into everything, and their squeals and shrieks had become commonplace. "Ceri, please."

Her personality was thundering back into her faster than I

would have believed possible, going from silence to short sentences in a matter of moments. There was a curious mix of modern and old-world charm in her speech that probably came from living with demons so long. She stopped in the threshold of my kitchen, wide-eyed as she took it all in. I didn't think it was culture shock. Most people had a similar reaction when seeing my kitchen.

It was huge, with both a gas and an electric stove so I could cook on one and stir spells on the other. The fridge was stainless steel and large enough to put a cow in. There was one sliding window overlooking the snowy garden and graveyard, and my beta, Mr. Fish, swam happily in a brandy snifter on the sill. Fluorescent lights illuminated shiny chrome and expansive counter space that wouldn't be out of place before the cameras of a cooking show.

A center island counter overhung with a rack of my spelling equipment and drying herbs gathered by Jenks and his family took up much of the space. Ivy's massive antique table took up the rest. Half of it was meticulously arranged as her office, with her computer—faster and more powerful than an industrial-sized package of laxative—color-coded files, maps, and the markers she used to organize her runs. The other half of the table was mine and empty. I wish I could say it was neatness, but when I had a run, I ran it. I didn't analyze it to death.

"Have a seat," I said casually. "How about some coffee?" *Coffee?* I thought as I went to the coffeemaker and threw out the old grounds. What was I going to do with her? It wasn't as if she was a stray kitten. She needed help. Professional help.

Ceri stared at me, her face returning to its numb state. "I . . ." she stammered, looking frightened and small in her gorgeous outfit. I glanced at my jeans and red sweater. I still had on my snow boots, and I felt like a slob.

"Here," I said as I pulled out a chair. "I'll make some tea." *Three steps forward, one back,* I thought when she shunned the chair I offered and took the one before Ivy's computer instead. Tea might be more appropriate, seeing as she was over a thousand years old. *Did they even have coffee in the Dark Ages?*

I was staring at my cupboards, trying to remember if we had a teapot, when Jenks and about fifteen of his kids came rolling in, all talking at once. Their voices were so high-pitched and rapid they made my head hurt. "Jenks," I pleaded, glancing at Ceri. She looked overwhelmed enough as it was. "Please?"

"They aren't going to do anything," he protested belligerently.

"Besides, I want them to get a good sniff of her. I can't tell what she is, she stinks of burnt amber so badly. Who is she, anyway, and what was she doing in our garden in her bare feet?"

"Um," I said, suddenly wary. Pixies had excellent noses, able to tell what species someone was just by smelling them. I had a bad suspicion that I knew what Ceri was, and I *really* didn't want Jenks to figure it out.

Ceri raised her hand as a perch, smiling beatifically at the two pixy girls who promptly landed on it, their green and pink silk dresses moving from the breeze stirred by their dragonfly wings. They were chattering happily the way pixy girls do, seemingly brainless but aware of everything down to the mouse hiding behind the fridge. Clearly Ceri had seen pixies before. That would make her an Inderlander if she was a thousand years old. The Turn, when we all came out of hiding to live openly with humans, had only been forty years ago.

"Hey!" Jenks exclaimed, seeing his kids monopolizing her, and they whirled up and out of the kitchen in a kaleidoscope of color and noise. Immediately he took their place, beckoning his oldest son, Jax, down to perch on the computer screen before her.

"You smell like Trent Kalamack," he said bluntly. "What are you?"

A wash of angst took me and I turned my back on them. *Damn, I was right. She was an elf.* If Jenks knew, he would blab it all over Cincinnati the moment the temperature got above freezing and he could leave the church. Trent didn't want the world to know that elves had survived the Turn, and he would drop Agent Orange on the entire block to shut Jenks up.

Turning, I frantically waved my fingers at Ceri, pantomiming zipping my mouth. Realizing she wouldn't have a clue what that meant, I put my finger to my lips. The woman eyed me in question, then looked at Jenks. "Ceri," she said seriously.

"Yeah, yeah," Jenks said impatiently, hands on his hips. "I know. You Ceri. Me Jenks. But what are you? Are you a witch? Rachel's a witch."

Ceri glanced at me and away. "I'm Ceri."

Jenks's wings blurred to nothing, the shimmer going from blue to red. "Yeah," he repeated. "But what species? See, I'm a pixy, and Rachel is a witch. You are . . ."

"Ceri," she insisted.

"Ah, Jenks?" I said as the woman's eyes narrowed. The question as to what the Kalamacks were had eluded pixies for the entirety of the family's existence. Figuring that out would give Jenks more prestige in the pixy world than if he took out an entire fairy clan by himself. I could tell he was on the edge of his patience when he flitted up to hover before her.

"Damn it!" Jenks swore, frustrated. "What the hell are you, woman?"

"Jenks!" I shouted in alarm as Ceri's hand flashed out, snagging him. Jax, his son, let out a yelp, leaving a cloud of pixy dust as he darted to the ceiling. Jenks's eldest daughter, Jih peeked around the archway from the hall ceiling, her wings a pink blur.

"Hey! Lego!" Jenks exclaimed. His wings made a furious clatter, but he wasn't going anywhere. Ceri had his pant leg between her thumb and forefinger. Her reflexes were better than even Ivy's if she had enough control to be that precise.

"I'm Ceri," she said, her thin lips tight as Jenks hovered, snared. "And even my demon captor had enough respect that he didn't curse at me, little warrior."

"Yes, ma'am," Jenks said meekly. "Can I go now?"

She raised one pale eyebrow—a skill I envied—then glanced at me for direction. I nodded emphatically, still shocked at how quick it had been. Not smiling, Ceri let him go.

"Guess you aren't as slow as I thought," Jenks said sullenly.

The ruffled pixy brought the scent of store-bought dirt to me as he retreated to my shoulder, and my brow furrowed when I turned my back on her to poke around under the counter for a teapot. I heard the soft familiar clink of pens, recognizing the sound of Ceri tidying Ivy's desk. Her centuries of slavery were showing again. The woman's mix of meek servitude and quick pride had me at a loss for how to treat her.

"Who is she?" Jenks whispered in my ear.

I crouched to reach into the cupboard, pulling out a copper teapot so badly tarnished that it was almost maroon. "She was Big Al's familiar."

"Big Al!" the pixy squeaked, rising up to land upon the tap. "Is that what you were doing out there? Tink's panties, Rachel, you're getting as bad as Nick! You know that's not safe!"

I could tell him now. Now that it was over. Very aware of Ceri listening behind us, I ran the water into the teapot and swirled it around to clean it. "Big Al didn't agree to testify against Piscary out of the goodness of its heart. I had to pay for it."

With a dry rasp of wings, Jenks moved to hover before me. Surprise, shock, and then anger cascaded over his face. "What did you promise him?" he said coldly.

"It's an it, not a him," I said. "And it's done." I couldn't look at him. "I promised to be its familiar if I was allowed to keep my soul."

"Rachel!" A burst of pixy dust lit the sink. "When? When is it coming to get you? We have to find a way out of this. There must be something!" He flew a bright path to my spell books under the center island counter and back. "Is there anything in your books? Call Nick. He'll know!"

Not liking his fluster, I wiped the water off the bottom of the teapot. My boot heels made a dull thumping on the linoleum as I crossed the kitchen. The gas ignited with a whoosh, and my face warmed from embarrassment. "It's too late," I repeated. "I'm its familiar. But the bond isn't strong enough for it to use me if I'm on this side of the ley lines, and as long as I can keep it from pulling me into the ever-after, I'll be okay." I turned from the stove, finding Ceri sitting before Ivy's computer, staring at me with rapt admiration. "I can say no. It's done."

Jenks came to a sputtering halt before me. "Done?" he said, too close to focus on. "Rachel, why? Putting Piscary away isn't worth that!"

"I didn't have a choice!" Frustrated, I crossed my arms before me and leaned against the counter. "Piscary was trying to kill me, and if I survived, I wanted him in jail, not free to come after me again. It's done. The demon can't use me. I tricked it."

"Him," Ceri said softly, and Jenks spun. I had forgotten she was there, she was so quiet. "Al is male. Female demons won't let themselves be pulled across the lines. That's how you can tell. Mostly."

I blinked, taken aback. "Al is male? Why did he keep letting me call him an it?"

She lifted her shoulder in a very modern show of confusion.

My breath came out in a puff and I turned back to Jenks. I started as I found him hovering right before my nose, his wings red. "You're an ass," he said, his tiny, smooth features creased in anger. "You should have told us. What if it had gotten you? What about Ivy and me? Huh? We would have kept looking for you, not knowing what had happened. At least if you had told us, we might have been able to find a way to get you back. Ever think of that, Ms. Morgan? We're a team, and you just stepped all over that!"

My next outburst died. "But there wasn't anything you could have done," I said lamely.

"How do you know?" Jenks snapped.

I sighed, embarrassed that a four-inch man was lecturing me—and had every right to. "Yeah, you're right," I said, slumping. Slowly my arms uncrossed. "I'm just . . . I'm just not used to having anyone I can depend on, Jenks. I'm sorry."

Jenks dropped three feet he was so surprised. "You . . . you agree with me?"

Ceri's head made a smooth turn to the open archway. Her empty expression went even more so. I followed her gaze to the dark hall, not surprised to find it holding Ivy's lithe silhouette, her hip cocked, hand on her thin waist, looking sleek in her body-tight leather.

Suddenly wary, I pulled myself from the counter and straightened. I hated it when she just appeared like that. I hadn't even felt the air pressure change when she opened the front door. "Hi, Ivy," I said, my voice still carrying its chagrin from Jenks.

Ivy's blank gaze matched Ceri's perfectly as she ran her brown eyes over the small woman sitting in *her* chair. She pushed herself into motion, moving with a living vampire's grace, her boots almost silent. Tucking her long, enviably straight black hair behind an ear, she went to the fridge and pulled out the orange juice. Dressed in her casual leather pants and black tuck-in shirt, she looked like a biker chick gone sophisticate. Her cheeks were red from the cold, and she looked chilled even though she still wore her short leather jacket.

Jenks hovered beside me, our argument forgotten in the more pressing problem of Ivy finding someone unexpected in her kitchen. My last guest she had pinned to the wall and threatened to bleed; Ivy didn't like surprises. That she was drinking orange juice was a good sign. It meant she had succumbed to that damned blood lust of hers, and Jenks and I would only have to deal with a guilt-strewn vampire instead of an irritable, guilt-strewn, and hungry vampire. She was a lot easier to live with now that she was practicing again.

"Ah, Ivy, this is Ceridwen," I offered. "She's staying with us until she finds her feet."

Ivy turned, leaning back against the counter to look predatory and sexy as she took the cap off the jug and drank right from the carton. *Like I'd say anything?* Ivy's gaze ran over Ceri, then flicked to Jenks's obvious agitation, and then to me. "So," she said, her melodious voice reminding me of torn gray silk on snow. "You wiggled out of your agreement with that demon. Good job. Nicely done."

My jaw dropped. "How did you know . . . ?" I stammered as Jenks yelped in surprise.

A faint smile, unusual but honest, pulled the corners of her mouth up. A flash of fang showed, her canines the same size as mine but sharp, like a cat's. She'd have to wait until she was dead to get the extended versions. "You talk in your sleep," she said lightly.

"You knew?" I said, floored. "You never said anything!"

"Nicely done?" Jenks's wings clattered like June bugs. "You think being a demon's familiar is a good thing? What train hit you on the way home?"

Ivy went to get a glass from the cupboard. "If Piscary had been released, Rachel would be dead by sunup," she said as she poured out juice. "So she's a demon's familiar? So what? She said the demon can't use her unless he pulls her into the ever-after. And she's alive. You can't do anything if you're dead." She took a sip of her drink. "Unless you're a vampire."

Jenks made an ugly sound and flew to the corner of the room to sulk. Jih took the opportunity to flit in to hide in the ladle hanging over the center counter, the tips of her wings showing a brilliant red above the copper rim.

Ivy's brown eyes met mine over her glass. Her perfect oval face was almost featureless as she hid her emotions behind the cool facade of indifference she maintained when there was someone in the room beside us two, Jenks included. "I'm glad it worked," she said as she set the glass on the counter. "Are you all right?"

I nodded, seeing her relief in the slight trembling of her long pianist fingers. She would never tell me how worried she had been, and I wondered how long she had stood in the hallway listening and collecting herself. Her eyes blinked several times, and her jaw clenched in an effort to stifle her emotion. "I didn't know it was tonight," she said softly. "I wouldn't have left."

"Thanks," I said, thinking Jenks was right. I had been an ass for not telling them. I just wasn't used to having anyone but my mother care.

Ceri was watching Ivy with a puzzled, rapt attention. "Partner?" she hazarded, and Ivy flicked her attention to the small woman.

"Yeah," Ivy said. "Partner. What's it to you?"

"Ceri, this is Ivy," I said as the small woman got to her feet.

Ivy frowned as she realized the precise order she kept her desk in had been altered.

"She was Big Al's familiar," I warned. "She needs a few days to find her feet is all."

Jenks made an eye-hurting noise with his wings, and Ivy gave me a telling look, her expression shifting to an annoyed wariness when Ceri came to stand before her. The small woman was peering at Ivy in confusion. "You're a vampire," she said, reaching to touch Ivy's crucifix.

Ivy sprang back with a startling quickness, her eyes flashing black.

"Whoa, whoa, whoa!" I said as I stepped between them, ready for anything. "Ivy, take it easy. She's been in the ever-after for a thousand years. She may not have seen a living vampire before. I think she's an Inderlander, but she smells like the ever-after so Jenks can't tell what she is." I hesitated, telling her with my eyes and my last sentence that Ceri was an elf, and therefore a loose cannon as far as magic was concerned.

Ivy's pupils had dilated to almost a full, vampire black. Her stance was domineering and sexually charged, but she had just slaked her blood lust and so was capable of listening. I shot a quick glance at Ceri, glad to see she wisely hadn't moved. "We all okay here?" I asked, my voice demanding they both back down.

Thin lips pressed tight, Ivy turned her back on us. Jenks dropped to my shoulder. "Nicely done," he said. "Got all your bitches in line, I see."

"Jenks!" I hissed, knowing Ivy had heard when her knuckles on her glass turned white. I flicked him off me, and laughing, he rose up and then back down to my shoulder.

Ceri was standing with her arms confidently at her side, watching Ivy grow more and more tense. "Oh-h-h-h-h," Jenks drawled. "Your new friend is gonna do something."

"Uh, Ceri?" I questioned, heart pounding as the petite woman went to stand beside Ivy at the sink, clearly demanding her attention.

Pale face tight with a repressed anger, Ivy turned. "What," she said flatly.

Ceri inclined her head regally, never taking her green eyes from Ivy's slowly dilating brown ones. "I apologize," she said in her high, clear voice, every syllable carefully pronounced. "I've slighted you." Her attention dropped to Ivy's elaborate crucifix on its silver chain about her neck. "You're a vampire warrior, and yet you can wear the Cross?"

Ceri's hand twitched, and I knew she wanted to touch it. Ivy knew it too. I watched, unable to interfere as Ivy turned to face her. Hip cocked, she gave Ceri a more in-depth once-over, taking in her dried tears, her exquisite ball gown, her bare feet, and her obvious pride and upright carriage. As I held my breath, Ivy took her crucifix off, the chain gathering her hair in front of her as she pulled it from around her neck.

"I'm a living vampire," she said as she put the religious icon in the elf's hand. "I was born with the vampire virus. You know what a virus is, don't you?"

Ceri's fingers traced the lines of the worked silver. "My demon let me read what I wished. A virus is killing my kin." She looked up. "Not the vampire virus. Something else."

Ivy's gaze darted to me, then returned to the small woman standing just a shade too close to her. "The virus changed me as I was forming in my mother's womb, making me some of both. I can walk under the sun and worship without pain," Ivy said. "I'm stronger than you," she added as she subtly put more space between them. "But not as strong as a true undead. And I have a soul." She said the last as if she expected Ceri to deny it.

Ceri's expression became empty. "You're going to lose it."

Ivy's eye twitched. "I know."

I held my breath, listening to the clock tick and the almost subliminal hum of pixy wings. Eyes solemn, the thin woman held the crucifix out to Ivy. "I'm sorry. That's the hell from which Rachel Mariana Morgan saved me."

Ivy looked at the cross in Ceri's hand, no emotion showing. "I'm hoping she can do the same for me."

I cringed. Ivy had pinned her sanity on the belief that there was a witch magic that might purge the vampire virus from her; that all it would take would be the right spell to let her walk away from the blood and violence. But there wasn't. I waited for Ceri to tell Ivy that no one was beyond redemption, but all she did was nod, her wispy hair floating. "I hope she can."

"Me, too." Ivy glanced at the crucifix Ceri was extending to her. "Keep it. It doesn't help anymore."

My lips parted in surprise, and Jenks landed upon my big hoop earrings as Ceri placed it about her neck. The elaborately tooled silver looked right against the rich purple and green of her formal gown. "Ivy—" I started, jerking when Ivy narrowed her eyes at me.

"It doesn't help anymore," she said tightly. "She wants it. I'm giving it to her."

Ceri reached up, clearly finding peace in the icon. "Thank you," she whispered.

Ivy frowned. "Touch my desk again, and I'll snap every one of your fingers."

Ceri took the threat with a light understanding that surprised me. It was obvious she had dealt with vampires before. I wondered where—since vampires couldn't manipulate ley lines and would therefore make lousy familiars.

"How about some tea?" I said, wanting something normal to do. Making tea wasn't normal, but it was close. The pot was steaming, and as I rummaged in a cupboard for a mug good enough for a guest, Jenks snickered, swinging my earring like a tire swing. His kids were flitting into the kitchen in twos and threes—much to Ivy's annoyance—pulled by the novelty of Ceri. They hovered over her, Jih taking the closest stance.

Ivy stood defensively before her computer, and after a moment's hesitation, Ceri sat in the chair farthest from her. She looked lost and alone as she fingered the crucifix about her neck. As I searched the pantry for a tea bag, I wondered how I was going to make this work. Ivy wasn't going to like another roommate. And where would we put her?

The accusing clatter of Ivy's pens was loud as she rearranged her pencil cup. "Got one," I said in relief as I finally found a tea bag. Jenks left me to bother Ivy, chased off my earring by the steam drifting up as I poured the boiling water into the mug.

"Here, Ceri," I said, waving the pixies away from her and setting it on the table. "Do you want anything with it?"

She looked at the cup as if she'd never seen one before. Eyes widening, she shook her head. I hesitated, wondering what I had done wrong. She looked like she was ready to cry again. "Is it okay?" I asked, and she nodded, her thin hand shaking as she took the mug.

Jenks and Ivy were staring at her. "You sure you don't want sugar or anything?" I asked, but she shook her head. Narrow chin trembling, she brought the cup to her lips.

Brow furrowed, I went to get the coffee grounds out of the

fridge. Ivy rose to rinse the carafe. She leaned close to me, running the water to blur her words as she muttered, "What's wrong with her? She's crying over her tea."

I spun. "Ceri!" I exclaimed. "If you want some sugar, it's okay!"

She met my gaze, tears streaming down her pale face. "I haven't had anything to eat for—a thousand years," she choked out.

I felt as if I had been punched in the gut. "Do you want some sugar?"

Still crying, she shook her head.

Ivy was waiting for me when I turned back around. "She can't stay here, Rachel," the vampire said, her brow tight.

"She'll be fine," I whispered, appalled that Ivy was ready to kick her out. "I'll bring my old cot down from the belfry and set it up in the living room. I've got some old T-shirts she can wear until I take her shopping."

Jenks buzzed his wings for my attention. "Then what?" he said from the spigot.

I gestured my frustration. "I don't know. She's much better already. She wasn't talking half an hour ago. Look at her now."

We all turned, finding Ceri sobbing quietly and drinking her tea in small reverent sips as the pixy girls hovered over her. Three were plating her long, fair hair and another was singing to her.

"Okay," I said as we turned back. "Bad example."

Jenks shook his head. "Rache, I really feel bad for her, but Ivy's right. She can't stay here. She needs professional help."

"Really?" I said belligerently, feeling myself warm. "I haven't heard of any group therapy sessions for retired demon familiars, have you?"

"Rachel . . ." Ivy said.

A sudden shout from the pixy children brought Jenks up from the spigot. His eyes went past us to his kids as they descended upon the mouse, who had finally made a dash for the living room and found itself in its own personal hell. "Excuse me," he said, flitting off to rescue it.

"No," I said to Ivy. "I'm not going to dump her in some institution."

"I'm not saying you should." Ivy's pale face had started to color, and the ring of brown about her eyes was shrinking as my body heat rose and my blood grew warm, triggering her instincts. "But she can't stay here. The woman needs normal, and Rachel? We aren't it."

I took a breath to protest, then let it out. Frowning, I glanced at Ceri. She was wiping her eyes, the hand curled about her mug shaking to make rings on the surface of her tea. My eyes went to the pixy children arguing over who was going to get to ride the mouse first. It was little Jessie, and the tiny pixy screamed in delight when the rodent darted out of the kitchen with her on its back. In a blur of gold sparkles, all but Jih followed. Maybe Ivy was right.

"What do you want me to do, Ivy?" I said, calming. "I'd ask my mom to take her in, but she's a step away from being in an institution herself."

Jenks buzzed back. "What about Keasley?"

Surprised, I looked at Ivy.

"The old guy across the street?" Ivy said warily. "We don't know anything about him."

Jenks landed on the sill beside Mr. Fish and put his hands on his hips. "He's old and on a fixed income. What more is there to know?"

As Ceri collected herself, I sifted the idea through my mind. I liked the old witch whose slow speech hid a sharp wit and high intelligence. He had stitched me up after Algaliarept had torn my neck. He had stitched up my will and confidence, too. The arthritic man was hiding something, and I didn't think his real name was Keasley any more than I believed his story that he had more medical equipment than a small emergency room because he didn't like doctors. But I trusted him.

"He doesn't like the law and he knows how to keep his mouth shut," I said, thinking it was perfect. Eyes pinched, I looked at Ceri talking to Jih in soft tones. Ivy's eyes were doubtful, and peeved, I pushed into motion. "I'm calling him," I added as I motioned to Ceri that I would be right back and went into the living room for the phone.

Three

"Ceri," Jenks said as I flipped the switch and got a pot of coffee going. "If tea makes you cry, you gotta try french fries. Come here, I'll show you how to use the microwave."

Keasley was on his way over. It might take him a while since he was racked by arthritis so badly that even most pain charms wouldn't touch it. I felt bad for pulling him out into the snow, but it would have been even more rude to descend upon his house.

With an intentness I didn't understand, Jenks perched himself on Ceri's shoulder and talked her through the task of microwaving frozen french fries. She bent to watch the little carton spin, my pink slippers on her feet looking overly large and awkward. Pixy girls swirled around her in a whirl of pastel silk and chatter, mostly ignored. The unending noise had driven Ivy into the living room, where she was currently hiding with her earphones on.

My head came up when the air pressure shifted. "'Ello?" came a strong raspy voice from the front of the church. "Rachel? The pixies let me in. Where are you ladies?"

I glanced at Ceri, recognizing her sudden apprehension. "It's Keasley, a neighbor," I said. "He's going to check you over. Make sure you're healthy."

"I'm fine," she said pensively.

Thinking this might be harder than I thought, I padded in my sock feet into the hallway to talk to him before he met Ceri. "Hi, Keasley, we're back here."

His hunched, wizened figure limped down the hallway, eclipsing the light. More pixy children escorted him, wreathing him in circles of sifting pixy dust. Keasley had a brown paper grocery bag in his hand, and he brought the cold scent of snow in with him, mixing pleasantly with a witch's characteristic redwood scent. "Rachel," he said, his brown eyes squinting up at me as he got closer. "How's my favorite redhead?"

"I'm good," I said, giving him a quick hug and thinking that after outwitting Algaliarept, good was an understatement. His overalls were worn and smelling of soap. I thought of him as the neighborhood's wise-old-man and a substitute grandfather figure all in one, and I didn't mind that he had a past he wasn't willing to share. He was a good person; that's all I needed to know.

"Come on in. I have someone I want you to meet," I said, and he slowed with a wary caution. "She needs your help," I said softly.

His thick lips pressed together, and the brown wrinkles of his face deepened. Keasley took a slow breath, his arthritic hands making the grocery bag crackle. He nodded, showing me a thinning spot in his tightly curled, graying hair. Blowing in relief, I led him into the kitchen, holding myself back so I could see his reaction to Ceri.

The old witch rocked to a halt as he stared. But upon seeing the delicate woman standing in pink fuzzy slippers beside the microwave in her elegant ball gown with a folder of steaming fries, I could understand why.

"I don't need a physician," Ceri said.

Jenks rose from her shoulder. "Hi, Keasley. You gonna check Ceri out?"

Keasley nodded, limping as he went to pull out a chair. He gestured for Ceri to sit, then carefully lowered himself into the adjacent seat. Wheezing, he set his bag between his feet, opening it to pull out a blood pressure cuff. "I'm not a doctor," he said. "My name is Keasley."

Not sitting, Ceri looked at me, then him. "I'm Ceri," she said, just above a whisper.

"Well, Ceri, it's nice to meet you." Setting the cuff on the table, he extended his arthritic-swollen hand. Looking unsure, Ceri awkwardly put her hand in his. Keasley shook it, smiling to show his coffee-stained teeth. The old man gestured to the chair, and Ceri arranged herself in it, reluctantly setting her fries down and warily eyeing the cuff.

"Rachel wants me to look you over," he said while he pulled more doctor stuff out.

Ceri glanced at me, sighing as she nodded in surrender.

The coffee had finished, and as Keasley took her temperature, checked her reflexes, her blood pressure, and made her say "Ahhhh," I took a cup into the living room for Ivy. She was sitting sideways in her cushy chair with her earphones on, head on one arm, feet draped over the other. Her eyes were shut, but she reached out without looking, taking the cup the instant I set it down. "Thank you," she mouthed, and still not having seen her eyes, I walked out. Sometimes Ivy gave me the creeps.

"Coffee, Keasley?" I asked as I returned.

The old man peered at the thermometer and turned it off. "Yes, thank you." He smiled at Ceri. "You're fine."

"Thank you, sir," Ceri said. She had been eating her fries while Keasley worked, and she looked glumly at the bottom of the carton.

Immediately Jenks was with her. "More?" he prompted. "Try some ketchup on them."

Suddenly Jenks's zeal to get her to eat french fries became very clear. It wasn't the fries he was interested in, it was the ketchup. "Jenks," I said tiredly as I took Keasley his coffee and leaned against the center island counter. "She's over a thousand years old. Even humans ate tomatoes then." I hesitated. "They did have tomatoes back then, right?"

The hum of Jenks's wings audibly dropped. "Crap," he muttered, then brightened. "Go ahead," he said to Ceri. "You try working the nuker this time without my help."

"Nuker?" she questioned, carefully wiping her hands on a napkin as she stood.

"Yeah. Don't they have microwaves in the ever-after?"

She shook her head, sending the tips of her fair hair floating. "No. I prepared Al's food with ley line magic. This is . . . old."

Keasley jerked, almost spilling his coffee. His eyes tracked Ceri's grace as she went to the freezer and, with Jenks's encouragement, pulled out a box of fries. She meticulously punched the buttons, her lip caught between her teeth. I thought it odd that the woman was over a thousand years old but thought the microwave was primitive.

"The ever-after?" Keasley said softly, and my attention returned to him.

I held my coffee before me with both hands, warming my fingers. "How is she?"

He shifted his shoulders. "She's healthy enough. Maybe a little underweight. Mentally she's been abused. I can't tell what or how. She needs help."

I took a deep breath, looking down into my cup. "I've got a big favor to ask."

Keasley straightened. "No," he said as he put his bag on his lap and started putting things in it. "I don't know who—or even what—she is."

"I stole her from the demon whose work you stitched up last fall," I said, touching my neck. "She was its—I mean, his—familiar. I'll pay for her room and board."

"That isn't it," he protested. Bag in hand, his tired brown eyes went worried. "I don't know anything about her, Rachel. I can't risk taking her in. Don't ask me to do this."

I leaned over the space between us, almost angry. "She has been in the ever-after the last millennium. I don't think she's out to kill you," I accused, and his leathery features shifted to a startled alarm. "All she needs," I said, flustered that I had found one of his fears, "is a normal setting where she can regain her personality. And a witch, a vampire, and a pixy living in a church running down bad guys isn't normal."

Jenks looked at us from Ceri's shoulder as the woman watched her fries warm. The pixy's face was serious; he could hear the conversation as clearly as if he was standing on the table. Ceri asked him a soft question, and he turned away, answering her cheerfully. He had chased all but Jih out of the kitchen, and it was blessedly quiet.

"Please, Keasley?" I whispered.

Jih's ethereal voice rose in song, and Ceri's face lit up. She joined in, her voice clear as the pixy's, managing only three notes before she started to cry. I stared as a cloud of pixies rolled into the kitchen, almost smothering her. From the living room came an irate shout as Ivy complained that the pixies were interfering with the stereo reception again.

Jenks yelled at his kids and all but Jih flitted out. Together they consoled Ceri, Jih soft and soothing, Jenks somewhat awkwardly. Keasley slumped, and I knew he'd do it. "Okay," he said. "I'll try it for a few days, but if it doesn't work, she's coming back."

"Fair enough," I said, feeling a huge weight slip off my chest.

Ceri looked up, her eyes still wet. "You didn't ask me my opinion."

My eyes widened and my face flamed. Her hearing was as good as Ivy's. "Um . . ." I stammered. "I'm sorry, Ceri. It's not that I don't want you to stay here—"

Heart-shaped face solemn, she nodded. "I am a stumbling

stone in a fortress of soldiers," she interrupted. "I'd be honored to stay with the retired warrior and ease his hurts."

Retired warrior? I thought, wondering what she saw in Keasley that I didn't. In the corner came a high-pitched argument between Jenks and his eldest daughter. The young pixy was wringing the hem of her pale green dress, her tiny feet showing as she pleaded with him.

"Now wait a moment," Keasley said, curling the top of his paper bag down. "I can take care of myself. I don't need anyone 'easing my hurts.' "

Ceri smiled. My slippers on her feet made a hush across the linoleum as she came to kneel before him. "Ceri," I protested, right along with Keasley, but the young woman batted our hands away, the suddenly sharp look in her green eyes brooking no interference.

"Get up," Keasley said gruffly as he sat before her. "I know you were a demon's familiar and this might be how he made you act, but—"

"Be still, Keasley," Ceri said, a faint glow of ever-after red blurring her pale hands. "I want to go with you, but only if you let me return your kindness." She smiled up at him, her green eyes losing their focus. "It will give me a feeling of self-worth I truly need."

My breath caught as I felt her tap the ley line out back. "Keasley?" I said, my voice high.

His brown eyes went wide and he froze where he sat as Ceri reached out and placed her hands upon the knees of his work-faded overalls. I watched his face go slack, the wrinkles sliding into themselves to make him look older. He took a deep breath, stiffening.

Kneeling before him, Ceri shivered. Her hands dropped from him. "Ceri," Keasley said, his raspy voice cracking. He touched his knees. "It's gone," he whispered, his tired eyes going watery. "Oh, dear child," he said, standing to help her rise. "I haven't been without pain for so long. Thank you."

Ceri smiled, tears leaking out as she nodded. "Neither have I. This helps."

I turned away, my throat tight. "I have some T-shirts you can wear until I take you shopping," I said. "Just keep my slippers. They'll get you across the street at least."

Keasley took her arm in one hand, his bag in the other. "I'll take her shopping tomorrow," he said as he headed for the hallway. "I haven't felt good enough to go to the mall in three years. It will do me good to get out." He turned to me, his old, wrinkled face transformed. "I'll send the bill to you, though. I can tell everyone she is my sister's niece. From Sweden."

I laughed, finding it was very close to a cry. This was working out better than I had hoped, and I couldn't stop smiling.

Jenks made a sharp noise, and his daughter slowly drooped to land upon the microwave. "All right, I'll ask!" he shouted, and she rose three inches, her face hopeful and her hands clasped before her. "If it's okay with your mother and it's okay with Keasley, it's okay with me," Jenks said, his wings a dismal blue.

Jih rose and fell in obvious nervousness as Jenks hovered before Keasley. "Um, do you have any plants at your house that Jih might tend?" he asked, looking terribly embarrassed. Brushing his blond hair from his eyes, he made a wry face. "She wants to go with Ceri, but I'm not letting her leave unless she can be productive."

My lips parted. I sent my eyes to Ceri, seeing by her held breath that she clearly wanted the company. "I've got a pot of basil," Keasley said reluctantly. "If she wants to stay when the weather breaks, she can work the garden, such as it is."

Jih squealed, pixy dust falling from her in a gold shimmer that turned to white.

"Ask your mother!" Jenks said, looking upset as the excited pixy girl zipped out. He landed on my shoulder, wings drooping. I thought I could smell autumn. Before I could ask Jenks, a shrill tide of pink and green flowed into the kitchen. Appalled, I wondered if there was a pixy in the church that wasn't in that four-foot circle surrounding Ceri.

Keasley's wrinkled face was filled with a stoic acceptance as he unrolled the bag of supplies and Jih dropped inside to make the trip safe from the cold. Above the crinkled top of the bag, the pixies all cried good-bye and waved.

Eyes rolling, Keasley handed the bag to Ceri. "Pixies," I heard him mutter. Taking Ceri's elbow, he nodded to me and headed into the hall, his pace faster and more upright than I'd ever seen it. "I have a second bedroom," he said. "Do you sleep at night or during the day?"

"Both," she said softly. "Is that all right?"

He grinned to show his coffee-stained teeth. "A napper, eh? Good. I won't feel so old when I drop off."

I felt happy as I watched them head to the sanctuary. This was going to be good in so many ways. "What's the matter, Jenks?" I said as he remained on my shoulder while the rest of his family accompanied Ceri and Keasley to the front of the church.

He sniffed. "I thought Jax would be the first one to leave to start his own garden."

My breath slipped from me in understanding. "I'm sorry, Jenks. She'll be fine."

"I know, I know." His wings shifted into motion, sending the scent of fallen leaves over me. "One less pixy in the church," he said softly. "It's a good thing. But no one told me it was going to hurt."

Four

Squinting over my sunglasses, I leaned against my car and scanned the parking lot. My cherry red convertible looked out of place among the scattering of minivans and salt-rusted, late model cars. At the back, away from potential scratches and dings, was a low-to-the-ground, gray sports car. Probably the zoo's p.r. person, as everyone else was either a part-time worker or a dedicated biologist who didn't care what they drove.

The early hour made it cold despite the sun, and my breath steamed. I tried to relax, but I could feel my gut tightening as my annoyance grew. Nick was supposed to meet me here this morning for a quick run in the zoo. It looked like he was going to be a no-show. Again.

I uncrossed my arms from in front of me and shook my hands to loosen them before I bent at the waist and put my palms against the ice-cold, snow-dusted parking lot. Exhaling into the stretch, I felt my muscles pull. Around me were the soft, familiar sounds of the zoo preparing to open, mixing with the scent of exotic manure. If Nick didn't show in the next five minutes, there wouldn't be enough time for a decent run.

I had bought us both runner passes months ago so we could run anytime from midnight to noon when the park was closed. I had woken up two hours earlier than usual for this. I was trying to make this work; I was trying to find a way to mesh my witch's noon-to-sunup schedule with Nick's human sunrise-to-midnight clock. It had never seemed to be a problem before. Nick used to try. Lately, it had been all up to me.

A harsh scraping pulled me upright. The trash cans were being rolled out, and my pique grew. Where was he? He couldn't have forgotten. Nick never forgot anything.

"Unless he wants to forget," I whispered. Giving myself a mental shake, I swung my right leg up to put my lightweight running shoe atop the hood. "Ow," I breathed as my muscles protested, but I leaned into it. I'd been slacking off on my workouts lately, as Ivy and I didn't spar anymore since she had resumed succumbing to her blood lust. My eye started to twitch, and I closed both of them as I deepened the stretch, grabbing my ankle and pulling.

Nick hadn't forgotten—he was too smart for that—he was avoiding me. I knew why, but it was still depressing. It had been three months, and he was still distant and hesitant. The worst thing was I didn't think he was dumping me. The man called demons into his linen closet, and he was afraid to touch me.

Last fall, I had been trying to bind a fish to me to satisfy some inane ley line class requirement and accidentally made Nick my familiar instead. Stupid, stupid, stupid.

I was an earth witch, my magic coming from growing things and quickened by heat and my blood. I didn't know much about ley line magic—except I didn't like it. I generally only used it to close protective circles when I was stirring a particularly sensitive spell. And to make the Howlers pay what they owed me. And occasionally to fend off my roommate when she lost control of her blood lust. And I had used it to knock Piscary flat on his can so I could beat him into submission with the leg of a chair. It had been this last one that tipped Nick from hot-and-heavy, maybe-this-is-the-one boyfriend, to phone conversations and cold kisses on my cheek.

Starting to feel sorry for myself, I pulled my right leg down and swung the left one up.

Ley line magic was heady in its rush of strength and could drive a witch insane, making it no accident that there were more black ley line witches than black earth witches. Using a familiar made it safer since the power of a ley line was filtered through the simpler minds of animals instead of through plants as earth magic did. For obvious reasons, only animals were used as familiars—at least on this side of the ley lines—and in truth, there were no witch-born spells to bind a human as a familiar. But being both fairly ignorant of ley line magic and rushed, I had used the first spell I found to bind a familiar.

So I had unknowingly made Nick my familiar—which we

were trying to undo—but then I made things immeasurably worse by pulling a huge amount of ley line energy through him to subdue Piscary. He had hardly touched me since. But that had been months ago. I hadn't done it again. He had to get over it. It wasn't as if I was practicing ley line magic. Much.

Uneasy, I straightened, blowing out my angst and doing a few side twists to send my ponytail bouncing. After having learned it was possible to set a circle without drawing it first, I had spent three months learning how, knowing it might be my only chance to escape Algaliarept. I had kept my practice to three in the morning, when I knew Nick was asleep—and I always drew directly off the line so it wouldn't go through Nick first—but maybe it was waking him up anyway. He hadn't said anything, but knowing Nick, he wouldn't.

The rattle of the gate opening brought me to a standstill and my shoulders slumped. The zoo was open, a few runners straggling out with red cheeks and exhausted, content expressions, still floating on a runner's high. *Damn it. He could have called.*

Bothered, I unzipped my belt pack and pulled out my cell phone. Leaning against the car and looking down to avoid the eyes of the passing people, I scrolled through my short list. Nick's was second, right after Ivy's number and right before my mom's. My fingers were cold, and I blew on them as the phone rang.

I took a breath when the connection clicked open, holding it when a recorded woman's voice told me the line was no longer in service. *Money?* I thought. Maybe that was why we hadn't been out for three weeks. Concerned, I tried his cell phone.

It was still ringing when the familiar choking rumble of Nick's truck grew loud. Exhaling, I snapped the cover closed. Nick's blue, beat-up Ford truck jostled off the main street and into the parking lot, maneuvering slowly, as the cars leaving were ignoring the lines and cutting across the expanse. I slipped the phone away and stood with my arms over my chest, legs crossed at my ankles.

At least he showed, I thought as I adjusted my sunglasses and tried not to frown. Maybe we could go out for coffee or something. I hadn't seen him in days, and I didn't want to ruin it with a bad temper. Besides, I had been worried sick the last three months about slipping my bargain with Al, and now that I had, I wanted to feel good for a while.

I hadn't told Nick, and the chance to come clean would be another weight off me. I lied to myself that I had kept quiet because

I was afraid he would try to take my burden—seeing as he had a chivalrous streak longer and wider than a six-lane highway—but in reality I was afraid he would call me a hypocrite since I was forever on him about the dangers of dealing with demons, and here I was, becoming one's familiar. Nick had an unhealthy lack of fear when it came to demons, thinking that as long as you handled them properly, they were no more dangerous than say . . . a pit viper.

So I stood and fidgeted in the cold as he parked his salt-stained, ugly truck a few slots down from mine. His indistinct shadow moved inside as he shuffled about, finally getting out and slamming the door with an intensity that I knew wasn't directed at me but necessary to get the worn latch to catch.

"Ray-ray," he said as he held his phone up and strode around the front. His lean height looked good and his pace was quick. A smile was on his face, its once-gauntness muted into a pleasant, rugged severity. "Did you just call?"

I nodded, letting my arms fall to my sides. Obviously he wasn't prepared to run, as he was dressed in faded jeans and boots. A thick fabric coat was unzipped to show a bland, flannel button-down shirt. It was neatly tucked in and his long face was clean-shaven, but he still managed to look mildly unkempt, with his short black hair a shade too long. He had a bookish mien instead of the hint of danger that I usually liked in my men. But maybe I found Nick's danger to be his intelligence.

Nick was the smartest man I knew, his brilliant jumps of logic hidden behind an understated appearance and a deceptively mild temperament. In hindsight, it was probably this rare mix of wicked intellect and harmless human that attracted me to him. Or possibly that he had saved my life by binding Big Al when he tried to rip out my throat.

And despite Nick's preoccupation with old books and new electronics, he wasn't a geek: his shoulders were too broad and his butt was too tight. His long, lean legs could keep up with me when we ran, and there was a surprising amount of strength in his arms, as evidenced by our once frequent, now distressingly absent, mock wrestling, which more often than not had turned into a more, er, intimate activity. It was the memory of our once-closeness that kept the frown off my face when he came around the front of his truck, his brown eyes pinched in apology.

"I didn't forget," he said, his long face looking longer as he tossed his straight bangs out of his way. There was a flash of a demon mark high on his brow, gained the same night I had gotten my first and remaining one. "I got caught up in what I was doing and lost track of time. I'm sorry, Rachel. I know you were looking forward to it, but I haven't even been to bed and I'm dead tired. Do you want to reschedule for tomorrow?"

I kept my reaction to a sigh, trying to stifle my disappointment. "No," I said around a long exhalation. He reached out, his arms going around me in a light hug. I leaned into the expected hesitancy of it, wanting more. The distance had been there so long that it almost felt normal. Pulling back, he shuffled his feet.

"Working hard?" I offered. This was the first time I had seen him in a week, not including the odd phone call, and I didn't just want to walk away.

Nick, too, didn't seem eager to leave. "Yes and no." He squinted into the sun. "I was up sifting through old messages on a chat-room list after finding a mention of that book Al took."

Immediately my attention sharpened. "Did you . . ." I stammered, pulse quickening.

My quick hope squished to nothing as he dropped his gaze and shook his head. "It was some freak wannabe. He doesn't have a copy. It was all made-up nonsense."

I reached out and briefly touched his arm, forgiving him for missing our morning run. "It's okay. We'll find something sooner or later."

"Yeah," he muttered. "But I'd rather it be sooner."

Misery hit me, and I froze. We had been so good together, and now all that was left was this awful distance. Seeing my depression, Nick took my hands, stepping forward to give me a loose embrace. His lips brushed my cheek as he whispered, "I'm sorry, Ray-ray. We'll manage something. I'm trying. I want this to work."

I didn't move, breathing in the smell of musty books and clean aftershave, my hands hesitantly going about him as I looked for comfort—and finally found it.

My breath caught and I held it, refusing to cry. We had been months searching for the counter curse, but Al wrote the book on how to make humans into familiars, and he had a very short print run of one. And it wasn't as if we could advertise in the papers for a ley line professor to help us, as he or she would likely turn me in for dealing in the black arts. And then I'd really be stuck. Or dead. Or worse.

Slowly Nick let go, and I stepped back. At least I knew it wasn't another woman.

"Hey, uh, the zoo is open," I said, my voice giving away my relief that the awkward distance he had been holding himself at finally seemed to be easing. "You want to go in and get a coffee instead? I hear their Monkey Mocha is to come back from the dead for."

"No," he said, but there was true regret in his voice, making me wonder if he had been picking up on my worry about Al all this time, thinking I was upset with him and drawing away. Maybe more of this was my fault than I had guessed. Maybe I could have forged a stronger union between us if I had told him instead of hiding it from him and driving him away.

The magnitude of what I might have done with my silence fell on me, and I felt my face go cold. "Nick, I'm sorry," I breathed.

"It wasn't your fault," he said, his brown eyes full of forgiveness, unaware of my thoughts. "I was the one that told him he could have the book."

"No, you see—"

He took me in a hug, silencing me. A lump formed in my throat, and I couldn't say anything as my forehead dropped to his shoulder. I should have told him. I should have told him right from the first night.

Nick felt the shift in me, and slowly, after a moment's thought, he gave me a tentative kiss on the cheek, but it was a tentativeness born from his long absence, not his usual hesitancy.

"Nick?" I said, hearing the coming tears in my voice.

Immediately he pulled back. "Hey," he said, smiling as his long hand rested on my shoulder. "I've got to go. I've been up since yesterday and I have to get some sleep."

I took a reluctant step back, hoping he couldn't tell how close to tears I was. It had been a long, lonely three months. At last something seemed to be mending. "Okay. You want to come over for dinner tonight?"

And finally, after weeks of quick refusals, he paused. "How about a movie and dinner instead? My treat. A real date . . . thing."

I straightened, feeling myself grow taller. "A date thing," I said, moving awkwardly foot-to-foot like a fool teenager asked to her first dance. "What do you have in mind?"

He smiled softly. "Something with lots of explosions, lots of guns . . ." He didn't touch me, but I saw in his eyes his desire to do so. ". . . tight costumes . . ."

I nodded, smiling, and he checked his watch.

"Tonight," he said, catching my eye as he headed back to his truck. "Seven o'clock?"

"Seven o'clock," I called back, my good feeling growing. He got in, the truck shaking as he slammed the door. The engine rumbled to life, and with a happy wave, he drove away.

"Seven o'clock," I said, watching the taillights flash before he jostled onto the street.

Five

Plastic hangers clattering, I stacked the clothes on the counter beside the cash register. The bored, bottle-dyed blonde with ear-length hair never looked up as her fingers manipulated those nasty metal clips. Gum snapping, she pointed her gun at everything, adding up my purchases for Ceri. She had a phone to her ear, head cocked, and her mouth never stopped as she chatted to her boyfriend about getting her roommate fried on Brimstone last night.

I eyed her in speculation, breathing in the fading aroma of the street drug lingering on her. She was dumber than she looked if she was dabbling in Brimstone, especially now. It had been coming in cut with a little something extra lately, leaving a rash of deaths spanning all the socioeconomic brackets. Maybe it was Trent's idea of a Christmas present.

The girl before me looked underage, so I could either sic Health and Inderland Services on her or haul her ass down to the I.S. lockup. The latter might be fun, but it would put a real crimp in my afternoon of solstice shopping. I still didn't know what to get Ivy. The boots, jeans, socks, underwear, and two sweaters on the counter were for Ceri. She was not going out with Keasley dressed in one of my T-shirts and pink fuzzy slippers.

The girl folded the last sweater, her bloodred manicure garish. Amulets clanked about her neck, but the complexion charm hiding her acne needed to be replaced. She must have been a warlock because a witch wouldn't be caught dead with a bass-ackward charm like that. I glanced at my wooden pinky ring. It might be small, but it was now potent enough to hide my freckles through a minor spell check. *Hack,* I thought, feeling vastly better.

A hum rose from nowhere, and I felt smug that I didn't jump like the register girl when Jenks all but fell onto the counter. He was wearing two black body stockings, one atop the other, and had a red hat and boots on against the chill. It was really too cold for him to be out, but Jih's leaving had depressed him, and he'd never been solstice shopping before. My eyes widened as I took in the doll he had lugged to the counter. It was three times his size.

"Rache!" he exclaimed, puffing as he pushed the black-haired, curvaceous plastic homage to adolescent boys' dreams upright. "Look what I found! It was in the toy department."

"Jenks . . ." I cajoled, hearing the couple behind me snicker.

"It's a Bite-me-Betty doll!" he exclaimed, his wings moving furiously to keep himself upright, his hands on the doll's thighs. "I want it. I want to get it for Ivy. It looks just like her."

Eyeing the shiny plastic leather skirt and red vinyl bustier, I took a breath to protest.

"Look, see?" he said, his voice excited. "You push the lever in her back, and fake blood squirts out. Isn't it great!"

I started when a gelatinous goo jumped from the blank-eyed doll's mouth, arching a good foot before hitting the counter. A red smear dripped down her pointy chin. The register girl eyed it, then hung up on her boyfriend. *He wanted to give this to Ivy?*

Pushing Ceri's jeans out of the way, I sighed. Jenks hit the lever again, watching in rapt attention as red squirted out with a rude sound. The couple behind me laughed, the woman hanging on his arm and whispering in his ear. Warming, I grabbed the doll. "I'll buy it for you if you stop that," I all but hissed.

Eyes bright, Jenks rose up to land on my shoulder, tucking in between my neck and my scarf to stay warm. "She's gonna love it," he said. "You watch."

Pushing it at the girl behind the counter, I glanced behind me at the tittering couple. They were living vamps, well-dressed and unable to go thirty seconds without touching each other. Knowing I was watching, the woman straightened the collar of his leather jacket to show off his lightly scarred neck. The thought of Nick brought a smile to me, the first time in weeks.

As the girl recalculated my total, I dug in my bag for my checkbook. It was nice having money. Real nice.

"Rache," Jenks questioned, "can you put a bag of M&M's in

there, too?" His wings sent a cold draft against my neck as he set them vibrating to generate some body heat. It wasn't as if he could wear a coat—not with those wings of his—and anything heavy was too limiting.

I snatched up a bag of overpriced candy whose hand-lettered cardboard sign said the sale would go to help rebuild the fire-damaged city shelters. I already had my total, but she could add it on. And if the vamps behind me had a problem with that, they could curl up and die twice. It was for orphans, for God's sake.

The girl reached for the candy and beeped it, giving me a snotty look. The register chirped to give me the new total, and as they all waited, I flipped to the check register. Freezing, I blinked. It had been balanced with neat tidy numbers. I hadn't bothered to keep a running total as I knew there was tons of money in it, but someone had. Then I brought it closer, staring. "That's it?" I exclaimed. "That's all I have left?"

Jenks cleared his throat. "Surprise," he said weakly. "It was just laying there in your desk, and I thought I'd balance it for you." He hesitated. "Sorry."

"It's almost gone!" I stammered, my face probably as red as my hair. The eyes of the register girl were suddenly wary.

Embarrassed, I finished writing out the check. She took it, calling her supervisor to run it through their system to make sure it was good. Behind me, the vamp couple started in with a snarky commentary. Ignoring them, I flipped through the check register to see where it went.

Almost two grand for my new desk and bedroom set, four more for insulating the church, and $3,500 for a garage for my new car; I wasn't about to let it sit out in the snow. Then there was the insurance and gas. A big chunk went to Ivy for my back rent. Another chunk went to my night in the emergency room for my broken arm as I hadn't had insurance at the time. A third chunk to *get* insurance. And the rest . . . I swallowed hard. There was money still in there, but I had enjoyed myself down from twenty thousand to high four figures in only three months.

"Um, Rache?" Jenks said. "I was going to ask you later, but I know this accounting guy. You want me to have him set up an IRA for you? I was looking at your finances, and you might need a shelter this year, seeing as you haven't been taking anything out for taxes."

"A tax shelter?" I felt sick. "There's nothing left to put into it."

Taking my bags from the girl, I headed for the door. "And what are you doing looking at my finances?"

"I'm living in your desk," he said wryly. "It's kind of all out there?"

I sighed. My desk. My beautiful solid-oak desk with nooks and crannies and a secret cubby at the bottom of the left-hand drawer. My desk that I had used for only three weeks before Jenks and his brood moved into it. My desk, which was now so thickly covered in potted plants that it looked like a prop for a horror movie about killer plants taking over the world. But it was either that or have them set up housekeeping in the kitchen cupboards. No. Not my kitchen. Having them stage daily mock battles among the hanging pots and utensils was bad enough.

Distracted, I tugged my coat closer and squinted at the bright light reflecting off the snow as the sliding doors opened. "Whoa, wait up!" Jenks shrilled in my ear when the blast of cold air hit us. "What the hell do you think you're doing, witch? Do I look like I'm made of fur?"

"Sorry." I made a quick left turn to get out of the draft and opened my shoulder bag for him. Still swearing, he dropped down to hide inside. He hated it, but there was no alternative. A sustained temp lower than forty-five degrees would throw him into a hibernation that would be unsafe to break until spring, but he should be all right in my bag.

A Were dressed in a thick wool coat that went to his boot tops edged from me with an uncomfortable look. When I tried to make eye contact, he pulled his cowboy hat down and turned away. A frown crossed me; I hadn't had a Were client since I made the Howlers pay me for trying to get their mascot back. Maybe I'd made a mistake there.

"Hey, give me those M&M's, okay?" Jenks grumbled up at me, his short blond hair framing delicate features reddened by the cold. "I'm starving here."

I obediently shuffled through the bags and dropped the candy in to him before pulling the ties to my shoulder bag shut. I didn't like bringing him out like this, but I was his partner, not his mom. He enjoyed being the only adult male pixy in Cincinnati not in a stupor. In his eyes, the entire city was probably his garden, as cold and snowy as it was.

I took a moment to dig my zebra-striped car key out from the front pocket. The couple that had been behind me in line passed me on their way out, flirting comfortably and looking like sex in leather. He had bought her a Bite-me-Betty doll, too, and they were laughing. My thoughts went to Nick again, and a warm stir of anticipation took me.

Putting my shades on against the glare, I went out to the sidewalk, keys jingling and bag held tight to me. Even making the trip in my bag, Jenks was going to get cold. I told myself I should make cookies so he could bask in the heat of the cooling oven. It had been ages since I'd made solstice cookies. I was sure I had seen some flour-smeared cookie cutters in a nasty zippy bag at the back of a cupboard somewhere. All I needed was the colored sugar to do it right.

My mood brightened at the sight of my car ankle-deep in crusty slush at the curb. Yeah, it was as expensive as a vampire princess to maintain, but it was mine and I looked really good sitting behind the wheel with the top down and the wind pulling my long hair back. . . . Not springing for the garage hadn't been an option.

It chirped happily at me as I unlocked it and dropped my bags in the unusable backseat. I folded myself into the front, setting Jenks carefully on my lap, where he might stay a little warmer. The heat went on full-bore as soon as I got the engine started. I tunked it into gear and was ready to pull out when a long white car slid up alongside in a slow hush of sound.

Affronted, I glared as it double-parked to block me in. "Hey!" I exclaimed when the driver got out in the middle of the freaking road to open the door for his employer. Ticked, I jammed it into neutral, got out of my car and jerked my bag farther up my shoulder. "Hey! I'm trying to leave here!" I shouted, wanting to bang on the roof of the car.

But my protests choked to nothing when the side door opened and an older man wearing scads of gold necklaces stuck his head out. His frizzed blond hair went out in all directions. Blue eyes glinting in suppressed excitement, he beckoned to me. "Ms. Morgan," he exclaimed softly. "Can I talk to you?"

I took my sunglasses off, staring. "Takata?" I stammered.

The older rocker winced, his face sliding into faint wrinkles as he glanced over the few pedestrians. They had noticed the limo, and with my outburst, the jig, as they say, was up. Eyes pinched in exasperation, Takata stretched out a long skinny hand, jerking me off my feet and into the limo. I gasped, holding my bag so I didn't squish Jenks as I fell into the plush seat across from him. "Go!"

the musician cried, and the driver shut the door and jogged to the front.

"My car!" I protested. My door was open and my keys were in the ignition.

"Arron?" Takata said, gesturing to a man in a black T-shirt tucked into a corner of the expansive vehicle. He slipped past me in a tang of blood that pegged him as a vamp. There was a flush of cold air as he got out, quickly thumping the door shut behind him. I watched through the tinted window as he slipped into my leather seats to look predatory with his shaved head and dark shades. I only hoped I looked half that good. The muffled sound of my engine revved twice, then we jerked into motion as the first of the groupies started patting the windows.

Heart pounding, I spun to look out the back window while we pulled away. My car was edging carefully past the people standing in the road shouting at us to come back. It worked its way into the clear, quickly catching up and running a red light to stay with us.

Stunned at how fast it had been, I turned.

The aging pop star was wearing outlandish orange slacks. He had a matching vest over a soothing earth-toned shirt. Everything was silk, which I thought was his only saving grace. God help him, even his shoes were orange. And socks. I winced. It kind of went with the gold chains and blond hair, which had been teased out until it was so big it could frighten small children. His complexion was whiter than mine, and I dearly wanted to pull out the wood-framed glasses that I had spelled to see through earth charms to know if he had hidden freckles.

"Uh, hi?" I stammered, and the man grinned, showing his impulsive, wickedly intelligent demeanor, and his tendency to find the fun in everything even if the world was falling apart around him. Actually, the innovative artist had done just that, his garage band making the jump to stardom during the Turn, capitalizing on the opportunity to be the first openly Inderland band. He was a Cincy hometown boy who had made good, and he returned the favor by donating the proceeds of his winter solstice concerts to the city's charities. It was particularly important this year, as a series of arson fires had decimated many of the homeless shelters and orphanages.

"Ms. Morgan," the man said, touching the side of his big nose. His attention went over my shoulder and out the back window. "Hope I didn't startle you."

His voice was deep and carefully schooled. Beautiful. I was a sucker for beautiful voices. "Um, no." Setting my shades aside, I unwound my scarf. "How are you doing? Your hair looks . . . great."

He laughed, easing my nervousness. We had met five years ago and had coffee over a conversation centering on the trials of curly hair. That he not only remembered me but also wanted to talk was flattering. "It looks like hell," he said, touching the long frizz that had been in dreadlocks when we last met. "But my p.r. woman says it ups my sales by two percent." He stretched his long legs out to take up almost the entirety of one side of the limo.

I smiled. "You need another charm to tame it?" I said, reaching for my bag.

My breath caught in alarm. "Jenks!" I exclaimed, jerking the bag open.

Jenks came boiling out. "About time you remembered me!" he snarled. "What the Turn is going on? I nearly snapped my wing falling onto your phone. You got M&M's all over your purse, and I'll be damned before I pick them up. Where in Tink's garden are we?"

I smiled weakly at Takata. "Ah, Takata," I started, "this is—"

Jenks caught sight of him. A burst of pixy dust exploded, lighting the car for an instant and making me jump. "Holy crap!" the pixy exclaimed. "You're Takata! I thought Rachel was pissing on my daisies about knowing you. Sweet mother of Tink! Wait until I tell Matalina! It's really you. Damn, it's really you!"

Takata reached over and adjusted a knob on an elaborate console, and heat poured out of the vents. "Yeah, it's really me. Do you want an autograph?"

"Hell, yes!" the pixy said. "No one will believe me."

I smiled, settling myself farther into the seat, my fluster vanishing at Jenks's star fawning. Takata tugged a picture of him and his band standing before the Great Wall of China from a dog-eared folder. "Who do I make it out to?" he said, and Jenks froze.

"Uh . . ." he stammered, his hovering wings going still. I shot my hand out to catch him, and his featherlight weight hit my palm. "Um . . ." he stuttered, panicking.

"Make it out to Jenks," I said, and Jenks made a tiny sound of relief.

"Yeah, Jenks," the pixy said, finding the presence of mind to flit over to stand on the photo as Takata signed it with an illegible signature. "My name is Jenks."

Takata handed me the picture to carry home for him. "Pleasure to meet you, Jenks."

"Yeah," Jenks squeaked. "Nice to meet you, too." Making another impossibly high noise to get my eyelids aching, he darted from me to Takata like an insane firefly.

"Park it, Jenks," I breathed, knowing the pixy could hear me even if Takata couldn't.

"My name is Jenks," he said as he lit atop my shoulder, quivering when I carefully put the photo in my bag. His wings couldn't stay still, and the come-and-go draft felt good in the stifling air of the limo.

I returned my gaze to Takata, taken aback at the empty look on his face. "What?" I asked, thinking something was wrong.

Immediately he straightened. "Nothing," he said. "I heard you quit the I.S. to go out on your own." He blew his air out in a long exhalation. "That took guts."

"It was stupid," I admitted, thinking of the death threat my past employer had set on me in retaliation. "Though I wouldn't change a thing."

He smiled, looking satisfied. "You like being on your own?"

"It's hard without a corporation backing you," I said, "but I've got people to catch me if I fall. I trust them over the I.S. any day."

Takata's head bobbed to make his long hair shift. "I'm with you on that." His feet were spread wide against the car's motion, and I was starting to wonder why I was sitting in Takata's limo. Not that I was complaining. We were on the expressway, looping about the city, my convertible trailing three car lengths behind.

"As long as you're here," he said suddenly, "I want your opinion on something."

"Sure," I said, thinking his mind jumped from topic to topic worse than Nick's. I loosened the tie on my coat. It was starting to get warm in there.

"Capital," he said, flipping open the guitar case beside him and pulling a beautiful instrument from the crushed green velvet. My eyes widened. "I'm going to release a new track at the solstice concert." He hesitated. "You did know I was playing at the Coliseum?"

"I've got tickets," I said, my flash of excitement growing. Nick had bought them. I had been worried he was going to cancel on me and I'd end up going to Fountain Square for the solstice as I usually did, putting my name in the lottery to close the ceremonial circle there. The large, inlaid circle had a "permit only" use status except for the solstices and Halloween. But now I had a feeling we would be spending our solstice together.

"Great!" Takata said. "I was hoping you would. Well, I have this piece about a vampire pining after someone he can't have, and I don't know which chorus works the best. Ripley likes the darker one, but Arron says the other fits better."

He sighed, showing an unusual bother. Ripley was his Were drummer, the only band member to have been with Takata for most of his career. It was said she was the reason everyone else only lasted a year or two before striking out on their own.

"I had planned on singing it live the first time on the solstice," Takata said. "But I want to release it to WVMP tonight to give Cincinnati a chance to hear it first." He grinned, to look years younger. "It's more of a high when they sing along."

He glanced at the guitar in his lap and strummed a chord. The vibration filled the car. My shoulders slumped, and Jenks made a choking gurgle. Takata looked up, his eyes wide in question. "You'll tell me which one you like better?" he asked, and I nodded. My own personal concert? Yeah, I could go for that. Jenks made that choking gurgle again.

"Okay. It's called 'Red Ribbons.'" Taking a breath, Takata slumped. Eyes vacant, he modified the chord he had been playing. His thin fingers shifted elegantly, and with his head bent over his music, he sang.

"Hear you sing through the curtain, see you smile through the glass. Wipe your tears in my thoughts, no amends for the past. Didn't know it would consume me, no one said the hurt would last." His voice dropped and took on the tortured sound that had made him famous. "No one told me. No one told me," he finished, almost whispering.

"Ooooh, nice," I said, wondering if he really thought I was capable of making a judgment.

He flashed me a smile, throwing off his stage presence that quickly. "Okay," he said, hunching over his guitar again. "This is the other one." He played a darker chord, sounding almost wrong. A shudder rippled its way up my spine, and I stifled it. Takata's posture shifted, becoming fraught with pain. The vibrating strings seemed to echo through me, and I sank back into the leather seats, the humming of the engine carrying the music right to my core.

"You're mine," he almost breathed, "in some small fashion. You're mine, though you know it not. You're mine, bond born of passion. You're mine, yet wholly you. By way of your will, by way of your will, by way of your will."

His eyes were closed, and I didn't think he remembered I was sitting across from him. "Um . . ." I stammered, and his blue eyes flashed open, looking almost panicked. "I think the first one?" I offered as he regained his composure. The man was more flighty than a drawer full of geckos. "I like the second better, but the first fits with the vampire watching what she can't have." I blinked. "What *he* can't have," I amended, flushing.

God help me, I must look like a fool. He probably knew I roomed with a vampire. That she and I weren't sharing blood probably hadn't made it into his report. The scar on my neck wasn't from her but from Big Al, and I tugged my scarf up to hide it.

He looked almost shaky as he put his guitar aside. "The first?" he questioned, seeming to want to say something else, and I nodded. "Okay," he said, forcing a smile. "The first it is."

There was another choked gurgle from Jenks. I wondered if he would recover enough to make more than that ugly sound.

Takata snapped the latches on his instrument case, and I knew the chitchat was over. "Ms. Morgan," he said, the rich confines of the limo seeming sterile now that it was empty of his music. "I wish I could say I looked you up for your opinion on which chorus I should release, but I find myself in a tight spot, and you were recommended to me by a trusted associate. Mr. Felps said he has worked with you before and that you had the utmost discretion."

"Call me Rachel," I said. The man was twice my age. Making him call me Ms. Morgan was ridiculous.

"Rachel," he said as Jenks choked again. Takata gave me an uncertain smile, and I returned it, not sure what was going on. It sounded like he had a run for me. Something that required the anonymity that the I.S. or the FIB couldn't provide.

As Jenks gurgled and pinched the rim of my ear, I straightened, crossed my knees, and pulled my little datebook out of my bag to try to look professional. Ivy had bought it for me two months ago in one of her attempts to bring order to my chaotic life. I only carried it to appease her, but setting up a run for a nationally renowned pop star might be the time to start using it. "A Mr. Felps recommended me to you?" I said, searching my memory and coming up blank.

Takata's thick expressive eyebrows were high in confusion. "He said he knew you. He seemed quite enamored, actually."

A sound of understanding slipped past me. "Oh, is he a living vamp, by chance? Blond hair. Thinks he's God's gift to the living and the dead?" I asked, hoping I was wrong.

He grinned. "You do know him." He glanced at Jenks, quivering and unable to open his mouth. "I thought he was pissing in my daisies."

My eyes closed as I gathered my strength. Kisten. Why didn't that surprise me? "Yeah, I know him," I muttered as I opened my eyes, not sure if I should be angry or flattered that the living vampire had recommended me to Takata. "I didn't know his last name was Felps."

Disgusted, I gave up on my attempt at being professional. Throwing my datebook back into my bag, I slouched in the corner, my movement less graceful than I hoped, as it was pushed along by the car's motion as we shifted lanes. "So what can I do for you?" I asked.

The older warlock straightened, tugging the soft orange of his slacks straight. I'd never known anyone who could look good in orange, but Takata managed it. "It's about the upcoming concert," he said. "I wanted to see if your firm was available for security."

"Oh." I licked my lips, puzzled. "Sure. That's no problem, but don't you have people for that already?" I asked, remembering the tight security at the concert I'd met him at. Vamps had to cap their teeth, and no one got in with more than a makeup spell. 'Course, once past security, the caps came off and the amulets hidden in shoes were invoked. . . .

He nodded. "Yes, and therein lies the problem."

I waited as he leaned forward, sending the scent of redwood to me. Long musician hands laced, he eyed the floor. "I arranged security with Mr. Felps as usual before I got into town," he said when his attention came back to me. "But a Mr. Saladan came to see me, claiming he's handling security in Cincinnati and that all monies owed to Piscary should be directed to him instead."

My breath came out in understanding. *Protection. Oh. I got it.* Kisten was acting as Piscary's scion since very few people knew that Ivy had displaced him and now held the coveted title. Kisten continued to handle the undead vampire's affairs while Ivy refused to. *Thank God.*

"You're paying for protection?" I said. "You want me to talk to Kisten and Mr. Saladan to get them to stop blackmailing you?"

Takata tilted his head back, his beautiful, tragic voice ringing out in laughter that was soaked up by the thick carpet and leather seats. "No," he said. "Piscary does a damned-fine job of keeping the Inderlanders in line. My concern is with Mr. Saladan."

Appalled, but not surprised, I tucked my red curls behind my ear, wishing I had done something with them that afternoon. Yeah, I used blackmail, but it was to keep myself alive, not make money. There was a difference. "It's blackmail," I said, disgusted.

He went solemn. "It's a service, and I don't begrudge a dime of it." Seeing my frown, Takata leaned forward to send his gold chains swinging, his blue eyes fixing on mine. "My show has an MPL, just like a traveling circus or fair. I wouldn't keep it one night if it wasn't for arranging protection at every city we play in. It's the cost of doing business."

MPL was short for Mixed Population License. It guaranteed that there was security in place to prevent bloodletting on the premises, a necessity when Inderlanders and humans mixed. If too many vampires gathered and one succumbed to his or her blood lust, the rest were hard-pressed to not follow suit. I was never sure how a slip of paper was enough to keep hunger-driven vampires' mouths to themselves, but establishments worked hard to keep an A rating on their MPLs since humans and living Inderlanders would boycott any place that didn't have one. It was too easy to end up dead or mentally bound to a vampire you didn't even know. And personally, I'd rather be dead than be a vampire's toy, my living with a vampire aside.

"It's blackmail," I said. We had just passed the bridge to cross the Ohio River. I wondered where we were going if it wasn't the Hollows.

Takata's thin shoulders moved. "When I'm touring, I'm at any one place for one night, maybe two. If someone starts trouble, we won't be around long enough to track them down, and every goth out there knows it. Where's the incentive for an excited vamp or Were to behave him- or herself? Piscary puts the word out that anyone causing trouble will answer to him."

I looked up, not liking that it made beautiful, simplistic sense.

"I have an incident-free show," Takata said, smiling, "and Piscary gets seven percent of the ticket sales. Everyone wins. Up to now, I've been very satisfied with Piscary's services. I didn't even mind he upped his cost to pay for his lawyer."

Snorting, I dropped my eyes. "My fault," I said.

"So I hear," the lanky man said dryly. "Mr. Felps was very impressed. But Saladan?" Takata grew concerned, his expressive fingers drumming out a complicated rhythm as his gaze went to the passing buildings. "I can't afford to pay both of them. There would be nothing left to rebuild the city's shelters, and that's the entire point to the concert."

"You want me to make sure nothing happens," I said, and he nodded. My eyes tracked the Jim Beam bottler just off the expressway while I took that in. Saladan was trying to muscle in on Piscary's turf now that the undead master vampire was put away for murder. Murders that I staked to him.

I tilted my head in a vain attempt to see Jenks on my shoulder. "I have to talk to my other partner, but I don't see a problem," I said. "There will be three of us. Me, a living vamp, and a human." I wanted Nick to go, even if he wasn't officially part of our firm.

"Me," Jenks squeaked. "Me too. Me too."

"I didn't want to speak for you, Jenks," I said. "It might be cold."

Takata chuckled. "With all that body heat and under those lights? No way."

"Then it's settled," I said, terribly pleased. "I'm assuming we get special passes?"

"Yes." Takata twisted to reach under the folder that held his band's pictures. "These will get you past Clifford. From there it shouldn't be a problem."

"Super," I said, delighted as I dug in my bag for one of my cards. "Here's my card in case you have to get in touch with me between then and now."

Things were starting to happen fast, and I took the wad of thick cardboard he gave me in return for my black business card. He smiled as he looked at it, and tucked it away in a front shirt pocket. Turning with that same soft look, he tapped a thick knuckle on the glass between the driver and us. I clutched my bag to me when we swerved to the shoulder.

"Thank you, Rachel," he said as the car stopped right there on the freeway. "I'll see you on the twenty-second about noon at the Coliseum so you can go over our security with my staff."

"Sounds good," I stammered as Jenks swore and dove for my bag when the door opened. Cold air blew in, and I squinted in the afternoon glare. Behind us was my car. *He was going to leave me right here?*

"Rachel? I mean it. Thank you." Takata extended his hand. I took, giving it a firm shake. His grip was tight, feeling thin and bony in mine. Professional. "I really appreciate it," he said as he released my hand. "You did good by quitting the I.S. You look great."

I couldn't help but smile. "Thank you," I said, letting the driver help me out of the limo. The vamp driving my car slipped past me and vanished into the darkest corner of the limo as I tightened the tie of my coat and draped my scarf about my neck again. Takata waved his good-bye as the driver shut the door. The small, tidy man nodded to me before turning around. I stood with my feet in the snow as the limo eased into the fast traffic and disappeared.

Bag in hand, I timed the traffic and slipped into my car. The heater was on full, and I breathed the scent of the vamp who had been driving it, pulling it deep into me.

My head hummed with the music Takata had shared with me. I was going to be working security at his solstice concert. It didn't get any better than that.

Six

I had gotten myself turned around and back over the Ohio River and into the Hollows, and still Jenks hadn't said anything. The starstruck pixy had parked himself on his usual spot atop the rearview mirror, watching the encroaching snow clouds turn the bright afternoon dark and depressive. I didn't think it was the cold that had turned his wings blue, as I had the heater cranked. It was embarrassment.

"Jenks?" I questioned, and his wings blurred to nothing.

"Don't say anything," he muttered, barely audible.

"Jenks, it wasn't that bad."

He turned, a look of self-disgust on him. "I forgot my name, Rache."

I couldn't help my smile. "I won't tell anyone."

The pink returned to his wings. "Really?" he asked, and I nodded. It didn't take a genius to realize it was important to the ego-driven pixy to be self-assured and in control. I was sure that's where his bad mouth and short temper came from.

"Don't tell Ivy," I said, "but the first time I met him, I fawned all over him. He could have taken advantage of me; used me like a tissue and thrown me away. He didn't. He made me feel interesting and important, even though I was working peon runs at the I.S. at the time. He's cool, you know? A real person. I bet he didn't think twice about you forgetting your name."

Jenks sighed, his entire body moving as he exhaled. "You missed your turn."

I shook my head, braking at a red light behind an obnoxious SUV I couldn't see around. The salt-stained bumper sticker read,

SOME OF MY BEST FRIENDS ARE HUMANS. YUM, and I smiled. Only in the Hollows. "I want to see if Nick is awake yet, as long as we're out," I explained. My eyes went to Jenks. "You'll be all right for a little longer?"

"Yeah," he said. "I'm okay, but you're making a mistake."

The light changed, and I almost stalled my car. We lurched through the intersection, slipping on the slush when I gunned it. "We talked today at the zoo," I said, feeling warm inside. "I think we're going to be okay. And I want to show him the backstage passes."

His wings made an audible hum. "You sure, Rachel? I mean, that was a big scare when you pulled that ley line through him. Maybe you shouldn't push it. Give him some space."

"I've given him three months," I muttered, not caring that the guy in the car behind me thought I was flirting with him as my eyes were on the rearview mirror. "Any more space and he'd be on the moon. I'm not going to rearrange his furniture, just show him the passes."

Jenks said nothing, his silence making me nervous. My worry shifted to puzzlement when I turned into Nick's parking lot and stopped beside his beat-up blue truck. There was a suitcase in the passenger seat. It hadn't been there this morning.

Lips parted, I glanced at Jenks, and he shrugged, looking unhappy. A cold feeling slipped into me. My thoughts flitted over our conversation at the zoo. We were going to the movies tonight. *And he was packed? He was going somewhere?*

"Get in my bag," I said softly, refusing to believe the worst. This wasn't the first time I had come over to find Nick gone or leaving. He had been in and out of Cincinnati a lot the last three months, me usually being unaware of it until he returned. And now his phone was disconnected and there was a packed bag in his truck? *Had I misread him?* If tonight was supposed to be a dump date, I was going to just die.

"Rachel . . ."

"I'm opening the door," I said as I stiffly put my keys into my bag. "You want to stay here and wait and hope it doesn't get too cold?"

Jenks flitted to hover before me. He looked worried despite his hands being on his hips. "Let me out as soon as we're inside," he demanded.

My throat tightened as I nodded, and he dropped down with a reluctant slowness. I carefully snugged the ties shut on my bag and got out, but a swelling feeling of hurt made me slam the door, and my little red car shook. Glancing into the bed of the truck, I realized it was dry and empty of snow. It seemed likely that Nick hadn't been in Cincinnati the last few days, either. No wonder I hadn't seen him last week.

Thoughts spinning, I paced up the slippery walk to the common door, yanking it open and taking the stairs, to leave successively smaller chunks of snow on the gray carpet. I remembered to let Jenks out at the top of the third-floor landing, and he hovered silently as he took in my anger.

"We were going out tonight," I said as I pulled my gloves off and jammed them in a pocket. "It's been staring at me in the face for weeks, Jenks. The hurried phone calls, the trips out of town without telling me, the lack of any intimate contact for God knows how long."

"Ten weeks," Jenks said, easily keeping up with me.

"Oh, really," I said bitterly, "thank you *so* much for that update."

"Easy, Rache," he said, spilling a trace of pixy dust in his wake from worry. "It might not be what you think."

I'd been dumped before. I wasn't stupid. But it hurt. Damn it, it still hurt.

There was nowhere for Jenks to land in the barren hallway, and he reluctantly lighted on my shoulder. Jaw clenched so hard it hurt, I made a fist to hammer on Nick's door. He had to be home—he didn't go anywhere without his truck—but before I could, the door swung open.

My arm dropped and I stared at Nick, my surprise mirrored on his long face. His coat was unzipped and a homemade hat of soft blue yarn was pulled tight to his ears. He took it off as I watched, shifting it and the keys in his grip to his other hand, which held a slick-looking briefcase at odds with his otherwise ragtag attire. His hair was tousled, and he smoothed it with a deft hand while he regained his composure. There was snow on his boots. *Unlike his truck.*

Keys jingling, he set the briefcase down. He took a breath, then let it slowly out. The guilt in his eyes told me I was right. "Hi, Ray-ray."

"Hi, Nick," I said, hitting the *k* with an excessive force. "I guess our date is off."

Jenks buzzed a greeting, and I hated the apologetic look he gave Nick. Four inches or six-foot-four, they were all in the same club. Nick didn't move to invite me in.

"Was tonight a dump dinner?" I asked abruptly, just wanting to be done with it.

His eyes widened. "No!" he protested, but his gaze flicked to the briefcase.

"Is it someone else, Nick? 'Cause I'm a big girl. I can take it."

"No," he repeated, his voice softer. He shifted, looking frustrated. He reached out, stopping just shy of my shoulder. His hand fell. "No."

I wanted to believe him. I really did. "Then what?" I demanded. *Why didn't he invite me in? Why did we have to do this in the freaking hallway?*

"Ray-ray," he whispered, his brow furrowed. "It's not you."

My eyes closed as I gathered my strength. *How many times had I heard that?*

His foot shoved the expensive briefcase into the hall, and my eyes flew open at the scraping sound. I stepped aside as he came out, shutting the door behind him. "It's not you," he said, his voice suddenly hard. "And it wasn't a dump dinner. I don't want to call it quits between us. But something came up, and frankly it's none of your business."

Surprised, my lips parted. Jenks's words flashed through me. "You're still afraid of me," I said, pissed that he didn't trust me to not pull a line through him again.

"I am not," he offered angrily. Motions stiff, he locked his door from the outside, turning to hold the key up between us. "Here," he said belligerently. "Take my key. I'll be out of town for a while. I was going to give it to you tonight, but since you're here, it will save me the trouble. I've stopped my mail, and the rent is paid up through August."

"August!" I stammered, suddenly afraid.

He glanced at Jenks. "Jenks, can Jax come over and watch my plants for me until I get back? He did a good job last time. It might only be a week, but the heat and electricity are on automatic draw in case it's longer."

"Nick . . ." I protested, my voice sounding small. *How had this turned around so fast?*

"Sure," Jenks said meekly. "You know, I think I'll go wait downstairs."

"No, I'm done." Nick picked up the briefcase. "I'm going to be busy tonight, but I'll swing by later to pick him up before I leave town."

"Nick, wait!" I said. My stomach clenched and I felt light-headed. I should've kept my mouth shut. I should've ignored the packed bag and played the stupid girlfriend. I should've gone to dinner and ordered lobster. My first real boyfriend in five years, and finally when things were starting to get back to normal, here I was, scaring him off. Just like all the others.

Jenks made an embarrassed sound. "Uh, I'll be by the front door," he said, vanishing down the stairwell to leave a trail of glowing pixy dust all the way to the next landing.

Long face tight in unhappiness, Nick pushed the key into my hand. His fingers were cold. "I can't—" He took a breath, meeting and holding my eyes. I waited, frightened at what he was going to say. Suddenly, I didn't want to hear it.

"Rachel, I was going to tell you this over dinner, but . . . I tried. I really did. I just can't do this right now," he said softly. "I'm not leaving you," he rushed to add before I could open my mouth. "I love you, and I want to be with you. Maybe for the rest of my life. I don't know. But every time you tap a line, I feel it, and it's as if I'm back in that FIB cruiser having an epileptic seizure from the line you pulled through me. I can't breathe. I can't think. I can't do anything. When I'm farther away, it's easier. I need to be away for a while. I didn't tell you because I didn't want you to feel bad."

Face cold, I could say nothing. He never told me I had made him seize. God help me, I hadn't known. Jenks had been with him. Why hadn't he told me?

"I have to catch my breath," he whispered, giving my hands a squeeze. "To go a few days without remembering that."

"I'll stop," I said, panicking. "I won't tap a line again. Nick, you don't have to leave!"

"Yes, I do." Dropping my hands, he touched my jawline. His smile was pained. "I want you to pull on a line. I want you to practice. Ley line magic is going to save your life someday, and I want you to become the best damned ley line witch Cincinnati has." He took a breath. "But I have to put some distance between us. Just for a while. And I have some business out of state. It has nothing to do with you. I'll be back."

But he had said August. "You're not coming back," I said, my throat closing. "You'll come for your books, and then you'll be gone."

"Rachel—"

"No." I turned away. The key was cold in my hand, cutting

into my palm. *Breathe,* I reminded myself. "Just go. I'll bring Jax over tomorrow. Just go."

I shut my eyes when he put a hand on my shoulder, but I wouldn't turn. They flashed open when he leaned closer and the scent of musty books and new electronics filled me. "Thank you, Rachel," he whispered, and there was the lightest touch of lips on mine. "I'm not leaving you. I'll be back."

I held my breath and stared at the ugly gray carpet. *I wouldn't cry, damn it. I wouldn't.*

I heard him hesitate, then the soft thumps of his boots on the stairs. My head started to hurt as the muted rumble of his truck vibrated the window at the end of the hall. I waited until I couldn't hear it anymore before I turned to follow him out, my steps slow and unseeing.

I'd done it again.

Seven

I pulled my car carefully into the tiny garage, turning off the lights and then the engine. Depressed, I stared at the spackled wall two feet in front of the grille. Silence soaked in, broken by the ticking of the engine cooling off. Ivy's bike rested quietly against the side wall, covered in a canvas tarp and stored for the winter. It was going to be dark soon. I knew I should get Jenks inside, but it was hard to find the will to unbuckle my belt and get out of the car.

Jenks dropped to the steering wheel with an attention-getting hum. My hands fell into my lap, shoulders slumping. "Well, at least you know where you stand now," he offered.

My frustration flared, then died, overwhelmed by a wave of apathy. "He said he's coming back," I said glumly, needing to believe the lie until I hardened myself to the truth.

Jenks wrapped his arms about himself, dragonfly wings still. "Rache," he cajoled. "I like Nick, but you're going to get two calls. One where he says he misses you and is feeling better, and the last when he says he's sorry and asks you to give his key to his landlord for him."

I looked at the wall. "Just let me be stupid and believe him for a while, okay?"

The pixy made a sound of wry agreement. He looked positively chilled, his wings almost black as he hunched, shivering. I'd pushed him past his limits by detouring to Nick's. I was definitely going to make cookies tonight. He shouldn't go to sleep cold like that. He might not wake up until spring.

"Ready?" I asked as I opened my bag, and he awkwardly

jumped down into it instead of flying. Worried, I debated if I should tuck my bag inside my coat. I settled on putting it in the department store bag and rolling the edges down as far as I could.

Only now did I open the door, being careful not to hit the edge of the garage. Bag in hand, I made my way on the shoveled path to the front door. A sleek black Corvette was parked at the curb, looking out of place and unsafe in the snowy streets. I recognized it as Kisten's, and my face tightened. I'd been seeing too much of him lately for my liking.

The wind bit at my exposed skin, and I glanced up at the steeple, sharp against the graying clouds. Mincing on the ice, I passed Kisten's mobile icon of masculinity and rose up the stone steps to the thick wooden double doors. There was no conventional lock, though there was an oak crossbar inside which I set every sunrise before I went to bed. Bending awkwardly, I scooped out a cup of pelletized de-icer from the open bag sitting beside the door and sprinkled it on the steps before the afternoon's snowmelt had a chance to freeze.

I pushed open the door, my hair drifting in the warm draft that billowed out. Soft jazz came with it, and I slipped inside to latch it softly behind me. I didn't particularly want to see Kisten—no matter how nice he was on the eyes—though I thought I should probably thank him for recommending me to Takata.

It was dark in the small foyer, the glow of dusk slipping in from the sanctuary beyond doing little to light it. The air smelled like coffee and growing things, sort of a mix between a plant nursery and coffeehouse. Nice. Ceri's things went atop the small antique table Ivy had swiped from her folks, and I opened up my bag, peering down to see Jenks looking up.

"Thank God," he muttered as he slowly lifted into the air. Then he hesitated, head cocked as he listened. "Where is everyone?"

I shrugged out of my coat and hung it up on a peg. "Maybe Ivy yelled at your kids again and they're hiding. Are you complaining?"

He shook his head. He was right, though. It was really quiet. Too quiet. Usually there were head-splitting shrills of pixy children playing tag, an occasional crash from a hanging utensil hitting the kitchen floor, or the snarls of Ivy chasing them out of the living room. The only peace we got were the four hours they slept at noon, and four hours again after midnight.

The warmth of the church was soaking into Jenks, and already his wings were translucent and moving well. I decided to leave Ceri's things where they were until I could get them across the street to her, and after stomping the snow off my boots beside the melting puddles Kisten had left, I followed Jenks out of the dark foyer and into the quiet sanctuary.

My shoulders eased as I took in the subdued lighting coming in through the knee-to-ceiling-high stained-glass windows. Ivy's stately baby grand took up one corner in the front, dusted and cared for but played only when I was out. My plant-strewn, rolltop desk was kitty-corner to it, way up in the front on the ankle-high stage where the altar once sat. The huge image of a cross still shadowed the wall above it, soothing and protective. The pews had been removed long before I moved in, leaving an echoing wooden and glass space redolent of peace, solitude, grace, and security. I was safe here.

Jenks stiffened, sending my instincts flaming.

"Now!" shrilled a piercing voice.

Jenks shot straight up, leaving a cloud of pixy dust hanging where he had been like an octopus inking. Heart pounding, I hit the hardwood floor, rolling.

Sharp patters of impacts hit the planks beside me. Fear kept me spinning until I found a corner. Heady, the strength of the graveyard's ley line surged through me as I tapped it.

"Rachel! It's my kids!" Jenks cried as a hail of tiny snowballs struck me.

Gagging, I choked on the word to invoke my circle, yanking back the cresting power. It crashed into me, and I groaned as twofold the ley line energy suddenly took up the same space. Staggering, I fell to a knee and struggled to breathe until the excess found its way back to the line. Oh God. It felt like I was on fire. I should have just made the circle.

"What in Tink's knickers do you think you're doing!" Jenks yelled, hovering over me as I tried to focus on the floor. "You should know better than to jump a runner like that! She's a professional! You're going to end up dead! And I'm going to let you rot where you fall. We're guests here! Get to the desk. All of you! Jax, I am *really* disappointed."

I took a breath. Damn. That really hurt. *Mental note: never stop a ley line spell midcast.*

"Matalina!" Jenks shouted. "Do you know what our kids are doing?"

I licked my lips. "It's okay," I said, looking up to find absolutely no one in the sanctuary. Even Jenks was gone. "I love my life," I muttered, and I worked myself carefully up from the floor in stages. The flaming tingle in my skin had subsided, and pulse hammering, I let go of the line completely, feeling the remaining energy flow out of my chi to leave me shaking.

With the sound of an angry bee, Jenks flew in from the back rooms. "Rachel," he said as he came to a halt before me. "I'm sorry. They found the snow that Kist brought in on his shoes, and he told them about snowball fights when he was a kid. Oh, look. They got you all wet."

Matalina, Jenks's wife, zipped into the sanctuary in a billow of gray and blue silk. Giving me an apologetic wince, she slipped under the crack in my rolltop desk. My head started to hurt and my eyes watered. Her scolding was so high-pitched that I couldn't hear it.

Tired, I straightened to my full height and tugged my sweater straight. Small spots of water showed where I'd been hit. If they had been fairy assassins with spells instead of pixies with snowballs, I'd be dead. My heart slowed, and I snatched up my bag from the floor. "It's okay," I said, embarrassed and wanting Jenks to shut up. "No biggie. Kids will be kids."

Jenks hovered in apparent indecision. "Yeah, but they're my kids, and we're guests. They'll be apologizing to you, among a few other things."

Gesturing it was okay, I stumbled down the dark hallway, following the smell of coffee. *At least no one had seen me rolling on the floor evading pixy snowballs,* I thought. But such commotions had become commonplace since the first hard frost and Jenks's family moved in. There was no way I could pretend I wasn't here now, though. Besides, they had probably smelled the flush of fresh air when I opened the door.

I passed the opposing his-and-her bathrooms that had been converted into a conventional bathroom and a combination bathroom/laundry room. The latter was mine. My room was on the right side of the hallway, Ivy's was directly across from it. The kitchen was next, and I made a left turn into it, hoping to grab some coffee and go hide in my room to avoid Kisten entirely.

I had made the mistake of kissing him in an elevator, and he never missed an opportunity to remind me of it. Thinking at the time I wouldn't live to see the sunrise, I had let my guard down and enjoyed myself, all but giving in to the lure of vampiric passion. Even worse? Kisten knew he had tipped me over the edge and that I had been a breath away from saying yes.

Exhausted, I elbowed the light switch and dropped my shoulder bag on the counter. Fluorescent lights flickered on, sending Mr. Fish into a frenzy of motion. Soft jazz and the rise and fall of conversation filtered in from the unseen living room. Kisten's leather coat was draped over Ivy's chair before her computer. There was a half-full pot of coffee, and after a moment's thought, I poured it into my gigantic mug. Trying to be quiet, I started a new batch. I didn't mean to eavesdrop, but Kisten's voice was as smooth and warm as a bubble bath.

"Ivy, love," he pleaded as I got the grounds out of the fridge. "It's only one night. An hour, maybe. In and out."

"No."

Ivy's voice was cold, the warning obvious. Kisten was pushing her past where I would, but they'd grown up together, the children of wealthy parents who expected them to join their families and have little vamp brats to continue Piscary's living-vampire line before they died and became true undead. It wouldn't happen—the marriage, not the dead part. They had already tried the cohabitation route, and while neither would say what happened, their relationship had cooled until all that was left was more of a warped sibling fondness.

"You don't have to do anything," Kisten persuaded, laying his fake British accent on heavy. "Just be there. I'll say everything."

"No."

Someone snapped off the music, and I silently pulled the silverware drawer open for the coffee scoop. Three pixy girls darted out, shrieking. I bit back my yelp, heart pounding as they vanished down the dark hallway. Motions quick from adrenaline, I poked around to find the scoop missing. I finally spotted it in the sink. Kisten must have made the coffee. If it had been Ivy, her asinine need for order would have had it washed, dried, and put away.

"Why not?" Kisten's voice had taken a petulant tone. "He's not asking for much."

Tight and controlled, Ivy's voice was seething. "I don't want that bastard in my head at all. Why would I let him see through my eyes? Feel my thoughts?"

The carafe hung from my fingers as I stood over the sink. I wished I wasn't hearing this.

"But he loves you," Kisten whispered, sounding hurt and jealous. "You're his scion."

"He doesn't love me. He loves me fighting him." It was bitter, and I could almost see her perfect, slightly Oriental features tighten in anger.

"Ivy," Kisten cajoled. "It feels good, intoxicating. The power he shares with you—"

"It's a lie!" she shouted, and I started. "You want the prestige? The power? You want to keep running Piscary's interests? Pretend you're still his scion? I don't care! But I'm not letting him in my head even to cover for you!"

I noisily ran the water into the carafe to remind them I was listening. I didn't want to hear more, and I wished they'd stop.

Kisten's sigh was long and heavy. "It doesn't work that way. If he really wants in, you won't be able to stop him, Ivy love."

"Shut. Up."

The words were so full of bound anger that I stifled a shudder. The carafe overflowed, and I jumped as water hit my hand. Grimacing, I shut the tap off and tipped the excess out.

There was a creak of wood from the living room. My stomach clenched. Someone had just pinned someone else to a chair. "Go ahead," Kisten murmured over the tinkling of the water pouring into the coffeemaker. "Sink those teeth. You know you want to. Just like old times. Piscary feels everything you do, whether you want him to or not. Why do you think you haven't been able to abstain from blood lately? Three years of denial, and now you can't go three days? Give it up, Ivy. He'd love to feel us enjoying ourselves again. And maybe your roommate might finally understand. She almost said yes," he goaded. "Not to you. To me."

I stiffened. That had been directed at me. I wasn't in the room, but I might as well have been.

There was another creak of wood. "Touch her blood and I'll kill you, Kist. I swear it."

I looked around the kitchen for a way to escape but it was too late as Ivy halted in the archway, with a scuff of boots. She hesitated, looking unusually ruffled as she gauged my unease in an instant with her uncanny ability to read body language. It made keeping secrets around her chancy at best. Anger at Kist had pinched her brow, and the aggressive frustration didn't bode well, even if it wasn't aimed at me. Her pale skin glowed a faint pink as she tried to calm herself, bringing the faint whisper of scar tissue on her neck into stark relief. She had tried surgery to minimize Piscary's physical sign of his claim on her, but it showed when she was upset. And she wouldn't accept any of my complexion charms. I had yet to figure that one out.

Seeing me unmoving by the sink, her brown eyes flicked from

my steaming mug of coffee to the empty pot. I shrugged and flicked the switch to get it brewing. What could I say?

Ivy pushed herself into motion, setting an empty mug on the counter. She smoothed her severely straight black hair, bringing herself back to at least looking calm and collected. "You're upset," she said, her anger at Kisten making her voice rough. "What's up?"

I pulled my backstage passes out and clipped them to the fridge with a tomato magnet. My thought went to Nick, then to rolling on the floor evading pixy snowballs. And mustn't forget the joy of hearing her threaten Kisten over my blood that she wasn't ever going to taste. *Golly, so much to choose from.* "Nothing," I said softly.

Long and sleek in her blue jeans and shirt, she crossed her arms and leaned against the counter beside the coffeemaker to wait for it to finish. Her thin lips pressed together and she breathed deeply. "You've been crying. What is it?"

Surprise stopped me cold. *She knew I had been crying? Damn.* It had only been three tears. At the stoplight. And I had wiped them away before they even dribbled out. I glanced at the empty hallway, not wanting Kisten to know. "I'll tell you later, okay?"

Ivy followed my gaze to the archway. Puzzlement crinkled the skin about her brown eyes. Then understanding crashed over her; she knew I'd been dumped. She blinked, and I watched her, relieved when the first flicker of blood lust at my new, available status quickly died.

Living vampires didn't need blood to remain sane, as undead vampires did. They still craved it, though, choosing whom they took it from with care, usually following their sexual preferences on the happy chance that sex might be included in the mix. But the taking of blood could range in importance from confirming a deep platonic friendship to the shallowness of a one-night stand. Like most living vamps, Ivy said she didn't equate blood with sex, but I did. The sensations a vampire could pull from me were too close to sexual ecstasy to think otherwise.

After twice being slammed into the wall by ley line energy, Ivy got the message that though I was her friend, I would never, *ever,* say yes to her. It had been easier after she resumed practicing, too, with her slaking her needs somewhere else and coming home satiated, relaxed, and quietly self-loathing for having given in again.

Over the summer she seemed to have turned her energies from trying to convince me that her biting me wasn't sex to ensuring that no other vampire would hit on me. If she couldn't have my blood, then no one could, and she had devoted herself in a disturbing, yet flattering, drive to keep other vampires from taking advantage of my demon scar and luring me into becoming their shadow. Living with her gave me protection from them—protection I wasn't ashamed to accept—and in return I was her unconditional friend. And whereas that might seem one-sided, it wasn't.

Ivy was a high-maintenance friend, jealous of anyone who attracted my attention, though she hid it well. She barely tolerated Nick. Kisten, though, seemed exempt, which made me oh-so-warm and fuzzy inside. And as I took up my coffee, I found myself hoping she would go out tonight and satisfy that damned blood lust of hers so she wouldn't be looking at me like a hungry panther the rest of the week.

Feeling the tension shift from anger to speculation, I looked at the unfinished pot brewing, thinking only of escaping the room. "You want mine?" I said. "I haven't drunk any."

My head turned at Kisten's masculine chuckle. He had appeared without warning in the doorway. "I haven't drunk any either," he said suggestively. "I'd like some if you're offering."

A flush of memory took me, of Kisten and me in that elevator: my fingers playing with the silky strands of his blond-dyed hair at the nape of his neck, the day-old stubble he cultivated to give his delicate features a rugged cast harsh against my skin, his lips both soft and aggressive as he tasted the salt on me, the feel of his hands at the small of my back pressing me into him. *Damn.*

I pulled my eyes from him, forcing my hand down from my neck where I had been unconsciously touching my demon scar to feel it tingle, stimulated by the vamp pheromones he was unconsciously putting out. *Double damn.*

Pleased with himself, he sat in Ivy's chair, clearly guessing where my thoughts were. But looking at his well-put-together body, it was hard to think of anything else.

Kisten was a living vamp, too, his bloodline going back as far as Ivy's. He had once been Piscary's scion, and the glow of sharing blood with the undead vampire showed in him still. Though he often acted the playboy by dressing in biker leather and affecting a bad British accent, he used it to hide his business savvy. He was smart. And fast. And while not as powerful as an undead vampire, he was stronger than his compact build and slim waistline suggested.

Today he was dressed conservatively in a silk shirt tucked into dark slacks, clearly trying to be the professional as he took on more of Piscary's business interests now that the vampire languished in prison. The only hints to Kisten's bad-boy side were the gunmetal gray chain he wore about his neck—twin to the pair Ivy wore about her ankle—and the two diamond studs he had in each ear. At least there were supposed to be two in each ear. Someone had torn one out to leave a nasty tear.

Kisten lounged in Ivy's chair with his immaculate shoes provocatively spread, leaning back as he took in the moods drifting about the room. I found my hand creeping up to my neck again, and I scowled. He was trying to bespell me, get in my head and shift my thoughts and decisions. It wouldn't work. Only the undead could bespell the unwilling, and he couldn't lean on Piscary's strength any longer to give him the increased abilities of an undead vampire.

Ivy pulled the brewed coffee out from under the funnel. "Leave Rachel alone," she said, clearly the dominant of the two. "Nick just dumped her."

My breath caught and I stared at her, aghast. I hadn't wanted him to know!

"Well . . ." Kisten murmured, leaning forward to put his elbows on his knees. "He was no good for you anyway, love."

Bothered, I put the island counter between us. "It's Rachel. Not love."

"Rachel," he said softly, and my heart pounded at the compulsion he put in it. I glanced out the window to the snowy gray garden and the tombstones beyond. What the Turn was I doing standing in my kitchen with two hungry vamps when the sun was going down? Didn't they have somewhere to go? People to bite, that weren't me?

"He didn't dump me," I said as I grabbed the fish food and fed Mr. Fish. I could see Kisten's reflection watching me in the dark window. "He's out of town for a few days. Gave me his key to check on everything and pick up his mail."

"Oh." Kisten glanced sidelong at Ivy. "A long excursion?"

Flustered, I set the fish food down and turned. "He said he was coming back," I protested, my face tightening as I heard the ugly truth behind my words. Why would Nick say he'd be coming back unless it had occurred to him *not* to?

As the two vamps exchanged more silent looks, I pulled a mundane cookbook out from my spell library and set it thumping onto the island counter. I'd promised Jenks the oven tonight. "Don't even try to pick me up on the rebound, Kisten," I warned.

"I wouldn't dream of it." The slow, soft tone of his voice said otherwise.

" 'Cause you're not capable of being half the man Nick is," I stupidly said.

"High standards, eh?" Kisten mocked.

Ivy perched herself on the counter by my ten-gallon dissolution vat of saltwater, wrapping her arms about her knees yet still managing to look predatory while she sipped her coffee and watched Kisten play with my emotions.

Kisten glanced at her as if for permission, and I frowned. Then he stood in a sliding sound of fabric, coming to lean on the island counter across from me. His necklace swung, pulling my attention to his neck, marked with soft, almost unseen, scars. "I like action movies," he said, and my breath came fast. I could smell the lingering aroma of leather on him under the dry scent of silk.

"So?" I said belligerently, peeved that Ivy had probably told him about Nick's and my weekend-long stints in front of the Adrenaline channel

"So, I can make you laugh."

I flipped to the most tattered, stain-splattered recipe in the book I'd swiped from my mom, knowing it was for sugar cookies. "So does Bozo the Clown, but I wouldn't date him."

Ivy licked her finger and made a tally mark in the air.

Kisten smiled to show the barest hint of fang, leaning back and clearly feeling the hit. "Let me take you out," he said. "A platonic first date to prove Nick wasn't anything special."

"Oh, please," I simpered, not believing he was stooping this low.

Grinning, Kisten turned himself into a spoiled rich boy. "If you enjoy yourself, then you admit to me that Nick was nothing special."

I crouched to get the flour. "No," I said when I rose to set it thumping on top of the counter.

A hurt look creased his stubbled face, put-on but still effective. "Why not?"

I glanced behind me at Ivy, silently watching. "You have money," I said. "Anyone can show a girl a good time with enough money."

Ivy made another tally mark. "That's two," she said, and he frowned.

"Nick was a cheap ass, huh," Kisten offered, trying to hide his ire.

"Watch your mouth," I shot back.

"Yes, Ms. Morgan."

The sultry submissiveness in his voice yanked my thoughts back to the elevator. Ivy once told me Kisten got off on playing the submissive. What I had found out was that a submissive vampire was still more aggressive than most people could handle. But I wasn't most people. I was a witch.

I put my eyes on his, seeing that they were a nice steady blue. Unlike Ivy, Kisten freely indulged his blood lust until it wasn't the overriding factor governing his life. "One hundred seventy-five dollars?" he offered, and I bent to get the sugar.

The man thought a cheap date was almost two hundred dollars?

"One hundred?" he said, and I looked at him, reading his genuine surprise.

"Our average date was sixty," I said.

"Damn!" he swore, then hesitated. "I can say damn, can't I?"

"Hell, yes."

From her perch on the counter, Ivy snickered. Kisten's brow pinched in what looked like real worry. "Okay," he said, deep in thought. "A sixty-dollar date."

I gave him a telling look. "I haven't said yes yet."

He inhaled long and slow, tasting my mood on the air. "You haven't said no, either."

"No."

He slumped dramatically, pulling a smile from me despite myself. "I won't bite you," he protested, his blue eyes roguishly innocent.

From under the island counter I pulled out my largest copper spell pot to use as a mixing bowl. It wasn't reliable any longer for spelling, as it had a dent from hitting Ivy's head. The palm-sized paint ball gun I stored in it made a comforting sound against the metal as I took it out to put back under the counter at ankle height. "And I should believe you because . . ."

Kisten's eyes flicked to Ivy. "She'll kill me twice if I do."

I went to get the eggs, milk, and butter out of the fridge, hoping neither of them sensed my pulse quickening. But I knew my temptation didn't stem from the subliminal pheromones they were unconsciously emitting. I missed feeling desired, needed. And Kisten had a Ph.D. in wooing women, even if his motives were one-sided and false. From the looks of it, he indulged in casual blood taking like some men indulged in casual sex. And I didn't want to become one of his shadows that he strung along, caught by the binding saliva in his bite to crave his touch, to feel his teeth sinking into me to fill me with euphoria. *Crap, I was doing it again.*

"Why should I?" I said, feeling myself warm. "I don't even like you."

Kisten leaned over the counter as I returned. The faultless blue of his eyes caught and held mine. It was obvious by his rakish grin that he knew I was weakening. "All the better reason to go out with me," he said. "If I can show you a good time for a lousy sixty bucks, think what someone you like could do. All I need is one promise."

The egg was cold in my hands, and I set it down. "What?" I asked, and Ivy stirred.

His smile widened. "No shirking."

"Beg pardon?"

He opened the tub of butter and dipped his finger into it, licking it slowly clean. "I can't make you feel attractive if you stiffen up every time I touch you."

"I didn't before," I said, my thoughts returning to the elevator. God help me, I had almost done him right there against the wall.

"This is different," he said. "It's a date, and I would give my eyeteeth to know why women expect men to behave differently on a date than any other time."

"Because you do," I said.

He gave a raised-eyebrow look to Ivy. Straightening, he reached across the counter to cup my jaw. I jerked back, brow furrowed.

"Nope," he said as he drew away. "I won't ruin my reputation by taking you out on a sixty-dollar date for nothing. If I can't touch you, it's a no-go."

I stared at him, feeling my heart pound. "Good."

Shocked, Kisten blinked. "Good?" he questioned as Ivy smirked.

"Yeah," I said, pulling the butter to me and scooping out about a half cup with a wooden spoon. "I didn't want to go out with you anyway. You're too full of yourself. Think you can manipulate anyone into doing anything. Your ego-testicle attitude makes me sick."

Ivy laughed as she unfolded herself and jumped lightly to the floor without a sound. "I told you," she said. "Pay up."

Shoulders shifting in a sigh, he twisted to reach his wallet in a back pocket, pulling out a fifty and shoving it into her hand. She raised a thin eyebrow and made another tally mark in the air. An unusual smile was on her as she stretched to drop it into the cookie jar atop the fridge.

"Typical," Kisten said, his eyes dramatically sad. "Try to do something nice for a person, cheer her up, and what do I get? Abused and robbed."

Ivy took three long steps to come up behind him. Curling an arm across his chest, she leaned close and whispered in his torn ear, "Poor baby." They looked good together, her silky sultriness and his confident masculinity.

He didn't react at all as her fingers slipped between the buttons of his shirt. "You would have enjoyed yourself," he said to me.

Feeling as if I'd passed some test, I pushed the butter off the spoon and licked my finger clean. "How would you know?"

"Because you enjoyed yourself just now," he answered. "You forgot all about that shallow, self-centered human who doesn't know a good thing when she bites him on his—" He looked at Ivy. "Where did you say she bit him, Ivy love?"

"His wrist." Ivy straightened and turned her back on me to retrieve her coffee.

"Who doesn't know a good thing when she bites him on his . . . wrist," Kisten finished.

My face was burning. "That's the last time I tell you anything!" I exclaimed to Ivy. And it wasn't as if I had drawn blood. Good God!

"Admit it," Kisten said. "You enjoyed talking with me, pitting your will against mine. It would have been fun," he said as he looked at me through his bangs. "You look like you could use some fun. Cooped up in this church for God knows how long. When was the last time you got dressed up? Felt pretty? Felt desirable?"

I stood very still, feeling my breath move in and out of me, balanced. My thoughts went to Nick leaving to go out of town without telling me, our cuddling and closeness that had ended with a shocking abruptness. It had been so long. I missed his touch making me feel wanted, stirring my passions and bringing me alive. I wanted that feeling back—even if it was a lie. Just for a night, so I wouldn't forget how it felt until I found it again.

"No biting," I said, thinking I was making a mistake.

Ivy jerked her head up, her face expressionless.

Kisten didn't seem surprised. A heady understanding was in his gaze. "No shirking," he said softly, his eyes alive and glinting. I was like glass to him.

"Sixty-dollar maximum," I countered.

Kisten stood, taking his coat from the back of the chair. "I'll pick you up at one A.M., night after tomorrow. Wear something nice."

"No playing on my scar," I said breathlessly, unable to find enough air for some reason. *What in hell was I doing?*

With a predatory grace, he shrugged into his coat. He hesitated, thinking. "Not one breath on it," he agreed. His thoughtful expression shifted to sly anticipation as he stood in the archway to the hall and held out his hand to Ivy.

Motions stiff, Ivy pulled the fifty back out of the cookie jar and gave it to him. He stood and waited, and she took another and slapped it into his hand.

"Thanks, Ivy love," he said. "Now I have enough for my date and a haircut, too." He met my eyes, holding them until I couldn't breathe. "See you later, Rachel."

The sound of his dress shoes seemed loud in the darkening church. I heard him say something to Jenks followed by the faint boom of the front door closing.

Ivy wasn't pleased. "That was a stupid thing to do," she said.

"I know." I wouldn't look at her, mixing the sugar and butter with a rough quickness.

"Then why did you do it?"

I kept stirring. "Maybe because unlike you, I like being touched," I said wearily. "Maybe because I miss Nick. Maybe because he's been gone the last three months and I've been too stupid to notice. Back off, Ivy. I'm not your shadow."

"No," she agreed, less angry than I expected. "I'm your roommate, and Kist is more dangerous than he lets on. I've seen him do this before. He wants to hunt you. Hunt you slow."

I stilled my motions and looked at her. "Slower than you?" I questioned bitterly.

She stared at me. "I'm not hunting you," she said, sounding hurt. "You won't let me."

Letting go of the spoon, I put my hands to either side of the bowl and bowed my head over it. We were the pair. One too afraid to feel anything lest she lose control of her ironclad hold on her emotions, and the other so hungry to feel anything that she'd risk her free will for one night of fun. How I had kept from being a vampire's flunky this long was a miracle.

"He's waiting for you," I said as I heard Kisten's car revving through the insulated walls of the church. "Go satiate yourself. I don't like it when you don't."

Ivy swung into motion. Not saying a word, she stiffly walked out, boots thumping on the hardwood floor. The sound of the church's door shutting was quiet. Slowly the ticking of the clock above the sink became obvious. Taking a slow breath, I pulled my head up, wondering how in hell I had become her keeper.

Eight

The rhythmic thumps of my running feet jolting up my spine were a pleasant distraction from my thoughts of Nick. It was bright, the sun glittering off the piles of snow to make me squint through my new sunglasses. I had left my old pair in Takata's limo, and the new ones didn't fit as well. This was the second day in a row that I had gotten up at an ungodly ten in the morning to come out and run, and by the Turn, I was going to run this time. Jogging after midnight wasn't as fun—too many weirdos. Besides, I had a date tonight with Kisten.

The thought zinged through me, and my pace increased. Each puffed breath was timed with my steps to make a hypnotic tempo luring me into a runner's high. I picked up the pace even more, reveling in it. An old witch couple was ahead of me doing a fast walk/run as I passed the bear exhibit. They were watching with a hungry interest. The bears, not the witches. I think that's why management let us runners in. We gave the large predators something to watch besides kids in strollers and tired parents.

Actually, our collective group of runners had taken it upon ourselves to adopt the Indochina tiger exhibit with just that in mind. The funds for their upkeep and health care came entirely from our special-pass fees. They ate very well.

"Track!" I exclaimed breathily in time with my steps, and the two witches slid aside, making a spot for me. "Thanks," I said as I passed them, catching their heavy redwood scent in the crisp, painfully dry air.

The sound of their companionable conversation quickly retreated. I spared a confused, angry thought for Nick. I didn't need him to run; I could run by myself. He hadn't run with me much lately anyway, not since I got my car and didn't need to bum a ride from him.

Yeah, right, I thought, my jaw clenching. It wasn't the car. It was something else. Something he wouldn't tell me about. Something that "frankly wasn't my business."

"Track!" I heard faintly from someone not far behind.

It was low and controlled. Whoever it was, they were keeping up with me with no trouble. All my warning flags went up. *Let's see if you can run,* I thought, taking a deep breath.

Different muscles eased into play like gears shifting as I pushed into a faster pace, my heart pounding and the cold air slicing in and out of me. I was already going at a good clip, my natural pace somewhere between a long distance run and a sprint. It had made me a favorite in the eight hundred meter in high school and had stood me in good stead when I worked for the I.S. and needed to run down the occasional tag. Now, my calves protested at the increased speed and my lungs began to burn. As I passed the rhinos and cut a left, I vowed to get out here more; I was going soft.

No one was ahead of me. Even the keepers were absent. I listened, hearing his pace increase to match mine. I snuck a quick look back as I made a sharp left.

It was a Were, somewhat short and lanky, sleek in matching gray running pants and long-sleeve shirt. His long black hair was held back with an exercise band, and there was no strain on his placid face as he kept up with me.

Crap. My heart gave an extra hard thump. Even without the cowboy hat and wool duster, I recognized him. *Crap, crap, crap.*

My pace quickened with a surge of adrenaline. It was the same Were. Why was he following me? My thoughts drifted back further than yesterday. I'd seen him before. Lots of befores. He was at the watch counter last week when Ivy and I were picking out a new perfume, to overpower my natural scent mixing with hers. He had been putting air into his tires three weeks ago when I was pumping gas and locked myself out of my car. And three months ago I'd seen him leaning against a tree when Trent and I talked at Eden Park.

My jaw clenched. *Maybe it's time we chatted?* I thought as I ran past the cat house.

There was a drop-off ahead by the eagles. I cut a right, leaning back as I went downhill. Mr. Were followed. As I thumped along behind the eagle exhibit, I took stock of what I had. In my belt pack were my keys, my phone, a mild pain amulet already invoked, and my minisplat gun loaded with sleepy time potions. No help there; I wanted to talk to him, not knock him out.

The path opened up into a wide deserted section. No one ran down here because the hill was such a killer to get back up. Perfect. Heart pounding, I went left to take the slope instead of heading for the Vine Street entrance. A smile curved over me as his pace faltered. He hadn't expected that. Leaning into the hill, I ran up it full tilt, seeming to be in slow motion. The path was narrow and snow-covered. He followed.

Here, I thought as I reached the top. Panting, I snuck a quick look behind me and jerked off the path and into the thick shrubbery. My lungs burned as I held my breath.

He passed me with the sound of feet and heavy breathing, intent on his steps. Reaching the top, he hesitated, looking to see which way I had gone. His dark eyes were pinched and the first signs of physical distress furrowed his brow.

Taking a breath, I leapt.

He heard me, but it was too late. I landed against him as he spun, pinning him against an old oak. His breath whooshed out as his back hit, his eyes going wide and surprised. My fingers went chokingly under his chin to hold him there, and my fist hit his solar plexus.

Gasping, he bent forward. I let go, and he fell to sit at the base of the tree, holding his stomach. A thin backpack slid up almost over his head.

"Who in hell are you and why have you been tailing me the last three months!" I shouted, trusting the odd hour and the closed status of the zoo to keep our conversation private.

Head bowed over his chest, the Were put a hand in the air. It was small for a man, and thick, with short powerful-looking fingers. Sweat had turned his spandex shirt a darker gray, and he slowly moved his well-muscled legs into a less awkward position.

I took a step back, my hand on my hip, lungs heaving as I recovered from the climb. Angry, I took off my sunglasses and hung them from my waistband and waited.

"David," he rasped as he looked up at me, immediately dropping his head while he struggled to take another breath. Pain and a hint of embarrassment had laced his brown eyes. Sweat marred his rugged face, thick with a black stubble that matched his long hair. "God bless it," he said to the ground. "Why did you have to hit me? What is it with you redheads, anyway, always having to hit things?"

"Why are you following me?" I shot at him.

Head still bowed, he put up a hand again, telling me to wait. I shifted nervously as he took a clean breath, then another. His hand dropped and he looked up. "My name is David Hue," he said. "I'm an insurance adjuster. Mind if I get up? I'm getting wet."

My mouth dropped open and I took several steps back onto the path as he rose and wiped the snow from his backside. "An insurance adjuster?" I stammered. Surprise washed the remnants of adrenaline from me. I put my arms about myself and wished I had my coat as the air suddenly seemed colder now that I wasn't moving. "I paid my bill," I said, starting to get angry. "I haven't missed one payment. You'd think for six hundred dollars a month—"

"Six hundred a month!" he said, his features shocked. "Oh, honey, we have to talk."

Affronted, I backed up farther. He was in his mid-thirties, I guessed from the maturity in his jaw and the barest hint of thickening about his middle that his spandex shirt couldn't hide. His narrow shoulders were hard with muscle that his shirt couldn't hide, either. And his legs were fabulous. Some people shouldn't wear spandex. Despite being older than I liked my men, David wasn't one of them.

"Is that what this is about?" I said, both ticked and relieved. "Is this how you get your clients? Stalking them?" I frowned and turned away. "That's pathetic. Even for a Were."

"Wait up," he said, lurching out onto the path after me in a snapping of twigs. "No. Actually, I'm here about the fish."

I jerked to a stop, my feet again in the sun. My thoughts zinged back to the fish I had stolen from Mr. Ray's office last September. *Shit.*

"Um," I stammered, my knees suddenly weak from more than the run. "What fish?" Fingers fumbling, I snapped my sunglasses open. Putting them on, I started walking for the exit.

David felt his middle for damage as he followed me, meeting my fast pace with his own. "See," he said almost to himself. "This is exactly why I've been following you. Now I'll never get a straight answer, I'll never settle the claim."

My stomach hurt, and I forced myself into a faster pace. "It was a mistake," I said, my face warming. "I thought it was the Howlers' fish."

David took off his sweatband, slicked his hair back, and replaced it. "Word is that the fish has been destroyed. I find that extremely unlikely. If you could verify that, I can write my report, send a check to the party Mr. Ray stole the fish from, and you'll never see me again."

I gave him a sidelong glance, my relief that he wasn't going to serve me with a writ or something very real. I had surmised that Mr. Ray had stolen it from someone when no one came after me for it. But this was unexpected. "Someone insured their fish?" I scoffed, not believing it, then realized he was serious. "You're kidding."

The man shook his head. "I've been following you trying to decide if you have it or not."

We had reached the entrance and I stopped, not wanting him to follow me to my car. Not that he didn't already know which one it was. "Why not just ask me, Mr. Insurance Agent?"

Looking bothered, he planted his feet widely with an aggressive stance. He was my height exactly—making him somewhat short for a man—but most Weres weren't big people on the outside. "You really expect me to believe you don't know?"

I gave him a blank look. "Know what?"

Running a hand across his thick bristles, he looked at the sky. "Most people will lie like the devil when they get ahold of a wishing fish. If you have it, just tell me. I don't care. All I want is to get this claim off my desk."

My jaw dropped. "A—A wishing . . ."

He nodded. "A wishing fish, yes." His thick eyebrows rose. "You really didn't know? Do you still have it?"

I sat down on one of the cold benches. "Jenks ate it."

The Were started. "Excuse me?"

I couldn't look up. My thoughts went back to last fall and my gaze drifted past the gate to my shiny red convertible waiting for me in the parking lot. I had wished for a car. Damn, I had wished for a car and gotten it. *Jenks ate a wishing fish?*

His shadow fell over me and I looked up, squinting at David's silhouette, black against the faultless blue of noon. "My partner and his family ate it."

David stared. "You're joking."

Feeling ill, I dropped my gaze. "We didn't know. He cooked it over an open fire and his family ate it."

His small feet moved in a quick motion. Shifting, he pulled a folded piece of paper and a pen from his backpack. As I sat with my elbows on my knees and stared at nothing, David crouched beside me and scribbled, using the smooth concrete bench as a desk. "If you would sign here, Ms. Morgan," he said as he extended the pen to me.

A deep breath sifted through me. I took the pen, then the paper. His handwriting had a stiff preciseness that told me he was meticulous and well-organized. Ivy would love him. Scanning it, I realized it was a legal document, David's handwritten addition stating that I had witnessed the destruction of the fish, unaware of its abilities. Frowning, I scrawled my name and pushed it back.

His eyes were full of an amused disbelief as he took the pen from me and signed it as well. I bit back a snort when he brought out a notarizing kit from his backpack and made it legal. He didn't ask for my identification, but hell, he'd been following me for three months. "You're a notary, too?" I said, and he nodded, returning everything to his backpack and zipping it up.

"It's a necessity in my line of work." Standing, he smiled. "Thank you, Ms. Morgan."

"No sweat." My thoughts were jumbled. I couldn't decide if I was going to tell Jenks or not. My gaze returned to David as I realized he was holding out his card. I took it, wondering.

"Since I've got you here," he said, moving so I wasn't looking into the sun to see him, "if you're interested in getting a better rate on your insurance—"

I sighed and let the card fall. *What a weenie.*

He chuckled, gracefully swooping to pick it up. "I get my health and hospitalization insurance for two fifty a month through my union."

Suddenly, I was interested. "Runners are almost uninsurable."

"True." He pulled a black nylon jacket out of his backpack and put it on. "So are field insurance adjusters. But since there are so few of us compared to the pencil pushers that make up the bulk of the company, we get a good rate. Union dues are one fifty a year. It gets you a discount on your insurance needs, car rentals, and all the steak you can eat at the yearly picnic."

That was too good to believe. "Why?" I asked, taking the card back.

He lifted his shoulder in a shrug. "My partner retired last year. I need someone."

My mouth opened in understanding. *He thought I wanted to be an insurance adjuster? Oh, ple-e-e-e-ease.* "Sorry. I've already got a job," I said, snickering.

David made an exasperated noise. "No. You misunderstand. I don't *want* a partner. I've driven off all the interns they've saddled me with, and everyone else knows better than to try. I've got two months to find someone, or they're going to shave my tail. I like my job, and I'm good at it, but I don't want a partner." He hesitated, his sharp gaze scanning the area behind me with professional intentness. "I work alone. You sign the paper, you belong to the union, you get a discount on your insurance, you never see me but for the yearly picnic, where we act chummy and do the three-legged race. I help you; you help me."

I couldn't stop my eyebrows from rising, and I shifted my attention from him to the card in my grip. Four hundred dollars less a month sounded great. And I'd be willing to bet they could beat what I was paying for my car insurance, too. Tempted, I asked, "What kind of hospitalization do you have?"

His thin lips curled up in a smile to show a hint of small teeth. "Silver Cross."

My head bobbed. It was designed for Weres, but it was flexible enough to work. A broken bone is a broken bone. "So," I drawled, leaning back, "what's the catch?"

His grin widened. "Your salary is deferred to me, as I'm the one doing all the work."

Ahhhh, I thought. He would get two salaries. This was a scam if I ever heard one. Smirking, I handed him his card back. "Thanks, but no thanks."

David made a disappointed sound, backing up with his card. "You can't blame me for trying. It was my old partner's suggestion, actually. I should have known you wouldn't go for it." He hesitated. "Your backup really ate that fish?"

I nodded, going depressed thinking about it. 'Least I got a car out of it first.

"Well . . ." He set the card down beside me, snapping it into the concrete. "Give me a call if you change your mind. The extension on the card will get you past my secretary. When I'm not in the field, I'm in the office from three to midnight. I might consider taking you on as an apprentice for real. My last partner was a witch, and you look like you have some chutzpah."

"Thanks," I said snidely.

"It's not as boring as it looks. And safer than what you're doing now. Maybe after you get beat up a few more times you'll change your mind."

I wondered if this guy was for real. "I don't work for people. I work for myself."

Nodding, he casually touched his head in a loose salute before he turned and walked away. I pulled myself straight as his trim figure slipped past the gate. He got in a gray two-seater across the lot from my little red car and drove off. I cringed, recognizing it and realizing he had watched Nick and me yesterday.

My butt was frozen from sitting on the concrete when I stood. I picked up his card, tearing it in half and going to a trash can, but as I held the ripped pieces over the hole, I hesitated. Slowly, I put them in my pocket.

An insurance adjuster? a small voice in my head mocked. Grimacing, I took the pieces out and dropped them in the can. Work for someone else again? No. Never.

Nine

Peace sat warm in me as I sprinkled the yellow sugar on the iced cookie shaped like the sun. Okay, so it was a circle, but with the sparkling sugar it could be the sun. I was tired of the long nights, and the physical affirmation of the turning seasons had always filled me with a quiet strength. Especially the winter solstice.

I set the finished cookie aside on the paper towel and took another. It was quiet but for music filtering in from the living room. Takata had released "Red Ribbons" to WVMP, and the station was playing it into the ground. I didn't care. The refrain was the one I had told him fitted with the theme of the song, and it pleased me I had played some small part in its creation.

All the pixies were sleeping in my desk for at least two more hours. Ivy probably wouldn't be up stumbling about in search of coffee for even longer. She had come in before sunrise looking calm and relaxed, self-consciously seeking my approval for having slaked her blood lust on some poor sap before falling into bed like a Brimstone addict. I had the church to myself, and I was going to squeeze every drop of solitude out of it that I could.

Swaying to the heavy beat of drums in a way I wouldn't if anyone were watching, I smiled. It was nice to be alone once in a while.

Jenks had made his kids do more than apologize to me, and I had woken this afternoon to a hot pot of coffee in a sparkling clean kitchen. Everything shone, everything was polished. They had even scoured the accumulated dirt out of the circle I had etched into the linoleum around the center island counter. Not a breath of dust or cobweb marred the walls or ceiling, and as I dipped my knife into the green icing, I vowed to try to keep it this clean all the time.

Yeah, right, I thought as I layered frosting on the wreath. I'd put it off until I was back to the same level of chaos that the pixies had dragged me out of. I'd give it two weeks, tops.

Timing my movements with the beat of the music, I placed three little hot candies to look like berries. A sigh shifted my shoulders, and I set it aside and took up the candle cookie, trying to decide whether to make it purple for aged wisdom or green for change.

I was reaching for the purple when the phone rang from the living room. I froze for an instant, then set the butter tub of frosting down and hustled after it before it could wake the pixies. They were worse than having a baby in the house. Snatching the remote from the couch, I pointed it at the disc player to mute it. "Vampiric Charms," I said as I picked up the phone and hoped I wasn't breathing hard. "This is Rachel."

"How much for an escort on the twenty-third?" a young voice asked, cracking.

"That depends on the situation." I frantically looked for the calendar and a pen. They weren't where I'd left them, and I finally dug through my bag for my datebook. I thought the twenty-third was a Saturday. "Is there a death threat involved or is it general protection?"

"Death threat!" the voice exclaimed. "All I want is a good-looking girl so my friends won't think I'm a dweeb."

My eyes closed as I gathered my strength. *Too late,* I thought, clicking the pen closed. "This is an independent runner service," I said tiredly, "not a bloodhouse. And kid? Do yourself a favor and take the shy girl. She's cooler than you think, and she won't own your soul in the morning."

The phone clicked off, and I frowned. This was the third such call this month. Maybe I should take a look at the yellow pages ad that Ivy bought.

I wiped my hands free of the last sugar and shuffled in the narrow cabinet that the message machine sat on, pulling out the phone book and dropping it on the coffee table. The red message light was blinking, and I tapped it, leafing through the heavy book to Private Investigators. I froze when Nick's voice came rolling out, guilty and awkward, telling me he had stopped by about six this morning and picked up Jax and that he would call me in a few days.

"Coward," I breathed, thinking it was one more crucifix tied to the coffin. He knew no one but the pixies would be up then. I vowed to enjoy myself on my date with Kisten, whether Ivy would have to kill him afterward or not. I jabbed the button to clear his message, then went back to the phone book.

We were one of the last listings, and as I found Vampiric Charms in a friendly font, my eyebrows rose. It was a nice ad, more attractive than the full-page ads around it, with a line drawing of a mysterious-looking woman in a hat and duster ghosted into the background.

" 'Fast. Discreet. No questions asked,' " I said, reading it. " 'Sliding scale. Payment options. Insured. Week, day, and hourly rates.' " Under it all were our three names, address, and phone number. I didn't get it. There was nothing here that would lead anyone to think bloodhouse or even a dating service. Then I saw the tiny print at the bottom saying to see the secondary entries.

I flipped through the thin sheets to the first one listed, finding the same ad. Then I looked closer; not at our ad, but the ones around it. Holy crap, that woman was hardly clothed, having the perky body of an animé cartoon. My eyes flicked to the heading. "Escort Service?" I said, flushing at the steamy, suggestive ads.

My gaze jerked to our advertisement again, the words taking on an entirely new meaning. No questions asked? Week, day, or hourly rates? *Payment options?* Lips pressed together, I shut the book, leaving it out to talk to Ivy about. No wonder we were getting calls.

More than a little irate, I unmuted the stereo and headed back into the kitchen, Steppenwolf's "Magic Carpet Ride" trying its best to lighten my mood.

It was the hint of a draft, the barest scent of wet pavement, that made my step hesitate and the palm streaking out at me past the archway to the kitchen miss my jaw.

"God bless it!" I swore as I dove past it into the kitchen instead of falling back into the cramped hall. Remembering Jenks's kids, I tapped the ley line out back but did nothing else as I fell into a defensive crouch between the sink and the island counter. I almost choked when I saw whom it was standing by the archway.

"Quen?" I stammered, not getting out of my stance as the lightly wrinkled, athletic man stared at me with no expression. The head of Trent's security was dressed entirely in black, his tight-fitting body stocking looking vaguely like a uniform. "What in hell are you doing?" I said. "I ought to call the I.S., you know that? And have them haul your ass out of my kitchen for illegal entry! If Trent wants to see me, he can come down here just like anyone else. I'll tell him he can suck dishwater, but he ought to have the decency to let me do it in person!"

Quen shook his head. "I have a problem, but I don't think you can handle it."

I made an ugly face at him. "Don't test me, Quen," I all but snarled. "You'll fail."

"We'll see."

That was all the warning I got as the man pushed off the wall, headed right for me.

Gasping, I dove past him instead of backward the way I wanted. Quen lived and breathed security. Backing away would only get me caught. Heart pounding, I grabbed my dented copper spell pot with white frosting in it and swung.

Quen caught it, yanking me forward. Adrenaline hurt my head as I let it go, and he tossed it aside. It made a harsh bong and spun into the hallway.

I snatched the coffeemaker and threw it. The appliance jerked back at its cord, and the carafe fell to shatter on the floor. He dodged, his green eyes peeved when they met mine, as if wondering what in hell I was doing. But if he got a grip on me, I was a goner. I had a cupboard of charms in arm's reach, but no time to invoke even one.

He gathered himself to jump, and remembering how he had evaded Piscary with incredible leaps, I went for my dissolution vat. Teeth gritted in effort, I tipped it over.

Quen cried out in disgust as ten gallons of saltwater cascaded over the floor to mix with the coffee and glass shards. Arms pinwheeling, he slipped.

I levered myself onto the island counter, stepping on frosted cookies and knocking over vials of colored sugar. Crouched to avoid the hanging utensils, I jumped feet first as he rose.

My feet hit him squarely in the chest and we both went down.

Where was everyone? I thought as my hip took the fall and I grunted in pain. I was making enough noise to wake the undead. But as such commotion was more common than silence these days, Ivy and Jenks would probably ignore it and hope it went away.

Slipping, I skittered from Quen. Hands reaching unseeing, I scrabbled for my paint ball gun kept purposely at crawling height. I yanked it out. Nested copper pots rolled noisily.

"Enough!" I shouted, arms stiff as I sat on my butt in saltwater, aiming at him. It was loaded with water-filled splat balls for practice, but he didn't know that. "What do you want?"

Quen hesitated, water making darker smears on his black pants. His eye twitched.

Adrenaline surged. He was going to risk it.

Instinct and practice with Ivy made me squeeze the trigger as he leapt onto the table to land like a cat. I tracked him, squeezing out every last splat ball.

His expression went affronted as he pulled himself to a crouching halt, his attention jerking from me to the six new splatters on his skintight shirt. Crap. I'd missed him once. Jaw clenched, his eyes narrowed in anger. "Water?" he said. "You load your spell gun with water?"

"Ain't you just lucky for that?" I snapped. "What do you want?" He shook his head, and my breath hissed in as I felt a dropping sensation in me. He was tapping the line out back.

Panic jerked me to my feet, and I flung my hair out of my eyes. From his vantage point on the table, Quen straightened to his full height, his hands moving as he whispered Latin.

"Like hell you will!" I shouted, throwing my splat gun at him. He ducked, and I snatched up whatever I could to throw it at him, desperate to keep him from finishing the charm.

Quen dodged the butter tub of frosting. It thunked into the wall to make a green smear. Grabbing the cookie tin, I ran around the counter, swinging it like a board. He dove off the table to avoid it, cursing at me. Cookies and red-hot candies went everywhere.

I followed him, grabbing him about the knees to bring us both down in a sodden splat. He twisted in my grip until his livid green eyes met mine. Hands scrabbling, I shoved saltwater soggy cookies into his mouth so he couldn't verbally invoke a charm.

He spit them at me, his deeply tanned, pockmarked face vehement. "You little canicula—" he managed, and I jammed some more into him.

His teeth closed on my finger, and I shrieked, jerking back. "You bit me!" I shouted, incensed. My fist swung, but he rolled to his feet, crashing into the chairs.

Panting, he stood. He was soaked, covered in water and sparkles of colored sugar. Growling an unheard word, he leapt.

I lurched upright to flee. Pain lanced through my scalp as he grabbed my hair and spun me around into an embrace, my back to his chest. One arm went chokingly around my neck. The other slipped between my legs, yanking me up onto one foot.

Furious, I elbowed him in the gut with my free arm. "Get your hands . . ." I grunted, hopping backward on one foot, "off my hair!" I reached the wall, and smashed him into it. His breath exploded out as I jabbed his ribs, and his grip around my neck fell away.

I spun to stiff-arm his jaw, but he was gone. I was staring at the yellow wall. Shrieking, I went down, my legs pulled out from under me. His weight landed on me, pinning me to the wet floor with my arms over my head.

"I win," he panted as he straddled me, his green eyes from under his short hair wild.

I struggled to no effect, ticked that it was going to be something as stupid as body mass that decided this. "You forgot something, Quen," I snarled. "I have fifty-seven roommates."

His lightly wrinkled brow furrowed.

Taking a huge breath, I whistled. Quen's eyes widened. Grunting in effort, I jerked my right hand free and slammed the heel of my hand at his nose.

He jerked back out of the way and I pushed him off me, rolling. Still on my hands and knees, I flipped my wet stringy hair out of the way.

Quen had gained his feet, but he wasn't moving. He was standing stock-still, cookie-smeared palms raised above his head in a gesture of acquiescence. Jenks was hovering before him, the sword he kept to fight off encroaching fairies aimed at Quen's right eye. The pixy looked pissed, dust spilling from him to make a steady sunbeam from him to the floor.

"Breathe," Jenks threatened. "Blink. Just give me a reason, you bloody freak of nature."

I stumbled upright as Ivy dove into the room, moving faster than I would have believed possible. Robe loose and flowing, she grabbed Quen by the throat.

The lights flickered and the hanging utensils swung as she slammed him into the wall beside the doorway. "What are you doing here?" she snarled, her knuckles white with pressure. Jenks had moved with Quen, his sword still touching the man's eye.

"Wait!" I exclaimed, worried they might kill him. Not that I'd mind, but then there'd be I.S. personnel in my kitchen, and paperwork. Lots of paperwork. "Slow down," I soothed.

My eyes flicked to Ivy, still holding Quen. There was frosting on my hand, and I wiped it off on my damp jeans as I caught my breath. Saltwater marked me and I had cookie crumbs and sugar in my hair. The kitchen looked like the Pillsbury Doughboy had exploded. I squinted at the purple frosting on the ceiling. *When had that happened?*

"Ms. Morgan," Quen said, then gurgled as Ivy tightened her grip. The music from the living room softened to talk.

I felt my ribs, wincing. Angry, I paced to where he hung in Ivy's hold. "Ms. Morgan?" I shouted, six inches from his reddening face. "Ms. Morgan? I'm Ms. Morgan now? What in hell is wrong with you!" I yelled. "Coming into my house. Ruining my cookies. Do you know how long it's going to take to clean this up?"

He gurgled again, and my anger started to slow. Ivy was staring at him with a shocking intensity. The scent of his fear had tripped her past her limits. She was vamping out at noon. This wasn't good, and I took a step back, suddenly sobered. "Um, Ivy?" I said.

"I'm okay," she said huskily, her eyes saying different. "Want me to bleed him quiet?"

"No!" I exclaimed, and I felt another drop in me. Quen was tapping a line. I took an alarmed breath. Things were spiraling out of control. Someone was going to get hurt. I could set a circle, but it would be around me, not him. "Drop him!" I demanded. "Jenks, you too!" Neither of them moved. "Now!"

Shoving him up the wall, Ivy dropped him and stepped away. He hit the floor in a slump, his hand at his neck as he coughed violently. Slowly he moved his legs into a normal position. Flipping his very black hair from his eyes, he looked up, sitting cross-legged and barefoot. "Morgan," he said roughly, his hand hiding his throat, "I need your help."

I glanced at Ivy, who was tightening her black silk robe about herself again. *He needed my help? Ri-i-i-i-ight.* "You okay?" I asked Ivy, and she nodded. The ring of brown left to her eyes was too thin for my comfort, but the sun was high, and the tension in the room was easing. Seeing my concern, she pressed her lips together.

"I'm fine," she reiterated. "You want me to call the I.S. now or after I kill him?"

My gaze ran over the kitchen. My cookies were ruined, sitting in soggy clumps. The globs of frosting on the walls were starting to run. Saltwater was venturing out of the kitchen, threatening to reach the living room rug. Letting Ivy kill him was looking really good.

"I want to hear what he has to say," I said as I slid open a drawer and put three dish towels in the threshold as a dike. Jenks's kids were peeking around the corner at us. The angry pixy rubbed his wings together to make a piercing whistle, and they vanished in a trill of sound.

Taking a fourth towel, I wiped the frosting off my elbow and went to stand before Quen. Feet spread wide and my fists on my hips, I waited. It must have been big if he was willing to risk Jenks figuring out he was an elf. My thoughts went to Ceri across the street, and my worry grew. I wasn't going to let Trent know she existed. He would use her some way—some very ugly way.

The elf felt his ribs through his black shirt. "I think you cracked them," he said.

"Did I pass?" I said snidely.

"No. But you're the best I've got."

Ivy made a sound of disbelief, and Jenks dropped down before him, staying carefully out of his reach. "You ass," the four-inch man swore. "We could have killed you three times over."

Quen frowned at him. "We. It was *her* I was interested in. Not *we.* She failed."

"So I guess that means you'll be leaving," I said, knowing I wouldn't be that lucky. I took in his subdued attire and sighed. It was just after noon. Elves slept when the sun was high and in the middle of the night, just like pixies. Quen was here without Trent's knowledge.

Feeling more sure of myself, I pulled out a chair and sat down before Quen could see my legs trembling. "Trent doesn't know you're here," I said, and he nodded solemnly.

"It's my problem, not his," Quen said. "I'm paying you, not him."

I blinked, trying to disguise my unease. Trent didn't know. Interesting. "You have a job for me that he doesn't know about," I said. "What is it?"

Quen's gaze went to Ivy and Jenks.

Peeved, I crossed my legs and shook my head. "We're a team. I'm not asking them to leave so you can tell me of whatever piss-poor problem you've landed yourself in."

The older elf's brow wrinkled. He took an angry breath.

"Look," I said, my finger jabbing out to point at him. "I don't like you. Jenks doesn't like you. And Ivy wants to eat you. Start talking."

He went motionless. It was then I saw his desperation, shimmering behind his eyes like light on water. "I have a problem," he said, fear the thinnest ribbon in his low, controlled voice.

I glanced at Ivy. Her breath had quickened and she stood with her arms wrapped about herself, holding her robe closed. She looked upset, her pale face even more white than usual.

"Mr. Kalamack is going to a social gathering and—"

My lips pursed. "I already turned down one whoring offer today."

Quen's eyes flashed. "Shut up," he said coldly. "Someone is interfering in Mr. Kalamack's secondary business ventures. The meeting is to try to come to a mutual understanding. I want you to be there to be sure that's all it is."

Mutual understanding? It was an I'm-tougher-than-you-so-get-out-of-my-city party. "Saladan?" I guessed.

Genuine surprise washed over him. "You know him?"

Jenks was flitting over Quen, trying to figure out what he was. The pixy was getting more and more frustrated, his shifts of direction becoming jerky and accented with sharp snaps of his dragonfly wings. "I've heard of him," I said, thinking of Takata. My eyes narrowed. "Why should I care if he assumes Trent's *secondary* business ventures? This is about Brimstone, isn't it?" I said. "Well, you can take a leap of faith and burn in hell. Trent is killing people, not that he hasn't done it before, but now he's killing them for no reason." Outrage pulled me to my feet. "Your boss is moth crap. I ought to bring him in, not protect him. And you," I said, louder, pointing, "are lower than moth crap for doing nothing while he does it!"

Quen flushed, making me feel vastly better about myself. "Are you that stupid?" he said, and I stiffened. "The bad Brimstone isn't from Mr. Kalamack; it's from Saladan. That's what this meeting is about. Mr. Kalamack is trying to get it off the streets, and unless you want Saladan taking over the city, you'd better start trying to keep Mr. Kalamack alive like the rest of us. Are you going to take the run or not? It pays ten thousand."

From Jenks came an eyeball-hurting pulse of ultrasonic surprise.

"Cash up front," Quen added, pulling a narrow wad of bills from somewhere on his person and throwing it at my feet.

I looked at the money. It wasn't enough. A million dollars wouldn't be enough. I shifted my foot, and it slid across the wet floor to Quen. "No."

"Take the money and let him die, Rache," Jenks said from the sun-strewn windowsill.

The black-clad elf smiled. "That's not how Ms. Morgan works." His pockmarked face was confident, and I hated the self-assured look in his green eyes. "If she takes the money, she'll protect Mr. Kalamack down to her last breath. Won't you?"

"No," I said, knowing I would. But I wasn't going to take his lousy ten grand.

"And you will take the money and the job," Quen said, "because if you don't, I'm going to tell the world about your summers at that little camp of his father's. You're the only person who has a ghost's chance in hell to keep him alive."

My face went cold. "Bastard," I whispered, refusing to feel afraid. "Why don't you just leave me alone? Why me? You just smeared me into the floor."

His eyes dropped from mine. "There will be vampires there," he said softly. "Powerful ones. There's the chance—" He took a breath and met my eyes. "I don't know if—"

I shook my head, somewhat reassured. Quen wouldn't tell. Trent would be mildly ticked if I was packed up and shipped off to Antarctica; he still had hopes of luring me to his payroll himself. "If you're afraid of vampires, that's your problem," I said. "I'm not going to let you make it mine. Ivy, get him out of my kitchen."

She didn't move, and I turned, my ire evaporating at the blank look on her face. "He's been bitten," she whispered, the wistful faltering in her voice shocking me. Hunched into herself, she leaned back against the wall, closed her eyes, and took a slow breath to scent him.

My lips parted in understanding. Piscary had bitten him, right before I clubbed the undead vampire into unconsciousness. Quen was an Inderlander, and so couldn't contract the vamp virus and be turned, but he might be mentally bound to the master vampire. I found my hand covering my neck, my face cold.

Big Al had taken the form and abilities of a vampire when he had torn open my neck and tried to kill me. He had filled my veins with the same potent cocktail of neurotransmitters that now ran through Quen. It was a survival trait to help ensure that vamps had a willing blood supply, and it turned pain into pleasure when stimulated by vampire pheromones. If the vamp had enough experience, they could sensitize the response such that they, and only they, could stimulate the bite into feeling good, binding the person to them alone and preventing easy poaching of their private supply.

Algaliarept hadn't bothered to sensitize the neurotransmitters—seeing as he was trying to kill me. I was left with a scar that any vamp could play on. I didn't belong to anyone, and as long as I kept vampire teeth on the right side of my skin, I wouldn't. In the ranking of the vampire world, an unbound bitee was the lowest of the low, a party favor, a pathetic remnant that was so beneath notice that any vampire could take what they wanted. Unclaimed property didn't last long, passed from vamp to vamp, soon drained of their vitality and will, left to rot in a confused loneliness of betrayal when the ugliness of their life started to show on their face. I'd be among their ranks if it wasn't for Ivy's protection.

And Quen had either been bitten and left unclaimed like me, or bitten and claimed by Piscary. As I stared in pity at the man, I decided he had a right to be afraid.

Seeing my understanding, Quen rose smoothly to his feet. Ivy tensed, and I raised my hand to tell her it was all right. "I don't know if the bite has bound me to him or not," Quen said, the evenness of his voice failing to hide the fear in him. "I can't risk Mr. Kalamack relying on me. I might . . . be distracted at a sensitive moment."

Waves of bliss and promises of pleasure coming from that bite might indeed be a large distraction, even in the midst of a fight. Pity pulled me forward. Tracks of sweat marred his lightly wrinkled face. He was as old as my father would be if he were still alive, with the strength of a twenty-year-old and the sturdiness only maturity imparted.

"Has any other vamp made your scar tingle?" I asked him, thinking it was a really personal question, but he had come to me.

Never dropping my gaze, he said, "I've yet to get into a situation where it might."

"Rache?" Jenks called, and there was a clatter of wings as he dropped to hover beside me.

"Then I don't know if Piscary bound you or not," I said, then froze as I realized my scar was tingling, sending hints of deeper feelings to bring me to a wide-eyed alertness. Quen stiffened. Our eyes met, and I knew by his frightened look that he was feeling it too.

"Rache!" Jenks shouted, his wings red as he got in my face

and forced me to back up. "Quen isn't the only one with a problem here!"

I followed his frightened gaze behind me to Ivy. "Oh . . . crap," I whispered.

Ivy had pressed herself into a corner, her robe falling open to show her black silk nightgown. Her awareness was lost, black eyes unseeing as her mouth worked. I froze, not knowing what was going on.

"Get him out of here," she whispered, a bead of saliva dropping from her teeth. "Oh, God, Rachel. He's not bound to anyone. Piscary . . . He's in my head." She took a gasping breath. "He wants me to take him. I don't know if I can stop. Get Quen out of here!"

I stared, not knowing what to do.

"Get him out of my head!" she moaned. "Get him out!" Horrified, I watched her slide down the wall to huddle with her hands over her ears. "Get him out!"

Heart pounding, I spun to Quen. My neck was a flaming mass of promise. I could see by his expression that his scar was alight and flaming. God help me, it felt good.

"Get the door," I said to Jenks. Grabbing Quen's arm, I pulled him into the hallway. From behind us came a frightening guttural groan. I broke into a run, dragging Quen behind me. Quen stiffened when we entered the sanctuary, breaking my hold.

"You're leaving!" I shouted, reaching for him. "Now!"

He was hunched and trembling, making the martial arts master look vulnerable. Lines from his internal struggle showed on his face. His eyes showed his broken spirit. "You will accompany Mr. Kalamack in my place," he said, his voice haggard.

"No, I won't." I reached for his arm.

Flashing alive, he sprang back. "You will accompany Mr. Kalamack in my place," he repeated, his face falling back into despair. "Or I will give in and go back into that kitchen." His face twisted, and I panicked that he might anyway. "He's whispering to me, Morgan. I can hear him through her. . . ."

My mouth went dry. My thoughts spiraled to Kisten. If I let him bind me to him, I could end up like this. "Why me?" I asked. "There's a university of people better at magic than I am."

"Everyone else relies on their magic," he panted, bent almost double. "You use it as a last resort. It gives you . . . the advantage." He gasped. "She's weakening. I can feel it."

"Okay!" I exclaimed. "I'll go, damn it! Just get out of here!"

A sound of agony, soft as a brush of wind, slipped from him. "Help me," he whispered. "I can't make myself move anymore."

Heart pounding, I grabbed his arm and dragged him to the door. Behind us was Ivy's tortured cry of anguish. My stomach twisted. What was I doing, going on a date with Kisten?

A bright stab of snow-reflected light lanced into the church as Jenks and his brood worked the elaborate pulley system we had rigged so they could open the door. Quen balked at the cold blast of air that sent the pixies hiding. "Get out!" I exclaimed in frustration and fear as I pulled him out onto the stoop.

A long Gray Ghost limo idled at the curb. My breath hissed in relief as Jonathan, Trent's number-one lackey, opened the driver's door and emerged. I never thought I'd be happy to see the shockingly tall, distasteful man. They were in this together, working behind Trent's back. This was a badder mistake than usual. I could feel it already.

Quen panted as I helped him lurch down the steps. "Get him out of here," I demanded.

Jonathan yanked open the passenger-side door. "Are you going to do it?" he said, his thin lips pressed tight as he took in my cookie-smeared hair and wet jeans.

"Yes!" I pushed Quen in. He fell onto the leather seat, collapsing like a drunk. "Go!"

The tall elf shut the door and stared at me. "What did you do to him?" he said coldly.

"Nothing! It's Piscary! Get him out of here!"

Apparently satisfied, he strode to the driver's side. With an odd quietness, the car accelerated. I stood on the icy sidewalk and shivered, watching it speed away until it turned a corner and was gone.

Pulse slowing, I wrapped my arms around myself. The winter sun was cold. Slowly I turned to go inside, not knowing what I'd find curled up on my kitchen floor.

Ten

I watched myself in the mirror above my new, solid-ash dresser as I put my hoop earrings in, the ones big enough for Jenks to ride on. The little black dress looked good on me, and the above-the-knee boots that went with it would keep me warm enough. I didn't think Kisten had planned a snowball fight in the park, as corny and cheap as that was. And he had said wear something nice. I stood sideways and checked myself out. This was nice. This was very nice.

Pleased, I sat on my bed and snapped my boots up, leaving the last few inches open so I could walk easier. I didn't want to get excited about going out with Kisten, but the chance to dress up and have a good time had been so infrequent lately that it was hard not to. I told myself that I could be going out with the girls and still feel like this. It wasn't Kisten; it was just going out.

Wanting a second opinion, I went clattering into the hall in search of Ivy. The memory of her fighting Piscary off in her mind was very real. The undead vampire had given up as soon as Quen was gone, but she had been very subdued the rest of the day, refusing to talk about it as she helped me clean the kitchen. She didn't want me going out with Kisten now, and I was inclined to agree with her that it was a stupid idea. But it wasn't as if I couldn't fight Kisten off. He had said he wouldn't bite me, and I wasn't about to let a moment of passion change my mind. Not now. Not ever.

I ran my hand down my sparkling party dress as I entered the living room, hesitating for Ivy's inspection. Curled up on the couch, she looked up from her magazine. I couldn't help but notice she was on the same page as when I had gone in to change thirty minutes ago.

"What do you think?" I said, making a slow circle and feeling tall in my spike-heeled boots.

She sighed, closing her magazine on her finger to mark the page. "I think it's a mistake."

My brow furrowed and I looked down at myself. "Yeah, you're right," I said as my thoughts went to my closet. "I'll put on something else."

I turned to leave, and she threw her magazine across the room to hit the wall before me. "That's not what I meant!" she exclaimed, and I spun, startled.

Ivy's oval face was creased and her thin eyebrows pinched as she sat up in her chair, fidgeting. "Rachel . . ." she cajoled, and I knew where this conversation was going.

"I'm not going to let him bite me," I said, becoming angry. "I'm a big girl. I can take care of myself. And after this afternoon, you can be damned sure his teeth aren't going to get anywhere near me."

Brown eyes worried, she curled her legs up under her to make herself look uncertain. It was a mien I didn't see on her very often. Her eyes closed as she took a breath as if gathering herself. "You look nice," she said, and I could almost feel my blood pressure drop. "Don't let him bite you," she added softly. "I don't want to have to kill Kisten if he binds you to him."

"You got it," I said, trying to lighten her mood as I walked out, knowing she might. It would be the only way to reliably break his hold on me. Time and distance would do it eventually, too, but Ivy wasn't one to take chances. And being bound to him after I had said no to her would be more than she could take. My heels clacked a little slower as I went back to my room to change into something more subdued. This outfit was asking for trouble.

Standing before my open closet, I pushed hangers around hoping something would jump out and say, "Wear me! Wear me!" I'd already been through everything and was starting to think I didn't have anything that wasn't too sexy and yet attractive enough for a night on the town. With all the money I'd spent filling my closet last month, there ought to have been something. My stomach tightened at the thought of my shrinking bank balance, but Quen had left his ten thousand on the kitchen floor. And I *had* agreed to baby-sit Trent . . .

The soft knock at my door startled me, and I spun, my hand to my collarbone.

"Um," Ivy said, her closed-lipped smile telling me she found something funny in having surprised me. "I'm sorry. I know you aren't going to let him bite you." She raised a long hand in a gesture of exasperation. "It's the vamp thing. That's all."

I nodded, understanding. I'd been living with Ivy long enough that her unconscious vampire instincts thought of me as her property even though her conscious mind knew different. It was why I didn't spar with her anymore, wash my clothes with hers, bring up ties of family and blood, or follow her out of the room if she abruptly left in the middle of a conversation for no apparent reason. All pushed her vampire-instinct buttons and would put us right back where we were seven months ago, fumbling about as we figured out how to live with each other.

"Here," Ivy said, coming one step into my room and holding out a fist-sized package wrapped in green foil and a purple bow. "It's an early solstice gift. I thought you might like to use it on your date with Kisten."

"Oh, Ivy!" I exclaimed, taking the elaborate, clearly store-wrapped package. "Thank you. I, ah, haven't wrapped yours yet. . . ." *Wrapped? I hadn't even bought it.*

"That's okay," she said, clearly flustered. "I was going to wait, but I thought you could use it. For your date," she fumbled. Eyes eager, she looked at the box in my hand. "Go on. Open it."

"Okay." I sat on my bed, carefully undoing the fabric and foil ribbon, as I might want to use it next year. The paper was embossed with the Black Kiss logo, and I slowed my fingers, wanting to prolong the suspense. The Black Kiss was an exclusive shop catering to vamps. I didn't even window-shop there. The associates knew by looking that I couldn't afford a hanky.

The paper came away to reveal a small wooden box, and inside that amid a cushion of crushed red velvet was a cut-glass perfume bottle. "Ooooh," I breathed. "Thank you." Ivy had been getting me perfume since I'd moved in as we tried to find a scent that covered up her lingering aroma on me and help her curb her vampiric tendencies. It wasn't the romantic gift one might think it was, but kind of a vampire antiaphrodisiac. My dresser was covered in castoffs of varying degrees of effectiveness. Actually, the perfume was more for her than me.

"It's really hard to find," she said, starting to look discomforted. "You have to special order it. My dad told me about it. I hope you like it."

"Mmmm," I said, opening it and dabbing some behind my ear and on my wrists. I breathed deeply, thinking it smelled like a green woods and dash of citrus: clean and crisp, with a hint of darker shadows. Scrumptious. "Oh, this is wonderful," I said, standing to give her a quick impromptu hug.

She held very still, and I busied myself at my dresser, pretending I didn't notice her surprise. "Huh," she said, and I turned, finding a bemused expression on her. "It works."

"What . . ." I said warily, wondering what I had put on.

Her gaze rove before settling on mine. "It blocks a vampire's sense of smell," she said. "At least the more sensitive aromas that run to the unconscious." She gave me a lopsided smile to make her look harmless. "I can't smell you at all."

"Cool," I said, impressed. "I should wear it all the time."

Ivy's expression went subtly guilty. "You could, but I got the last bottle, and I don't know if I could find it again."

I nodded. She meant it was more expensive than a gallon of water on the moon. "Thank you, Ivy," I said earnestly.

"You're welcome." Her smile was genuine. "Happy early solstice." Her attention went to the front of the church. "He's here."

The rumble of an idling car filtered in through my thin stained-glass window. I took a deep breath and glanced at my bedside clock. "Right on time." I turned to her, pleading with my eyes for her to get the door.

"Nope." She grinned to show an unconscious slip of teeth. "You get it."

She turned and left. I looked down at myself, thinking what I had on was grossly inappropriate, and now I had to answer the door in it. "Ivy . . ." I complained as I followed her out. She never slowed, holding her hand up in refusal as she walked into the kitchen.

"Fine," I muttered, boot heels clicking to the front of the church. I flicked on the lights in the sanctuary in passing, the high, dim glow doing little to brighten the gloom. It was after one in the morning, and the pixies were all safe and snug in my desk until about four, when they would wake up. There was no light in the foyer, and I wondered if we ought to do something about that as I pushed open one side of the heavy wooden door.

With the soft sound of shoes grinding on rock salt, Kisten shifted back.

"Hi, Rachel," he said, his eyes taking in my clothes. A faint stiffening of the skin about his eyes told me I had guessed correctly; I wasn't dressed for whatever he had planned. I wished I knew what he had on under the luscious gray wool coat he was wearing. It went all the way to his boot tops and looked classy. He had shaved, too—his usual day-old stubble gone—giving him a polished look I wasn't used to seeing on him.

"This isn't what I'm wearing," I said by way of greeting. "Come on in. I just need a minute to change."

"Sure." Past him at the curb was his black Corvette, the light snow melting as it hit. He edged in past me, and I pulled the door thumping shut behind him.

"Ivy's in the kitchen," I said, starting back to my room, his soft steps following right behind me. "She had a bad afternoon. She won't talk to me, but she might talk to you."

"She called me," he said, the careful cadence of his words telling me he knew about Piscary asserting his dominance over her. "You're going to put on different boots, right?"

I jerked to a stop at the door to my room. "What's wrong with my boots?" I said, thinking they were the only thing that I was going to keep on. Ah . . . the only thing from this outfit, not the only thing total.

He looked at them, his dyed-blond eyebrows high. "They're what, five inches?"

"Yeah."

"It's icy. You're going to slip and break your ass." His blue eyes widened. "I mean your rear end."

A smile crossed my face at the thought that he was trying to clean up his mouth for me. "They make me as tall as you, too," I said smugly.

"I noticed." He hesitated. With a little jiggle, he whisked past me and into my room.

"Hey!" I protested as he went right to my closet. "Get out of my room!"

Ignoring me, he pushed all the way to the back where I put everything I didn't like. "I saw something here the other day," he said, making a small exclamation as he leaned to tug at something. "Here," he said, holding out a pair of drab black boots. "Start with these."

"Those?" I complained as he set them aside and stuck his

arms back into my closet. "There's no heel to those at all. And they're four years old and out of style. And what were you doing in my closet?"

"That's a classic boot," Kisten said, affronted. "It never goes out of style. Put them on." He shuffled about again, pulling something out by feel, as he couldn't possibly see anything back there. My face warmed when I saw an old suit I'd forgotten I had. "Oh, this is just ugly," he said, and I snatched it out of his hands.

"It's my old interview suit," I said. "It's supposed to be ugly."

"Throw it away. But keep the pants. You're wearing them tonight."

"I am not!" I protested. "Kisten, I am fully capable of picking out my own clothes!"

Silently he raised his eyebrows, then went right back in to get a black long-sleeve shirt, from my don't-go-there section, that my mother bought for me three years ago. I hadn't the heart to give it away as it was silk, even though it was so long it hung mid-thigh on me. The neckline was too low, and it made my small chest look even flatter.

"This too," he said, and I shook my head.

"No," I said firmly. "It's too long, and it's something my mother would wear."

"Then your mother has better taste than you," he said in good humor. "Wear a camisole under it, and for God's sake, don't tuck it in."

"Kisten, get out of my closet!"

But he reached back in, bowing his head over something small in his hands as he rocked back. I thought it might be that ugly purse with the sequins I wished I had never bought, but I went mortified when he turned with an innocuous looking book. It had no title and was bound with a soft brown leather. The glint in Kisten's eyes told me he knew what it was.

"Give me that," I said, reaching out for it.

A wicked grin on him, Kisten held it up over his head. I could probably still get it, but I'd have to climb him. "Well, well, well . . ." he drawled. "Ms. Morgan. You have shocked and delighted me. Where did you get a copy of Rynn Cormel's guide to dating the undead?"

I pressed my lips together and fumed, stymied. Hip cocked, I could do nothing as he took a distancing step back and flipped through it.

"Have you read it?" he asked, then made a surprised *Mmmm*

sound as he paused at a page. "I forgot about that one. I wonder if I can still do that."

"Yes, I've read it." I extended my hand. "Give it here."

Kisten pulled his attention from the pages, his long masculine hands cradling the book open. His eyes had gone black just a wee bit, and I cursed myself as a thrill of excitement went through me. Damn vamp pheromones.

"Ooooh, it's important to you," Kisten said, glancing out the door when Ivy banged something in the kitchen. "Rachel . . ." he said, his voice softer as he moved a step closer. "You know all my secrets." Without looking, his fingers dog-eared a page. "What drives me crazy. What instinctively tips me over—the—edge . . ."

He said the last word carefully, and I stifled a delicious shudder.

"You know how to . . . manipulate me," he murmured, the book dangling from an inattentive hand. "Do witches have a manual?"

He had somehow gotten within two feet of me, and I didn't remember him moving. The smell of his wool coat was strong, and under that was the heady scent of leather. Flustered, I snatched the book away, and Kisten dropped back a step. "Don't you wish," I muttered. "Ivy gave it to me so I would stop pushing her buttons. That's all it is." I shoved it under my pillow, and his smile widened. Damn it, if he touched me, I was going to slug him.

"That's where it belongs," he said. "Not a closet. Keep it close for quick reference."

"Get out," I said, pointing.

Long coat drifting about his shoe tops, he moved to the door, his every motion holding a confident seductive grace. "Put your hair up," he said as he sauntered through the archway. A grin came over him, showing me his teeth. "I like your neck. Page twelve, third paragraph down." He licked his lips, hiding the flash of fang even as I saw it.

"Out!" I shouted, taking two steps and slamming the door.

Fuming, I turned to what he had laid out on my bed, glad I'd made it that afternoon. A faint tingling at my neck drew my hand up, and I pressed my palm into it, willing it away. I stared at my pillow, then hesitantly pulled the book out. Rynn Cormel had written it? Cripes, the man had single-handedly run the country during the Turn, and he had enough time to write a vampire sex manual, too?

The scent of lilac rose as I opened it at the dog-eared page. I was prepared for anything, having been through the book twice and finding myself more appalled than turned on, but it was only about the use of necklaces to send messages to your lover. Apparently the more you covered your neck, the more you were inviting him or her to rip it open. The gothic metallic lace that was so popular lately was like walking around in a teddy. Going completely bare at the neck was almost as bad—a delicious claim of vampiric virginity and a complete and utter turn-on.

"Huh," I muttered, closing the book and dropping it on my new bedside table. Maybe a reread was in order. My gaze went to the outfit Kisten had chosen for me. It looked frumpy, but I'd try it on, and when Ivy told him I looked like I was forty, he could wait another ten minutes while I changed back.

Motions quick, I took off my boots and tossed them thumping aside. I had forgotten that the gray slacks were lined with silk, and they made a pleasant sensation slipping over my legs. I chose a black halter top—without Kisten's help—and put the long shirt on over it. It didn't do a thing to show off my curves, and I turned to my mirror, frowning.

I froze at my reflection, shocked. "Damn," I whispered. I had looked good before in my black dress and boots. But in this? In this I looked . . . sophisticated. Remembering page twelve, I fumbled for my longest gold chain and looped it over my head. "Double damn," I breathed, shifting to see myself from a different angle.

My curves were gone, hidden behind the simple straight lines, but the subdued statement of the modest slacks, silk shirt, and gold chain screamed confidence and casual wealth. Now my pale skin was softly alabaster instead of sickly white, and my athletic build appeared sleek. It was a new look for me. I didn't know I could do high-class wealthy.

I hesitantly pulled my hair up off my neck and held it atop my head. "Whoa," I breathed, when it turned me from sophisticated to elegant. Looking this good outweighed the embarrassment of letting Kisten know he could dress me better than I could dress myself.

Digging in a drawer, I found and invoked my last amulet to tame the frizz of my hair, then put my hair up, pulling a few strands to drape artfully before my ears. I dabbed on a bit more of my new perfume, checked my makeup, hid my hair-taming amulet behind my shirt, then grabbed a small clasp purse, as my shoulder bag would ruin everything. The lack of my usual charms gave me a moment of pause, but it was a date, not a run. And if I had to fight Kisten off, I'd be using ley line magic anyway.

My flat-heeled boots were subdued as I left my room and followed the soft give-and-take murmurs of Kisten and Ivy into the amber-lit sanctuary. I hesitated at the doorway, looking in.

They had woken the pixies, who were flitting everywhere, concentrating about Ivy's grand piano as they played tag among the wires and stops. There was a faint hum of sound shifting the air, and I realized the vibrations from their wings were making the strings resonate.

Ivy and Kisten stood by the archway to the foyer. She had that same uneasy, defiant look on her that she'd been wearing earlier when she refused to talk to me. Kisten was bent close, clearly concerned, with his hand on her shoulder.

I cleared my throat for their attention, and Kisten's hand fell. Ivy's posture shifted back to her usual equanimity, but I could see her shattered confidence underneath.

"Oh, that's better," Kisten said as he turned, his eyes lighting briefly on my necklace.

He had unbuttoned his coat, and I ran my eyes appreciatively over him as I approached. No wonder he had wanted to dress me. He looked fabulous: navy Italian pinstripe suit, shiny shoes, hair slicked back and smelling faintly of soap . . . and smiling at me with an attractive self-assurance. His usual chain was a quick flash hidden behind the collar of his starched white shirt. A tasteful tie was snugged up to his neck, and a watch fob ran from a vest pocket through a buttonhole and then to the other vest pocket. Looking at his trim waist, broad shoulders, and slender hips, there was nothing to argue with. Nothing at all.

Ivy blinked as she took me in. "When did you buy that?" she asked, and I smiled widely.

"Kist picked it out of my closet," I said brightly, and that would be the only admission of my lack of polish he was going to get.

It was a date, so I went to stand beside Kisten; Nick would have gotten a kiss, but as Ivy and Jenks were hovering—and in Jenks's case, literally—a little discretion was in order. More importantly, he wasn't Nick.

Jenks landed on Ivy's shoulder. "Do I need to say anything?" the pixy asked Kisten, his hands on his hips to look like a protective father.

"No, sir," Kisten said, entirely serious, and I fought to keep a smile from me. The picture of a four-inch pixy threatening a six-foot living vampire would have been ridiculous if Kisten weren't taking him seriously. Jenks's warning was real and very enforceable. The only thing more unstoppable than fairy assassins were pixies. They could rule the world if they wanted.

"Good," Jenks said, apparently satisfied.

I stood by Kisten and rocked back and forth on my flat heels twice, staring at everyone. No one said a word. This was really weird. "Ready to go?" I finally prompted.

Jenks snickered and flitted off to corral his kids back into the desk. Ivy gave Kisten a last look, and walked out of the sanctuary. Sooner than I would have expected, the TV blared. I ran my eyes over Kisten, thinking he looked as far away from his biker image as a goat is to a tree.

"Kisten," I said, putting a hand to my necklace. "What does this . . . say?"

He leaned close. "Confidence. Not looking for anything, but naughty behind closed doors."

I stifled a thrill-invoked shudder when he pulled away. *Okay. That . . . works.*

"Let me help you with your coat," he said, and a sound of dismay came from me as I followed him into the foyer. My coat. My ugly, ugly coat with the fake fur around the collar.

"Ouch," Kisten said, his brow furrowed in the dim light seeping in from the sanctuary as he saw it. "Tell you what." He shrugged out of his coat. "You can wear mine. It's unisex."

"Now wait up," I protested, taking a step back before he could put it on me. "I'm smarter than that, fang-boy. I'll end up smelling like you. This is a platonic date, and I'm not going to break rule number one by mixing our scents before I even step out of my church."

He grinned, his white teeth glinting in the dim light. "Got me dead to rights," he admitted. "But what are you going to wear? That?"

A wince pulled my face tight while I looked at my coat. "All right," I agreed, not wanting to ruin my new facade of elegance with fake fur and nylon. And there was my new perfume . . . "But I'm not putting this on to intentionally mix our scents. Understand?"

He nodded, but his smile made me think otherwise, and I let him help me slip into it. My gaze went distant as its heavy weight eased over my shoulders, comforting and warm. Kisten might not be able to smell me, but I could smell Kisten, and his lingering body warmth sank into me. Leather, silk, and the barest hint of a clean-scented aftershave made a mix I was hard-pressed not to sigh into. "Will you be okay?" I asked, seeing he had only his suit jacket.

"The car is already warm." He intercepted my reach for the door, his hand touching mine atop the handle. "Allow me," he said gallantly. "You're my date. Let me act like it."

Thinking he was being silly, I nevertheless let him open the door and take my arm as he helped me down the steps lightly dusted with snow. The snow had started shortly after sundown, and the ugly gray splotches kicked up by the snowplows were covered in pristine white. The air was crisp and cold, and there was no wind.

I wasn't surprised when he maneuvered to open the car door for me, and I couldn't help but feel special as I arranged myself. Kisten shut the door and hustled around to the front. The leather seats were warm, and there was no cardboard tree hanging from the rearview mirror. I took a quick look at the discs in the console as he got in. They ranged from Korn to Jeff Beck, and he even had one of singing monks. *He* listened to singing monks?

Kisten settled himself. As soon as the car started, he flipped the heater on full. I sank into the seat, relishing the deep rumble of the engine. It was markedly stronger than my little car, vibrating through me like thunder. The leather, too, was of a higher quality, and the mahogany on the dash was real, not fake. I was a witch; I could tell.

I refused to compare Kisten's car to Nick's drafty, ugly truck, but it was hard not to. And I liked being treated special. Not that Nick didn't make me feel special, but this was different. It was fun to get dressed up, even if we ended up eating at Mickey-d's. Which was a very real possibility as Kisten had only sixty dollars to spend.

Glancing at him sitting beside me, I realized I didn't care.

Eleven

"So," I said slowly as I fought to keep myself from reaching for the handle of the door to keep it from swinging open when we went over a railroad track. "Where are we going?"

Kisten gave me a sideways smile, the lights from the car behind us illuminating him. "You'll see."

My eyebrows rose, and I took a breath to press for details when a soft chirping came from his pocket. My playful mood faltered into one of exasperation as he gave me an apologetic look and reached for his phone.

"I hope this isn't going to happen all night," I muttered, putting my elbow on the door handle and staring at the dark. "Just turn around and take me home if it is. Nick never took a call when we were on a date."

"Nick wasn't trying to run half the city, either." Kisten flipped the silver top up. "Yes," he said, his sharp annoyance pulling my elbow from the door and my attention back to him. The muted, tiny sound of pleading filtered out. In the background I could hear thumping music. "You're kidding." Kisten flicked his attention from the road to me and back to the road. His eyes held a mix of hassle and disbelief. "Well get out there and open the floor."

"I tried that!" the tiny voice shouted. "They're animals, Kist. Bloody savages!" The voice subsided into an unrecognizable high-pitched panic.

Kisten sighed as he looked at me. "Okay, okay. We'll stop in. I'll take care of it."

The voice on the other end gushed in relief, but Kisten didn't bother to listen, flipping the phone closed and tucking it away.

"Sorry, love," he said in that ridiculous accent. "One quick stop. Five minutes. I promise."

And it had started off so well, too. "Five minutes?" I questioned. "Something's got to go," I threatened, half serious. "Either the phone or that accent."

"Oh!" he said, putting his hand to his chest dramatically. "Wounded to the quick." He looked askance at me, clearly relieved I was taking this as well as I was. "I can't do without my phone. The accent goes . . ." He grinned. ". . . my love."

"Oh, please," I moaned, enjoying the light banter. I had been walking on eggshells around Nick so long, afraid to say anything lest I make things worse. Guess I didn't have to worry about that anymore.

I wasn't surprised when Kisten turned toward the waterfront. I had already surmised the trouble was at Piscary's Pizza. Since losing its Mixed Public License last fall, it had gone to a strictly vamp cliental, and from what I heard, Kisten was actually turning a profit. It was the only reputable establishment in Cincinnati without an MPL to do so. "Savages?" I questioned when we pulled into the parking lot of the two-story restaurant.

"Mike is being histrionic," Kisten said as he parked in a reserved spot. "It's only a bunch of women." He got out of the car and I sat tight, my hands in my lap as his door shut. I would have expected him to leave the car running for me. My head jerked up when he opened my door, and I stared blankly at him.

"Aren't you coming in?" he said, hunched as the cold breeze off the river shifted his bangs. "It's freezing out here."

"Ah, should I?" I stammered, surprised. "You lost your MPL."

Kisten reached for my hand. "I don't think you need to be worried."

The pavement was icy, and I was glad that I was wearing flat boots as I got out of his car. "But you don't have an MPL," I said again. The parking lot was full, and watching vampires bleeding each other couldn't be a pleasant sight. And if I willingly went in there knowing it lacked an MPL, the law wouldn't help me if anything went wrong.

Kisten's coat was long, dragging while he held my arm and escorted me to the canopy covered entrance. "Everyone in there knows you beat Piscary into unconsciousness," he said softly, inches from my ear to make me very aware of his breath on my cheek. "None of them would dare even think to do that. And you could have killed him but you didn't. It takes more guts to let a vampire live than to kill one. No one will mess with you." He opened the door, and light and music spilled out. "Or is it the blood you're worried about?" he questioned as I balked.

I fixed my eyes on his and nodded, not caring if he saw my apprehension.

Expression distant, Kisten gently led me forward. "You won't see any," he said. "Everyone here came to relax, not feed the beast. This is the only place in Cincinnati where vampires can go in a public setting and be themselves without having to live up to some human's, witch's, or Were's idea of what they should be and how they should act. There won't be any blood unless someone cuts a finger opening a beer."

Still unsure, I let him guide me in, stopping just inside the door while he knocked the snow from his dress shoes. The heat of the place struck me first, and I didn't think it was all coming from the fireplace at the far end of the room. It had to be pushing eighty, the warmth carrying the pleasant aroma of incense and dark things. I breathed deeply as I untied Kisten's coat, and it seemed to settle in my brain, relaxing me the way a hot bath and a good meal did.

A stirring of unease ruined the feeling when a living vamp came forward with an unsettling quickness. His shoulders looked as wide as I was tall, and he massed three hundred pounds if he was an ounce. But his eyes were sharp, revealing a quick intelligence, and he moved his muscular bulk with the sexy grace most living vamp's had. "I'm sorry," he said in an iron-pumping-gym accent as he came close. His hand was reaching out—not to touch but clearly indicating that I should leave. "Piscary's lost its MPL. Vamps only."

Kisten slid behind me and helped me slip his coat off. "Hi, Steve. Any trouble tonight?"

"Mr. Felps," the large man exclaimed softly, his speech taking on a well-educated accent to match the intelligence his eyes couldn't hide. "I wasn't expecting you until later. No. No trouble apart from Mike upstairs. We're all quiet down here." Brown eyes apologetic, he glanced at me. "Sorry, ma'am. I didn't know you were with Mr. Felps."

Seeing a golden opportunity to pry, I smiled. "Does Mr. Felps often bring young women not of the vampiric persuasion to his club?" I asked.

"No, ma'am," the man said so naturally that I had to believe him. His words and actions were so innocuous and unvampiric, that I had to sniff twice to make sure he was one. I hadn't realized how much of the vampire identity stemmed from attitude. And as I scanned the lower floor, I decided it was like any upscale restaurant, more mundane than when it had its MPL.

The wait staff was appropriately dressed with most of their scars hidden, and they moved with an efficient quickness that wasn't the least provocative. My gaze roved over the pictures above the bar, faltering when I saw a blurry shot of Ivy in her biker leather, riding her cycle with a rat and a mink perched on the gas tank. *Oh God. Someone had seen us.*

Kisten gave me a wry look upon seeing where my eyes were. "Steve, this is Ms. Morgan," he said as he handed my borrowed coat to the bouncer. "We aren't staying long."

"Yes, sir," the man said, then stopped in his tracks and turned. "Rachel Morgan?"

My smile grew wider. "Pleasure to meet you, Steve," I said.

A rush of fluster ran through me as Steve took my hand and kissed the top of it. "The pleasure is mine, Ms. Morgan." The large vampire hesitated, gratitude passing behind his expressive eyes. "Thank you for not killing Piscary. It would have made Cincinnati hell."

I chuckled. "Aw, it wasn't just me; I had help bringing him in. And don't thank me yet," I said, not sure if he was serious or not. "Piscary and I have an old argument, and I simply haven't decided if it's worth the effort to kill him or not."

Kisten laughed, but it sounded somewhat forced. "All right, all right," he said as he pulled my hand from Steve's. "That's enough. Steve, will you have someone get my long leather coat from downstairs? We're leaving as soon as I open the floor."

"Yes, sir."

I couldn't hide my smile as Kisten moved his grip to my elbow and subtly guided me to the stairway. I decided that though he kept touching me, it wasn't for any ulterior motive—yet—and I could tolerate him moving me around like a Barbie doll. It kinda went with my sophisticated look tonight and made me feel special.

"Good God, Rachel." His whisper in my ear made me shiver. "Don't you think you have enough of a badass attitude already without dumping blood on the floor?"

Steve was already gossiping to the help, and heads were turning to watch Kisten escort me to the second floor. "What?" I said, smiling confidently at anyone who would meet my eyes. I looked good. I felt good. Everyone could tell.

Kisten pulled me close to put his hand at the small of my back. "Do you really think it was a good idea to tell Steve that Piscary lives only because you haven't decided if you want to kill him or not? What kind of an image do you think that gives you?"

I smiled at him. I felt good. Relaxed. Like I had been sipping wine all afternoon. It had to be the vamp pheromones, but my demon scar had yet to even twinge. This was something else. Apparently there was nothing more relaxed and comfortable than a sated vampire, and they apparently liked to share the feeling. How come Ivy never felt like this? "Well, I did say I had help," I admitted, wondering if my words were slurring. "But killing Piscary is gonna move to the top of my wish list if he ever gets out of prison."

Kisten said nothing, peering at me with his brow furrowed, and I wondered if I had said something bad. But he had given me Egyptian embalming fluid that night, thinking it would knock Piscary out. He had said he wanted me to kill him. Maybe he'd changed his mind?

The music coming from the second floor grew louder the higher we rose up the stairway. It was a steady dance beat, and as it thumped into me, I found myself wanting to move to it. I could feel my blood humming, and I swayed as Kisten pulled me to a halt at the top of the stairs.

It was warmer up there, and I fanned myself. The huge plate-glass windows that had once overlooked the Ohio River had been replaced with walls, unlike the openings remaining downstairs. The dining tables had been removed to leave a building-wide, high-ceilinged open space ringed with tall cocktail tables pressed against the walls. There were no chairs. At the far end was a long bar. Again no chairs. Everyone was standing.

Above the bar just below the ceiling was a dark loft where the DJ and light-show panel was. Behind that was what looked like a pool table. A harried-looking tall man was standing in the center of the dance floor with a cordless mike, pleading to the mixed crowd of vampires: living and dead, men and women, all dressed similar to what I had been wearing earlier. It was a vamp dance club, I decided, wanting to cover my ears against the loud catcalls.

The man with the mike caught sight of Kisten, and his long face lifted in relief. "Kisten!" he said, his miked utterance turning heads and causing a cheer from the surrounding women in skimpy party dresses. "Thank God!"

The man beckoned to him, and Kisten took my shoulders.

"Rachel?" he questioned. "Rachel!" he exclaimed, pulling my attention from the pretty spinning lights above the floor. His blue eyes went worried. "Are you okay?"

I nodded, my head bobbing up and down. "Yup, yup, yup," I said, giggling. I felt so warm and relaxed. I liked Kisten's dance club.

Kisten's brow furrowed. He glanced at the overdressed man everyone was laughing at, then back to me. "Rachel, this will only take a moment. Is that okay?"

I was watching the lights again, and he turned my chin to look at him. "Yes," I said, moving my mouth slowly so it would come out right. "I'll wait right here. You go open the floor." Someone bumped me, and I almost fell into him. "I like your club, Kisten. It's fab."

Kisten stood me upright, waiting until I had my balance before letting go. The crowd had started to chant his name, and he raised a hand in acknowledgment. They redoubled their calls, and I put my hands over my ears. The music pounded into me.

Kisten gestured to someone at the bottom of the stairs, and I watched Steve take them two at a time, moving his hulking size like it was nothing. "Is she what I think she is?" Kisten asked the big man as he came close.

"Ye-e-e-e-ah," the big man drawled as they both peered at me. "She's blood-sugared. But she's a witch." Steve's eyes left me and fixed on Kisten. "Isn't she?"

"Yes," Kisten said, almost having to shout over the noise from the people for him to take the mike. "She's been bitten, but she's not bound to anyone. Maybe that's why."

"Vampy, vampy pher . . . uh . . . pher—" I licked my lips, frowning. "Pheromones," I said, my eyes wide. "Mmmm, nice. How come Ivy never feels like this?"

"Because Ivy is a tightass." Kisten frowned. A sigh shifted him, and I reached for his shoulders. He had nice shoulders, all hard with muscle and possibility.

Kisten took my hands from him and held them before me. "Steve, stay with her."

"Sure, boss," the big vampire said, moving to stand beside and slightly behind me.

"Thanks." Kisten peered into my eyes, holding them. "I'm sorry, Rachel," he said. "This isn't your fault. I didn't know this would happen. I'll be right back."

He shifted away, and I reached out after him, blinking at the tumult that rose as he took the center of the room. Kisten stood for a moment, looking sexy in his Italian suit as he gathered his thoughts with his head bowed and waited. He was working the crowd before he even said a word; I couldn't help but be impressed. A closed-lipped, roguish smile quirked his mouth when he pulled his head up, eyeing them from under his blond bangs. "Holy shit," he whispered into the mike, and the crowd cheered. "What the hell are you all doing here?"

"Waiting for you!" a female voice shouted.

Kisten grinned, moving his body suggestively as he nodded in the direction of the voice. "Hey, Mandy. You here tonight? When did they let you out?"

She screamed happily at him, and he smiled. "You are a ba-a-a-ad bunch of vixens, you know that? Giving Mickey a hard time. What's wrong with Mickey? He's good to you."

The women cheered, and I covered my ears, almost falling over as my balance shifted. Steve took my elbow.

"Well, I was trying to go out on a date," Kisten said, dropping his head dramatically. "My first one in I don't know how long. You see her, over there by the stair?"

A huge spotlight slammed into me, and I winced, squinting. The heat from it made my skin tingle, and I straightened, almost falling when I waved. Steve caught my arm, and I smiled up at him. I leaned into him, and he shook his head good-naturedly, running a finger along the underside of my jaw before gently standing me upright.

"She's a little out of it tonight," Kisten said. "You are all enjoying yourself *far* too much, and it's rubbing off on her. Who knew witch runners needed to party like us?"

The noise redoubled, and the pace of the lights quickened, racing over the floor and up the walls and ceilings. My breath came faster as the beat of the music grew.

"But you know what they say," Kisten said over the rhythm. "The bigger they are—"

"The better it is," someone yelled.

"The more they need to party!" Kisten shouted over the laughs. "So take it easy on her, okay? She just wants to relax and have some fun. No pretenses. No games. I say any witch with enough balls to bring down Piscary and let him live has long enough fangs to party with. Are you all A-positive with that?"

The second floor exploded into sound, pressing me into Steve. My eyes warmed as my emotions swung from one extreme to the other. They liked me. How cool was that?

"Then let's get this party started!" Kisten yelled, spinning to the DJ nest behind him. "Mickey, give me the one I want."

The women screamed their approval, and I watched in slack-jawed surprise when the floor was suddenly covered in women, their eyes wild and their motions sharp. Short revealing dresses, high heels, and extravagant makeup was the rule, though there were a few older vampires dressed as classy as me. The living barely outnumbered the undead.

Music rolled from the speakers in the ceiling, loud and insistent. A heavy beat, a tinny snare drum, a corny synthesizer, and a raspy voice. It was Rob Zombie's "Living Dead Girl," and as I stared in disbelief, the varying motions of the clean-limbed and scantily clad female vamps shifted to the rhythmic, simultaneous movements of a choreographed dance.

They were line dancing. Oh—my—God. The vampires were line dancing.

Like a school of fish, they swayed and moved together, feet thumping with the strength to shake the dust from the ceiling. Not a one made a mistake or misstep. I blinked as Kisten did a Michael Jackson to move to the front, looking indescribably alluring in his confidence and suave movements, following it up with a Staying Alive. The women behind him followed him exactly after the first gesture. I couldn't tell if they had practiced or if their quicker reactions allowed them such a seamless improvisation. Blinking, I decided it didn't matter.

Lost in the power and intensity, Kisten all but glowed, riding the combined agreement of the vampires behind him. Numb from an overload of pheromones, music, and lights, I felt myself go hazy. Every motion had a liquid grace, every gesture was precise and unhurried.

The noise beat at me, and as I watched them party with a wild abandonment, I realized that it stemmed from the chance to be as they wanted to be without fear of anyone reminding them that they were vampires and therefore *had* to be dark and depressed and carry a mysterious danger. And I felt privileged to be respected enough to see them as they wished they could be.

Swaying, I leaned into Steve while the base line beat my mind into a blessed numbness. My eyelids refused to stay open. A thunder of noise shook through me, then subsided to mutate into a faster beat of different music. Someone touched my arm, and my eyes opened.

"Rachel?"

It was Kisten, and I smiled, giddy. "You dance good," I said. "Dance with me?"

He shook his head, glancing at the vampire who was holding me upright. "Help me get her outside. This is fucking weird."

"Bad, bad mouth," I slurred, my eyes closing again. "Watch your mouth."

A giggle escaped me, and it turned into a delighted shriek when someone picked me up to carry me cradled in his arms. I shivered as the noise lessened, and my head thumped into someone's chest. It was warm, and I snuggled closer. The thundering beat softened to casual conversation and the clatter of china. A heavy blanket covered me, and I made a sound of protest when someone opened a door and cold air hit me.

The music and laughter behind me subsided into an icy silence broken by twin steps crunching on grainy snow and the chiming of a car. "Do you want me to call someone?" I heard a man ask as an uncomfortably cold draft made me shiver.

"No. I think all she needs is some air. If she isn't right by the time we get there, I'll call Ivy."

"Well, take it easy, boss," the first voice said.

I felt a drop, and then the cold of a leather seat pressed against my cheek. Sighing, I snuggled deeper under the blanket that smelled of Kisten and leather. My fingers were humming, and I could hear my heartbeat and feel my blood moving. Even the thump of the door closing did nothing to stir me. The sudden roar of the engine was soothing, and as the car's motion pushed me into oblivion, I could have sworn I heard monks singing.

Twelve

The familiar rumble of driving over railroad tracks woke me, and my hand shot out to grab the handle before the door could jiggle open. My eyelids flashed apart when my knuckles smacked into the unfamiliar door. Oh yeah. I wasn't in Nick's truck; I was in Kisten's Corvette.

I froze, slumped and staring at the door with Kisten's leather coat draped over me like a blanket. Kisten took a slow breath, and the volume of the music dropped. He knew I was awake. My face warmed, and I wished I could pretend I was still passed out.

Depressed, I sat up and put Kisten's long coat on the best I could in the tight confines of the car. I wouldn't look at him, gazing out the window to try to place where in the Hollows we were. The streets were busy, and the clock on the dash said it was nearing two. I had passed out like a drunk in front of a fair slice of Cincinnati's upper-middle-class vampires, high on their pheromones. They must have thought I was a weak-willed, skinny witch who couldn't hold her own.

Kisten shifted in his seat as he eased to a halt at a light. "Welcome back," he said softly.

Lips pressed tight, I subtly felt my neck to make sure everything was the way I'd left it. "How long was I out?" I asked. *This is going to do wonders for my reputation.*

Kisten moved the gearshift out and back into first. "You didn't pass out. You fell asleep." The light changed and he inched up on the car in front of us to bully it into moving. "Passing out implies a lack of restraint. Falling asleep is what you do when you're tired." He glanced at me as we went through the intersection. "Everyone gets tired."

"No one falls asleep in a dance club," I said. "I passed out." My mind sifted through the memories, clear as holy water instead of mercifully blurred, and my face flamed. Sugared, he had called it. I had been blood-sugared. I wanted to go home. I wanted to go home, crawl into the priest hole the pixies had found in the belfry stairway, and just die.

Kisten was silent, the tensing of his body while he drove telling me he was going to say something as soon as he double-checked it against his patronizing meter. "I'm sorry," he said, surprising me, but the admission of guilt fed my anger instead of pacifying it. "I was an ass for taking you into Piscary's before finding out if witches could get blood-sugared. It never occurred to me." His jaw clenched. "And it's not as bad as you think."

"Yeah, right," I muttered, hand searching under the seat until I found my clasp purse. "I bet it's halfway across the city by now. 'Hey, anybody want to go over to Morgan's tonight and watch her get sugared? All it takes is enough of us having fun and down she goes! Whoo hoo!' "

Kisten's attention was riveted on the road. "It wasn't like that. And there were over two hundred vamps in there, a good portion undead."

"And that's supposed to make me feel better?"

Motions stiff, he pulled his phone from a pocket, punched a button, and handed it to me.

"Yeah?" I questioned into the phone, almost snarling. "Who is this?"

"Rachel? God, are you okay? I swear I'll kill him for taking you into Piscary's. He said you got sugared. Did he bite you?"

"Ivy!" I stammered, then glared at Kisten. "You told Ivy? Thanks a hell of a lot. Want to call my mom next?"

"Like Ivy wouldn't find out?" he said. "I wanted her to hear it from me. And I was worried about you," he added, stopping my next outburst.

"Did he bite you!" Ivy said, jerking my attention from his last words. "Did he?"

I turned back to the phone. "No," I said, feeling my neck. *Though I don't know why. I was* such *an idiot.*

"Come home," she said, and my anger shifted to rebellion. "If someone bit you, I could tell. Come home so I can smell you."

A sound of disgust came from me. "I'm not coming home so you can smell me! Everyone there was really nice about it. And it felt good to let go for five stinking minutes." I scowled at Kisten, seeing why he had given me Ivy to talk to. The manipulative bastard smiled. How could I stay angry with him when I was defending him?

"You got blood-sugared in five minutes?" Ivy sounded horrified.

"Yeah," I said dryly. "Maybe you ought to try it. Go sit and soak up the pheromones at Piscary's. They might not let you in, though. You might kill everyone else's buzz."

Her breath caught, and I immediately wished I could take it back. *Shit.* "Ivy . . . I'm sorry," I said quickly. "I shouldn't have said that."

"Let me talk to Kisten," came her soft voice.

I licked my lips, feeling like dirt. "Sure."

Fingers cold, I handed the phone to him. His unreadable eyes met mine for a flash. He listened for a moment, muttered something I didn't catch, then ended the call. I watched him for any hint of his mood as he tucked the little silver phone away behind his wool coat.

"Blood-sugared?" I questioned, thinking I ought to know what happened. "You want to tell me what that is exactly?"

His hands shifted on the wheel and he took a more relaxed position. The come-and-go flashes from the streetlights made eerie shadows on him. "It's a mild depressant," he said, "that vampires kick out when they're sated and relaxed. Sort of like an afterglow? It came as a surprise the first time a few of the newest undead got sugared shortly after Piscary's went to an all-vamp clientele. It did them a world of good, so I took out the tables upstairs and put in a light show and DJ. Made it into a dance club. Everyone got sugared after that."

He hesitated as we made a sharp turn into an enormous parking lot down by the riverfront. Piles of snow rose six feet up at the edges. "It's a natural high," he said as he downshifted and drove slowly to the small cluster of cars parked by a large brightly lit boat at the dock. "Legal, too. Everyone likes it, and they've started self-policing themselves, kicking out anyone who comes in looking for a quick bleed and protecting the ones who come in hurting and fall asleep like you did. It's making a difference, too. Go ask that FIB captain of yours. Violent crimes being perpetrated by single young vamps have dropped."

"No kidding," I said, thinking it sounded like an informal vampire support group. *Maybe Ivy should go. Nah. She'd ruin it for everyone else.*

"You wouldn't have been so receptive if you hadn't needed it so much," he said, parking at the outskirts.

"Oh, so it *is* my fault," I said dryly.

"Don't," he said, his words harsh as he yanked the parking brake up. "I let you yell at me once already tonight. Don't try to flip this back on me. The more you need it, the harder it hits you is all. That's why no one thought anything less of you—and maybe they think a little more."

Taken aback, I made an apologetic face. "Sorry." I kinda liked that he was too smart to be manipulated by wicked female logic. It made things more interesting. Slowly he relaxed, turning off the heater and the softly playing disc.

"You were hurting inside," he said as he took the singing monk CD out and put it in its case. "From Nick. I've watched you hurt since you drew on that line through him and he got scared. And they got a kick out of seeing you unwind." He smiled with a distant look. "It made them feel good that the big bad witch who beat up Piscary trusted them. Trust is a feeling we don't get very often, Rachel. Living vampires lust after it almost as much as blood. That's why Ivy is ready to kill anyone who threatens your friendship with her."

I said nothing, staring as it started to make sense.

"You didn't know that, did you?" he added, and I shook my head, uncomfortable with digging into the whys of my relationship with Ivy. The car was getting cold, and I shivered.

"And showing your vulnerability probably upped your reputation, too," he said. "That you didn't feel threatened by them and let it happen."

I looked at the boat sitting before us, decorated with blinking holiday lights. "I didn't have a choice."

He reached out and adjusted the collar of his coat about my shoulders. "Yes, you did."

Kisten's hand fell from me, and I gave him a weak smile. I wasn't convinced, but at least I didn't feel like so much of a fool. My mind went over the events, the slow slide from a relaxed state into sleep, and the attitudes of those around me. There hadn't been any laughter at my expense. I had felt comforted, cared for. Understood. And there hadn't been a flicker of blood lust coming from any of them. I hadn't known vampires could be like that.

"Line dancing, Kisten?" I said, feeling my lips quirk into a wry smile.

A nervous laugh came from him and he bowed his head. "Hey, ah, could you not tell anyone about that?" he asked, the rims of his ears reddening. "What happens at Piscary's stays at Piscary's. It's an unwritten rule."

Being stupid, I reached out and ran a finger over the arch of his blood-reddened ear. He beamed, shifting to take my hand and brush his lips against my fingers. "Unless you want to get yourself banned from there as well," he said.

A shiver went through me at his breath on my fingers, and I pulled my hand away. His speculative look went right to my core, pulling my stomach into knots of anticipation. "You looked good out there," I said, not caring if it was a mistake. "Do you have a karaoke night?"

"Mmmm," he murmured, shifting in his seat to fall into his bad-boy slump against the door. "Karaoke. There's an idea. Tuesdays are slow. We never get enough people to get a good buzz going. That might be just the thing."

I turned my attention to the boat to hide my smile. The image of Ivy on stage singing "Round Midnight" flitted through me and was gone. Kisten's attention followed mine to the boat. It was one of those remade riverboats, two stories tall and almost entirely enclosed. "I'll take you home if you want," he said.

Shaking my head, I tightened the tie on his coat, and the scent of leather puffed up. "No, I want to see how you pay for a dinner cruise on an iced-over river with only sixty dollars."

"This isn't dinner. This is the entertainment." He went to toss his hair artfully aside, then stopped mid-movement.

The lights in my head started to go on. "It's a gambling boat," I said. "That's not fair. Piscary owns all the gambling boats. You won't have to pay for a thing."

"It's not Piscary's boat." Kisten got out of the car and came around to my side. Looking good in his wool coat, he opened my door and waited for me to get out.

"Oh," I said, more lights turning on. "We're here checking out the competition?"

"Something like that." He bent to look at me. "Coming? Or are we going to leave?"

If he wasn't going to get his chips for free, it would be legal under our arrangement. And I'd never gambled before. It might be fun. Accepting his hand, I let him help me out of the car.

His pace was rapid as we hustled to the railed gangplank. A man in a parka and gloves waited at the foot of the ramp, and as Kisten talked with him, I glanced at the boat's waterline. Rows of bubbles kept the riverboat from becoming iced in. It was probably more expensive than taking the boat out for the winter, but city regulations stipulated you could only gamble on the river. And even though the boat was tied to the dock, it *was* on the water.

After speaking into a radio, the big man let us pass. Kisten put a hand on the small of my back and pushed me forward. "Thanks for letting me borrow your coat," I said as my boots clattered up and we found ourselves on the covered walkway. Tonight's snow made a white icing, and I brushed it off the railing to make slushy clumps in the open water.

"My pleasure," he said, pointing to a half wood, half glass door. There was an etched intertwined pair of capital S's on it, and I shuddered when a shimmer of ley line force passed through me when Kisten opened the door and we crossed the threshold. It was probably the casino's antitampering charm, and it gave me the willies, like I was breathing air coated in oil.

Another big man in a tux—a witch, by the familiar scent of redwood—was there to greet us, and he took both Kisten's and my coat. Kisten signed the guest book, putting me down as "guest." Peeved, I wrote my name below his with big loopy flourishes, taking up three entire lines. The pen made my fingers tingle, and I looked at the metal barrel before I set it down. All my warning flags went up, and while Kisten bought a single chip with most of our date allowance, I made a precise line through both my and Kisten's name to prevent our signatures from possibly being used as a focusing object for a ley line charm.

"And you did that because . . ." Kisten questioned as he took my arm.

"Trust me." I smiled at the stone-faced witch in a tux handling the guest book. There were subtler ways to prevent such thefts of focusing objects, but I didn't know them. And that I had just insulted the host didn't bother me at all. Like I would ever be back there again?

Kisten had my arm so I was free to nod, as if I was important to anyone who looked up from his or her gaming. I was glad Kisten had dressed me; I'd have looked like a whore here in what I had picked out. The oak and teak paneling was comforting, and the rich green carpet felt scrumptious on my feet, clear through my boots. The few windows were draped with deep burgundy and black fabric, pulled aside to show the lights of Cincinnati. It was warm with the scent of people and excitement. The clatter of chips and bursts of sound quickened my pulse.

The low ceiling could have been claustrophobic, but it wasn't. There were two tables of blackjack, a craps table, a wheel, and an entire bank of one-armed bandits. In the corner was a small bar. Most of the staff was of the witch or warlock persuasion, if my gut instinct was right. I wondered where the poker table was. Upstairs, perhaps? I didn't know how to play anything else. Well, I could play blackjack, but that was for sissies.

"How about some blackjack?" Kisten said as he subtly guided me that way.

"Sure," I said, smiling.

"Do you want a drink?"

I glanced at the surrounding people. Mixed drinks were the rule, except for the one guy with a beer. He was drinking it out of the bottle, and it ruined his entire look, tux aside. "Dead Man's Float?" I asked as Kisten helped me up onto a stool. "Double shot of ice cream?"

The hovering waitress nodded, and after getting Kisten's order, the older witch left. "Kisten?" My gaze rose, drawn by an enormous disk of gray metal hanging from the ceiling. Ribbons of a shiny metal radiated from it like a sunburst, running to the edges of the ceiling. It could have been a decoration, but I'd be willing to bet the metal continued behind the wood paneling and even under the floor. "Kisten, what is that?" I whispered as I nudged him.

His gaze flicked to the disk. "Probably their security system." His eyes met mine and he smiled. "Freckles," he said. "Even without your spells, you're the most beautiful woman here."

I blushed at his compliment—sure now that the enormous disk was more than art deco—but when he turned back to the dealer, I frantically looked at the mirror wall by the stairway. My shoulders slumped as I saw me in my sophisticated outfit with freckles and my hair starting to frizz. The entire boat was a no-spell zone—at least for us earth witches using amulets—and I suspected that big purple disk had something in there to hinder ley line witches, too.

Just having the boat on the water was some protection against ley line tampering since you couldn't tap a line over the water unless you went the roundabout way through a familiar. In all likelihood, the boat's security system dampened already invoked ley line spells and would detect anyone tapping a line through a familiar to invoke a new one. I had once had a smaller version on my long-gone I.S. issue cuffs.

While Kisten made nice with the dealer over his paltry fifty-dollar chip, I sat back and studied the people. There were about thirty, all well-dressed and most older than Kisten and I. A frown crossed me as I realized Kisten was the only vamp here: witches, Weres, and a few red-eyed humans up past their bedtime, but no vampires.

That struck me as wrong, so while Kisten doubled his money with a few hands, I unfocused my attention, wanting to see the room with my second sight. I didn't like using my second sight, especially at night when I could see an overlay of the ever-after, but I'd rather suffer a bad case of the heebie-jeebies than not know what was happening. I spared a thought wondering if Algaliarept would know what I was doing, than decided there was no way he could unless I tapped a line. Which I wouldn't.

Settling myself, I closed my eyes so my little used second sight wouldn't have to compete with my more mundane vision, and with a mental shove, I opened my mind's eye. Immediately the wisps of my hair that had worked themselves free moved in the wind that always blew in the ever-after. The memory of the ship dissolved to nothing, and the broken landscape of the demon city took its place.

A soft sound of disgust slipped from me, and I reminded myself just why I never did this so close to the center of Cincinnati; the demon city was broken and ugly. The waning crescent moon was probably up now, and there was a definite red glow to the bottoms of the clouds, seeming to light the stark cascade of broken buildings and vegetation-stained rubble with a haze that covered everything and made me feel slimy somehow. It was said the demons lived belowground, and seeing what they had done to their city—built on the same ley lines as Cincinnati—I didn't wonder why. I'd seen the ever-after once during the day. It wasn't much better.

I wasn't in the ever-after, just viewing it, but I still felt uncomfortable, especially when I realized the reason everything looked clearer than usual was because I was coated in Algaliarept's black aura. Reminded of my slipped bargain, I opened my eyes, praying that Algaliarept wouldn't find a way to use me through the lines as he had threatened.

The gambling boat was just the way I left it, the noises that had been keeping me mentally connected to reality taking on meaning again. I was using both my visions, and before my second sight could become overwhelmed and lost, I hurriedly looked around.

My gaze was immediately drawn to the metal disk in the ceiling, and my mouth twisted in distaste. It pulsated with a thick purple smear, coating everything. I would have bet that this was what I had felt when I crossed the threshold.

It was everyone's aura that interested me most, though. I couldn't see mine, even when I looked in the mirror. Nick had once told me it was yellow and gold—not that anyone could see it under Al's now. Kisten's was a healthy, warm, orangy red shot through with slices of yellow concentrating about his head, and a smile quirked my lips. He used his head to make decisions, not his heart; I wasn't surprised. There was no black in it, though almost everyone else's in the room was streaked with darkness, I realized as I scanned the floor.

I stifled a twitch when I found a young man in the corner watching me. He was in a tux, but it had a comfortable look on him, not the stiff, uptight demeanor of the doorman or the professional dullness of the dealers. And the full glass by his hand said patron, not wait staff. His aura was so dark, it was hard to tell if it was a deep blue or deep green. A hint of demon black ran through it, and I felt a wash of embarrassment that if he was looking at me with his second sight—which I was sure he was—he could see me coated in Algaliarept's black slime.

Leaning back with his chin on his inward-curled fingertips, he fixed his gaze on mine from across the room, evaluating. He was deeply tanned—a neat trick in midwinter—and combined with the faint highlights in his straight black hair, I guessed he was from out of state and somewhere warm. Of average build and average looks, he didn't strike me as particularly attractive, but his confident assurance warranted a second look. He appeared wealthy, too, but who didn't in a tux?

My eyes slid from him to the guy swilling beer, and I decided tux-trash could be done after all. And with that thought making me smile, I turned back to surfer boy.

He was still watching me, and upon seeing my smile, he matched it, tilting his head in speculation and inviting conversation. I took a breath to shake my head, then stopped. Why in hell not? I was fooling myself that Nick was coming back. And my date with Kisten was a one-night-only offer.

Wondering if his trace of black was from a demon mark, I narrowed my concentration to try to see past his unusually dark aura. As I did, the purple glow coming from the ceiling disk brightened to take on the first tinges of yellow.

The man started, his attention jerking to the ceiling. Shock marred his clean-shaven face. An abrupt call went through the room from about three different places, and at my forgotten elbow, Kisten swore as the dealer said this hand had been tampered with and that all play was suspended until he could break a new deck.

I lost my second sight completely then, as the witch manning the guest book pointed me out to a second man, clearly security by his serious lack of any emotional expression.

"Oh crap," I swore, turning my back on the room and picking up my Dead Man's Float.

"What?" Kisten said irately while he stacked his winnings according to color.

I winced, meeting his eyes over the rim of my glass. "I think I made a boo-boo."

Thirteen

"What did you do, Rachel?" Kisten said flatly, stiffening as he looked over my shoulder.

"Nothing!" I exclaimed. The dealer gave me a tired look and broke the seal on a fresh deck of cards, and I didn't turn when I felt a presence loom heavy behind me.

"Is there a problem?" Kisten said. His attention was fixed a good three feet above my head. Slowly I turned, finding a really, really big man in a really, really big tux.

"It's the lady I need to talk with," his voice rumbled.

"I didn't do anything," I said quickly. "I was just looking over, um, the security. . . ." I finished weakly. "Just as a professional interest. Here. Here's one of my cards. I'm in security myself." I fumbled in my clasp purse for one, handing it to him. "Really, I wasn't going to tamper with anything. I didn't tap a line. Honest."

Honest? How lame was that? My black business card looked small in his thick hands, and he glanced at it once, quickly reading it. He made eye contact with a woman at the foot of the stairs. She shrugged, mouthing, "She didn't tap a line," and he turned to me. "Thank you, Ms. Morgan," the man said, and my shoulders eased. "Please don't assert your aura over the house spells." He didn't smile at all. "Any more interference and we will ask you to leave."

"Sure, no problem," I said, starting to breathe again.

He walked away, and play resumed around us. Kisten's eyes were full of annoyance. "Can't I take you anywhere?" he said dryly, putting his chips into a little bucket and handing them to me. "Here. I have to use the little boys' room."

I stared blankly as he gave me a warning look before he ambled off, leaving me alone in a casino with a bucket of chips and no idea what to do with them. I turned to the blackjack dealer, and he arched his eyebrows. "Guess I'll play something else," I said as I slipped from the stool, and he nodded.

Clutch purse tucked under my arm, I glanced over the room with my chips in one hand and my drink in the other. Surfer boy was gone, and I stifled a sigh of disappointment. Head down, I looked at the chips, seeing they were engraved with the same intertwined S's. Not even knowing the monetary value of what I had, I drifted to the excitement of the craps table.

I smiled at two men who slid apart to make a spot for me, setting my drink and chips on the lower rim of the table while I tried to figure out why some people were happy at the five that was rolled and some were upset. One of the witches who'd made room for me was standing too close, and I wondered when he would inflict his pickup line on me. Sure enough, after the next roll he gave me a sloppy grin and said, "Here I am. What are your last two wishes?"

My hand trembled and I forced it to remain unmoving. "Please," I said. "Just stop."

"Oh, nice manners, babe," he said loudly, trying to embarrass me, but I could embarrass myself a hell of a lot easier than he could.

The chatter of the game seemed to vanish as I focused on him. I was ready to let him have it, my self-respect wounded to the quick, when surfer boy appeared. "Sir," he said calmly, "that was the worst line I've ever heard, not only insulting but showing a severe lack of forethought. You're obviously bothering the young woman. You should leave before she does permanent damage to you."

It was protective, yet implied I could take care of myself, not an easy thing to accomplish in one paragraph, much less one sentence. I was impressed.

One-line-wonder took a breath, paused, and with his eyes rising over my shoulder, he changed his mind. Muttering, he took his drink and his buddy on the other side of me and left.

My shoulders eased and I found myself sighing as I turned to surfer boy. "Thank you," I said, taking a closer look at him. His eyes were brown and his lips were thin, and when he smiled, the expression encompassed both of them, full and honest. There was some Asian heritage in his not-too-distant past, giving him straight black hair and a small nose and mouth.

He ducked his head, seemingly embarrassed. "No thanks needed. I had to do something to redeem all men for that line." His strong-jawed face took on a false sincerity. "What're your other two wishes?" he asked, chuckling.

I laughed, ending it by looking at the craps table as I thought of my big teeth.

"My name is Lee," he said, stepping into the silence before it became awkward.

"Rachel," I said, relieved when he extended his hand. He smelled like sand and redwood, and he slipped his thin fingers into my grip to meet my pressure with an equal force. Our hands yanked apart and my eyes jerked to his when a slip of ley line energy equalized between us.

"Sorry," he said as he tucked his hand behind his back. "One of us must be low."

"It's probably me," I said, refusing to wipe my hand. "I don't keep line energy in my familiar."

Lee's eyebrows rose. "Really? I couldn't help but notice you looking at the security."

Now I was really embarrassed, and I took a sip of my drink and turned to lean with my elbows on the upper railing about the table. "That was an accident," I said as the amber dice rolled past. "I didn't mean to trip the alarms. I was just trying to get a closer look at—um—you," I finished, certainly as red at my hair. *Oh God, I was screwing this up royally.*

But Lee seemed amused, his teeth white in his suntanned face. "Me too."

His accent was nice. West Coast, perhaps? I couldn't help but like his easy demeanor, but when he took a sip of his white wine, my gaze fixed to his wrist peeping from behind his cuff and my heart seemed to stop. It was scarred. It was scarred exactly like mine. "You have a demon sca—" His eyes jerked to mine, and my words cut off. "Sorry."

Lee's attention flicked to the nearby patrons. None seemed to have heard. "It's okay," he said softly, his brown eyes pinched. "I got it by accident."

I put my back against the railing, understanding now why my demon-tainted aura hadn't scared him off. "Don't we all?" I said, surprised when he shook his head. My thoughts went to Nick, and I bit my lower lip.

"How did you get yours?" he asked, and it was my turn to be nervous.

"I was dying. He saved me. I owe him for safe passage through the lines." I didn't think it necessary to tell Lee that I was the demon's familiar. "How about you?"

"Curiosity." Eyes squinting, he frowned at a past memory.

Curious myself, I gave him another once-over. I wouldn't say Al's real name and break the contract we had come to when I had bought a summoning name from him, but I wanted to know if it was the same demon. "Hey, uh, does yours wear crushed green velvet?" I asked.

Lee jerked. His brown eyes went wide under his sharply cut bangs, and then a smile born of shared trouble came over him. "Yes. He talks in a British accent—"

"And has a thing for frosting and french fries?" I interrupted.

Lee ducked his head and chuckled. "Yes, when he isn't morphing into my father."

"How about that?" I said, feeling an odd kinship. "It's the same one."

Tugging his sleeve down to cover the mark, Lee rested his side against the craps table. "You seem to have a knack for ley lines," he said. "Are you taking instruction from him?"

"No," I said forcefully. "I'm an earth witch." I twiddled my finger with my ring amulet and touched the cord of the one around my neck that was supposed to defrizz my hair.

His attention went from the scar on my wrist to the ceiling. "But you . . ." he drawled.

I shook my head and sipped my drink, my back to the game. "I told you it was an accident. I'm not a ley line witch. I took a class is all. Well, half of one. The instructor died before the class was finished."

He blinked in disbelief. "Dr. Anders?" he blurted. "You had a class with Dr. Anders?"

"You knew her?" I pulled myself straighter.

"I've heard of her." He leaned close. "She was the best ley line witch east of the Mississippi. I came out here to take classes from her. She was supposed to be the best."

"She was," I said, depressed. She was going to help get Nick unbound as my familiar. Now, not only was the spell book gone, but she was dead and all her knowledge with her. I jerked upright as I realized I had been wool gathering. "So, you're a student?" I asked.

Lee rested his elbows on the rail, watching the dice skitter and roll behind me. "Road scholar," he said shortly. "I got my degree years ago from Berkeley."

"Oh, I'd love to see the coast some time," I said, playing with my necklace and wondering how much of this conversation had turned into exaggeration. "Doesn't the salt make everything difficult?"

He shrugged. "Not so much for ley line witches. I feel bad for earth witches, locked into a path that has no power."

My mouth dropped open. No power? Hardly. Earth magic's strength stemmed from ley lines as much as ley line witches' spells. That it was filtered through plants made it more forgiving, and perhaps slower, but no less powerful. There wasn't a ley line charm written that could physically change a person's form. Now that was power. Chalking it up to ignorance, I let it slide lest I drive him away before I got a chance to know just how big of a jerk he was, first.

"Look at me," he said, clearly recognizing that he had stuck his foot so far down his throat that his toes might wiggle out of his ass. "Here I am bothering you, when you probably want to pl[illegible] some before your boyfriend gets back."

"He's not my boyfriend," I said, not as excited as I could be for the subtle inquiry as to my attached status. "I told him he couldn't take me out on a decent date for sixty dollars, and he accepted the challenge."

Lee ran his eyes over the casino. "How's it going?"

I sipped my drink, wishing the ice cream hadn't melted. Behind me there was a loud cheer as something good happened. "Well, so far I've gotten sugared and passed out in a vamp dance club, insulted my roommate, and tripped the security system of a casino boat." I lifted a shoulder in a half shrug. "Not bad, I guess."

"It's early yet." Lee's gaze followed the rolling dice behind me. "Can I buy you a drink? I've heard the house wine is good. Merlot, I think it is."

I wondered where this was going. "No thanks. Red wine . . . doesn't sit well with me."

He chuckled. "I'm not particularly fond of it either. It gives me migraines."

"Me too," I exclaimed softly, truly surprised.

Lee tossed his bangs from his eyes. "Now, if I had said that, you would have accused me of dropping you a line." I smiled, feeling shy all of a sudden, and he turned to the cheering at the table. "You don't gamble, do you?" he said.

I glanced behind me and then back to him. "It shows, huh?"

He put a hand on my shoulder and turned me around.

"They've rolled three fours in a row, and you haven't noticed," he said softly, almost in my ear.

I did nothing to either discourage or encourage him, the sudden pounding of my heart not telling me what to do. "Oh, is that unusual?" I said, trying to keep my voice light.

"Here," he said, motioning to the craps man. "New roller," he called loudly.

"Oh, wait," I protested. "I don't even know how to bet."

Not to be deterred, Lee took my little chip bucket and guided me to the head of the table. "You roll, I'll bet for you." He hesitated, brown eyes innocent. "Is that . . . okay?"

"Sure," I said, grinning. What did I care? Kisten had given me the chips. That he wasn't there to spend them with me wasn't my problem. Teaching me how to throw craps was what he was supposed to be doing, not some guy in a tux. Where was he, anyway?

I glanced over the assembled faces around the table as I took the dice. They felt slippery—like bone in my hand—and I shook them.

"Wait . . ." Lee reached out and took my hand in his. "You have to kiss them first. But only once," he said, his voice serious though his eyes glinted. "If they think they'll get loved all the time, they won't put out."

"Right," I said, his hands falling when I pulled the dice to my lips but refused to touch them. I mean, really. Yuck. People shuffled their chips around, and heart faster than the game warranted, I threw the dice. I eyed Lee, not the dice, as they skittered and danced.

Lee watched in rapt attention, and I thought that though he wasn't pretty like Kisten, he was far more likely to be on a magazine cover than Nick. Just an average guy, and a witch with a degree. My mother would love me to bring this one home. Something had to be wrong with him. *Besides his demon mark?* I thought dryly. God, save me from myself.

The watching people had various reactions to the eight I rolled. "Not good?" I asked Lee.

His shoulders rose and fell as he took the dice the craps man pushed to him. "It's okay," he said. "But you have to roll an eight again before a seven comes up to win."

"Oh," I said, pretending I understood. Mystified, I threw the dice. This time they came up nine. "Keep going?" I said, and he nodded.

"I'll place some one-roll bets for you," he said, then paused. "If that's okay?"

Everyone was waiting, so I said, "Sure, that will be great."

Lee nodded. His brow furrowed for a moment, then he set a pile of red chips on a square. Someone snickered, leaning to whisper "Innocent slaughter" in their neighbor's ear.

The dice were warm in my hand, and I sent them rolling. They bounced off the wall, coming to halt. It was an eleven, and everyone at the table groaned. Lee, though, was smiling. "You won," he said, putting a hand on my shoulder. "See?" He pointed. "Odds are fifteen-to-one of rolling an eleven. I figured you'd be a zebra."

My eyes widened as the predominate color of my pile of chips went from red to blue as the craps man piled a stack on them. "Beg pardon?"

Lee set the dice in my hand. "When you hear hoofbeats, look for horses. That would be the common rolls in this case. I knew you'd roll something odd. A zebra."

I grinned, rather liking the idea, and the dice flew from me almost before he moved my chips to another square. My pulse quickened, and as Lee explained the details of odds and betting, I rolled again, and again, and again, the table becoming louder and more excited. It wasn't long before I caught on. The risk, the question of what would happen and the breathless wait until the dice settled, was akin to being on a run, only better because here it was little plastic chips on the line, not my life. Lee switched his tutorial to other ways to wager, and when I dared to make a suggestion, he beamed, gesturing that the table was mine.

Delighted, I took over the betting, letting it ride where it was while Lee put a hand on my shoulder and whispered the odds of throwing this and that. He smelled like sand. I could feel his excitement through the thin material of my silk shirt, and the warmth of his fingers seemed to linger on my shoulder when he shifted to put the dice in my hand.

I looked up when the table cheered my latest roll, surprised that almost everyone was clustered about us and that we had somehow become the center of attention. "Looks like you have it." Lee smiled as he took a step back.

Immediately my face went slack. "You're leaving?" I asked as the red-cheeked guy drinking beer pressed the dice into my hand and urged me to throw them.

"I need to go," he said. "But I couldn't resist meeting you." Leaning close, he said, "I enjoyed teaching you craps. You're a very special woman, Rachel."

"Lee?" Confused, I set the dice down and the people around the table groaned.

Lee slid the dice into his hand and put them in mine. "You're hot. Don't stop."

"Do you want my phone number?" I asked. *Oh God, I sounded desperate.*

But Lee smiled, his teeth hidden. "You're Rachel Morgan, the I.S. runner who quit to work with the last living Tamwood vamp. You're in the phone book—in four places, no less."

My face flamed, but I managed to stop myself before I told everyone I wasn't a hooker.

"Till next time," Lee said, raising his hand and inclining his head before he walked away.

Setting the dice down, I backed from the table so I could watch him vanish up the stairway at the back of the boat, looking good in his tux and purple sash. It matched his aura, I decided. A new shooter took my place, and the noise returned.

My good mood soured, I retreated to a table by a cold window. One of the wait staff brought me my three buckets of chips. Another set a fresh Dead Man's Float on a linen napkin. A third lit the red candle and asked me if I needed anything. I shook my head, and he eased away. "What's wrong with this picture?" I whispered as I rubbed my fingers into my forehead. Here I was dressed up like a young rich widow, sitting alone in a casino with three buckets of chips. Lee had known who I was and never let on? Where in hell was Kisten?

The excitement at the craps table nosedived, and people started pulling away in twos and threes. I counted to a hundred, then two hundred. Angry, I stood, ready to cash in my chips and find Kisten. Little boys' room, my ass. He was probably upstairs playing poker—without me.

Chip buckets in hand, I jerked to a stop. Kisten was coming down the stairs, movements sharp and quick with a living vampire's speed. "Where have you been?" I demanded when he came even with me. His face was tight and I could see a line of sweat on him.

"We're leaving," he said shortly. "Let's go."

"Hold up." I jerked out of the grip he had on my elbow. "Where've you been? You left me all alone. Some guy had to teach me how to throw craps. See what I won?"

Kisten glanced down at my buckets, clearly not impressed.

"The tables are fixed," he said, shocking me. "They were entertaining you while I talked to the boss."

I felt as if I'd been punched in the gut. I jerked back when he went for my elbow again. "Stop trying to drag me around," I said, not caring that people were watching. "And what do you mean, you were talking to the boss?"

He gave me an exasperated look, the first hints of stubble showing on his chin. "Can we do this outside?" he said, obviously in a hurry.

I glanced at the big men coming down the stairway. This was a gambling boat. It wasn't Piscary's. Kisten was handling the undead vampire's affairs. He was here leaning on the new guy in town, and he had brought me in case there was trouble. My chest tightened in anger as it all started to come together, but discretion was the wiser part of valor.

"Fine," I said. My boots made muted thumps in time with my pulse as I headed for the door. I dropped my buckets of chips on the counter and smiled grimly at the chip lady. "I want my winnings donated to the city fund for rebuilding the burned orphanages," I said tightly.

"Yes, ma'am," the woman said politely, weighing them out.

Kisten took a chip from the pile. "We're going to cash this one out."

I plucked it from his fingers, mad at him for having used me like this. This was where he wanted Ivy to go with him. And I had fallen for it. Whistling, I tossed the chip to the craps dealer. He caught it, inclining his head in thanks.

"That was a hundred-dollar chip!" Kisten protested.

"Really?" Ticked, I took another, throwing it after the first. "I don't want to be a cheap ass," I muttered. The woman handed me a receipt for $8,750, donated to the city's fund. I stared at it for a moment, then tucked it in my clutch purse.

"Rachel," Kisten protested, his face going red behind his blond hair.

"We're keeping nothing." Ignoring Kisten's coat that the doorman was holding for me, I blew out the door with its double S's. One for Saladan, perhaps? *God, I was a fool.*

"Rachel . . ." Anger made Kisten's voice hard as he leaned out the door after me. "Come back here and tell her to cash one of them out."

"You gave me the first ones, and I won the rest!" I shouted from the foot of the ramp, my arms wrapped around me in the falling snow. "I'm donating all of them. And I'm pissed at you, you bloodsucking coward!"

The man at the foot of the ramp snickered, steeling his face into impassivity when I glared at him. Kisten hesitated, then closed the door and came down after me, my borrowed coat over his arm. I stomped to his car, waiting for him to unlock the door for me or tell me to call a cab.

Still putting on his coat, Kisten stopped beside me. "Why are you mad at me?" he said flatly, his blue eyes starting to go black in the dim light.

"That is Saladan's boat, isn't it?" I said furiously, pointing. "I may be slow, but I eventually catch on. Piscary runs the gambling in Cincinnati. You came out here looking for Piscary's cut. And Saladan turned you down, didn't he? He's moving in on Piscary's turf, and you brought me as backup knowing I would fight for your ass if things got out of control."

Incensed, I ignored his teeth and his strength and put my face inches from his. "Don't you *ever* trick me into backing you up again. You could have gotten me killed with your little games. I don't get a second chance, Kisten. Dead is dead for me!"

My voice echoed off the nearby buildings. I thought of the ears listening from the boat, and my face burned. But I was angry, damn it, and this was going to be settled before I got back in Kisten's car. "You dress me up to make me feel special," I said, my throat tight and my anger high. "Treat me as if taking me out was something you wanted to do for me even if it was only in the hope of sinking your teeth in, and then I find out it's not even that but *business*? I wasn't even your first choice. You wanted Ivy to come with you, not me! I was your *alternate plan.* How cheap do you think that makes me feel?"

He opened his mouth, then shut it.

"I can understand you using me as a second-choice date because you're a man and therefore a jerk!" I exclaimed. "But you knowingly brought me out here into a potentially dangerous situation without my spells, without my charms. You said it was a date, so I left everything at home. Hell, Kisten, if you wanted backup, I would have!

"Besides," I added, my anger starting to slow since he seemed to actually be listening instead of spending the time formulating excuses. "It would have been fun knowing what was going on. I could have pumped people for information, stuff like that."

He stared at me, surprise mirrored in his eyes. "Really?"

"Yeah, really. You think I became a runner for their dental plan? It would've made for more fun than having some guy teach me craps. That was your job, by the way."

Kisten stood next to me, a dusting of snow starting to accumulate on his leather coat draped over his arm. His face was long and unhappy in the dim light from a streetlamp. He took a breath, and my eyes narrowed. It escaped him in a quick sound of defeat. I could feel my blood racing, and my body was both hot and cold from my anger and the cutting wind off the river. I liked even less that Kisten could probably read my feelings better than I could.

His eyes with their growing rim of blue flicked past me to the boat. As I watched, they flashed to black, chilling me. "You're right," he said shortly, his voice tight. "Get in the car."

My anger flamed back. *Son of a bitch . . .* "Don't patronize me," I said tightly.

He reached out, and I jerked away before he could touch me. Black eyes looking soulless in the dim light, he turned his reach for me into opening my door. "I'm not," he said, his motions edging into that eerie vamp quickness. "There are three men coming off the boat. I can smell gunpowder. You were right, I was wrong. Get in the damn car."

Fourteen

Fear flashed through me, and sensing it, Kisten took a breath as if I had slapped him. I froze, reading in his rising hunger that I had more to worry about than the feet booming down the gangplank. Heart pounding, I got in the car. Kisten handed me my coat and his keys. My door thumped shut, and while he crossed in front of his car, I jammed the key into the ignition. Kisten got in, and the sudden rumble came simultaneously with him shutting his door.

The three men had shifted direction, their pace quickening as they headed for an early model BMW. "They'll never catch us in that," Kisten scoffed. Wipers going to push off the snow, he put the car in gear, and I braced against the dash when he punched it. We skidded, fishtailing into the street and running a late yellow light. I didn't look behind us.

Kisten slowed as the traffic increased, and pulse hammering, I wiggled into his coat and put on my seat belt. He flicked the heater on high, but it only blew cold air. I felt naked without my charms. Damn it, I should have brought something, but it was supposed to have been a date!

"I'm sorry," Kisten said as he cut a sudden left. "You were right."

"You *idiot*!" I shouted, my voice harsh in the close confines of the car. "Don't you *ever* make my decisions for me, Kisten. Those men had guns, and I had nothing!" Fading adrenaline made my words louder than I had intended, and I glanced at him, suddenly sobered as I remembered the black of his eyes when my fear had hit him. He might look safe, dressed in his Italian suit and his hair slicked back—but he wasn't. He could shift between one heartbeat and the next. *God, what was I doing here?*

"I said I was sorry," Kisten said again, not looking from the road as the lit buildings, hazy with snow, passed. There was more than a hint of bother in his tone, and I decided to stop shouting at him even if I was still pissed and shaking. Besides, he wasn't cowering, begging for forgiveness, and his confident admission of having made a mistake was nice for a change.

"Don't worry about it," I said sourly, not yet ready to forgive him, but not wanting to talk about it anymore, either.

"Shit," he said, his jaw clenching as he watched the rearview mirror instead of the road in front of him. "They're still following us."

I twitched, managing to not turn and look, satisfying myself with what I could see in the side mirror. Kisten took a sudden right and my lips parted in disbelief. The road ahead of us was empty, a dark tunnel of nothing compared to the lights and the security of commerce behind us. "What are you doing?" I asked, hearing a tinge of fear in my voice.

His eyes were still on the road behind us when the dark Cadillac jerked out in front of us, blocking the road as it spun sideways.

"Kisten!" I shouted, bracing my arms against the dash. A tiny shriek escaped me as he swore and jerked the wheel. My head smacked the window and I bit back a cry of pain. Breath held, I felt the wheels lose contact with the pavement and we slipped on the ice. Still swearing, Kisten reacted with his vamp reflexes, the car fighting him. The little Corvette gave a final little hiccup of motion as it found the curb and we swayed to a shaken halt.

"Stay in the car." He reached for the door. Four men in dark suits were getting out of the Cadillac ahead of us. Three were in the BMW behind us. All witches, probably, and here I was, with only a couple of vanity charms. *This was going to look really good in the obituaries.*

"Kisten, wait!" I said.

Hand on the door, he turned. My chest clenched at the blackness in his eyes. *Oh God, he had vamped out.*

"It will be okay," he said, his voice a black-earth, rich rumble that went to my core and gripped my heart.

"How do you know?" I whispered.

A blond-dyed eyebrow shifted up so slightly, I wasn't sure it even moved. "Because if they kill me, then I'd be dead and I'll hunt them down. They want to—talk. Stay in the car."

He got out and shut the door. The car was still running, the thrum of the engine tightening my muscles one by one. Falling snow hit the windshield to melt, and I turned off the wipers. "Stay in the car," I muttered, fidgeting. I glanced behind me, seeing the three guys from the BMW moving closer. Kisten was lit to a stark severity as he crossed in front of his lights, approaching the four men with his palms forward with a casualness that I knew was false. "Like hell I'm going to stay in the car," I said, reaching for the handle and lurching into the cold.

Kisten turned. "I told you to stay in the car," he said, and I pushed down my fear at the starkness in his expression. He had already divorced himself from what was going to happen.

"Yeah, you did," I shot back, forcing my arms down. It was cold and I shivered.

He hesitated, clearly torn. The approaching men spread out. We were surrounded. Their faces were shadowed but confident. All they needed was a bat or crowbar to thump against their hand to make it complete. But they were witches. Their strength was in their magic.

My breath came slow, and I rocked forward on my flat boots. Feeling the stir of adrenaline, I moved into the car's headlights and put my back to Kisten's.

The black hunger in his eyes seemed to pause. "Rachel, please wait in the car," he said his voice making my skin crawl. "This won't take long, and I don't want you to get cold."

He didn't want me to get cold? I thought, watching the three guys from the BMW behind us settle in to make a living fence. "There are seven witches here," I said softly. "It only takes three to make a net, and one to hold it once it's in place."

"True, but it only takes me three seconds to drop a man."

The men in my sight faltered. There was a reason the I.S. didn't send witches to bring in a vampire. Seven against one might do it, but not without someone getting really hurt.

I risked a glance over my shoulder to see that the four guys from the Cadillac were looking at the man in the long coat who had gotten out from the BMW. *Top guy*, I thought, thinking he was too confident as he adjusted his long coat and jerked his head to the men around us. The two in front of Kisten started forward and three dropped back. Their lips were moving and their hands were gesturing. The hair on the back of my neck pricked at the sudden rise of power.

At least three ley line witches, I guessed, then went cold as one of the advancing men pulled out a gun. Crap. Kisten could come back from the dead, but I couldn't.

"Kisten . . ." I warned, my voice rising and my eyes fixed on the gun.

Kisten moved, and I jumped. One moment he was next to me, and the next he was among the men. There was a pop of a gun. Gasping, I ducked, blinding myself in the Corvette's headlights. Crouched, I saw one guy was down, but not the one with the gun.

Encircling us, almost lost in the glare, the ley line witches muttered and gestured, their net tightening when they took a step in. My skin tingled as the lacework fell over us.

Moving too fast to readily follow, Kisten grabbed the wrist of the man with the gun. The snap of bone was clear in the cold, dry air. My stomach lurched as the man screamed and fell to his knees. Kisten followed it up with a powerful blow to his head. Someone was shouting. The gun fell, and Kisten caught it before it hit the snow.

With a flick of his wrist, Kisten sent the gun arching to me. It glinted in the headlights as I lurched forward to catch it. The heavy metal landed in my grip. It was hot, surprising me. There was another pop of a gun, and I jerked. The gun fell to the snow.

"Get that weapon!" the man in the long coat at the outskirts shouted.

I peeked over the hood of Kisten's Corvette, seeing he had a gun, too. My eyes widened as I saw the black shadow of a man coming at me. There was a ball of orange ever-after in his hand. My breath hissed as he smiled and threw it at me.

I hit the pavement, the snow-covered ice making a hard landing. The ever-after exploded into a shower of sulfur-smelling sparkles as it struck Kisten's car and ricocheted away. Cold slush seeped against me, the shock clearing my head.

From the ground, I put my palms against the cold pavement and levered myself up. My clothes . . . My clothes! My silk-lined pants were covered in filthy gray snow. "Look what you made me do!" I shouted, furious as I shook the cold slop from me.

"You son of a bitch!" Kisten cried, and I spun to see three witches down in a messy circle about him. The one that had thrown the ever-after made a pained motion, and Kisten savagely kicked him. *How had he gotten there so fast?* "You burned my paint job, you mother!"

As I watched, Kisten's mien shifted in a breathless instant.

Eyes black, he lunged at the closest gesturing ley line witch. The man's eyes widened, but he had no time for more.

Kisten's fist rammed into his face, rocking his head back. There was an ugly sounding crunch, and the witch crumpled. Arms slack, he arched backward through the air, landing to skid into the headlights of the Cadillac.

Spinning before the first had stopped moving, Kisten landed before the next, turning in a tight circle. His dress shoes smacked into the back of the startled witch's knees. The man cried out as his legs buckled. The sound cut off with a frightening suddenness when Kisten stiff armed his throat. My stomach clenched at the gurgle and crackle of cartilage.

The third witch backpedaled into a run. *Mistake. Terrible, terrible mistake.*

Kisten paced the ten feet between them in half a heartbeat. Grabbing the fleeing witch, he spun him in a circle, never letting go of his arm. The pop of his arm dislocating hit me like a slap. I put a hand to my stomach, sickened. It had taken a moment's thought, and nothing more.

Kisten stopped before the last witch standing, an aggressive eight feet back. I shuddered, remembering Ivy looking at me like that. He had a pistol, but I didn't think it was going to help him.

"You going to shoot me?" Kisten snarled.

The man smiled. I felt him tap a line. My breath came quick to shout a warning.

Kisten jerked forward, catching the man about the throat. The man's eyes bulged in fear as he struggled for air. The pistol dropped, his hand hanging useless. Kisten's shoulders tensed, his aggression shining from him. I couldn't see his eyes. I didn't want to. But the man he held could, and he was terrified.

"Kisten!" I shouted, too afraid to interfere. *Oh God. Please no. I don't want to see this.*

Kisten hesitated, and I wondered if he could hear my heart pounding. Slowly, as if fighting himself, Kisten pulled the man closer. The witch was gasping, struggling to breathe. Headlights glinted on the spit frothing at the corner of his mouth, and his face was red.

"Tell Saladan I'll be seeing him," Kisten almost growled.

I jerked when Kisten's arm thrust out and the witch went flying. He landed against a defunct light post, and the shock reverberated up the pole to make the light flicker on. I was afraid to move as Kisten turned. Seeing me standing in the falling snow lit by the car's headlights, he paused. Eyes that awful black, he brushed a spot of dampness from his coat.

Poised and tense, I tore my gaze from him to follow his attention when he glanced over the carnage, brightly lit from the three pair of headlights and the one streetlamp. Men sprawled everywhere. The one with the dislocated shoulder had vomited and was trying to get to a car. From down the street a dog barked and a curtain fluttered against a lit window.

I put a hand to my stomach, nauseous. I had frozen. Oh God, I had frozen, unable to do anything. I had let myself get stupid because my death threats were gone. But because of what I did, I would always be a target.

Kisten strode into motion, the ring of blue around his black pupils a thin rim. "I told you to stay in the car," he said, and I stiffened as he took my elbow and led me to his Corvette.

Numb, I didn't resist. He wasn't angry with me, and I didn't want to make him any more aware of my pounding heart and lingering fear. But a tingle of warning brought me stiff. Jerking out of Kisten's grip, I turned, eyes wide and searching.

From under the streetlamp the broken man slitted his eyes, his face ugly in pain. "You lose, bitch," he said, then mouthed a savage word in Latin.

"Look out!" I cried, pushing Kisten away from me.

He fell back, catching his balance with his vampire grace. I went sprawling when my boots slipped. A raw scream shocked through me. Heart pounding, I scrambled up, my eyes going first to Kisten. He was all right. It was the witch.

My hand went to my mouth, horrified as his ever-after–smeared body writhed on the snow-covered sidewalk. Fear slithered through me as the kicked-up snow took on a tinge of red. He was bleeding through his pores. "God save him," I whispered.

He shrieked, then shrieked again, the harsh sound striking a primal chord in me. Kisten strode to him quickly. I couldn't stop him; the witch was bleeding, screaming in pain and fear. He was pushing every button Kisten had. I turned away, a trembling hand resting on the rumbling warm hood of the Corvette. I was going to get sick. I knew it.

My head jerked up as the man's terror and pain ended in a sodden crack. Kisten stood from his crouch, a horrible, angry look on him. The dog barked again, filling the icy night with the sound of alarm. A pair of dice rolled from the man's slack hand, and Kisten picked them up.

I couldn't think anymore. Kisten was suddenly next to me, his hand on my elbow hustling me to the car. I let him move me, glad he hadn't succumbed to his vampiric instincts, and wondering why he hadn't. If anything, his vampire aura was completely washed away, his eyes normal and his reactions only mildly fast.

"He's not dead," he said, handing me the dice. "None of them are dead. I didn't kill anyone, Rachel."

I wondered why he cared what I thought. Taking the pieces of plastic, I gripped them until my fingers ached. "Get the gun," I whispered. "My fingerprints are on it."

Not acknowledging he heard me, he tucked my coat in out of the door and shut it.

The sharp tang of blood drew my attention down, and I forced my hand open. The dice were sticky. My gut twisted, and I held a winter-cold fist to my mouth. They were the pair I had used in the casino. The entire room had seen me kiss them; he tried to use them as a focal object. But I hadn't made a link to them and so the black charm swung back to its maker instead.

I stared out the window trying not to hyperventilate. That was supposed to be me there, limbs contorted and sprawled in a smear of blood-melted snow. I had been a wild card in Saladan's game, and he had been prepared to take me out to tip the balance back to his men. And I had done nothing, too frozen by my lack of charms and shock to even make a circle.

There was a flash of brighter light as Kisten stepped in front of the car's headlights, bending to come up with the weapon. His eyes met mine—tired and weary—until a soft movement behind him brought him spinning around. Someone was trying to leave.

I made a small moan as Kisten took incredibly long, fast steps and had him, jerking him upright, feet dangling. A whimper came from the man, going right to my core as he pleaded for his life. I told myself that to pity him was foolish, that they had planned worse for me and Kisten. But all Kisten did was talk to him, faces touching as the vampire whispered into his ear.

In a splurge of motion, Kisten threw him onto the hood of the Cadillac, wiping the weapon off on the hem of the witch's coat. Finished, he dropped the gun and turned away.

Kisten's back was hunched when he stomped back to the car, making him a bad mix of anger and worry. I said nothing as he got in and turned the wipers on. Still silent, he jerked the gearshift back and forth, maneuvering the car to get out of the box the two cars had made.

I held onto the door handle and said nothing as our momentum shifted, stalled, and shifted again. Finally there was only clear road ahead of us, and Kisten floored it. My eyes widened as the wheels spun and we started to drift on the ice to the left, but then the tires caught and we lurched forward. We left the way we had come, in a sliding sound of racing engine.

I kept silent as Kisten drove, his motions quick and sudden. The lights abruptly brightened around us, falling onto his face, lined with stress. My stomach was tense and my back hurt. He knew I was trying to figure out how to react.

Watching him had been both exhilarating and scary as all hell. Living with Ivy had taught me vamps were as changeable as a serial killer, fun and captivating one moment, aggressive and dangerous the next. I knew it, but seeing it had been a shocking reminder.

Swallowing hard, I looked at my posture, seeing I was wound up tighter than a chipmunk on speed. Immediately I forced my clasped hands apart and my shoulders down. I stared at the bloody dice in my hand and Kisten muttered, "I wouldn't do that to you, Rachel. I wouldn't."

The rhythm of the wipers was slow and steady. *Maybe I should've stayed in the car.*

"There're hand wipes in the console."

His voice carried the softness of an apology. Dropping my eyes before he could meet them, I flipped open the console and found some tissues. My fingers were shaking as I wrapped the dice up and, after a moment of hesitation, dropped them into my clutch purse.

Digging deeper, I found the wipes. Unhappy, I handed Kisten the first, then cleaned my hands with the second. Kisten easily drove the snowy, busy streets and meticulously cleaned his cuticles at the same time. When finished, he held out his hand for my used wipe, and I gave it to him. There was a little trash bag hanging behind my seat, and he effortlessly reached back and threw them both away. His hands were as steady as a surgeon's, and I curled my fingers under my palms to hide their trembling.

Kisten resettled himself, and I could almost see him force the tension from him as he exhaled. We were halfway across the Hollows, the lights of Cincinnati sharp before us.

"Snap, crackle, pop," he said lightly.

Bewildered, I looked at him. "I beg your pardon?" I said, glad my voice was even. Yeah, I had watched him down a coven of black art witches with the effortless grace of a predator, but if he wanted to discuss breakfast cereals now, I'd go along with it.

He smiled with his lips closed, a hint of an apology, or perhaps guilt, in the back of his blue eyes. "Snap, crackle, pop," he said. "Bringing them down sounded like a bowl of cereal."

My eyebrows rose and a wry smile came over me. With a small movement, I stretched my feet to the floor vent. If I didn't laugh, I was going to cry. And I didn't want to cry.

"I haven't done too well tonight, have I?" he said, his eyes back on the road.

I didn't say anything, not sure what I felt.

"Rachel," he said softly. "I'm sorry you had to see that."

"I don't want to talk about it," I said, recalling the man's terrified, agony-laced screams. I had known Kisten did ugly things because of who he was and who he worked for, but seeing it left me both repelled and fascinated. I was a runner; violence was part of my existence. I couldn't blindly label what happened as bad without casting my own profession into darkness.

Though his eyes had been black and his instincts wound tight, he had acted quickly and decisively, with a grace and succinct movement that I envied. Even more, throughout it all, I had felt Kisten's attention lightly on me, always aware of where I was and who was threatening me.

I had frozen, and he had kept me safe.

Kisten accelerated smoothly into the intersection before us when the light turned green. He sighed, clearly unaware of my thoughts as he took the turn to head to the church. The glowing clock on the dash read three-thirty. Going out didn't sound like fun anymore, but I was still shaking, and if he didn't feed me, I was going to end up eating cheese crackers and leftover rice for dinner. Yuck. "Mickey-d's?" I prompted. *It was just a date, for God's sake. One platonic . . . date.*

Kisten's head jerked up. Lips parted in wonder, he almost rammed the car ahead of us, slamming on the brakes at the last moment. Used to the way Ivy drove, I simply braced myself and rocked forward and back.

"You still want to have dinner?" he asked while the guy before us shouted unheard insults through his rearview mirror.

I shrugged. I was coated in dirty snow slime, my hair was

falling down about my ears, my nerves were shot—if I didn't get something in my stomach, I was going to get snippy. Or sick. Or worse.

Kisten settled back, a thoughtful expression smoothing his pinched features. A wisp of his usual, cocky self glimmered in his slumping posture. "Fast food is all I can afford—now," he grumbled lightly, but I could see he was relieved I wasn't demanding he take me home. "I was planning on using some of those winnings to take you up to Carew Tower for a sunrise dinner."

"The orphans need the money more than I need an overpriced dinner at the top of Cincinnati," I said. Kisten laughed at that, the sound making it easy to stifle my last thread of lingering caution. He kept me alive when I had frozen. It wasn't going to happen again. Ever.

"Hey, uh, is there any way you might see to not tell Ivy about . . . that?" he asked.

I smiled at the unease in his voice. "It'll cost you, fang-boy."

A small noise escaped him and he turned, his eyes wide in mock concern. "I'm in the position to offer you a super-sized shake for your silence," he intoned, and I stifled a shiver at the play menace he had put in it. Yeah, color me stupid. But I was alive, and he had kept me safe.

"Make it chocolate," I said, "and you've got yourself a deal."

Kisten's smile widened, and he gripped the wheel with more surety.

I settled back into the heated leather cushions, stifling the small, oh-so-small, thought of concern. *What. Like I was going to tell Ivy anyway?*

Fifteen

The crunch of ice and salt was loud as Kisten escorted me to my door. His car was parked at the curb in a puddle of light, diffuse from the falling snow. I rose up the steps, wondering what would happen in the next five minutes. It was a platonic date, but it was a date. That he might kiss me had me nervous.

I turned as I reached the door, smiling. Kisten stood beside me in his long wool coat and shiny shoes, looking good with his hair falling over his eyes. The sifting snow was beautiful, and it was gathering on his shoulders. The ugliness of the night's trouble drifted in and out of my thoughts. "I had a good time," I said, wanting to forget it. "Mickey-d's was fun."

Kisten's head drooped and a small chuckle escaped him. "I've never pretended to be health inspectors to get a free meal before. How did you know what to do?"

I winced. "I, uh, flipped burgers during high school until I dropped a charm into the fry vat." His eyebrows rose and I added, "I got fired. I don't know what the big deal was. Nobody got hurt, and the woman looked better with straight hair."

He laughed, turning it into a cough. "You dropped a potion in the fry vat?"

"It was an accident. The manager had to pay for a day at a spa, and I got pushed off the broomstick. All she needed was a salt bath to break the spell, but she was going to sue."

"I can't imagine why . . ." Kisten rocked to his toes and down, his hands behind his back as he looked up through the snow at the steeple. "I'm glad you had a good time. I did, too." He took a step back, and I went still. "I'll stop by sometime tomorrow night to pick up my coat."

"Hey, um, Kisten?" I said, not knowing why. "Do you . . . want a cup of coffee?"

He came to a graceful halt with one foot on the next step down. Turning back, he smiled, his pleased expression reaching all the way to his eyes. "Only if you let me make it."

"Deal." My pulse was just a shade faster as I opened the door and preceded him in. The sound of slow jazz met us, drifting up from the living room. Ivy was home, and I hoped she had already been out and back from her twice-weekly fix. A soulfully sung "Lilac Wine" made a soft mood, accentuated by the darkness of the sanctuary.

I shuffled off Kisten's coat, the sound of the silk lining a soft hush as it slid from me. The sanctuary was dim and silent, the pixies snug in my desk though they ought to have been up by now. Wanting to preserve the mood, I slipped off my boots while Kisten hung his coat beside the one he had let me borrow.

"Come on back," I whispered, not wanting to wake the pixies. Kisten's smile was soft as he followed me into the kitchen. We were quiet, but I knew Ivy had heard us when she turned the music down a shade. Tossing my clutch purse to my side of the table, I felt like someone else as I padded in my stocking feet to the fridge for the coffee. I caught sight of my reflection in the window. If you ignored the snow stains and falling hair, I didn't look too bad.

"I'll get the coffee," I said, searching the fridge as the sound of tinkling water intruded on the jazz. Grounds in hand, I turned to find him looking relaxed and comfortable in his pin-striped suit as he stood at the sink and cleaned the new coffee carafe. His mind was entirely on his task, seemingly unaware that I was in the same room while he threw out the old grounds and pulled a filter from the cupboard with a smooth, unthinking motion.

After an entire four hours with him without one flirting comment or sexual/blood innuendo, I felt comfortable. I hadn't known he could be like this: normal. I watched him move, seeing him with his thoughts on nothing. I liked what I saw, and I wondered what it would be like to be this way all the time.

As if feeling my eyes on him, Kisten turned. "What?" he asked, smiling.

"Nothing." I glanced at the black hallway. "I want to check on Ivy."

Kisten's lips parted to show a glimpse of teeth as his smile widened. "Okay."

Not sure why that seemed to please him, I gave him a last, high-eyebrow look and headed into the candlelit living room. Ivy was sprawled across her cushy suede chair, her head on one arm, her legs draped over the other. Her brown eyes flicked to mine as I entered, taking in the smooth, elegant lines of my clothes all the way to my feet in their nylons.

"You've got snow all over you," she said, her expression and position unchanging.

"I, uh, slipped," I lied, and she accepted that, taking my nervousness as embarrassment. "Why are the pixies still asleep?"

She snorted—sitting up to put her feet on the floor—and I sat on the matching couch across from her with the coffee table between us. "Jenks kept them up after you left so they wouldn't be awake when you got home."

A thankful smile came over me. "Remind me to make him some honey cakes," I said, leaning back and crossing my legs.

Ivy slumped into her chair, mirroring my posture. "So . . . how was your date?"

My eyes met hers. Very aware of Kisten listening from the kitchen, I shrugged. Ivy often acted like a cloying ex-boyfriend, which was really, really weird. But now that I knew it stemmed from her need to keep my trust, it was a bit easier to understand, though still odd.

She took a slow breath, and I knew she was scenting the air to make sure no one had bitten me at Piscary's. Her shoulders eased, and I rolled my eyes in exasperation.

"Hey, um," I started. "I'm really sorry about what I said earlier. About Piscary's?" Her eyes jerked to mine and I quickly added, "You want to go sometime? Together, I mean? I think if I stay downstairs, I won't pass out." My eyes pinched, not knowing why I was doing this except if she didn't find a way to relax soon, she was going to snap. I didn't want to be around for that. And I'd feel better if I was there to keep an eye on her. I had a feeling she would pass out quicker than I had.

Ivy shifted in the chair, moving back where she was when I came in. "Sure," she said, her voice not giving me a clue to her thoughts as she looked at the ceiling and closed her eyes. "We haven't had a girls' night out in a while."

"Great."

I settled back into the cushions to wait for Kisten. From the stereo, a soft-spoken voice dripping sex whispered as the songs changed. The scent of brewing coffee became obvious. A smile came over me as Takata's newest single came on. They were playing it even on the jazz stations. Ivy opened her eyes. "Backstage passes," she said, smiling.

"Al-l-l-l-l-l the way backstage," I countered. She had already agreed to work the concert with me, and I was eager to introduce her to Takata. But then I thought of Nick. No chance he'd be going now. Maybe I could ask Kisten to help us. And since he was posing as Piscary's scion, he would be doubly effective as a deterrent. Kinda like a cop car parked in the median. I looked at the black archway, wondering if he'd say yes if I asked, and if I wanted him there.

"Listen." Ivy held up a finger. "This is my favorite part. That low thrum goes all the way to my gut. Hear the pain in her voice? This has got to be Takata's best CD yet."

Her voice? I thought. Takata was the only one singing.

"You're mine, in some small fashion," Ivy whispered, her eyes closed, the inner pain showing on her brow making me uneasy. "You're mine, though you know it not. You're mine, bond born of passion . . ."

My eyes widened. She wasn't singing what Takata was. Her words were interlaced with his, an eerie backdrop that set my skin to crawl. That was the chorus he wasn't going to release.

"You're mine, yet wholly you," she breathed. "By the way of your will—"

"Ivy!" I exclaimed, and her eyes flashed open. "Where did you hear that?"

She looked blankly at me as Takata continued, singing of bargains made in ignorance.

"That's the alternate chorus!" I said, sitting up to the edge of the couch. "He wasn't going to release that."

"Alternate chorus?" she said as Kisten came in, setting the tray with three cups of coffee on the table beside the thick red candles and pointedly sitting next to me.

"The lyrics!" I pointed to the stereo. "You were singing them. He wasn't going to release those. He told me. He was going to release the other ones."

Ivy stared at me as if I had gone insane, but Kisten groaned, hunching to put his elbows on his knees and his head in his hands. "It's the vamp track," he said, his voice flat. "Damn. I thought something was missing."

Bewildered, I reached for my coffee. Ivy sat up and did the same. "Vamp track?" I said.

Kisten's head came up. His expression was resigned as he brushed his blond bangs back. "Takata puts a track in his music that only the undead can hear," he said, and I froze, my mug halfway to my lips. "Ivy can hear it because she's Piscary's scion."

Ivy's face went white. "You can't hear her?" she asked. "Right there," she said, looking at the stereo as the refrain came back on. "You can't hear her singing between Takata?"

I shook my head, feeling uneasy. "All I can hear is him."

"The drum?" she asked. "Can you hear that?"

Kisten nodded, leaning back with his coffee and looking sullen. "Yes, but you're hearing a hell of a lot more than we are." He set his cup down. "Damn it," he swore. "Now I'll have to wait until I'm dead and hope to find an old copy laying around." He sighed in disappointment. "Is it good, Ivy? Her voice is the eeriest thing I've ever heard. She's in every CD, but she's never listed in the credits." He slumped. "I don't know why she doesn't burn her own album."

"You can't hear her?" Ivy said, her words a sharp staccato. She set the cup down hard enough to spill, and I stared, surprised.

Kisten made a wry face and shook his head. "Congratulations," he said bitterly. "Welcome to the club. Wish I was still in it."

My pulse quickened as Ivy's eyes flashed into anger. "No!" she said, standing.

Kisten glanced up, his eyes wide, only now realizing Ivy wasn't pleased.

Ivy shook her head, wire-tight. "No," she said adamantly. "I don't want it!"

Understanding pulled me straight. That she could hear it meant that Piscary's grip on her was tightening. I looked at Kisten and his expression went worried. "Ivy, wait," he soothed as her usually placid face went ugly with anger.

"Nothing is mine anymore!" she exclaimed, her eyes flashing to black. "It was beautiful, and now it's ugly because of him. He's taking everything, Kist!" she shouted. "Everything!"

Kisten stood, and I froze as he went around the table and reached for her. "Ivy . . ."

"This is going to stop," she said, knocking his hand aside with a quick jerk before he could touch her. "Right now."

My jaw dropped as she strode from the room with a vampire

quickness. The candles flickered, then steadied. "Ivy?" I set my coffee down and stood, but the room was empty. Kisten had darted out after her. I was alone. "Where are you going. . . ." I whispered.

I heard the muffled rumble of Ivy's sedan start, borrowed from her mother for the winter. In an instant she was gone. I went into the hall, the soft thump of Kisten shutting the door and his steps on the hardwood floor clear in the silence.

"Where's she going?" I asked him as he came even with me at the top of the hallway.

He put a hand on my shoulder in a silent suggestion that I go back into the living room. In my stocking feet I felt the difference in our height keenly. "To talk to Piscary."

"Piscary!" Alarm brought me to a standstill. I pulled out of his light grip and stopped in the hall. "She can't talk to him alone!"

But Kisten gave me a mirthless smile. "She'll be fine. It's high time she talks to him. As soon as she does, he'll back off. That's why he's been bothering her. This is a good thing."

Not convinced, I returned to the living room. I was very conscious of him behind me, silent, close enough to touch. We were alone, if you didn't count the fifty-six pixies in my desk. "She'll be all right," he said under his breath as he followed me, shoes silent on the gray carpet.

I wanted him to leave. I was emotionally whipped, and I wanted him to leave. Feeling his eyes on me, I blew out the candles. In the new darkness, I gathered the coffee cups onto the tray in the hopes that he would take the hint. But as my gaze rose to the hallway, a thought stopped me cold. "Do you think Piscary can make her bite me? He almost made her bite Quen."

Kisten shifted into motion, his fingers brushing mine as he took the tray from me in the smoke-scented air. "No," he said, clearly waiting for me to go into the kitchen before him.

"Why not?" I padded into the brightly lit room.

Squinting at the new glare, Kisten slid the tray beside the sink and dumped the coffee to make brown puddles in the white porcelain sink. "Piscary was able to exert such an influence on her this afternoon because he caught her off guard. That, and she didn't have any set behavior to fight it. She's been battling her instincts to bite you since you were partners in the I.S. Saying no has gotten easy. Piscary can't make her bite you unless she gives in first, and she won't give in. She respects you too much."

I opened the dishwasher, and Kisten stacked the cups in the top rack. "Are you sure?" I asked softly, wanting to believe.

"Yes." His knowing smile made him a bad boy in an expensive suit again. "Ivy takes pride in denying herself. She values her independence more than I do, which is why she fights him. It'd be easier if she'd give it up. He'd stop forcing his dominance then. It's not degrading to let Piscary see through your eyes, channel your emotions and desires. I found it uplifting."

"Uplifting." I leaned against the counter in disbelief. "Piscary exerting his will over her and making her do things she doesn't want to is 'uplifting'?"

"Not when you put it like that." He opened the cupboard under the sink and pulled out the dish detergent. I briefly wondered how he knew it was there. "But Piscary is being a pain in the ass only because she's resisting him. He likes her fighting him."

I took the bottle from him and filled the little cup in the door of the dishwasher.

"I keep telling her that being Piscary's scion doesn't make her less, but more," he said. "She doesn't lose any of herself, and gains so much. Like the vampire track, and having almost the full strength of an undead without any of the drawbacks."

"Like a soul to tell you it's wrong to view people as walking snack bars," I said tartly, snapping the door shut.

A sigh slipped from him, the fine fabric of his suit bunching at his shoulders when he took the bottle of soap from me and set in on the counter. "It's not like that," he said. "Sheep are treated like sheep, users are used, and those who deserve more receive everything."

Arms crossed over my chest, I said, "And who are you to make that decision?"

"Rachel." He sounded weary as he cupped my elbows in his hands. "They make the decision themselves."

"I don't believe that." But I didn't pull away, and I didn't push his hands off me. "And even if they do, you take advantage of it."

Kisten's eyes went distant, falling from mine as he gently pulled my arms into a less aggressive posture. "Most people," he said, "are desperate to be needed. And if they don't feel good about themselves or think they're undeserving of love, some will fasten upon the worst possible way to satisfy that need to punish themselves. They're the addicts, the shadows both claimed and unclaimed, passed like the fawning sheep they make themselves into as they search for a glimmer of worth, knowing it's false even as they beg for it. Yes, it is ugly. And yes, we take advantage of those who let us. But which is worse, taking from someone who wants you to, knowing in your soul that you're a monster, or taking from an unwilling person and proving it?"

My heart pounded. I wanted to argue with him, but everything he had said, I agreed with.

"And then there are those who relish the power they have over us." Kisten's lips thinned from a past anger, and he dropped his hands from me. "The clever ones who know that our need to be accepted and trusted runs so deep it can be crippling. Those who play upon that, knowing we will do almost anything for that invitation to take the blood we desperately crave. The ones who exult in the hidden domination a lover can exert, feeling it elevates them to an almost godlike status. Those are the ones who want to be us, thinking it will make them powerful. And we use them, too, casting them aside with less regret than the sheep unless we grow to hate them, upon which we make them one of us in cruel restitution."

He cupped my jaw with his hand. It was warm, and I didn't pull away. "And then there are the rare ones who know love, who understand it. Who freely give of themselves, demanding only a return of that love, that trust." His faultless blue eyes never blinked, and I held my breath. "It can be beautiful, Rachel, when there is trust and love. No one is bound. No one loses his or her will. No one becomes less. Both become more than they can be alone. But it is so rare, so beautiful when it happens."

I shivered, wondering if he was lying to me.

The soft touch of his hand down my jaw as he pulled away sent my blood humming. But he didn't notice, his attention on the coming dawn visible out the window. "I feel bad for Ivy," he whispered. "She doesn't want to accept her need for belonging, even as it charts her every move. She wants that perfect love but thinks she isn't deserving of it."

"She doesn't love Piscary," I whispered. "You said there was no beauty without trust and love."

Kisten's eyes met mine. "I wasn't talking about Piscary."

His attention went to the clock above the sink, and when he took a backward step, I knew he was leaving. "It's getting late," he said, his distant voice telling me he was already mentally somewhere else. Then his eyes cleared and he was back. "I enjoyed our date," he said as he drew away. "But next time, there isn't going to be a limit on what I can spend."

"You're assuming there's going to be a next time?" I said, trying to lighten the mood.

He met my smile with his own, the new bristles on his face catching the light. "Maybe."

Kisten started for the front door, and I automatically followed to see him out. In my stockings, my feet were as soundless as his on the hardwood floor. The sanctuary was quiet, not a peep from my desk. Still not having said anything, Kisten shrugged into his wool coat.

"Thank you," I said as I handed him the long leather coat that he had let me borrow.

His teeth were a glimmer in the dark foyer. "My pleasure."

"For the night out, not the coat," I said, feeling my nylons go wet from the snowmelt. "Well, thanks for letting me use your coat, too," I stammered.

He leaned closer. "Again, my pleasure," he said, the faint light a glimmer in his eyes. I stared, trying to tell if his eyes were black from desire or shadow. "I *am* going to kiss you," he said, his voice dusky, and my muscles tensed. "No shirking."

"No biting," I said, deadly serious. Anticipation bubbled up inside me. But it was from me, not my demon scar, and accepting that was both a relief and a fear—I couldn't pretend it was the scar. Not his time.

His hands enfolded my lower jaw, both rough and warm. I inhaled as he drew closer, his eyes closing. The scent of leather and silk was strong, the hint of something deeper, primal, tugging at my instincts making me not know what to feel. Eyes open, I watched him lean in, my heart pounding with the anticipation of his lips on mine.

His thumbs shifted, following the curve of my jaw. My lips parted. But the angle was wrong for a full kiss, and my shoulders eased when I realized he was going to kiss the corner of my mouth.

Relaxing, I leaned forward to meet him, flashing into a near panic when his fingertips moved farther back, burying themselves in my hair. Adrenaline pounded through me in a cold wash as I realized he wasn't headed for my mouth at all.

He was going to kiss my neck! I thought, freezing.

But he stopped just shy, exhaling when his lips found the soft hollow between my ear and jaw. Relief mixed with fear, making me incapable of anything. The remnants of the adrenaline scouring through me made my pulse thunder. His lips were gentle, but his hands about my face were firm with restrained need.

A cool warmth took the place of his lips when he pulled away, yet he held himself poised for a moment, then another. My heart beat wildly, and I knew he could feel it almost as if it were his own. His breath came in a slow exhalation that I mirrored.

In the sound of rustling wool, Kisten stepped back. His eyes found mine, and I realized my hands had risen and were about his waist. They fell from him reluctantly, and I swallowed hard, shocked. Though he hadn't touched my lips or neck, it had been one of the most exhilarating kisses I'd ever experienced. The thrill of not knowing what he was going to do had put me in a tizzy that a full-mouthed kiss never could have.

"That's the damnedest thing," he said softly, a puzzled arch to his eyebrow.

"What?" I questioned breathily, still not having shaken off the feeling.

He shook his head. "I can't smell you at all. It's kind of a turn-on."

I blinked, unable to say a word.

"'Night, Rachel." A new smile hovered about him as he shifted another step back.

"Good night," I whispered.

He turned and opened the door. The chill air shocked me out of my daze. My demon scar hadn't made a single twinge, dormant. *That,* I thought, *was frightening. That he could do this to me without even playing upon my scar. What in hell was wrong with me?*

Kisten gave me a final smile from the landing, the snowy night a beautiful backdrop. Turning, he walked down the icy steps, his footsteps crunching on the salt.

Bewildered, I shut the door behind him, wondering what had happened. Still feeling unreal, I dropped the locking bar, then reopened it upon remembering Ivy was out.

Arms clasped about myself, I headed for my bedroom. My thoughts were full of what Kisten had told me about how people dictated their own fate when letting a vampire bind them. That people paid for the ecstasy of vampire passion with different levels of dependency ranging from food to equal. *What if he was lying?* I thought. *Lying to trick me into letting him bind me to him?* But then a more frightening thought pulled my feet to a halt and made my face go cold.

What if he was telling the truth?

Sixteen

Boots thumping in the hallway, I followed Ivy to the front door. Her tall frame moved with a preoccupied grace, predatorial as always in her tasteful leather pants. She might get away solstice shopping in leather, but I had opted for jeans and a red sweater. Even so, we both looked good. Shopping with Ivy was fun. She always treated for cookies, and dodging the offers for dates took on a delicious sense of danger, as she attracted *all* sorts of people.

"I've got to be back by eleven," she said as we entered the sanctuary and she swung her long hair back. "I've got a run tonight. Someone's underage daughter was lured into a bloodhouse, and I'm going in to get her out."

"You want some help?" I asked, buttoning my coat and hitching my bag higher up my shoulder while I walked.

Pixies were clustered at the stained-glass windows, hovering at the lighter colors and squealing at something outside. A harsh smile came over Ivy. "No. It won't take much."

The hard anticipation on her pale oval face worried me. She had come back from visiting Piscary in a very bad mood. Clearly it hadn't gone well, and I had a feeling she was going to take her frustration out on whoever had abducted that girl. Ivy was rough with vampires who preyed on the underage. Someone was going to spend their holiday in traction.

The phone rang, and Ivy and I froze, looking at each other. "I'll get it," I said. "But if it's not a run, I'll let the machine pick it up."

She nodded, heading out the door with her purse. "I'll warm up the car."

Taking a quick breath, I jogged to the back of the church. On the third ring the machine engaged. The outgoing message spewed its spiel, and my face tightened. Nick had recorded it for me—I thought it posh for it to appear that we employed a male secretary. Though now, seeing as we were listed with professionals of another sort, it probably only added to the confusion.

My frown deepened when the outgoing message cut off and Nick's voice continued. "Hey, Rachel?" he said hesitantly. "Are you there? Pick up if you are. I . . . I was hoping you'd be home. It's what, about six there?"

I forced my hand to pick up the phone. *He was in a different time zone?* "Hi, Nick."

"Rachel." The relief was thick in his voice, in stark contrast to my flat tone. "Good. I'm glad I caught you."

Caught me. Yeah. "How are you doing?" I asked, trying to keep the sarcasm from my voice. I was still stinging, hurt and confused.

He took a slow breath. I could hear water in the background and a hiss of something cooking. The soft clink of glasses and the murmur of conversation intruded. "I'm doing okay," he said. "I'm doing good. I slept really well last night."

"That's great." *Why in hell didn't you tell me my ley line practice was waking you up? You could have been sleeping well here, too.*

"How are you doing?" he asked.

My jaw hurt, and I forced my teeth apart. *I'm confused. I'm hurt. I don't know what you want. I don't know what I want.* "Fine," I said, thinking of Kisten. At least I knew what he wanted. "I'm fine." My throat hurt. "Want me to get your mail, or will you be home soon?"

"I've got a neighbor picking it up. But thanks."

You didn't answer my question. "Okay. Do you know if you'll be back by the solstice, or should I give your ticket to . . . someone else?" I hadn't meant to hesitate. It just happened. It was obvious Nick had heard it, too, given his silence. A seagull cried in the background. He was on a beach? He was at a bar on a beach and I was dodging black charms in cold slush?

"Why don't you do that," he said finally, and I felt as if someone punched me in the gut. "I don't know how long I'm going to be here."

"Sure," I whispered.

"I miss you, Rachel," he said, and I closed my eyes.

Please don't say it, I thought. *Please.*

"But I'm feeling much better. I'll be home soon."

It was exactly what Jenks had told me he would say, and my throat closed up. "I miss you, too," I said, feeling betrayed and lost all over again. He said nothing, and after three heartbeats, I stepped into the breach. "Well, Ivy and I are going shopping. She's in the car."

"Oh." He sounded relieved, the bastard. "I won't keep you. Um, I'll talk to you later."

Liar. "All right. 'Bye."

"I love you, Rachel," he whispered, but I hung up as if I hadn't heard. I didn't know if I could answer him anymore. Miserable, I pulled my hand from the receiver. My red nail polish looked bright against the black plastic. My fingers were trembling and my head hurt.

"Then why did you leave instead of telling me what's wrong?" I asked the empty room.

I exhaled with a measured slowness to try to wash the tension from me. I was going shopping with Ivy. I wouldn't ruin it by brooding about Nick. He was gone. He wasn't coming back. He felt better when he was a time zone away from me; why would he come back?

Hitching my bag higher up my shoulder, I headed for the front. The pixies were still clustered at the windows in small knots. Jenks was somewhere else, for which I was grateful. He'd only tell me "I told you so" if he had heard my conversation with Nick.

"Jenks! You have command of the ship!" I shouted as I opened the front door, and a smile, faint but real, crossed me when a piercing whistle emanated from my desk.

Ivy was in the car already, and my eyes were drawn across the street to Keasley's house, pulled by the sound of kids and a dog barking. My steps slowed. Ceri was in his yard, wearing the jeans I had dropped off earlier and an old coat of Ivy's. Bright red mittens and a matching hat made a vivid splash against the snow as she and about six kids ranging from ten to eighteen rolled snowballs around. A mountain was taking shape in the corner of Keasley's small lot. Next door were four more kids doing the same. It looked like there was going to be a snowball fight before too much longer.

I waved to Ceri, then Keasley—who was standing on his porch watching with an intent hunch that told me he'd like to be down there, too. Both of them waved back, and I felt warm. I'd done something good.

I lifted the door latch of Ivy's borrowed Mercedes, slipping in to find it still blowing cold air from the vents. It took forever for the big four-door sedan to warm up. I knew Ivy didn't like driving it, but her mother wouldn't lend her anything else and a cycle in slush was asking for stitches. "Who was it?" Ivy asked as I angled the vent off me and buckled myself in. Ivy drove as if she couldn't be killed, which I thought was a little ironic.

"Nobody."

She gave me a telling look. "Nick?"

Lips pressed together, I set my bag on my lap. "Like I said, nobody."

Not looking behind her, Ivy pulled away from the curb. "Rachel, I'm sorry."

The sincerity in her gray silk voice pulled my head up. "I thought you hated Nick."

"I do," she said, not at all apologetic. "I think he's manipulative and withholds information that might get you hurt. But you liked him. Maybe . . ." She hesitated, her jaw tightening and relaxing. "Maybe he's coming back. He does . . . love you." She made an ugly sound. "Oh God, you made me say it."

I laughed. "Nick isn't that bad," I said, and she turned to me. My eyes flicked to the truck we were about to rear-end at a stoplight, and I braced myself against the dash.

"I said he loved you. I didn't say he trusted you," she said, her eyes on me as she braked smoothly to a halt ending with our grille six inches from his bumper.

My stomach clenched. "You don't think he trusts me?"

"Rachel," she cajoled, inching forward as the light changed but the truck didn't move. "He leaves town without telling you? Then doesn't tell you when he's coming back? I don't think some*one* has come between you, I think some*thing* has. You scared the hell out of him, and he's not enough of a man to admit it, deal with it, and get over it."

I said nothing, glad when we started moving again. I hadn't just scared him, I had made him seize. It must have been awful. No wonder he left. Great, now I'd feel guilty all day.

Ivy jerked the wheel and shifted lanes. A horn blew, and she eyed the driver in the rearview mirror. Slowly the car put space between us, pushed back by the force of her gaze. "Do you mind if we stop at my folks' house for a minute? It's on the way."

"Sure." I stifled a gasp when she cut a right in front of the truck we'd just passed. "Ivy, you may have lightning reflexes, but the guy driving that truck just had kittens."

She snorted, dropping back two whole feet off the bumper of the car now ahead of us.

Ivy made an obvious effort to drive normally through the busier areas of the Hollows, and slowly I relaxed my death grip on my bag. It was the first time we'd been together and away from Jenks in about a week, and neither one of us knew what to get him for the solstice. Ivy was tending to the heated doghouse she had seen in a catalog; anything to get him and his brood out of the church. I'd settle for a lockbox we could cover with a rug and pretend was an end table.

As Ivy drove, slowly the yards grew larger and the trees taller. The houses began moving back from the street until only their roofs showed from behind stands of evergreens. We were just inside the city limits, right next to the river. It really wasn't on the way to the mall, but the interstate wasn't far, and with that, the city was wide-open.

Ivy pulled unhesitatingly into a gated drive. Twin tracks made a black trail on the dusting of snow that had fallen since it had been plowed. I leaned to look out the window, never having seen her parents' house. The car slowed to a halt before an old, romantic-looking three-story home painted white with hunter green shutters. A little red two-seater was parked out front, dry and free of snow.

"You grew up here?" I asked as I got out. The two names on the mailbox gave me pause until I remembered vampires maintained their names after marriage to keep living bloodlines intact. Ivy was a Tamwood, her sister was a Randal.

Ivy slammed her door and dropped her keys into her black purse. "Yeah." She looked to holiday lights making a tasteful, subdued display. It was getting dusky. The sun was only about an hour from setting, and I was hoping we would be gone before then. I didn't particularly want to meet her mom.

"Come on in," she said, her boots thumping on the brushed steps, and I followed her onto the covered porch. She opened the door, shouting, "Hi! I'm home!"

A smile curved over me as I hesitated just outside to stomp the snow off. I liked hearing her voice so relaxed. Coming inside, I shut the door and breathed deeply. Cloves and cinnamon—someone had been baking.

The large entryway was all varnished wood and subtle shades of cream and white. It was as stark and elegant as our living room was warm and casual. A runner of cedar bough made graceful loops up the railing of the nearby stairway. It was warm, and I unbuttoned my coat and stuffed my gloves in the pockets.

"That's Erica's car outside. She's probably in the kitchen," Ivy said, dropping her purse on the small table beside the door. It was polished so highly that it looked like black plastic.

Taking her coat off, she draped it over an arm and headed for a large archway to the left, coming to a halt at a thumping of feet on the steps. Ivy looked up, her placid face shifting. It took me a moment to realize she was happy. My gaze followed her to a young woman slumping downstairs.

She looked to be about seventeen, dressed in a skimpy goth short skirt to show her midriff, with black fingernails and lipstick. Silver chains and bangles swung everywhere as she hopped down the stairs, bringing that dog-eared page to mind. Her black hair was cut short and styled into wild spikes. Maturity hadn't yet finished filling her out, but I could tell already that she was going to look exactly like her big sister apart from being six inches shorter: lean, sleek, predatory, and with just enough oriental cast to make her exotic. Nice to know it ran in the family. Of course, right now she looked like a teenage vamp out of control.

"Hi, Erica," Ivy said, reversing her steps and waiting for her at the foot of the stairs.

"My God, Ivy," Erica said, her high voice heavy on the valley girl accent. "You *have* to talk to Daddy. He's being total Big Brother. Like, *I* don't know the difference between good Brimstone and bad Brimstone? Listening to him, you'd think I was still two, crawling around in diapers trying to bite the dog. God! He was in the kitchen," she continued, her mouth going as she eyed me up and down, "making Mom her organically grown, earth-friendly, politically correct *stinking* cup of tea, when I can't go out one night with my friends. It's so *unfair*! Are you staying? She'll be up rattling the windows soon."

"No." Ivy drew back. "I'm here to talk to Dad. He's in the kitchen?"

"Basement," Erica said. Mouth finally stopping, she sent her gaze over me again as I stood in a bemused wonder at how fast she talked. "Who's your friend?" she asked.

A faint smile curled up the corners of Ivy's mouth. "Erica, this is Rachel."

"Oh!" the young woman exclaimed, her brown eyes that were almost hidden behind her black mascara going wide. She stepped forward and grabbed my hand, pumping it up and down enthusiastically with her bangles jingling. "I shoulda known! Hey, I saw you at Piscary's," she said, giving me a whack on the shoulder that sent me forward a step. "Man, you were sugared up good. Riding the short bus. Walking with the ghost. I didn't recognize you." Her eyes traveled over my jeans and winter coat. "You had a date with Kisten? Did he bite you?"

I blinked, and Ivy laughed nervously. "Hardly. Rachel doesn't let anyone bite her." She took a step to her sister, giving her a hug. I felt good when the young woman returned it with a careless attention, apparently not knowing or caring how rarely Ivy touched anyone. The two pulled apart, and Ivy's features stilled. She took a breath, nostrils widening.

Erica grinned like the cat who ate the canary. "Guess who I picked up at the airport?"

Ivy straightened. "Skimmer's here."

It was almost a whisper, and Erica all but danced back a step. "Came in on a morning flight," she said, as proud as if she had landed the plane herself.

My eyes widened. Ivy was wire-tight. Breath catching, she spun to an archway at the sound of a door closing. A feminine voice echoed, "Erica? Is that my cab?"

"Skimmer!" Ivy took a step to the archway, then rocked back. She looked at me, more alive than I'd seen her in a long time. A small scuff at the archway pulled her attention from me. Emotion cascaded over her, and the happiness settled in to stay, telling me that Skimmer was one of the few people Ivy felt comfortable to be herself around.

So there were two of us, I thought, turning to follow her gaze to a young woman standing in the threshold. I felt my brows rise in speculation as I took in what had to be Skimmer. She was dressed in faded jeans and a crisp, white button-down shirt to make a nice mix of casual sophistication. Understated black boots brought her height to about mine. Slim and well-proportioned, the blond woman stood with a confident grace typical of living vampires.

She had a single silver chain about her neck, and her blond hair was pulled back in a simple ponytail to accentuate a bone structure that models could spend a small fortune on plastic surgery to find. I stared at her eyes, wondering if they were really that blue or if they just seemed that way because of her incredibly long eyelashes. Her nose was small and turned up at the end to give her smile a look of shy confidence.

"What are you doing here?" Ivy said, her face alight as she went to greet her. The two women gave each other a long hug. My lips parted and I froze at the lingering kiss before they parted. *Okay . . .*

Ivy slipped me a glance, but she was smiling when she turned back to Skimmer, smiling, still smiling, with her hands on the woman's elbows. "I can't believe you're here!" she said.

Skimmer glanced at me once before focusing on Ivy. She looked like she had enough confidence and smarts to break horses, teach aboriginal children, and dine out at a five-star restaurant all in one day. *And she and Ivy had kissed? Not just a peck, but a real . . . kiss?*

"I'm out here on business," she said. "Long-term business," she added, her pleasant voice thick with a pleased emotion. "A year, I'm guessing."

"A year! Why didn't you call me? I would have picked you up!"

The woman took a step back, and Ivy's hold on her fell away. "I wanted to surprise you," she said, her smile rising to encompass her blue eyes. "Besides, I wasn't sure of your situation. It's been so long," she finished softly.

Her eyes fell on me, and I warmed in my new understanding. *Aw, crap on toast. How long had I been living with Ivy? How could I have not known? Was I blind or just stupid?*

"Damn," Ivy swore, still obviously excited. "It's good to see you. What are you out here for? Do you need a place to stay?"

My pulse quickened and I tried to keep my worry from showing. Two of them together in the church? Not good. Even more disturbing was that Skimmer seemed to relax at her offer, losing interest in me and focusing entirely on Ivy.

Erica stood beside me, grinning mischievously. "Skimmer came out to work for Piscary," she said, clearly eager to tell what she thought was good news, but my face went cold. "It's all arranged. She looks to him now." Twirling her necklaces, the young vampire beamed. "Just like I always thought she should."

Ivy took a breath and held it. Wonder crossed her, and she reached out to touch Skimmer's shoulder as if not believing she was really there. "You look to Piscary?" she breathed, and I wondered what the significance was. "Who or what did he give for you?"

Skimmer shrugged, lifting one narrow shoulder and letting it fall. "Nothing yet. I've been trying the last six years to wiggle into his camarilla, and if I work this right, it will be permanent." She dropped her head briefly, her eyes alight and eager when they rose. "I'm staying at Piscary's place meantime," she said, "but thanks for the offer to bunk with you."

Piscary's, I thought, my worry strengthening. That was where Kisten was living. This was getting better and better. Ivy, too, seemed to have to think about that. "You left your place with Natalie to run Piscary's restaurant?" she asked, and Skimmer laughed. It was comfortable and pleasant, and the volumes that were left unsaid made me uneasy.

"No. Kist can have that job," she said lightly. "I'm here to get Piscary out of prison. My permanent inclusion into Piscary's camarilla is contingent upon it. If I win my case, I stay. If I lose, I go back home."

I froze. *Oh my God. She was Piscary's lawyer.*

Skimmer hesitated at Ivy's lack of response. Ivy turned to me, a panicked look on her face. I watched the wall come down, sealing everything away. Her happiness, her joy, her excitement at reuniting with an old friend; it was all gone. Something slipped between us, and I felt my chest tighten. Erica's bangles clanked as the young vampire clearly realized something was wrong but not understanding. Hell, I didn't think I understood.

Suddenly wary, Skimmer glanced from me to Ivy. "So, who's your friend?" she asked into the awkward silence.

Ivy licked her lips and turned to face me more fully. I shifted forward, not knowing how to react. "Rachel," Ivy said, "I'd like you to meet Skimmer. We roomed together for our last two years of high school out on the West Coast. Skimmer, this is Rachel, my partner."

I took a breath, trying to decide how I should handle this. My hand went out to shake hers, but Skimmer walked past it, taking me into an expansive hug.

I tried not to stiffen, determined to go with the flow until I had a chance to talk to Ivy about just what we were going to do about this. Piscary couldn't get out of prison; I'd never sleep again. My arms went about her in a loose generic hug, and I froze when the woman put her lips under my ear and breathed, "Pleasure to meet you."

Adrenaline jolted through me as my demon scar flashed into waves of heat. Shocked, I shoved her away, collapsing to a defensive posture. The living vampire fell back, surprise making her long lashes and blue eyes look enormous. She caught her balance a good five feet away. Erica gasped, and Ivy was a black blur coming between us.

"Skimmer!" Ivy shouted, her voice almost panicked as she stood with her back to me.

My heart pounded and sweat broke out. The flaming promise on my neck hurt, it was so strong, and I put a hand to it, feeling betrayed and shocked.

"She's my business partner!" Ivy exclaimed. "Not my blood partner!"

The slim woman stared at us, flashing into a red-faced embarrassment. "Oh God," she stammered, hunching into a slightly submissive posture. "I'm sorry." She put a hand to her mouth. "I am really, really sorry." She looked at Ivy, who was slowly relaxing. "Ivy, I thought you'd taken a shadow. She smells like you. I was just being polite." Skimmer's gaze darted to me as I tried to slow my heartbeat. "You asked me to stay with you. I thought—God, I'm sorry. I thought she was your shadow. I didn't know she was your . . . friend."

"It's all right," I lied, forcing myself upright. I didn't like the way she had said "friend." It implied more than what we were. But I currently wasn't up to trying to explain to Ivy's old roommate that we weren't sharing blood or a bed. Ivy wasn't much help, standing with a deer-in-the-headlights look. And I had this weird feeling I was still missing something. *God, how did I get to this place?*

Erica was standing by the foot of the stairs, her eyes wide and her mouth open. Skimmer looked distressed as she tried to cover her error, smoothing her hands on her pants and touching her hair. She took a deep breath. Still flushed, she stiffly extended her hand in an obvious show of intent and stepped forward. "I'm sorry," she said as she halted before me. "My name is Dorothy Claymor. You can call me that if you want to. I probably deserve it."

I managed to dredge up a stilted smile. "Rachel Morgan," I said, shaking her hand.

The woman froze, and I pulled away. She looked at Ivy, the pieces falling into place.

"The one who put Piscary in prison," I added, just to be sure she knew where I stood.

A sick smile came over Ivy. Dropping back a step, Skimmer's gaze went between us. Confusion made her cheeks bright red. This was a mess. This was a sticky, stinking mess of crap, and the levels were steadily rising.

Skimmer swallowed hard. "It's a pleasure to meet you." Hesitating, she added, "Boy, this is awkward."

I felt my shoulders ease at her admission. She was going to do what she had to do, and I was going to do what I had to do. And Ivy? Ivy was going to go insane.

Erica moved forward, the jingling of her jewelry sounding loud. “Hey, ah, does anyone want a cookie or something?”

Oh yeah. A cookie. That would make everything better. Dunked in a shot of tequila, maybe? Or better yet, just the bottle? Yeah, that ought to do it.

Skimmer forced a smile. Her crisp mien was wearing thin, but she was holding up well considering she had left her home and master to rekindle a relationship with her high school girlfriend who was rooming with the woman who had put her new boss behind bars. *Join us next time for* Days of the Undead *when Rachel learns her long lost brother is really a crown prince from outer space.* My life was so screwed up.

Skimmer glanced at her watch—I couldn’t help but notice it had diamonds on it in place of numbers. “I’ve got to go. I’m meeting with—someone in about an hour.”

She was going to meet someone in about an hour. Just after the sun went down. Why didn’t she just say Piscary?

“You need a ride?” Ivy said, sounding almost wistful, if she would ever let that particular emotion come from her.

Skimmer looked from Ivy to me and back to Ivy, hurt and disappointment flickering in the back of her eyes. “No,” she said softly. “I’ve got a cab coming.” She swallowed, trying to scrape herself back together. “Actually, I think that’s it now.”

I didn’t hear anything, but I didn’t have a living vampire’s hearing.

Skimmer shifted awkwardly forward. “It was nice meeting you,” she said to me, then turned to Ivy. “I’ll talk to you later, sweets,” she said, eyes closed as she gave her a long hug.

Ivy was still in a shocked quandary, and she returned it looking numb.

“Skimmer,” I said as they broke apart and the shaken, subdued woman took a thin jacket from the hall closet and put it on. “This isn’t what you think.”

She stopped with her hand on the doorknob, looking at Ivy for a long moment with deep regret. “It’s not what I think that matters,” she said as she opened the door. “It’s what Ivy wants.”

I opened my mouth to protest, but she left, latching the door softly behind her.

Seventeen

Skimmer's departure left an awkward silence. As the cab accelerated down the drive, I looked at Ivy standing in the sterile white entryway with its elegant decorations that utterly lacked any warmth. Guilt was thick on her. I knew it was from the reminder that she still harbored the belief that someday I'd be her scion—apparently with a little extra something on the side. It was a position that I think Skimmer had moved out here hopefully to fill.

Not sure what I was feeling, I faced her. "Why did you let her think we were lovers?" I said, shaking inside. "God, Ivy. We aren't even sharing blood, and she thinks we're lovers."

Ivy's face closed, the barest tightening of her jaw giving away her emotion. "She doesn't think that at all." She strode out of the room. "Do you want some juice?" she called back.

"No," I said softly as I followed her deeper into the house. I knew if I pressed the issue right now, she would likely become more closed. This conversation wasn't over, but having it in front of Erica wasn't a good idea. My head hurt. Maybe I could get her to talk about it over coffee and cheesecake while we were shopping. Maybe I should move to Timbuktu, or the Tennessee mountains, or somewhere else where there weren't any vampires. (Don't ask. It's weird, even for Inderlanders—which is saying a lot.)

Erica was tight on my heels, her mindless chatter an obvious attempt to cover up the issues that Skimmer had raised. Her bright voice filled the sterile house with life as she trailed after us through large dim rooms full of hardwood furniture and cold drafts. I made a mental note to never get Erica and Jenks in the same room. No wonder Ivy didn't have a problem with Jenks. Her sister was cut from the same cloth.

Ivy's boots were slow on the polished floor when we left a dark blue formal dining room and entered a brightly lit, spacious kitchen. I blinked. Ivy met my startled gaze and shrugged. I knew that Ivy had remodeled the church's kitchen before I had moved in, and as I looked around, I realized she had patterned it after the one she grew up with.

The room was nearly as spacious, that same center island counter taking up the middle. Cast-iron pots and metal utensils hung over it instead of my ceramic spoons and copper spell vats, but it made the same comfortable spot to lean against. There was a heavy antique table—twin to ours—against the near wall, right where I'd expect it. Even the cupboards were the same style, and the counters had an identical color. The floor, though, was tile instead of linoleum.

Past the sink where I had a single window overlooking the graveyard, there was a bank of windows that showed a long snowfield running down to the gray ribbon of the Ohio River. Ivy's parents owned a lot of property. You could graze cattle down there.

A kettle steamed on the stove, and as Ivy moved it off the burner, I dropped my bag on the table where my chair would be if I was home. "This is nice," I said wryly.

Ivy gave me a cautious look, clearly glad I had shelved the pending discussion about Skimmer. "It was cheaper to do both kitchens at once," she said, and I nodded. It was warm, and I took my coat off, draping it on the back of the chair.

Stretching to show the small of her back, Erica stood on one foot to reach a glass jar half full of what looked like sugar cookies. Leaning against the counter, she ate one, offering Ivy another but none to me. I had a feeling they weren't sugar cookies but those awful cardboard-tasting disks that Ivy had kept shoving down my throat last spring when I was recovering from a massive blood loss. Sort of a vampire pick-me-up that helped support their—ah—lifestyle.

A muffled thumping grew louder, and I turned to what I had thought was a pantry door. It creaked opened to show a staircase leading down. A tall gaunt man was coming up and out of the shadows. "Hi, Dad," Ivy said, and I straightened, smiling at the softness in her voice.

"Ivy . . ." The man beamed as he set a tray with two tiny

empty cups down on the table. His voice was gravely, matching his skin: rough and pebbly. I recognized the texture as scars left from the Turn. It had affected some more than others, and witches, pixies, and fairies not at all. "Skimmer's here," he said gently.

"I saw her," Ivy said, and he hesitated at the lack of anything more.

He looked tired, his brown eyes content as he gave Ivy a quick hug. Gently waving black hair framed his serious face softly lined with what looked like worry rather than age. It was obvious that this was where Ivy got her height. The living vampire was tall, with a refinement that turned his gaunt frame pleasing rather than unattractive. He was wearing jeans and a casual shirt. Small, almost unseen lines scarred his neck, and his arms showing past his rolled-up sleeves had the same marks on the underside. It must be hard being married to an undead.

"I'm glad you came home," the man said, his eyes flicking briefly to me and the cross on my charm bracelet before settling back on his daughter with an obvious warmth. "Your mother will be up in a bit. She wants to talk to you. Skimmer put her in a rare mood."

"No." Ivy dropped back out of his touch. "I wanted to ask you something, is all."

He nodded once, his thin lips falling into a resigned disappointment. I felt a slight tingle from my demon scar as he poured the steaming water into a second teapot. The clanking of the porcelain was loud. Arms crossed before me, I leaned to rest against the table to distance myself. I hoped the tingle was a lingering sensation from Skimmer and didn't stem from Ivy's dad. I didn't think it was him. He looked too calm to be fighting a need to slake his hunger.

"Dad," Ivy said, seeing my unease. "This is Rachel. Rachel, this is my dad."

As if aware my scar was tingling, Ivy's dad stayed at the other end of the kitchen, taking the cookies from Erica and putting them back into the cookie jar. The girl huffed, then grimaced at her dad's raised eyebrow. "It's a pleasure to meet you," he said, his attention returning to me.

"Hello, Mr. Randal," I said, not liking the way he was eyeing Ivy and me standing beside each other. I suddenly felt as if I was on a date, meeting the parents, and I flushed. I didn't like his knowing smile. Apparently neither did Ivy.

"Stop it, Dad." Ivy pulled out a chair and sat. "Rachel is my roommate, not my live-in."

"You'd better make sure Skimmer knows that." His narrow chest moved as he breathed deeply to take in the emotions on the air. "She came out here for you. Left everything. Think hard before you walk away from that. She has good breeding behind her. An unbroken millennium line is hard to find."

Tension slammed back into me and I felt myself stiffen.

"Oh God," Erica moaned, her hand back in the cookie jar. "Don't start, Daddy. We just had an ugly in the hallway."

Smiling to show teeth, he reached across to take the cookie from her and ate a bite. "Don't you have to be to work soon?" he said when he swallowed.

The young vampire jiggled. "Daddy, I want to go to the concert. All my friends are."

My eyebrows rose. Ivy shook her head with the smallest of movements, a private answer to my question as to whether we should tell him we were going and that we'd keep an eye on her.

"No," her father said, brushing the crumbs from himself as he finished his cookie.

"But, Daddy . . ."

Opening the jar, he took out three more. "You don't have enough control—"

Erica puffed, slumping against the counter. "My control is fine," she said sulkily.

He straightened, the first hints of steel tightening his face. "Erica, your hormones are jumping up and down right now. One night you have control in a stressful situation, the next you lose it while you're watching TV. You aren't wearing your caps like you're supposed to, and I don't want you to accidentally bind someone to you."

"Daddy!" she cried, flushing a dull, embarrassed red.

Getting two glasses from the cupboard, Ivy snickered. My uneasiness faded slightly.

"I know . . ." her father said, his head bowed and a hand raised. "A lot of your friends have shadows, and it looks like fun having someone trailing behind you, seeking your attention and always there. You're the center of their world, and they see only you. But Erica, bonded shadows are a lot of work. They aren't pets you can give to a friend when you tire of them. They need reassurance and attention. You're too young to have that kind of responsibility."

"Daddy, stop!" Erica said, clearly mortified. I sat as Ivy got a carton of orange juice from the fridge. I wondered how much of this was for Erica and how much of it was his way of trying to scare me off from his eldest daughter. It was working. Not that I needed any encouragement.

The living vampire's face went stern. "You're being careless," he said, his gravely voice harsh. "Taking risks that might put you in a place you don't want to be yet. Don't think I don't know you take your caps off as soon as you leave this house. You aren't going to that concert."

"That's not fair!" she shouted, spiked hair bobbing. "I'm pulling all A's *and* working part-time. It's *just* a *concert!* There won't even be any Brimstone there!"

He shook his head as she huffed. "Until that bad Brimstone is off the streets, you will be home before sunrise, young lady. I'm not going down to the city tombs to identify and bring a member of my house home. I've done that once, and I'm not ready to do it again."

"Daddy!"

Ivy handed her father a glass of juice, then sat down with her drink in the chair adjacent to mine. Crossing her legs at the knees, she said, "I'm going to the concert."

Erica gasped, her jewelry tinkling as she jumped. "Daddy!" she cried. "Ivy's going. I won't take any Brimstone and I won't bite anyone. I promise! Oh God! Please let me go!"

Eyebrows high, Ivy's dad looked at Ivy. She shrugged, and Erica held her breath. "If it's all right with your mother, it's all right with me," he finally said.

"Thank you, Daddy!" Erica squealed. She flung herself at him, almost knocking her taller father down. In a clatter of boots, she yanked the door to the stairwell open and thumped downstairs. The door arched closed, and Erica's shouts grew muffled.

The man sighed, his thin shoulders moving. "Just how long were you going to let her beg before you told me you were going?" he asked wryly.

Her eyes on her juice, Ivy smiled. "Long enough that she will listen to me when I tell her to wear her caps or I'll change my mind."

A chuckle rose. "You learn well, young grasshopper," he said, affecting a strong accent.

There was a thumping on the stairs and Erica burst out, eyes black in excitement, chains swinging. "She said yes! Gotta go! Love you, Daddy! Thanks, Ivy!" She made a pair of bunny ears with her fingers, crooking them as she said, "Kiss, kiss!" and darted out of the room.

"Do you have your caps?" her father shouted after her.

"Yes!" she called back, her voice faint.

"Take some of those necklaces off, young lady!" he added, but the door slammed. The quiet was a relief, and I met Ivy's smile with bemused wonder. Erica could really fill a room.

Ivy's father put his glass down. His face seemed to take on more wrinkles, and I could see the strain his body was enduring to supply the blood his undead wife needed to stay sane.

I watched Ivy shift her fingers on her glass to spin it where it sat. Slowly her smile faded. "Has she been to see Piscary?" she asked softly, the sudden worry in her voice drawing my attention. This was why Ivy had come to talk to her dad, and as I thought of Erica's carefree, wild innocence in Piscary's manipulative embrace, I worried, too.

Ivy's dad, though, didn't seem to have a problem with it, taking a slow sip of juice before answering, "Yes. She visits him every two weeks. As is respectful." My brow pinched at the implied question, and I wasn't surprised when he followed up with, "Have you?"

Ivy stilled the fingers encircling her glass. Uncomfortable, I looked for a way to excuse myself and go hide in the car. Ivy glanced at me, then her father. He leaned back, waiting. From outside came the rumble of Erica's car, fading to leave the hum of the clock on the oven the only sound. Ivy took a breath. "Dad, I made a mistake."

I felt Ivy's dad's eyes land on me, even though I was staring out the window trying to divorce myself from the conversation. "We should talk about this when your mother is available," he said, and I took a quick breath.

"You know," I said as I got up, "I think I'll go wait in the car."

"I don't want to talk about it with Mom, I want to talk about it with you," Ivy said crossly. "And there's no reason Rachel can't hear this."

The hidden request in Ivy's voice stopped me short. I sank back down, ignoring the obvious disapproval from her dad. This wasn't going to be fun. Maybe she wanted my opinion of the conversation to balance out her own. I could do that for her.

"I made a mistake," Ivy said softly. "I don't want to be Piscary's scion."

"Ivy . . ." There was a tired weariness in that one word. "It's time to start taking on your responsibilities. Your mother was his scion before she died. The benefits—"

"I don't want them!" Ivy said, and I watched her eyes closely, wondering if the ring of brown about her pupil was shrinking. "Maybe if he wasn't in my head all the time," she added, moving her juice away. "But I can't take it anymore. He just keeps pushing."

"He wouldn't if you would go see him."

Ivy sat straighter, eyes on the table. "I did go see him. I told him that I wasn't going to be his scion and to get out of my head. He laughed at me. He said I had made a choice and now I had to live and die by it."

"You did make a choice."

"And now I'm making another one," she shot back, her eyes lowered submissively but her voice determined. "I'm not going to do it. I don't want to run Cincinnati's underground, and I won't." She took a deep breath, her eyes rising to his. "I can't tell if I like something anymore because *I* like it or because Piscary likes it. Dad, will you talk to him for me?"

My eyes widened at her pleading tone. The only time I had heard it before was when she thought she was dead and was begging me to keep her safe. My jaw clenched as I remembered. God, that had been awful. When I looked up at his continued silence, I was startled to find Ivy's dad watching me. His lips were pressed tight and his gaze was angry, as if this was my fault.

"You're his scion," he said, his eyes accusingly on mine. "Stop shirking your duties."

Ivy's nostrils flared. I really didn't want to be here, but if I moved, I would only draw attention to myself. "I made a mistake," she said angrily. "And I'm willing to pay the cost to get out of it, but he's going to start hurting people to make me do what he wants. That's not fair."

He made a scoffing laugh and rose. "Did you expect anything different? He's going to use everything and everyone he can to manipulate you. He's a master vampire." Putting his hands on the table, he leaned toward Ivy. "It's what they do."

Cold, I sent my gaze down to the river below. It didn't matter if Piscary was in jail or not. All he had to do was say the word, and his minions would not only bring Ivy in line but get me out of his hair as well. Expensive, but effective.

But Ivy pulled her head up, shaking it in reassurance before turning her damp eyes to her father. "Dad, he said he's going to start calling on Erica."

The man's face went ashen to make the small fever scars stand out starkly. Relief that Piscary wasn't targeting me flashed through me, then guilt that I could feel such a thing. "I'll talk to him," he whispered, the worry in his voice for his innocent, so-alive daughter clear.

I felt sick. In their conversation were the dark, ugly shadows of the hidden pacts older children made to each other to protect a younger, innocent sibling from an abusive parent. The feeling solidified when her dad repeated softly, "I'll talk to him."

"Thank you."

All of us seemed to draw away in an uncomfortable silence. It was time to go. Ivy stood first, quickly followed by me. I grabbed my coat from the back of the chair and shrugged into it. Ivy's dad rose slowly, seeming twice as tired as when we came in. "Ivy," he said as he came close. "I'm proud of you. I don't agree with what you're doing, but I'm proud of you."

"Thanks, Dad." Smiling a close-lipped smile in relief, she gave him a hug. "We gotta go. I've got a run tonight."

"Darvan's girl?" he asked, and she nodded, the hint of guilt and fear on her still. "Good. You keep doing what you're doing. I'll talk to Piscary and see what I can work out."

"Thanks."

He turned to me. "It was a pleasure meeting you, Rachel."

"Same here, Mr. Randal." I was glad the vampire talk seemed to be over. We could all pretend to be normal again; hide the ugliness under the five-thousand-dollar rug.

"Wait, Ivy. Here." The man reached into his back pocket and pulled out a worn wallet, turning himself from a vampire into just another dad.

"Dad," Ivy protested. "I've got my own money."

He smiled with half his mouth. "Think of it as a thank-you for watching Erica at the concert. Have lunch on me."

I said nothing as he shoved a hundred dollar bill into Ivy's hand, pulling her forward into a one-armed hug. "I'll call you tomorrow morning," he said softly.

Ivy's shoulders lost their usual upright posture. "I'll come by. I don't want to talk over the phone." She shot me a forced, close-lipped smile. "Ready to go?"

I nodded, giving Ivy's dad a head bob as I followed her out into the dining room and to the front door. Knowing how good vamp hearing was, I kept my mouth shut until the elegantly carved door thumped shut behind us and our feet were again on the snow.

It had grown dusky, and the snowdrifts seemed to glow in the light reflected off the sky.

Erica's car was gone. Key's jingling, Ivy hesitated. "Hold up," she said, boots squeaking in the snow as she went to where the red car had been parked. "I think she ditched her caps."

I stood by my open door and waited while Ivy came to a standstill beside the wheel marks. Eyes closed, she flung her hand as if throwing something, and then strode to the other side of the drive. As I watched in a mystified silence, she searched the snow. Bending at the waist twice, she picked something up. She came back and got into the car without comment.

I followed her in and fastened my belt, wishing it were darker so I didn't have to watch her drive. At my questioning silence, Ivy held out her hand and dropped two bits of hollow plastic into my grip. The car started, and I aimed the vents at me, hoping the engine was still warm. "Caps?" I asked, looking at them small and white in my palm as Ivy pulled away. *How on earth did she find these in the snow?*

"Guaranteed to keep from breaking skin," Ivy said, her thin lips pressing together. "And with that, she can't accidentally bind anyone to her. She's supposed to wear them until Dad says so. And at this rate, she's going to be thirty before that happens. I know where she works. Mind if we drop them off?"

I shook my head, extending them back to her. Ivy checked both ways at the end of the drive before pulling out in front of a blue station wagon, wheels spinning in the slush. "I've got an empty caps case in my purse. Would you put them in there for me?"

"Sure." I didn't like digging around in her purse, but if I didn't, she'd do it while driving, and my stomach was in enough knots already. I felt odd as I put Ivy's purse on my lap and opened it up. It was disgustingly tidy. Not a single used tissue or lint-covered candy.

"Mine is the one with the colored glass on it," Ivy said, watching the road with half her attention. "I should have a plastic one in there, somewhere. The disinfectant is probably still good. Dad would kill her if he knew she threw them in the snow. They cost as much as her summer camp last year in the Andes."

"Oh." My three summers spent at Kalamack's Make-A-Wish camp for dying children suddenly looked pale. Shifting past a small container that looked like an elaborately decorated pillbox was a thumb-sized white vial. I unscrewed the top to find it full of a bluish liquid.

"That's the one," Ivy said, and I dropped them in. They floated, and when I went to stick my pinky in to sink them, she added, "Just put the top on and give it a shake. They'll sink."

I did just that, dropping the vial into her purse and setting it beside her.

"Thanks," Ivy said. "The time I 'lost' mine, he grounded me for a month."

I gave her a weak smile, thinking it was kind of like losing your glasses or retainer . . . or maybe your diaphragm. *Oh God. Did I really want to know all this?*

"You still wear caps?" I said, curiosity getting the better of me. She didn't seem to be embarrassed about it. Maybe I should just go with it.

Ivy shook her head, signaling an instant before she crossed two lanes of traffic to get to the expressway's on-ramp. "No," she said as I clutched the door handle. "Not since I was seventeen. But I keep them in case—" She cut her words off. "Just in case."

Just in case what? I wondered, then decided I didn't want to know. "Uh, Ivy?" I questioned as I tried not to figure out where she was going to force herself into traffic. I held my breath while we merged and, from behind us, horns blew. "What the heck does bunny ears and 'kiss, kiss' mean?"

She stared at me, and I made a peace sign and crooked my fingers twice in quick succession. An odd smile quirked the corners of her mouth. "Those aren't bunny ears," she said. "Those are fangs."

I thought about that, then flushed. "Oh."

Ivy chuckled. I eyed her for a moment, then deciding there would be no better time, I took a slow breath. "Um, about Skimmer . . ."

Her good mood vanished. She shot me a look, then put her eyes back on the road. "We were roommates." A faint flush came over her, telling me it was more than that. "We were *very* close roommates," she added carefully, as if I hadn't already figured it out. Ivy hit the brakes hard to avoid a black BMW that wanted to pen her in behind a minivan. Accelerating quickly, she darted around to the right, leaving him behind.

"She came out here because of you," I said, feeling my blood quicken. "Why didn't you tell her we aren't like that?"

Her grip on the wheel tightened. "Because . . ." She took a soft breath and tucked her hair behind her ear. It was a nervous tic that I didn't see very often. "Because I didn't want to," she said as she settled in behind a red Trans-Am doing fifteen over the posted limit.

Eyes worried, she looked at me, ignoring the green minivan that both the Trans-Am and we were roaring up on. "I'm not going to apologize, Rachel. The night you decide taking and giving blood isn't sex, I'm going to be there. I'll take what I can until you do."

Horribly uncomfortable, I shifted in my seat. "Ivy . . ."

"Don't," she said lightly as she yanked the car to the right, hitting the gas to dart ahead of both of them. "I know how you feel about it. I can't change your mind. You're going to have to figure it out for yourself. Skimmer being here doesn't change anything." She slipped in front of the van, giving me a soft smile that convinced me even more that blood was sex. "And then you'll spend the rest of your life kicking yourself for waiting so long to take that chance."

Eighteen

The commercial cut in, the volume jarring me as I sat on the couch. Sighing, I pulled my knees to my chin and hugged my legs. It was early, just after two in the morning, and I was trying to find the gumption to go make something to eat. Ivy was still on her run, and even with the awkward conversation in the car, I was hoping she'd be home early enough so we could go out. Warming up a potpie and eating alone had all the appeal of pulling the skin off my shins.

Grabbing the remote, I muted the TV. This was depressing. I was sitting on the couch on a Friday night watching *Die Hard*, alone. Nick should have been there with me. I missed him. I think I missed him. I missed something. Maybe I just missed being held. Was I that shallow?

Tossing the remote down, I realized a voice was coming from the front of the church. I sat up; it was a man's voice. Alarmed, I tapped the line out back. Between one breath and the next, my center filled. With the force of the line running through me, I gathered myself to rise, only to sink down when Jenks flew into the room at head height. The soft hum of his wings told me in an instant that whatever was up front wasn't going to kill me *or* put money in my pocket.

Eyes wide, he landed on the lampshade. The dust sifting from him floated upward with the rising heat of the bulb. He was usually tucked in my desk asleep at this hour, which was why I was having my pity party now so I could sulk without interference. "Hey, Jenks," I said as I let go of the line and the unfocused magic left me. "Who's here?"

His face became worried. "Rachel, we might have a problem."

I eyed him sourly. I was sitting alone watching *Die Hard.* That was a problem, not whatever had come waltzing in our door. "Who is it?" I said flatly. "I already ran off the Jehovah's Witnesses. You would think living in a church, they might get the idea, but no-o-o-o."

Jenks frowned. "Some Were in a cowboy hat. He wants me to sign a paper saying I ate that fish we stole for the Howlers."

"David?" I jerked out of the chair and headed for the sanctuary.

Jenks's wings were a harsh buzz as he flew beside me. "Who's David?"

"An insurance adjustor." My brow furrowed. "I met him yesterday."

Sure enough, David was standing in the middle of the empty room, looking uncomfortable in his long coat and hat pulled down over his eyes. Pixy children were watching from under the crack of the rolltop desk, their pretty faces all lined up in a row. He was on a cell phone, and upon seeing me, he muttered a few words, closed the cover, and tucked it away.

"Hello, Rachel," he said, cringing as his voice echoed. His eyes ran over my casual jeans and red sweater, and then went to the ceiling as he shifted from foot to foot. It was obvious he wasn't comfortable in the church, like most Weres, but it was psychological not biological.

"I'm sorry to bother you," he said as he took off his hat and crushed it in a tight grip. "But hearsay won't stand up in this case. I need your partner to verify he ate that wishing fish."

"Holy crap! It was a wishing fish!" There was a chorus of shrill cries from the desk. Jenks made a harsh sound, and the faces lining the crack scattered back into the shadows.

David took a trifolded paper from a pocket of his duster and unfolded it atop Ivy's piano. "If you could sign here?" he said, then straightened, his eyes suspicious. "You *did* eat it?"

Jenks looked scared, his wings a blue so dark they were almost purple. "Yeah. We ate it. Are we going to be all right?"

I tried to hide my smile, but David grinned, his teeth looking white in the dim light of the sanctuary. "I think you'll be fine, Mr. Jenks," he said, clicking open a pen and holding it out.

My eyebrows rose. David hesitated, looking from the pen to the pixy. The pen was the larger of the two. "Ummm," he said, shifting on his feet.

"I've got it." Jenks zipped to the desk, returning with a pencil lead. I watched him carefully write his name, the ultrasonic chatter from the desk making my eyes hurt. Jenks rose, pixy dust sifting from him. "Hey, uh, we aren't in any trouble, are we?"

The pungent scent of ink assailed me, and David looked up from notarizing it. "Not from our end of things. Thank you, Mr. Jenks." He looked at me. "Rachel."

A soft rattling of the windows from an air-pressure shift brought both our heads up. Someone had opened the back door to the church. "Rachel?" came a high voice, and I blinked.

It was my mom? Bewildered, I looked at David. "Ah, it's my mom. Maybe you ought to go. Unless you want her to bully you into taking me on a date."

David's face went startled as he tucked the paper away. "No. I'm done. Thanks. I probably should have called first, but it *is* normal business hours."

My face warmed. I had just added ten thousand to my bank account, courtesy of Quen and his "little problem." I could sit on my butt and sulk for one night if I wanted. And I wasn't going to prep the charms I'd be using on said run tonight. Spelling after midnight under a waning moon was asking for trouble. Besides, how I arranged my day was not his business.

Bothered, I looked at the back of the church, not wanting to be rude but not wanting my mom to play twenty questions with David, either. "I'll be right there, Mom!" I shouted, then turned to Jenks. "Will you see him out for me?"

"Sure thing, Rache." Jenks rose up to head height to accompany David into the foyer.

" 'Bye, David," I said, and he gave me a raised-hand good-bye and put his hat on.

Why does it all happen at once? I thought, hustling to the kitchen. My mom visiting unannounced would top off an already perfect day. Tired, I entered the kitchen to find her with her head in my fridge. From the sanctuary came the boom of the front door closing.

"Mom," I said, trying to keep my voice pleasant. "It's great to see you. But it's business hours." My thoughts went to my bathroom, wondering if my undies were still atop the dryer.

Smiling, she straightened, peeking at me from around the door of the fridge. She was wearing sunglasses, and they looked really odd with her straw hat and sundress. *Sundress? She was in a sundress? It was below twenty out there.*

"Rachel!" Smiling, she shut the door and opened her arms. "Give me a hug, honey."

Thoughts whirling, I absently returned her embrace. Maybe I should call her psychologist and make sure she was still making her appointments. An odd smell clung to her, and as I pulled away, I said, "What is that you're wearing? It smells like burnt amber."

"That's because it is, love."

Shocked, my eyes went to her face. Her voice had dropped several octaves. Adrenaline shook me. I jerked back, only to find a white-gloved hand gripping my shoulder. I froze, unable to move as a ripple of ever-after cascaded over her, revealing Algaliarept. *Oh, crap. I was dead.*

"Good evening, familiar," the demon said, smiling to show me flat blocky teeth. "Let's find a ley line and get you home, hmm?"

"Jenks!" I shrieked, hearing my voice harsh with terror. Leaning back, I swung my foot up, kicking him square in the 'nads.

Al grunted, his red, goat-slitted eyes widening. "Bitch," he said, reaching down and grabbing my ankle.

Gasping, I went down as he yanked me onto my butt. I hit with a thump, panicking. As I kicked ineffectively at him, he dragged me out of the kitchen and into the hall.

"Rachel!" Jenks shrilled, black pixy dust sifting from him.

"Get me a charm!" I shouted as I grabbed the archway and hung on. *Oh God. He had me. If he got me to a line, he could physically drag me to the ever-after, me saying no or not.*

Arms tensing, I fought to hold onto the wall long enough for Jenks to open my charm cupboard and grab one. I didn't need a finger stick; my lip was already bleeding from the fall.

"Here," Jenks cried, hovering at ankle height to look me right in the eye. He had the cord to a sleep charm in his grip. His eyes were frightened and his wings were red.

"Don't think so, witch," Al said, giving me a jerk.

Pain sliced through my shoulder, and my grip was torn away. "Rachel!" Jenks exclaimed as my fingernails scraped the hardwood floor and then the carpet in the living room.

Al muttered Latin, and I cried out as an explosion blew the back door off its hinges.

"Jenks! Get out! Get your kids safe!" I shouted when cold air raced in to replace the air the explosion had blown out. Dogs barked as I slid down the stairs on my stomach. Snow, ice, and rock salt scraped my middle and my chin. I stared up at the shattered doorframe as David's silhouette showed black against the light. I held my hand out for the charm Jenks had dropped. "The charm!" I screamed when he clearly had no idea what I wanted. "Throw me the charm!"

Al came to a halt. His English riding boots making prints on the unshoveled walk, he turned. *"Detrudo,"* he said, clearly a trigger word for a curse imprinted on his memory.

I gasped as a black and red shadow of ever-after struck David, throwing him into the far wall and out of my sight. "David!" I called as Al started dragging me again.

Wiggling, I twisted so I was on my butt and not my stomach. I cut a small swath through the snow behind Al as he pulled me kicking to the wooden gate at the front of the garden that led to the street. Al couldn't use the ley line in the graveyard to drag me into the ever-after, as it was entirely encircled by holy ground that he couldn't cross. The nearest ley line I knew about was eight blocks away. *I had a chance,* I thought, the cold snow soaking my jeans.

"Let go!" I demanded, kicking the back of Al's knees with my one free foot.

His leg buckled and he stopped, his irate look clear in the light from the streetlamp. He couldn't turn misty to avoid the strikes since I would be able to slip his grip. "What a canicula you are," he said, taking both ankles with one hand and continuing.

"I don't want to go!" I shouted, grabbing onto the edges of the gate as we passed through it. We jerked to a stop, and Al sighed.

"Let go of the fence," he said, sounding tired.

"No!" My muscles started to shake as I fought to keep unmoving while Al pulled. I had only one ley line charm imprinted on my subconscious, but trapping Al and me in a circle would get me nowhere. He could break it as easily as I, now that his aura would be tainting it.

A cry slipped from me when Al gave up trying to drag me through the gate and he picked me up and threw me over his shoulder. My breath exploded out of me as his muscle-hard shoulder cut into my middle. He stank of burnt amber, and I fought to get free.

"This would be a lot easier," he said as I jabbed my elbows between his shoulder blades to no effect, "if you would accept that I have you. Just say you'll come willingly, and I can pop us into a line from here and it will save you a lot of embarrassment."

"I'm not worried about embarrassment!" I stretched to reach a passing limb of a tree, my breath coming out in relief as I snagged one. Al jerked back, pulled off balance.

"Oh, look," he said as he yanked me free and my palms came away scraped and bleeding. "Your wolfie friend wants to play."

David, I thought, twisting to see past Al's shoulder. As I struggled to breathe, I saw a huge shadow standing at the center of the lamp-lit, snow-packed street. My mouth dropped. He had Wered. He had Wered in less than three minutes. God, that must have hurt.

And he was huge, having retained his entire human mass. His head would come to my shoulder, I'd guess. Black silky fur, more like hair, shifted in the cold wind. His ears were flat against his head, and an impossibly low warning growl came from him. Feet the size of my spread hands dug into the snow as he barred our way. He gave an indescribably deep warning bark, and Al chuckled. Lights were coming on in adjacent houses and curtains were being peeked around. "She's legally mine," Al said lightly. "I'm carting her home. Don't even try."

Al started down the street, leaving me torn between screaming for help and admitting I was a goner. A car was coming, its lights throwing everything into stark relief. "Good doggie," Al muttered as we passed David with a good ten feet between us. Looking harsh in the light from the headlamps, David bowed his head, and I wondered if he had given up, knowing he could do nothing. But then his head came up and he started after us.

"David, there's nothing you can do! David, no!" I shrieked when his slow lope shifted into a full run. Eyes lost in a killing frenzy, he barreled right for me. Sure, I didn't want to be pulled into the ever-after, but I didn't want to be dead, either.

Swearing, Al turned around. *"Vacuefacio,"* he said, his white-gloved hand outstretched.

I twisted on his shoulder to see. A black ball of force shot from him, meeting David's silent attack two feet in front of us. David's huge feet skidded, but he ran right into it. Yelping, he rolled, tumbling into a snow pile. The scent of singed hair rose and was gone.

"David!" I cried, not feeling the cold that pinched me. "Are you all right?"

I yelped as Al dumped me on the ground, a blocky hand squeezing my shoulder until I cried out in pain. The thick sheet of compressed snow on the pavement melted up through me, and my rear went numb with hurt and cold. "Idiot," Al grumbled to himself. "You've got a familiar, why by your mother's ashes aren't you using her?"

He smiled at me, thick eyebrows high in anticipation. "Ready to work, Rachel, love?"

My breath froze in me. Panicking, I stared up at him, feeling my face go pale and my eyes go wide. "Please don't," I whispered.

He grinned all the wider. "Hold this for me," he said.

A scream of pain ripped from me as Al tapped a line, sending its strength thundering into me. My muscles jerked and a spasm shook me until my face hit the pavement. I was on fire, and I clenched into a fetal position, hands over my ears. Scream upon scream beat upon me. I couldn't block them out. They hammered at me, the only thing that was real besides the agony in my head. Like an explosion, the force of the line ran through me, settling into my center, spilling over to set my limbs on fire. My brain felt as if it had been dipped in acid, and all the time, that awful screaming racked my ears. I was on fire. I was burning.

I suddenly realized the screaming was coming from me. Huge, racking sobs took their place as I managed to stop. An eerie, keening wail rose, and I managed to stop that, too. Panting, I opened my eyes. My hands were pale and shaking in the light from the car. They weren't charred. The scent of burnt amber wasn't my skin peeling away. It was all in my head.

Oh God. My head felt like it was three places at once. I was hearing everything twice, smelling everything twice, and having thoughts that weren't my own. Al knew everything I was feeling, everything I was thinking. I could only pray that I hadn't done this to Nick.

"Better?" Al said, and I jerked as if whipped, hearing his voice in my head as well as my ears. "Not bad," he said, yanking me unresisting to my feet. "Ceri passed out with only half that much, and it took her three months to stop making that awful noise."

Numb, I felt spittle slip from me. I couldn't remember how to wipe it away. My throat hurt and the cold air I sucked into me seemed to burn. I could hear dogs barking and a car engine. The light from its headlamps wasn't moving, and the snow sparkled. I hung loose in Al's grip, feet trying to move as he began walking again. He dragged me out from in front of the car, and in a slippery squeak of snow and ice, it sped away.

"Come along, Rachel, love," Al said in the new darkness, clearly in a good mood as he pulled me over a snowplowed hill and onto the shoveled walk. "Your wolf has given up, and unless you submit to me, we have a good bit of city to walk before I can get you to a ley line."

Stumbling, I lurched after Al, my feet in my socks long cold and unresponsive. His hand gripped my wrist in a shackle stronger than any metal. Al's shadow stretched behind us to where David panted, shaking his head as if to clear it. I could do nothing, feeling nothing as David's lips pulled back from his muzzle. Silently, he lunged. Numb and uncaring, I watched as if from a distance. Al, though, was very much aware.

"Celero fervefacio!" he exclaimed, angry, and I screamed as the curse burned through me. The force of Al's magic exploded from his outstretched hand and struck David. In a flash, the snow melted underneath the Were, and he writhed on the black circle of pavement. I screamed from the agony, catching it—smothering it—hearing it trail into the keen of a banshee.

"Please . . . no more," I whispered, spit falling from me to melt a spot of snow. I stared at the dirty white, thinking it was my soul, pitted and sullied, paying for Al's black magic. I couldn't think. The pain burned through me still, becoming a familiar hurt.

The sound of frightened people pulled my bleary gaze up. The neighborhood was watching from doors and windows. I'd probably make the news. A sharp bang drew my attention to the house we had passed, an elegant snow castle with turrets and towers gracing one corner of the yard. The light from the open door spilled over the trampled snow, falling almost to Al and me. I caught my breath at Ceri standing in the threshold, Ivy's crucifix about her neck. Her nightgown flowed to the porch, white and billowy. Her unbound hair floated about her, coming almost to her waist. Her posture was stiff with anger. "You," she said, her voice ringing clear over the snow.

From behind me came a warning yip, and I felt a tug of a pull. Through Al's knowledge, I instinctively knew that Ceri had set a circle around Al and me. A futile sob escaped me, but I fastened on the feeling like a hungry cur on trash. I had felt something that wasn't from Al. The demon's own emotion of annoyance was quick behind my depression, covering it up until I forgot what I felt like. From Al, I knew the circle was useless. You can make a circle without drawing it first, but only a drawn circle is strong enough to hold a demon.

Al didn't even bother to slow down, dragging me into the sheet of ever-after.

My breath hissed in as the force Ceri had put in the circle

flowed into me. I screamed as a new wave of fire coated my skin. It ran from where I first touched the field, flowing like liquid to cover me. Pain searched for my center. It found it, and I screamed again, twisting out of Al's grip as it found my chi full and bursting. The ever-after rebounded, scouring through me to settle in the only place it could force room: my head. Sooner or later it would be too much and I'd go insane.

I clenched into myself. The rough sidewalk scraped my thigh and shoulder as I convulsed. Slowly it became bearable, and I was able to stop screaming. The last one trailed off into a moan that silenced the dogs. *Oh God, I was dying. I was dying from the inside out.*

"Please," I begged Ceri, knowing she couldn't hear me. "Don't do that again."

Al yanked me upright. "You're an *excellent* familiar," he encouraged, his face split in a wide grin. "I'm so proud of you. You managed to stop screaming again. I think I'll make you a cup of tea when we get home and let you nap before I show you off to my friends."

"No . . ." I whispered, and Al chuckled at my defiance even before the word escaped me. I could have no thoughts without him knowing them first. Now I realized why Ceri had numbed her emotion, preferring to have none rather than share them with Al.

"Wait," Ceri said, her voice ringing clear over the snow as she ran down the porch steps, past the chain-link fence, and into the yard before us.

I sagged in Al's grip as he stopped to look at her. Her voice flowed over me, soothing my skin and mind alike. My eyes warmed at the hint of respite from the pain, and I almost sobbed in relief. She looked like a goddess. She granted release from pain.

"Ceri," Al said warmly, his attention only half on David as he circled us, his hackles raised and a frightening savagery in his eyes. "You're looking well, love." His eyes traveled over the elaborate castle of snow behind her. "Miss your homeland?"

"I am Ceridwen Merriam Dulciate," she said, the command in her voice like a whip. "I'm not your familiar. I have a soul. Give me the respect that calls for."

Al snickered. "I see you found your ego. How does it feel to be growing old again?"

I saw her stiffen. She came to stand before us, and I could see her guilt. "I don't fear it anymore," she said softy, and I wondered if an unaging life was what Al had lured her into being his familiar with. "It's the way of the world. Let Rachel Mariana Morgan go."

Al threw his head back and laughed, showing his thick, flat teeth to the cloudy sky. "She is mine. You're looking well. Care to come back? You could be sisters. How nice is that?"

Her mouth twitched. "She has a soul. You can't force her."

Panting, I hung from where Al held me. If he got me into a line, whether I had a soul or not wouldn't matter. "Yes, I can," Al said, cementing it into fact. His brow furrowed, and he jerked his attention to David. I had seen him circling us in a wide path, trying to make a physical circle with his footsteps with which he could bind Al. The demon's eyes narrowed. *"Detrudo,"* he said, gesturing.

I gasped, jerking as a thread of ever-after flowed from me to work Al's charm. Head erect, I choked back whatever awful sound was going to come out of my raw throat. I managed to keep silent as it raced from me, but all my efforts to stay quiet did no good when a wave of ever-after surged in from a line to replace what Al had used. Again fire immolated my center, overflowing and making my skin burn, finally settling in my thoughts. I couldn't think. There was nothing but hurt in me. I was burning. My very thoughts, my soul, were burning.

Shocked, I fell to my knees, the pain from the icy sidewalk going almost unnoticed as a cry of misery escaped me. My eyes were open, and Ceri cringed, standing barefoot before us in the snow. A shared pain was mirrored in her eyes, and I fastened on them, finding peace in their green depths. She had survived this. I could survive this. I would survive this. *God, help me find a way to survive this.*

Al laughed as he felt my resolve. "Good," he encouraged. "I appreciate your effort to be silent. You'll get there. Your god can't help you, but call for him anyway. I'd like to meet him."

I took a shuddering breath. David was a shaking puddle of silky fur in the snow some distance from where he had been. I was screaming when the spell hit him and didn't see him knocked aside. Ceri went to him when he rose, grasping his muzzle in both hands and peering into his eyes. She looked dwarfed beside him, his absolute blackness looking dangerous and somehow right beside her frailty, dressed in flowing white. "Give this to me," she whispered as she gazed unafraid into his eyes, and David's ears pricked.

Dropping his face, she paced forward until she was standing where David's footprints left off. Keasley joined her, buttoning his thick fabric coat as he moved from my right to halt beside her. He took her hand, murmuring, "It's yours," before letting go, and they both stepped back.

I wanted to weep but didn't have the strength. They couldn't help me. I admired Ceri's confidence, her proud and impassioned stance, but it was misplaced. I might as well be dead.

"Demon," she said, her voice chiming through the still air like a bell. "I bind you."

Al jerked as a sheet of smokey blue ever-after blossomed over us, and his face reddened. *"Es scortum obscenus impurua!"* he shouted, letting me go. I stayed where I fell, knowing he wouldn't have released me if I could escape. "How dare you use what I taught you to bind me!"

Panting, I pulled my head up, only now realizing why she had touched David and then Keasley. David had started the circle, Ceri had made a second portion of it, and Keasley had made the third. They had given her permission to bind their paths together as one. The circle had been made; he was caught. And as I watched him pace to the edge of the bubble and a victorious Ceri, I thought it wouldn't take much for him to decide to kill me out of spite.

"Moecha putida!" he shouted, hammering on the force between them. "Ceri, I will tear your soul from you again, I swear it!"

"Et de," she said, her narrow chin high and her eyes glinting, "*acervus excerementum*. You can jump to a line from here. Leave now before the sun rises so we can all go back to bed."

Algaliarept took a slow breath, and I shuddered at the bound anger in the movement. "No," he said. "I'm going to widen Rachel's horizons, and you will listen to her scream as she learns to take the full capacity of what I demand."

He could draw more through me? I thought, feeling my lungs press together as I temporarily lost the will to breathe. *There was worse than this?*

Ceri's confidence faltered. "No," she said. "She doesn't know how to store it properly. Any more, and her mind will bend. She'll be insane before you teach her how to make your tea."

"You don't need to be sane to make tea or do my toast upon one side," he snarled. Snatching my arm, he jerked me unresisting to my feet.

Ceri shook her head, standing in the snow as if it were summer. "You're being petty. You've lost her. She outsmarted you. You're a sore loser."

Al pinched my shoulder, and I gritted my teeth, refusing to cry out. It was only pain. It was nothing compared to the steady burning of the ever-after he was forcing me to hold for him. "Sore loser!" he shouted, and I heard the cries of fear from the people in the shadows. "She can't hide on holy ground forever. If she tries, I'll find a way to use her through the lines."

Ceri glanced at David, and I closed my eyes in despair. She thought he could do it. God help me. It was only a matter of time before he figured out how. My gamble to save my soul was going to fail. "Go away," she said, pulling her attention from David. "Go back to the ever-after and leave Rachel Mariana Morgan in peace. No one here has called you."

"You can't banish me, Ceri!" he raged, jerking me upright until I fell into him. "My familiar opened a summoning path for me to follow when she tapped a line. Break this circle and let me take her as is my right!"

Ceri took an exultant breath. "Rachel! He acknowledged you called him. Banish him!"

My eyes widened.

"No!" Algaliarept shouted, sending a flow of ever-after into me. I nearly passed out, the waves of pain washing through me building upon themselves until there was nothing left but agony. But I took a breath, smelling the stink of my burned soul.

"Algaliarept," I choked out, my voice a ragged gasp. "Return to the ever-after."

"You little bitch!" he snarled, backhanding me. The force of the blow picked me up, throwing me into Ceri's wall. I landed in a crumpled heap, unable to think. My head hurt and my throat was raw. The snow under me was cold. I snuggled into it, burning.

"Go away. Go away *now,*" I whispered.

The overwhelming ever-after energy humming through my brain vanished in a clock-tick. I moaned at its absence. I heard my heart beat, pause, and beat again. It was all I could do to keep breathing, empty with just my own thoughts in my head. It was gone. The fire was gone.

"Get her out of the snow," I heard Ceri say urgently, her voice easing into me like ice water. I tried to open my eyes, failing. Someone picked me up, and there was the warmth of body heat. It was Keasley, a small part of me decided, as I recognized the smell of redwood and cheap coffee. My head thumped into him and my chin dropped to my chest. I felt small cool hands upon my forehead, and with Ceri singing to me, I felt myself shift into movement.

Nineteen

"Oh God," I whispered, my words sounding as raw as my throat felt. It was a raspy utterance, more like gravel in a tin pail than a voice. My head hurt, and a wet washcloth smelling of Ivory soap was over my eyes. "I don't feel so good."

Ceri's cool hand touched my cheek. "I'm not surprised," she said wryly. "Keep your eyes shut. I'm going to change your compress."

Around me was the soft breathing of two people and a very big dog. I vaguely remembered being carried in, wavering on passing out but never quite managing it, hard as I tried. I could tell by the smell of my perfumes that Keasley had put me in my room, and the pillow under my head had a familiar, comfortable feel. The heavy weight of the afghan I kept at the foot of my bed was draped over me. *I was alive. Go figure.*

Ceri lifted the damp washcloth from me, and despite her warning, I cracked my lids. "Ow . . ." I moaned as the light from a candle on the dresser seemed to pierce my eyes, going all the way to the back of my skull and ricocheting. My headache tripled.

"She told you to keep your eyes shut," Jenks said sardonically, but the relief in his voice was obvious. The click of David's nails intruded, shortly followed by a warm snuff in my ear.

"She's fine," Ceri said softly, and he retreated.

Fine? I thought, concentrating on my breathing until the light bouncing around in my head lost momentum and died. *This was fine?*

The throbbing in my head retreated to a mild agony, and when

I heard a soft puff of breath and the biting scent of blown-out candle reached me, I opened my eyes again.

In the streetlight leaking past my curtains, I could see Ceri on a kitchen chair beside my bed. A pan of water was on her lap, and I cringed when she set it on Ivy's vampire dating guide, out where everyone could see it. On my other side stood Keasley, a hunched shadow. Perched on the bedpost, Jenks glowed a dull amber, and lurking in the background was David taking up half the floorspace with his wolf bulk.

"I think we're back in Kansas, Toto," I murmured, and Keasley harrumphed.

My face was damp and cold, and a draft from the broken door mixed with the musty smell of the heater blowing from the vent. "Jenks!" I croaked when I remembered the wash of winter air that had hit him. "Are your kids all right?"

"Yeah, they're fine," he said, and I slumped back to the pillow. My hand crept up to hold my throat. It felt as if it was bleeding inside.

"David?" I questioned softer. "How about you?"

His panting increased as he pushed Keasley out of the way to snuff warm and moist in my ear. His jaws opened. Ceri gasped when David gripped my entire face in his mouth.

Adrenaline cut through the pain. "Hey!" I exclaimed, struggling as he gave me a gentle shake and let go. Heart pounding, I froze at the soft growl rumbling up and the wet nose nudging my cheek. Making a doggie huff, he padded into the hall.

"What in hell does that mean?" I said, heart jackhammering against my chest.

Jenks rose in a sprinkling of pixy dust that made me squint. It wasn't bright, but my eyes hurt that bad. "He's glad you're okay," he said, his tiny features serious.

"This is okay?" I said, and from the sanctuary came an odd, yodeling bark of laughter.

My throat hurt, and I held a hand to it as I sat up. There was Were spit on my face, and I wiped it off with the damp washcloth and set it over the edge of the pan. My muscles hurt. Hell, everything hurt. And I hadn't liked my head being in David's mouth at all.

The sound of manicured nails clacking on the floorboards drew my attention to the dark hallway as he trotted past headed for the back of the church. His backpack and clothes were in his mouth, and his coat trailed behind like a downed animal.

"Jenks," Ceri said softly. "See if he's going to change here or if he'd like some help getting his things in his satchel."

Jenks rose up, falling back at a short negative bark from the living room.

Jaw clenched against a Texas-sized headache, I decided it was likely he'd change back before leaving. It was illegal to Were in public outside of the three days around the full moon. Once the restriction had only been tradition; now it was law to make humans feel better. What Weres did in their own homes was their own business. I was confident no one would say anything about him shifting to help save me from a demon, but he couldn't drive his car in the shape he was in, and catching a ride on a bus wasn't going to happen.

"Well," Keasley said as he sat on the edge of my bed, "let's take a look at you."

"Ow . . ." I exclaimed when he touched my shoulder and the bruised muscle sent a stab of pain through me. I pushed his hand off me, and he shifted closer.

"I'd forgotten what a pain-in-the-butt patient you are," he said, reaching out again. "I want to know where you're hurting."

"Stop," I croaked, trying to slap his knobby arthritic hands. "My shoulder hurts where Al pinched it. My hands hurt where I scraped them, my chin and stomach hurt where he dragged me down the steps. My knees hurt from . . ." I hesitated. ". . . falling in the road. And my face hurts where Al slapped me." I looked at Ceri. "Do I have a black eye?"

"You will in the morning," she said softly, wincing in sympathy.

"And my lip is cut," I finished, touching it. The faint scent of bane joined the smell of snow. David was turning back, nice and slow. He'd have to after the hurt he must have endured to shift so quickly before. I was glad he had some bane. The herb was a mild pain depressant and sedative to make it easier. Too bad it only worked on Weres.

Keasley groaned as he rose. "I'll get you a pain amulet," he said, shuffling into the hallway. "Mind if I make some coffee? I'm staying until your roommate is back."

"Make it two amulets," I said, not knowing if it would help my head. Pain amulets worked only on physical pain, and I had a feeling this was more of an echo left from channeling so much ley line force. *Was this what I'd done to Nick?* No wonder he had left.

I squinted when the light flicked on in the kitchen and a slice of it spilled into my room. Ceri watched me carefully, and I nodded to tell her it was okay. Patting my hand atop the coverlet, she murmured, "Tea would be easier for you to stomach than coffee." Her solemn green eyes went to Jenks. "Will you stay with her?"

"Yeah." His wings flashed into motion. "Baby-sitting Rachel is what I do third best."

I sneered at him, and Ceri hesitated. "I won't be long," she said, rising to leave in the soft sound of bare feet on wood.

The comfortable rhythm of conversation drifted in from the kitchen, and I awkwardly pulled my afghan up about my shoulders. Every muscle ached as if I had been in a fever. My feet were cold in my soggy socks, and I was probably making a damp spot on my bed from my snow-wet clothes. Depressed, my eyes landed on Jenks atop the bedpost at my feet.

"Thanks for trying to help," I said. "You sure you're okay? He blew the door right off."

"I should have been faster with that amulet." His wings turned a dismal blue.

I shrugged, immediately wishing I hadn't when my shoulder started throbbing. *Where was Keasley with my charms?* "They might not even work on demons."

Jenks flitted close to land on the bump of my knee. "Damn, Rache. You look like crap."

"Thanks."

The heavenly scent of coffee started to mix with the musty heater. A shadow eclipsed the light from the hallway, and I creakily turned to see Ceri. "Eat these while your tea is brewing," she said, setting down a plate with three of Ivy's cookies on them.

My lips curled down in a frown. "Do I have to?" I complained. "Where's my amulet?"

"Where's my amulet?" Jenks mocked in a high falsetto. "God, Rachel. Suck it up."

"Shut up," I muttered. "You try channeling a demon's ley line and see if you even survive. I bet you'd explode in a flash of pixy dust, you little twit."

He laughed, and Ceri frowned at us as if we were children. "I've got it right here," she said, and I leaned forward so she could drape the cord over my head. A blessed relief soaked in to ease my muscles—Keasley must have invoked it for me—but my headache remained, all the worse now that there was nothing to distract me from it.

"I'm sorry," Ceri said. "It's going to take a good day." When I didn't say anything, she shifted to the door, adding, "I'll get your tea." She walked out, a scuffing pulling my gaze up. "Excuse me," she murmured, gazing at the floor when she almost ran into David. The Were looked tired, seeming older as he adjusted the collar of his coat. His stubble was thicker, and the thick spice of bane was heavy on him. "Would you like some tea?" she said, and my eyebrows rose as her usual confidence shifted to meek awe.

David shook his head, accepting her submissive mien with a grace that made him seem noble. Head still lowered, she edged past him and went into the kitchen. Jenks and I exchanged wondering looks as he came in and dropped his backpack. Nodding to Jenks, he pulled the kitchen chair farther away from me and sat down, leaning back with his arms crossed and eyeing me speculatively from under his cowboy hat.

"You want to tell me what that was all about before I go?" he said. "I'm starting to think there's a good reason no one will insure you."

I made an embarrassed face and took a cookie. "Remember that demon that testified to put Piscary behind bars?"

His eyes widened. "Son of my mother's bitch!"

Jenks laughed, his voice tinkling like wind chimes. "Damn stupid of her if you ask me."

Ignoring Jenks, I met David's shocked look: part worry, part pain, part disbelief. "He came to collect his due for services rendered," I said. "Which he got. I'm his familiar, but I still have my soul, so he can't cart me off to the ever-after unless I let him." I looked to the ceiling, wondering what kind of a runner I was going to be if I couldn't tap a line after sunset without bringing demons down on me.

David made a soft whistle. "No tag is worth that."

My eyes flicked to his. "Ordinarily I'd agree with you, but at the time, Piscary was trying to kill me and it seemed like a good idea."

"Good idea, hell. It was damn stupid," Jenks muttered, clearly of the belief that if he had been there, things never would have degraded that far. He might have been right.

Feeling as if I had a hangover, I took a bite of cookie. The dry things made me hungry and nauseated at the same time. "Thank you for helping me," I said, brushing the crumbs away. "He would have had me if you hadn't done something. Are you going to be okay? I've never seen anyone Were that fast before."

Leaning forward, he shifted his backpack to rest between his feet. I watched his eyes stray to the door, and I knew he wanted to leave. "My shoulder hurts, but I'll be all right."

"I'm sorry." I finished the first cookie and started on another. It seemed as if I could feel it starting to hum through me. "You ever need anything, you tell me. I owe you big. I know how bad it hurts. Last year I went from witch to mink in three seconds. Twice in one week."

His breath hissed and lines appeared in his brow. "Ouch," he said, respect in his eyes.

I smiled, a new warmth growing in me. "You aren't kidding. But you know, it's likely going to be the only time I'll ever be that skinny and have a fur coat."

A faint smile came over him. "Where does the extra mass go, anyway?"

There was only one cookie left, and I forced myself to eat it slowly. "Back to a ley line."

His head bobbed. "We can't do that."

"I noticed. You make one hell of a big wolf, David."

His smile widened. "You know what? I changed my mind. Even if you ever want to go into insurance, don't call me."

Jenks dropped to the empty plate so I wouldn't have to keep shifting my head to see both of them. "That will be the day," he snickered. "I can just see Rachel in a gray business suit with a briefcase, her hair in a bun and glasses on her nose."

I laughed, immediately falling into a coughing jag. Arms clasped about me, I hunched into myself, shaking with rough, hacking coughs. My throat felt like it was on fire, but that paled next to the throbbing ache in my head that exploded at the sudden movement. That pain amulet bumping about my neck wasn't doing much good.

David patted my back in concern. The hurt from my shoulder broke through the amulet, and my stomach roiled. Eyes watering, I fended him off. Ceri came in, making soft admonishments as she set a mug of tea down and put a hand on my shoulder. Her touch seemed to calm the spasm, and gasping, I let her ease me back into the pillows she propped up behind me. Finally I stopped and met her gaze.

Her shadowy face was pinched in concern. Behind her, Jenks and David watched. I didn't like David seeing me like this, but it wasn't as if I had much choice. "Drink your tea," she said, holding it up to me and putting my hand around it.

"My head hurts," I complained, taking a sip of the bland brew. It wasn't real tea, but something with flowers and weeds in it. What I wanted was a cup of that coffee, but I didn't want to hurt Ceri's feelings. "I feel like run-over crap," I complained.

"You look like run-over crap," Jenks said. "Drink your tea."

It was tasteless but soothing. I took another swallow, scraping up a smile for Ceri. "Mmmm. Good," I lied.

She straightened, clearly pleased as she picked up the wash-basin. "Drink it all. Do you mind if Keasley tacks a blanket over your door to stop the draft?"

"That would be great. Thanks," I said, but she didn't leave until I took another sip.

Her shadow left the hall, and my smile fell into a grimace. "This stuff is tasteless," I whispered. "Why does everything good for me have to be tasteless?"

David glanced at the empty doorway and the light spilling in. Jenks flew to land on his shoulder as the Were unzipped his back-pack. "I've got something that might help," David said. "My old partner used to swear by it. Begged me for some when he partied-too-hearty."

"Whoa!" Hand over his nose, Jenks flitted upward. "How much bane you got in there, Johnny Appleseed?"

David's smile grew sly. "What?" he said, his brown eyes innocent. "It's not illegal. And it's organic. No carbs, even."

The familiar spicy scent of bane rose thicker in the small room, and I wasn't surprised when David brought out a cellophane bag with a zippy top. I recognized the name brand: Wolf's Head Organic. "Here," he said as he took the cup out of my hand and set it on my bedside table.

Hiding what he was doing from the hallway, he shook a good tablespoon into my drink. Running his eyes over me, he shook in a little more. "Try it now," he said, handing it to me.

I sighed. Why was everyone giving me stuff? All I wanted was a sleep charm or maybe one of Captain Edden's strange aspirins. But David looked so hopeful, and the smell of bane was more appealing than rosehips, that I stirred it with my pinky. The crushed leaves sank to leave the tea a richer color. "What good will this do?" I asked as I took a sip. "I'm not a Were."

David dropped the bag into his backpack and zipped it shut. "Not much. Your witch metabolism is too slow for it to really work. But my old partner was a witch, and he said it helped with his hangovers. It's got to taste better, if nothing else."

He stood to leave, and I sipped again, agreeing. My jaw relaxed; I hadn't even known I had been clenching it. Warm and smooth, the bane tea slipped down my throat with a mixed taste of ham broth and apples. My muscles seemed to unknot, like taking a shot of tequila. A sigh slipped from me, and the soft weight of Jenks landing on my arm pulled my eyes to his.

"Hey, Rache? You okay?"

I smiled and took another swallow. "Hi, Jenks. You're all sparkly."

Jenks's face blanked, and David looked up from working the buttons closed on his coat. His brown eyes were questioning.

"Thanks, David," I said, hearing my voice slow, precise, and low. "I owe you, okay?"

"Sure." He picked up his backpack. "You take care of yourself."

"I will." I gulped half my tea, and it slid down to make a warm spot in me. "I don't feel too bad right now. Which is good, seeing as I have a date with Trent tomorrow, and if I don't go, his security officer is gonna kill me."

David jerked to a stop in the threshold. From beyond him came the *tap-tap-tap* of Keasley hammering a blanket over the door. "Trent Kalamack?" the Were questioned.

"Yeah." I took another drink, swirling the tea with my pinky until the bane made a whirlpool and shifted the brew even darker. "He's going to talk to Saladan. His security officer is making me go with him." I squinted up at David, the light from the hallway seeming bright but not painful. I wondered where David's tattoos were. Weres always had tattoos, don't ask me why.

"Have you ever met Trent?" I asked.

"Mr. Kalamack?" David rocked back into the room. "No."

I squirmed under my afghan and focused on my cup. David's partner was right. This stuff was great. I didn't hurt anywhere. "Trent is a prick," I said, remembering what we were talking about. "I've got the goods on him, and he's got the goods on me. But I don't have anything on his security officer, and if I don't do this, he's going to tell."

Jenks hovered, making an uncertain swoop from David to the door and back to me. David eyed him, then asked, "Tell what?"

I leaned closer, my eyes widening as my tea threatened to slop when I moved faster than I thought I should. Frowning, I finished it off, not minding the bits of leaves that came with it. Smiling, I leaned close, enjoying the smell of musk and bane. "My secret," I whispered, wondering if David would let me hunt for his tattoos if

I asked. He looked great for an older guy. "I've got a secret, but I'm not going to tell you."

"I'll be back," Jenks said, swooping close. "I want to know what she put in that tea."

He zipped out, and I blinked, watching the sparkles of his pixy dust settle. I'd never seen so many before, and they were the colors of the rainbow. Jenks must have been worried.

"Secret?" David prompted, but I shook my head and the light seemed to brighten.

"I'm not going to tell. I don't like the cold."

David put his hands on my shoulders and eased me into the pillows. I smiled up at him, happy when Jenks flew in. "Jenks," David said softly. "Has she been bitten by a Were?"

"No!" he protested. "Unless it was before I met her."

My eyes had slid shut, and they opened when David shook me. "What?" I protested, pushing at him when he peered at me, his liquid brown eyes too close to mine. Now he reminded me of my dad, and I smiled at him.

"Rachel, honey," he said. "You been bitten by a Were?"

A sigh came from me. "Nope. Never you and never Ivy. No one bites me but mosquitoes, and I squish them. Little bastards."

Jenks hovered backward and David drew away. I closed my eyes, listening to them breathe. It seemed awfully loud. "Shhhh," I said. "Quiet."

"Maybe I gave her too much," David said.

Ceri's soft padding of feet seemed loud. "What . . . What did you do to her?" she asked, her voice sharp, pulling my eyes open.

"Nothing!" David protested, his shoulders hunched. "I gave her some bane. It shouldn't have done this. I've never seen it do this to a witch before!"

"Ceri," I said, "I'm sleepy. Can I go to sleep?"

Her lips pursed, but I could tell she wasn't angry with me. "Yes." She tugged the coverlet to my chin. "Go to sleep."

I slumped back, not caring that I was still wearing wet clothes. I was really, really tired. And I was warm. And my skin was tingling. And I felt like I could sleep for a week.

"Why didn't you ask me before you gave her bane?" Ceri asked sharply, her words a whisper but very clear. "She's already on Brimstone. It's in the cookies!"

I knew it! I thought, trying to open my eyes. *Boy, I was going to let Ivy have it when she got home.* But she wasn't, and I was tired, so I did nothing. I'd had it with people getting me drunk. I swear, I wasn't going to eat anything I didn't make myself ever again.

The sound of David's chuckle seemed to set my skin to tingle where the coverlet didn't come between him and me. "I got it now," he said. "The Brimstone upped her metabolism to where the bane is going to do some real good. She's going to sleep for three days. I gave her enough to knock a Were out for a full moon."

A jerk of alarm went through me. My eyes flashed open. "No!" I said, trying to sit up as Ceri pushed me into the pillows. "I have to go to that party. If I don't, Quen will tell!"

David helped her, and together they kept my head on the pillow and my feet under the afghan. "Take it easy, Rachel," he soothed, and I hated that he was stronger than I. "Don't fight it, or it's going to come back up on you. Be a good little witch and let it work itself out."

"If I don't go, he'll tell!" I said, hearing my blood race through my ears. "The only thing I have on Trent is that I know what he is, and if I tell, Quen will freaking kill me!"

"What!" Jenks shrieked, his wings clattering as he rose.

Too late, I realized what I had said. *Shit.*

I stared at Jenks, feeling my face go white. The room went deathly still. Ceri's eyes were round with question, and David stared in disbelief. I couldn't take it back.

"You know!" Jenks shouted. "You know what he is, and you didn't tell me? You witch! You knew? You knew! Rachel! You . . . you . . ."

Disapproval was thick in David's eyes, and Ceri looked frightened. Pixy children peeked around the doorframe. "You knew!" Jenks yelled, pixy dust sifting from him in a golden sunbeam. His kids scattered in a frightened tinkling sound.

I lurched upright. "Jenks—" I said, hunching into myself as my stomach clenched.

"Shut up!" he shouted. "Just shut the hell up! We're supposed to be partners!"

"Jenks . . ." I reached out. I wasn't sleepy anymore, and my gut twisted.

"No!" he said, a burst of pixy dust lighting my dim room. "You don't trust me? Fine. I'm outta here. I gotta make a call. David, can I and my family bum a ride from you?"

"Jenks!" I tossed the covers from me. "I'm sorry! I couldn't tell you." *Oh God, I should have trusted Jenks.*

"Shut the hell up!" he exclaimed, then flew out, pixy dust flaming red in his path.

I stood to follow. I took a step, then reached for the doorframe, my head swinging to look at the floor. My vision wavered and my balance left me. I put a hand to my stomach. "I'm going to be sick," I breathed. "Oh God, I'm going to be sick."

David's hand was heavy on my shoulder. Motions firm and deliberate, he pulled me into the hall. "I told you it was going to come back up on you," he muttered while he pushed me into the bathroom and elbowed the light on. "You shouldn't have sat up. What is it with you witches? Think you know everything and never listen to a damn thing."

Needless to say, he was right. Hand over my mouth, I just made it to the toilet. Everything came up: the cookies, the tea, dinner from two weeks ago. David left after my first retch, leaving me alone to hack and cough my way into the dry heaves.

Finally I got control over myself. Knees shaking, I rose and flushed the toilet. Unable to look at the mirror, I rinsed my mouth out, gulping water right from the tap. I had thrown up all over my amulet, and I took it off, rinsing it under a steady stream of water before setting it beside the sink. All my hurts came flowing back, and I felt like I deserved them.

Heart pounding and feeling weak, I splashed water off my face and looked up. Past my raggedy looking reflection, Ceri stood in the doorway, her arms clasped about her. The church was eerily silent. "Where's Jenks?" I rasped.

Her eyes fell from mine, and I turned around. "I'm sorry, Rachel. He left with David."

He left? He couldn't leave. It was freaking twenty out.

There was a soft scuff, and Keasley shuffled to stand beside her.

"Where did he go?" I asked, shivering as the lingering bane and Brimstone churned inside.

Ceri's head drooped. "He asked David to take him to a friend's house, and the entire sídh left in a box. He said he couldn't risk his family anymore, and . . ." Her gaze went to Keasley, her green eyes catching the fluorescent light. "He said he quit."

He left? I lurched into motion, headed for the phone. Didn't want to risk his family, my ass. He had killed two fairy assassins this spring, letting the third live as a warning to the rest. And it wasn't the cold. The door was going to be fixed, and they could always stay in Ivy's or my room until it was. He left because I had lied to him. And as I saw Keasley's wrinkled grim face behind Ceri's, I knew I was right. Words had been said that I hadn't heard.

Stumbling into the living room, I looked for the phone. There was only one place he'd go: the Were who had despelled my stuff last fall. I had to talk to Jenks. I had to tell him I was sorry. That I had been an ass. That I should have trusted him. That he was right to be angry with me and that I was sorry.

But Keasley intercepted my reach, and I drew back at his old hand. I stared at him, cold in the thin protection the blanket had put between me and the night. "Rachel . . ." he said as Ceri drifted to a melancholy stop in the hall. "I think . . . I think you should give him a day at least."

Ceri jerked, and she looked down the hallway. Faint on the air I heard the front door open, and the blanket moved in the shifting air currents.

"Rachel?" came Ivy's voice. "Where's Jenks? And why is there a Home Depot truck unloading sheet plywood in our drive?"

I sank down onto a chair before I fell over. My elbows went on my knees, and my head dropped into my hands. The Brimstone and bane still warred within me, making me shaky and weak. Damn. What was I going to tell Ivy?

Twenty

The coffee in my oversized mug was cold, but I wasn't going to go into the kitchen for more. Ivy was banging around there, baking more of her vile cookies despite us having already gone over that I wasn't going to eat them and was madder than a troll with a hangover that she'd been slipping me Brimstone.

The clatter of my pain amulet against the complexion charm hiding my bruised eye intruded as I set my mug aside and reached for the desk lamp. It had gotten dusky while Ceri tried to teach me how to store line energy. Cheery yellow light spilled over the plants strewn on my desk, the glow just reaching Ceri sitting on a cushion she had brought over from Keasley's. We could have done this in the more comfortable living room, but Ceri had insisted on hallowed ground despite the sun being up. And it was quiet in the sanctuary. Depressingly so.

Ceri sat cross-legged on the floor to make a small figure in jeans and a casual shirt under the shadow of the cross. A pot of tea sat beside her, steaming though my own mug was long cold. I had a feeling she was using magic to keep it warm, though I had yet to catch her at it. A delicate cup was cradled reverently in her thin hands—she had brought that from Keasley's, too—and Ivy's crucifix glimmered about her neck. The woman's hands were never far from it. Her fair hair had been plaited by Jenks's eldest daughter that morning, and she looked at peace with herself. I loved seeing her like this, knowing what she had endured.

There was a thump from the kitchen followed by the clatter of the oven door shutting. A frown crossed me, and I turned to Ceri as she prompted, "Are you ready to try again?"

Setting my sock-footed feet firmly on the floor, I nodded. Quick from practice, I reached out with my awareness and touched the line out back. My chi filled, taking no more or less than it ever did. The energy flowed through me much like a river flows through a pond. I had been able to do this since I was twelve and accidentally threw Trent into a tree at his father's Make-A-Wish camp. What I had to do was pull some of that energy out of the pond and lift it to a cistern in my mind, so to speak. A person's chi, whether human, Inderlander, or demon, could hold only so much. Familiars acted as extra chi that a magic user could draw on as his or her own.

Ceri waited until I gestured I was ready before she tapped the same line and fostered more into me. It was a trickle instead of Algaliarept's deluge, but even so, my skin burned when my chi overflowed and the force rippled through me, seeking somewhere to puddle. Going back to the pond and river analogy, the banks had overflowed and the valley was flooding.

My thoughts were the only place it could settle, and by the time it found them, I had made the tiny three-dimensional circle in my imagination that Ceri had spent most of the afternoon teaching me how to craft. Shoulders easing, I felt the trickle find the small enclosure. Immediately the warm sensation on my skin vanished as the energy my chi couldn't hold was drawn into it like mercury droplets. The bubble expanded, glowing with a red smear that took on the color of my and Al's aura. Yuck.

"Say your trigger word," Ceri prompted, and I winced. It was too late. My eyes met hers, and her thin lips twitched. "You forgot," she accused, and I shrugged. Immediately she stopped forcing energy into me, and the excess ran out in a brief spark of heat back to the line. "Say it this time," she said tightly. Ceri was nice, but she wasn't a particularly patient teacher.

Again she made ley line energy overflow my chi. My skin warmed, the bruise from where Algaliarept slapped me throbbing. The amperage, if you will, was a touch more than usual, and I thought that it was Ceri's not-so-subtle encouragement to get it right this time.

"Tulpa," I whispered, hearing it in my mind as well as my ear. The word choice wasn't important. It was building the association between the word and the actions that were. Latin was generally used, as it was unlikely that I would say it accidentally, triggering the spell by mistake. The process was identical to when I had learned to make an instant circle. The word tulpa wasn't Latin—it hardly qualified as English—but how often was it used in conversation?

Faster this time, the energy from the line found my enclosure and filled it. I pulled my gaze to Ceri and nodded for more. Green eyes serious in the dim light from the heat lamp on my desk, she returned it. My breath seeped out and my focus blurred when Ceri upped the level and a flash of warmth tingled over my skin. "Tulpa," I whispered, pulse quickening.

The new force found the first. My spherical protection circle within my unconsciousness expanded to take it in. Again my focus cleared, and I nodded to Ceri. She blinked when I gestured for more, but I wasn't going to let Al knock me out with an overload of force. "I'm fine," I said, then stiffened when the bruised skin around my eye throbbed, burning with the sensation of a sunburn even through the pain amulet. "Tulpa," I said, slumping as the heat vanished. *See,* I told my frazzled brain. *It's an illusion. I'm not really on fire.*

"That's enough," Ceri said uncomfortably, and I pulled my chin up from my chest. The fire was gone from my veins, but I was exhausted and my fingers were trembling.

"I don't want to sleep tonight until I can hold what he pushed into me," I replied.

"But, Rachel . . ." she protested, and I raised a hand slowly in denial.

"He's going to come back," I said. "I can't fight him if I'm convulsing in pain."

Face pale, she bobbed her head, and I jerked as she forced more into me. "Oh God," I whispered, then said my trigger word before Ceri could stop. This time I felt the energy flow like acid through me, following new channels, pulled by my word rather than finding its way to my bubble by accident. My head jerked up. Eyes wide, I stared at Ceri as the pain vanished.

"You did it," she said, looking almost frightened as she sat cross-legged before me.

Swallowing, I pulled my legs under me so she wouldn't see my knees tremble. "Yeah."

Unblinking, she held her cup in her lap. "Let it go. You need to recenter yourself."

I found my arms were wrapped around myself. Forcing them down, I exhaled. Letting go of the energy spindled in my head sounded easier than it was. I had enough force in me to throw Ivy into the next county. If it didn't flow back to my chi and then the line using the gently seared channels that Ceri had been burning through my nervous system, it was really going to hurt.

Steeling myself, I set my will around the bubble and squeezed. Breath held, I waited for the pain, but the ley line energy smoothly returned to my chi and then the line, leaving me shaking from spent adrenaline. Enormously relieved, I brushed my hair out of my eyes and put my gaze on Ceri. I felt awful: tired, exhausted, sweaty, and shaking—but satisfied.

"You're improving," she said, and a thin smile crossed me.

"Thanks." Taking my mug, I took a sip of cold coffee. She was probably going to ask me to pull it off the line by myself next; I wasn't yet ready to try. "Ceri," I said as my fingers trembled. "This isn't that hard compared to the benefits. Why don't more people know this?"

She smiled, her dusky shape in the shadow of the lamp going sage looking. "They do in the ever-after. It's the first thing—no, the second thing—that a new familiar is taught."

"What's the first?" I asked before I remembered I really didn't want to know.

"The death of self-will," she said, and my expression froze at the ugliness in how casually she said it. "Letting me escape, knowing how to be my own familiar, was a mistake," she said. "Al would kill me if he could to cover it up."

"He can't?" I said, suddenly frightened that the demon might try.

Ceri shrugged. "Maybe. But I have my soul, black as it is. That's what's important."

"I suppose." I didn't understand her cavalier attitude, but I hadn't been Al's familiar for a millennium. "I don't want a familiar," I said, glad Nick was so distant he couldn't feel any of this. I was sure if he was close enough, he would've called to make sure I was okay. I think.

"You're doing well." Ceri sipped her tea and glanced at the dark windows. "Al told me it took me three months to get to where you are now."

I looked at her, shocked. There was no way I could be better than her. "You're kidding."

"I was fighting him," she said. "I didn't want to learn, and he had to force me into it, using the absence of pain as a positive reinforcement."

"You were in pain for three months?" I said, horrified.

Her eyes were on her thin hands, laced about her teacup. "I

don't remember it. It was a long time ago. I do remember sitting at his feet every night, his hand soft on my head while he relaxed as he listened to me cry for the sky and trees."

Imagining this beautiful wisp of a woman at Algaliarept's feet suffering his touch was almost too much to bear. "I'm sorry, Ceri," I whispered.

She jerked, as if only now realizing she had said it aloud. "Don't let him take you," she said, her wide eyes serious and solemn. "He liked me, and though he used me as they all use their familiars, he did like me. I was a coveted jewel in his belt, and he treated me well so I would be useful and at his side for a longer time. You, though . . ." Her head bowed, breaking our eye contact and pulling her braid over her shoulder. "He will torment you so hard and so fast that you won't have time to breathe. Don't let him take you."

I swallowed, feeling cold. "I wasn't planning on it."

Her narrow chin trembled. "You misunderstand. If he comes for you and you can't fight him off, make him so angry that he kills you."

Her sincerity struck me to the core. "He's not going to give up, is he?" I said.

"No. He needs a familiar to keep his standing. He won't give up on you unless he finds someone better. Al is greedy and impatient. He'll take the best he can find."

"So all this practice is making me a more attractive target?" I said, feeling sick.

Ceri squinted apologetically. "You need it to keep him from simply stunning you with a massive dose of ley line force and dragging you into a line."

I gazed at the darkening windows. "Damn," I whispered, not having considered that.

"But being your own familiar will help in your profession," Ceri said persuasively. "You'll have the strength of a familiar without the liabilities."

"I suppose." I set my mug aside, gaze unfocused. It was getting dark, and I knew she wanted to be home before the sun set. "Do you want me to try it alone?" I prompted hesitantly.

Her attention flicked to my hands. "I'd advise a small rest. You're still shaking."

I looked at my fingers, embarrassed that she was right. Curling them into a fist, I gave her a sheepish smile. She took a sip of her tea—clearly willing herself to be patient when I had no control over the situation—and I jumped when she whispered, *"Consimilis calefacio."*

She had done something; I had felt a drop in the line, even though I wasn't connected to it. Sure enough her gaze meeting mine was bright in amusement. "You felt that?" she said around a beautiful laugh. "You're getting very attached to your line, Rachel Mariana Morgan. It belongs to the whole street, even if it is in your backyard."

"What did you do?" I asked, not wanting to delve into what she had meant by that. She held her cup up in explanation, and my smile grew. "You warmed it up," I said, and she bobbed her head. Slowly my smile faded. "That's not a black charm, is it?"

Ceri's face lost its expression. "No. It's common ley line magic that acts on water. I will not add to the smut on my soul, Rachel. I'll be hard pressed to get rid of it as it is."

"But Al used it on David. It almost cooked him," I asserted, feeling sick. People were mostly water. Heat that up and you could cook them from the inside. *God, I was sick for even thinking of it.*

"No," she reassured me. "It was different. This one works only on things without auras. The curse strong enough to break through an aura is black and needs a drop of demon blood to twist. The reason David survived was because Al was drawing on a line through you, and he knew you couldn't handle the lethal amount—yet."

I thought about that for a moment. If it wasn't black, there was no harm in it. And being able to warm up my coffee without the microwave would blow Ivy away. "Is it hard to do?"

Ceri's smile blossomed. "I'll walk you through it. Give me a moment; I have to remember how to do it the long way," she said, extending her hand for my mug.

Oh, gotta slow to the witch's pace, I thought, leaning forward and handing it to her. But seeing as it was most likely the charm she used three times a day to cook Al's meals, she could probably do it in her sleep.

"It's sympathetic magic," she explained. "There's a poem to help remember the gestures, but the only two words you *have* to say are Latin. And it needs a focal object to direct the magic where to go," she explained, and took a sip of my cold coffee, making a face. "This is swill," she muttered, her words awkward as she spoke around the drop on her tongue. "Barbaric."

"It's better when it's hot," I protested, not having known you could hold a focal object in your mouth and still have it be effective. She could do the spell without it, but then she would have to throw the spell at my cup. This was easier, and less likely to spill my coffee, too.

Her face still showing her distaste, she raised her thin, expressive hands. "From candles burn and planet's spin," she said, and I moved my fingers, mimicking her gesture—I suppose if you used your imagination, it kind of looked like lighting a candle, though how her suddenly dropping hand related to spinning planets was beyond me. "Friction is how it ends and begins."

I jumped when she brought her hands together to make a loud pop, simultaneously saying, *"Consimilis."*

Similar, I thought, thinking it might be a catch phrase for sympathetic magic. And the pop might be an audible show of air molecules undergoing friction. In sympathetic magic, it didn't matter how nebulous the relationship was as long as it was real.

"Cold to hot, harness within," she continued, making another unfamiliar gesture, but I recognized the next finger movement from when I used a ley line charm to break the Howlers' bat in practice. Perhaps it was the motion that tapped into the focal object for direction. Huh. Maybe there was some sense to this ley line stuff after all.

"Calefacio!" she said happily, invoking the charm and setting it all into motion.

I felt a mild drop through me as the charm pulled energy from the line to excite the water molecules in the cup, warming the coffee. "Wow," I breathed when she handed me back my mug, softly steaming. "Thanks."

"You're welcome," she said. "You have to regulate the ending temperature yourself by how much line energy you put into it."

"The more energy, the hotter it gets?" I took a careful sip, deciding it was perfect. It must have taken her years to gain this much proficiency.

"Depending on the amount you have to warm up," Ceri whispered, her eyes distant in memory. "So be careful with your bathwater until you know what you're doing." Visibly pulling herself back to the present, she turned to me. "Are you settled now?"

Adrenaline zinged through me, and I set my warm coffee down. *I can do this. If Ceri can warm her tea and spindle line energy in her head, then so can I.*

"Fill your center," she encouraged. "Then pull some from it as if you're going to work a spell as you say your invocation word."

I tucked a curl behind my ear and settled myself. Exhaling, I closed my eyes and I tapped the line, feeling the pressures equalize in an instant. Setting my mind to the poised calmness I cultivated when I said a ley line charm, a curious, new sensation tingled through me. A tinge of energy flowed in from the line, replacing what I had unconsciously pulled from my chi. *Tulpa,* I thought, hope bringing me tight.

My eyes flew open as a wash of force flowed in from the line to replace what had darted from my chi to my head. In a torrent, the line raced through me and settled in my thoughts. My enclosure expanded to take it in. Shocked, I did nothing to stop it.

"Enough!" Ceri cried, rising to her knees. "Rachel, let go of the line!"

I jerked, pulling my focus from the ley line. There was a brief swish of warmth through me as a dribble of force backwashed from my thoughts to my chi, topping it off. Breath held, I froze in my chair, staring at her. I was afraid to move, there was so much energy in my head.

"Are you all right?" she said, not settling back down, and I nodded.

From the kitchen came a faint, "You okay in there?"

"We're fine!" I carefully shouted back, then looked at Ceri. "We're fine, right?"

Green eyes wide, she bobbed her head, not dropping my gaze for an instant. "You're holding a lot of energy outside your center," she said. "But I've noticed your chi doesn't hold as much as mine. I think . . ." She hesitated. "I think an elf's chi can hold more than a witch's, but witches seem to be able to hold more in their thoughts."

I could taste the energy in me, tinfoil-like on my tongue. "Witches make better batteries, huh?" I quipped weakly.

She laughed, her clear voice going up to the dusky rafters. I wished there were pixies up there to dance amid the sound. "Maybe that's why witches abandoned the ever-after sooner than elves," she said. "Demons seem to prefer witches over elves or humans for their familiars. I thought it was because there were so few of us, but maybe not."

"Maybe," I said, wondering how long I could hold all this force without spilling it. My nose tickled. I desperately didn't want to sneeze.

Ivy's boots in the hallway intruded, and we both turned as she strode toward us with her purse over her shoulder and a plate of cookies in her hand. "I'm headed out," she said lightly, tossing her hair over her shoulder. "Want me to walk you home, Ceri?"

Immediately Ceri stood. "That's not necessary."

Ire flickered in Ivy's eyes. "I know it's not necessary."

Ivy's plate of steaming cookies hit the desktop before me in a harsh clatter. My eyebrows rose, and I swung my feet to the floor. Ivy wanted to talk to Ceri alone—about me. Bothered, I tapped my fingernails in a sharp staccato. "I'm not eating those," I said flatly.

"It's medicinal, Rachel," she said, her voice heavy with threat.

"It's Brimstone, Ivy," I shot back. Ceri shifted from foot to foot in obvious discomfort, but I didn't care. "I can't believe you gave me Brimstone," I added. "I arrest people who do Brimstone; I don't share rent with them." *I was not going to tag Ivy. I didn't care if she broke every law in the I.S. handbook. Not this time.*

Ivy's stance went aggressive, her hip cocked and her lips almost bloodless. "It's medicinal," she said sharply. "It's specially processed and the amount of stimulant in it is so low you can't even smell it. You can't smell Brimstone, can you? Can you?"

The ring of brown about her pupils had shrunk, and I dropped my gaze, not wanting to trip her into pulling an aura. Not now, with the sun almost down. "There was enough in it to jerk the bane into play," I said sullenly.

Ivy, too, calmed, knowing she had reached her limits. "That wasn't my fault," she said softly. "I never gave you enough to even trigger a Brimstone dog."

Ceri raised her narrow chin. There was no remorse in her green eyes. "I apologized for that," she said tightly. "I didn't know it was illegal. It wasn't the last time I gave it to someone."

"See?" Ivy said, gesturing to Ceri. "She didn't know, and that insurance guy was only trying to help. Now shut up, eat your cookies, and stop making us feel bad. You've got a run tomorrow and you need your strength."

Leaning back in my swivel chair, I pushed the plate of vamp cookies away. I wasn't going to eat them. I didn't care that what I had kept down yesterday had upped my metabolism so my black eye was already turning yellow and my cut lip was healed. "I'm fine."

Ivy's usually placid face clouded over. "Fine," she said sharply.

"Fine," I shot back, crossing my legs and turning so I was eyeing her askance.

Ivy's jaw clenched. "Ceri, I'll walk you home."

Ceri glanced between us. Face empty of emotion, she bent to get her teapot and cup. "I'll take care of my dishes first," she said.

"I can do that," I rushed to say, but Ceri shook her head, watching her feet so as not to spill as she made her way to the kitchen. I frowned, not liking her doing domestic work. It was too much like what I imagined Algaliarept had forced on her.

"Let her do it," Ivy said when the sound of Ceri's steps ended. "It makes her feel useful."

"She's royalty," I said. "You do know that, don't you?"

Ivy glanced into the dark hallway as the sound of running water filtered out. "Maybe a thousand years ago. Now she's nothing, and she knows it."

I made a puff of air. "Don't you have any compassion? Doing my dishes is degrading."

"I have a lot of compassion." A flicker of anger set Ivy's thin eyebrows high. "But the last time I looked, there weren't any openings for princesses in the want ads. What is she supposed to do to give her life meaning? There aren't any treaties for her to make, no rulings to judge, and her biggest decision is to have eggs or waffles for breakfast. There's no way to give herself a feeling of worth with her old royalty crap. And doing dishes isn't degrading."

I leaned back in my chair in a show of acquiescence. She was right, but I didn't like it. "So you have a run?" I prompted when the silence stretched.

Ivy sent one shoulder up and down. "I'm going to talk to Jenks."

"Good." I met her eyes, relieved. *Something we could talk about without arguing.* "I stopped at that Were's house this afternoon. The poor guy wouldn't let me in. The pixy girls had been at him. His hair was solid cornrows." I had woken up one morning with my hair braided into the fringe of my afghan. Matalina had made them apologize, but it took me forty minutes to untangle myself. I would give just about anything to wake up like that again.

"Yeah, I saw him," Ivy said, and I sat up from my slouch.

"You've been over there?" I asked, watching Ivy get her coat from the foyer and return. She slipped it on, the short leather jacket making a soft hush of silk against silk.

"I've been over there twice," she said. "The Were won't let me in, either, but one of my friends is taking him out on a date so Jenks will have to answer the door, the little prick. Typical little man. He has an ego the size of the Grand Canyon."

I chuckled, and Ceri came in from the back. Her borrowed coat was over her arm and the shoes that Keasley bought her were in her grip. I wasn't going to tell her to put them on. She could walk in the snow barefoot as far as I was concerned. Ivy, though, gave her a pointed look.

"You going to be all right for a while?" Ivy asked as Ceri dropped her shoes to the floor and snugged her feet into them.

"Good God," I muttered, twisting the chair back and forth. "I'll be fine."

"Stay on holy ground," she added as she gestured for Ceri to head out. "Don't tap a line. Eat your cookies."

"Not going to happen, Ivy," I said. *Pasta. I wanted pasta in alfredo sauce.* That's what Nick had cooked up for me the last time Ivy was bent on shoving these things down my throat. I couldn't believe she'd been slipping me Brimstone. *Yes, I could.*

"I'll call you in about an hour to make sure you're all right."

"I won't answer," I said, irritated. "I'm going to take a nap." I stood and stretched until my sweater and halter top rose to show my belly button. It would have gotten a wolf whistle from Jenks, and the silence in the rafters was depressing.

Ceri came forward with her cushion to give me a hug goodbye. It startled me, and I hesitantly returned it. "Rachel can take care of herself," she said proudly. "She's been holding enough ever-after to blow a hole in the roof for the last five minutes and has forgotten about it."

"Holy crap!" I exclaimed, feeling my face warm. "I am, aren't I!"

Ivy sighed as she strode to the church's front door. "Don't wait up for me," she called over her shoulder. "I'm having dinner with my folks and won't be home until after sunup."

"You should let it go," Ceri said as she edged after Ivy. "At least when the sun is down. Someone else might summon him, and if they don't banish him properly, he'll come looking for you. He might try to knock you out by adding to what you're holding now." She shrugged in a very modern gesture. "But if you stay on holy ground, you should be all right."

"I'll let it go," I said absently, my thoughts whirling.

Ceri smiled shyly. "Thank you, Rachel," she said softly. "It's good to feel needed."

I jerked my attention back to her. "You're welcome."

The scent of cold snow filtered in. I looked up seeing Ivy standing impatiently in the threshold of the open door, the fading light making her a threatening silhouette in tight leather. "'By-y-y-y-ye, Rachel," she prompted mockingly, and Ceri sighed.

Turning, the slender woman made her unhurried way to the door, kicking off her shoes at the last moment and going barefoot out onto the icy cement steps.

"How can you stand the cold?" I heard Ivy say before the door shut behind them.

I soaked in the silence and the dusky light. Reaching over, I clicked off the desk lamp and it seemed to brighten outside. I was alone—for what was probably the first time—in my church. No roommate, no boyfriend, no pixies. Alone. My eyes closed, and I sat on the slightly raised stage and breathed. I could smell plywood over the almond scent of Ivy's stupid cookies. A soft pressure behind my eyes reminded me I was still holding that ball of ever-after, and with a nudge of my will, I broke the three-dimensional circle in my thoughts and the energy flowed back to the line in a warm wash.

I opened my eyes and headed for the kitchen, my sock feet soundless. I wasn't going to take a nap; I was going to make brownies as part of Ivy's present. There was no way I could compete with thousand-dollar perfume: I had to take the handmade-goodie track.

Detouring into the living room, I searched for the remote. The smell of plywood was almost an assault, and I glanced at the window Ivy had sketched on the panel, freehanding the view of the graveyard. I clicked on the stereo and Offspring's "Come Out and Play" spilled out. Grinning, I cranked it. "Wake the dead," I said, tossing the remote and dancing into the kitchen.

While the bouncy music lured me into a better mood, I pulled out my dented spell pot, which I couldn't use for spelling anymore, and the recipe book I had swiped from my mom. Thumbing through it, I found Grandma's fudgy brownie recipe penciled in beside the gourmet recipe that tasted like cardboard. Timing my motions with the music, I got out the eggs, sugar, vanilla, and dumped them on the center island counter. I had the chocolate chips melting on the stove and the evaporated milk measured out when the air shifted and the front door slammed. The egg in my hand slipped, cracking as it hit the counter.

"Forget something, Ivy?" I shouted. Adrenaline stabbed

through me as my gaze went from the broken egg to everything scattered over the kitchen. I'd never get it hidden before she made it back here. *Couldn't that woman stay away for even an hour?*

But it was Kisten's voice that answered.

Twenty-one

"It's me, Rachel," Kisten called, his voice faint over the music blaring from the living room. I froze, the memory of the kiss he'd given me keeping me where I stood. I must have looked like an idiot when he turned the corner and stopped in the threshold.

"Ivy's not here?" he said, his eyes giving me the once-over. "Shoot."

I took a breath to settle myself. "Shoot?" I questioned, sliding the cracked egg off the counter and into the bowl. *I didn't think anyone said shoot anymore.*

"Can I say shit?"

"Hell, yes."

"Shit, then." His gaze went from me to the kitchen, lacing his hands behind his back as I picked the bigger chunks of shell out.

"Hey, would you, ah, turn the music down for me?" I said, sneaking a glance at him when he nodded and walked out. It was Saturday, and he was dressed casually in leather boots and faded jeans that were nice and tight. His short leather coat was open, and a burgundy silk shirt showed a wisp of chest hair. *Just enough,* I thought as the music softened. I could smell his coat. I was a sucker for the scent of leather. *This might be a problem.*

"Are you sure Ivy didn't send you over to baby-sit?" I questioned as he returned and I wiped the egg slime off on a damp dishcloth.

He chuckled and sat in Ivy's chair. "No." He hesitated. "Is she going to be gone for a while, or can I wait?"

I didn't look up from the recipe, not liking how he had said that. There had been more inquiry in his voice than the question warranted. "Ivy went to talk to Jenks." I ran my finger down the page without looking at the words. "Then she's having dinner with her folks."

"Sunup," he murmured, and I felt my warning flags go up. All of them.

The clock above the sink ticked, and I took the melted chocolate off the stove. I wasn't about to stand with my back to him, so I set it on the counter between us, crossing my arms in front of me and putting my backside against the sink. Watching me, he tossed his hair out of his eyes. I took a breath to tell him to go, but he interrupted.

"Are you all right?"

I stared blankly at him, then remembered. "Oh! The demon—thing," I muttered, embarrassed as I touched the pain charms about my neck. "You heard about that, huh?"

He smiled with half his mouth. "You made the news. And I had to listen to Ivy for three solid hours while she bitched about not being here at the time."

Going back to my recipe, I rolled my eyes. "Sorry. Yeah. I'm okay. A few scrapes and bruises. Nothing major. But I can't tap a line after sundown anymore." I didn't want to tell him I wasn't entirely safe after dark either, unless I was on holy ground . . . which the kitchen and living room weren't. "It's really going to put a crimp in my runs," I said sourly, wondering how I was going to get around this latest mountain. Oh well. It wasn't as if I relied on ley line magic. I was an earth witch after all.

Kisten didn't seem to think it mattered much either, if his casual shrug meant anything. "I'm sorry to hear Jenks left," he said, stretching his legs out and crossing his boots at his ankles. "He was more than an asset to your company. He's a good friend."

My face screwed up into an unpleasant expression. "I should have told him what Trent was when I figured it out."

Surprise cascaded over him. "You know what Trent Kalamack is? No shit?"

Jaw clenched, I dropped my eyes to the recipe book and nodded, waiting for him to ask it.

"What is he?"

I stayed silent, my eyes fixed on the page. The soft sound of him moving pulled my gaze up.

"Never mind," he said. "It doesn't matter."

Relieved, I gave the chocolate a clockwise stir. "It matters to Jenks. I should have trusted him."

"Not everyone needs to know everything."

"You do if you're four inches tall with wings."

He got up, drawing my attention as he stretched. With a soft, satisfied sound, his shoulders eased and he collapsed in on himself. Taking his coat off, he headed to the fridge.

I tapped the spoon on the side to flick most of the chocolate off. My brow furrowed. Sometimes it was easier to talk to a stranger. "What am I doing wrong, Kisten?" I said, frustrated. "Why do I drive the people I like away?"

He came out from behind the fridge door with the bag of almonds I'd bought last week. "Ivy's not leaving."

"Those are mine," I said, and he paused until I gestured sourly that he could have them.

"I'm not leaving," he added, mouth gently moving as he ate one.

I exhaled noisily, dumping the measured sugar into the chocolate. He looked really good over there, and memories kept intruding: thoughts of us dressed up and enjoying ourselves, the spark his black eyes drew through me when Saladan's heavies lay broken in the street, Piscary's elevator with me wrapped around him wanting to feel him taking everything I had. . . .

The crunch of the sugar against the pan was loud as I stirred. *Damn vamp pheromones.*

"I'm glad Nick left," Kisten said. "He wasn't good for you."

I kept my head down, but my shoulders tensed. "What do you know about it?" I said, tucking a long red curl behind my ear. I looked up, finding him calmly eating my almonds. "Nick made me feel good. I made him feel good. We had fun together. We liked the same movies, the same places to eat. He could keep up with me when we ran at the zoo. Nick was a good person, and you have no right to pass judgment on him." I snatched a damp dishcloth, wiping up my spilled sugar and shaking it into the sink.

"You may be right," he said as he jiggled a handful of nuts into his palm and rolled the bag shut. "But I find one thing fascinating." He put a nut between his teeth and crunched through it noisily. "You put him in the past tense."

My mouth dropped open. Torn between anger and shock, my face went cold. In the living room, the music changed to something fast and bouncy—and totally inappropriate.

Kisten cracked the fridge open, set the nuts back into the door, and closed it. "I'll wait for Ivy for a while. She might come back with Jenks—if you're lucky. You have a tendency to demand more of a person than most are willing to give." He shook the nuts still left in his hand as I sputtered. "Kind of like a vampire," he added as he picked up his coat and walked out.

My hand was dripping, and I realized I was squeezing the dishcloth so hard that water was seeping out. I threw it into the sink, furious and depressed. Not a good combination. From the living room, happy pop music bounced and skittered. "Will you turn that off!" I shouted. My jaw ached where I was clenching it, and I forced my teeth to part when the music stopped. Fuming, I measured out the sugar and dumped it in. I reached for the spoon, a sound of frustration coming from me as I remembered I had already added the sugar. "Damn it back to the Turn," I muttered. Now I'd have to make a double batch.

Spoon held tightly, I tried to stir it in. Sugar went everywhere, spilling over the edge. My teeth gritted, and I stomped back to the sink for the dishcloth.

"You don't know squat," I whispered as I scraped the spilled sugar into a little pile. "Nick might come back. He said he was. I have his key."

I pushed the gathered sugar into the cup of my hand, hesitating before I dumped it into the bowl with the rest. Brushing the last of the grit from my fingers, I looked at the dark hallway. Nick wouldn't give me his key if he wasn't coming back.

Music started up, soft with a steady beat. My eyes narrowed. I never said he could put something else in. Angry, I took a step toward the living room, then jerked to a halt. Kisten had left in the middle of a conversation. He had taken food with him. Crunchy food. According to Ivy's dating book, that was a vampiric invitation. And following him would be saying I was interested. Even worse, he knew I knew.

I was still staring at the hallway when Kisten walked past. He backpedaled to a stop as he saw me there with a blank look on my face.

"I'll wait in the sanctuary," he said. "Is that okay with you?"

"Sure," I whispered.

His eyebrows rose, and with that same little smile, he ate an almond. "Okay." Kisten vanished down the dark hallway, his boots silent on the hardwood floor.

I turned away and stared at the night-blackened window. I counted to ten. I counted to ten again. I counted to ten a third time, finding myself in the hallway by the time I reached seven. *I'll go in, say my piece, and leave,* I promised myself when I found him at the piano, his back to me as he sat on the bench. He pulled himself straight as my feet scuffed to a halt.

"Nick is a good man," I said, my voice shaking.

"Nick is a good man," he agreed, not turning around.

"He makes me feel wanted, needed."

Kisten slowly spun. His stubble caught the faint light filtering in from the street. The outline of his wide shoulders tapered down to his slim waist, and I mentally shook myself at how good he looked. "He used to." His low, smooth voice sent a shiver through me.

"I don't want you to talk about him anymore," I said.

He gazed at me for a heartbeat, then said, "Okay."

"Good." I took a quick breath, turned and walked out.

My knees were shaking, and listening for any steps behind me, I took a right into my room. Heart pounding, I reached for my perfume. The one that hid my scent.

"Don't."

Gasping, I turned, finding Kisten behind me. Ivy's bottle slipped from my fingers. His hand darted out, and I jumped as it enfolded mine, imprisoning the precious bottle safe within my grip. I froze. "I like the way you smell," he whispered, far, far too close.

My stomach clenched. I could risk bringing Al down on me by tapping a line to knock him unconscious, but I didn't want to. "You need to get out of my bedroom," I said.

His blue eyes looked black in the dim light. The faint glow from the kitchen made him an alluring, dangerous shadow. My shoulders were so tense they hurt as he opened my hand and took the perfume from me. The click as it hit my dresser jerked me straight. "Nick isn't coming back," he said, unaccusing and blunt.

My breath slipped from me, and I closed my eyes. *Oh God.* "I know."

My eyes jerked open when he took my elbows. I froze, waiting for my scar to flash into play, but it didn't. He wasn't trying to bespell me. A foolish part of me respected that, and like an idiot, I did nothing instead of telling him to get the hell out of my church and away from me.

"You need to be needed, Rachel," he said, inches away as his breath shifted my hair. "You live so brightly, so honestly, that you need to be needed. You're hurting. I can feel it."

"I know."

His solemn eyes took on a shade of pity. "Nick is human. No matter how he tries, he'll never understand you entirely."

"I know." I swallowed hard. There was a wet warmth in my eyes. My jaw tightened until my head hurt. *I will not cry.*

"He can't give you what you need." Kisten's hands slipped to my waist. "He'll always be just a little afraid."

I know. My eyes closed, opening as I let him pull me closer.

"And even if Nick learns to live with his fear," he said earnestly, his eyes asking me to listen, "he won't ever forgive you for being stronger than he is."

A lump formed in my throat. "I . . . I have to go," I said. "Excuse me."

His hands fell from me, and I pushed past him and into the hall. Confused and wanting to scream at the world, I strode into the kitchen. I stopped, seeing among the pots and flour a huge aching emptiness that had never been there before. Arms wrapped about myself, I lurched into the living room. I had to get the music off. It was beautiful. I hated it. I hated everything.

Snatching up the remote, I pointed it at the player. Jeff Buckley. I couldn't handle Jeff in the state I was in. Who in hell put Jeff Buckley in my player? Clicking it off, I tossed the remote to the couch. Adrenaline jerked me straight as the remote hit, not the suede of Ivy's couch, but someone's hand.

"Kisten!" I stammered as he turned the music back on, watching me with half-lidded eyes. "What are you doing?"

"Listening to music."

He was calm and wire-tight, and panic struck me at his calculating surety. "Don't sneak up on me like that," I said, my breath coming short. "Ivy never sneaks up on me."

"Ivy doesn't like who she is." His eyes were unblinking. "I do."

He reached out. Breath coming in a quick surge, I knocked his arm aside. Tension sang through me as he jerked me forward, holding me to him. Panic, then anger, flashed. There wasn't a twinge from my scar. "Kisten!" I exclaimed, trying to move. "Let me go!"

"I'm not trying to bite you," he said softly, his lips brushing my ear. "Stop it."

His voice was firm, soothing. There was no blood lust in it. My thoughts flashed back to waking up in his car to the sound of singing monks. "Let go!" I demanded, strung out and feeling like I was either going to hit him or start to cry.

"I don't want to. You're hurting too much. How long has it been since someone held you? Touched you?"

A tear leaked out and I hated that he saw it. Hated he knew I was holding my breath.

"You need to feel, Rachel." His voice grew soft, pleading. "This is killing you slowly."

I swallowed the lump in my throat. He was seducing me. I wasn't such an innocent that I knew he wouldn't try. But his hands upon my arms were warm. And he was right. I needed another's touch, ached for it, damn me to hell. I had almost forgotten how it felt to be needed. Nick had given that back to me, that tiny thrill of excitement knowing someone was wanting to touch you, wanting you and you alone to touch him.

I had endured more short-term relationships than a socialite has shoes. Either it was my I.S. job, or my wacko mother pushing for commitment, or that I attracted jerks who simply saw a redhead as a potential notch on their broomstick. Maybe I was a crazy bitch demanding trust without being able to give it. I didn't want another one-sided relationship, but Nick was gone and Kisten smelled good. He made me feel the pain less.

My shoulders eased, and he exhaled as he felt me stop fighting him. Eyes closing, I dropped my forehead into his shoulder as my folded arms made a small space between us. The music was soft and slow. I wasn't crazy. I could trust. I did trust. I had trusted Nick, and he had left.

"You'll leave," I breathed. "They all leave. They get what they want, and they leave. Or they find out what I can do, and then they leave."

His arms about me tightened for an instant, then relaxed. "I'm not going anywhere. You already scared the hell out of me when you took Piscary down." He buried his nose in my hair and breathed in my scent. "And I still am here."

Lulled by his body warmth and his touch, my tension trickled away. Kisten altered my balance—and I moved with him. Moving, hardly moving, our weight shifted as the slow and seductive music lured me into swaying with him.

"You can't hurt my pride," Kisten whispered, his fingers tracing the middle of my back. "I've lived my entire life with people stronger than I. I like that, and have no shame in being the weaker one. I'll never be able to cast a spell, and I don't give a shit that you can do something I can't."

The music and our almost-not-moving started a warm spot in me. Licking my lips, I slipped my arms from between us to find they felt natural about his waist. My heartbeat quickened and my eyes were wide as I stared at the wall, my breath slipping in and out of me in an unreal evenness. "Kisten . . ."

"I'll always be here," he said softly. "You can never fill my need, never drive me away, no matter how much you give me. The good or the bad. I'll always be hungry for emotion, always and forever, and I can feel you hurting. I can turn it to joy. If you'll let me."

I swallowed as he drew us to a stop. He pulled back, and with a gentle touch on my jaw, he tilted my head so he could see my eyes. The pulsing beat of the music pattered on my mind, numbing and soothing. His gaze was heady. "Let me do this," he whispered, deeply dangerous. But with his words, he put me in a position of power. I could say no.

I didn't want to.

My thoughts pinged through me too fast to be realized. His hands felt good, and his eyes held passion. I wanted what he could give me—what he promised. "Why?" I whispered.

His lips parted and he breathed, "Because I want to. Because you want me to."

I didn't look from him. His pupils never shifted, never grew. My grip on him became firmer as my arms pressed into him. "There will be no sharing of blood, Kisten. Ever."

His breath came and went, and his hands tightened. Expression dusky with the knowledge of what was to come, he leaned closer. "One," he said as he kissed the corner of my mouth. "Step." He kissed the other side. "At a time," he continued as he kissed me gently, so gently it made me ache for more. "My love," he finished.

A stab of desire went right to my core. My eyes closed. *Oh God. Save me from myself.*

"I make no promises," I whispered.

"I don't ask for any," he said. "Where are we going?"

"I don't know." My hands drifted downward from his waist. We were swaying to the music again. I felt alive, and as we almost-danced, a hint of fire came from my demon scar.

"Can I do this?" Kisten asked, moving closer so more of our bodies touched. I knew he was asking my permission to play upon my scar, to willingly let him bespell me. That he asked gave me a feeling of security I knew was probably false.

"No. Yes. I don't know." *So torn.* It felt good, just my body touching his, his arms about my waist, a new demand in their strength. "I don't know. . . ."

"Then I won't." *Where were we going?* Exhaling, he ran his hands down my arms, lacing his fingers in mine. Gently he pulled my hands to the small of his back, holding them there as we swayed, shifting to the slow, seductive music.

A shiver rose inside me. The scent of leather grew thick and warm. Where he touched sent a sliver of heat to tingle my fingers. My head dropped into the hollow between his neck and shoulder. I wanted to put my lips there, knowing what he would feel, knowing how he would taste if I dared. But I didn't, contenting myself to send my breath there instead, afraid of what he would do if my lips touched him.

Heart pounding, I moved his hands to the small of my back and I left them there, moving, pressing, massaging. My hands rose to twine my fingers behind his head. My thoughts touched upon us in the elevator when I thought Piscary was going to kill me. It was too much to resist, the memory of my demon scar alive and alight.

"Please," I whispered, my lips brushing his neck to make him tremble. His torn earlobe was inches from me, tempting. "I want you to." Pulling my gaze up, I searched his eyes, seeing but not fearing the narrowing band of blue. "I trust you. But I don't trust your instincts."

A deep understanding and relief pinched his eyes. His hands dropped lower, caressing until they found the top of my legs, then reversed their motion, moving, always moving, as we swayed. "I don't trust them either," he said, fake accent utterly gone. "Not with you."

My breath caught as his fingers traced from my back to my front, a whisper against my jeans. Tugging at the top button. Hinting. "I'm wearing caps," he said. "The vampire has been defanged."

Startled, my lips parted as he smiled, showing me that his sharp canines were indeed capped. It sent a surge of heat through me, disquieting and thought provoking. Sure, he couldn't draw blood, but now I'd let him explore a hell of a lot more of me. And he knew it. But safe? No. He was more dangerous now than if he hadn't capped his teeth.

"Oh God," I whispered, knowing I was lost as he nuzzled his head into the hollow of my shoulder and gently kissed me. Eyes closing, I sent my fingers into his hair, clenching as his kiss shifted, moving to the very edge of my collarbone where my scar started.

Waves of demand pulsed from it, and my knees buckled.

"Sorry," Kisten breathed huskily as he caught my elbows and kept me upright. "I didn't know it was that sensitive. Just how much saliva did you get dosed with?"

His lips were off my neck and by my ear. Almost panting, I leaned into him. The blood in me pounded, wanting me to do something. "I almost died," I said. "Kisten . . ."

"I'll be careful," he said, the tenderness going right to my core. I willingly followed his lead as he sat me on the couch, nestling me between the back and the arm. Taking his hands, I pulled Kisten down beside me. My scar was tingling and waves of promise scoured me. *Where were we going?*

"Rachel?"

I heard the same question in his voice, but I didn't want to answer. Smiling, I pulled him closer across the couch. "You talk too much," I whispered, and covered my mouth with his.

A soft sound came from him as his lips pushed back, his stubble rough. Fingers spaced wide across my cheek, he held me still as I pulled his weight farther down upon me. Nudging my hip, he made room for his knee between me and the back of the couch.

My skin tingled where his fingers touched my jaw. I slipped a hesitant tongue between his lips, and my breath came quick as he darted his tongue deep into me. He tasted faintly of almonds, and when he moved to draw away, I twined my fingers at the nape of his neck to keep him there just a moment longer. He made a surprised sound, pushing more aggressively. Now I pulled back, running my tongue across the smoothness of his teeth as I went.

Kisten shuddered, the tremor felt clearly as he supported his weight over me. I didn't know how far I wanted to go. But this? This was good. I couldn't lead him on, promising more than I could give. "Wait . . ." I said reluctantly, meeting his gaze.

But seeing him above me, breathless with his passion held in check, I hesitated. His eyes were black, heady with desire and need. I searched for and found a carefully checked blood lust. His shoulders were tense under his shirt, a hand was firm against my side, his thumb massaging under my halter. The look of wanting in him sent adrenaline to my core, rousing me more than his rough and gentle touch that rose higher to find my breast. *Oh, to be wanted, needed.*

"What?" he said, poised and waiting.

The hell with it. "Never mind," I said, playing with the hair about his ear.

His soft hand under my halter top went still. "You want me to stop?"

A second stab of feeling struck though me. I felt my eyes close. "No," I breathed, hearing a hundred well-thought-out convictions die in that word. Heart pounding, I slipped my amulets from me and dropped them to the carpet—I wanted to feel everything—but it wasn't until I reached for his belt buckle that he understood.

A low guttural sound escaped him, and he dropped his head to mine. His weight was a welcomed warmth pressing on me as his lips found my demon scar and gently mouthed it.

Fire spilled like molten stone through me to my groin, and I gasped as the sensation rebounded and multiplied. The dull aches from my recent demon attack mutated into pleasure, courtesy of the old vampire saliva he was playing upon. I couldn't think. I couldn't breathe. My hands jerked out from where I had been trying to undo his pants, and I clutched his shoulder. "Kisten," I breathed when I was able to take a shuddering breath.

But he didn't let up, pushing me down until my head was on the arm of the couch. My fingers dug into him as gentle teeth replaced his lips. A groan escaped me, and he worked the scar, his teeth soft and his breath harsh. I wanted him. I wanted all of him.

"Kisten . . ." I pushed at him. I had to ask first. I had to know.

"What?" he said flatly as he pushed my shirt and halter out of the way and his fingers found my breast and began moving, promising more.

In the gap between us, I finally got his belt undone. I gave a tug, and I heard a rivet snap through. His head dropped back to me, and before he could find my neck again and send me into an unaware ecstasy, I undid his zipper and sent my hands searching. *God save me,* I thought as I found him, the smooth skin tight under my questing fingers. "You've had sex with a witch before?" I whispered, pushing his jeans down and running my hand across his backside.

"I know what I'm getting into," he said breathily.

I felt myself melt into the couch as my thoughts and shoulders eased. My hands found him again, and he exhaled long and slow. "I didn't want to assume—" I said, then gasped as he dropped his weight lower and pulled my shirt up. "I didn't want you to be surprised. . . . Oh God. Kisten," I panted, almost frantic with need as his lips moved from under my jaw to my collarbone and then to my breast. Waves of promise rose high, and I arched my back as he pulled, his hands warm against my skin. *Where was he? I couldn't reach that far.*

He silenced my whisper as he lifted his face and kissed me. Now I could reach, and my breath slipped from me in bliss as I grasped him and sent my fingers moving lower. "Kisten . . ."

"You talk too much," he said, his lips moving against my skin. "You ever have sex with a vamp?" he said, his eyes half closed, watching me.

I exhaled as he turned his attention to my neck again. His fingers traced the path his lips were going to take, and waves of ecstasy rolled through me when they did. "No," I panted as I yanked his jeans down. I'd never get them off over his boots. "Anything I should be aware of?"

He ran his hands under my breast, again tracing the path his lips soon followed. Back arched, I tried not to moan with need as I reached down, trying to find all of him. "We bite," he said, and I cried out when he did just that, gently pinching me between his teeth.

"Get my pants off before I kill you," I panted, almost insane with desire.

"Yes, ma'am," he growled, and his stubble scraped me as he pulled away.

I took a much needed deep breath, following him up to push him back down and straddle him. His hands worked my zipper as I fumbled with the buttons of his shirt. A sigh escaped me when I got the last one undone and sent my hands over him, my fingers tracing up and across the definition of his abs and chest. I leaned over him, my hair hiding what I was doing as my lips hop-skipped from his middle to the hollow at his neck. I lingered there, hesitantly, daring to run my teeth against his skin, pulling against it with a slight pressure. Under me, he shivered, and his hands, working my jeans down my hips, shook.

Eyes wide, I pulled away, thinking I had gone too far.

"No," he whispered, putting his hands on my waist to keep me there. His face was strained with emotion. "Don't stop. It's . . . I won't break your skin." His eyes flashed open. "Oh God, Rachel. I promise I won't break your skin."

The passion in his voice struck me. Abandoning myself, I pinned him to the couch, knees to either side. Lips searching, I found his neck, turning my kisses into something more substantial. His heavy breaths and light hands drove my desire into pulsing demands, pounding through me in time with my heartbeat. Teeth replaced my lips, and his breath grew ragged.

His hands grasped my waist, and I was lifted up enough that I could push my jeans off. They caught on my socks, and with a cry of impatience, I pulled my lips from him long enough to kick them off. Then I was back, my skin warm where it touched him under me. I leaned over him, holding his neck unmoving as I used my teeth against his skin instead of my lips.

Kisten's breath came in a shuddering sound. "Rachel," he breathed, his hands firm against my middle as he sent his hand downward, searching.

A low sound, barely audible, came from me as his fingers brushed me. In his touch, I felt his need flash into demand. My eyes closed and I sent one hand downward, finding him.

Feeling him against me, I shifted forward, then back. Our breath slipped out in tandem as we joined. Heavy and potent, my want and relief rose. He slipped deep inside me. *Soon, God help me, if it wasn't soon, I was going to die.* His soft breathing rose to swirl in my thoughts, sending surges from my neck to my groin.

My heart pounded, and his fingers traced my neck, resting atop my pulsing skin. We moved together, a pace steady with promise. His free arm wrapped about me, holding me closer, its weight both imprisoning and secure.

"Give me this," he whispered, drawing me closer, and I willingly bent to his will, letting his lips find my demon scar.

My breath came in a loud gasp. I shuddered, our rhythm shifting. He held me close as the waves of desire built upon themselves. His lips on my neck became teeth, hungry, demanding. There was no pain, and I urged him to do what he would. A small part of me knew if he hadn't his caps, I would have been bitten. It only drove me to a more desperate need. I heard myself cry out, and his grip trembled, becoming tighter.

Wild with passion, I clutched his shoulders. It was there, I only needed to catch it. My breath came fast against his neck. There was nothing but him, and me, and our bodies moving together. His rhythm shifted, and feeling his passions beginning to crest, I found his neck and sent my teeth into him again.

"Harder," he whispered. "You can't hurt me. I promise you can't hurt me."

It tipped me over the edge, and as I played pretend with my vampire, I lunged hungrily into him with no thought of what I'd leave behind.

Kisten groaned, his arms tightening around me. His head

pushed mine aside, and with a guttural sound, he buried his face in my neck.

I cried out as his lips found my scar. Fire struck my body alight. With that, fulfillment crashed upon me and I climaxed. Wave after wave rose, each building on the one before. Kisten shuddered, his motion under me ceasing as his passions crested an instant after my own. My breath came in a pained sound and I trembled, unable to move, fearing and wanting the last tingling jolts. "Kisten?" I managed as they faded to nothing and I found myself panting against him.

His grip about me hesitated and his hands fell away. My forehead dropped to his chest, and I took a shaking breath, exhausted and spent. I could do nothing as I lay atop him, my eyes half closed. Slowly I realized my back was cold and that Kisten's hand was tracing a warm path up and down my spine. I could hear his heartbeat and smell our scents mingling. Muscles trembling with fatigue, I pulled my head up to find his eyes shut and a contented smile on him.

My breath caught. *Holy shit. What had I just done?*

Kisten's eyes opened, finding mine. They were clear and blue, the black of his pupil normal and calming. "Now you're afraid?" he said. "It's a little late for that."

His gaze lingered on my black eye—only now seeing it with my amulets on the floor. I pulled myself up from him, immediately falling back as it was cold. My limbs started shaking. "Um, that was fun," I said, and he laughed.

"Fun," he said, running a finger down my jawline. "My wicked witch thought that was *fun*." His smile wouldn't leave him. "Nick was a fool to let you go."

"What do you mean?" I said, shifting to move, but his hands held me to him.

"I mean," he said softly, "that you are the most erotic woman I've ever touched. That you're both a wide-eyed innocent and an experienced slut all at the same time."

I stiffened. "If this is your attempt at pillow talk, it sucks eggs."

"Rachel," he cajoled, the heavy look of satisfied tenderness the only thing keeping me where I was. *That and I didn't think I could stand up quite yet.* "You have no idea how arousing it is to have your tiny little teeth on me, struggling to break through, tasting without tasting. An innocent, experienced and hungry all at the same time."

I raised my eyebrows, blowing a strand of hair out of my eyes. "You had this all planned, didn't you?" I accused. "Thought you could come in here and seduce me like you do everyone else?" It wasn't as if I could be angry, lying atop him as I was, but I tried.

"No. Not like everyone else," he said, the glint in his eyes going right to my core. "And yes, I came over here fully intending to seduce you." He lifted his head and whispered in my ear, "It's what I'm good at. Just like you're good at evading demons and kicking ass."

"Kicking ass?" I questioned as he dropped his head back to the arm of the couch. His hand was exploring again, and I didn't want to move.

"Yeah," he said, and I jumped as he found a ticklish spot. "I like a woman who takes care of herself."

"Not much of a white knight on a horse, huh?"

He raised one eyebrow. "Oh, I could," he said. "But I'm a lazy son of a bitch."

I laughed at that, and he joined me with his own chuckle as his grip about my waist tightened. With a little lurch, he lifted me from him. "Hold on," he said as he stood, swinging me into the cradle of his arms as if I was a five-pound bag of sugar. With his vamp strength, he held me with one arm and hoisted his pants up loose about his hips. "Shower?"

My arms were laced about his neck, and I inspected it for bite marks. There wasn't a one, though I knew I had bit down hard enough to leave them. I also knew without looking that he hadn't made a visible mark on me despite his roughness. "That sounds great," I said as he shuffled forward, his jeans still unzipped.

"I'll get you a shower," he said as I looked behind me to my amulets, pants, and one sock strewn on the floor. "And then we'll open all the windows and air the church out. I'll help you finish making your fudge, too. That will help."

"It's brownies."

"Even better. That uses the oven." He hesitated before my bathroom door, and feeling cared for and wanted in his arms, I pushed it open with my foot. The man was strong. I'd give him that. This was as satisfying as the sex. Well, almost.

"You have scented candles, don't you?" he asked as I flicked on the light with my toe.

"I have two X-chromosomes," I said dryly as he set me atop

the washer and pulled off my last sock. "I have a candle or two." *He was going to help me into the shower? How sweet.*

"Good. I'll get one going in the sanctuary. Tell Ivy you put it there in the window for Jenks, and you can keep it going until sunup."

A whisper of unease pulled me straight, and my motions grew slow as I pulled my sweater over my head and dropped it onto the washer. "Ivy?" I questioned.

Kisten leaned against the wall and took off his boots. "You don't mind telling her?"

His boot thumped into the far wall, and my face went cold. *Ivy. Scented candles. Airing out the church. Making brownies to scent the air. Washing his scent off me. Swell.*

Smiling his bad-boy smile, Kisten padded to me in his socks and open jeans. His wide hand cupped my jaw and he leaned close. "I don't mind if she knows," he said, and I didn't move, enjoying the warmth. "She's going to find out eventually. But I'd break it to her gently if I were you, not dump it on her." He gave me a soft kiss on the corner of my mouth. His hand trailed reluctantly from me as he backed up and opened the door to the shower.

Crap, I'd forgotten about Ivy. "Yeah," I said distantly, recalling her jealousy, her dislike of surprises, and how badly she reacted to both. "You think she's going to be upset?"

Kisten turned, his shirt off and water beading on his hand from feeling the temperature. "Upset? She's going to be as jealous as a green apple that you and I have a physical way to express our relationship and she doesn't."

Frustration filled me. "Damn it, Kisten. I'm not going to let her bite me so she knows I like her. Sex and blood. Blood and sex. It's the same thing, and I can't do that with Ivy. I'm not wired that way!"

He shook his head, a sad smile on him. "You can't say blood and sex are the same thing. You've never given blood to another. You have nothing to base your view on."

I frowned. "Every time a vamp puts his eyes on me looking for a snack, it feels sexual."

He came forward, wedging his body between my knees, pressing close up to the washer. His hand went out, and he pushed my hair back over my shoulder. "Most living vampires who are looking for a quick fix find a willing partner faster when they stir them sexually. But Rachel, the meaning behind the giving and receiving blood isn't supposed to be based on sex but respect and love. That you can't be moved by the promise of great sex is why Ivy gave up that tack with you so quickly. But she's still hunting you."

I thought of all the facets of Ivy that Skimmer's appearance had forced me to openly acknowledge. "I know."

"Once she gets over her initial anger, I think she'll be all right with us dating."

"I never said I was dating you."

He smiled knowingly and touched my cheek. "But if I took your blood, even in accident or a moment of passion?" Kisten's blue eyes pinched in worry. "One scratch and she'd stake me. The entire city knows she's put a claim on you, and God help the vamp that gets in her way. I took your body. If I touch your blood, I'm dead twice."

I went cold. "Kisten, you're scaring me."

"You should be scared, little witch. She's going to be the most powerful vampire in Cincinnati someday, and she wants to be *your* friend. She wants you to be *her* savior. She thinks you'll either find a way to kill the vamp virus in her so she can die with her soul intact, or be her scion so she can die knowing that you'll be there to take care of her."

"Kisten. Stop."

Smiling, he kissed my forehead. "Don't worry. Nothing has changed from yesterday. Tomorrow will be the same. She's your friend, and she won't ask anything you can't give."

"That doesn't help."

He shrugged, and with a last touch on my side, he took a step back. Steam billowed out from the crack in the door as Kisten shimmied out of his jeans and leaned into the shower to adjust the temperature again. My eyes ran from his well-toned calves to his tight behind to his broad back, lightly muscled. All thoughts of Ivy's coming anger vanished. *Damn.*

As if feeling my eyes on him, he turned, catching me ogling him.

The steam eddied about him. Drops of moisture from the showerhead clung to his stubble. "Let me help you get your camisole off," he said, the timbre of his voice shifting.

I ran my eyes down him again, grinning as I brought my gaze up. *Double damn.*

He slipped his hands behind my back, and with a little help on my part, he nudged me forward to the edge of the dryer and slipped my halter top off. Wrapping my legs around him, I laced my hands behind his neck and tucked my chin into the hollow of his neck. God help me, he was beautiful. "Kisten?" I questioned as he nuzzled my hair out of the way and found the ticklish spot behind my ear. A warm feeling started in my middle, stemming from where his lips touched me, demanding I recognize it. Accept it. Call it a good thing.

"Do you still have that tight leather biker outfit?" I asked, kind of embarrassed.

Lifting me off the washer and carrying me into the shower, he laughed.

Twenty-two

I smiled as the music ended, to leave a comfortable silence. The ticking of the clock above the sink became loud in the candlelit air. My eyes went to the hand jerking about the dial. It was creeping up on four in the morning, and I had nothing to do but sit and daydream about Kisten. He had left about three to handle the crowd at Piscary's, leaving me warm, content, and happy.

We had spent the entire early evening together eating BLTs and junk food, ransacking Ivy's and my music collection and then using her computer to burn a CD of our favorites. In retrospect, I think it had been the most enjoyable evening of my entire adult life as we laughed over each other's memories and I realized I enjoyed sharing more than my body with him.

Every candle I owned was lit as insurance that I'd be able to pick the time I told Ivy about my new arrangement with Kisten, and their glow added to the peace instilled by the soft burble of potpourri over the stove and the slight lethargy from the pain amulet about my neck. The air smelled of ginger, popcorn, and brownies, and as I sat at Ivy's table with my elbows to either side of me, I played with my amulets and wondered what Kisten was doing.

Much as I didn't want to admit it, I really liked him, and that I could have gone from fear to dislike to attraction and interest in less than a year left me concerned and embarrassed. It wasn't like me to overlook my healthy distrust of vampires because of a tight butt and a charming demeanor.

Living with a vampire might have something to do with it, I thought, dipping my hand into the nearby bowl of popcorn and eating a piece because it was there, rather than out of any need to satisfy hunger. I didn't think my new attitude was because of my scar; I had liked Kisten before the sex, or there wouldn't have been any—and he hadn't played upon it to influence me, either.

Wiping my fingers free of the salt, I stared into nothing. I had been thinking of Kisten differently since he'd dressed me up and made me feel good. *Maybe,* I thought, picking out another kernel. Maybe I could find something with a vampire that I'd never been able to hold on to with a witch, warlock, or human.

Chin in the cup of my palm, I sent my fingers lightly over the demon scar as I recalled his careful attention as he shampooed my hair and soaped my back, and how good it felt to be able to return the favor. He had let me hog the showerhead most of the time. That kind of stuff was important.

The sound of the front door opening jerked my attention to the clock. *Ivy was home? Already?* I had wanted to be tucked in bed pretending sleep when she came in.

"You up, Rachel?" she said, loud enough to be heard and soft enough to not wake me.

"Kitchen," I called back. Nervous, I glanced at the potpourri. It was enough. Kisten had said it was. Standing, I flicked on the overhead light and resettled myself. As the fluorescent bulbs flickered on, I tucked my amulets behind my sweater and listened to her thump about in her room. Her steps in the hall were quick and stilted.

"Hi," I said when she walked in, a vision of tight leather and tall boots. A black satchel was over one arm, and a silk-wrapped package about the size of a broken fishing pole was in her hand. My eyebrows rose as I realized she had put on makeup. Her image was both professional and sexy. Where was she going this late? And dressed like that?

"What happened with dinner with the folks?" I prompted.

"Change of plans." Setting her stuff beside me on the table, she crouched to dig in a lower drawer. "I came to get a few things, then I'm gone." Still at knee level, she smiled at me to show teeth. "I'll be back in a couple of hours."

"Okay," I said, slightly confused. She looked happy. She actually looked happy.

"It's cold in here," she said as she pulled out three of my wooden stakes and set them clattering on the counter by the sink. "It smells like you had the windows open."

"Um, it must be from our plywood door." My brow furrowed

as she stood, tugging the hem of her leather jacket down. Crossing the room with a speed just shy of eerie, she unzipped the satchel and jammed the stakes into it. I silently watched her, wondering.

Ivy hesitated. "Can I use them?" she asked, mistaking my silence for disapproval.

"Sure. Keep them," I said, wondering what was up. I hadn't seen her in this much leather since she took that run to liberate a vamp child from a jealous ex. And I really didn't want a stake back if it had been used.

"Thanks." Boot heels clacking on the linoleum, she went to the coffeemaker. Her oval face creased in annoyance as she peered at the empty carafe.

"You have a run?" I asked.

"Sort of." Her enthusiasm dimmed, and I watched her throw the old grounds away.

Curiosity got the better of me, and I flicked back the silk covering to see what was under it. "Holy crap!" I exclaimed as I found a shiny length of steel smelling faintly of oil. "Where did you get a sword!"

"Nice, isn't it." Not turning, she added three scoops of coffee to the filter and set it to brew. "And you can't trace it like bullets or charms."

Oh, such a warm and fuzzy thought. "Can you use it?"

Ivy pushed herself from the counter. I leaned back in my chair as she shook the wrap off, grasping the handle of the thin sword and pulling it from the back sheath. It came free with a whisper of ringing steel that tickled my inner ear. Like collapsing silk, her posture melted into a classic pose, her free arm arched over her head and her sword arm bent and extended. Her face was empty as she looked at the wall, her black hair swinging to a slow stop.

I had a freaking vampire samurai warrior for a roommate. This was getting better and better. "And you know how to use it, too," I said faintly.

She flashed me a smile as she stood and wedged it back into its sheath. "I took lessons from fifth grade through high school," she said as she set it on the table. "I grew so fast that it was hard to keep my balance. I kept running into things. Mostly people who irritated me. Adolescence is when the faster reflexes kick in. The practice helped, and I stuck with it."

I licked the salt off my fingers and pushed the popcorn away. I was willing to bet the classes had a good section devoted to self-control. Feeling more relaxed since the candles seemed to be working, I stretched my legs out under the table, wanting some of the coffee. Ivy rummaged in an upper cupboard to bring out her thermos. I eyed the dripping coffee, hoping she wasn't going to take it all.

"Well," she said as she filled the metal vacuum bottle with hot water to warm it up. "You look like the vamp who bled the cat."

"Beg pardon?" I said, stomach clenching.

She turned and dried her hands off on a dishcloth. "Did Nick call?"

"No," I said flatly.

Her smile widened. Swinging her hair out of her way, she said, "Good." Then, softly, she repeated, "That's good."

This was not where I wanted the conversation to go. Rising, I wiped my palms on my jeans and padded in my bare feet to turn the flame up under the potpourri. Ivy yanked open the fridge and came out with the cream cheese and a bag of bagels. The woman ate as if calories couldn't stick to her. "No Jenks?" I asked, though the answer was obvious.

"No Jenks. He did talk to me, though." Her eyes were pinched with frustration. "I told him I knew what Trent was, too, and to get over it. Now he won't talk to me, either." She popped the lid on the cream cheese and scraped a knifeful across her bagel. "Do you think we should put an ad in the paper?"

My head rose. "To replace him?" I stammered.

Ivy took a bite and shook her head. "Just shake him up," she said around her full mouth. "Maybe if he sees our ad for pixy backup, he'll talk to us."

Frowning, I sat down in my spot and slouched, extending my legs to put my bare feet on her unused chair. "I doubt it. It would be just like him to tell us to take a flying leap."

Ivy lifted one shoulder and let it fall. "It's not like we can do anything until spring."

"I suppose." God, this was depressing. I had to find a way to apologize to Jenks. Maybe if I sent him a clown-delivered telegram. Maybe if I was the clown. "I'll talk to him again," I said. "Take him some honey. Maybe if I get him drunk, he'll forgive me for being such an ass."

"I'll pick some up while I'm out," she offered. "I saw some gourmet honey made from Japanese cherry blossoms." Dumping the water from the thermos, she refilled it with the entire carafe of coffee, sealing the heavenly scent in metal and glass.

Biting back my disappointment, I pulled my feet off her chair.

Obviously she had been thinking about how to soothe Jenks's pride as well. "So where are you going this late with a thermos of coffee, a bag of stakes, and that sword?" I asked.

Ivy leaned against the counter with the sleek grace of a black panther, the half-eaten bagel perched on her fingertips. "I have to lean on some uppity vamps. Keep them up past their bedtime. The sword is for show, the stakes to remember me by, and the coffee is for me."

I made a face, imagining just how nasty it could be to have Ivy keep you up. Especially if she applied herself. But then my eyes widened as I put two and two together. "You're doing this for Piscary?" I said, sure I was right when she turned to look out the window.

"Yup."

Silently I waited, hoping she'd say something. She didn't. I ran my attention over her, taking in her closed posture. "Your dad worked something out?" I hinted.

She sighed and turned to me. "As long as I handle Piscary's affairs, the bastard won't be dipping into my head." She looked at her half-eaten bagel. Frowning, she clacked her boots to the trash and threw it away.

I said nothing, surprised she had capitulated so easily. Apparently hearing in my silence an accusation that wasn't there, her smooth face went ashamed. "Piscary agreed to let me continue using Kisten as my frontman," she said. "He likes the notoriety, and anyone who is important will know that whatever he says is really coming from me—I mean, Piscary. I don't have to do anything unless Kisten runs into something he can't handle. Then I'll go in as the muscle to bail him out."

My memories returned to Kisten taking down seven witches with the ease and nonchalance of breaking a candy bar. I couldn't imagine anything he couldn't handle, but then again, he wouldn't be able to go up against undead vampires without leaning on Piscary's strength. "And you're okay with this?" I said stupidly.

"No," she said, crossing her arms before her. "But it's what my dad came up with, and if I can't accept how he helped me, I shouldn't have asked for it."

"Sorry," I muttered, wishing I had kept my mouth shut.

Apparently mollified, Ivy crossed the kitchen and put the thermos in with the stakes. "I don't want Piscary in my head," she said, giving her satchel a shake to settle everything before zipping it closed. "As long as I do what he says, he'll stay out; and he'll leave Erica alone. Kisten should be his scion, not me," she muttered. "He wants it."

I absently agreed, and her fingers on the bag went still, her face carrying a shadow of the pain I recognized from the night Piscary had raped her in more ways than one. A chill struck through me as her nostrils flared and her focus went distant. "Kisten was here," she said softly.

My skin tightened. *Damn. I hadn't been able to keep it from her for even a night.* "Uh, yeah," I said as I pulled myself straighter in my chair. "He was here looking for you." *About half the day ago.* The chill inside me deepened when her focus narrowed, reading my unease. Her head shifted to look at the potpourri on the stove. *Double damn.*

Lips pressed tight, she walked out, heels clacking.

The wood chair scraped loudly as I stood. "Um, Ivy?" I called, following her out.

My breath caught and I jerked to a stop when I almost ran into her in the dark hallway on her way back from the sanctuary. "Excuse me," she muttered, shifting around me with a vamp's speed. Her posture was tense, and in the light leaking in from the kitchen, I could see her eyes were dilated. *Crap. She was vamping out.*

"Ivy?" I said to the empty hall, as she had walked into the living room. "About Kisten—"

My words choked off and I halted, my feet edging the gray carpet in the candlelit living room. Ivy stood with a ridged stiffness before the couch. The couch Kisten and I had had sex on. Emotions cascaded over her, frightening in their rapidity: dismay, fear, anger, betrayal. I jumped when she jerked into motion, jabbing at the CD-check button.

The five CDs came rolling halfway out. Ivy stared at them, stiffening. "I'll kill him," she said, her fingers touching Jeff Buckley.

Shocked, I opened my mouth to protest, finding my words dying to nothing at the anger, black and heavy, in her tight expression.

"I'll kill him twice," she said. She knew. Somehow she knew.

My heart pounded. "Ivy," I started, hearing the fear in my voice. And with that, I jerked her instincts into play. Gasping, I backpedaled, far too slow.

"Where is it?" she hissed, her eyes wide and wild as she reached for me.

"Ivy . . ." My back hit the wall of the hallway, and I knocked her hand aside. "He didn't bite me."

"Where is it!"

Adrenaline surged. Smelling it, she jerked her hand out, reaching. Her eyes were black and lost. It was only our former sparring that kept her grip from landing as I blocked her reach and dove under her arm to come to a stand in the middle of the candlelit living room.

"Back off, Ivy!" I exclaimed, trying not to fall into a defensive crouch. "He didn't bite me!" But I didn't have time to breathe before she was on me, jerking the collar of my sweater.

"Where did he bite you?" she said, her gray voice trembling. "I'll kill him. I'll freaking kill him! I can smell him all over you!"

Her hand jerked to the hem of my sweater.

It tripped me over the panic line, and instinct took over. "Ivy! Stop!" I shouted. Frightened, I tapped the line. She reached for me, face twisted in anger. The line filled my chi, wild and out of control. A burst of energy flamed from my hands, burning them, as I hadn't harnessed it with a charm.

We both cried out as a black and gold sheet of ever-after expanded from me, knocking Ivy back into the plywood door. She slid to the floor in an awkward heap, her arms over her head and her legs askew. The windows shook at the boom. I rocked back, then caught my balance. Anger replaced my fear. I didn't care if she was all right or not.

"He didn't bite me!" I shouted, spitting my hair out of my mouth as I stood over her. "Okay? We had sex. All right? God help you, Ivy. It was only sex!"

Ivy coughed. Red-faced and gasping, she found her breath. The plywood sheet behind her was cracked. Shaking her head, she peered up at me, clearly not focusing yet. She didn't get up. "He didn't bite you?" she rasped, her face shadowy in the candlelight.

My legs trembled from adrenaline. "No!" I exclaimed. "You think I'm stupid?"

Clearly shaken, she looked askance at me. Taking a slow breath, she wiped her lower lip with the back of her hand. My gut tightened as it came away red with blood. Ivy stared at it, then gathered her legs under her and got to her feet. I breathed easier when she reached for a tissue, wiping her hand off and crumpling it into a ball.

She reached out, and I sprang back. "Don't touch me!" I said, and she raised a hand in acquiescence.

"Sorry." She looked at the cracked plywood, then winced as she felt her back. Carefully she tugged her coat down. Eyes going to mine, she took a slow breath. My heart pounded in time to the pain in my head. "You slept with Kisten and he didn't bite you?" she asked.

"Yes. And no, he didn't bite me. And if you *ever* touch me again, I'm walking out the front door, forever. Damn it, Ivy. I thought we were clear on this!"

I expected an apology or something, but all she did was eye me speculatively and ask, "Are you sure? You might not even notice if he cut your inner lip."

Goose bumps rose, and I ran my tongue across the inside of my mouth. "He wore caps," I said, feeling ill for how easily he could have tricked me. But he hadn't.

Ivy blinked. Slowly she sat on the edge of the couch, her elbows on her knees and her forehead cupped in the cradle of her hands. Her thin body looked vulnerable in the light from the three candles on the table. Crap. It suddenly occurred to me that not only did she want a closer relationship with me, but that Kisten was her old boyfriend. "Ivy? Are you okay?"

"No."

I cautiously sat on the chair across from her, the corner of the table between us. By any standards, this was a complete shitfest. I cursed silently, then reached out. "Ivy. God, this is awkward."

She jumped at the weight of my hand on her arm, looking up with frighteningly dry eyes. I pulled back, laying my hand like a dead thing in my lap. I knew I shouldn't touch her when she wanted more. But to sit and do nothing was so cold.

"It just kind of happened."

Ivy touched her lip to see that it had stopped bleeding. "It was just sex? You didn't give him your blood?"

The vulnerability in her voice struck me. My head bobbed. I felt like a doll, my eyes wide and my thoughts empty. "I'm sorry," I said. "I didn't think you and Kisten . . ." I hesitated. This wasn't about the sex, but the blood she thought I had given him. "I didn't think you and Kisten had a formal relationship anymore," I fumbled, unsure if I was putting it right.

"I don't share blood with Kisten but for the rare occasion when he's been dumped and needs some TLC," she said, her gray silk voice soft. Still she wouldn't look up. "Blood is not sex, Rachel. It's a way to show you care for someone. A way to show . . . you love them."

It was barely a whisper. My breath grew fast. I felt we were balanced on a knife's edge, and it scared the crap out of me. "How can you say sex isn't blood, when you'll have sex with anyone?" I said, adrenaline making my voice harsher than I intended. "Good God, Ivy, when was the last time you had sex *without* blood?"

Only now did she bring her head up, shocking me with the fear in her eyes. She was afraid, and not because she thought I'd given my blood to Kisten. She was afraid of the answers I was demanding. I don't think she had faced them before, even in the chaos her desires had left her in. I felt hot, then cold. Pulling my knees to my chin, I tucked my bare heels against me.

"Okay," she said with the last of her exhaled breath, and I knew the next thing she said would be stark honesty. "You have a good point. I usually include blood with sex. I like it that way. It's a rush. Rachel, if you would only . . ." she said, her hands coming up from her knees.

I felt myself pale. I shook my head, and she changed her mind about what she was going to say. She seemed to deflate, all the tension pooling out of her. "Rachel, it's not the same," she finished weakly, brown eyes pleading.

My thoughts went to Kist. The twinge from my scar dove to my groin and brought my breath even faster. Swallowing, I forced the feeling from me. I pulled back, glad the table was between us. "That's what Kisten says, but I can't separate it. And I don't think you can either."

Ivy's face went red, and I knew I was right.

"Damn it, Ivy. I'm not saying it's wrong they're the same," I said. "Hell, I've been living with you for seven months. Don't you think by now you'd know if I thought it was? But that's not the way I'm put together. You're the best friend I've ever had, but I'm not going to share a pillow with you, and I'm never going to let anyone taste my blood." I took a breath. "I'm not put together that way, either. And I can't live my life avoiding a real relationship with someone because it might hurt your feelings. I told you it's not going to happen between us, and it's not. Maybe . . ." I felt sick. "Maybe I should move out."

"Move out?"

It was a breathy sound of dismay, and the warmth of tears stung my eyes. I stared at the wall, jaw clenched. The last seven months had been the most frightening, scary, and best months of my life. I didn't want to leave—and not just because she was protecting me from another vampire biting and claiming me—but staying here wasn't fair to either of us if she couldn't let it go.

"Jenks is gone," I said, my voice low so it wouldn't shake. "I just slept with your old boyfriend. It's not fair to stay here if there is never going to be anything more than friendship between us. Especially now that Skimmer is back." I looked at the broken door, hating myself. "We should just call everything quits."

God, why was I almost crying? I couldn't give her any more, and she desperately needed it. Skimmer could; Skimmer wanted to. I should leave. But when I looked up, I was shocked to see the candlelight glinting upon a ribbon of moisture under her eye.

"I don't want you to go," she said, and the lump in my throat thickened. "A good friendship is reason enough to stay, isn't it?" she whispered, her eyes so full of pain that a tear leaked out of me.

"Damn it," I said, wiping a finger under my eye. "Look what you made me do."

I jerked when she reached across the table and took my wrist. My eyes were riveted to hers as she pulled it to her and touched my tear-damp fingertips to her lips. Her eyes closed and her lashes fluttered. A zing of adrenaline struck me. My pulse quickened, the memory of vampire-induced ecstasy high in my thoughts. "Ivy?" I said weakly, pulling away.

She let go. My heart pounded as she took a slow breath, tasting the air with her senses, running my emotions through her incredible brain, reading the balance of what I might and might not do. I didn't want to know what her calculations totaled to.

"I'll pack my things," I said, frightened that she might know more about me than I did.

Her eyes opened. I thought I saw a faint glimmer of strength. "No," she said, the first hint of her iron will returning. "We're both crap when we're alone, and I'm not just talking about the stupid firm. I promise I won't ask anything of you except to be my friend. Please . . ." She took a breath. "Please don't go because of this, Rachel. Do what you want with Kist. He's a good man and I know he won't hurt you. Just . . ." She held her breath, her determination faltering. "Just be here when I come home tonight?"

I nodded. I knew she wasn't just asking about tonight. And I didn't want to leave. I loved it here: the kitchen, the witch's garden, the cool-factor of living in a church. That she valued our friendship meant a lot to me, and after avoiding true friendship for years because of what had happened to my dad, having a best friend meant a lot to me too. She had once threatened to withdraw her desperately needed protection from me if I left. This time, she hadn't. I was afraid to look for the reason, afraid that it might stem from that tiny thrill I had felt when she had tasted my tears.

"Thank you," she said, and I froze as she leaned forward over the table to give me a quick hug. The scent of almonds and leather filled my senses. "If Kisten can convince you that blood isn't sex," she said, "promise to tell me?"

I stared at her. The memory of Skimmer kissing her flashed through me and was gone.

Apparently satisfied, she let go, stood, and went into the kitchen.

"Ivy," I breathed, too numb and strung out to speak louder, knowing she could hear me. "How many rules are we breaking?"

She hesitated as she appeared in the hallway, satchel and sword in hand, shifting from foot to foot and not answering me. "I'll be back after sunrise. Maybe we can have a late dinner? Gossip about Kisten over lasagna? He's actually a nice guy—he'll be good for you." Giving me an awkward smile, she left.

Her voice had held a faint ribbon of regret, but I didn't know if it was for having lost me or Kisten. I didn't want to know. I stared at the carpet, not seeing the candles or smelling the scent of wax and perfume as the faint boom of the door shifted the air. How had my life gotten this screwed up? All I had wanted to do was quit the I.S., help a few people, make something of myself and my degree. Since then I had found and driven away my first real boyfriend in years, insulted a pixy clan, become Ivy's golden ring, and had sex with a living vampire. That wasn't even counting the two death threats I'd survived or the precarious situation with Trent. What the hell was I doing?

Rising, I stumbled into the kitchen, face cold and legs feeling like rubber. Looking up at the sound of running water, I froze. Algaliarept was at the sink filling the teapot, its tarnished copper beading with condensation.

"Good evening, Rachel," he said, smiling to show me flat teeth. "Hope you don't mind me making a pot of tea. We have a lot to do before the sun comes up."

Oh God. I'd forgotten about that.

Twenty-three

"Damn!" I swore, backpedaling. The sanctuary. If I could reach holy ground, he couldn't touch me. I shrieked as a heavy hand fell on my shoulder. Spinning, I clawed at his face. It went misty, and I lurched when his grip vanished. In an instant he had my ankle and jerked me off my feet. "Let go!" I shouted when I hit the floor, my voice harsh as I kicked him.

He spun me sliding into the fridge. His long face took on a sun-starved complexion and his red goat eyes turned eager over his smoked glasses. I scrambled up, and he lunged, grabbing me with his white-gloved hand and giving me a shake to rattle my teeth. He shoved me, and I landed against the center island counter like a rag doll. Turning, I put my back against it, wide-eyed and heart beating fast. I was so stupid. I was *so stupid!*

"If you run again, I'll call you in breach of our agreement," he said calmly. "That's your warning. Please run. It will make everything so-o-o-o much simpler."

Shaking, I held onto the counter for balance. "Go away," I said. "I didn't summon you."

"It's not that simple anymore," he said. "It took me a day in the library, but I found precedence." His precise accent became even more officious, and he put the back of his knuckles to his velvet green frock and quoted, " 'If said familiar is stationed at a beta site by way of loan or similar event, the master may seek the familiar out to perform duties.' You opened the door by tapping a line," he added. "And since I have a task for you, I'm here until you finish it."

I felt sick. "What do you want?" There was a spell pot on my counter full of an amber liquid smelling of geranium. I hadn't counted on him bringing his work to me.

"What do you want—master," Al prompted, smiling to show me his thick, blocky teeth.

I tucked my hair behind my ear. "I want you to get the hell out of my kitchen."

His smile never flickered as, with a powerful motion, he backhanded me. I stifled a gasp, lurching for balance. Adrenaline surged as he gripped my shoulder, keeping me upright.

"Funny, funny girl," he murmured, his British elegance chilling me and his beautiful chiseled looks turning harsh. "Say it."

The sharp taste of blood edged my tongue. My back pressed into the counter painfully. "What do you want, oh gracious master from my ass."

I didn't have time to duck as the flat of his hand swung. Pain shocked through my cheek, and I hit the floor. Al's silver-buckled boots edged my vision. He was wearing white stockings, and there was lace where they met the bottom of his trousers.

Nausea rose. I touched my cheek, feeling it burn and hating him. I tried to rise, unable to when he put a foot on my shoulder and forced me down. Hating him all the more, I tossed my hair aside so I could see him. *What difference did it make?* "What do you want, master?"

I felt like I was going to vomit.

His thin lips curled up in a smile. Tugging the lace from his sleeves, he bent to solicitously help me up. I refused, but he yanked me up so fast that I found myself pressed against him, breathing in the scent of crushed velvet and burnt amber. "I want this," he whispered, running a hand up under my sweater, searching.

My heart raced. Stiffening, I clenched my teeth. *I'll kill him. Somehow, I'll kill him.*

"Such a touching conversation with your roommate," he said, and I twitched, as his voice had shifted to Ivy's. Ever-after zinged through me as his appearance shifted while still touching me. Red goat eyes stared at me from Ivy's perfect face. Lean and tight, the image of her body wrapped in leather pressed against me, pinning me to the counter. The last time, he had bitten me. *Oh, God. Not again.*

"But maybe you want this instead," he said with her gray silk voice, and sweat started at the small of my back. Her long straight hair brushed my cheek, the silky whisper pulling an unstoppable shiver from my skin. Feeling it where our bodies touched, he leaned close until I recoiled.

"Don't pull away," he said with her voice, and my resolve grew. He was slime. He was a bastard. I'd kill him for this. "I'm sorry, Rachel. . . ." he breathed, long fingers burning into tingles where they touched, tracing a line from my shoulder to my hip. "I'm not angry. I understand you're afraid. But the things I could teach you—if you knew the heights of passion we could find." His breath shuddered. Ivy's arms were around me cool and light—gentling me to him against my will. I could smell her rich scent of dark incense and ash. He had her perfectly.

"Let me show you?" the vision of Ivy whispered, and I closed my eyes. "Just a taste . . . I know I can change your mind."

It was pleading, heavy with her vulnerable desires. It was everything she hadn't said, everything she wouldn't. My eyes opened as my scar flashed to life. *God, no.* Fire raced to my groin. Knees buckling, I tried to push away. Demon-red eyes shifted to a liquid brown, and his grip grew firmer, pulling me closer until his breath came and went on my neck. "Gently, Rachel," her voice whispered. "I could be so gentle. I could be everything a man can't be. Everything you want. Just one little word, Rachel. Tell me you will?"

I couldn't . . . I couldn't deal with this right now. "Didn't you have something for me to do?" I said. "The sun will be up soon and I need to get to bed."

"Slowly," he crooned, Ivy's breath smelling of oranges. "There's only one first time."

"Let go of me," I said tightly. "You aren't Ivy and I'm not interested."

Ivy's passion-filled black eyes narrowed, but Al's attention was over my shoulder and I didn't think it was anything I had said. He let go of me, and I stumbled to catch my balance. A shimmer of ever-after cascaded over him, melting his features back to his usual vision of a young British lord of the eighteenth century. The glasses were back to hide his eyes, and he adjusted them on his thin-bridged nose. "How grand," he said, his accent shifting as well. "Ceri."

There was the distant boom of the front door crashing open. "Rachel!" came her voice, high and frightened. "He's this side of the lines!"

Heart pounding, I spun. I took a breath to warn her, but it was too late. My outstretched hand fell as she lurched into the room, her simple white dress furling about her bare feet as she stopped in the archway. Green eyes wide and soulful, she put a hand to her chest atop Ivy's crucifix. "Rachel . . ." she breathed, dismay slumping her shoulders.

Al took a step and she spun in a dancer's circle, toe pointed and unbound hair furling. She recited an unheard poem laced with darkness, and a ripple of line energy cascaded between us. White-faced and holding her arms, she stared at him, trembling within her small circle.

The stately demon beamed, adjusting the lace about his collar. "Ceri. How splendid to see you. I miss you, love," he almost purred.

The young woman's chin trembled. "Banish him, Rachel," she said, her fear obvious.

I tried to swallow, failing. "I tapped a line. He found precedence. He has a task for me."

Her eyes widened. "No . . ."

Al frowned. "I haven't been in the library in a thousand years. They were whispering behind my back, Ceri. I had to renew my card. It was most embarrassing. Everyone knows you're gone. Zoë is making my tea. It's the most awful tea I've ever had—he can't hold the sugar spoon with only two digits. Do come back." His pleasant face creased into a smile. "I'll make it worth your soul."

Ceri jerked. Chin high, she said haughtily, "My name is Ceridwen Merriam Dulciate."

A rough sound of mirth escaped him. Taking off his glasses, he leaned an elbow against the counter. Mocking gaze on mine, he murmured, "Ceri, be a dear and make a spot of tea?"

My face went slack as Ceri dropped her head and took a step. Al chuckled when she made a cry of self-disgust and stopped at the edge of her circle. Tiny fists clenched, she fumed.

"Old habits die hard," he mocked.

Bile bubbled up. Even now she was his. "Leave her alone," I snarled.

From nowhere, a white-gloved hand struck me. I spun into the counter, jaw burning. Gasping, I hunched over it with my hair falling about my face. I was getting tired of this.

"Don't hit her!" Ceri said, her voice high and virulent.

"Does it bother you?" he said lightly. "Pain moves her more than fear. Which is good—pain keeps a person alive longer than fear."

My hurt turned to anger. Eyebrows high, he dared me to

protest as I found my breath. His goat eyes slid to the head-sized vat he had brought with him. "Let's get started, shall we?"

I looked at the pot, recognizing the brew by the smell. It was the one to make a person into a familiar. Fear chilled me, and I wrapped my arms about myself. "I'm already coated with your aura," I said. "Making me take more isn't going to make a difference."

"I didn't ask for your opinion."

I sprang back as he moved. Grinning, he extended the basket that had appeared in his hand. I could smell wax. "Set the candles," he ordered, amused at my quick reaction.

"Rachel . . ." Ceri whispered, but I couldn't look at her. I had promised to be his familiar, and now I would be. Miserable, my thoughts went to Ivy as I set the milky green candles at the spots marked by black nail polish. Why couldn't I make good choices?

My grip on the last candle trembled. It had gouges on it, as if something had tried to break the circle by going through it. Something with big nasty claws.

"Rachel!" Al barked, and I jumped. "You didn't set them with their place names."

Still holding the last candle, I stared blankly. Past him, Ceri nervously licked her lips.

"You don't know their place names," Al added, and I shook my head, not wanting to be hit again, but Al only sighed. "I'll set them myself when I light them," he grumbled, his pale face taking on a ruddy tinge. "I expected more of you than this. Apparently you've been spending most of your time with earth magic, neglecting your ley line arts."

"I'm an earth witch," I said. "Why would I bother?"

Ceri jerked as Al threatened to smack me again, her almost translucent hair swirling. "Let her go, Algaliarept. You don't want her for a familiar."

"Offering to take her place?" he mocked, and I took a fearful breath that she might.

"No!" I shouted, and he laughed.

"Don't fret, Rachel, love," he crooned, and I flinched when he ran a gloved finger across my jawline, tracing the path down my arm to my hand to take the last candle from me. "I keep my familiars until something better comes along, and despite you being as ignorant as a frog, you're capable of holding almost twice the line energy that she can." He leered. "Lucky you."

Clapping his white-gloved hands once, he spun to make his coattails furl. "Now. Watch closely, Rachel. You'll be lighting my candles tomorrow. These are words that move mortals and gods alike, making all equal and capable of keeping my circle whole against even Newt."

Swell.

"Salax," he said as he lit the first candle from the pencil-thick red taper that had appeared in his gloved hand. *"Aemulatio,"* he said as he lit the second. *"Adfictatio, cupidus,* and my favorite, *inscitia,"* he said as he lit the last one. Smiling, the still-glowing taper vanished. I felt him tap a line, and with a translucent swirl of red and black, his circle rose to arch closed over our heads. My skin prickled from its strength, and I clasped my arms about myself.

These are a few of my favorite things, I heard patter through my mind, and I stifled a hysterical giggle. I was going to be a demon's familiar. There was no way out of it now.

Al's head jerked up at the ugly choking sound, and Ceri's face went still. "Algaliarept," she pleaded. "You're pushing her too hard. Her will is too strong to bend easily."

"I'll break my familiars the way I see fit," he said calmly. "A little grounding, and she'll be as right as rain in the desert." One hand on his hip and the other cupping his chin, he eyed me speculatively. "Time for your bath, love."

Algaliarept snapped his fingers with a showman's flair. His hand opened, and a cedar-slatted bucket appeared hanging from it. My eyes widened as he threw its contents at me.

Cold water smacked into me. My breath whooshed out in an affronted yelp. It was saltwater, stinging my eyes and dribbling into my mouth. Reality washed through me, clearing my head. He was making sure I didn't have any potions in me to contaminate the coming spell. "I don't use potions, you big green turd!" I shouted, shaking my arms in my sodden sleeves.

"See?" Al was clearly pleased. "All better."

The slight ache of my ribs intruded as my pain charm broke. Most of the water was soaking my spell book library. If I survived this, I'd have to air them all out. What a jerk.

"Ooooh, your eye is doing nicely," he said as he reached forward to touch it. "Eating your roommate's Brimstone, are we? Wait until you try the real stuff. It will knock your socks off."

I jerked back when his gloved hand brushed my skin with the scent of lavender, but Al's hand dropped lower to grasp my hair. Shrieking, I swung my foot up. He caught it, moving faster than I could follow. Ceri watched in pity as I fought, helpless. Holding my foot high, he forced me against the counter. His glasses had been knocked aside, and he smiled at me with a domineering delight. "The hard way," he whispered. "Marvelous."

"No!" I exclaimed as a pair of sheers suddenly glinted in his hand.

"Hold still," he said, dropping my foot and pinning me against the counter.

I wiggled and spit at him, but he had me against the counter and I could do nothing. I panicked as I heard metal sheering. He let go by turning misty, and I fell to the floor.

Hand clutching my hair, I scrambled to my feet. "Stop it! Just stop it!" I shouted, alternating my attention between his glee and the chunk he had cut from my hair. Damn it, it was at least four inches long. "Do you know how long it takes to grow my hair out!"

Al gave Ceri a sidelong glance as the scissors disappeared and he dropped my hair into the potion. "She's worried about her hair?"

My gaze shot to the red strands floating on top of Al's brew, and as I stood there in my soggy sweater, I went cold. That vat of potion wasn't for Al to give me more of his aura. It was for me giving him mine. "Oh, hell no!" I exclaimed, backing up. "I'm not giving you my aura!"

Al plucked a ceramic spoon from the rack hanging over the center island counter and pushed the strands of hair down. He had a refined elegance in his velvet and lace, every inch of him as trim and debonair as inhumanly possible. "Is that a refusal, Rachel?" he murmured. "Please tell me it was?"

"No," I whispered. There was nothing I could do. Nothing.

His smile went wider. "Now your blood to quicken it, love."

Pulse pounding, I looked from the needle between his finger and thumb to the vat. If I ran, I was his. If I did this, he could use me through the lines. Damn, damn, and double damn.

Numbing my thoughts, I took the tarnished silver needle. My mouth went dry as its heavy weight filled my grip. It was as long as my palm and elaborately tooled. The tip was copper so the silver wouldn't interfere with the charm. Peering closer, I felt my stomach turn. There was a naked twisted body writhing around the barrel. "God save me," I whispered.

"He's not listening. He's too busy."

I stiffened. Al had come up behind me and was whispering in my ear.

"Finish the potion, Rachel." His breath was hot on my cheek, and I couldn't move as he pulled my hair back. A shudder rippled through me as he tilted his head and bent closer. "Finish it . . ." he breathed, his lips brushing my skin. I could smell starch and lavender.

Teeth gritted, I gripped the needle and stabbed it into me. My held breath came out, and I held it again. I thought I heard Ceri crying.

"Three drops," Al whispered, nuzzling my neck.

My head hurt. Blood pounding, I held my finger over the vat and massaged three drops into it. The scent of redwood rose, briefly overpowering the cloying stench of burnt amber.

"Mmmm, richer." His hand wrapped around mine, taking the needle back. It vanished in a smear of ever-after, and his grip shifted to my bleeding finger. "Give me a taste?"

I jerked back as far from him as I could, my arm stretched out between us. "No."

"Leave her alone!" Ceri pleaded.

Slowly Al's grip loosened. He watched me, a new tension rising in him.

I wrestled my hand away and put another step between us. I clutched my arms about me, cold despite the heater blowing on my bare feet.

"Get on the mirror," he said, his face expressionless behind his smoked glasses.

My gaze shot to it waiting for me on the floor. "I—I can't," I whispered.

His thin lips pressed together, and I gritted my teeth to keep silent when he picked me up and set me on it. I inhaled, eyes widening when I felt like I slipped two inches into the mirror. "Oh God, oh God," I moaned, wanting to reach for the counter, but Al was in the way, grinning.

"Push your aura off," he said.

"I can't," I panted, feeling myself hyperventilate.

Al pulled his glasses down his thin nose and looked at me over them. "Doesn't matter. It's dissolving like sugar in the rain."

"No," I whispered. My knees started shaking and the pounding in my head worsened. I could feel my aura slipping away and Al's taking a stronger hold on me.

"Capital and fine," Al said, his goat eyes on the mirror.

My gaze followed his, and I clutched at my stomach. I could see myself in it. My face was covered in Al's aura, black and empty. Only my eyes showed, a faint glow flickering about them. It was my soul, trying to make enough aura to put between Al's aura and me. It wasn't enough as the mirror sucked it all up and I could feel Al's presence sink into me.

I found I was panting. I imagined what it must have been like for Ceri, her soul utterly gone and Al's aura seeping into her like this all the time, alien and wrong.

I shook. Hands clasped over my mouth, I looked frantically for something to throw up in. Gagging, I lurched off the mirror. I would not spew. I wouldn't.

"Marvelous," Al said as I hunched over, my teeth clenched and my bile rising. "You got all of it. Here. I'll just slip it into the vat for you."

His voice was cheery and bright, and as I peered at him from around my hair, Al dropped the mirror into the potion. The brew flashed to clear. Just like I knew it would.

Ceri was sitting on the floor, crying with her head on her knees. She pulled her head up, and I thought she looked all the more beautiful for her tears. I only looked ugly when I cried.

I jumped when a thick yellowed tome hit the counter beside me. The light through the window was starting to brighten, but the clock said it was only five. Almost three hours before the sun would rise to end this nightmare, unless Al ended it sooner.

"Read it."

Looking down, I recognized it. It was the book I had found in my attic, the one that Ivy claimed wasn't among the ones she planted up there for me, the very same one that I had given to Nick to hold for me after I accidentally used it to make him my familiar and the same book that Al had tricked away from us. The one Algaliarept wrote to make people into demon familiars. *Shit.*

I swallowed hard. My fingers looked pale as I put them on the text, running down to find the incantation. It was in Latin, but I knew the translation. "Some to you, but all to me," I whispered. "Bound by ties made so by plea."

"Pars tibi, totum mihi," Al said, grinning. *"Vinctus vinculuis, prece fractis."*

My fingers started shaking. "Moon made safe, ancient light made sane. Chaos decreed, taken tripped if bane."

"Luna servata, lux sanata. Chaos statutum, pejus minutum. Go on. Finish."

There was only one line left. One line, and the spell would be complete. Nine words, and my life would be a living hell whether I was on this side of the lines or not. I took a breath. Then another. "Lee of mind," I whispered. My voice trembled, and it was getting harder to breathe. "Bearer of pain. Slave until the worlds are slain . . ."

Al's grin widened and his eyes flashed black. *"Mentem tegens, malum ferens,"* he intoned. *"Semper servus. Dum duret—mundus."*

With an eager impatience, Al pulled his gloves from his hands and plunged his hands into the vat. I jerked. A twang reverberated through me, followed by gut-wrenching dizziness. Black and smothering, the charm wrapped about my soul, numbing me.

Red-knuckled hands dripping, Al steadied himself against the counter. A shimmer of red cascaded over him, and his image blurred before settling. He blinked, seemingly shaken.

I took a breath, then another. It was done. He had my aura for good—all but what my soul was desperately trying to replace to insinuate between my being and Al's aura still coating me. Maybe in time it would get better, but I doubted it.

"Good," he said, tugging his sleeves down and wiping his hands off on a black towel that had appeared in his grip. White gloves materialized, hiding his hands. "Good and done. Capital."

Ceri cried softly, but I was too drained to even look at her.

My cell phone chirped from my bag on the far counter, sounding absurd.

The last of Al's fleeting disquiet vanished. "Oh, do let me answer," he said, breaking the circle as he went to get it.

I shuddered as I felt a slight pull from my empty center as the energy went back through Al and into the line it originated from. Al's eyebrows were high in delight when he turned with my cell phone in his gloved hand. "I wonder who it is?" he simpered.

Unable to stand any longer, I slipped to the floor, my back to the counter as I hugged my knees. The vent air was warm on my bare feet, but my damp jeans soaked up the cold. I was Al's familiar. Why was I even bothering to keep the air moving in and out of my lungs?

"That's why they take your soul," Ceri whispered. "You can't kill yourself if they have your will."

I stared, only now understanding.

"Hello-o-o-o?" Al purred, leaning against the sink, the pink cylinder looking odd against his old world charm. "Nicholas Gregory Sparagmos! What a delight!"

My head came up. "Nick?" I breathed.

Al held a long hand over the receiver and simpered. "It's your boyfriend. I'll field it for you. You look tired." Wrinkling his nose, he turned to the phone. "Feel that, did you?" he said cheerfully.

"Something missing, now is there? Be careful what you wish for, little wizard."

"Where's Rachel!" came Nick's voice, thin and tinny. He sounded panicked, and my heart sank. I reached out, knowing Al wouldn't give the phone to me.

"Why, she's at my feet," Al said, grinning. "Mine, all mine. She made a mistake, and now she's mine. Send her flowers for her grave. It's all you can do."

The demon listened for a moment, emotions flickering over him. "Oh, don't be making promises you can't keep. It is so-o-o-o lower class. As it happens, I'm not in need of a familiar anymore, so I won't be responding to your little summons; don't call me. She saved your soul, little man. Too bad you never told her how much you loved her. Humans are so stupid."

He broke the connection with Nick in mid-protest. Snapping the phone closed, he dropped it back in my bag. It started ringing immediately, and he tapped it once. My phone played its obnoxious good-bye song and shut off.

"Now." Al clapped his hands. "Where were we? Ah yes. I'll be right back. I want to see it work." Red eyes glowing in delight, he vanished with a small shift of air.

"Rachel!" Ceri cried. She fell into me, dragging me out of the broken circle. I pushed at her, too depressed to try to get away. It was coming. Al was going to fill me with his force, making me feel his thoughts, turning me into a copper-top battery that could make his tea and do his dishes. The first of my helpless tears dribbled out, but I couldn't find the will to hate myself for them. I knew I should be crying. I had gambled my life to put Piscary away and lost.

"Rachel! Please!" Ceri pleaded, her grip on my arm hurting as she tried to drag me. My damp feet made a squeaking noise, and I pushed at her, trying to get her to stop.

A red bubble of ever-after popped into existence where Al had pinged out. The air pressure violently shifted, and both Ceri and I clasped our hands to our ears.

"Damn it all to heaven and back!" Al swore, his velvet green frock open and in disarray. His hair was wild and his glasses were gone. "You did everything right!" he shouted, gesturing violently. "I've got your aura. You've got mine. Why can't I reach you through the lines!"

Ceri knelt behind me, her arm protectively about me. "It

didn't work?" she quavered, pulling me back a little more. Her wet finger traced a quick circle about us.

"Do I look like it worked?" he exclaimed. "Do I look happy to you?"

"No," she breathed, and her circle expanded about us, black-smeared but strong. "Rachel," she said, giving me a squeeze. "You're going to be okay."

Al went still. Deathly quiet, he turned, his boots making a soft sound against the flooring. "No, she isn't."

My eyes widened at his frustrated anger. *Oh God. Not again.*

I stiffened as he tapped a line and sent it crashing into me. With it came a whisper of his emotion, satisfied and anticipatory. Fire coursed through me, and I screamed, pushing Ceri away. Her bubble burst in a glittering sensation of hot needles, adding to my agony.

Curled into a fetal position, I frantically thought the word, *Tulpa,* slumping in relief as the torrent coursed through me and settled in the sphere in my head. Panting, I slowly pulled my head up. Al's confusion and frustration filled me. My anger grew until it overshadowed his emotions.

Al's thoughts in mine shifted to stark surprise. Vision blurring as what I was seeing conflicted with what my brain said was true, I stumbled to my feet. Most of the candles were out, knocked over to make puddles of wax and scenting the air with smoke. Al felt my defiance through our link, and his face turned ugly when my pride for having learned to store energy seeped into him. "Ceri . . ." he threatened, his goat eyes narrowing.

"It didn't work," I said, my voice low as I watched him from around my stringy wet hair. "Get out of my kitchen."

"I'm going to have you, Morgan," Al snarled. "If I can't take you by right, I'll by god beat you into submission and pull you in, broken and bleeding."

"Oh yeah?" I came back with. I glanced at the pot that had held my aura. His eyes widened in surprise as he knew my thought the instant I had it. The bond now went both ways. He had made a mistake.

"Get out of my kitchen!" I exclaimed, dumping the line energy he had forced me to hold back through our familiar link and into him. I jerked upright as it all flowed from me and into him, leaving me empty. Al stumbled backward, shocked.

"You *canicula!*" he cried, his image blurring.

Staggering to remain upright, he tapped the line, adding more force.

Eyes narrowing, I set my thoughts to loop it right back at him. Whatever he was going to send into me was going to end up right back in him.

Al choked as he sensed what I was going to do. There was a sudden wrench in my gut and I stumbled, catching myself against the table as he broke the live connection between us. I stared at him across the kitchen, breath rough. This was going to be settled right here and now. One of us was going to lose. And it wasn't going to be me. Not in my kitchen. Not tonight.

Al put one foot behind him, taking a deceptively relaxed stance. He ran a hand over his hair, smoothing it. His round smoked glasses appeared, and he buttoned his frock. "This isn't working," he said flatly.

"No," I rasped. "It isn't."

Safe in her circle, Ceri snickered. "You can't have her, Algaliarept, you big stupid," she mocked, making me wonder at her word choice. "You made the familiar gate swing both ways when you forced her to give you her aura. You're her familiar as much as she is yours."

Al's momentary placid face blossomed into anger. "I've used this spell a thousand times to milk auras, and this has never happened before. And I am *not* her familiar."

I watched, feeling tense and ill as a three-legged stool appeared behind Al. It looked like something Attila the Hun would have used, with a red velvet cushion and horsehair fringe going to the floor. Not bothering to see if it was behind him, he sat, his expression puzzled.

"That's why Nick called," I said, and Al gave me a patronizing look. When he took my aura, it broke the bond I had with Nick. He had felt it. *Aw, crap. Al was my familiar?*

Ceri gestured that I should join her in her circle, but I couldn't chance that Al might hurt her in the instant it would take to reform it. Al, though, was preoccupied with his own thoughts.

"This isn't right," he mumbled. "I've done this before with hundreds of witches with souls and it's never forged a bond this strong. What's so different about . . ."

My stomach dropped as all visible emotion drained from him. He glanced at the clock above the sink, then me. "Come here, little witch."

"No."

He pressed his lips together and stood.

Gasping, I backpedaled, but he had my wrist and pulled me to the island counter. "You've done this spell before," he said as he squeezed my pricked finger, making it bleed again. "When you made Nicholas Gregory Sparagmos your familiar. It was your blood in the brew, little witch, that invoked it?"

"You know it was." I was too drained to be frightened anymore. "You were there." I couldn't see his eyes, but my reflection in his glasses looked ugly and pale with wet stringy hair.

"And it worked," he said thoughtfully. "It didn't just bind you, it bound you tight enough for you to draw a line through him?"

"That's why he left," I said, surprised I could still feel the pain.

"Your blood kindled the spell fully. . . ." Speculation was thick in his goat eyes as he looked at me from over his glasses. He drew my hand up, and though I tried to wiggle free of him, he licked the blood from my finger with a cold, tingling sensation. "So subtly scented," he breathed, his eyes never leaving mine. "Like perfumed air your lover has walked through."

"Let go," I said, pushing at him.

"You should be dead," he said, his voice full of wonder. "How is it that you're still alive?"

Jaw clenched, I worked at his grip on me, trying to get my fingers between him and my wrist. "I work hard at it." With a gasp, I fell back as he released his hold.

"You work hard at it." Smiling, he took a step back and gave me a once-over. "The mad have a grace all their own. I must go start a study group."

Frightened, I hunched over my wrist and held it.

"And I will have the likes of you as my own, Rachel Mariana Morgan. Count on it."

"I'm not going into the ever-after," I said tightly. "You'll have to kill me first."

"You don't have a choice," he intoned, chilling me. "You tap a line when the sun is down, and I'll find you. You can't make the circle that can keep me out. If you aren't on holy ground, I'll beat you silly and drag you into the ever-after. And from there, you will not escape."

"Try it," I threatened, reaching behind me to find the meat-tenderizing hammer hanging on the overhead rack. "You can't touch me unless you go solid, and it's going to hurt, red man."

Brow furrowed in concern, Al hesitated. The thought flitted through me that it must be like swatting at a wasp. Timing is everything.

Ceri was wearing a smile I didn't understand. "Algaliarept," she said softly. "You made a mistake. She found a loophole in your contract, and now you'll accept it and leave Rachel Mariana Morgan alone. If you don't, I'm going to start a school on holding line energy."

The demon's face went blank. "Ah, Ceri? Wait a moment, love."

Hammer in hand, I backed up until her bubble was cold at my back. Her hand reached out, and I jumped when she pulled me in, her circle flashing up almost before I knew it had fallen. My shoulders eased at the shimmer of black between us and Al. There was only the faintest glimmer of pale blue from her damaged aura visible through the smut Al had left on her. I patted her hand as she gave me a relieved, sideways hug. "Is that a problem?" I asked, not understanding why Al was so upset.

Ceri was positively smug. "I escaped him knowing how. He'll get in trouble for it. Big trouble. I'm surprised he hasn't been called up on it yet. But then, no one knows." She turned her mocking green eyes on Al. "Yet."

I felt an odd stab of alarm as I took in the savage satisfaction on her. She had known this all along, simply waiting until the information could best be used. The woman was more contriving than Trent, and she didn't seem to have a problem gambling with people's lives, either, mine included. Thank God she was on my side. *She was, wasn't she?*

Al raised a protesting hand. "Ceri, we can talk about this."

"In a week," she said confidently, "there won't be a ley line witch in Cincinnati that won't know how to be their own familiar. In a year, the world will be closed to you and your kind, and *you* will have to answer for it."

"Is it that big of a deal?" I asked as Al adjusted his glasses and shifted from foot to foot. It was cold away from the vent, and I shivered in my damp clothes.

"It's harder to lull a person into foolish choices if they can fight back," Ceri said. "If it gets out, their pool of potential familiars will be weak and undesirable in a matter of years."

My mouth dropped open. "Oh."

"I'm listening," Al said, sitting with an uncomfortable stiffness.

Hope so strong it was almost painful raced through me. "Take your demon mark off me, break the familiar bond, agree to leave me alone, and I won't tell."

Al snorted. "Not shy about asking for things, are you?"

Ceri gave my arm a warning squeeze and let go. "Let me do this. I've written most of his nonverbal contracts the last seven hundred years. Can I speak for you?"

I looked at her, her eyes alight and savage with her need for revenge. Slowly I set the hammer down. "Sure," I said, wondering just what, exactly, I had saved from the ever-after.

She pulled herself straighter, an official air falling over her. "I propose that Al will take his mark off you and break the familiar bonds between you both, in return for your solemn vow to not teach anyone how to hold line energy. Furthermore, you and your kin by blood or the laws of man shall remain free of reprisal from the demon known as Algaliarept and his agents in this world or the ever-after from now until the two worlds collide."

I tried to find enough spit to swallow, failing. I never would have thought of that.

"No," Al said firmly. "That's three things to my one, and I'll not lose my hold on the likes of her completely. I want a way to recoup my loss. And if she crosses the lines, I don't care what agreement we have, she's mine."

"Can we force him?" I said softly. "I mean, we do have him over a barrel?"

Al chuckled. "I could call Newt in to arbitrate if you like. . . ."

Ceri went pale. "No." Taking a steadying breath, she looked at me, her confidence cracked but not shattered. "What of the three can you bear to keep?"

I thought of my mother and my brother Robbie. Nick. "I want him to break the familiar bonds," I said, "and I want him to leave me and my kin by blood or law alone. I'll keep the demon mark and settle up later."

Algaliarept brought his foot up and propped his ankle atop a bent knee. "Clever, clever witch," he agreed. "If she breaks her word, she forfeits her soul."

Ceri's eyes went serious. "Rachel, if you teach *anyone* how to hold line energy, your soul belongs to Algaliarept. He can pull you into the ever-after at his will and you are his. Do you understand?"

I nodded, believing for the first time that I might see the sunrise again. "What happens if he breaks his word?"

"If he harms you or your kin—by his own volition—Newt will put Algaliarept in a bottle and you have a genie. It's standard boilerplate, but I'm glad you asked."

My eyes widened. I looked from Al to her. "No shit?"

She smiled at me, her hair floating as she tucked it behind an ear. "No shit."

Al harrumphed, and we jerked our attentions back to him. "What about you?" he said, clearly annoyed. "What do you want for keeping your mouth shut?"

The satisfaction of getting something back from her former captor and tormentor was in Ceri's eyes. "You will take back the stain on my soul that I took in your stead, and you will not seek reprisal against me or my kin in body or law from now until the two worlds collide."

"I'm not taking back a thousand years of curse imbalance," Al said indignantly. "That's why you were my damn familiar." He put both feet on the floor and leaned forward. "But I won't have it said I'm not agreeable. You keep the smut, but I'll let you teach one person how to hold line energy." A smile, contriving and satisfied, filled his unholy eyes. "One child. A girl child. Your daughter. And if she tells anyone, her soul is forfeit to me. Immediately."

Ceri paled, and I didn't understand. "She can tell one of her daughters, and so on," she countered, and Al smiled.

"Done." He stood. The glow of ever-after energy hovered about him like a shadow. Lacing his fingers together, he cracked his knuckles. "Oh, this is grand. This is good."

I looked at Ceri in wonder. "I thought he'd be upset," I said softly.

She shook her head, clearly worried. "He still has a hold on you. And he's counting on one of my kin to forget the seriousness of the arrangement and make a mistake."

"The familiar bonds," I insisted, glancing at the dark window. "He breaks them now?"

"The time of dissolution was never stated," Al said. He was touching the things he had brought into my kitchen, making them disappear in a smear of ever-after.

Ceri drew herself up. "It was tacitly implied. Break your hold, Algaliarept."

He looked over his glasses at her, smiling when he put a hand before and behind him and made a mocking bow. "It is a small thing, Ceridwen Merriam Dulciate. But you can't think less of me for trying."

Humming, he adjusted his frock. A bowl cluttered with bottles and silver implements appeared on the island counter. There was a book atop it all, small with a handwritten title, the script elegant and looping. "Why is he so happy?" I whispered.

Ceri shook her head, the tips of her hair moving after her head stopped. "I've only seen him like this when he discovers a secret. I'm sorry, Rachel. You know something that makes him very happy."

Swell.

Holding the book at reading height, he rifled through it, a scholarly air about him. "I can break a familiar bond as easy as snapping your neck. You, though, will have to do it the hard way; I'm not going to waste a stored curse on you. And since I'll not have you knowing how to break familiar bonds, we will add a little something. . . . Here it is. Lilac wine. It starts with lilac wine." His eyes met mine over the book. "For you."

A flash of cold went through me as he beckoned me out of the circle, a small, smoky purple bottle appearing behind his long fingers.

I took a quick breath. "You'll break the bonds and leave?" I said. "Nothing extra?"

"Rachel Mariana Morgan," he admonished. "Do you think so little of me?"

I glanced at Ceri, and she nodded for me to go. Trusting her, not Al, I stepped forward. She broke the circle as I did, setting it in place immediately behind me.

He uncorked the bottle, pouring out a glimmering drop of amethyst into a tiny cut crystal cup the size of my thumb. Putting a gloved finger to his thin lips, he extending it. Grimacing, I took it. My heart pounded. I had no choice.

Coming close with an eagerness I didn't trust, he showed me the open book. It was in Latin, and he pointed at a handwritten set of instructions. "See this word?" he said.

I took a breath. "*Umb—*"

"Not yet!" Al shouted, making me start, heart pounding. "Not until the wine coats your tongue, stupid. My god, you think you'd never twisted a curse before!"

"I'm not a ley line witch!" I exclaimed, my voice harsher than it probably should be.

Al's eyebrows rose. "You could be." His eyes went to the glass in my grip. "Drink it."

I glanced at Ceri. At her encouragement, I let the tiny amount pass my lips. It was sweet, making my tongue tingle. I could feel it seeping into me, relaxing my muscles. Al tapped the book, and I looked down. *"Umbra,"* I said, holding the drop on my tongue.

The wild sweetness went sour. "Auck," I said, leaning forward to spit it out.

"Swallow . . ." Al warned softly, and I started when he clamped a hand under my chin and tilted my head back so I couldn't open my mouth.

Eyes tearing, I swallowed. My pounding heart echoed in my ears. Al leaned closer, his eyes going black as he loosened his grip on me and my head drooped. My muscles went loose and watery, and when he let go of me, I fell to the floor.

He didn't even try to catch me, and I landed in a pained crumple. My head hit the floor and I took a quick breath. Closing my eyes, I gathered myself, wedging my palms under me and sitting up. "Thanks a hell of a lot for the warning," I said angrily, looking up and not finding him.

Confused, I stood to find Ceri sitting at the table with her head in her hands and her bare feet tucked under her. The fluorescent light was off, and a single white candle sent a soft glow into the gloom of a cloudy dawn. I stared at the window. *The sun was up? I must have passed out.* "Where is he?" I breathed, blanching when I saw it was almost eight.

She pulled her head up, shocking me with how weary she seemed. "You don't remember?"

My stomach rumbled, and there was an uneasy lightness to it. "No. He's gone?"

She turned to face me squarely. "He took back his aura. You took back yours. You broke the bond with him. You cried and called him a son of a bitch and told him to leave. He did—after he struck you so hard you lost consciousness."

I felt my jaw, then the back of my head. It felt about the same: really, really bad. I was damp and cold, and I got up, clasping my arms around me. "Okay." I felt my ribs, deciding nothing was broken. "Anything else I ought to know?"

"You drank an entire carafe of coffee in about twenty minutes."

That might explain the shakes. It had to be that. Outsmarting demons was becoming old hat. I sat beside Ceri, exhaling in a long breath. Ivy would be home soon. "You like lasagna?"

A smile blossomed over her. "Oh, yes, please."

Twenty-four

My sneakers were silent on the flat carpet of Trent's back hallways. Both Quen and Jonathan were with me, leaving me trying to decide if they were escort or prison guard. We had already woven through the Sunday-silent public areas of his offices and conference rooms that Trent hid his illegal activities behind. Publicly, Trent controlled a good portion of the transportation that ran through Cincinnati, coming in from all directions and leaving the same: railways, roadways, and even a small municipal airport.

Privately, Trent ran a good deal more, using those same transportation systems to get his illegal genetic products out and expanding his Brimstone distribution. That Saladan was cutting into his business in his hometown probably cheesed the man off to no end. It was a finger in the air if anything was. And tonight ought to be an education as Trent either broke that finger off and jammed it into one of Saladan's convenient orifices or took a hit. I didn't like Trent, but I'd keep him alive if it was the latter.

Though I don't know why, I thought as I followed Quen. It was barren down here, lacking even the institutional holiday decorations that graced the front. The man was slime. He had hunted me down like an animal the time he caught me stealing evidence from his secondary office, and my face warmed when I realized we were in the hallway that led to that very room.

A half step ahead of me, Quen was tense, dressed in his vaguely uniformlike black body stocking. He had a snug black and green jacket on over it today, making him look like Scotty might beam him up at any moment. My hair brushed my neck, and I purposely shifted my head to feel the tips tickle my shoulders. I had gotten it cut that afternoon to match the chunk Al had taken out, and the cream rinse the stylist had used wasn't doing much to tame it.

My garment bag with the outfit Kisten had picked out for me was over my shoulder, back from the cleaners. I had even remembered the jewelry and boots. I wasn't going to put them on until I knew I was taking this run. I suspected Trent might have other ideas—and my jeans and sweatshirt with the Howlers' logo looked out of place beside Jonathan's tailored elegance.

The distasteful man hung an irritating three steps behind us. He had met us at the steps of Trent's main building and remained a silent, accusing, professionally cold presence since. The man was six-ten if he was a foot, his features pointy and sharp. An aristocratic, hawklike nose gave him an air of smelling something offensive. His eyes were a cold blue, and his carefully styled black hair was graying. I hated him, and I was trying really hard to overlook that he had tormented me when I was a mink trapped in Trent's office for three unreal days.

Warming at the memory, I took off my coat as we walked, struggling, as neither man offered to take my garment bag. There was a definite moistness to the air the farther back we went. Faint to the point of being almost subliminal was the sound of running water, piped in from who knew where. My steps slowed when I recognized the doorway to Trent's secondary office. Behind me, Jonathan stopped. Quen continued without pause, and I hurried to catch up.

Jonathan clearly wasn't pleased. "Where are you taking her?" he asked belligerently.

Quen's steps grew stiff. "To Trenton." He never turned around or changed his pace.

"Quen . . ." Jonathan's voice was thick in warning. I glanced mockingly back, pleased to see his long wrinkled face showing worry rather than his perpetual stuck-up sneer. Brow furrowed, Jonathan hastened forward as we halted before the arched wooden door at the end of the hall. The overly tall man pushed in front, placing a hand atop the heavy metal latch as Quen reached for it. "You aren't taking her in there," Jonathan warned.

I shifted my garment bag in a sound of sliding nylon, my eyes going from one to the other as the political currents passed between them. Whatever was behind the door was good.

The smaller, more dangerous man narrowed his eyes, and the

pox scars went white in his suddenly red face. "She is going to keep him alive tonight," he said. "I'm not going to make her change and wait for him in a secondary office like a paid whore."

Jonathan's blue eyes went even more determined. My pulse quickened, and I stepped out from between them. "Move," Quen intoned, his surprisingly deep voice resonating through me.

Flustered, Jonathan stepped back. Quen pulled it open, the muscles in his back tensing. "Thank you," he said insincerely as the door swung out, slow with inertia.

My lips parted; the door was a freaking six inches thick! The sound of running water chattered out, accompanied by the scent of wet snow. It wasn't cold, though, and I peered past Quen's narrow shoulders to see a soft mottled carpet and a wall paneled in a dark wood that had been oiled and rubbed until it glistened with golden depths. *This,* I thought as I followed Quen in, *had to be Trent's private quarters.*

The short hallway immediately expanded into a second-story walkway. My feet stopped as I looked out over the large room below us. It was impressive, maybe 130 feet long, half as much wide, and twenty feet tall. We had come out on the second floor, which hugged the ceiling. Below, amid the rich carpet and woods, were casually placed seating arrangements of couches, chairs, and coffee tables. Everything was in soft earth tones, accented with maroon and black. A fireplace the size of a fire truck took up one wall, but what drew my attention was the floor-to-ceiling window that stretched the entirety of the wall across from me, letting in the dusky light of early evening.

Quen touched my elbow, and I started down the wide carpeted stairs. I kept one hand on the banister since I couldn't look away from the window, fascinated. Window, not windows, as it seemed to be one plate of glass. I didn't think glass that large was structurally sound, but there it was, looking as if it was only a few millimeters thick with no distortion. It was as if nothing was there.

"It's not plastic," Quen said softly, his green eyes on the view. "It's ley line energy."

My eyes jerked to his, reading the truth in his eyes. Seeing my wonder, a faint smile edged his Turn-scarred features. "It's everyone's first question," he said, showing how he knew where my thoughts had been. "Sound and air are the only things to pass through."

"It must have cost a fortune," I said, wondering how they got the usual red haze of ever-after out of it. Beyond it was a stunning vista of Trent's private, snow-slumped gardens. A crag of stone rose almost as high as the roof, a waterfall cascading over it to leave thickening bands of ice to glint in the last of the day's light. The water pooled into a natural-looking basin that I would have bet wasn't, turning into a stream that meandered through the well-established evergreens and shrubs until it vanished.

A deck gray with age and swept clear of snow stretched between the window and the landscaping. As I slowly descended to the lower level, I decided the round disk of cedar flush with the deck and leaking steam was probably a hot tub. Nearby was a sunken area with seating for backyard parties. I had always thought Ivy's grill with its gleaming chrome and huge burners was over the top, but whatever Trent had was probably obscene.

My feet found the first floor, and my gaze dropped to my feet as it suddenly seemed I was walking on loam instead of carpet. "Nice," I breathed, and Quen indicated that I should wait at the nearest gathering of chairs.

"I'll tell him," the security officer said. He shot Jonathan what I thought was a warning look before he retraced his steps to the second floor to vanish into an unseen area of the house.

I laid my coat and garment bag on a leather couch and made a slow spin on my heel. Now that I was downstairs, the fireplace looked even bigger. It wasn't lit, and I thought I could probably stand up in the hearth without stooping. At the opposite end of the room was a low stage with built-in amps and a light display. A nice-sized dance floor spread before it, surrounded by cocktail tables.

Hidden and cozy under the shelter of the second-story overhang was a long bar, the well-oiled wood and chrome gleaming. There were more tables here, bigger and lower. Huge planters full of dark green foliage that could flourish in the dimmer light surrounded them to give a measure of privacy that the large open floor plan lacked.

The noise from the waterfall had quickly retreated into an unnoticed background babble, and the stillness of the room soaked into me. There were no attendants, no one moving through the room on other business, not even one holiday candle or dish of sweets. It was as if the room was caught under a storybook spell, waiting to be woken. I didn't think the room had been used for what it was designed for since Trent's father died. Eleven years was a long time to be silent.

Feeling peace in the quiet of the room, I took a slow breath and turned to find Jonathan eyeing me with obvious distaste. The faint tension in his jaw sent my eyes to where Quen had vanished. A faint smile quirked the corner of my mouth. "Trent doesn't know you two cooked this up, does he?" I said. "He thinks Quen is going with him tonight."

Jonathan said nothing, the twitch in his eye telling me I was right. Smirking, I dropped my shoulder bag to the floor beside the couch. "I bet Trent could throw a hell of a party," I prompted, hoping for something. Jonathan was silent, and I wove past a low coffee table to stand with my hands on my hips to look out the "window."

My breath made the sheet of ever-after ripple. Unable to resist, I touched it. Gasping, I jerked my hand back. An odd, drawing sensation pulled through me, and I clutched my hand within the other as if I'd been burned. It was cold. The sheet of energy was so cold that it burned. I looked behind me to Jonathan, expecting to see him smirking, but he was staring at the window, his long face slack in surprise.

My gaze followed his, my stomach tightening as I realized the window wasn't clear anymore, but swirling with amber shades of gold. Damn. It had taken on the color of my aura. Clearly Jonathan hadn't expected this. My hand ran through my short hair. "Ah . . . Oops."

"What did you do to the window?" he exclaimed.

"Nothing." I took a guilty step back. "I just touched it, that's all. Sorry."

Jonathan's hawklike features took on more ugliness. Steps long and jerky, he strode to me. "You hack. Look what you did to the window! I will not allow Quen to entrust Mr. Kalamack's safety to you tonight."

My face warmed, and finding an easy outlet for my embarrassment, I let it turn to anger. "This wasn't my idea," I snapped. "And I said I was sorry about the window. You should be lucky I'm not suing for pain and suffering."

Jonathan took a loud breath. "If he comes to any harm because of you, I'll—"

Anger flashed through me, fed by the memory of three days in hell as he tormented me. "Shut up," I hissed. Ticked that he was taller than me, I stepped up onto a nearby coffee table. "I'm not in a cage anymore," I said, keeping enough presence of mind not to poke him in the chest with a finger. His face went startled, then choleric. "The only thing between your head and my foot becoming real close and personal right now is my questionable professionalism. And if you *ever* threaten me again, I'll slam you halfway across the room before you can say number-two pencil. Got it, you tall freak of nature?"

Frustrated, he clenched his long thin hands tight.

"Go ahead, elf-boy," I seethed, feeling the line energy I had spindled in my head earlier almost spill over to fill my body. "Give me a reason."

The sound of a closing door jerked our attentions to the second-story walkway. Jonathan visibly hid his anger and took a step back. Suddenly I felt really stupid on top of the table. Trent came to a startled halt above us in a dress shirt and pants, blinking. "Rachel Morgan?" he said softly to Quen, standing beside and a little behind him. "No. This isn't acceptable."

Trying to scrape something from the situation, I threw one hand extravagantly into the air. Putting the other on my hip, I posed like a prop girl showing off a new car. "Ta-da!" I said brightly, very conscious of my jeans, sweatshirt, and the new haircut I wasn't particularly fond of. "Hi, Trent. I'm your baby-sitter tonight. Where do your folks hide the good booze?"

Trent's brow furrowed. "I don't want her there. Put on your suit. We leave in an hour."

"No, Sa'han."

Trent had turned to walk away, but he jerked to a stop. "Can I speak to you for a moment," he said softly.

"Yes, Sa'han," the smaller man murmured deferentially, not moving.

I hopped off the table. Did I know how to make a good first impression or what?

Trent frowned, his attention going from an unrepentant Quen to Jonathan's nervous stance. "You're both in on this," he said.

Jonathan laced his hands behind his back, subtly shifting himself another step from me. "I trust Quen's judgment, Sa'han," he said, his low voice rising clear in the empty room. "I do not, however, trust Ms. Morgan's."

Affronted, I huffed at him. "Go suck on a dandelion, Jon."

The man's lips twitched. I knew he hated the shortened name. Trent, too, wasn't happy. Glancing at Quen, he started down the stairway with a fast, even pace, half dressed in his dark designer suit and looking like a cover model for GQ. His wispy blond hair had been slicked back, and his shirt pulled slightly across his shoulders as he descended to the lower floor. The spring in his step and the glint in his eye told me more clearly than anything that elves were at their best the four hours around sunup and sundown.

A deep green tie was draped casually across the back of his neck, not yet fastened into place. God help me, but he looked good, everything anything of the female persuasion could ever want: young, handsome, powerful, confident. I wasn't pleased that I liked the way he looked, but there it was.

Question high in his expression, Trent shook his sleeves down and buttoned the cuffs with a preoccupied quickness as he came down the stairs. The top two buttons of his shirt were undone, making an intriguing sight. His head came up as he reached the lower landing, and he paused for a heartbeat when he saw the window.

"What happened to the ward?" he questioned.

"Ms. Morgan touched it." Jonathan had the smug glee of a six-year-old tattling on his older sibling. "I'd advise against Quen's plans. Morgan is unpredictable and dangerous."

Quen shot him a dark look that Trent missed since the man was buttoning the top of his shirt. "Lights full," Trent said, and I squinted when huge lights in the ceiling flickered on one by one to make it bright as day. My stomach clenched as I looked at the window. Crap. I had broken it but good. Even my streaks of red were in it, and I didn't like that the three of them would know I had that much tragedy in my past. But at least Al's black was gone. *Thank God.*

Trent came closer, his smooth face unreadable. The clean smell of aftershave drifted from him as he stopped. "It did this when you touched it?" he asked, his gaze going from my new haircut to the window.

"I, uh, yeah. Quen said it was a sheet of ever-after. I thought it was a modified protection circle."

Quen ducked his head and stepped closer. "It's not a protection circle, it's a ward. Your aura and the aura of the person who set it up must resonate to a similar frequency."

His young features creased in worry, Trent squinted at it. An unshared thought passed through him, and his fingers twitched. I eyed the tell, knowing he thought it more than odd, and significant. It was a notion that solidified when Trent glanced at Quen and something of a security nature passed between them. Quen made a small shrug, and Trent took a slow breath.

"Have someone from maintenance look at it," Trent said. Tugging at his collar, he added loudly, "Lights revert." I froze when the glare vanished and my eyes tried to adjust.

"I don't agree with this," Trent said in the soothing dimness, and Jonathan smiled.

"Yes, Sa'han," Quen said softly. "But you will take Morgan or you will not be going."

Well, well, well, I thought, as the rims of Trent's ears went red. I hadn't known Quen had the authority to tell Trent what to do. Clearly, though, it was a right seldom invoked, and never without consequences. Beside me, Jonathan looked positively ill.

"Quen . . ." Trent started.

The security officer took a firm stance, looking over Trent's shoulder at nothing with his hands laced behind his back. "My vampire bite makes me unreliable, Sa'han," he said, and I winced at his obvious pain of openly admitting it. "I'm no longer sure of my effectiveness."

"Damn it, Quen," Trent exclaimed. "Morgan has been bitten, too. What makes her any more sure than you?"

"Ms. Morgan has been living with a vampire for seven months and hasn't succumbed," Quen said stiffly. "She has developed a series of defensive strategies for combating a vamp trying to bespell her. I haven't, yet, and so I'm no longer reliable in questionable situations."

His scarred face was tight with shame, and I wished Trent would shut up and just go with it. This confession was killing Quen.

"Sa'han," he said evenly. "Morgan can protect you. I cannot. Don't ask me to do this."

I fidgeted, wishing I was somewhere else. Jonathan glared at me as if it were my fault. Trent's face was pained and worried, and Quen flinched when he put a comforting hand upon his shoulder. With a reluctant slowness, Trent let his hand fall away. "Get her a corsage and see if there's something suitable for her to wear in the green suite. She looks about the same size."

The flash of relief that crossed Quen was replaced by a deeper self-doubt that looked wrong and worrisome. Quen appeared broken, and I wondered what he was going to do if he felt he couldn't protect Trent anymore. "Yes, Sa'han," he murmured. "Thank you."

Trent's gaze fell on me. I couldn't tell what he was thinking, and I felt cold and uneasy. The feeling strengthened when Trent nodded once to Quen and said, "Do you have a moment?"

"Of course, Sa'han."

The two of them headed into one of the unseen downstairs rooms to leave me with Jonathan. The unhappy man gave me a look rife with disgust. "Leave your dress here," he said. "Follow me."

"I have my own outfit, thanks," I said picking up my shoulder bag, coat, and my garment bag from where I had left them and following him to the stairs. At the foot of the stairs, Jonathan turned. His cold eyes traveled over me and my garment bag, and he sniffed patronizingly.

"It's a nice outfit," I said, warming when he snickered.

He took the steps quickly, forcing me to scramble to keep up. "You can look like a whore if you like," he said. "But Mr. Kalamack has a reputation." He eyed me over his shoulder as he reached the top. "Hurry up. You don't have much time to get presentable."

Seething, I took two steps for every one of his as he cut a sharp right into a large common room holding a comfortable, more normal-sized living room. There was an efficiency at the back, and what looked like a breakfast nook. One of Trent's live-shot video feeds showed a second view of the dim garden. Several heavy-looking doors opened up onto the area, and I was guessing this was where Trent did his "normal" living. I became sure of it when Jonathan opened the first one to show a small sitting room opening onto an extravagant bedroom. It was decorated entirely in shades of green and gold, managing to look wealthy without dipping into gaudy. Another fake window past the bed showed the forest, dusky and gray with twilight.

I assumed that the other doors led to other such suites of rooms. All the wealth and privilege couldn't hide that the entire area was set up to be very defensible. There probably wasn't a real window in the place other than the one downstairs covered in ley line energy.

"Not that way," Jonathan all but barked as I took a step to the bedroom. "That's the bedroom. Stay out of it. The changing room is over here."

"Sorry," I said sarcastically, then hitched my garment bag higher atop my shoulder and followed him into a bathroom. At least I thought it was a bathroom. There were so many plants it was hard to tell. And it was the size of my kitchen. The multitude of mirrors reflected the lights that Jonathan flicked on until I was squinting. The glare seemed to bother him, too, since he worked the bank of switches until the multitude of bulbs reduced to one over the commode and one over the single sink and expansive counter. My shoulders eased in the dimmer light.

"This way," Jonathan said as he passed through an open archway. I followed, stopping short just inside. I suppose it was a closet, as there were clothes in it—expensive-looking women's clothes—but the room was huge. A rice-paper screen took up one corner with a vanity against the back of it. A small table with two chairs was tucked to the right of the door. To the left was a trifold mirror. All it needed was a wet bar. Damn. I was *so* in the wrong line of work.

"You can change here," Jonathan said through his nose. "Try not to touch anything."

Ticked, I dropped my coat on a chair and hung my garment bag on a convenient hook. Shoulders tight, I unzipped the bag and turned, knowing Jonathan was judging me. But my eyebrows rose at his surprised look while he took in the outfit Kisten had put together for me. Then his expression returned to its usual ice. "You aren't wearing that," he said flatly.

"Shove it up your ass, Jon," I snapped.

Movements stilted, he strode to a set of sliding mirror doors, opening them to pull out a black dress as if he knew exactly where it was. "You will wear *this,*" he said, thrusting it at me.

"I'm not wearing that." I tried to make my voice cold, but the dress was exquisite, made of a soft fabric cut low down the back and flatteringly high in the front and around the neck. It would fall to my ankles to make me look tall and elegant. Swallowing back my envy, I said, "It's cut too low in back to hide my splat gun. And it's too tight to run in. That's a lousy dress."

His extended arm dropped, and it was all I could do to keep from wincing when the beautiful fabric puddled on the carpet. "You pick one out, then."

"Maybe I will." I stepped hesitantly to the closet.

"The evening dresses are in that one," Jonathan said, sounding patronizing.

"Duh . . ." I mocked, but my eyes widened and my hand went out to touch. God help me, they were all beautiful, each having an understated elegance. They were organized by color, and matching shoes and purses were carefully arranged underneath. Some had hats in the rack above them. My shoulders slumped when I touched a flaming red dress, but Jonathan's whispered, "whore" encouraged me to keep moving. My eyes left it reluctantly.

"So, Jon," I said as he watched me shuffle through the dresses. "Either Trent is a cross-dresser or he enjoys bringing size eight tall women to his house wearing evening gowns and sending them home in rags." I eyed him. "Or does he just knock them up and knock them off?"

Jonathan's jaw clenched and his face flushed. "These are for Miss Ellasbeth."

"Ellasbeth?" My hands fell from a purple dress that would cost me a month of runs. *Trent had a girlfriend?* "Oh, hell no! I'm not wearing another woman's dress without asking."

He snickered, his long face taking on a hint of annoyance. "They belong to Mr. Kalamack. If he says you can wear them, you can."

Not fully reassured, I turned back to my search. But all my apprehensions vanished when my hands touched a soft filmy gray. "Oh, look at this," I breathed, pulling the top and skirt from the closet and holding them triumphantly up, as if he gave a flying flip.

Jonathan looked from the cabinet of scarves, belts, and purses he had just opened. "I thought we threw that out," he said, and I made a face, knowing he was trying to make me feel like it was ugly. It wasn't. The tight bustier and matching skirt were elegant, the fabric soft to the touch and thick enough for winter without being binding. It was a shimmering black once I got it into the light. The skirt went to the floor, but was split in a multitude of narrow bands from the knees so it would flutter about my ankles. And with the slits that high, my splat gun in its thigh holster would be an easy reach. It was perfect.

"Is it suitable?" I asked as I took it to the hanger and hung it over my outfit. I looked up when he was silent, finding his face twisted.

"It will do." He raised his watchband to his wrist, pushing a button and speaking into the spiffy-keen communicator I remembered was there. "Make the corsage black and gold," he muttered. Glancing at the door, he added to me, "I'll get the matching jewelry from the safe."

"I have my own jewelry," I said, then hesitated, not wanting to see what my imitation stuff would look like against fabric such as this. "But okay," I amended, unable to meet his eyes.

Jonathan harrumphed. "I'll send someone to do your makeup," he added as he walked out.

That was downright insulting. "I can touch up my own makeup, thank you," I said loudly after him. I was wearing mundane makeup atop the complexion spell that hid the remnants of my still healing black eye, and I didn't want anyone to touch it.

"Then I only have to get the stylist to do something with your hair," came echoing back.

"My hair is fine!" I shouted. I looked in one of the mirrors, touching the loose curls starting to frizz. "It's fine," I added, softer. "I just had it done." But all that I heard was Jonathan's sniggering laughter and the sound of a door opening.

"I'm not going to leave her alone in Ellasbeth's room," came Quen's gravely voice in answer to Jonathan's mutter. "She'd kill her."

My eyebrows rose. Did he mean I would kill Ellasbeth, or Ellasbeth would kill me? That kind of detail was important.

I turned when Quen's silhouette took up the doorway to the bathroom. "You baby-sitting me?" I said as I grabbed my slip and nylons and took the black dress behind the screen.

"Miss Ellasbeth isn't aware you're on the grounds," he said. "I didn't think it necessary to tell her, as she's returning home, but she's been known to change her plans without notice."

I eyed the rice paper between Quen and me, then kicked off my sneakers. Feeling vulnerable and short, I shimmied out of my clothes, folding them instead of letting them sit in a crumpled heap as I usually did. "You're really big on that need-to-know kick, aren't you?" I said, and I heard him speak softly to someone who had just come in. "What is it you aren't telling me?"

The second, unseen person left. "Nothing," Quen said shortly.

Yeah, right.

The dress was lined in silk, and I stifled a moan as it eased over me. I looked down at the hem, deciding that it would fall right when I put my boots on. Brow pinching, I hesitated. My boots weren't going to work. I'd have to hope Ellasbeth was a size eight shoe and that tonight's butt kicking could be accomplished in heels. The bustier gave me a smidgen of trouble, and I finally gave up trying to zip it the last inch.

I gave myself one last look, tucking my complexion amulet between me and my waistband. Splat gun in my thigh holster, I came round the screen. "Zip me up, honey?" I said lightly, earning what I thought was a seldom-given smile from Quen. He nodded, and I showed him my back. "Thanks," I said when he finished.

He turned to the table and chairs, stooping to pick up a corsage that hadn't been there when I went behind the screen. It was a black orchid bound with a gold and green ribbon. Straightening, he took the pin from it, hesitating as he looked at the narrow strap. Right off I knew his dilemma, and I wasn't going to help him a bit.

Quen's scarred face pinched. Eyes on my dress, his lips pressed together. "Excuse me," he said, reaching forward. I froze, knowing he wouldn't touch me unless he had to. There was enough fabric to attach it, but he would have to put his fingers between that pin and me. I exhaled, collapsing my lungs to give him a smidgen more room.

"Thank you," he said softly.

The back of his hand was cold, and I stifled a shiver. Trying not to fidget, I sent my attention to the ceiling. A faint smile crossed me, growing as he got the orchid fastened and stepped away with an exhalation of relief.

"Something funny, Morgan?" he said sourly.

I dropped my head, watching him from around my drooping bangs. "Not really. You reminded me of my dad—for a minute there."

Quen adopted a look both disbelieving and questioning. Shaking my head, I grabbed my shoulder bag from the table and went to sit at the vanity against the screen. "See, we had this big seventh-grade dance, and I had a strapless dress," I said as I brought out my makeup. "My dad wouldn't let my date pin the flower on, so he did it himself." My focus blurred, and I crossed my legs. "He missed my prom."

Quen remained standing. I couldn't help but notice he had put himself where he could see me and the door both. "Your father was a good man. He'd be proud of you tonight."

Quick and painful, my breath caught. Slowly I let it out, my hands resuming their primping. I really wasn't surprised Quen had known him—they were the same age—but it hurt nonetheless. "You knew him?" I couldn't stop myself from asking.

The look he gave me through the mirror was unreadable. "He died well."

Died well? God, what was it with these people?

Angry, I turned in my seat to see him directly. "He died in a cruddy little hospital room with dirt in the corners," I said tightly. "He was supposed to stay alive, damn it." My voice was even, but I knew it wouldn't stay that way. "He was supposed to be there when I got my first job, then lost it three days later after I slugged the boss's son when he tried to feel me up. He was supposed to be there when I graduated from high school and then college. He was supposed to be there to scare my dates into behaving so I wouldn't have to find my own way home from wherever the prick dumped me when he found I'd fight back. But he wasn't, was he? No. He died doing something with Trent's father, and no one has the balls to tell me what great thing it was that was worth screwing up my life for."

My heart pounded, and I stared at Quen's quiet, pox-scarred face. "You've had to be your own keeper for a long time," he said.

"Yeah." Lips pressed tight, I turned back to the mirror, my foot bobbing up and down.

"What doesn't kill you—"

"Hurts." I watched his reflection. "It hurts. It hurts a lot." My black eye throbbed under my higher blood pressure, and I reached to touch it. "I'm strong enough," I said bitterly. "I don't want to be any stronger. Piscary is a bastard, and if he gets out of prison, he's going to die twice." I thought of Skimmer, hoping she was as bad a lawyer as she was good a friend to Ivy.

Quen's feet shifted, but he didn't move. "Piscary?"

The question in his voice brought my gaze up. "He said he killed my dad. Did he lie to me?" *Need to know. Did I finally "need to know" according to Quen?*

"Yes and no." The elf's eyes flicked to the doorway.

I spun in the chair. He could tell me. I think he wanted to. "Well, which is it?"

Quen ducked his head and took a symbolic step back. "It's not my place."

Heart pounding, I stood, my hands clenched into fists. "What happened?" I demanded.

Again Quen looked toward the bathroom. A light flicked on and a beam spilled into the room to diffuse into nothing. An effeminate man's voice chattered seemingly to itself, filling the air with a bright presence. Jonathan answered back, and I looked at Quen in a panic, knowing he wouldn't say anything in front of him.

"It was my fault," Quen said softly. "They were working together. I should have been there, not your father. Piscary killed them as sure as if he had pulled the trigger."

Feeling unreal, I stepped close enough to see the sweat on him. It was obvious he had overstepped his bounds telling me even this much. Jonathan came in trailing a man dressed in tight black and shiny boots. "Oh!" the small man exclaimed, hustling to the vanity with his fishing-tackle boxes. "It's red! I *adore* red hair. And it's natural, too. I can tell from here. Come sit, dove. The things I can do for you! You won't recognize yourself."

I spun to Quen. Tired eyes haunted looking, he stepped away, leaving me breathless. I stood, staring, wanting more, knowing I wouldn't get it. Damn it, Quen's timing sucked, and I forced my hands to remain at my side instead of throttling him.

"Sit your fanny down!" the stylist exclaimed when Quen inclined his head at me and walked out. "I only have half an hour!"

Frowning, I gave Jonathan's mocking expression a tired look, then sat down in the chair and tried to explain to the man that I liked it the way it was, and could he just give it a quick brush through? But he hissed and shushed me, pulling out bottle after bottle of spray and odd-looking instruments whose use I couldn't even guess. I knew it was a battle already lost.

Twenty-five

I settled into the seat of Trent's limo, crossing my legs and arranging one of the narrow panels of my skirt to cover my knee. The shawl I was using instead of a coat slid down my back, and I let it stay there. It smelled like Ellasbeth, and my subtler perfume couldn't compete.

The shoes were a half size too small, but the dress fit perfectly: the bustier tight but not confining, and the skirt riding high on my waist. My thigh holster was as subtle as dandelion fluff, completely unseen. Randy had styled my shorter hair up off my neck, binding it with thick gold wire and vintage beads into an elaborate coiffure that had taken the man twenty minutes of unending prattle to fix. But he was right. I felt completely unlike myself and *expe-e-e-e-ensive.*

This was the second limo I'd been in that week. Maybe it was a trend. If so, I could handle that. Jittery, I glanced at Trent staring out at the huge trees as we approached the gatehouse, their black trunks standing out against the snow. He seemed a thousand miles away, not even aware I was sitting next to him. "Takata's car is nicer," I said, breaking the silence.

Trent twitched, recovering smoothly. The reaction made him look as young as he was. "Mine's not a rental," he said.

I shrugged, foot jiggling as I looked out the smoked window.

"Warm enough?" he asked.

"What? Oh. Yes, thank you."

Jonathan drove us past the guardhouse without slowing, the rising bar reaching its apex the second we passed under it. It closed equally fast. I fidgeted, checking my clutch purse for my charms, feeling for the press of my splat gun, and touching my hair. Trent was looking out the window again, lost in his own world, which had nothing to do with me.

"Hey, sorry about the window," I said, not liking the silence.

"I'll send you a bill if it can't be fixed." He turned to me. "You look nice."

"Thank you." I sent my eyes over his silk-lined wool suit. He wasn't wearing an overcoat, and it was tailored to show off every inch of him. His boutonniere was a tiny black bud rose, and I wondered if he had grown it himself. "You wash up good yourself."

He gave me one of his professional smiles, but there was a new glint to it, and I thought it might actually have a tinge of real warmth.

"The dress is beautiful," I added, wondering how I was going to get through tonight without resorting to talk about the weather. I leaned to tug my nylons straight.

"That reminds me." Trent twisted to dip a hand into a pocket. "These go with it." He held out his hand, dropping a heavy set of earrings into my palm. "There's a necklace, too."

"Thanks." I tilted my head to take out my simple hoops, dropping them into my clutch purse and snapping it closed. Trent's earrings were a series of interlocking circles, and heavy enough to be real gold. I worked them into place, feeling their unfamiliar weight.

"And the necklace . . ." Trent held it up, and my eyes widened. It was gorgeous, made of interlaced rings the size of my thumbnail and matching the earrings. They made a delicate lace panel, and I would have labeled it goth but for its richness. A wooden pendant in the shape of the Celtic rune for protection hung from the nadir, and I hesitated in my reach. It was beautiful, but I suspected its peekaboo lace would make me a veritable vampire slut.

And Celtic magic gave me the willies. It was a specialized art, much of it depending upon one's belief, not if you did the spell right or not. More of a religion than magic. I didn't like mixing religion and magic—it made for terribly strong forces when something unmeasurable mixed its will with that of the practitioner's intent, making the results not necessarily in line with what was expected. It was wild magic, and I preferred mine nicely scientific. If you invoke the help of a higher being, you can't complain when things don't go to your plan, but to its.

"Turn around," Trent said, and my eyes darted to his. "I'll put it on you. It has to be snug for it to look right."

I was not about to show Trent I was squeamish, and as protection charms were fairly reliable, I took the simple fake gold cord from around my neck and dropped it into my clutch bag with my earrings. I wondered if Trent knew what wearing this was saying, deciding he probably did and thought it was a big joke.

Tension tightened my shoulders as I gathered strands of hair that Randy had pulled for effect. The necklace settled about my neck in a heavy feeling of security, still warm from his pocket.

Trent's fingers touched me, and I yelped in surprise as a surge of ley line energy rose through me and into him. The car swerved and Trent's fingers jerked away. The necklace hit the carpeted floor with a tinkle of metal. Hand to my throat, I stared at him.

He had put himself into the corner. The amber light from the ceiling glinted to make shadows on him. Eyeing me with a look of annoyance, he scooted forward and scooped the necklace from the floor, jiggling it until it hung properly across one hand.

"Sorry," I said, heart pounding and my hand still covering my neck.

Trent frowned, meeting Jonathan's gaze in the rearview mirror before gesturing for me to turn back around. I did, very conscious of him behind me. "Quen said you've been working on your ley line skills," Trent said while he draped the metal over me again. "It took me a week to learn how to keep my familiar's energy from trying to equalize when I touched another practitioner. Of course I was three at the time, so I had an excuse."

His hands fell from me, and I settled into the supple cushions. His expression was smug, his usual professionalism gone. It wasn't any of his business that this was the first time I had tried to spindle line energy in me as a matter of convenience. I was ready to bag it. My feet hurt, and thanks to Quen, I wanted to go home, eat a carton of ice cream, and remember my dad.

"Quen knew my dad," I said sullenly.

"So I hear." He looked not at me but the passing view as we made our way into the city.

My breath came faster, and I shifted in my seat. "Piscary said he killed my dad. Quen implied there was more to it than that."

Trent crossed his legs and unbuttoned his suit coat. "Quen talks too much."

Tension pulled my stomach tight. "Our fathers were working together?" I prompted. "Doing what?"

His lip twitched, and he ran a hand across his hair to make

sure it was lying flat. From the driver's seat, Jonathan coughed in warning. *Right. Like his threats meant anything to me?*

Trent shifted in the seat to look at me, his face holding a shade of interest. "Ready to work with me?"

I cocked an eyebrow at him. *Work* with *me. Last time it was work* for *me.*

"No." I smiled though I wanted to step on his foot. "Quen seems to blame himself for my dad's death. I find that fascinating. Especially when Piscary claimed responsibility."

A sigh came from Trent. His hand went out to steady himself when we eased onto the interstate. "Piscary killed my father outright," he said. "Your father was bitten while trying to help him. Quen was supposed to be there, not your father. That's why Quen went to help you subdue Piscary. He felt he needed to take your father's place, seeing as he believes it was his fault your father wasn't there to help you himself."

My face went cold, and I pushed myself back into the leather seat. I had thought Trent had sent Quen to help me; Trent had nothing to do with it. But a niggling thought surfaced through my confusion. "But my father didn't die of a vampire bite."

"No," Trent said carefully, his eyes on the growing skyline. "He didn't."

"He died when his red blood cells started attacking his soft tissues," I prompted, waiting for more, but Trent's posture went closed. "That's all I'm getting, isn't it?" I said flatly, and the man gave me half a smile, charming and sly.

"My offer of employment is ever open, Ms. Morgan."

It was hard, but I managed to keep a somewhat pleasant expression on my face as I slumped in the seat. I suddenly felt like I was being lulled, lured into places that I once vowed I'd never go: places like working for Trent, sex with a vampire, crossing the street without looking. All of them you could get away with, but eventually you were going to get blasted by a bus. *What in hell was I doing in a limo with Trent?*

We had passed into the Hollows, and I sat up, taking more interest. The holiday lights were thick, primarily green, white, and gold. The silence stretched. "So-o-o, who is Ellasbeth?"

Trent shot me a poisonous look, and I smiled sweetly. "Not my idea," he said.

How very interesting, I thought. *I found a nerve. Wouldn't it be fun to stomp on it?* "Old girlfriend?" I guessed brightly. "Live-in? Ugly sister you hide in the basement?"

Trent's expression had returned to its professional emptiness, but his restless fingers were ever-moving. "I like your jewelry," he said. "Maybe I should have had Jonathan put it into the house safe while we were gone."

I put a hand to his necklace, feeling it warm from my body. "I was wearing crap, and you know it." Damn it, I had enough of his gold on me to make a set of false teeth for a horse.

"We can talk about Nick, then." Trent's soothing voice carried a derisive edge. "I'd much rather talk about Nick. It was Nick, wasn't it? Nick Sparagmos? He's moved out of the city, I hear, after you sent him into an epileptic seizure." Hands clasped at his knee, he gave me a telling look, pale eyebrows high. "What *did* you do to him? I never could find that out."

"Nick is fine." I pulled my hands down before they could play with my hair. "I'm watching his apartment while he's away on business." I looked out the window, reaching behind me to pull the shawl back up over my shoulders. He could sling mud better than the best rich-bitch at school. "We need to discuss what it is I'm supposed to be protecting you against."

From the driver's seat came Jonathan's snort. Trent, too, chuckled. "I'm not in need of protection," he said. "If I was, Quen would be here. You're a semifunctioning decoration."

Semifunctioning . . . "Yeah?" I shot back, wishing I could say I was surprised.

"Yeah," he said right back, the word sounding odd coming from him. "So sit where you're put and keep your mouth shut."

Face warming, I moved so that my knees almost touched his thigh. "Listen to me, Mr. Kalamack," I said sharply. "Quen is paying me good money to keep your ass above the grass, so don't leave the room without me and don't get into my line of sight with the bad guys. Got it?"

Jonathan turned into a parking lot, and I had to brace myself when he applied the brakes too sharply. Trent glanced at him, and I watched their gazes lock through the rearview mirror. Still angry, I looked out to find ugly piles of snow a good six feet high. We were down by the riverfront, and my shoulders tensed at the gambling boat with its stacks steaming slightly. Saladan's gambling boat? Again?

My thoughts went back to my night with Kisten and the guy in a tux who had taught me craps. *Shit.* "Hey, uh, do you know what Saladan looks like?" I asked. "Is he a witch?"

The hesitancy in my tone was probably what caught Trent's

attention, and while Jonathan parked in the long spot reserved for a car of this length, he eyed me. "He's a ley line witch. Black hair, dark eyes, my age. Why? Are you worried? You should be. He's better than you."

"No." *Crap. Or should I say craps?* Grabbing my clutch purse, I slumped back into the cushions when Jonathan opened the door and Trent got out with a grace that had to be practiced. A blast of cold air replaced him, making me wonder how Trent could stand there as if it was summer. I had a feeling I'd already met Saladan. *Idiot!* I berated myself. But showing Lee I wasn't afraid of him after his failed little black charm would be extremely satisfying.

Becoming eager for the encounter, I slid across the bench seat to the open door, jerking back when Jonathan slammed it in my face. "Hey!" I shouted, adrenaline making my head hurt.

The door opened, and Jonathan gave me a satisfied smirk. "Sorry, ma'am," he said.

Past him was Trent, a tired look on his face. Holding my borrowed shawl close, I watched Jonathan as I slid out. "Why, thank you, Jon," I said brightly, "you freaking bastard."

Trent ducked his head, hiding a smile. I jerked the shawl higher, and making sure I kept my line energy where it was supposed to be, I took Trent's arm so he could help me up the icy ramp. He stiffened to pull away, and I grabbed his arm with my free hand, pinching my purse between us. It was cold, and I wanted to get inside. "I'm wearing heels for you," I muttered. "The least you can do is make sure I don't fall on my can. Or are you afraid of me?"

Trent said nothing, his posture shifting into an uneasy acceptance as we went, step for step, across the parking lot. He turned to look over his shoulder at Jonathan, indicating that he should stay with the car, and I simpered at the tall unhappy man, giving him Erica's crooked-bunny-ear kiss good-bye. It was fully dark now, and the wind blew bits of snow against my legs, bare but for my nylons. Why hadn't I insisted on borrowing a coat? I wondered. This shawl was worthless. And it stank like lilac. I hated lilac.

"Aren't you cold?" I questioned, seeing Trent seemingly as warm as if it was July.

"No," he said, and I remembered Ceri walking in the snow with a similar tolerance.

"Must be an elf thing," I muttered, and he chuckled.

"Yup," he said, my eyes jerking to his at the casual word. They were bright with amusement, and I glanced at the beckoning ramp.

"Well, I'm frozen through," I grumbled. "Can we move a little faster?"

He quickened his pace, but I was still shivering by the time we got to the entry door. Trent solicitously held it for me, ushering me in ahead of him. Letting go of his arm, I went inside, my hands clasping my upper arms to try to warm myself. I gave the doorman a brief smile, and got a stoic, blank look. Taking my shawl off, I held it between two fingers to the coat attendant, wondering if I could conveniently leave it here—by accident, of course.

"Mr. Kalamack and Ms. Morgan," Trent said, ignoring the guestbook. "We're expected."

"Yes, sir." The doorman gestured for someone to take his place. "Right this way."

Trent offered me his arm. I hesitated, trying to read his quiet face and failing. Taking a breath, I linked my arm in his. As my fingers brushed the top of his hand, I made a conscious effort to maintain my level of line energy when I felt a slight pull from my chi. "Better," he said, his eyes searching the busy game room as we followed the doorman. "You're improving by leaps and bounds, Ms. Morgan."

"Shove it, Trent," I said, smiling at the people who looked up when we entered. His hand was warm under my fingers, and I felt like a princess. There was a lull in the noise, and when the conversations rose again, they had an excitement that couldn't be laid entirely at the feet of gambling.

It was warm, and the air pleasantly scented. The disk hanging over the center of the room seemed quiet, but I imagined if I bothered to look at it with my second sight that it would be pulsating with that ugly purple and black. I glanced at my reflection to see if my hair was behaving under the stylist's sprays and wires, glad the yellow of my black eye was still hidden behind the mundane makeup. Then I looked again.

Damn! I thought, slowing. Trent and I looked fantastic. No wonder people were staring. He was trim and debonair, and I was elegant in my borrowed dress with my hair up off my neck and bound with that heavy gold wire. Both of us were confident, both of us were smiling. But even as I thought we made the perfect couple, I realized that though we were together, each of us was alone. Our strengths were not dependent upon each other, and while that wasn't bad, it didn't lend itself to being a couple. We were simply standing next to each other looking good.

"What is it?" Trent asked, gesturing that I should go up the stairs ahead of him.

"Nothing." Gathering my slit skirt as best I could, I went up the narrow carpeted stairway after the doorman. The sound of gaming people went faint, turning into a background hum to stir my subconscious. A cheer rose, and I wished I could be down there, feeling my heart pound in the breathless wait to see what the dice would show.

"I thought they'd search us," Trent said softly so the man escorting us couldn't hear.

I shrugged. "For what? Did you see that big disk on the ceiling?" He glanced behind us, and I added, "It's a huge spell damper. Kind of like the charms I used to have on my cuffs before you burned them all to hell, but it affects the whole boat."

"Didn't you bring a weapon?" he whispered as we reached the second floor.

"Yes," I said through my teeth, smiling. "And I could shoot someone with it, but the potions won't take effect until whoever it is leaves the boat."

"What good is it then?"

"I don't kill people, Trent. Get over it." *Though I might make an exception for Lee.*

I saw his jaw tighten and relax. Our escort opened a narrow door, gesturing for me to enter. I stepped in, finding Lee looking pleasantly surprised as he brought his attention from the paperwork on his desk. I tried to keep my expression neutral, the memory of that man writhing on the street under a black charm aimed at me making me angry and ill all at the same time.

A tall woman stood behind him, leaning to breathe upon his neck. She was leggy and lean, dressed in a black jumpsuit with bell-bottom hems. The neckline went almost to her navel. Vamp, I decided, when her eyes dropped to my necklace and she smiled to show me small, pointy canines. My scar twinged, and my anger slowed. Quen wouldn't have stood a chance.

Eyes alight, Lee rose and tugged the coat of his tux straight. Physically pushing the vampire out of his way, he came out from around the desk. Trent entered, and his gaze became even more animated. "Trent!" he exclaimed, striding forward with his hands extended. "How are you, old man!"

I stepped back as Trent and Lee warmly clasped hands. *You've got to be kidding me.*

"Stanley," he said, smiling, and it finished falling into place. *Stanley, long for Lee.*

"Damn!" Lee said, pounding Trent on the back. "How long has it been? Ten years?"

Trent's smile flickered, his annoyance at that back slap nearly undetectable but for the slight tightening in his eyes. "Almost that. You look good. Still hitting the waves?"

Lee ducked his head, a roguish grin turning him into a scalawag despite him being in a tux. "Now and again. Not as much as I like. My damn knee has been giving me trouble. But you look good. Got some muscle on you now. Not that skinny boy trying to keep up with me."

Trent's eyes flicked to mine, and I gave him a mute look. "Thanks."

"Word is you're getting married."

Married? I was wearing his fiancée's dress? Oh, this was getting better and better.

Lee brushed his hair out of his eyes and sat against the desk. The vamp behind him started to rub his shoulders in a sultry, whore-bitch sort of a way. She hadn't taken her eyes off me, and I didn't like it. "Anyone I know?" Lee prompted, and Trent's jaw clenched.

"A beautiful young woman named Ellasbeth Withon," he said. "From Seattle."

"Ah." Brown eyes wide, Lee smiled as if he was laughing at Trent. "Congratulations?"

"You've met her," Trent said sourly, and Lee chuckled.

"I've heard of her." He made a pained face. "Am I invited to the wedding?"

I puffed impatiently. I had thought we came here to knock heads, not have a reunion. Ten years would put them in their late teens. College? And I didn't like being ignored, but I supposed that was standard for hired help. At least whore-bitch hadn't been introduced either.

"Of course," Trent said. "The invitations will go out as soon as she decides between the eight options she's narrowed it down to," he said dryly. "I'd ask you to be my best man, if I thought you'd ever get on a horse again."

Lee pulled himself off the desk and out of the vamp's reach. "No, no, no," he protested, going to a small cabinet and bringing out two glasses and a bottle. "Not again. Not with you. My God, what did you whisper into that beast's ear, anyway?"

Trent smiled, a real one this time, and took the offered shot glass. "Fair is fair, surfer dude," he said, and I blinked at the accent he affected. "Seeing as you almost drowned me."

"Me?" Lee sat back on the desk, one foot off the floor. "I had nothing to do with that. The canoe had a leak. I didn't know you couldn't swim."

"That's what you keep saying." Trent's eye twitched. Taking a tiny sip, he turned to me. "Stanley, this is Rachel Morgan. She's my security tonight."

I beamed a false smile. "Hello, Lee." I held out my hand, careful to keep my ley line energy reined, though with the memory of that man's screams echoing through me, it was hard not to give him a jolt. "Nice to see the upstairs this time."

"Rachel," Lee said warmly, turning my hand to kiss the top of it instead of shaking it. "You can't imagine how bad I felt for getting you mixed up in that ugly business. I'm so pleased you came away from it unscathed. I trust you're being compensated properly tonight?"

I yanked my hand back before his lips touched it, making a show of wiping it off. "No apologies needed. But I'd be remiss for not thanking you for teaching me how to play craps." My pulse quickened and I stifled the urge to slug him. "Want your *dice back?*"

The vampire slid behind him, her hands going possessively atop his shoulders. Lee kept his smile in place, seemingly oblivious to my barb. *God, the man had been bleeding from his pores, and that had been aimed at me. Bastard.*

"The orphanage was most grateful for your donation," Lee said smoothly. "They put a new roof on with it, so I'm told."

"Fantastic," I said, honestly pleased. Beside me, Trent fidgeted, clearly dying to interrupt. "I'm always glad when I can help those less fortunate."

Lee took the vampire's hands in his and moved her to stand beside him.

Trent took my arm while they were distracted. "You bought the new roof?" he breathed.

"Apparently," I muttered, noting he was surprised about the roof, not the scuffle in the streets.

"Trent, Rachel," Lee said as he held the vampire's hand in his. "This is Candice."

Candice smiled to show her teeth. Ignoring Trent, she fixed her brown eyes on my neck, a red tongue edging the corner of her mouth. Exhaling, she eased closer. "Lee, sweetheart," she said, and I gripped Trent's arm tighter when her voice ran like ripples over my scar. "You told me I'd be entertaining a man." Her smile went predatory. "But this is okay."

I forced a breath. Waves of promise were coming from my neck, making my knees weaken. My blood pounded and my eyes almost slipped shut. I took a breath, then another. It took all my experience with Ivy to keep from responding. She was hungry, and she knew what she was doing. If she had been undead, I would have been hers. As it was, even with my scar she couldn't bespell me unless I let her. And I wasn't going to.

Aware of Trent watching, I gained control of myself, though I could feel the sexual tension rising in me like fog on a damp night. My thoughts slid to Nick, then Kisten, where they lingered to make things worse. "Candice," I said softly, leaning closer. *I wouldn't touch her. I wouldn't.* "It's nice to meet you. And I will break off your teeth and use them to pierce your belly button if you even as much as look at my scar again."

Candice's eyes flashed to black. The warmth in my scar died. Angry, she drew away, her hand atop Lee's shoulder. "I don't care if you are Tamwood's plaything," she said, trying to be all Queen of the Damned, but I lived with a truly dangerous vampire and her efforts were pathetic. "I can take you down," she finished.

My jaw clenched. "I live with Ivy. I'm not her plaything," I said softly, hearing a muted cheer from downstairs. "What does that tell you?"

"Nothing," she said, her pretty face going ugly.

"And nothing is exactly what you're going to get from me, so back off."

Lee stepped between us. "Candice," he said, putting a hand on the small of her back and pushing her to the door. "Do me a favor, sweetheart. Get Ms. Morgan some coffee, will you? She's working tonight."

"Black, no sugar," I said, hearing my voice rasp. My heart was pounding and sweat had broken out. Black witches I could handle. Skilled, hungry vampires were a little harder.

Unkinking my fingers from Trent's arm, I pulled away. His face was quiet as he looked at me and then the vamp Lee was escorting to the door. "Quen . . ." he whispered.

"Quen wouldn't have had a chance," I said, my heart slowing. If she had been an undead, neither would I. But Saladan wouldn't have been able to convince an undead vampire to back him, lest

Piscary find out and kill him or her twice. There was honor among the dead. Or maybe it was just fear.

Lee said a few words to Candice, and the woman slunk out into the hall, giving me a sly smile before she left. Red heels were the last I saw of her. My thoughts spun when I noticed she had an anklet identical to Ivy's. There couldn't be more than one like that without a reason—perhaps Kisten and I ought to chat.

Not knowing what it meant, if anything, I sat in one of the green upholstered chairs before I fell over from the fading adrenaline. Hands clasped to hide their faint trembling, I thought of Ivy and the protection she gave me. No one had made a play for me like that in months, not since the vamp at the perfume counter had mistaken me for someone else. If I had to fight that off every day, it would only be a matter of time before I became a shadow of myself: thin, anemic, and belonging to someone. Or worse, belonging to anyone.

The sound of sliding fabric pulled my attention to Trent as he sat in the second chair. "You all right?" he breathed when Lee shut the door behind Candice with a firm thump.

His voice was soothing, surprising me. Forcing myself to straighten, I nodded, wondering why he cared, or even if he did. Exhaling, I forced my hands open and loose.

Bustling with efficiency, Lee edged back around his desk and sat. He was smiling to show his white teeth amid his suntanned face. "Trent," he said, leaning back in his chair. It was larger than ours, and I think it put him several inches taller. *Subtle.* "I'm glad you came to see me. We should talk before anything gets more out of hand than it has."

"Out of hand?" Trent didn't move, and I watched his concern for me melt into nothing. Green eyes hard, he set his shot glass on the desk between them, the soft click sounding louder than it should. Never looking from Saladan's sloppy grin, he took over the room. This was the man who killed his employees in his office and got away with it, the man who owned half the city, the man who thumbed his nose at the law, living above it in his fortress in the middle of an old-growth, planned-out forest.

Trent was angry, and I suddenly didn't mind that they were ignoring me.

"You derailed two of my trains, caused a near strike of my trucking line, and burned down my primary public relations effort," Trent said, a wisp of his hair starting to float.

I stared at him while Lee shrugged. *Primary public relations effort? It had been an orphanage. God, how cold could you be?*

"It was the easiest way to get your attention." Lee sipped his drink. "You've been inching your way past the Mississippi the last ten years. Did you expect anything less?"

Trent's jaw tightened. "You're killing innocent people with the potency of the Brimstone you're putting on the streets."

"No!" Lee barked, pushing the glass from him. "There are no innocents." Thin lips pressed together, he leaned forward, angry and threatening. "You crossed the line," he said, shoulders tense under his tux. "And I wouldn't be here culling your weak clientele if you stayed on your side of the river as agreed."

"My father made that agreement, not me. I've asked your father to lower the levels he allows in his Brimstone. People want a safe product. I give it to them. I don't care where they live."

Lee fell back with a sound of disbelief. "Spare me the benefactor crap," he simpered. "We don't sell to anyone who doesn't want it. And Trent? They want it. The stronger, the better. The death levels even out in less than a generation. The weak die off, the strong survive, ready and willing to buy more. To buy stronger. Your careful regulation weakens everyone. There's no natural balance, no strengthening of the species. Maybe that's why there are so few of you left. You've killed yourself by trying to save them."

I sat with my hands deceptively slack in my lap, feeling the tension rise in the small room. *Culling weak clientele? Strengthening the species?* Who in hell did he think he was?

Lee made a quick movement, and I twitched.

"But the bottom line," Lee said, easing back when he saw me move, "is that I'm here because you are changing the rules. And I'm not leaving. It's too late for that. You can hand everything over to me and graciously move off the continent, or I will take it, one orphanage, one hospital, one train station, street corner, and bleeding-heart innocent at a time." He took a sip of his drink and cradled it in his laced hands. "I like games, Trent. And if you remember, I won whatever we played."

Trent's eye twitched. It was his only show of emotion. "You have two weeks to get out of my city," he said, his voice a smooth ribbon of calm water hiding a deadly undertow. "I'm going to maintain my distribution. If your father wants to talk, I'm listening."

"Your city?" Lee flicked his eyes over me, then back to Trent. "Looks to me like it's split." He arched his thin eyebrows. "Very dangerous, very attractive. Piscary is in prison. His scion is ineffective. You're vulnerable from the veneer of honest businessman you hide behind. I'm going to take Cincinnati and the distribution net you have so painstakingly developed, and use it as it ought to be. It's a waste, Trent. You could control the entire Western Hemisphere with what you have, and you're pissing it away on half-strength Brimstone and biodrugs to dirt farmers and welfare cases that won't ever make anything of themselves—or anything for you."

A seething anger warmed my face. I happened to be one of those welfare cases, and though I would probably be shipped off to Siberia in a biocontainment bag if it ever got out, I bristled. Trent was scum, but Lee was disgusting. I opened my mouth to tell him to shut up about things he didn't understand when Trent touched my leg with his shoe in warning.

The rims of Trent's ears had gone red, and his jaw was tight. He tapped at the arm of the chair, a deliberate show of his agitation. "I do control the Western Hemisphere," Trent said, his low, resonating voice making my stomach clench. "And my welfare cases have given me more than my father's paying customers—Stanley."

Lee's tanned face went white in anger, and I wondered what was being said that I didn't understand. Perhaps it hadn't been college. Maybe they had met at "camp."

"Your money can't force me out," Trent added. "Ever. Go tell your father to lower his Brimstone levels and I'll back off from the West Coast."

Lee stood, and I stiffened, ready to move. He placed his hands spread wide, bracing himself. "You overestimate your reach, Trent. You did when we were boys, and nothing has changed. It's why you almost drowned trying to swim back to shore, and why you lost every game we played, every race we ran, every girl we made a prize." He was pointing now, underscoring his words. "You think you're more than you are, having been coddled and praised for accomplishments that everyone else takes for granted. Face it. You're the last of your kind, and it's your arrogance that put you there."

My eyes shifted between them. Trent sat with his legs comfortably crossed and his fingers laced. He was absolutely still. He was incensed, none of it showing but for the hem of his slacks trembling. "Don't make a mistake you can't walk away from," he said softly. "I'm not twelve anymore."

Lee backed up, a misplaced satisfaction and confidence in him as he eyed the door behind me. "You could have fooled me."

The door latch shifted and I jerked. Candice walked in, an

institutional-white mug of coffee in her hand. "Excuse me," she said, her kitten-soft voice only adding to the tension. She slunk between Trent and Lee, breaking their gazes on each other.

Trent shook out his sleeves and took a slow breath. I glanced at him before reaching for the coffee. He looked shaken, but it was from repressing his anger, not fear. I thought of his biolabs and Ceri safely hiding with an old man across the street from my church. Was I making choices for her that she should be making for herself?

The mug was thick, the warmth of it seeping into my fingers when I took it. My lip curled when I realized she had put cream in it. Not that I was going to drink it. "Thanks," I said, making an ugly face right back at her when she took a sexually charged pose atop Lee's desk, her legs crossed at the knee.

"Lee," she said, leaning to make a provocative show. "There is a slight problem on the floor that needs your attention."

Looking annoyed, he pushed her out of his way. "Deal with it, Candice. I'm with friends."

Her eyes went black and her shoulders stiffened. "It's something you need to attend. Get your ass downstairs. It won't wait."

I flicked my gaze to Trent, reading his surprise. Apparently the pretty vamp was more than decoration. *Partner?* I wondered. She sure was acting like it.

She cocked one eyebrow at Lee in mocking petulance, making me wish I could do the same. I still hadn't bothered to learn how. "Now, Lee," she prompted, slipping off the desk and going to hold the door for him.

His brow furrowed. Brushing his short bangs from his eyes, he pushed his chair back with excessive force. "Excuse me." Thin lips tight, he nodded to Trent walked out, his feet thumping on the stairway.

Candice smiled predatorily at me before she slipped out after him. "Enjoy your coffee," she said, closing the door. There was a click as it locked.

Twenty-six

I took a deep breath, listening to the silence. Trent shifted his legs to put his ankle atop a knee. Eyes distant and worried, he chewed on a lower lip, looking nothing like the drug lord and murderer he was. Funny, you couldn't tell by looking.

"She locked the door," I said, jumping at the sound of my own voice.

Trent lifted his eyebrows. "She doesn't want you to wander. I think it's a good idea."

Snarky elf, I thought. Stifling a frown, I went to the small round window looking out across the frozen river. Using the flat of my hand, I wiped the condensation from it and took in the varied skyline. Carew Tower was lit up with holiday lights, glowing with the gold, green, and red film they covered the top floor windows with so they would shine like huge bulbs. It was clear tonight, and I could even see a few stars through the city's light pollution.

Turning, I put my hands behind my back. "I don't trust your friend."

"I never have. You'll live longer that way." Trent's tight jaw eased and the green of his eyes went a little less hard. "Lee and I spent our summers together when we were boys. Four weeks at one of my father's camps, four weeks at his family's beach house on a manmade island off the coast of California. It was supposed to foster goodwill between our families. He's the one who set the ward on my great window, actually." Trent shook his head. "He was twelve. Quite an accomplishment for him at the time. Still is. We had a party. My mother fell into the hot tub, she was so tipsy. I should replace it with glass now that we're—having difficulties."

He was smiling in a bittersweet memory, but I had stopped listening. Lee set the ward? It had taken the color of my aura, just like the disk in the game room. Our auras resonated to a similar frequency. Eyes squinting, I thought about our shared aversion to red wine. "He has the same blood disease I do, doesn't he?" I said. It couldn't be a coincidence. Not with Trent.

Trent's head jerked up. "Yes," he said cautiously. "That's why I don't understand this. My father saved his life, and now he's squabbling over a few million a year?"

Few million a year. Pocket change for the rich and filthy. Restless, I glanced at Lee's desk, deciding I had nothing to learn by sifting through the drawers. "You, ah, monitor the levels of Brimstone you produce?"

Trent's expression went guarded, then, as if making a decision, he ran a hand across his hair to make it lie flat. "Very carefully, Ms. Morgan. I'm not the monster you'd like me to be. I'm not in the business of killing people; I'm in the business of supply and demand. If I didn't produce it, someone else would, and it wouldn't be a safe product. Thousands would die." He glanced at the door and uncrossed his legs to put both feet on the floor. "I can guarantee it."

My thoughts went to Erica. The thought of her dying under the flag of being a weak member of the species was intolerable. But illegal was illegal. My hand smacked into his gold earrings as I tucked a strand of hair behind my ear. "I don't care how pretty the colors are that you paint your picture with, you're still a murderer. Faris didn't die because of a bee sting."

His brow furrowed. "Faris was going to give his records to the press."

"Faris was a frightened man who loved his daughter."

I put a hand on my hip and watched him fidget. It was very subtle: the tension in his jaw, the way he held his manicured fingers, the lack of any expression.

"So why don't you kill me?" I asked. "Before I do the same?" My heart pounded, and I felt as if I was at a cliff's edge.

Trent broke his persona of professional, well-dressed drug lord with a smile. "Because you won't go to the press," he said softly. "They will bring you down with me, and survival is more important than the truth to you."

My face warmed. "Shut up."

"It's not a failing, Ms. Morgan."

"Shut up!"

"And I knew eventually you'd work with me."

"I won't."

"You already are."

Stomach churning, I turned away. I gazed unseeing over the frozen river. A frown creased my brow. It was so silent I could hear the thumping of my heart—why was it that quiet?

I spun, hands gripping my elbows. Trent looked up from arranging the crease in his pants. His gaze was curious at the frightened look I knew I had. "What?" he said carefully.

Feeling unreal and disconnected, I took a step to the door. "Listen."

"I don't hear anything."

I reached out and wiggled the knob. "That's the problem," I said. "The boat is empty."

There was a heartbeat of silence. Trent rose, his suit making a pleasant hush. He looked more concerned than alarmed as he shook his sleeves down and came forward. Nudging me out of the way, he tried the handle.

"What, you think it's going to work for you when it won't work for me?" I said, grabbing his elbow and pulling him out from in front of the door. Balancing on one foot, I held my breath and kicked at the jamb, thankful that even luxury boats tried to keep everything as light as possible. My heel went right through the thin wood, my foot catching. The strips of my beautiful dress dangled and waved as I hopped ungainly backward to disentangle myself.

"Hey! Wait!" I exclaimed when Trent picked the splinters from the hole and reached through to unlock it from the outside. Ignoring me, he opened the door and darted into the hall.

"Damn it, Trent!" I hissed, snatching up my clutch purse and following him. Ankle hurting, I caught up with him at the foot of the stairs. Reaching out, I jerked him back, sending his shoulder into the wall of the narrow passage. "What are you doing?" I said, inches away from his angry eyes. "Is this how you treat Quen? You don't know what's out there, and if you die, I'm the one that's going to suffer, not you!"

He said nothing, his green eyes choleric and his jaw tight.

"Now get your scrawny ass behind mine, and keep it there," I said, giving him a shove.

Sullen and worried, I left him there. My hand wanted to reach for my splat gun, but as long as that purple disk was up and running, the potions in it wouldn't do anything but tick someone off as I got a nasty concoction of monkshood and spiderwort all over their nice dress clothes. A faint smile curved over my face. I didn't mind doing this the physical way.

What I could see of the room was empty. I listened, hearing nothing. Crouching to put my head at knee level, I peeked around the corner. I was down here for two reasons. First, if anyone was waiting to hit me, they'd have to adjust their swing, giving me time to get out of the way. Second, if I were hit, I wouldn't have so far to go to find the floor. But as I took in the elegant room, my stomach churned. The floor was littered with bodies.

"Oh my God," I said softly as I rose. "Trent, he killed them." *Was that it? Was Lee going to frame us for murder?*

Trent pushed past me, slipping my grasping reach easily. He crouched by the first body. "Knocked out," he said flatly, his beautiful voice turned to steel.

My horror turned to confusion. "Why?" I scanned the floor, guessing they had fallen where they stood.

Trent rose. His eyes went to the door. I agreed. "Let's get out of here," I said.

His steps behind me were quick as we hustled to the foyer to find it predictably locked. Through the frosted glass I could see cars in the parking lot, Trent's limo parked where we left it. "I got a bad feeling about this," I muttered, and Trent pushed me aside to look.

I stared at the thick wood, knowing I wouldn't be able to kick through that. Tense, I dug through my clutch purse. While Trent wasted his energy trying to break a window with a bar stool, I punched speed dial number one. "It's bulletproof glass," I said as the phone rang.

He lowered the stool and ran a hand over his wispy hair to make it perfect again. He wasn't even breathing hard. "How do you know?"

I shrugged, turning sideways for some privacy. "It's what I would have used." I returned to the gaming room as Ivy picked up. "Hey, Ivy," I said, refusing to lower my voice lest I give Mr. Elf the impression I hadn't planned this. "Saladan locked us in his gambling boat and ran away. Could you come on out and jimmy the door for me?"

Trent was peering out at the parking lot. "Jonathan is there. Call him."

Ivy was saying something, but Trent's voice was louder. I covered the receiver with a hand and said to Trent, "If he was still conscious, don't you think that he might be a little curious as to why Lee left and already have come to take a look?"

Trent's face went a little whiter.

"What?" I said as I focused back on Ivy. She was almost frantic.

"Get out!" she shouted. "Rachel, Kist had a bomb put on the boiler. I didn't know that's where you were going! Get out!"

My face went cold. "Um, I gotta go, Ivy. Talk to you later."

As Ivy yelled, I closed the cover to my phone and tucked it away. Turning to Trent, I smiled. "Kisten is blowing up Lee's boat as an object lesson. I think we need to leave."

My phone started ringing. I ignored it, and the call—Ivy?—was shunted into voice mail. Trent's confidence melted away to leave an attractive, well-dressed young man trying to show he wasn't afraid. "Lee wouldn't let anyone burn his boat," he said. "He doesn't work that way."

I clutched my arms about myself, scanning the room for something—anything—to help me. "He burned down your orphanage."

"That was to get my attention."

I looked at him, tired. "Would your *friend* let his boat burn and take you with it if Piscary was blamed for it? Heck of an easy way to take over the city."

Trent's jaw tightened. "The boiler room?" he asked.

I nodded. "How did you know?"

He headed for a small door behind the bar. "It's what I would have done."

"Swell." I followed him, my pulse quickening as I stepped around the unconscious people. "Where are we going?"

"I want to look at it."

I stopped dead in my tracks as Trent turned to go down a ladder backward. "You can dismantle a bomb?" It would be the only way to save everyone. There had to be a dozen people.

From the bottom of the ladder, Trent peered up at me, looking odd in his dress suit among the filth and clutter. "No. I just want to look at it."

"Are you nuts!" I exclaimed. "You want to look at it? We have to get out of here!"

Trent's upturned face was placid. "It might have a timer on it. Are you coming?"

"Sure," I said, stifling a laugh; I was pretty sure it would come out sounding hysterical.

Trent wove through the boat with a disturbing lack of urgency.

I could smell hot metal and smoke. Trying not to snag my dress, I peered into the dimness. "There it is!" I shouted, pointing. My finger was shaking, and I dropped my hand to hide it.

Trent strode forward and I followed, hiding behind him when he crouched before a metal box with wires coming out of it. He reached to open it, and I panicked. "Hey!" I cried, grabbing his shoulder. "What the Turn are you doing? You don't know how to turn it off!"

He caught his balance without getting up, looking at me in annoyance, every hair on his head still perfect. "That's where the timer will be, Morgan."

I swallowed hard, peering over his shoulder as he carefully opened the lid. "How much time?" I whispered, my breath sending his wispy hair drifting.

He stood, and I took a step back. "About three minutes."

"Oh, hell no." My mouth went dry, and my phone started ringing. I ignored it. Leaning, I looked closer at the bomb, starting to feel a little unsteady.

Trent pulled on a watch fob to bring out an antique-looking timepiece and set the modern timer on it. "We've got three minutes to find a way off."

"Three minutes! We can't find a way off the boat in three minutes. The glass is bulletproof, the doors are thicker than your head, and that big purple disk will soak up any spell we throw at it!"

Trent's eyes were cold on me. "Get ahold of yourself, Morgan. Hysterics won't help."

"Don't tell me what to do!" I exclaimed, my knees starting to shake. "I think best when I'm having hysterics. Just shut up and let me have them!" Arms wrapped around myself, I glanced at the bomb. It was hot down there, and I was sweating. Three minutes. What in hell could you do in three minutes? Sing a little song. Dance a little dance. Make a little love. Find a new romance. *Oh God. I was making up poetry.*

"Maybe he has an escape route in his office?" Trent suggested.

"And that's why he locked us in there?" I said. "Come on." I grabbed his sleeve and pulled. "We don't have enough time to find a way off." My thoughts went to the purple disk in the ceiling. I had influenced it once. Maybe I could bend it to my will. "Come on!" I repeated as his sleeve slipped through my fingers when he refused to move. "Unless you want to stay and watch numbers count down. I might be able to break the no-spell zone Lee has on his boat."

Trent rocked into motion. "I still say we can find a weak point in his security."

I headed up the ladder, not caring if Trent noticed I wasn't wearing undies or not. "Not enough time." Damn it, why didn't Kisten tell me what he was doing? I was surrounded by men who kept secrets from me. Nick, Trent, and now Kisten. Could I pick 'em or what? And Kist was killing people. I didn't want to like a guy who killed people. What was *wrong* with me?

Heart pounding as if marking the reducing seconds, we went back to the gaming room. It was silent and still. Waiting. My mouth twisted at the sight of the sleeping people. They were dead. I couldn't save them and Trent. I didn't even know how I was going to save myself.

The disk above me looked innocuous enough, but I knew it was still functioning when Trent glanced at it and paled. I guessed he was using his second sight. "You can't break that," he said. "But you don't need to. Can you make a protection circle big enough for both of us?"

My eyes widened. "You want to ride it out in a protection circle? You *are* crazy! The minute I hit it, down it goes!"

Trent looked angry. "How big, Morgan?"

"But I tripped the alarms last time just looking at it!"

"So what!" he exclaimed, his confidence cracking. It was nice to see him shaken, but under the circumstances, I couldn't enjoy it. "Trip the alarms! The disk doesn't stop you from tapping a line and making a spell. It only catches you when you do. Make the damned circle!"

"Oh!" I looked at him in understanding, my first wild hope dying. I couldn't tap a line to make a protection circle. Not sitting on water as I was. "Um, you make it," I said.

He seemed to start. "Me? It takes me a good five minutes with chalk and candles."

Frustrated, I groaned. "What kind of an elf are you!"

"What kind of a runner are you?" he shot back. "I don't think your boyfriend will mind if you tap a line through him to save your life. Do it, Morgan. We're running out of time!"

"I can't." I spun in a tight circle. Through the unbreakable glass, Cincinnati glowed.

"Screw your damned honor, Rachel. Break your word to him or we're dead!"

Miserable, I turned back to him. *He thought I was honorable?*

"That's not it. I can't draw on a line through Nick anymore. The demon broke my link with him."

Trent went ashen. "But you gave me a shock in the car. That was too much for what a witch can hold in his or her chi."

"I'm my own familiar, okay!" I said. "I made a deal with a demon to be its familiar so it would testify against Piscary, and I had to learn how to store ley line energy for it. Oh, I've got tons of energy, but a circle requires you stay connected to a line. I can't do it."

"You're a demon's familiar?" His face looked horrified, frightened, scared of me.

"Not anymore!" I shouted, angry to have to admit it had even happened. "I bought my freedom. Okay? Get off my case! But I don't have a familiar, and I can't tap a line over water!"

From my bag came the faint sound of my phone ringing. Trent stared at me. "What did you give it for your freedom?"

"My silence." My pulse hammered. What difference did it make if Trent knew? We were both going to die.

Grimacing as if having decided something, Trent took off his coat. Shaking his sleeve down, he undid the cuff link and pushed his sleeve past his elbow. "You aren't a demon's familiar?" It was a soft, worried whisper.

"No!" I was shaking. As I watched in slack-eyed confusion, he grabbed my arm just below the elbow. "Hey!" I shouted, pulling away.

"Deal with it," he said grimly. Gripping my arm harder, he used his free hand to force me to take his wrist in the same grip acrobats use when working the trapeze. "Don't make me regret this," he muttered, and my eyes widened when a rush of line energy flowed into me.

"Holy crap!" I gasped, almost falling. It was wild magic, having the uncatchable flavor of the wind. He had joined his will to mine, tapping a line through his familiar and giving it to me as if we were one. The line coming through him and into me had taken on a tinge of his aura. It was clean and pure with the taste of the wind, like Ceri's.

Trent groaned, and my eyes shot to his. His face was drawn and sweat had broken out on him. My chi was full, and though the extra energy was looping back to the line, apparently the stuff I had spindled already in my head was burning through him.

"Oh God," I said, wishing there was a way I could shift the balance. "I'm sorry, Trent."

His breath came in a ragged gasp. "Make the circle," he panted.

Eyes jerking to his timepiece swinging from its fob, I said the invocation. We both staggered as the force running through us ebbed. I didn't relax at all as the bubble of ley line energy blossomed about us. I glanced at his watch. I couldn't see how much time was left.

Trent tossed his hair from his eyes, not letting go of my arm. Eyes looking haggard, he ran his gaze over the gold smeared bubble over us to the people beyond. His expression went empty. Swallowing hard, he shifted his grip tighter. Clearly it wasn't burning him any longer, but the pressure would steadily build to its previous levels. "It's really big," he said, looking at the shimmer. "You can hold an undrawn circle this big?"

"I can hold it," I said, avoiding his eyes. His skin pressing against mine was warm and there were tingles coming from it. I didn't like the intimacy. "And I wanted it large so we have some leeway when the shock hits us. As soon as you let go or I touch it—"

"It falls," Trent finished for me. "I know. You're babbling, Morgan."

"Shut up!" I exclaimed, nervous as a pixy in a room full of frogs. "You may be used to having bombs blow up around you, but this is my first time!"

"If you're lucky, it won't be the last," he said.

"Just shut up!" I snapped. I hoped my eyes weren't as scared looking as his. If we survived the blast, there was still the aftermath to get through. Falling chunks of boat and icy water. Great. "Um, how long?" I asked, hearing my voice shake. My phone was ringing again.

He glanced down. "Ten seconds. Maybe we should sit down before we fall."

"Sure," I said. "That's probably a good ide—"

I gasped as a boom shook the floor. I reached for Trent, desperate that our grip on each other not break. The floor pushed up at us, and we fell. He clutched at my shoulder, pulling me into him to keep me from rolling away. Pressed against him, I could smell silk and aftershave.

My stomach dropped, and a flash of fire burst around us. I screamed as my ears went numb. In an unreal, soundless motion, the boat broke apart as we rose. The night became smears of black sky and red fire. The tingle of the circle breaking washed over me. Then we fell.

Trent's grip was torn away, and I cried out when fire raced over me. My explosion-numbed ears filled with water and I couldn't breathe. I wasn't burning, I was drowning. It was cold, not hot. Panicking, I fought against the heavy water pushing at me.

I couldn't move. I didn't know which way was up. The dark was full of bubbles and chunks of boat. A faint glow to my left caught my attention. I gathered myself and aimed for it, telling my brain it was the surface even though it seemed to be sideways, not up.

God, I hoped it was the surface.

I burst from the water, my ears still not working. The cold struck me, freezing. I gasped, the air like knives in my lungs. I took another thankful breath. I was so cold it hurt.

Pieces of boat were still falling, and I tread water, thankful that I wore a dress I could move in. The water tasted like oil, and the swallow I had taken in hung heavy in me.

"Trent!" I shouted, hearing it as if through a pillow. "Trent!"

"Here!"

I shook the wet hair from my eyes and turned. Relief went though me. It was dark, but through the floating ice and wood, I saw Trent. His hair was plastered against him, but he looked unhurt. Shivering, I kicked off the one heel that I still had on and started toward him. Bits of boat were making the odd splash. How could it still be falling? I wondered. There was enough flotsam between us to build two boats.

Trent started forward with a professional looking stroke. Apparently he had learned to swim. The glimmer of fire on the icy water brightened around us. Looking up, I gasped. Something big and burning had yet to come down.

"Trent!" I shouted, but he didn't hear me. "Trent, look out!" I screamed, pointing. But he wasn't listening. I dove, trying to escape.

I was flung as if smacked. The water around me turned red. I lost most of the air from my lungs when something hit me, bruising my back. The water saved me, though, and with my lungs aching and my eyes smarting, I followed my exhaled breath to the surface.

"Trent!" I called as I emerged from the icy water and into the burning cold of the night. I found him holding a cushion that was rapidly filling with water. His eyes met mine, unfocused. The light from the burning boat was dimming, and I swam for him. The dock was gone. I didn't know how we were going to get out of there.

"Trent," I said, coughing when I reached him. My ears were ringing, but I could hear myself. I spit the hair out of my mouth. "Are you okay?"

He blinked as if trying to focus. Blood seeped from under his hairline, making a brown streak in his fair hair. His eyes closed, and I watched in horror when his grip on the cushion went slack. "No, you don't," I said, reaching out before he could slip under.

Shivering, I wrapped an arm about his neck, tucking his chin against the inside of my elbow. He was breathing. My legs were going slow from the cold and my toes were cramping. I looked for help. Where in hell was the I.S.? Someone must have seen that explosion.

"Never around when you need them," I muttered, shoving a chunk of ice as large as a chair out of my way. "Probably out giving someone a ticket for selling expired charms." The dock was gone. I had to get us out of the water, but the break wall was three feet of concrete. The only way out was to get back onto the ice and walk to another dock.

A sound of desperation came from me as I struck out for the edge of the hole the blast had ripped in the ice. I'd never make it even with the slow current. The water was starting to creep higher up me, and my movements were slower and harder to make. I wasn't cold anymore, either, and that scared the hell out of me. I could probably make it . . . if I weren't dragging Trent.

"Damn it all to hell!" I shouted, using my anger to keep moving. I was going to die here, trying to save his ass. "Why didn't you tell me what you were doing, Kisten!" I exclaimed, feeling my tears like fire leaking out of me as I swam. "Why didn't I tell you where I was going?" I yelled back at myself. "I'm a dumbass. And your stupid watch is fast, Trent! Did you know that? Your stupid . . ." I took a sobbing breath. ". . . watch is fast."

My throat hurt, but the motion seemed to warm me. The water felt positively balmy now. Panting, I stopped swimming, treading water. My vision blurred when I realized I was almost there. A big chunk of ice was in my way, though, and I'd have to swim around it.

Taking a resolute breath, I shifted my leaden arm and kicked my legs. I couldn't feel them anymore, but I assumed they were moving since the eight-inch-thick shelf of ice seemed to be moving closer. The last of the light from the burning boat made little red smears on the ice as I reached out and touched it. My hand slid cleanly away to pull in snow, and I sank. Adrenaline pounded through me and I kicked back to the surface. Trent sputtered and coughed.

"Oh, Trent," I said, water filling my mouth. "I forgot you were here. You first. Come on. Up on the ice."

Using the questionable leverage of what looked like part of the casino's bar, I got Trent halfway up onto the frozen river. Tears slipped down my face as I was now able to use both arms to keep myself afloat. I hung for a moment, my hands unfeeling in the snow while I rested my head atop the ice. I was so tired. Trent wasn't drowning. I had done my job. Now I could save myself.

I reached up to pull myself onto the ice—and failed. Snow fell in to make puddles of slush. Switching tactics, I tried to lever my leg up. It wouldn't move. I couldn't move my leg.

"Okay," I said, not as scared as I thought I ought to be. The cold must have numbed everything—even my thoughts felt blurry. I was supposed to be doing something, but I couldn't remember what. I blinked as I saw Trent, his legs still in the water.

"Oh, yeah," I whispered. I had to get out of the water. The sky above me was black, and the night was silent but for the ringing in my ears and the faint sound of sirens. The light from the fires was dim and going dimmer. My fingers wouldn't work, and I had to use my arms like clubs to pull a chunk of boat closer. Concentrating to not lose my thought, I pushed it under to buoy me up. A groan slipped from me when, with its help, I managed to slip a leg up onto the ice. I rolled awkwardly and lay panting. The wind was like fire on my back, and the ice was warm. I'd done it.

"Where is everyone?" I breathed, feeling my flesh hard against the cold ice. "Where's Ivy? Where's the fire department? Where's my phone?" I giggled as I remembered it was at the bottom of the river with my purse, then sobered as I thought of the unconscious people drifting downward through the icy water in their best finery to join it. Hell, I'd kiss even Denon, my old, despised boss from the I.S., if he showed up.

That reminded me. "Jonathan," I whispered. "Oh, Jo-o-o-o-onathan," I sang. "Where are you? Come out, come out, wherever you are—you tall freak of nature."

I lifted my head, glad I was pointed in the right direction. Squinting past my stringy hair, I could see a light where the limo sat. The headlights were aimed at the river, shining to show the destruction and thc sinking bits of boat. Jonathan's silhouette stood at the quay. I could tell it was him because he was the only person I knew who was that tall. He was looking the wrong way. He'd never see me, and I couldn't shout anymore.

Damn it. I was going to have to get up.

I tried. I really did. But my legs wouldn't work and my arms just lay there, ignoring me. Besides, the ice was warm, and I didn't want to get up. Maybe if I shouted he'd hear me.

I took a breath. "Jonathan," I whispered. Oh hell, this wasn't going to work.

I took another breath. "Jonathan," I said, hearing it around my ringing ears. I pulled my head up, watching as he didn't move to look. "Never mind," I said, letting my head fall back onto the ice. The snow was warm, and I pressed into it. "This is nice," I mumbled, but I don't think it made it past my thoughts into real words.

It felt as if the world was spinning, and I could hear the slosh of water. Snuggling into the ice, I smiled. I hadn't slept well for days. I exhaled, drifting off into nothing, enjoying the warmth of the sun that was suddenly shining on the ice. Someone curled their arms around me, and I felt my head thump into a soggy chest as I was lifted.

"Denon?" I heard myself murmur. "Come here, Denon. I owe you a big . . . kiss . . ."

"Denon?" someone echoed.

"I'll carry her, Sa'han."

I tried to open my eyes, swirling back into nothing when I felt myself move. I drowsed, not awake but not quite not asleep. Then I was still, and I tried to smile and go to sleep. But a faint pinch and throb kept intruding on my cheek, and my legs hurt.

Irritated, I pushed at the ice, finding it was gone. I was sitting up, and someone was slapping me. "That's enough," I heard Trent say. "You're going to leave a mark."

The pinch vanished to leave just the throbbing. *Jonathan was slapping me?* "Hey, you freakin' bastard," I breathed. "You hit me again and I'll take care of your family planning."

I could smell leather. My face screwed up as feeling started to come back into my legs and arms. Oh God, it hurt. I opened my eycs to find Trent and Jonathan peering down at me. Blood seeped from Trent's hairline and water dripped from his nose. Above their heads was the interior of the limo. I was alive? How did I get to the car?

"'Bout time you found us," I breathed, my eyes closing.

I heard Trent sigh. "She's okay."

I suppose. Maybe. Compared to being dead, I guess I was okay.

"Pity," Jonathan said, and I heard him shift away from me. "It would have simplified things if she wasn't. Not too late to slip her in the water with the rest."

"Jon!" Trent barked.

His voice was as hot as my skin felt. I was freaking burning up.

"She saved my life," Trent said softly. "I don't care if you like her or not, but she has earned your respect."

"Trenton—" Jonathan started.

"No." It was cold. "She has *earned* your respect."

There was a hesitation, and I would have drifted off to nothing if the pain in my legs would let me. And my fingers were on fire.

"Yes, Sa'han," Jonathan said, and I jerked awake.

"Get us home. Call ahead and have Quen draw a bath for her. We have to get her warmer than this."

"Yes, Sa'han." It was slow and reluctant. "The I.S. is here. Why don't we leave her with them?"

I felt a small pull upon my chi as Trent tapped a line. "I don't want to be seen here. Just don't get in anyone's way and we won't be noticed. Hurry up."

My eyes wouldn't listen to me anymore, but I heard Jonathan get out and shut the door. There was another thump when he got in the driver's door and the car eased into motion. The arms around me tightened, and I realized I was in Trent's lap, the warmth of his body doing more than the air to warm me. I felt the softness of a blanket against me. I must have been swaddled up right tight; I couldn't move my legs or arms.

"I'm sorry," I murmured, giving up on trying to open my eyes. "I'm getting water all over your suit." Then I giggled, thinking that had sounded really pathetic. He was already soaked. "Your Celtic charm isn't worth a damn," I whispered. "I hope you kept your receipt."

"Shut up, Morgan," Trent said, his voice distant and preoccupied.

The car picked up speed, and the sound seemed to lull me. *I could relax,* I thought as I felt the tingling of circulation in my limbs. I was in Trent's car, wrapped in a blanket, and held in his arms. He wouldn't let anything hurt me.

He wasn't singing, though, I mused. *Shouldn't he be singing?*

Twenty-seven

The warm water I was sitting in was nice. I had been in it long enough to prune twice, but I didn't care. Ellasbeth's sunken tub was fab. I sighed, leaning my head back and staring at the ten-foot ceilings framed by the potted orchids lining the bathtub. Maybe there was something to this drug lord business if you got to have a tub like this. I'd been in it for over an hour.

Trent had called Ivy for me even before we reached the city's limits. I'd talked to her myself not too long ago, telling her I was okay and was soaking in warm water and wasn't getting out until hell froze over. She had hung up on me, but I knew we were okay.

Dragging my fingers through the bubbles, I adjusted Trent's borrowed pain amulet hanging about my neck. I didn't know who had invoked it; maybe his secretary? All my charms were at the bottom of the Ohio River. My smile faltered as I remembered the people I hadn't been able to save. I would not feel guilty that I breathed and they didn't. Their deaths were laid at Saladan's feet, not mine. Or maybe Kisten's. Damn it. What was I going to do about that?

I closed my eyes and said a prayer for them, but they jerked open when a faint cadence of brisk steps grew louder. They quickly grew closer, and I froze as a thin woman dressed smartly in a cream-colored suit clacked and clicked in over the bathroom tile unannounced. There was a department store bag over her arm. Her steely gaze was fixed on the doorway to the changing room, and she never saw me as she vanished into it.

It had to be Ellasbeth. Crap. What was I supposed to do? Wipe the bubbles from my hand and offer to shake hers? Frozen, I stared at the door. My coat was on one of the chairs and my garment bag was still hanging by the changing screen. Pulse quickening, I wondered if I could reach the green towel before she realized she wasn't alone.

The faint rustling stopped, and I shrank down into the bubbles when she strode back in, house afire. Her dark eyes were narrowed in anger and her high cheekbones were red. Posture stiff, she halted, bag still over her arm and apparently forgotten. Her thick, waving blond hair was held back to give her narrow face a stark beauty. Lips tight, she held her head high, her eyes fixing vehemently upon me as soon as she cleared the archway.

So that's what it looked like when hell froze over.

"Who are you?" she said, her strong voice domineering and cold.

I smiled, but I knew it looked rather sickly. "Ah, I'm Rachel Morgan. Of Vampiric Charms?" I started to sit up, then changed my mind. I hated the question that had crept into my tone, but there it was. 'Course it might have been there because I was naked except for bubbles, and she was standing in four-inch heels and a casually tasteful outfit that Kisten might pick out for me if he took me shopping in New York.

"What are you doing in my bathtub?" She gazed disparagingly at my healing black eye.

I reached for a towel and dragged it in with me, covering myself. "Trying to warm up."

Her mouth twitched. "I don't wonder why," she said sharply. "He's a cold bastard."

I sat up in a rush of water as she walked out. "Trenton!" her voice rang out, harsh against the peace I had been wallowing in.

My breath puffed out, and I looked at the soaked towel clinging to me. Sighing, I got up and opened the drain with my foot. The water swirling about my calves settled and began to escape. Ellasbeth had thoughtfully left all the doors open, and I could hear her shouting at Trent. She wasn't far away. Perhaps as close as the common room. Deciding that as long as I could hear her out there, it was probably safe enough to get dried off in here, I wrung out the soaked towel and grabbed two new ones from the warmer.

"God save you, Trenton," came her voice, bitter and abusive. "Couldn't you even wait until I was gone before bringing in one of your whores?"

I reddened and my motions to dry my arms grew rough.

"I thought you *had* left," Trent said calmly, not helping matters. "And she's not a whore, she's a business associate."

"I don't care what you call her, she's in my rooms, you bastard."

"There wasn't anywhere else to put her."

"There are eight bathrooms this side of the wall, and you put her in mine?"

I was glad my hair was somewhat dry, and that it smelled like Ellasbeth's shampoo made me feel all peachy-keen. Hopping ungainly on one foot, I tried to get my underwear on, thankful I had only been wearing the nylons that I brought from home when I went into the drink. My skin was still damp and everything was sticking. I almost went down when my foot got stuck halfway into my jeans leg, and lurching, I caught myself against the counter.

"Damn you, Trenton! Don't even try to say *that* is business!" Ellasbeth was shouting. "There's a naked witch in my bathtub, and you're sitting in your robe!"

"No, you listen to me." Trent's voice was iron hard, and I could hear his frustration even from two rooms away. "I said she's a business associate, and that's what she is."

Ellasbeth made a harsh bark of laughter. "From Vampiric Charms? She told me the name of her bloodhouse herself!"

"She's a runner, if it's any of your business," Trent said so coldly I could almost see his clenched jaw. "Her partner is a vampire. It's a play on words, Ellasbeth. Rachel was my security escort tonight, and she fell into the river saving my life. I wasn't going to drop her at her office half dead from hypothermia like an unwanted cat. You told me you were taking the seven o'clock flight out. I thought you were gone, and I wasn't about to put her in my rooms."

There was a moment of silence. I shimmied into my sweatshirt. Somewhere on the bottom of the river was several thousand dollars of soft ribbon gold from Randy's coiffure and one earring. At least the necklace had survived. Maybe the charm worked only on the necklace.

"You were on that boat. . . . The one that blew up . . ." It was softer, but there wasn't a hint of apology in her sudden concern.

In the silence, I fumbled at my hair, grimacing. Maybe if I had half an hour I could do something with it. Besides, there was no way to recover from the first stellar impression I'd made. Taking a steadying breath, I squared my shoulders and padded in my sock feet to the common room. Coffee. I could smell coffee. Coffee would make everything better.

"You can understand my confusion," Ellasbeth was saying as I hesitated by the door, unnoticed but able to see them. Ellasbeth stood beside the round table in the breakfast nook, looking meek in the way a tiger looks when it realizes it can't eat the man with the whip. Trent was seated, wearing a green robe edged in maroon. There was a professional-looking bandage on his forehead. He looked bothered—as he should with his fiancée accusing him of cheating.

"That's the closest to an apology I'm going to get, isn't it?" Trent said.

Ellasbeth dropped the department store bag and put a hand on her hip. "I want her out of my rooms. I don't care who she is."

Trent's eyes fell on mine as if drawn to them, and I winced apologetically. "Quen is taking her home after a light dinner," he said to her. "You're welcome to join us. As I said, I thought you had left."

"I changed to a vamp flight so I could shop longer."

Trent glanced back at me again to tell Ellasbeth that they weren't alone. "You spent six hours in the stores and have only one bag?" he said, the faintest accusation in his voice.

Ellasbeth followed his gaze to me, quickly masking her anger with a pleasant expression. But I could see her frustration. It remained to be seen how it would show itself. I was betting on hidden barbs and slights disguised as compliments. But I would be nice as long as she was.

Smiling, I came out in my jeans and Howlers sweatshirt. "Hey, uh, thanks for the pain amulet and letting me get cleaned up, Mr. Kalamack." I stopped beside the table, the awkwardness as thick and choking as bad cheesecake. "No need to bother Quen. I'll call my partner to come and get me. She's probably banging on your gatehouse already."

Trent made a visible effort to purge the anger from his posture. Elbows on the table so the sleeves of his robe fell to show the fair hair upon his arms, he said, "I'd rather have Quen take you home, Ms. Morgan. I don't particularly want to talk to Ms. Tamwood." He glanced at Ellasbeth. "Do you want me to call the airport for you, or are you staying another night?"

It was entirely devoid of any invitation. "I'll be staying," she said tightly. Bending at the waist, she picked up her bag and walked to her door. I watched her quick stilted steps, seeing in them a dangerous combination of callous disregard and ego.

"She's an only child, isn't she?" I said as the sound of her heels was lost on the carpet.

Trent blinked, his lips parting. "Yes, she is." Then he gestured for me to sit. "Please."

Not really sure I wanted to eat with the two of them, I gingerly sat on the chair opposite Trent. My gaze went to the fake window spanning the entirety of the wall that the small, nearby sunken living room took up. It was just after eleven according to the clocks I had seen, and it was dark with no moon. "Sorry," I said, my gaze flicking to the archway to Ellasbeth's rooms.

His jaw tightened for an instant, then relaxed. "Can I get you some coffee?"

"Sure. That would be great." I was almost faint from hunger, and the heat of my bath had drained me. I looked up with wide eyes as a matronly woman in an apron made her unhurried way out of the small kitchen tucked in at the back of the room. It was partially open to the seating arrangement, but I hadn't noticed her until now.

Giving me a smile that encompassed all her face, the woman set a mug of that heavenly scented coffee in front of me before topping off Trent's smaller teacup with an amber brew. I thought I could smell gardenias, but I wasn't sure. "Bless you," I said as I wrapped my hands around it and breathed in the steam.

"You're welcome," she said with the professional warmth of a good waitress. Smiling, she turned to Trent. "What will it be tonight, Mr. Kalamack? It's almost too late for a proper dinner."

As I blew on the surface of my coffee, my thoughts went to the different schedules of witches and elves, thinking it interesting that one of our species was awake at all times and that dinner happened about the same time for both of us.

"Oh, let's make it light," Trent said, clearly trying to ease the mood. "I have about three pounds of Ohio River sitting in me somewhere. How about a breakfast instead? The usual, Maggie."

The woman nodded, the white hair clipped close to her head not moving at all. "And how about you, dear?" she asked me.

I glanced between Trent and the woman. "What's the usual?"

"Four eggs over easy and three slices of rye toast done on one side."

I felt myself blanch. "That's eating light?" I said before I could stop my mouth.

Trent arranged his jammies' collar, peeking from behind his robe. "High metabolism."

My thoughts went back to how he and Ceri never seemed to get cold. The temperature of the river, too, hadn't affected him. "Um," I said as I realized she was still waiting. "The toast sounds good, but I'll pass on the eggs."

Eyebrows high, Trent took a sip of his tea, eyeing me over the rim. "That's right," he said, his voice unaccusing. "You don't tolerate them well. Maggie, let's go with waffles."

Shocked, I leaned back in my chair. "How did you . . ."

Trent shrugged, looking good in his bathrobe and bare feet. He had nice feet. "You don't think I know your medical history?"

My wonder died as I recalled Faris dead on his office floor. *What in hell was I doing here eating dinner with him?* "Waffles would be great."

"Unless you'd like something more traditional for dinner. Chinese doesn't take long. Would you rather have that? Maggie makes fabulous wontons."

I shook my head. "Waffles sound good."

Maggie smiled, turning to putter back into the kitchen. "Won't be but a moment."

I put my napkin in my lap, wondering how much of this let's-be-nice-to-Rachel scene was because Ellasbeth was in the next room listening and Trent wanted to hurt her for accusing him of cheating. Deciding I didn't care, I put my elbows on the table and took a sip of the best coffee I'd ever tasted. Eyes closing in the rising steam, I moaned in delight. "Oh God, Trent," I breathed. "This is good."

The sudden thump of heels on carpet pulled my eyes open. It was back.

I straightened in my chair as Ellasbeth came in, her dress coat open to show a starched white shirt and a peach-colored scarf. My gaze went to her ring finger and I blanched. You could run a city on the sparkle that thing put out.

Ellasbeth sat beside me, a shade too close for my liking. "Maggie?" she said lightly. "I'll have tea and biscuits, please. I ate while out."

"Yes, ma'am," Maggie said as she leaned through the open archway. Her tone lacked utterly in any warmth. Clearly Maggie didn't like Ellasbeth, either.

Ellasbeth fixed a smile to her face, setting her long, fragile-looking fingers on the table to best show off her engagement ring. *Bitch.* "Seems we got off the horse on the wrong side, Ms. Morgan," she said cheerfully. "Have you and Trenton known each other long?"

I didn't like Ellasbeth. I think I'd be pretty upset myself if I came home and found a girl in Nick's bathtub, but after seeing her shouting at Trent, I couldn't find any sympathy for her. Accusing someone of cheating is harsh. My smile faltered as I realized I had almost done the same thing to Nick. I had accused him of dumping me, asking if there was someone else. There was a difference, but not much. Shit. I had to apologize. That he hadn't told me where he'd been going the last three months while avoiding me didn't seem like enough reason anymore. At least I hadn't called him any names. Jerking myself from my thoughts, I smiled at Ellasbeth.

"Oh, Trent and I go back a long way," I said lightly, twirling a curl of my hair about my finger and remembering its new shortness. "We met at camp as children. Sort of romantic when you think about it." I smiled at Trent's suddenly blank look.

"Really?" She turned to Trent, the hint of a tiger growling in her voice's soft cadence.

Sitting up, I tucked my legs under me to sit cross-legged, running my finger across the rim of the mug suggestively. "He was such a cub when he was younger, full of fire and spirit. I had to fight him off, the dear boy. That's where he got that scar on his lower arm."

I looked at Trent. "I can't believe you haven't told Ellasbeth! Trent, you aren't still embarrassed about that, are you?"

Ellasbeth's eye twitched, but her smile never faltered. Maggie set a delicate looking cup full of an amber liquid by her elbow and quietly walked away. Her carefully shaped eyebrows high, Ellasbeth took in Trent's silent posture and his lack of denial. Her fingertips made one rolling cadence against the table in agitation. "I see," she said, then stood. "Trenton, I do believe I will catch a flight out tonight after all."

Trent met her gaze. He looked tired and a bit relieved. "If that is what you want, love."

She leaned close to him, her eyes on me. "It's to give you the chance to settle your affairs—sweetness," she said, her lips shifting the air about his ear. Still watching me, she lightly kissed his cheek. There was no feeling in her eyes beyond a vindictive glint. "Call me tomorrow."

Not a flicker of emotion crossed Trent. Nothing. And its very absence chilled me. "I'll count the hours," he said, his voice giving no clue either. Both of their eyes were on me as his hand rose to touch her cheek, but he didn't kiss her back. "Should Maggie pack up your tea?"

"No." Still watching me, she straightened, her hand lingering possessively on his shoulder. The picture they made was both beautiful and strong. And united. I remembered the reflection of Trent and me at Saladan's boat. Here was the bond that had been lacking between us. It wasn't love, though. It was more of . . . My brow furrowed. . . . a business merger?

"It was a pleasure meeting you, Rachel," Ellasbeth said, pulling my thoughts back to the present. "And thank you for accompanying my fiancé tonight. Your services are undoubtedly well-practiced and appreciated. It's a shame he won't be calling upon them again."

I leaned across the table to shake her offered hand with a neutral pressure. I think she had just called me a whore—again. I suddenly didn't know what was going on. *Did he like her, or didn't he?* "Have a nice flight out," I said.

"I will. Thank you." Her hand slipped from mine and she drew a step back. "Walk me to the car?" she asked Trent, her voice smooth and satisfied.

"I'm not dressed, love," he said softly, still touching her. "Jonathan can take your bags."

A flicker of annoyance crossed her, and I flashed her a catty smile. Turning, she walked out to the hallway overlooking the great room. "Jonathan?" she called, her heels clacking.

My God. The two played mind games with each other as if it was an Olympic sport.

Trent exhaled. Putting my feet on the floor, I made a wry face. "She's nice."

His expression went sour. "No she isn't, but she's going to be my wife. I'd appreciate it if you wouldn't imply anymore that we are sleeping together."

I smiled, a real one this time. "I just wanted her to leave."

Maggie bustled close, putting down table settings and taking away Ellasbeth's teacup and saucer. "Nasty, nasty woman," she muttered, her motions quick and sharp. "And you can sack me if you want, Mr. Kalamack, but I don't like her and I never will. You watch. She'll bring some woman with her who will take over my kitchen. Rearrange my cupboards. Push me out."

"Never, Maggie," Trent soothed, his posture shifting to a companionable ease. "We all have to make the best of it."

"Oh, worra, worra, worra," she mumbled as she made her way back into the kitchen.

Feeling more relaxed now that Ellasbeth was gone, I took another sip of that wonderful coffee. "*She's* nice," I said, looking at the kitchen.

His green eyes boyishly soft, he nodded. "Yes, she is."

"She's not an elf," I said, and his eyes jerked to mine. "Ellasbeth is," I added, and his look went closed again.

"You're getting uncomfortably adept, Ms. Morgan," he said, leaning away from me.

Putting my elbows to either side of the white plate, I rested my chin on the bridge my hands made. "That's Ellasbeth's problem, you know. She feels like she is a broodmare."

Trent shook out his napkin and put it on his lap. His robe was slowly coming undone to show a pair of executive-looking pajamas. It was somewhat of a disappointment—I'd been hoping for boxers. "Ellasbeth doesn't want to move to Cincinnati," he said, unaware that I was sneaking glances at his physique. "Her work and friends are in Seattle. You wouldn't be able to tell by looking at her, but she's one of the world's best nuclear transplant engineers."

My surprised silence brought his attention up, and I stared at him.

"She can take the nucleus of a damaged cell and transplant it into a healthy one," he said.

"Oh." Beautiful and smart. She could be Miss America if she learned how to lie better. But it sounded really close to illegal genetic manipulation to me.

"Ellasbeth can work from Cincinnati as easily as Seattle," Trent said, mistaking my silence for interest. "I've already financed the university's research department to update their facilities. She's going to put Cincinnati on the map for her developments, and she's angry that she's being forced to move instead of me." He met my questioning eyes. "It's not illegal."

"Tomato, tomatto," I said, leaning back when Maggie set a crock of butter and a pitcher of steaming syrup on the table and walked away.

Trent's green eyes met mine and he shrugged.

The scent of cooking batter drifted close, heady with promise, and my mouth watered as Maggie returned with two steaming plates of waffles. She set one before me, hesitating to make sure I was pleased. "This looks wonderful," I said, reaching for the butter.

Trent adjusted his plate while he waited for me. "Thanks, Maggie. I'll take care of the settings. It's getting late. Enjoy the rest of your evening."

"Thank you, Mr. Kalamack," Maggie said, clearly pleased as she rested a hand atop his shoulder. "I'll clean up the spills before I go. More tea or coffee?"

I looked up from pushing the butter to Trent. They were both waiting for me. "Um, no," I said as I glanced at my mug. "Thank you."

"This is fine," Trent echoed.

Maggie nodded as if we were doing something right before she returned to the kitchen humming. I smiled when I recognized the odd lullaby, "All the Pretty Little Horses."

Lifting a lid to a covered container, I found it full of crushed strawberries. My eyes widened. Tiny whole ones the size of my pinky nail made a ring around the rim as if it was June, not December, and I wondered where he had gotten them. I eagerly ladled berries on top of my waffle, looking up when I realized Trent was watching me. "You want some of these?"

"When you're done with them."

I went to take another scoop, then hesitated. Dropping the spoon back in, I pushed them across the table. The small noise of clinking silverware seemed loud as I poured the syrup. "You do know the last man I saw in a robe, I beat into unconsciousness with a chair leg," I quipped, desperate to break the silence.

Trent almost smiled. "I'll be careful."

The waffle was crisp on the outside and fluffy on the inside, easily cut with a fork. Trent used a knife. I carefully put the perfect square into my mouth so I wouldn't dribble. "Oh God," I said around my full mouth and giving up on manners. "Is it because we almost died that this tastes so good, or is she the best cook on earth?"

It was real butter, and the maple syrup had the dusky flavor that said it was a hundred percent real. Not two percent, not seven percent; it was real maple syrup. Remembering the stash of maple candy I once found while searching Trent's office, I wasn't surprised.

Trent put an elbow on the table, his eyes on his plate. "Maggie puts mayonnaise in them. It gives them an interesting texture."

I hesitated, staring at my plate, then deciding if I couldn't taste it, there wasn't enough egg to worry about. "Mayonnaise?"

A faint sound of dismay came from the kitchen. "Mr. Kalamack . . ." Maggie came out, wiping her hands on her apron. "Don't be giving my secrets away, or you'll find tea leaves in your brew tomorrow," she scolded.

Leaning to look over his shoulder, he widened his smile to become an entirely different person. "Then I'll be able to read my fortune. Have a good night, Maggie."

Harrumphing, she walked out, passing the sunken living room and making a left turn at the walkway overlooking the great hall. Her steps were almost soundless, and the closing of the main door was loud. Hearing running water in the new silence, I ate another bite.

Drug lord, murderer, bad man, I reminded myself. But he wasn't talking, and I was starting to feel uncomfortable. "Hey, I'm sorry about the water in your limo," I offered.

Trent wiped his mouth. "I think I can handle a little dry cleaning after what you did."

"Still," I said as my gaze slid to the crock of strawberries. "I'm sorry."

Seeing my eyes flick from the fruit to him, Trent made a questioning face. He wasn't going to offer them to me, so I reached out and took them. "Takata's car isn't nicer than yours," I said, upending the container over the remains of my waffle. "I was just jerking you around."

"I figured that out," he said wryly. He wasn't eating, and I looked up to see him with knife and fork in hand, watching me scrape the last of the strawberries out with my butter knife.

"What?" I said as I put the crock down. "You weren't going to have any more."

He carefully cut another square of waffle. "You've been in contact with Takata, then?"

I shrugged. "Ivy and I are working security at his concert next Friday." I wedged a small bite into my mouth and closed my eyes as I chewed. "This is really good." He didn't say anything, and my eyes opened. "Are you—ah—going?"

"No."

Turning back to my plate, I glanced at him from around my hair. "Good." I ate another bite. "The man is something else; when we talked, he was wearing orange pants. And he's got his hair out to here." I gestured, showing Trent. "But you probably know him. Personally."

Trent was still working on his waffle with the steady pace of a snail. "We met once."

Content, I slid all the strawberries off the remnants of my waffle and concentrated on them. "He picked me up off the street, gave me a ride, dumped me off on the expressway." I smiled. "At least he had someone bring my car along. Have you heard his early release?" *Music. I could always keep the conversation going if it was about music. And Trent liked Takata. I knew that much about him.*

" 'Red Ribbons'?" Trent asked, an odd intentness to his voice.

Nodding, I swallowed and pushed my plate away. There were no more strawberries, and I was full. "Have you heard it?" I asked, settling back in my chair with my coffee.

"I've heard it." Leaving a shallow wedge of waffle uneaten, Trent set his fork down and pushed it symbolically away. His hands went to his tea and he leaned back in his chair. I went to take a sip of coffee, freezing as I realized Trent had mirrored both my posture and my motion.

Oh, crap. He likes me. Mirroring motions was classic in the body language of attraction. Feeling as if I'd stumbled into somewhere I didn't want to go, I intentionally leaned forward and put the flat of my arm on the table, my fingers encircling my warm mug of coffee. *I wouldn't play this game. I wouldn't!*

" 'You're mine, yet wholly you,' " Trent said dryly, clearly oblivious to my thoughts. "The man has no sense of discretion. It's going to catch up with him someday."

Eyes distant and unaware, he put the flat of his arm on the table. My face went cold and I choked, but it wasn't because of what he had done. It was because of what he had said. "Holy crap!" I swore. "You're a vamp's scion!"

Trent's eyes jerked to mine. "Excuse me?"

"The lyrics!" I sputtered. "He didn't release those. It's on the vamp track only undead vampires and their scions can hear. Oh my God! You've been bitten!"

Lips pressed together, Trent picked up his fork and cut a triangle of waffle, using it to sop up the last of the syrup on his plate. "I'm not a vampire's scion. And I've never been bit."

My heart pounded and I stared. "Then how do you know them? I heard you. I heard you say them. Straight off the vamp track."

He arched his thin eyebrows at me. "How do you know about the vamp track?"

"Ivy."

Trent rose. Wiping his fingers clean, he tightened his robe and crossed the room to the casual living-room pit with the wall-sized TV and stereo. I watched him pluck a CD from atop a shelf and drop it into a player. While it spun up, he punched in a track and "Red Ribbons" came from hidden speakers. Though it was soft, I could feel the base line thumping into me.

Trent showed a tired acceptance as he turned with a set of wireless headphones. They were professional looking, the type that fit over your ears instead of resting on them. "Listen," he said, extending them to me. I drew back suspiciously, and he wedged them on my head.

My jaw dropped and my eyes flew to his. It was "Red Ribbons," but it wasn't the same song. It was incredibly rich, seeming to go right to my brain, skipping my ears. It echoed within me, swirling behind and through my thoughts. There were impossible highs, and rumbling lows that set my tongue tingling. It was the same song, but there was so much more.

I realized I was staring at my plate. What I had been missing was beautiful. Pulling in a breath of air, I drew my head up. Trent had sat again, watching. Stunned, I reached to touch the headphones, reassuring myself that they were really there. The vamp track was indescribable.

And then the woman started to sing. I looked at Trent, feeling panicked, it was so beautiful. He nodded with a Cheshire cat smile. Her voice was lyrical, both rough and tragic. It pulled emotion from me I wasn't aware I could feel. A deep painful regret. Unrequited need. "I didn't know," I whispered.

As I listened to the end, unable to take the headphones off, Trent took our plates to the kitchen. He came back with an insulated pot of tea, topping off his cup before sitting down. The track ended, leaving only silence. Numb, I slid the headphones off and set them by my coffee.

"I didn't know," I said again, thinking that my eyes must look haunted. "Ivy can hear all that? Why doesn't Takata release them sounding like that?"

Trent adjusted his position in his chair. "He does. But only the undead can hear it."

I touched the headphones. "But you—"

"I made them after finding out about the vamp track. I wasn't sure they would work with witches. I gather by your expression that they did?"

My head bobbed loosely. "Ley line magic?" I questioned.

A smile, almost shy, flickered over him. "I specialize in misdirection. Quen thinks it a waste of time, but you'd be surprised what a person will do for a pair of those."

I pulled my eyes from the headphones. "I can imagine."

Trent sipped his tea, leaning back in speculation. "You don't . . . want a pair, do you?"

I took a breath, frowning at the faint taunt in his voice. "Not for what you're asking, no." Setting my mug of coffee at arm's length, I stood. His earlier behavior of mimicking my motions was suddenly abundantly clear. He was an expert in manipulation. He had to know what signals he was sending. Most people didn't—at least consciously—and that he had tried to lay the groundwork to try to romance my help when money wouldn't buy it was contemptible.

"Thanks for dinner," I said. "It was fabulous."

Surprise brought Trent straight. "I'll tell Maggie you enjoyed it," he said, his lips tightening. He'd made a mistake, and he knew it.

I wiped my hands off on my sweatshirt. "I'd appreciate that. I'll get my things."

"I'll tell Quen you're ready to go." His voice was flat.

Leaving him sitting at the table, I walked away. I caught a glimpse of him as I turned and went into Ellasbeth's rooms. He was touching the headphones, his posture unable to hide his annoyance. The bandage on his head and his bare feet made him look vulnerable and alone.

Stupid lonely man, I thought.

Stupid ignorant me for pitying him.

Twenty-eight

I scooped my shoulder bag up from the bathroom floor, making a slow circuit to be sure I'd gotten everything. Remembering my garment bag, I went to retrieve it and my coat from the changing room. My jaw dropped at the open phone book on the low table and my face flamed. She had it open to escorts, not independent runners. "She thinks I'm a hooker," I muttered, ripping the page out and jamming it into my jeans pocket. Damn it, I didn't care that we both did legit escort service occasionally, Ivy was going to take it out. Ticked, I shrugged into my ugly coat with the fake fur about the collar, snatched up my unworn outfit, and left, almost running into Trent on the open walkway. "Whoa! Sorry," I stammered, taking two steps back.

He tightened the tie on his robe, his eyes empty. "What are you going to do about Lee?"

The night's events rushed back, making me frown. "Nothing."

Trent rocked back, surprise making him look young. "Nothing?"

My focus blurred as I recalled the people scattered where they fell past my saving. Lee was a butcher. He could have gotten them out but had left them so it would look like a hit by Piscary. Which it was, but I couldn't believe that Kisten would do that. He must have warned them. He had to have. But Trent was standing before me, his green eyes questioning.

"It's not my problem," I said, and pushed past him.

Trent was right behind me, his bare feet silent. "He tried to kill you."

Not slowing, I said over my shoulder, "He tried to kill you. I got in the way." *Twice.*

"You're not going to do anything?"

My gaze went to the huge window. It was hard to tell in the dark, but I thought it was clear again. "I wouldn't say that. I'm going to go home and take a nap. I'm tired."

I headed for that six-inch-thick door at the end of the walkway. Trent was still behind me. "You don't care he's going to flood Cincinnati with unsafe Brimstone, killing hundreds?"

My jaw tightened as I thought of Ivy's sister. The jarring from my steps went up my spine. "You'll take care of him," I said dryly. "Seeing as it touches your *business interests.*"

"You have no desire to seek revenge. None whatsoever."

His voice was thick with disbelief, and I stopped. "Look. I got in his way. He's stronger than me. You, on the other hand . . . I'd just as soon see you fry, elf-boy. Maybe Cincinnati would be better without you."

Trent's smooth face went blank. "You don't seriously believe that."

Shifting my garment bag, I exhaled. "I don't know what I believe. You aren't honest with me. Excuse me. I have to go home and feed my fish." I walked away, headed for the door. I knew the way to the front, and Quen would probably catch up with me somewhere in between.

"Wait."

The pleading tone in his voice pulled me to a stop, my hand touching the door. I turned as Quen appeared at the foot of the stairway, his face worried and threatening. Somehow, I didn't think it was because I was about to go wandering through the Kalamack compound, but of what Trent might say. My hand fell from the doorknob. *This might be worth staying for.*

"If I tell you what I know of your father, will you help me with Lee?"

At the ground floor, Quen shifted. "Sa'han—"

Trent's brow furrowed defiantly. *"Exitus acta probat."*

My pulse quickened and I adjusted the fake fur collar of my coat. "Hey! Keep it English, boys," I snapped. "And the last time you said you would tell me about my dad, I came away with his favorite color and what he liked on his hot dog."

Trent's attention went to the floor of the great room and Quen. His security officer shook his head. "Would you like to sit down?" Trent said, and Quen grimaced.

"Sure." Eyeing him warily, I retraced my steps and followed him to the ground floor. He settled himself in a chair tucked between the window and a back wall, his comfortable posture telling me this was where he sat when he was in this room. He had a view of the dark waterfall, and there were several books, their ribbon bookmarks giving evidence of past afternoons in the sun. Behind him on the wall were four tattered Visconti tarot cards, each carefully protected behind glass. My face went cold as I realized that the captive lady on the Devil card looked like Ceri.

"Sa'han," Quen said softly. "This is not a good idea."

Trent ignored him, and Quen retreated to stand behind him, where he could glower at me.

I put my garment bag over a nearby chair and sat, my legs crossed at the knees and my foot bobbing impatiently. Helping Trent with Lee would be a small thing if he told me anything of importance. Hell, I was taking the bastard out myself as soon as I got home and whipped up a few charms. Yeah, I was a liar, but I was always honest with myself about it.

Trent edged to the end of his seat, his elbows on his knees and his gaze on the night. "Two millennium ago, the tide turned in our effort to reclaim the ever-after from the demons."

My eyes widened. Foot stilling, I took my coat off. This might take a while to get to my dad. Trent met my gaze, and seeing my acceptance of this roundabout way, he eased back in a squeak of leather. Quen made a pained sound deep in his throat.

"The demons saw their end coming," Trent said softly. "In an unusual effort of cooperation, they set aside their internal squabblings for supremacy and worked to twist a curse upon all of us. We didn't even realize it had happened for almost three generations, not recognizing the higher fatality percentage of our newborn for what it was."

I blinked. The demons were responsible for the elves' failure? I thought it had been their habit of hybridizing with humans.

"Infant mortality increased exponentially each generation," Trent said. "Our tenuous grip on victory slipped from us in tiny coffins and the sound of mourning. Eventually we realized they had twisted a curse on us, changing our DNA so that it spontaneously broke, each generation becoming progressively worse."

My stomach roiled. Genetic genocide. "You tried to repair the damage by hybridizing with humans?" I asked, hearing the smallness of my voice.

His eyes flicked from the window to me. "That was a last ditch effort to save something until a way could be developed to fix it. It was ultimately a disaster, but it did keep us alive until we improved the genetic techniques to arrest and ultimately repair most of the degradation. When the Turn made it illegal, the labs went underground, desperate to save the few of us who managed to survive. The Turn scattered us, and I find a confused child about every other year."

Feeling unreal, I whispered, "Your hospitals and orphanages." I had never guessed there was a motive other than public relations behind them.

Trent smiled faintly upon seeing the understanding in my eyes. Quen looked positively ill, his wrinkles sliding into each other, his hands behind his back, staring at nothing in a silent protest. Trent eased forward again. "I find them sickly and dying, and they're always grateful for their health and the chance to seek out more of their kin. It's been a thin line the last fifty years. We're balanced. This next generation will save or damn us."

The thought of Ceri intruded, squelched. "What does this have to do with my dad?"

A quick nod bobbed his head. "Your father was working with mine trying to find an old sample of elven DNA in the ever-after that we could use as a pattern. We can fix what we know is wrong, but to make it better, to bring the infant mortality down to where we can survive without medical help, we needed a sample from someone that died before the curse was twisted. Something that we can pattern the repairs upon."

A sound of disbelief escaped me. "You need a sample over two thousand years old?"

He lifted one shoulder in a half shrug. His shoulders didn't seem as wide in the robe, and he looked comfortably vulnerable. "It's possible. There were many pockets of elves that practiced mummification. All we need is one cell even marginally perfect. Just one."

My eyes flicked to a stoic Quen, then him. "Piscary almost killed me trying to find out if you hired me to go into the ever-after. It's not going to happen. I'm not going there." I thought of Al waiting for me, my agreement worthless on his side of the lines. "No way."

An apologetic slant came into Trent's eyes as he watched me from across the coffee table. "I'm sorry. I didn't mean for Piscary to focus on you. I would have rather told you the entire story last year when you quit the I.S., but I was concerned . . ." He took a slow breath. "I didn't trust you to keep your mouth shut about our existence."

"You trust me now?" I said, thinking of Jenks.

"Not really, but I have to."

Not really, but I have to. What the hell kind of an answer is that?

"We're too few to let the world know we exist," Trent was saying, his eyes on his laced fingers. "It would be too easy for a zealot to pick us off, and I have enough trouble with Piscary trying to do just that. He knows the threat we will pose to his standing if our numbers increase."

My mouth twisted and I pushed back into the leather. Politics. It was always political. "Can't you just untwist the curse?"

His face was weary as he turned to the window. "We did when we discovered what had happened. But the damage remains, and would be worsening if we didn't find every elven child and fix what we can."

My lips parted in understanding. "The camp. That's why you were there?"

He shifted reluctantly in his chair, looking suddenly nervous. "Yes."

I pressed back farther into the cushions, not knowing if I wanted him to answer my next question. "Why . . . why was I at that camp?"

Trent's stiff posture eased. "You have a somewhat unusual genetic defect. A good five percent of the witch population has it—a recessive gene which is harmless unless they pair up."

"One in four chance?" I guessed.

"If both parents have it. And if the two recessive genes pair up, it kills you before your first birthday. My father managed to keep it suppressed in you until you were old enough to handle a full course of treatment."

"He did this a lot?" I asked, my stomach knotting. I was alive because of illegal genetic manipulation. It was what I had guessed, but now I knew for sure. Maybe I shouldn't let it bother me. The entire elf race relied on illegal medicine to remain in existence.

"No," Trent said. "Records indicate that with very few exceptions, he allowed infants with your affliction to die, their parents not knowing there was a cure. It's rather expensive."

"Money," I said, and Trent's jaw clenched.

"If the decision was based on money, you wouldn't have seen your first birthday," he said tightly. "My father didn't take one cent for saving your life. He did it because he was friends with your father. You and Lee are the only two running about under the sun that he pulled back from that death, and that was because of friendship. He didn't take a dime for saving either of you. Personally, I'm starting to think he made a mistake."

"This isn't making me want to help you," I said snidely, but Trent gave me a tired look.

"My father was a good man," he said softly. "He wouldn't refuse to help your father save your life when your father had already devoted his life to help him save our entire race."

Frowning, I put a hand to my stomach. I didn't like what I was feeling. My father didn't sacrifice his life in exchange for mine—which was a good thing. But he wasn't the upright, honest, hardworking I.S. runner I had thought. He had willingly helped Trent's father with his illegal activities long before I got sick.

"I'm not a bad person, Rachel," Trent said. "But I will eliminate anyone who threatens to stop the flow of money coming in. My research to repair the damage the demons did to my people's genome isn't cheap. If we could find an old enough sample, we could fix it completely. But it has degraded to the point where we don't know even the color of the pieces anymore."

My thoughts lighted on Ceri, and I steeled my face. The thought of her and Trent meeting was intolerable. Besides, she was only a thousand years old.

Trent's smooth features went tired with a worry far beyond his years. "If the money stops, the next generation of elves will start to slip again. Only if we find a sample from before the curse was twisted can we fix it completely and my species will have a chance. Your father thought it was a task worth dying for."

My eyes flicked to the tarot card with Ceri's likeness and I kept my mouth shut. Trent would use her like a tissue and throw her away.

Trent leaned back, his gaze going sharp on mine. "Well, Ms. Morgan," he said, managing to appear in control even wearing a robe and pj's. "Have I given you enough?"

For a long moment I looked at him, watching his jaw slowly tighten when he realized I was balancing and not knowing which way I was going to jump. Feeling cocky and self-assured, I raised my eyebrows. "Oh hell, Trent. I was going after Lee anyway. What do you think I was doing in your bathtub for two hours? Washing my hair?"

I had no choice but to tag Lee after he tried to blow me up. If I didn't, every mark I put behind bars was going to come out gunning for me.

Trent's face went annoyed. "You've got it figured out already, don't you?" he asked, irritation thick in his river-gray voice.

"Mostly." I beamed, and Quen sighed, clearly having seen beforehand that I was going to snooker his boss but good. "I just need to call my insurance agent and set it up."

Knowing I had gotten the better of Trent was worth more than he could ever line my pockets with, and I snorted when Quen whispered, "Her insurance agent?"

Still sitting, I pointed a finger at Trent. "I've got two things for you to do. Two things, then you back off and let me work. I'm not doing this as a committee. Understand?"

Eyebrows high, Trent said flatly, "What do you want?"

"First, I want you to go to the FIB and tell them Lee knocked out all those people and locked the doors knowing there was a bomb on the boat."

Trent laughed, his warm voice taking on a biting edge. "What is that going to get you?"

"They'll go looking for him. He'll go underground. A warrant will be filed, and with that, I have a legal right to pick him up."

Trent's eyes widened. Behind him, Quen nodded. "That's why . . ." Trent murmured.

I couldn't help my smile. "You can run from the law, but standing up your insurance adjustor?" I shook my head. "Not a good idea."

"You're going to get in to kill him posing as an insurance agent?"

I wished I could say I was surprised. *God, he was so arrogant.* "I don't kill people, Trent. I haul their asses to lockup, and I need a reason for keeping him there. I thought he was your friend."

A hint of uncertainty flickered over Trent. "I thought he was, too."

"Maybe his girlfriend knocked him on the head and forced him into leaving?" I said, not believing it. "Wouldn't you feel bad if you killed him, then found out he had tried to save you?"

Trent gave me a weary look. "Always seeing the best in a person, Ms. Morgan?"

"Yeah. Except with you." I started making a mental list of who I had to tell I was alive: Kisten, Jenks—if he'd listen—Ceri, Keasley . . . Nick? Oh God, my mom. *That one ought to be fun.*

Pushing his fingers into his forehead, Trent sighed. "You have no idea how this works."

Affronted, I puffed at him and his smarter-than-thou attitude. "Work with me here, huh? Letting the bad guy live might be good for your soul."

He didn't look convinced; he looked patronizing. "Letting Lee live is a mistake. His family won't like him in jail. They'd rather have him dead than be an embarrassment."

"Well isn't that just too bad. I'm not going to kill him, and I'm not going to let you kill him, either, so sit down, shut up, hold on, and watch how real people solve problems."

Trent shook his head to make his hair float about his red-rimmed ears. "What's arresting Lee going to get you? His lawyers will have him out before he can sit on a jail-cell cot."

"Voice of experience?" I mocked, seeing as I almost had him there last fall.

"Yes," he said darkly. "The FIB has my fingerprints on file, thanks to you."

"And the I.S. has a sample of my DNA for identification purposes. Suck it up."

Quen made a soft sound, and I suddenly realized we were arguing like children.

Looking peeved, Trent settled back in his chair and laced his fingers over his middle. Fatigue pulled at him. "Admitting I was on that boat is going to be difficult. We weren't seen leaving. And it would be hard to explain how we survived and everyone else died."

"Be inventive. Maybe the truth?" I said cockily. *Pushing Trent's buttons was kinda fun.* "Everybody knows he's trying to jerk Cincinnati out from under you and Piscary. Go with it. Just leave me dead in the river."

Trent eyed me carefully. "You're going to tell your FIB captain you're alive, yes?"

"That's one of the reasons you're going to file with the FIB and not the I.S." My gaze went to the stairway as Jonathan's tall form started down it. He seemed irritated, and I wondered what was up. No one said anything as he approached, and I wished I hadn't pushed Trent so far. The man didn't look happy. It would be just like him to kill Lee out from under me. "You want Saladan out of the city?" I said. "I'll do that for you for free. All I want is you to file a complaint and pay for the lawyer to keep him in prison. Can you do that for me?"

His face went empty as thoughts he didn't want to share with me passed through his mind. Nodding slowly, he beckoned Jonathan closer.

Taking that as a yes, I felt my shoulders ease. "Thanks," I muttered as the tall man bent to whisper in Trent's ear and Trent's gaze shot to me. I strained to hear, getting nothing.

"Keep him at the gate," Trent said, glancing at Quen. "I don't want him on the grounds."

"Who?" I said, wondering.

Trent stood and tightened the tie on his robe. "I told Mr. Felps I'd arrange for your return, but he seems to think you're in need of rescuing. He's waiting for you at the gatehouse."

"Kisten?" I stifled a jerk. I'd be glad to see him, but I was afraid of the answers he would have for me. I didn't want him to have planted that bomb, but Ivy had said he did. *Damn it, why did I always fall for the bad boys?*

While the three men waited, I stood and gathered my things, hesitating before I stuck my hand out. "Thank you for your hospitality . . . Trent," I said, pausing only briefly as I tried to decide what to call him. "And thanks for not letting me freeze to death," I added.

A soft smile quirked the corners of his lips at the hesitation, and he met my firm grip with his own. "It was the least I could do, seeing as you kept me from drowning," he answered. His brow furrowed, clearly wanting to say more. Breath held, he changed his mind and turned away. "Jonathan, will you accompany Ms. Morgan to the gatehouse? I want to talk to Quen."

"Of course, Sa'han."

I glanced back at Trent as I followed Jonathan to the stairs, my mind already on what I had to do next. I'd call Edden first, at his home number, soon as I got to my Rolodex. He might still be up. Then my mother. Then Jenks. This was going to work. It had to.

But as I quickened my pace to keep up with Jonathan, a wash of concern went though me. Sure, I was going to get in to see Saladan, but then what?

Twenty-nine

Kisten had the heat on full, and the warm air shifted a strand of my shorter hair to tickle my neck. I reached to turn it down, thinking he was laboring under the false assumption that I was still suffering from hypothermia and warmer was better. It was stifling, the sensation only strengthened by the darkness we drove through. I cracked the window and eased back as the cold night slipped in.

The living vamp snuck a look at me, jerking his gaze back to the headlight-lit road as soon as our eyes met. "Are you okay?" he asked for the third time. "You haven't said a word."

Shaking my open coat to make a draft, I nodded. He had gotten a hug at Trent's gate, but it was obvious he felt the hesitation. "Thanks for picking me up," I said. "I wasn't too keen on Quen taking me home." I ran my hand across the door handle of Kisten's Corvette, comparing it to Trent's limo. I liked Kisten's car better.

Kisten blew out his breath in a long exhalation. "I needed to get out. Ivy was driving me crazy." He glanced away from the dark road. "I'm glad you told her as soon as you did."

"You talked?" I asked, surprised and a little worried. *Why couldn't I like nice men?*

"Well, she talked." He made an embarrassed noise. "She threatened to cut off both my heads if I jerked your blood out from under her."

"Sorry." I looked out the window, becoming more upset. I didn't want to have to walk away from Kisten because he had meant for those people to die in some stupid power struggle they weren't aware of. He took a breath to say something, and I interrupted with a quick, "Would you mind if I used your phone?"

His expression wary, he pulled his shiny phone from a belt holster and handed it to me. Not particularly happy, I called information and got the number for David's company, and for a few dollars more, they connected me. Why not? It wasn't my phone.

While Kisten silently drove, I worked my way through their automated system. It was almost midnight. He ought to have been in, unless he was on a run or had gone home early. "Hi," I said when I finally got a real person. "I need to talk to David Hue?"

"I'm sorry," an older woman said with an overabundance of professionalism. "Mr. Hue isn't here presently. Can I give you to one of our other agents?"

"No!" I said before she could dump me back into the system. "Is there a number I can reach him at? It's an emergency." *Note to self: never, ever throw anyone's card away again.*

"If you'd like to leave your name and number—"

What part of "emergency" didn't she understand? "Look," I said with a sigh. "I really need to talk to him. I'm his new partner, and I lost his extension. If you could just—"

"You're his new partner?" the woman interrupted. The shock in her voice gave me pause. Was David that hard to work with?

"Yeah," I said, flicking a glance at Kisten. I was sure he could hear both ends of the conversation with his vamp ears. "I really need to talk to him."

"Ah, can you hold for a moment?"

"You bet."

Kisten's face brightened in the glare of oncoming cars. His jaw was fixed and his eyes were riveted to the road.

There was a crackling of the phone being passed, then a cautious, "This is David Hue."

"David," I said, smiling. "It's Rachel." He didn't say anything, and I rushed to keep him on the line. "Wait! Don't hang up. I've got to talk to you. It's about a claim."

There was the sound of a hand going over the phone. "It's okay," I heard him say. "I'll take this one. Why don't you make an early night of it? I'll close down your computer."

"Thanks, David. I'll see you tomorrow," his secretary said faintly, and after a long moment, his voice came back on the line.

"Rachel," he said warily. "Is this about the fish? I've already filed the claim. If you've perjured me, I'm going to be very upset."

"What is it with you thinking the worst of me?" I questioned, miffed. My eyes slid to Kisten as he gripped the wheel tighter. "I made a mistake with Jenks, okay? I'm trying to fix it. But I've got something you might be interested in."

There was a short silence. "I'm listening," he said cautiously.

My breath puffed out in relief. Fidgeting, I dug for a pen in my shoulder bag. Opening my datebook, I clicked my pen open. "Ah, you work by commission, right?"

"Something like that," David said.

"Well, you know that boat that exploded?" I snuck a glance at Kisten. The light from the oncoming traffic made little glints in his stubble as he clenched his jaw.

There was a rattling of computer keys in the background. "Still listening . . ."

My pulse quickened. "Does your company own the policy on it?"

The sound of keys quickened and vanished. "Seeing as we insure everything Piscary isn't interested in, probably." There was another spurt of tapping keys. "Yes. We have it."

"Great," I sighed. *This was going to work.* "I was on it when it exploded."

I heard the squeak of a chair through the line. "Somehow that doesn't surprise me. You saying it wasn't an accident?"

"Ah, no." I flicked a glance at Kisten. His knuckles gripping the wheel were white.

"Really." It wasn't a question, and the sound of tapping keys started up again, shortly followed by the hum of a printer.

I shifted in Kisten's heated leather seats and stuck the end of the pen in my mouth. "Would I be correct that your company doesn't pay out when property is destroyed—"

"Because of acts of war or gang-related activity?" David interrupted. "No. We don't."

"Fantastic," I said, not thinking it necessary to tell him I was sitting next to the guy who had arranged the whole thing. *God, please let Kisten have an answer for me.* "How would you like me to come down there and sign a paper for you?"

"I'd like that really fine." David hesitated, then added, "You don't strike me as the kind of woman who commits acts of random kindness, Rachel. What do you want out this?"

My gaze ran down Kisten's clenched jaw to his strong shoulders, then lingered on his hands gripping the wheel as if he was trying to squeeze the iron out of it. "I want to be with you when you go out to adjust Saladan's claim."

Kisten jerked, apparently only now understanding why I was talking to David. The silence on the other end of the line was thick. "Ah . . ." David murmured.

"I'm not going to kill him; I'm going to arrest him," I quickly offered.

The thrum of the engine rumbling up through my feet shifted and steadied.

"It's not that," he said. "I don't work with anyone. And I'm not working with you."

My face burned. I knew he thought very little of me after finding I had kept information from my own partner. But it was David's fault it came out. "Look," I said, turning away from Kisten as he stared at me. "I just saved your company a wad of money. You get me in when you go to adjust his claim, then back out of the way and let me and my team work." I glanced at Kisten. Something had shifted in him. His grip on the wheel was loose and his face was empty.

There was a short silence. "And afterward?"

"Afterward?" The moving lights made Kisten's face unreadable. "Nothing. We tried working together. It didn't work out. You get an extension on finding a new partner."

There was a long silence. "That's it?"

"That's it." I clicked my pen closed and threw it and my datebook into my bag. *Why did I even try to be organized?*

"Okay," he finally said. "I'll bark down the hole and see what comes up."

"Fantastic," I said, genuinely glad, though he seemed less than pleased. "Hey, in a few hours I'm going to have died in that explosion, so don't worry about it, okay?"

A tired sound escaped him. "Fine. I'll call you tomorrow when the claim comes in."

"Great. I'll see you then." David's lack of excitement was depressing. The phone clicked off without him saying good-bye, and I closed it and handed it back to Kisten. "Thanks," I said, feeling very awkward.

"I thought you were turning me in," Kisten said softly.

Mouth falling open, I stared, only now understanding his previous tension. "No," I whispered, feeling afraid for some reason. He had sat there and done nothing as he thought I was turning him in?

Shoulders stiff and eyes on the road, he said, "Rachel, I didn't know he was going to let those people die."

My breath caught. I forced it out, then took another. "Talk to me," I said, feeling light-headed. I stared out the window, hands in my lap and my stomach clenched. *Please, let me be wrong this time?*

I looked across the car, and after his eyes flicked to the rearview mirror, he pulled off to the side of the road. My gut clenched. Damn it, why did I have to like him? Why couldn't I like nice men? Why did the power and personal strength that attracted me always seem to translate into callous disregard for other people's lives?

My body shifted forward and back when he came to a sudden halt. The car shook as traffic continued to pass us at eighty miles an hour, but here it was still. Kisten shifted in his seat to face me, reaching over the gearshift to cradle my hands in my lap. His day-old stubble glinted in the lights from the oncoming traffic across the median, and his blue eyes were pinched.

"Rachel," he said, and I held my breath hoping he was going to tell me it had all been a mistake. "I arranged to have that bomb strapped to the boiler."

I closed my eyes.

"I didn't intend for those people to die. I called Saladan," he continued, and I opened my eyes when a passing truck shook us. "I told Candice there was a bomb on his boat. Hell, I told her where it was and that if they touched it, it would detonate. I gave them plenty of time to get everyone off. I wasn't trying to kill people, I was trying to make a media circus and sink his business. It never occurred to me he would walk away and leave them to die. I misjudged him," he said, a bitter recrimination in his voice, "and they paid for my shortsightedness with their lives. God, Rachel, if I even guessed he would do that, I'd have found another way. That you were on that boat . . ." He took a breath. "I almost killed you. . . ."

I swallowed hard, feeling the lump in my throat grow less. "But you've killed people before," I said, knowing the problem wasn't tonight but a history of belonging to Piscary and having to carry out his will.

Kisten leaned back though his hands never left mine. "I killed my first person when I was eighteen."

Oh God. I tried to pull away, but he gently tightened his grip. "You need to hear this," he said. "If you want to walk away, I want you to know the truth so you don't come back. And if you stay, then it's not because you made a decision based on too little information."

Steeling myself, I looked at his eyes, gauging them sincere, and perhaps carrying a hint of guilt and past hurt. "You've done this before," I whispered, feeling afraid. I was one in a string of women. They had all left. Maybe they were smarter than me.

He nodded, his eyes closing briefly. "I'm tired of being hurt, Rachel. I'm a nice guy who just happened to kill his first person at eighteen."

I swallowed, taking my hands back under the pretense of tucking my hair behind an ear. Kisten felt me draw away and turned to look out the front window, placing his hands back on the wheel. I had told him not to make my decisions for me; I suppose I deserved every sordid detail. Stomach twisting, I said, "Go on."

Kisten stared at nothing as the traffic passed, accentuating the point of stillness in the car. "I killed my second about a year later," he said, his voice flat. "She was an accident. I managed to keep from ending anyone else's life again until last year when—"

I watched him as he took a breath and exhaled. My muscles trembled, waiting for it.

"God, I'm sorry, Rachel," he whispered. "I swore I'd try to never have to kill anyone again. Maybe that's why Piscary doesn't want me as his scion now. He wants someone to share the experience, and I won't do it. He was the one who actually killed them, but I was there. I helped. I held them down, kept them busy while he gleefully butchered them one by one. That they deserved it hardly seems justification anymore. Not with the way he did it."

"Kisten?" I said hesitantly, pulse fast.

He turned, and I froze, trying not to be frightened. His eyes had gone black in the memory. "That feeling of pure domination is a twisted, addictive high," he said, the lost hunger in his voice chilling me. "It took me a long time to learn how to let go of that so I could remember the inhuman savagery of it, hidden by the jolt of pure adrenaline. I lost myself with Piscary's thoughts and strength flooding me, but I know how to wield it now, Rachel. I can be both his scion and a just person. I can be his enforcer and a gentle lover. I know I can walk the balance. He's punishing me right now, but he'll take me back. And when he does, I'll be ready."

What the hell was I doing here?

"So," I said, hearing my voice tremble. "That's it?"

"Yeah. That's it," he said flatly. "The first was under Piscary's orders to make an example of someone luring underage kids. It was excessive, but I was young and stupid, trying to prove to Piscary that I'd do anything for him, and he took enjoyment from seeing me agonize about it later. The last time was to stop a new camarilla from forming. They were advocating a return to pre-Turn traditions of abducting people no one would miss. The woman." His eyes flicked to me. "That's the one that haunts me. That's when I decided to be honest when I could. I swore I'd never end another innocent's life again. It doesn't matter that she lied to me . . ." His eyes closed and his grip on the wheel trembled. The light from across the median showed the lines of pain on his face.

Oh God. He had killed someone in a passionate rage.

"And then I ended sixteen lives tonight," he whispered.

I was so stupid. He admitted to killing people—people the I.S. probably would thank him for getting rid of, but people nevertheless. I had come into this knowing he wasn't the "safe boyfriend," but I'd had the safe boyfriend and always ended up hurt. And despite the brutality he was capable of, he was being honest. People had died tonight in a horrible tragedy, but that hadn't been his intent.

"Kisten?" My eyes dropped to his hands, his short round nails carefully kept clean and close to his fingertips.

"I had the bomb set," he said, guilt making his voice harsh.

I hesitantly reached to take his hands from the wheel. My fingers felt cold against his. "You didn't kill them. Lee did."

His eyes were black in the uncertain light when he turned to me. I sent my hand behind his neck to pull him closer, and he resisted. He was a vampire, and that wasn't an easy thing to be—it wasn't an excuse, it was a fact. That he was being forthright meant more to me than his ugly past. And he had sat there while he thought I was turning him in and did nothing. He had ignored what he believed and trusted me. I would try to trust him.

I couldn't help but feel for him. Watching Ivy, I had come to the conclusion that being a master vampire's scion was very much like being in a mentally abusive relationship where love had been perverted by sadism. Kisten was trying to distance himself from his master's sadistic demands. He *had* distanced himself, he had distanced himself so far that Piscary had dumped him for a soul even more desperate for acceptance: my roommate. *Swell.*

Kisten was alone. He was hurting. He was being honest with me—I couldn't walk away. We had both done questionable things, and I couldn't label him as evil when I was the one with the demon mark. Circumstances had made our choices for us. I did the best I could. So did he.

"It wasn't your fault they died," I said again, feeling as if I had found a new way to see. Before me lay the same world, but I was looking around corners. *What was I becoming? Was I a fool to trust, or a wiser person finding the capacity to forgive?*

Kisten heard the acceptance of his past in my voice, and the relief reflected in his face was so strong that it was almost painful. My hand on his neck slid forward, drawing him closer over the console. "It's okay," I whispered as his hands slipped from my fingers and took my shoulders. "I understand."

"I don't think you can. . . ." he insisted.

"Then we'll deal with it when I do." Tilting my head, I closed my eyes and leaned to find him. His grip on my shoulder eased, and I found myself reaching after him, drawn in as our lips touched. My fingers pressed into his neck, urging him closer. A jolt struck through me, bringing my blood to the surface, tingling through me as his kiss deepened, promising more. It didn't stem from my scar, and I drew his hand to it, almost gasping when his fingertips traced the light, almost unseen scar tissue. The thought of Ivy's dating guide flitted through me, and I saw it all in an entirely new way. *Oh God, the things I could do with this man.*

Maybe I needed the dangerous man, I thought as a wild emotion rose in me. Only someone who had done wrong could understand that, yes, I did questionable things too, but that I was still a good person. If Kisten could be both, then maybe that meant I could be, too.

And with that, I abandoned all pretense of thought. His hand feeling my pulse and my lips pulling on his, I sent my tongue hesitantly between his lips, knowing a gentle inquiry would strike a hotter chord than a demanding touch. I found a smooth tooth, and I curled my tongue around it, teasing.

Kisten's breath came fast and he jerked away.

I froze as he was suddenly not there, the heat of him still a memory on my skin. "I'm not wearing my caps," he said, the black swelling in his eyes and my scar pulsing in promise. "I was so worried about you, I didn't take the time to . . . I'm not . . ." He took a shaking breath. "God, you smell good."

Heart pounding, I forced myself back into my seat, watching him as I tucked my hair behind an ear. I wasn't sure I cared if he had his caps on or not. "Sorry," I said breathlessly, blood still pounding through me. "I didn't mean to go that far." *But you just sort of pull it out of me.*

"Don't be sorry. You're not the one who's been neglecting—things." Blowing his breath out, Kisten tried to hide his heady look of want. Under the rougher emotions was a soft look of grateful understanding and relief. I had accepted his ugly past, knowing his future might not be any better.

Saying nothing, he put the car in first and accelerated. I held the door until we slid back onto the road, glad nothing had changed though everything was different.

"Why are you so good to me?" he said softly as we picked up speed and passed a car.

Because I think I could love you? I thought, but I couldn't say it yet.

Thirty

My head came up at the faint sound of knocking. Giving me a warning look, Ivy stood, stretching for the kitchen's ceiling. "I'll get it," she said. "It's probably more flowers."

I took a bite of cinnamon toast and muttered around my full mouth, "If it's food, bring it back, will you?"

Sighing, Ivy walked out, both sexy and casual in her black exercise tights and a thigh-length baggy sweater. The radio was on in the living room, and I had mixed feelings about the announcer talking about the tragedy of the boat explosion early last night. They even had a clip of Trent telling everyone I had died saving his life.

This was really odd, I thought as I wiped butter from my fingers. Things had been showing up on our doorstep. It was nice to know I would be missed, and I hadn't known I had touched so many lives. It wasn't going to be pretty when I came out of the closet as being alive, though—kind of like standing someone up at the altar and having to give all the presents back. 'Course, if I died tonight, I'd go to my grave knowing just who my friends were. I kinda felt like Huck Finn.

"Yeah?" Ivy's wary voice came back through the church.

"I'm David. David Hue," came a familiar voice, and swallowing the last bite of toast, I ambled up to the front of the church. I was starving, and I wondered if Ivy was slipping Brimstone into my coffee to try to build my body's reserves after that dunk in the river.

"Who is she?" Ivy asked belligerently as I entered the sanctuary and found them on the landing, the lowering sun coming in past their feet.

"I'm his secretary," a tidy woman at David's side said, smiling. "Can we come in?"

My eyes widened. "Whoa, whoa, whoa," I said, waving my hands in protest. "I can't watch two of you and bring in Lee."

David ran his eyes down my casual sweater and jeans, his eyes thick with a calculating evaluation. They lingered on my shortened hair, dyed a temporary brown just this afternoon as he had suggested over the phone. "Mrs. Aver isn't going to come with us," he said, making what was probably an unconscious nod of approval. "I thought it prudent that your neighbors see me arrive with a woman as well as leave with one. You're close to the same body build."

"Oh." *Idiot,* I thought. *Why didn't I think of that?*

Mrs. Aver smiled, but I could tell she thought I was an idiot, too. "I'll just pop into your bathroom and change, and then I'll go," she said brightly. Taking a step into the room, she set her slim briefcase beside the piano bench and hesitated.

Ivy started. "This way," she said, indicating that the woman should follow her.

"Thank you. You're so kind."

Making a small face for all the hidden undercurrents, I watched Mrs. Aver and Ivy leave, the former making a lot of noise in her bland black heels, the latter silent in her slippers. Their conversation ended with the click of my bathroom door shutting, and I turned to David.

He looked like a completely different Were outside of his spandex running pants and shirt. And nowhere near the same person the time I saw him leaning against a park tree in a duster that went to his boot tops and a cowboy hat pulled over his eyes. His heavy stubble was gone, to leave sun-roughed cheeks, and his long hair was styled and smelled of moss. Only the highest ranking Weres could carry off polish and not look like they were trying, but David managed it. The three-piece suit and manicured fingernails helped. He looked older than his athletic physique would testify, with a pair of glasses perched on his nose and a tie snugged up to his neck. Actually, he looked really good—in a professional, educated sort of way.

"Thanks again for helping me get in to see Saladan," I said, feeling awkward.

"Don't thank me," he said. "I'm getting a huge bonus." He set his expensive-looking suitcase on the piano bench. He seemed preoccupied—not angry with me, but wary and disapproving. It made me uncomfortable. Sensing me watching him, he looked up. "Mind if I do a little prep paperwork?"

I shifted back a step. "No. Go right ahead. You want some coffee?"

David looked at Jenks's desk and hesitated. Brow furrowing, he sat astride the piano bench and opened his briefcase up before him. "No thanks. We won't be here that long."

"Okay." I retreated, feeling his dissatisfaction heavy on me. I knew he didn't like that I had lied to my partner by omission, but all I needed was for him to get me in to see Lee. I hesitated at the top of the hallway. "I'll go change. I wanted to see what you were wearing."

David looked up from his paperwork, his brown eyes distant as he tried to do two things at once. "You'll be wearing Mrs. Aver's clothes."

My eyebrows rose. "You've done this before."

"I told you the job was a lot more interesting than you would think," he said to his papers.

I waited for him to say something more, but he didn't, so I went to find Ivy, feeling awkward and depressed. He hadn't said a word about Jenks, but his disapproval was clear.

Ivy was busy with her maps and pens when I entered, saying nothing as I poured a cup of coffee for me, and then her. "What do you think of David?" I asked, setting her cup beside her.

Her head went down and she tapped a colored pen on the table. "I think you'll be okay. He seems to know what he's doing. And it's not like I won't be there."

Leaning against the counter, I held my mug with both hands and took a long sip. Coffee slid down, easing my jitters. Something in Ivy's posture caught my attention. Her cheeks were a shade red. "I think you like him," I said, and her head jerked up. "I think you like older men," I added. "Especially older men in suits that bite and can plan better than you."

At that, she did flush. "And I think you should shut up."

We both started at the soft knock on the archway to the hall. It was Mrs. Aver, and it was embarrassing that neither of us had heard her come out of the bathroom. She was dressed in my robe, her clothes over one arm. "Here you go, honey," she said as she handed me her gray suit.

"Thanks." I set my coffee down and took it.

"If you would, drop them off at Weres-'N-Tears dry cleaners. They do a good job getting out blood and stitching up small rips. Do you know where that is?"

I looked at the matronly woman standing before me in my fuzzy blue robe, her long brown hair down about her shoulders. She looked to be about the same size as me, if a bit hippy. My hair was a shade darker, but it was close enough. "Sure," I said.

She smiled. Ivy was back at her maps, ignoring us, her foot silently moving. "Great," the Were said. "I'm going to change and say 'bye to David before I leave on four feet." Flashing me a toothy grin, she sashayed to the hallway, hesitating. "Where's your back door?"

Ivy stood up with a noisy scrape of a chair. "It's broken. I'll get it for you."

"Thank you," she said with that same polite smile. They left, and I slowly I brought the woman's clothes to my nose. They were still warm from her body heat, and the faint scent of musk mixed with a light meadowy smell. My lips curved downward at the idea of wearing someone else's clothes, but the entire idea was to smell like a Were. And it wasn't as if she had brought me rags to put on. The lined wool suit must have cost her a bundle.

Steps slow and measured, I went to my room. That dating guide was still out on my dresser, and I looked at it with a mix of depression and guilt. What had I been thinking, wanting to read it again with the idea to drive Kisten wild? Miserable, I shoved it in the back of my closet. God help me, I was an idiot.

Resigned, I slipped out of my jeans and sweater. Soon the clack of nails in the hallway intruded, and as I put on my nylons, there was the pained sound of nails being pulled from wood. The new door wouldn't be in until tomorrow, and it wasn't as if she could slip out a window.

I was feeling very unsure about this, and it wasn't anything I could really pinpoint. *It wasn't going in charmless,* I thought as I shimmied into the gray skirt and tucked the white blouse in. Ivy and Kisten would be bringing in everything I needed; my duffel bag of spells was already packed and waiting in the kitchen. And it wasn't because I was going up against someone better in ley line magic. I did that all the time.

I shrugged into the jacket, slipping the warrant for Lee into an inner pocket. Wedging my feet into the low heels I had pulled from the back of my closet, I stared at my reflection. Better, but still it was me, and I reached for the contact lenses that David had couriered over earlier.

As I blinked and teared the thin brown bits of plastic into place, I decided that my unease was because David didn't trust me. He didn't trust my abilities, and he didn't trust me. I'd never had a partner relationship where I was the one under doubt. I had been thought of as an airhead before, and a flake, even incompetent, but never untrustworthy. I didn't like it. But looking back over what I had done to Jenks, it was probably deserved.

Movements slow and depressed, I styled my shorter hair up into a spare, businesslike bun. I put my makeup on heavy, using a base that was too dark, and so having to give my hands and neck a good layer as well. It covered my freckles, though, and with an unhappy feeling, I twisted my wooden pinky ring off; the charm was broken. With the darker makeup and the brown contact lenses, I looked different, but the clothes really turned the trick. And as I stood before my mirror and looked at myself in my dull boring suit and a dull boring hairstyle, and a dull boring look on my face, I didn't think even my mother would recognize me.

I dabbed a drop of Ivy's expensive perfume on me—the one that hid my scent—then followed it up with a splash of a musky perfume Jenks once said smelled like the underside of a log: earthy and rich. Clipping Ivy's phone onto my waist, I went into the hall, my heels making an unusual amount of noise. The soft sound of Ivy and David in conversation pulled me into the sanctuary, where I found them at her piano. I really wished Jenks were with us. It was more than needing him for reconnaissance and camera detail. I missed him.

David and Ivy looked up at the sound of my feet. Ivy's mouth dropped open. "Bite me and slight me," she said. "That is the most god-awful thing I think I've seen you wear. You actually look respectable."

I smiled weakly. "Thanks." I stood there gripping my hands in a fig-leaf posture as David ran his gaze over me, the slight easing of his brow the only sign of his approval. Turning away, he tossed his papers into his briefcase and snapped it shut. Mrs. Aver had left hers behind, and I picked it up when David indicated I should. "You'll bring my spells?" I asked Ivy.

She sighed, turning her gaze to the ceiling. "Kisten is on his way over. I'll go over it with him one more time, then we lock up the church and leave. I'll give you a ping when we're in place." She looked at me. "You do have my spare phone?"

"Ah . . ." I touched it on my waist. "Yes."

"Good. Go," she said as she turned and walked away. "Before I do something stupid like give you a hug."

Depressed and unsure, I headed out. David was behind me, his pace silent but his presence obvious by the faint scent of fern. "Sunglasses," he murmured when I reached for the door handle, and I paused to put them on. I pushed the door open, squinting from the late sun as I picked my way through the sympathy offerings ranging from professional flower arrangements to crayon-bright pages torn from coloring books. It was cold, the crisp air refreshing.

The sound of Kisten's car pulled my head up, and my pulse jackhammered. I froze on the steps and David almost ran into me. His foot bumped a squat vase, and it rolled down the steps to the sidewalk, spilling water and the single budded red rose it held.

"Someone you know?" he asked, his breath warm on my ear.

"It's Kisten." I watched him park and get out. *God, he looked good, all trim and sexy.*

David's hand went onto my elbow, pushing me into motion. "Keep going. Don't say anything. I want to see how your disguise holds up. My car is across the street."

Liking the idea, I continued down the stairs, stopping only to pick up the vase and set it on the lowest stair. It was actually a jelly-jar glass, with a pentagram of protection on it, and I made a soft sound of recognition as I tucked the red rose back into it and straightened. I hadn't seen one of those in years.

I felt a flutter in my stomach when Kisten's steps grew loud.

"Bless you," he said as he passed me, thinking I had put the flower there, not just picked it up. I opened my mouth to say something, closing it as David pinched my arm.

"Ivy!" Kisten shouted, hammering on the door. "Let's go! We're going to be late!"

David escorted me across the street and to the other side of his car, his hand firmly under my elbow—it was slick, and the heels I had on weren't made for ice. "Very nice," he said, sounding begrudgingly impressed. "But it's not as if you've slept with him."

"Actually," I said as he opened the door for me, "I have."

His eyes jerked to mine and a shocked look of revulsion crossed him. From inside the church came a faint, "You're fucking kidding! That was her? No fucking way!"

I pushed my fingers into my forehead. At least he didn't swear like that when I was around. My eyes went to David, the width of the door between us. "It's the species thing, isn't it?" I said flatly.

He said nothing. Jaw clenched, I told myself that he could think what he wanted. I didn't have to live up to his standards. Lots of people didn't like it. Lots of people didn't give a flip. Who I slept with should have nothing to do with our professional relationship.

Mood worsening, I got in and closed my door before he could do it. My belt clicked shut, and he slid behind the wheel and started his little gray car up. I didn't say a word as he pulled out and headed for the bridge. David's cologne became cloying, and I cracked the window.

"You don't mind going in without your charms?" David asked.

His tone lacked the expected disgust, and I seized on that. "I've gone in charmless before," I said. "And I trust Ivy to get them to me."

His head didn't move, though his eyes tightened in the corners. "My old partner never was without his charms. I'd laugh at him when we'd go in and he'd have three or four of them hanging around his neck. 'David,' he'd say, 'this one's for seeing if they're lying. This one's for knowing if they're under a disguise. And this one's for telling me if they're carrying a bunch of energy around in their chi and are ready to blast us all to hell.' "

I glanced at him, my mood softening. "You don't mind working with witches."

"No." He took his hand off the wheel when we rumbled over a railroad track. "His charms saved me a lot of pain. But I can't tell you the number of times he spent fumbling for the right spell when a good right cross would have settled things faster."

We crossed the river into Cincinnati proper, and the buildings made flickering come-and-go shadows on me. He was prejudiced only when sex came into the picture. I could handle that. "I'm not going in completely helpless," I said, warming slightly. "I can make a protection circle around myself if I have to. But I'm really an earth witch. Which might make things difficult as it's harder to bring someone in if you can't do the same magic." I made a face he didn't see. "Then again, there's no way I can beat Saladan at ley line magic, so it's just as well I'm not even going to try. I'll get him with my earth charms or my foot in his gut."

David brought the car to a slow halt at a red light. Face showing the first signs of interest, he turned to me. "I heard you brought down three ley line assassins."

"Oh, that." I warmed. "I had help with that. The FIB was there."

"You brought Piscary down yourself."

The light changed, and I appreciated him not creeping up on the car ahead of us until it moved. "Trent's security officer helped me," I admitted.

"He distracted him," David said softly. "You were the one who clubbed him into unconsciousness."

Pressing my knees together, I turned to look at him straight on. "How do you know?"

David's heavy jaw tightened and relaxed, but he didn't look from the street. "I talked to Jenks this morning."

"What!" I exclaimed, almost hitting my head on the ceiling. "Is he okay? What did he say? Did you tell him I was sorry? Will he talk to me if I call him?"

David glanced askance at me as I held my breath. Saying nothing, he made a careful turn onto the parkway. "No to everything. He's very upset."

I settled in my seat, flustered and worried.

"You need to thank him if he ever talks to you again," David said tightly. "He thinks the world of you, which is the main reason I didn't go back on my agreement to get you in to see Saladan."

My gut twisted. "What do you mean?"

He hesitated while he passed a car. "He's hurt you didn't trust him, but he didn't say one bad word about you, even stood up for you when I called you a flighty airhead."

My throat tightened and I stared out the passenger-side window. *I was such an ass.*

"He's of the backward opinion that he deserved being lied to, that you didn't tell him because you felt he couldn't keep his mouth shut and that you were probably right. He left because he thought he let you down, not the other way around. I told him you were a fool, and that any partner who lied to me would end up with their throat torn out." David made a puff of scorn. "He kicked me out. Four-inch man kicked me out. Told me if I didn't help you like I said I would, he'd track me down when the weather broke and give me a lobotomy when I slept."

"He could do it," I said, my voice tight. I could hear the threatened tears in it.

"I know he could, but that's not why I'm here. I'm here because of what he didn't say. What you did to your partner is deplorable, but so honorable a soul wouldn't think highly of someone who didn't deserve it. I can't see why he does, though."

"I've been trying to talk to Jenks for the last three days," I said around the lump in my throat. "I'm trying to apologize. I'm trying to fix this."

"That's the other reason I'm here. Mistakes can be fixed, but if you do it more than once, it's no longer a mistake."

I said nothing, my head starting to hurt as we passed a river-overlook park and pulled onto a side street. David touched his collar, and I read in his body posture that we were almost there. "And it was sort of my fault it came out," he said softly. "Bane has a tendency to make you loose in the lips. I'm sorry about that, but it was still wrong of you."

It didn't matter how it came out. Jenks was furious with me, and I deserved it.

David signaled and turned into a cobbled drive. I tugged at my gray skirt and adjusted my jacket. Wiping my eyes, I sat upright and tried to look professional, not like my world was falling down around me and all I had to depend on was a Were who thought I was the lowest of the low. I'd have given anything to have Jenks on my shoulder making wisecracks about my new haircut or how I smelled like the bottom of an outhouse. Anything.

"I'd keep my mouth shut if I were you," David said darkly, and I bobbed my head, thoroughly depressed. "My secretary's perfume is in the glove box. Give your nylons a good spray. The rest of you smells okay."

I obediently did as he said, my usual hot abhorrence to take direction from someone squelched in that he thought so little of me. The musty scent of the perfume overpowered the car, and David rolled his window down, grimacing. "Well, you did say . . ." I muttered when the cold air pooled at my ankles.

"It's going to be quick once we get in there," David said, his eyes watering. "Your vamp partner has five minutes tops before Saladan gets angry about the claim and kicks us out."

I held Mrs. Aver's briefcase on my lap tighter. "She'll be there."

David's only response was a muttered rumble. We wound up a short drive that looped about itself. It had been plowed and swept, and the red clay bricks were damp with snowmelt. At the top of it was a stately house painted white with red shutters and tall, narrow windows. It was one of the few older mansions that had been refurbished without losing its charm. The sun was behind the house, and David parked in the shadows behind a black pickup truck and cut the engine. A curtain at a front window shifted.

"Your name is Grace," he said. "If they want identification, it's in your wallet inside your briefcase. Here." He handed me his glasses. "Wear them."

"Thanks." I set the plastic lenses on my nose, learning that David was farsighted. My head started to hurt and I pulled them lower so I could look at the world over them instead of through them. I felt awful, the butterflies in my stomach as heavy as turtles.

A sigh shifted him, and he reached between our seats for his briefcase in the back. "Let's go."

Thirty-one

"David Hue," David said coolly, sounding bored and a little irritated as we stood in the entryway of the old mansion. "I have an appointment."

I, not we, I thought, keeping my eyes down and trying to stay in the background while Candice, the vamp that had been all over Lee on his boat, cocked her jeans-clad hip and looked at his business card. There were two more vamps behind her in black suits that screamed security. I didn't mind playing the meek subordinate; if Candice recognized me, it would get really bad, really quick.

"That was me you talked to," the shapely vampire said around a bothered sigh. "But after the recent ugliness, Mr. Saladan has retired to . . . a less public environment. He's not here, much less taking appointments." Smiling to show her teeth in a politically polite threat, she handed his card back. "I'll be glad to talk to you, though."

My heart pounded and I stared at the Italian tile. He was here—I could almost hear the rattle of chips—but if I didn't get in to see him, this was going to be a lot more difficult.

David looked at her, the skin about his eyes tightening, then picked up his briefcase. "Very well," he said shortly. "If I can't speak with Mr. Saladan, my company has no recourse but to assume our understanding of terrorist activity is correct and we will deny payment on the claim. Good day, ma'am." He barely glanced at me. "Come on, Grace. Let's go."

Breath catching, I felt my face pale. If we walked out of here, Kisten and Ivy would be headed into a trap. David's steps were loud as he went for the door, and I reached out after him.

"Candice," came Lee's irate, buttery voice from the second-story railing above the grand staircase. "What are you doing?"

I spun, David taking my elbow in warning. Lee stood by the upper landing, a drink in one hand, a folder and pair of wire-rimmed glasses in the other. He was wearing what looked like a suit without the coat, his tie loose about his neck but still tidy.

"Stanley, honey," Candice purred, falling into a provocative slump against the small table by the door. "You said no one. Besides, it's just a little boat. How much could it be worth?"

Lee's dark eyes pinched as he frowned. "Almost a quarter million—dear. They're insurance agents, not I.S. operatives. Do a spell check on them and show them up. They're required by law to keep everything confidential, including that they were even here." He looked at David and tossed his surfer-boy bangs out of his way. "Am I right?"

David smiled up at him with that shared, good-old-boys' look that I hated. "Yes, sir," he said, his voice echoing against the flat white of the open vestibule. "We couldn't do our work without that little constitutional amendment."

Lee put his hand up in acknowledgment, turned, and vanished down the open hall. A door creaked shut, and I jerked as Candice grabbed my briefcase. Adrenaline pulled me straight, and I clutched it to me.

"Relax, Grace," David said patronizingly as he took it from me and handed it to Candice. "This isn't unusual."

The two vamps in the background came forward, and I forced myself to not move. "You'll have to forgive my assistant," David said while he put our cases on the table by the door and opened first his and spun it around, then mine. "Breaking in a new assistant is hell."

Candice's expression went mocking. "Were you the one to give her the black eye?"

I flushed, my hand going to touch my cheekbone and my gaze falling to my ugly shoes. Apparently the darker makeup didn't work as well as I thought.

"You have to keep your bitches in line," David said lightly. "But if you hit them right, you only have to hit them once."

My jaw clenched, and I warmed as Candice laughed. I watched from under my lowered brow while a vamp pawed through my briefcase. It was full of stuff only an insurance adjustor would have: a calculator with more tiny buttons than a leprechaun's dress boots, notepads, coffee-stained folders, useless little calendars to stick on your fridge, and pens with smiley faces on them. There were receipts from places like sub shops and Office Depot. God, it was awful. She glanced at my fake business cards with an absent-minded interest.

While David's briefcase got the same scrutiny, Candice sauntered into a back room. She came back with a pair of wire-rimmed glasses, which she made a show of scrutinizing us through. My heart pounded as she then brought out an amulet. It was glowing a warning red.

"Chad, honey," she murmured. "Back up. Your spell is interfering."

One of the vamps flushed and retreated. I wondered what Chad-honey had a spell for that would turn his ears that particular color. My breath slipped from me when the amulet shifted green, making me grateful that I'd gone in under a mundane disguise. Beside me, David's fingers twitched. "Can we move this faster?" he said. "I have other people to see."

Candice smiled and twirled the amulet on her finger. "Right this way."

With a quickness seemingly born from irritation, David snapped his briefcase closed and dragged it from the small table. I did the same, relieved when the two vamps vanished into a back room following the smell of coffee. Candice headed up the stairs with a slow pace, her hips going as if they were going to gyrate off her. Trying to ignore her, I followed.

The house was old, and now that I was getting a better look at it, not well-maintained. Upstairs, the carpet was thinning, and the pictures hanging in the open hallway overlooking the vestibule were so ancient they probably came with the house. The paint above the wainscoting was that icky green popular before the Turn, and it looked repulsive. Someone with little imagination had used it to cover the eight-inch floorboards carved with ivy and hummingbirds, and I spared a pained thought at the grandeur hidden behind ugly paint and synthetic fibers.

"Mr. Saladan," Candice said in explanation as she opened a black-varnished door. Her smile was catty, and I followed David in, keeping my eyes down when I passed her. I held my breath, praying that she couldn't tell it was me, hoping she wouldn't come in. But why would she? Lee was an expert in ley line magic. He didn't need protection from two Weres.

It was a good-sized office done in oak paneling. High ceilings and the thick framework about the tall block of windows was the only evidence that the room had started out as a bedroom before becoming an office. Everything else had been covered and disguised with chrome and light oak that was only a few years old. I was a witch; I could tell.

The windows behind the desk went to the floor, and the low sun spilled in over Lee as he rose from his desk chair. A bar cart was in one corner, and an entertainment center took up most of the opposite wall. Two comfortable chairs were arranged before his desk, leaving one ugly one in a far corner. There was a huge wall mirror and no books. My opinion of Lee hit rock bottom.

"Mr. Hue," Lee said warmly as he extended his tanned hand over the expanse of the modern-looking desk. His suit coat was hanging from a nearby hat tree, but he had at least snugged his tie up. "I've been expecting you. Sorry about the mix-up downstairs. Candice can be protective at times. You can understand, seeing as boats seem to be exploding around me."

David chuckled, sounding a little like a dog. "Not a problem, Mr. Saladan. I won't take much of your time. It's a courtesy call to let you know how your claim is being processed."

Smiling, Lee held his tie to himself and sat, indicating we should do the same. "Can I get you a drink?" he asked as I settled myself in the supple leather chair and put my briefcase down.

"No, thank you," David said.

Lee hadn't given me more than a cursory glance, not even offering to shake my hand. The "men's club" air was thick enough to chew on, and whereas I normally would have charmingly asserted myself, this time I gritted my teeth and pretended I didn't exist like a good little bitch at the bottom of the hierarchy.

While Lee added ice to his drink, David donned a second pair of glasses and opened his briefcase atop his lap. His clean-shaven jaw was tight and I could smell his leashed excitement growing. "Well," he said softly, bringing out a sheaf of papers. "I regret to inform you that, after our initial inspection and our preliminary interviews with a survivor, my company has declined making a settlement."

Lee dropped a second cube of ice into his drink. "Excuse me?" He spun on a shiny heel. "Your *survivor* has too much at stake to come forth with any information contrary to it being an accident. And as for your inspection? The boat is at the bottom of the Ohio River."

David bobbed his head. "Quite so. But the boat *was* destroyed during a citywide power struggle, and thus its destruction falls under the terrorism clause."

Making a bark of disbelief, Lee sat behind his desk. "That boat is brand-new. I've only made two payments on it. I'm not going to take the loss. That's why I insured it."

David put a stapled pack of papers on the desk. Peering over his glasses, he dug out a second paper, closed his briefcase, and signed it. "This is also notice that your premiums on your other properties we insure will be increasing by fifteen percent. Sign here, please."

"Fifteen percent!" Lee exclaimed.

"Retroactive to the beginning of the month. If you would like to cut me a check, I am prepared to accept payment."

Damn, I thought. David's company played hardball. My thoughts shifted from Lee to Ivy. This was going south really fast. Where was her call? They had to be in place by now.

Lee wasn't happy. Jaw tight, he laced his fingers together and set them on the desk. His face went red from behind his black bangs and he leaned forward. "You need to look in your briefcase, little pup, and find a check in there for me," he said, his Berkeley accent growing pronounced. "I'm not accustomed to being disappointed."

David snapped his briefcase shut and set it gently on the floor. "You need to broaden your horizons, Mr. Saladan. It happens to me all the time."

"Not me." Round face wrathful, Lee got to his feet. The tension rose. I eyed Lee, then David, looking confident even though he was seated. Neither man was going to back down.

"Sign the paper, sir," David said softly. "I'm just the messenger. Don't get the lawyers into this. Then they're the only ones who get any money and you become uninsurable."

Lee took a hasty breath, his dark eyes pinched in anger.

I jumped at the sudden ring of my phone. My eyes widened. It was playing the theme to the Lone Ranger. I scrambled to turn it off, not knowing how. *God help me.*

"Grace!" David barked, and I jumped again. The phone slipped from my fingers. I fumbled after it, face flaming. My emotions warred between panic that they were both looking at me and my relief that Ivy was ready.

"Grace, I told you to turn that phone off when we were in the drive!" David yelled.

He stood, and I looked at him in helplessness. He snatched the phone out of my hands. The music cut off and he threw it back at me.

My jaw clenched as it hit my palm with a sharp snap. I'd had enough. Seeing my hot anger, David moved between me and Lee, gripping my shoulder in warning. Ticked, I knocked his arm away. But my anger caught when he smiled and winked at me.

"You're a good operative," he said softly as Lee punched a button on his intercom and had a hushed conversation with what sounded like a very upset Candice. "Most of the people I work with would have gone for my throat at the front door with that subordinate-bitch comment. Dig your feet in. We can get a few more minutes out of this conversation, and I still need him to sign my form."

I nodded, though it was hard. The compliment helped.

Still standing, Lee reached for his coat and slipped his arms into it. "I'm sorry, Mr. Hue. We will have to continue this at another opportunity."

"No, sir." David stood unmoving. "We will finish this now."

There was a commotion in the hallway, and I rose when Chad, the vampire with the charm, stumbled in. Seeing David and me, he swallowed down his first, probably frantic, words.

"Chad," Lee said, the faintest bother in his expression as he took in the vamp's disheveled appearance. "Will you see Mr. Hue and his assistant to their car?"

"Yes, sir."

The house was quiet and I stifled a smile. Ivy once took out an entire floor of FIB agents. Unless Lee had a hell of a lot of people hidden about, it wouldn't be long until I had my charms and Lee would be wearing handcuffs.

David didn't move. He stood before Lee's desk, his Were mien growing. "Mr. Saladan." He pushed the form forward with two fingers. "If you would?"

Red spots started on Lee's round cheeks. Taking a pen from an inner jacket pocket, he signed the paper, making his name big and unreadable. "Tell your superiors that I will be compensated for my loss," he said, leaving it on the desk for David to pick up. "It would be a shame if your company found itself in financial straits by a number of your more expensive properties becoming damaged."

David picked up the paper and tucked it in his briefcase. Standing beside and a little behind him, I felt his tension rise and saw him shift his balance to the balls of his fcct. "Is that a threat, Mr. Saladan? I can transfer your claim to our complaint department."

A soft boom thumped against my inner ear, and Chad jiggled on his feet. It was a distant explosion. Lee looked at a wall as if he could see through it. My eyebrows rose. Ivy.

"Just one more signature." David brought out a trifolded paper from a coat pocket.

"Our time is done, Mr. Hue."

David stared at him, and I could almost hear the growl. "It won't take but—a moment. Grace, I need your signature, here. Then Mr. Saladan's . . . here."

Surprised, I stepped forward, head lowered to the paper David smoothed out on the desk. My eyes widened. It stated that I was a witness to seeing the bomb on the boiler. I thought it wrong that David's company was more worried about the boat than the people who died on it. But that was insurance for you.

I took the pen, glancing up at David. He made a small shrug, a new, hard glint to his eyes. Despite his anger, I think he was enjoying this.

Heart pounding, I signed it as Rachel. I listened for any sound of battle as I handed the pen to David. They had to be close, and there might not be any indication that they were in the house if all went well outside. Lee was tense, and my stomach tightened.

"And you, sir." It was sarcastic, and David turned the paper to him. "Sign, and I can close your file and you'll never have to see me again."

I wondered if that was his standard line as I reached into an inner pocket of my borrowed jacket and pulled out the warrant Edden had brought over that afternoon.

Motions rough and belligerent, Lee signed the paper. Beside me, I heard the softest rumble of satisfaction from David. It was only then that Lee looked at my signature. The man went white under his tan. His thin lips parted. "Son of a bitch," he swore, his eyes rising to me, then Chad in the corner.

Smiling, I gave Lee my warrant. "This one's from me," I said cheerfully. "Thanks, David. Do you have what you need?"

David took a step back, tucking his form away. "He's all yours."

"Son of a bitch!" Lee said again, a disbelieving smile quirking his lips. "You just don't know when to stay dead, do you?"

My breath hissed in and I jerked as I felt him tap a line.

"Get down!" I shouted, shoving David out of the way and lurching back.

Pinwheeling, David hit the floor. I slid almost to the door. The air crackled and a thump reverberated through me. On all fours, I jerked my gaze to the ugly purple stain dripping to the floor. *What the Turn was that?* I thought, scrambling up and tugging my skirt to my knees.

Lee gestured to Chad, who looked cowed. "Well, get them!" he said, sounding disgusted.

Chad blinked, then strode to David.

"Not him, you idiot!" Lee shouted. "The woman!"

Chad yanked himself to a stop, turned, then reached for me.

Where in hell was Ivy? My demon scar flamed to pleasure, and while it was rather distracting, I nevertheless had no problem jamming the heel of my palm into Chad's nose, jerking back when the cartilage tore. I hated the feel of breaking noses. It gave me the willies.

Chad cried out in pain, hunching over and holding his blood-soaked hands to his face. I followed him down, giving him an elbow on the back of his neck, which he conveniently put in my reach. In three seconds Chad was down.

Rubbing my elbow, I looked up to find David watching in wide-eyed interest. I was between Lee and the door. Smiling, I tossed the hair that had escaped my bun out of my eyes. Lee was a ley line witch; chances were that he was a coward when it came to physical pain. He wouldn't jump out that window unless he had to.

Lee thumbed an intercom. "Candice?" His voice was a mix of anger and threat.

Panting, I licked my thumb and pointed to Lee. "David, you might want to leave. This is going to be dicey."

My good mood grew when Kisten's voice came out of the speaker along with the pained sounds of a catfight. "Candice is busy, old man." I recognized the sound of Ivy's attack, and Kisten made a noise of sympathy. "Sorry, love. You shouldn't have strayed. Oh, that *had* to hurt." Then he was back, his fake accent heavy and amused. "Perhaps I could help you?"

Lee clicked off the intercom. He adjusted his coat, watching me. He looked confident. Not good. "Lee," I said, "we can do it easy, or hard."

There was a thumping of feet in the hallway, and I fell back to David when five men came spilling in. Ivy wasn't with them. Neither were my charms. They did have a lot of guns, though, all pointed at us. *Damn.*

Lee smiled and came out from behind his desk. "I'm all for easy," he said, so smug I wanted to slap him.

Chad was starting to move, and Lee nudged him in the ribs. "Get up," he said. "The Were has a paper in his jacket. Get it."

Stomach churning, I backed up as Chad staggered to his feet, blood dripping on his cheap suit. "Just give it to him," I warned when David tensed. "I'll get it back."

"No, I don't think you will," Lee said as David handed it to Chad and the vamp passed the now blood-smeared paper to Lee. White teeth gleaming, he tossed his hair and smiled. "Sorry to hear about your accident."

I glanced at David, hearing our coming death in his words.

Lee wiped the blood off on Chad's coat. Folding it twice, he tucked it in a jacket pocket. Headed for the door, he said casually, "Shoot them. Take out the bullets, then dump them under the ice downriver from the dock. Clean up the room. I'm going out for an early dinner. I'll be back in two hours. Chad, come with me. We need to talk."

My heart pounded and I could smell David's rising tension. His hands were opening and closing as if they hurt. Maybe they did. I gasped at the sound of safeties going off.

"Rhombus!" I shouted, my word lost in the thunder of weapons discharging.

I staggered as my thoughts tapped the nearest line. It was the university's, and it was huge. I smelled gunpowder. Straightening, I patted at myself frantically. Nothing hurt but my ears. David's face was white but there was no pain in his eyes. A shimmer of molecule-thin ever-after shone around us. The four men were straightening from their own crouches. I had gotten the circle up in time and their bullets had ricocheted right back at them.

"What do we do now?" one asked.

"Hell if I know," the tallest said.

From the floor of the vestibule came Lee's shout, "Just fix it."

"You!" came Ivy's faint demand. "Where's Rachel!"

Ivy! Frantic, I looked at my circle. It was a trap. "Can you take two of them?" I asked.

"Give me five minutes to Were, and I can take them all," David all but growled.

The noise of fighting drifted up. It sounded like there were a dozen people down there, and one angry vampire. One of the men looked at the others and ran out. Three left. The pop of a gun downstairs brought me straight. "We don't have five minutes. Ready?"

He nodded.

Face twisting, I broke my link to the line and the circle fell. "Go!" I exclaimed.

David was a blur beside me. I went for the smallest, knocking his weapon aside with a foot as he tried to backpedal. It was my training against his slower magic, and my training won. His gun skittered across the floor, and he dove for it. *Idiot.* Following him down, I elbowed his kidney. He gasped and turned to face me, far short of the gun. God, he looked young.

Teeth gritted, I picked up his head and slammed it into the ground. His eyes closed and his body went slack. Yeah, it was crude, but I was in kind of a hurry.

The crack of a weapon discharging pulled me around. "I'm fine!" David barked, popping up with a Were's quickness from a crouch and jabbing a small, powerful fist at the last witch standing. Eyes rolling to the back of his head, the witch dropped the gun from slack fingers and toppled to fall on the first man David had downed. Damn, he was fast!

My heart pounded and my ears rang. We had brought them down with only one shot fired. "You got two," I said, exhilarated at the joined effort. "Thanks!"

Breathing hard, David wiped his lip and swooped to get his briefcase. "I need my paper."

We stepped over the downed witches. David went out before me. He stopped, eyes narrowing at the man on the balcony taking aim at Ivy. Grunting, he swung his briefcase. It smacked into the witch's head. Staggering, the man turned. I spun on one foot, slamming my foot into his solar plexus. His arms pinwheeled as he fell back into the railing.

I didn't stop to see if he was down or not. Leaving David to wrestle for the gun, I ran down the stairs. Ivy was fending off Candice. My bag of charms was at Ivy's feet. There were three bodies sprawled on the tile floor. Poor Chad wasn't having a very good day.

"Ivy!" I called when she threw Candice into the wall and had a moment. "Where's Lee!"

Her eyes were black and her lips were pulled back from her teeth. With a high scream of outrage, Candice came at her. Ivy jumped for the chandelier, her foot connecting with Candice's jaw to rock the vampire back. There was a creak from the ceiling.

"Look out!" I cried from the bottom step as Ivy swung to land with an unreal grace and the chandelier fell. It shattered, sending broken glass and crystal everywhere.

"Kitchen!" Ivy panted from a hunched crouch. "He's in the garage. With Kisten."

Candice looked at me, hatred in her black eyes. Blood ran from her mouth, and she licked it. Her gaze went to the duffel bag of spells. She tensed to run for it—and Ivy jumped.

"Go!" Ivy shouted, grappling with the smaller vampire.

I went. Heart pounding, I ran around the ruin of the chandelier, scooping up my charms in passing. From behind me came a scream of terror and pain. I skidded to a stop. Ivy had Candice pinned to the wall. My face went cold. I'd seen it before. *God help me. I'd lived it.*

Candice bucked and fought, a new frenzy in her motions as she tried to get free. Ivy held her still, as unmoving as a steel girder. Piscary's strength made her unstoppable, and Candice's fear was feeding her blood lust. A rattle of gunfire came from the unseen garage. I tore my gaze from them, frightened. Ivy had vamped out. Absolutely and totally. She had lost herself.

Mouth dry, I ran through the empty kitchen to the garage door. Candice screamed again, the terrifying sound ending in a gurgle. I hadn't wanted this. I hadn't wanted this at all.

I spun at a scuffling noise behind me, but it was David. His face was white, and he never slowed down as he paced to me. There was a weapon in his grip.

"Is she . . ." I asked, hearing my voice shake.

His hand went on my shoulder and he pushed me into motion. Lines marked his face, and he looked old. "Just go," he said raggedly. "She's got your back."

The sound of men's voices in the garage rose, then fell. There was a spat of gunfire. Crouched by the door, I shuffled through my duffel bag. I put a slew of amulets around my neck and tucked my cuffs into my waistband. My splat gun was heavy in my hand, fourteen little babies in a row ready for sleep in the reservoir, enough propellant to shoot them all.

David peeked around the door, then ducked back. "Five men with Saladan behind a black car on the far end of the garage. I think they're trying to get it started. Your boyfriend is around the corner. We can reach him with a quick run." He looked at me as I fumbled at my charms. "Good God! What are all those for?"

My boyfriend? I thought, crawling to the doorway with my charms dragging under me. *Well, I* had *slept with him.* "One is for pain," I whispered. "One is for slowing down bleeding. One is for detecting black charms before I walk into them, and one—"

My words cut off as the car started. *Shit.*

"Sorry I asked," David muttered, close behind me.

Heart pounding, I risked an upright, hunched walk, taking a deep breath of the dark, garage-cold air as I ducked behind a bullet-dinged silver Jag. Kisten's head swung up. He was on the floor with a hand pressed to his lower chest. Pain glazed his eyes, and his face was pale under his blond-dyed hair. Blood seeped from under his hand, and I went cold from more than the unheated garage. Four men were down beside him. One moved, and he kicked him in the head until he didn't move anymore.

"Better and better," I whispered, making my way to Kisten. The garage door whined into motion, and the shouts from the car were loud over the revving engine. But Kisten was the only thing I cared about right now.

"Are you okay?" I dropped two charms over his head. I felt sick. He wasn't supposed to have gotten hurt. Ivy wasn't supposed to have been tripped into draining someone. Nothing was supposed to have gone this way.

"Get him, Rachel," he said, managing a pained-looking grimace. "I'll live."

The car's tires squealed as it backed up. Panicking, I looked from Kisten to the car, torn.

"Get him!" Kisten insisted, his blue eyes crinkled in pain.

David eased Kisten to the garage floor. One hand pressing Kisten's hand against the wound, he sent the other searching his jacket. Pulling out his phone, David flipped it open and punched 911.

Kisten nodded, his eyes closing as I stood. The car had backed up into the turnaround spot and was jerking into motion. It stalled. Mad as all hell, I stomped out after it.

"Lee!" I shouted. The car's engine sputtered and caught, its wheels spinning on the wet cobbles. My jaw gritted. Tapping a line, I clenched my fist. Line energy coursed through me, filling my veins with the staggering feeling of strength. My eyes narrowed. "Rhombus," I said, fingers splayed as I gestured.

My knees buckled and I screamed when the pain from the line energy required to make such a large circle raged through me, burning when I couldn't channel it all at once. There was an ugly noise of folding metal and squealing tires. The sound raked through me, fixing in my memory to haunt my nightmares. The car had hit my circle, but the car broke, not me.

I caught my balance and continued forward as men piled out of the smashed vehicle. Never slowing, I took aim with my splat gun, squeezing the trigger with a methodical slowness. Two went down before the first of the bullets went cutting through the air beside my head.

"You shooting at me?" I screamed. "You shooting at me!" I dropped the gunman with a charm, leaving Lee and two men. One put his hands in the air. Lee saw him, then with no hesitation, shot him. The pop of the gun jerked through me as if I had been hit.

The witch's face went ashen, and he collapsed to the cobbled drive, leaning against the car and trying to hold his blood into him.

Anger shocked through me and I halted. Seething, I aimed at Lee and squeezed.

Drawing himself up, he whispered Latin and gestured. I lurched to the side, but he had been going for the ball and it deflected to the right. Still crouched, I shot again. Lee's eyes went patronizing as he deflected it too. The movements of his hands took on a more sinister mien, and my eyes widened. *Shit, I had to end this now.*

I lunged at him, yelping when the last vampire slammed into me. We went down in a tangle, me fighting furiously to keep him from getting a hold on me. With a last grunt and savage kick, I broke free, rolling to my feet. Panting, I backed away. My sparring with Ivy came back in a mixed slurry of hope and despair. I had never managed to best her. Not really.

Silent, the vampire attacked. I dove to the side, skinning my elbow as Mrs. Aver's suit tore through. He was on me, and I rolled, head covered with my arms, kicking him off when I caught my breath. The tingle of my circle zinged through me. I had run into it and it had fallen. Immediately I lost connection with the line, making me feel empty.

I jumped to my feet, swerving to avoid the vamp's leg swing. *Damn it, he wasn't even trying!* My splat gun was behind him, and when he came at me, I collapsed out of his reach, rolling to get it. Fingers grasping, my breath exploded out as the cool metal settled in my grip.

"Got you, you bastard!" I shouted, spinning to plug him right in the face.

His eyes widened, then rolled up. Stifling a shriek, I rolled out of the way as his momentum tipped him forward. There was a sodden thump as he hit the cobbled drive. Blood seeped out from under his cheek. He'd broken something.

"Sorry you work for such a dick," I breathed as I got up, then did a double take. My face went slack and I let my gun slip to dangle from a finger. I was surrounded by eight men, all of them a good ten feet back. Lee stood behind them, looking obnoxiously satisfied as he adjusted the button on his coat. I grimaced and tried to catch my breath. Oh yeah. I had broken the circle. *Shit on crap, how many times did I have to tag this guy?*

Panting and hunched in pain, I saw David and Kisten unmoving under three guns in the garage. There were eight surrounding me. Add in the five I'd just downed. Kisten had gotten at least four. Mustn't forget the original guys upstairs. I didn't even know how many Ivy had taken out. The man was ready for a freaking war.

Slowly I straightened. I could handle that.

"Ms. Morgan?" Lee's voice sounded odd among the dripping snowmelt coming off the garage's overhang. The sun was behind the house, and I shivered now that I wasn't moving. "Anything left in your little gun?"

I looked at it. If I had counted right—and I thought I had—there were eight charms in there. Eight charms that were useless as Lee could deflect them all. And even if he didn't, I stood little chance in taking that many men without getting nailed. *If I played by the rules . . .*

"I'm dropping the gun," I said, then carefully, slowly, opened the reservoir and dumped the blue splat balls out before I tossed it to him. Seven tiny spheres bounced, rolling in the cracks of the red cobbled drive to come to a stop. Seven in the open; one in my hand. *God, this had to work. Just don't bind my hands. I had to keep my hands.*

Shaking, I put my hands in the air and backed away, a tiny splat ball dropping down my sleeve to make a cold spot at my elbow. Lee gestured, and the surrounding men converged. One grabbed my shoulder, and I struggled not to hit him. *Placid, meek. No need to tie me up.*

Lee got in my face. "Stupid, stupid girl," he sneered, touching his forehead under his short dark bangs where a new cut spread.

He pulled his hand back, and I forced myself to not move, taking it as he backhanded me. Seething, I pulled myself straight where the momentum had shifted me. The surrounding men laughed, but my hands behind my back were moving, the splat ball rolling to find my palm as I finished. My eyes flicked from Lee to my splat balls on the cobbles. Someone bent to pick one up. "You're wrong," I said to Lee, breathing hard. "I'm a stupid, stupid witch."

Lee's attention followed mine to the splat balls. *"Consimilis,"* I said, tapping a line.

"Get down!" Lee exclaimed, pushing the men around him out of the way.

"Calefacio!" I shouted, elbowing the witch holding me and rolling to the ground. My circle snapped into existence around me with a quick thought. There was a sharp pop, and a scattering of blue-colored shrapnel peppered the outside of my bubble. The plastic balls had burst from the heat, sending superheated sleep potion everywhere. I looked up from between my arms. Everyone was down but Lee, having put enough men between him and the flying potions. In the garage, Ivy stood panting over the last three vamps. We had gotten them. All that was left was Lee. And he was mine.

A smile curved over me as I stood and broke my circle, taking the energy back into my chi. "Just you and me, surfer boy," I said, tossing the splat ball I had used for a focusing object and catching it. "Care to throw the dice?"

Lee's round face went still. He held himself unmoving, and then, without a glimmer of emotion, tapped a line.

"Son of a bitch," I swore, lunging. I slammed into him, knocking him flat on the cobbles. Teeth gritted, he gripped my wrist, squeezing until the splat ball rolled from me.

"You will shut up!" I shouted from atop him, jamming my arm into his throat so he couldn't speak. He fought me, bringing his hand up to smack my cheek.

My breath hissed out in a pained gasp as he hit the bruise Al gave me. Catching his wrist, I snapped my cuffs on him. Spinning him over, I wrenched his arm out from under him. Knee on his back, pinning him to the pavement, I snapped the other ring about his other wrist.

"I am tired of your crap!" I exclaimed. "Nobody tries to put a black charm on me, and nobody traps me in a boat with a bomb. Nobody! You hear me? Who in hell do you think you are, coming into my city and trying to take over?" Rolling him over, I snatched David's paper from behind his coat. "And this isn't yours!" I said, holding it high like a trophy.

"Ready for a little trip, witch?" Lee said, his eyes dark with hate and blood leaking from his mouth.

My eyes widened as I felt him pull more from the ley line he was already linked to. "No!" I shouted, realizing what he was doing. *The cuffs were FIB issue,* I thought, kicking myself. They were FIB issue, lacking the core of solid silver that the I.S. issue cuffs came standard with. He could jump. He could jump to a line if he knew how. And apparently he did.

"Rachel!" Ivy shrieked, her voice and the light cutting off with a terrifying suddenness.

A sheet of ever-after coated me. I choked, pushing Lee away, clawing at my mouth, unable to breathe. My heart beat wildly as his magic raced through me, etching the lines both physical and mental that defined me. The blackness of never flooded me, and I panicked as I felt myself exist in splinters everywhere but nowhere sure. I teetered on madness, unable to breathe, unable to think.

I screamed as I snapped back into myself with a wrench and the blackness retreated to the pit of my soul. I could breathe.

Lee kicked at me, and I rolled away to my hands and knees, thanking God I had them again. Cold rock bit through my nylons, and I sucked in the air, gasping, gagging at the choking smell of ash. The wind whipped my hair into my face. My exposed skin went icy. Heart pounding, I looked up, knowing by the ruddy light coating the rubble I knelt in that we weren't in Lee's drive anymore.

"Oh . . . crap," I whispered as I took in the setting sun glowing through the remains of shattered buildings.

I was in the ever-after.

Thirty-two

The frost-rimmed rocks beside me slid, and I jerked out of the way before Lee's foot could connect with my ribs again. Red and small, the sun crept behind the shadow of a broken building. It looked like Carew Tower. Nearby were the remnants of what might be a fountain. *We were at Fountain Square?* "Lee," I whispered, frightened. "We have to get out of here."

There was a *ping*, and Lee brought his arms out from behind his back. His suit was dirty and it looked out of place amid the destruction. The soft and certain clink of a falling rock pulled my head around, and he threw the handcuffs at it. We weren't alone. *Damn.*

"Lee!" I hissed. *Oh God. If Al found me, I was dead.* "Can you get us home?"

He smiled, brushing the hair out of his eyes. Slipping on the loose rubble, he scanned the ragged horizon. "You don't look well," he said, and I winced at how loud his voice was against the cold rocks. "First time in the ever-after?"

"Yes and no." Shivering, I got up and felt my scraped knees. I'd put a run in my nylons, and blood was seeping out. I was standing in a line. I could feel it humming, could almost see it—it was that strong. Clasping my arms about myself, I jerked at the sound of sliding rock. I wasn't thinking of tagging him; I was thinking of escape. But I couldn't travel the lines.

Another rock fell, bigger. I spun, eyes searching the frost-smeared rubble.

Hands on his hips, Lee squinted up at the red-bottomed clouds as if the cold didn't bother him. "Lesser demons," he said. "Fairly harmless unless you're hurt or ignorant."

I inched away from the fallen rock. "This isn't a good idea. Let's go back and we can finish this like normal people."

He brought his gaze to me. "What will you give me?" he mocked, thin eyebrows high.

I felt like the time my date drove me to a farmhouse and stranded me, telling me if I didn't put out, I could find my own way back. I broke his finger to get the key for his truck and cried all the way home. My mom called his mom and that was the end of it except for the endless ribbing I took at school. Maybe I'd have gotten some respect if my dad had beat up his dad, but that hadn't been an option at that point. I didn't think breaking Lee's finger would get me home this time. "I can't," I whispered. "You killed all those people."

Shaking his head, he sniffed. "You hurt my reputation. I'm going to be rid of you."

My mouth went dry when I realized where this was headed. He was going to give me to Algaliarept, the bastard. "Don't do this, Lee," I said, frightened. My head jerked up at the rapid scrabbling of claws. "We both owe him," I said. "He can take you just as easily."

Lee kicked chunks of rock from his feet to make a clear spot. "No-o-o-o, the word on both sides of the lines is he wants *you.*" Eyes black in the red light, Lee smiled. "But just in case, I'm going to soften you up a little first."

"Lee," I whispered, hunched from the cold as he started to mutter Latin. The glow of the line energy in his hand lit his face with ugly shadows. I tensed in sudden panic. There was nowhere to run in the three seconds I had.

My breath caught at the sudden clatter of things hiding. I jerked my attention up to see a sphere of energy headed right for me. If I made a circle, Al would feel it. If I deflected it, Al would know. So like an idiot, I froze, and it smacked right into me.

Fire rippled over my skin. My head flung back, mouth open as I fought for air. It was simply line energy, overflowing my chi. *Tulpa,* I thought as I fell, giving it somewhere to go.

Immediately the fire died, racing to the sphere already up and waiting in my head. Something in me seemed to shift, and I knew I had made a mistake. The things around us squealed and vanished.

I heard a gentle pop. Heart pounding, I straightened. My breath caught, and I slowly let it out in a steaming ribbon of white moisture. Al's jaunty silhouette was black against the setting sun as he stood atop a broken building, his back to us.

"Shit," Lee swore. "What the hell is he doing here already?"

I spun to Lee and the soft hiss of metallic chalk against pavement. It was a ley line witch's version of duct tape, and it would make a very secure circle. My heart pounded as a shimmer of black and purple rose between us. Blowing hard, Lee tucked his chalk away and smiled confidently at me.

Shivering violently, I looked over the sunset-red slumps of broken rock. I didn't have anything to make a circle with. I was a dead witch. I was on Al's side of the lines; my previous contract didn't mean anything.

Al turned at the sensation of Lee's circle going up. But it was my eyes that his fixed on. "Rachel Mariana Morgan," he drawled, clearly pleased as a cascade of ley line energy washed over him and his attire shifted to what I thought was an English riding outfit, complete with whip and shiny, calf-high boots. "What *did* you do to your hair?"

"Hi, Al," I said, backing up. I had to get out of there. *There's no place like home,* I thought, feeling the hum of the line I was standing in and wondering whether it would help if I clicked my heels. Lee had flown over the rainbow, why, oh why, the hell couldn't I?

Satisfaction all but glowed from Lee. My gaze went from him to Al as the demon carefully picked his way down the slide of rubble to the floor of the large square.

The square, I thought, hope catching in my throat. Spinning, I tried to place myself, tripping as I pushed rocks with my foot, searching. If this was a mirror of Cincinnati, then this was Fountain Square. And if this was Fountain Square, then there was a humdinger of a circle all laid out between the street and the parking garage. But it was really, really big.

My breath came fast when my foot revealed a battered arc of purple inlay. *It was the same. It was the same!* Frantic, I realized Al was almost to the floor of the square. I quickly tapped the nearby line. It flowed into me with the mirror-bright taste of clouds and tinfoil. *Tulpa,* I thought, desperate to gather enough power to close a circle this size before Al realized what I was doing.

I stiffened as a torrent of line energy flooded me. Groaning, I dropped to one knee. His aristocratic face going slack, Al drew himself upright. He saw my intent in my eyes. "No!" he cried, lunging forward as I reached to touch the circle and say my word of invocation.

A gasp slipped from me as, with the feeling of being poured

out of myself, a shimmering wave of translucent gold swam up from the ground, bisecting rocks and slumped rubble, arching to a humming close high over my head. Staggering, I fell back, my mouth gaping open as I stared up at it. *Holy crap, I had closed Fountain Square circle.* I had closed a circle thirty feet across that had been designed for seven witches to set comfortably, not one. Though apparently one could do it if properly motivated.

Al skidded to a halt, arms swinging to avoid running into the circle. A faint bong of reverberation echoed in the dusky air, crawling over my skin like dust. My eyes widened and I stared. Bells. Big, deep, resonant bells. There really were bells, and my circle had rung them.

Adrenaline shook my knees, and they rang again. Al stood to look peeved a mere three feet from the edge, head cocked and thin lips pressed tight as he listened to the third peal die away. The power of the line running through me ebbed, settling into a soft hum. The silence of the night was frighteningly profound.

"Nice circle," Al said, sounding impressed, bothered, and interested. "You're going to be grand fun at tractor pulls."

"Thanks." I twitched when he took off his glove and tapped my circle to make rippled dimples waver across it. "Don't touch it!" I blurted, and he chuckled—tapping, tapping, ever moving, looking for a weak spot. It was a huge circle; he might find one. *What had I done?*

My hands tucked into my armpits for warmth, I looked at Lee, still in his circle, doubly safe within mine. "We can still get out of here," I said, hearing my voice tremble. "Neither one of us needs to be his familiar. If we—"

"How stupid can you be?" Lee edged his foot across his circle, dissolving it. "I want to be rid of you. I want to pay off my demon scar. Why, on God's green earth, would I save you?"

Shivering, I felt the wind bite at me. "Lee!" I said, turning to keep Al in my sight as he moved to the back of my circle, still testing. "We have to get out of here!"

His small nose wrinkling at the scent of burnt amber, Lee laughed. "No. I'm going to beat you into a pulp, and then I'm going to give you to Algaliarept, and he's going to call my debt paid." Cocky and self-assured, he looked at Al, who had stopped pushing at my circle and was now standing with a beatific smile. "Is that satisfactory?"

A lump of fear settled heavy in my belly as a wicked, contriving smile spread over Al's chiseled face. An elaborately detailed rug and a maroon velvet chair from the eighteenth century appeared behind him, and still smiling, Al settled himself, the last of the sun making him a red smear among the broken buildings. Crossing his legs, he said, "Stanley Collin Saladan, we have an agreement. Give me Rachel Mariana Morgan, and I will indeed call your debt paid."

I licked my lips, and they went cold in the bitter wind. Around us came the soft scrabblings as things crept closer, called by me ringing the city's bells and lured by the promise of darkness. A soft plink of stone brought me spinning around. *Something was in here with us.*

Lee smiled, and I wiped my hands off on my borrowed dress suit and stood straighter. He was right to feel confident—I was an earth witch without her charms up against a ley line master—but he didn't know everything. Al didn't know everything. Hell, I didn't know everything, but I knew something they didn't. And when that ugly red sun set behind the broken buildings, it wasn't going to be me who was Al's familiar.

I wanted to survive. Right now it didn't matter if giving Lee to Al in my stead was right or not. Later, when I was curled up with a cup of cocoa and shaking with the memory of this, would be soon enough to decide. But to win, I'd first have to lose. This was really going to hurt.

"Lee," I said, trying one last time. "Take us out of here!" *God, please let me be right!*

"You're such a girl," he said, tugging his dirt-stained suit straight. "Always whining and expecting to be rescued."

"Lee! Wait!" I shouted as he took three steps and threw a ball of purple haze.

I dove to the side. It skimmed past at chest height to hit the remnants of the fountain. With a rumble, a section of it cracked and broke away. Dust rose, red in the darkening air.

When I turned, Lee had my business card in his grip—the one I had given the bouncer at his boat. *Shit. He had a focusing object.* "Don't," I said. "You won't like how it ends."

Lee shook his head, his lips moving as he whispered. *"Doleo,"* he said clearly, the invocation word vibrating the air, and with my card in his grip, he gestured.

Jerking straight, I caught my harsh gurgle before it came from me. Gut-twisting pain doubled me over. Breathing through it, I staggered to my feet. I couldn't think to come back with anything. I staggered forward to try to free myself from pain. If I could hit him, it might stop. If I could get my card, he couldn't target me but would have to throw his spells.

I crashed into Lee. We went down, stones jabbing me. Lee kicked out, and I rolled as Al applauded, white-gloved hands a soft patting. Pain clouded me; thinking was impossible. *Illusion,* I told myself. It was a ley line charm. Only earth magic could inflict real pain. *It was an illusion.* Panting, I forced the charm from me with pure will. I wouldn't feel it.

My bruised shoulder throbbed, hurting worse than it actually did. I fastened on the real pain, willing the phantom agony away. Hunched, I saw Lee from around my hair, now completely fallen out of that stupid bun. *"Inflex,"* Lee said, grinning as his moving fingers finished his spell, and I cringed, waiting for something to happen, but nothing did.

"Oh, I say!" Al exclaimed from his rock. "First rate. Capital!"

I wove on my feet, fighting the last shadows of pain. I was in the line again. I could feel it. If I knew how to trip the lines, I could end this right now. *Bibbity bobbity boo,* I thought. *Alakazam.* Hell, I'd even twitch my nose if I thought it would work. But it didn't.

The rustle around me grew. They were becoming bolder as the sun threatened to set. A rock fell behind me, and I spun. My foot slipped. Crying out, I went down. Nausea hit me as my ankle twisted. Gasping, I clutched at it, feeling tears of pain start.

"Brilliant!" Al applauded. "Bad luck is extremely difficult. Take the charm off her. I don't want a klutz in my kitchen."

Lee gestured and a brief whirlwind smelling of burnt amber lifted through my hair. My throat tightened as the charm broke. My ankle throbbed and the cold rocks bit at me. He had cursed me with bad luck? *Son of a bitch . . .*

Jaw gritted, I reached for a rock to pull myself up. I had blasted Ivy before with raw ever-after, and I didn't need a focusing object if I threw it at him. Anger growing, I pulled upright, reaching into my memory for the how of it. It had always been instinctive before. The fear and anger helped, and as I staggered to my feet, I pushed the ever-after from my chi into my hands. They burned, but I held it, pulling more energy off the line until my outspread hands felt like they were charring. Furious, I compressed the raw energy in my hands to baseball size. "Bastard," I whispered, stumbling as I threw it at him.

Lee dived to the side, and my gold ball of ever-after hit my circle. My eyes widened when a cascade of tingles raced through me as my bubble broke.

"Damn it all to hell!" I shouted, not having thought ahead enough to realize my aura-laced spell would break my circle. Terrified, I spun to Al, thinking if I couldn't get it back up in time I'd be fighting both of them. But the demon was still seated, staring over my shoulder with his goat-slitted eyes wide. He looked over his glasses, mouth hanging open.

I spun in time to see my spell hit a nearby building. A faint *boom* shook my feet. I put a hand to my mouth as a chunk the size of a bus flaked off and fell with an unreal slowness.

"You stupid witch," Lee said. "It's coming right for us!"

I turned and ran, hands reaching as I scrabbled my way across the rubble, hands numb on the frost-cracked rocks. The ground shook, dust rose thick in the air. I staggered and fell.

Hacking and coughing, I got up, shaking. My fingers hurt and I couldn't move them. I turned to find Lee on the other side of the new rockfall, hatred and a touch of fear in his eyes.

Latin came from him. My eyes were fixed upon the card in his moving fingers, heart pounding as I waited, helpless. He gestured, and my card burst into flame.

It flashed like gunpowder. I cried out and turned away, hands over my eyes. The shrieks of the minor demons beat upon me. I reeled backward, balance gone. Red smears coated my vision. My eyes were open and tears streamed down my face, but I couldn't see. I couldn't see!

There was the sound of sliding rocks, and I yelped as someone cuffed me. I blindly lashed out, almost falling as the heel of my hand met nothing. Fear settled into me, debilitating. I couldn't see. He had taken my sight!

A hand shoved me over, and I fell, swinging my leg. I felt it hit him, and he went down. "Bitch," he gasped, and I shrieked when he yanked out a handful of my hair and scrabbled away.

"More!" Al said cheerfully. "Show me your best!" he encouraged.

"Lee!" I cried. "Don't do this!" The red wasn't clearing. *Please, please let it be illusion.*

Dark words came from Lee, sounding obscene. I smelled a strand of my hair burn.

My heart clenched in sudden doubt. I wasn't going to make it. He was going to all but kill me. There was no way to win this. Oh, God . . . what had I been thinking?

"You gave her doubt," Al said wonderingly from the blackness. "That's a very complex charm," he breathed. "What else? Can you divine?"

"I can look backward," Lee said nearby, panting.

"Oh!" Al said gleefully. "I have a marvelous idea! Make her recall her father's death!"

"No . . ." I whispered. "Lee, if you have any compassion. Please."

But his hated voice started whispering, and I groaned, falling into myself as a mental pain cut through the physical. My dad. My dad gasping his last. The feel of his dry hand in mine, the strength gone. I had stayed, refusing to leave for anything. I was there when his breaths stopped. I was there when his soul was freed, leaving me to fend for myself far, far too early. It had made me strong, but it had left me flawed.

"Dad," I sobbed, my chest hurting. He had tried to stay, but couldn't. He had tried to smile, but it was broken. "Oh, Dad," I whispered, softer as the tears welled. I had tried to keep him there with me, but I hadn't been able to.

A black depression rose from my thoughts, pulling me into myself. He had left me. I was alone. He had gone. No one had ever come close to filling the void. No one ever would.

Sobbing, the miserable memory of that awful moment when I realized he was gone filled me. It wasn't when they pulled me from him at the hospital, but two weeks later when I broke the school's eight hundred meters record and I looked into the stands for his proud smile. He was gone. And that was when I knew he was dead.

"Brilliant," Al whispered, his cultured voice soft beside me.

I did nothing as a gloved hand curved under my jaw and tilted my head up. I couldn't see him as I blinked, but I felt the warmth of his hand. "You broke her utterly," Al said in wonder.

Lee's breathing was harsh. Clearly it had taken a lot out of him. I couldn't stop crying, the tears dribbling down my cheeks, cold in the wind. Al let go of my jaw, and I curled into a ball in the rubble at his feet, uncaring of what might happen next. *Oh God, my dad.*

"She's yours," Lee said. "Take my mark off."

I felt Al's arms go around me, lifting me up. I couldn't help but press into him. I was so cold, and he smelled like Old Spice. Though I knew it was Al's twisted cruelty, I clutched at him and sobbed. I missed him. God, I missed him. "Rachel," came my dad's voice, pulled from my memory, and I cried all the harder. "Rachel," it came again. "Is there nothing left?"

"Nothing," I said around my sobbing breaths.

"Are you sure?" my dad said, gentle and caring. "You tried so hard, my little witch. You really fought him with everything and failed?"

"I failed," I said between my sobs. "I want to go home."

"Shhhh," he soothed, his hand cool against me in my darkness. "I'll get you home and put you to bed."

I felt Al shift into motion. I was broken, but I wasn't done. My mind rebelled, wanting to sink deeper into nothingness, but my will survived. It was either Lee or me, and I wanted my cup of cocoa on Ivy's couch and a theme book of rationalizations.

"Al," I whispered. "Lee should be dead." It was easier to breathe. The memory of my father's death was slipping back into the hidden folds of my brain. They had been buried there so long that they found their places easily, one by one filed away for lonely nights by myself.

"Hush, Rachel," Al said. "I see what you intended by letting Lee trounce you, but you can kindle demon magic fully. There has never been a witch that can do that." He laughed, his glee chilling me. "And you're mine. Not Newt's, not anyone else's but mine."

"What about my demon mark?" Lee protested, several steps back, and I wanted to cry for him. He was so dead, and he didn't know it yet.

"Lee can," I whispered. I could see the sky. Blinking profusely, I saw a dark shadow of Al holding me silhouetted against the red-smeared clouds. Relief slipped into me, pushing out the last of my doubt to leave a shimmer of hope underneath. Ley line charms of illusion only worked short-term unless they were given a permanent place to reside in silver. "Taste him," I said. "Taste his blood. Trent's father fixed him, too. He can kindle demon magic."

Al jerked to a stop. "Bless me thrice. There are two of you?"

I shrieked as I fell, crying out as my hip hit a rock.

From behind me, I heard Lee's shout of fear and shock. Turning where Al had dropped me, I peered over the rubble and rubbed my eyes to make out Al drawing a sharp nail across Lee's arm. Blood welled, and I felt sick. "I'm sorry, Lee," I whispered, hugging my knees to myself. "I'm so sorry."

Al made a low sound deep in his throat of pleasure. "She's right," he said as he brought a finger from his lips. "And you're better at ley line magic than she is. I'll take you instead."

"No!" Lee screamed, and Al jerked him closer. "You wanted her! I gave you her!"

"You gave her to me, I took off your demon mark, and now I'm taking you. You can both kindle demon magic," Al said. "I could spend decades fighting a scrawny, high-maintenance familiar like her and never wedge the spells you already know into her cotton-fluffed head. Ever try twisting a demon curse?"

"No!" Lee cried, fighting to get away. "I can't!"

"You will. Here," Al said, dropping him down onto the ground. "Hold this for me."

I covered my ears and curled into myself as Lee screamed, then screamed again. It was high and raw, scraping across my skull like a nightmare. I felt like I was going to vomit. I had given Lee to Al to save my life. That Lee tried to do the same to me didn't make me feel better.

"Lee," I said, tears leaking out. "I'm sorry. God, I'm sorry."

Lee's voice cut off as he passed out. Al smiled, turning on a heel to me. "Ta, love. I don't like to be on the surface when it gets dark. All the best of luck to you."

My eyes widened. "I don't know how to get home!" I cried.

"Not my problem. 'Bye now."

I sat up, chilled as the stones I was sitting on seemed to soak into me. Lee came to with an ugly gibbering sound. Tucking him under an arm, Al gave me a nod and vanished.

A stone slid down to roll to my feet. I blinked, wiping my eyes to only get rock dust and chips of stone in them. "The line," I whispered, remembering. Maybe if I got into the line. Lee had jumped from outside of a line, but maybe I had to learn to walk before I could run.

A movement at the edge of my awareness caught my attention. Heart pounding, I whipped my head around, seeing nothing. Steadying myself, I wedged myself up, gasping when white-hot knives stabbed my ankle to take my breath away. I slipped back to the ground. Jaw gritted, I decided I would just crawl over there.

I reached out, seeing Mrs. Aver's business suit coated in the dust and frost it had scraped from the surrounding rocks. Gripping an outcrop, I pulled myself forward, managing a halfway upright position. My body was shaking with cold and fading adrenaline. The sun was almost down. A sliding of rocks urged me on. They were getting closer.

A soft pop pulled my head up. A tumble of pebbles and rocks came from everywhere as the lesser demons scrambled into hiding. My breath slipped from me as, from around my hair, I saw a small figure in dark purple sitting cross-legged before me, a narrow staff as long as I was tall laying across its lap. A robe draped it. Not a bathrobe, but a classy mix of a kimono and something a desert sheik would wear, all billowy with the suppleness of linen. A round hat with straight sides and a flat top was perched on its head. Squinting in the fading light, I decided there was an inch or so of air between the gold trim and the ground. *Now what?*

"Who in hell are you?" I said, pulling myself forward another step, "and will you be taking me home instead of Al?"

"Who in hell are you?" it echoed, its voice a mix of rough lightness. "Yes. That fits."

It wasn't hitting me with that carved black stick, or putting a charm on me, or even making ugly faces, so I ignored it and dragged myself forward another foot. There was a crackle of paper, and wondering, I tucked David's trifolded paper into my waistband. *Yeah, he'd probably want this back.*

"I'm Newt," it said, seemingly disappointed I was ignoring it. There was a rich accent that I couldn't place, an odd way of saying the vowels. "And no, I'm not taking you home. I already have a demon familiar. Algaliarept is right; you're almost worthless right now."

A demon for a familiar? Ooooh, that had to be good. Grunting, I pulled myself forward. My ribs hurt, and I pressed a hand into them. Panting, I looked up. A smooth face, not young, not old—sort of . . . nothing—met me. "Ceri is afraid of you," I said.

"I know. She's very perceptive. Is she well?"

Fear slid through me. "Leave her alone," I said, jerking back as it pushed my hair out of my eyes. Its touch seemed to sink into me though I felt fingertips firm on my forehead. I stared at its black eyes as it peered at me, unruffled and curious.

"Your hair ought to be red," it said, smelling of crushed dandelions. "And your eyes are green like my sisters', not brown."

"Sisters?" I wheezed, considering I might give it my soul if it would give me a pain amulet. God, I hurt all over, inside and out. I sat back on my heels out of its reach. Newt had an eerie grace, its outfit giving no hint to gender. There was a necklace of black gold about its neck—again, the design neither masculine nor feminine. My gaze dropped to its bare feet, hovering above the rubble. They were narrow and slim, somewhat ugly. Masculine? "Are you a boy or a girl?" I finally asked, not sure.

Newt's brow furrowed. "It makes a difference?"

Muscles trembling, I pulled my hand to my mouth and sucked at a spot where the rock had pinched me. *It did to me.* "Don't get me wrong, but why are you just sitting there?"

The demon smiled, making me think the reason couldn't be good. "There are a few side bets as to whether you will learn how to use the lines before sunset. I'm here so no one cheats."

A stab of adrenaline cleared my head. "What happens when the sun goes down?"

"Anyone can have you."

A rock slid from a nearby pile, and I pushed into motion. "But you don't want me."

It shook its head, drifting back. "Maybe if you told me why Al took the other witch instead of you, I might. I . . . don't remember."

Newt's voice sounded worried, making me wonder. Too much ever-after in the brainpan perhaps? I didn't have time to deal with a crazy demon, no matter how powerful it was. "Read the papers. I'm busy," I said, pulling myself forward.

I jerked when a boulder the size of a car fell two feet in front of me. The ground shook and bits of rock chips stung my face. I stared at it, then Newt, who was smiling as it adjusted its grip on its staff to look pleasant and innocuous. My head hurt. *Okay, maybe I had a little time.* "Ah, Lee can kindle demon magic," I said, not seeing any reason to tell it I could too.

Newt's black eyes widened. "Already?" it said, then its face clouded, not angry with me, but at itself. I waited for it to move the rock. It didn't. Taking a deep breath, I started to go around Newt, as it seemed the demon had forgotten I was there. The sense of danger flowing from the slight figure was growing, building on itself to tighten my gut and make my skin crawl. I was getting the distinct impression that I was still alive because a very powerful demon was curious, nothing more.

Hoping Newt would forget about me, I inched myself forward, trying to ignore the pain in my ankle. I slipped, sucking in my breath as the flat of my arm hit a rock, sending a shiver of pain up it. The boulder was right in front of me, and gathering myself, I wedged my knees under me. My ankle was burning agony as I gained my feet and held the rock for balance.

There was a brush of air, and Newt was beside me. "Do you want to live forever?"

The question sent a shiver through me. Damn it, Newt was becoming more interested, not less. "No," I whispered. Hand outstretched, I limped from the rock.

"I didn't either, until I tried it." The redwood staff clunked to the ground as Newt moved to keep even with me, black eyes eerily more alive than anyone else's I'd ever seen. My skin crawled. Something was wrong with Newt—really wrong. I couldn't put my finger on it until I realized that the minute I took my attention from Newt, I forgot what the demon looked like. Apart from those eyes.

"I know something Algaliarept doesn't," Newt said. "I remember now. You like secrets. You're good at keeping them, too. I know all about you; you're afraid of yourself."

I gritted my jaw as my ankle gave a twinge as I slipped on a rock. The line was just ahead. I could feel it. The sun had sunk below the horizon, halfway gone. It took seven minutes to sink once it touched the earth. Three and a half minutes. I could hear a gathering of breath from the lesser demons. *God, help me find a way out of this.*

"You should be afraid of you," Newt said. "Want to know why?"

I pulled my head up. Newt was bored out of his or her mind and looking for amusement. I didn't want to be interesting. "No," I whispered, becoming more frightened.

An evil smile crossed Newt, emotions shifting faster than a vampire hyped up on Brimstone. "I think I will tell Algaliarept a joke. And when he's done ripping that witch apart for what he lost, I'll trade for that mark you owe him and make it mine."

I started to shake, unable to stop my hands from trembling. "You can't do that."

"I can. I might." Newt twirled the staff idly, hitting a rock so it ricocheted into the dark. There was a catlike yelp of pain and a scattering of sliding rock. "And then I'll have two," the demon said to itself, "because you won't be able to figure out how to travel the lines and will have to buy a trip out of here. From me."

There was a cry of outrage from the watchers behind the rocks, quickly squelched.

Horrified, I came to a jerky stop, feeling the line right ahead of me.

"You want to survive," Newt intoned, its voice dropping in pitch. "You'll do anything for it. Anything."

"No," I whispered, terrified because Newt was right. "I saw Lee do it. I can do it too."

Black eyes glinting, Newt set the butt of its staff down. "You won't figure it out. You won't believe; not yet. You have to make a deal . . . with me."

Frightened, I wavered on my feet, and with the next step, I stumbled into the line, feeling as if it was a stream, warm and generous, filling me up. Almost panting, I teetered, seeing the eyes around me narrow with greed and anger. I hurt. I had to get out of there. The power of the line hummed through me, peaceful and comforting. *There's no place like home.*

Newt's expression went mocking, its pupil-black eyes spiteful. "You can't do it."

"I can," I said, my vision darkening as I almost passed out. From the deepest shadows glittered green eyes. Close. Very close. The power of the line hummed through me. *There's no place like home, there's no place like home, there's no place like home,* I thought desperately, pulling energy into me, spindling it in my head. I had traveled the lines with Lee. I had seen how he had done it. All it took was him thinking about where he wanted to be. I wanted to be home. Why wasn't it working?

My knees shook as the first dark shape came out to stand with an unreal thinness, slow and hesitant. Newt looked at it, then turned slowly to me, one eyebrow raised. "One favor, and I'll send you back."

Oh God. Not another one. "Leave me alone!" I shouted, the rough edges of a rock scraping my fingers as I flung it at an approaching form and almost fell over. A gasp sounding like a sob came from me as I caught my balance. The lesser demon ducked, then straightened. Three more pairs of eyes glowed behind it.

I jumped as Newt suddenly was before me. The light was gone. Black eyes slammed into me, delving into my soul and clenching until fear squeezed out to bubble up. "You can't do it. No time to learn," Newt said, and I shuddered. Here was power, raw and swirling. Newt's soul was so black it was almost unseen. I could feel its aura press against me, starting to slip into mine with the force of Newt's will. It could take me over if it wanted. I was nothing. My will was nothing.

"Owe me or die in this squalid pile of broken promises," Newt said. "But I can't send you through the lines with a thin tie called home. Home won't do it. Think on Ivy. You love her more than that damn church," it said, its honesty more cutting than any physical pain.

Crying out in angry, high voices, the shadows bunched and lunged.

"Ivy!" I shouted, accepting the bargain and willing myself to her: the smell of her sweat when we sparred, the taste of her Brimstone cookies, the sound of her steps, and the rise of her eyebrows when she was trying not to laugh.

I recoiled as Newt's black presence was suddenly in my head. *How many mistakes can one life survive?* echoed crystallinelike in my mind, but whose thought it was I didn't know.

Newt pressed the air from my lungs, and my mind shattered. I was everywhere and nowhere. The perfect disconnection of the line raced through me, making me exist in every line on the continent. *Ivy!* I thought again, starting to panic until I remembered her, fastening on her indomitable will and the tragedy of her desires. *Ivy. I want to go to Ivy.*

With a savage, jealous thought, Newt snapped my soul back together. Gasping, I covered my ears as a loud pop shook me. I fell forward, my elbows and knees smacking into gray tile. People screamed, and I heard the crash of metal. Papers flew, and someone shouted to call the I.S.

"Rachel!" Ivy cried.

I looked up past my falling hair to see I was in what looked like a hospital hallway. Ivy was sitting in an orange plastic chair, her eyes red and her cheeks blotchy, shock in her wide brown eyes. David was beside her, dirty and disheveled, Kisten's blood on his hands and chest. A phone rang and went unanswered.

"Hi," I said weakly, my arms starting to tremble. "Uh, could one of you maybe check me in? I don't feel so good."

Ivy stood, reaching out. I tipped forward. My cheek hit the tile. The last thing I remember was my hand touching hers.

Thirty-three

"Coming!" I called out, my pace quickening as I strode through the dusky sanctuary to the door, my snow boots thumping to leave small inverse divots of snow behind. The huge dinner bell that was our doorbell clanked again, and I picked up the pace. "I'm coming. Don't ring the bell again or the neighbors will call the I.S., for God's sake."

The reverberations were still echoing when I reached for the handle, the nylon of my coat making a sliding sound. My nose was cold and my fingers were frozen, the warmth of the church not having had enough time to warm them up. "David!" I exclaimed, opening the door to find him on the softly lit stoop.

"Hi, Rachel," he said, looking comfortably attractive with his glasses, long coat, thick stubble, and his cowboy hat dusted with snow. The bottle of wine in his hand helped. An older man stood beside him in a leather jacket and jeans. He was taller than David, and I eyed his lightly wrinkled but trim physique in question. A wisp of snow-white hair peeped from under his hat. There was a twig in his grip, unquestionably a symbolic offering for the solstice bonfire out back, and I realized he was a witch. *David's old partner?* I thought. A limo idled softly behind them, but I was guessing they had come in the blue four-door parked in front of it.

"Rachel," David said, drawing my gaze back to them. "This is Howard, my old partner."

"Pleased to meet you, Howard," I said, extending my hand.

"The pleasure is mine." Smiling, he slipped off a glove to extend a softly wrinkled, freckled hand. "David told me all about you, and I invited myself. I hope you don't mind."

"Not at all," I said earnestly. "The more, the merrier."

Howard pumped my hand up and down three times before releasing it. "I had to come," he said, green eyes glinting. "The chance to meet the woman who can outrun David *and* put up with his working style doesn't come along very often. You two did good with Saladan."

His voice was deeper than I expected, and the feeling of being evaluated strengthened. "Thank you," I said, mildly embarrassed. I shifted back from the doorway in invitation. "We're all back by the fire. Come on in. It's easier to go through the church than stumble through the garden the back way."

Howard slipped inside in a whiff of redwood while David knocked the snow from his boots. He hesitated, looking up at the new sign above the door. "Nice," he said. "Just get it?"

"Yeah." Mood going soft, I leaned out to look up at it. The deeply engraved brass plaque had been bolted to the front of the church above the door. It had come with a light, and the single bulb lit the stoop in a soft glow. "It's a solstice gift for Ivy and Jenks."

David made a sound of approval laced with understanding. I flicked my attention from him back to the sign. VAMPIRIC CHARMS; LLC. TAMWOOD, JENKS, AND MORGAN. I loved it, and I hadn't minded paying extra to make it a rush order. Ivy's eyes had gotten very wide when I pulled her out on the stoop that afternoon to see it. I thought she was going to cry. I'd given her a hug right there on the landing as it was obvious she wanted to give me one but was afraid I'd take it the wrong way. She was my friend, damn it. I could hug her if I wanted.

"I'm hoping it helps stop the rumors about me being dead," I said, ushering him in. "The paper was really quick to print my obituary, but because I'm not a vamp, they won't put anything in the risen-again announcements unless I pay for it."

"Imagine that," David said. I could hear the laughter in his voice, and I gave him a dry look as he stomped his boots a final time and came in. "You look good for a dead witch."

"Thanks."

"Your hair is almost back to normal. How about the rest of you?"

I shut the door, flattered at the sound of concern in his voice. Howard stood in the middle of the sanctuary, his eyes ranging over Ivy's piano and my desk. "I'm doing okay," I said. "My stamina is shot, but it's coming back. My hair, though?" I tucked a curl of reddish-brown hair behind an ear and the soft knit hat my mother had given me that afternoon. "The box said it washes out in five shampoos," I said sourly. "I'm still waiting."

Somewhat peeved at the reminder of my hair, I led the way into the kitchen, the two men trailing behind. Actually, my hair was the least of my worries. Yesterday I had found a scar with a familiar circle-and-slash pattern on the arch of my left foot; Newt's claim of a favor. I owed two demons, but I was alive. I was alive and was no one's familiar. And finding the mark there had been better than waking up with a big N tattooed on my forehead.

David's steps faltered as he saw the plates of goodies laid out on the table. Ivy's workspace had been pushed into a three-by-three-foot section, the rest was full of cookies, fudge, cold cuts, and crackers. "Help yourself," I said, refusing to get worked up about things currently out of my control. "Do you want to nuke your wine before we go out?" I asked, eating a slice of salami. "I've got a pitcher to warm it up in." I could use my new charm, but it wasn't reliable, and I was tired of burning my tongue.

The clunk of the wine as it hit the table was loud. "You drink it warm?" David said, sounding appalled as he looked at the microwave.

"Ivy and Kisten do." Seeing the Were hesitate, I gave the pot of spiced cider on the stove a quick stir. "We can warm up half and put the rest in a snow bank if you want," I added.

"Sure," David said, his short fingers manipulating the foil-wrapped top.

Howard began filling a plate, but at David's pointed look, he started. "Mmmm!" the older witch said abruptly, plate in hand. "Mind if I go out back and introduce myself?" He wiggled the twig sandwiched between his hand and the foam plate in explanation. "I haven't been to a solstice burning in a long time."

A smile came over me. "Go right on out. The door is through the living room."

David and Howard exchanged another look, and the witch found his way. I heard a soft rise of voices in greeting as he opened the door. David exhaled slowly. Something was up.

"Rachel," he said. "I've got a paper for you to sign."

My smile froze. "What did I do?" I blurted. "Was it breaking Lee's car?"

"No," he said, and my chest tightened when his eyes dropped. *Oh God. It must be bad.*

"What is it?" I set the spoon in the sink and turned, gripping my elbows.

David unzipped his coat and pulled out a trifolded paper and handed it to me. Taking his bottle, he started to open it. "You don't have to sign it if you don't want to," he said, glancing at me from under his cowboy hat. "I won't be offended. Really. You can say no. It's okay."

I went cold, then hot, as I read the simply worded statement, wonder in me as I looked up and met his anxious eyes. "You want me to be a member of your pack?" I stammered.

"I don't have one," he rushed to explain. "You'd be the only one in it. I'm a registered loner but my company won't fire someone with tenure if they're an alpha male or female."

I could say nothing and he rushed to fill the silence.

"I, uh, feel bad for trying to bribe you," he said. "It's not like we're married or anything, but it gives you the right to get your insurance through me. And if either of us is hospitalized, we have access to the medical records and have a say as to what happens if the other is unconscious. I don't have anyone to make those kind of decisions for me, and I'd rather have you than a court or my siblings." He shrugged with one shoulder. "You can come to the company picnic, too."

My gaze fell to the paper, then rose to his stubbled face, then back to the paper. "What about your old partner?"

He peeked over the paper to look at the print. "It takes a female to make a pack."

"Oh." I stared at the form. "Why me?" I asked, honored he'd ask but bewildered. "There must be lots of Were women who would jump at the chance."

"There are. And that's just it." Dropping back, he rested against the island counter. "I don't want a pack. Too much responsibility. Too many ties. Packs grow. And even if I went into this with another Were with the understanding that it was an agreement on paper and nothing else, she would expect certain things, and so would her kin." He looked at the ceiling, his eyes showing his age. "And when those things weren't provided, they would start to treat her like a whore instead of an alpha bitch. I won't have that problem with you." He met my eyes. "Will I?"

I blinked, starting slightly. "Ah, no." A smile quirked the corner of my mouth. *Alpha bitch? That sounded about right.* "Gotta pen?" I asked.

David exhaled with a soft puff, relief in his eyes. "We need three witnesses."

I couldn't stop grinning. Wait until I told Ivy. She'd have kittens.

We both spun to the window as a whoosh of flame and a shout rose high. Ivy threw a second bough of evergreen on the bonfire, and the fire billowed up again. She was taking to my family's tradition of a solstice fire with an unsettling enthusiasm.

"I can think of three people off the top of my head," I said, jamming it into a back pocket.

David nodded. "We don't have to do it tonight. But the fiscal year is coming up, and we'll want to file it before then so you can start your benefits and get a line in the new catalog."

I was on tiptoe to reach a pitcher for the wine, and David reached up and got it for me. "There's a catalog?" I asked as I dropped to my heels.

His eyes were wide. "You want to remain anonymous? That costs extra, but okay."

I shrugged, not knowing. "What's everyone going to say when you show up at the company picnic with me?"

David poured half the wine into the pitcher and set it to heat in the microwave. "Nothing. They all think I'm rabid anyway."

The smile wouldn't leave me as I ladled out a mug of spiced cider. His motive might be slanted—wanting the extra security for his job—but we would both benefit. So it was with a much improved mood that we headed for the back door, his warmed wine and half-empty bottle in his hands, and my spiced cider in mine. The heat of the church had taken the chill from me, and I led the way into the living room.

David's steps slowed while he took in the softly glowing room. Ivy and I had decorated, and purple, red, gold, and green were everywhere. Her leather stocking had looked lonely on the mantel, so I had bought a red and green knit one with a bell on the toe, embracing any holiday that got me presents. Ivy had even hung a little white stocking for Jenks that she had taken from her sister's doll collection, but the jar of honey wouldn't come close to fitting in it.

Ivy's Christmas tree glowed in the corner, looking ethereal. I'd never had one before, and I felt honored she had let me help her decorate it with tissue-paper-wrapped ornaments. We had made a night of it as we listened to music and ate the popcorn that never made it onto a string.

There were only two things under it: one for me, one for Ivy, both from Jenks. He was gone, but his presents to us had been left behind in opposite bedrooms.

I reached for the handle of the new door, a lump in my throat. We had opened them already—neither one of us were good at waiting. Ivy had sat and stared at the Bite-me-Betty doll, her jaw clenched and her breathing almost nonexistent. I hadn't been much better, all but crying upon finding the pair of cell phones in their foam box. One was for me, the other, much smaller one, was for Jenks. According to the receipt still in the box, he had activated it last month and even put himself on speed dial on mine.

Yanking open the door, I held it for David, my jaw clenched. I'd get him to come back. If I had to hire a pilot to write my apology in the sky, I would get him to come back.

"David," I said as he passed. "If I give you something, will you take it to Jenks?"

He glanced at me from the first step down. "Maybe," he said warily.

I grimaced. "It's just some seeds. I couldn't find anything in my language of flowers book that said, 'I'm sorry. I'm an ass,' so I went with forget-me-nots."

"Okay," he said, sounding more sure. "I can do that."

"Thanks." It was a whisper, but I was sure he heard me over the calls at his arrival.

I took the heated wine from David and placed it near the fire. Howard looked content talking to Keasley and Ceri, sneaking unsure glances at Takata lurking in the more-certain shadows of the oak tree. "Come on over," I said to David as Kisten tried to get his attention. Ivy's sister was prattling next to him, and he looked exhausted. "I want you to meet Takata."

The midnight air was crisp, almost painfully dry, and I smiled at Ivy when I saw her trying to explain to Ceri the art of making a s'more. The puzzled elf didn't understand how layering chocolate between a sugary grain product and spun confection could possibly taste good. Her words, not mine. I was sure her opinion would change after she ate one.

I felt Kisten's eyes on me from around the lowering flames and I stifled a shiver. The come-and-go light played on his face, not unattractively thinner after his stint in the hospital. My thoughts of Nick had waned to a soft ache under the living vamp's attentions. Kist was here, and Nick wasn't. The reality was, Nick hadn't truly been here for months. He hadn't called or sent a solstice card, and he had intentionally left no way for me to reach him. It was time to move on.

Takata shifted his perch atop the picnic table in case we wanted to sit. The concert earlier tonight had gone off without a hitch, and since Lee wasn't around, Ivy and I watched from backstage.

Takata had dedicated "Red Ribbons" to our firm, and half the crowd had waved their lighters in tribute thinking I was still dead.

I had only been joking when I invited him to my bonfire, but I was glad he came. He seemed to relish that no one was fawning over him as he sat contentedly in the background. I recognized that distant look on his lined face from when Ivy was planning a run, and wondered if his next album might have a song about sparks among the frost-blackened arms of an oak.

"Takata," I said as we approached, and he came back to himself. "I'd like you to meet David Hue. He's the insurance adjustor who helped me get to Saladan."

"David," Takata said, taking off his glove before extending his thin long hand. "Nice to meet you. It looks like you escaped unscathed from Rachel's latest run."

David smiled warmly without showing his teeth. "Pretty much," he said as he released his hand and rocked back a step. "Though I wasn't sure when those handguns showed up." Making a mock shudder, he shifted so his front would be warmed by the flames. "Too much for me," he said softly.

I was glad he wasn't wide-eyed and stammering, or squealing and jumping up and down like Erica had done until Kisten collared her and dragged her away.

"David!" Kisten called when my thoughts pulled my eyes to him. "Can I talk to you about my boat? How much do you think it would cost to insure her through you?"

A sound of pain slipped from David. "The price of being in insurance," he said softly.

My eyebrows rose. "I think he just wants to get someone between him and Erica. The girl does *not* shut up."

David pushed himself into motion. "You won't leave me alone too long will you?"

I grinned. "Is that one of my responsibilities as a member of your pack?" I said, and Takata's eyes widened.

"As a matter of fact, it is." Raising his hand to Kisten, he ambled to him, stopping to nudge a log back into the flames with the toe of his boot as he went. Howard was laughing at him from across the fire, his green eyes glinting.

I looked to find Takata's thick eyebrows high. "Member of his pack?" he questioned.

Nodding, I sat beside Takata on top of the picnic table. "For insurance purposes." Setting my spiced cider down, I put my elbows on my knees and sighed. I loved the solstice, and not just for the food and parties. Cincinnati dropped all of its lights from midnight until sunrise, and it was the only time I ever saw the night sky as it was supposed to be. Anyone thieving during the blackout was dealt with hard, curtailing any problems.

"How are you doing?" Takata said, surprising me. I had almost forgotten he was there. "I heard you were hospitalized."

I smiled sheepishly, knowing I was starting to look tired after screaming for two-plus hours at Takata's concert. "I'm okay. They weren't ready to release me, but Kisten was just down the hall, and after they caught us, ah, experimenting with the controls for the bed, they decided we both were well enough to be on the streets." *Crabby old night nurse. By the amount of fuss she made, one would have thought we were committing some kind of kinky—well, crabby old night nurse, anyway.*

Takata eyed me as I flushed and pulled my knit hat down lower over my ears. "There's a limo out front," I said to change the subject. "Want me to tell them to go away?"

His gaze went up into the black branches. "They can wait. They have food in there."

Nodding, I relaxed. "You want some warm wine?"

He started, his wide eyes looking shocked. "No. No thanks."

"More spiced cider, then?" I offered. "Here. I haven't had any of mine."

"Just put a swallow in there," he said, extending his empty cup, and I poured half of my drink into his. I felt kinda special, sitting next to Takata with half my drink in his mug, but I stiffened as a faint twang reverberated through me. I froze, not knowing what it was, and Takata's eyes met mine.

"You felt it too?" he said, and I nodded, feeling uneasy and a little worried.

"What was it?"

Takata's wide mouth turned into a huge smile as he laughed at me. "The circle at Fountain Square. Happy Solstice." He raised his cup, and I automatically touched mine to it.

"Happy Solstice," I echoed, thinking it odd that I had felt it. I never had before. But then, maybe having closed it myself once made me sensitive to it.

Feeling as if all was right with the world, I sipped my cider, finding David's eyes pleading with me over the rim of my mug. Erica's mouth was going nonstop, and Kisten was gripping his shoulder, trying to have a conversation around her. "Excuse me," I said as I slid from the table. "David needs rescuing."

Takata chuckled, and I made my unhurried way past the fire. Though he never stopped talking to David, Kisten's eyes were on me, and I felt a warm spot start in my middle.

"Erica," I said, coming even with them. "Takata wants to play a song for you."

Takata jerked upright, giving me a panicked look when the young woman squealed. Both Kisten and David slumped in relief as she darted around the fire to him. "Thank God," Kisten whispered, and I sat down in her spot. "That girl never shuts up."

Snorting, I eased closer, pushing into his thigh, hinting. He curved an arm around me, as I wanted, pulling me close. Kisten exhaled softly, and a shiver rippled over me. I knew he felt it when my scar started tingling. "Stop it," I whispered, embarrassed, and his grip tightened.

"I can't help it," he said on an intake of breath. "When is everyone going to be leaving?"

"Sunup," I said, setting my drink down. "Absence makes the heart grow fonder."

"It's not my heart that misses you," he breathed, and a second shiver passed through me.

"So," Kisten said loudly when David started to look uncomfortable. "Rachel tells me you asked her to be your absent partner so you could get two salaries and she could get a good rate on her insurance."

"Ah, yes . . ." David stammered, looking down so his hat hid his eyes. "About that . . ."

I jumped as Kisten's cold hand worked its way under my coat and touched the skin at my waist. "I like that," he murmured, not talking about how his fingers were tracing small circles to warm my middle. "Inventive. My kind of man."

David's head came up. "Would you excuse me," he muttered, sending a quick hand to fiddle with his glasses. "I haven't said hello to Ceri and Keasley yet."

I chuckled, and Kisten pulled me closer. "You do that, Mr. Peabody," Kisten said.

The short Were jerked to a stop, gave him a warning frown, then continued, stopping to get a glass of his wine on the way.

My smile slowly faded. The scent of leather became obvious, mixing with the hard aroma of burning ash, and I snuggled closer into Kisten. "Hey," I said softly, my gaze fixed on the fire. "David wants me to sign a paper. Make me part of his pack."

His breath caught. "You're kidding," he said, pushing me

away so he could focus on me. His blue eyes were wide and his face surprised and wondering.

Looking at my cold fingers, I slipped them into his. "I'd like you to witness it."

"Oh." His gaze went to the fire and he shifted his arm to lean a smidgen away.

I grinned in understanding and laughed. "No, you idiot," I said, pushing on his arm. "It's a pack membership, not an inter-species bond. I'm not marrying the guy, for the Turn's sake. It's only a legal agreement so I can get my insurance through him and his company won't fire him. He'd ask a Were woman, but he doesn't want a pack, and that's what he'd get if he asked one."

Kisten exhaled long and slow, and I could feel the softness return to his grip. "Good," he said, pulling me closer. "'Cause you're my alpha bitch, babe, and no one else's."

I gave him a telling look, which was hard to do seeing as I was almost in his lap. "Babe?" I said dryly. "You know what I did to the last guy who called me that?"

Kisten jerked me closer. "Maybe later, love," he whispered to start a delicious tingle in me. "We don't want to shock your friends," he added, and I followed his gaze to where Howard and Keasley were laughing while Ceri tried to eat her s'more without getting messy.

"Will you witness the paper for me?" I asked.

"Sure." His grip around me tightened. "I think making ties is a good thing." His arm slipped from me, and I followed his gaze to see Ivy glaring at us. "Ivy might not, though."

Suddenly concerned, I pulled away. Ivy got to her feet, and with steps quick and long, she strode up the porch steps and into the church. The back door shut hard enough to make the wreath fall off.

Not noticing, Erica sprang into a flurry of motion to move a bench closer to the fire. The conversation grew excited, and Keasley and Ceri drifted over when Takata finally pulled out the guitar he brought with him but had been ignoring. He settled himself, long fingers moving slowly from the cold as he strummed. It was nice. Really nice. The only thing missing was Jenks's wiseass remarks and a sprinkling of pixy dust.

I sighed, and Kisten's lips brushed my ear. "You'll get him back," he breathed.

Surprised he knew where my thoughts were, I said, "Are you sure?"

I felt him nod. "Come springtime and he can get out again,

he'll be back. He thinks too much of you to not listen once his pride starts to heal. But I know all about big egos, Rachel. You're going to have to grovel."

"I can do that," I said in a small voice.

"He thinks it's his fault," Kisten continued.

"I'll convince him otherwise."

His breath was a puff behind my ear. "That's my girl."

I smiled at the stirring of feelings he was instilling in me. My gaze went to the shadow of Ivy in the kitchen, then back to the impromptu music. One down. Two more to go. And they were likely going to be the hardest ones. It wasn't as if I could ask Ceri or Keasley. There was a spot on that form for a Social Security number. Ceri didn't have one, and I knew without asking Keasley wouldn't want to put his down. I had a suspicion by the lack of government checks that he was playing dead.

"Could you excuse me?" I murmured as Ivy's shadow behind the glass was eclipsed by a swirl of mist from the hot water she was running into the sink. Kisten's hold loosened. Takata's blue eyes met mine before I turned away, an unknown emotion in them.

I paused to put the cedar wreath back on its hook before I went in. The warmth of the church hit me, and I took my hat off and tossed it to the black hearth. I entered the kitchen to find Ivy leaning against the counter, her head down and her hands gripping her elbows.

"Hi," I said, hesitating in the threshold.

"Let me see the contract," she said, extending her hand and her head coming up.

My lips parted. "How did . . ." I stammered.

A faint, sour smile crossed her and was gone. "Sound carries well over flame."

Embarrassed, I pulled it out of my pocket, feeling it both cold from the night and warm from my body. She took it, her brow furrowed. Turning her back on me, she unfolded it. I fidgeted. "Um, I need three witnesses," I said. "I'd like you to be one of them."

"Why?"

She didn't turn around and her shoulders were tense. "David doesn't have a pack," I said. "It's harder to fire him if he does. He gets to keep his job working solo, and I can get my insurance through him. It's only two hundred a month, Ivy. He's not looking for anything more than that or he would have asked a Were woman."

"I know. My question is why do you want *my* signature?" Paper in hand, she turned, the empty look on her face making me uncomfortable. "Why is it important to you that *I* sign it?"

I opened my mouth, then shut it. My thoughts touched on what Newt had said. Home hadn't been a strong enough pull, but Ivy was. "Because you're my partner," I said, warming. "Because what I do affects you."

Ivy silently plucked a pen from her pencil cup and clicked it open. I suddenly felt awkward, realizing that David's little paper granted him something she wanted: a recognizable connection with me.

"I did a background check on him when you were in the hospital," she said. "He's not hooking up with you to help him out with a preexisting problem."

My eyebrows rose. I hadn't thought about that. "He said this was a no-strings-attached affair." I hesitated. "Ivy, I live with you," I said, trying to reassure her that our friendship didn't need a paper or signature to be real, and both our names were above the door. Both of them.

She was silent, her face empty of emotion, her brown eyes still. "You trust him?"

I nodded. I had to go with my gut feeling here.

The barest smile appeared on her. "Me too." Pushing a plate of cookies aside, she wrote her name on the first line in a careful but almost illegible signature.

"Thanks," I said, and she handed it back. My gaze went past her as the back door opened. Ivy looked up, and I recognized a softening in her gaze when Kisten's familiar footsteps thumped on the rug beside the door, knocking off the snow. He came into the kitchen, David on his heels.

"Are we signing the paper or not?" Kisten said, the tension in his voice telling me he was ready to argue with Ivy if she was balking.

Ivy clicked her pen open and shut so fast that it hummed. "I already did. Your turn."

He squared his shoulders, grinning as he took the pen when she extended it, adding his masculine signature under hers. His Social Security number was next, and he handed the pen to David.

David edged between them, looking small beside their tall grace. I could see his relief as he wrote his full name. My pulse increased and I took the pen, pulling the paper closer.

"So," Kisten said when I signed it. "Who are you going to ask to be the third witness?"

"Jenks," Ivy and I said together, and I looked up. Our eyes met and I clicked the pen closed.

"Will you ask him for me?" I said to David.

The Were picked up the paper, carefully folding it and tucking it away in an inner coat pocket. "You don't want to ask someone else? He might not."

I glanced at Ivy and straightened, tucking a curl of hair behind my ear. "He's a member of this firm," I said. "If he wants to spend the winter sulking in a Were's basement, that's fine with me, but he had better get his little pixy butt back here when the weather breaks or I'm going to be royally pissed." I took a deep breath, adding, "And maybe this will convince him he's a valued member of the team and that I'm sorry."

Kisten took a shuffling step back.

"I'll ask him," David said.

The back door opened and Erica tumbled in, her cheeks red and her eyes snapping. "Hey! Come on! He's ready to play! God save you, he's warmed up and ready to play, and you're inside eating? Get your asses out here!"

Ivy's attention went from the snow she had tracked in to my eyes. David lurched into motion, pushing the flighty goth vamp out before him. Kisten followed, the noise of their conversation heady with the sound of companionship. Takata's music rose, and my eyes widened when Ceri's ethereal voice was set to a carol older than even she. She indeed sang in Latin. My eyebrows rose and I looked at Ivy.

Ivy zipped her coat up and got her mittens from the counter. "You really okay with this?" I asked her.

She nodded. "Asking Jenks to sign that paper might be the only way to hammer it into his thick skull that we need him."

I made a face and went before her as I tried to come up with a way to convey to Jenks how wrong I had been to not trust him. I had slipped Algaliarept's snare, managing to not only get rid of one of my demon marks but also break my familiar bond with Nick, too—not that it mattered now. I had gone out on a date with the city's most powerful bachelor and had breakfast with him. I had rescued a thousand-year-old elf, learned how to be my own familiar, and discovered I could throw a mean craps game. Not to mention I found you could have sex with a vampire and not get bitten. Why did I have the feeling that getting Jenks to talk to me was going to be harder than all that put together?

"We'll get him back," Ivy murmured behind me. "We *will* get him back."

Thumping down the snow-covered stairs and going into the music and star-filled night, I swore we would.

A FISTFUL OF CHARMS

To the man who invariably says, "Really? Okay," instead of, "You want to do what?"

Acknowledgments

I'd like to thank Gwen Hunter for helping me with the med stuff on the bridge, and TB, who read through my diving sequences. If anything doesn't jive, it wasn't from these two ladies but me pushing the envelope. And of course, a very large thank you to my agent, Richard Curtis, and to my editor, Diana Gill, without whom the Hollows would have stayed in my imagination alone.

One

The solid thud of David's car door shutting echoed off the stone face of the eight-story building we had parked beside. Leaning against the gray sports car, I shaded my eyes and squinted up at its aged and architecturally beautiful columns and fluted sills. The uppermost floor was golden in the setting sun, but here at street level we were in a chill shadow. Cincinnati had a handful of such landmark buildings, most abandoned, as this one appeared to be.

"Are you sure this is the place?" I asked, then dragged the flat of my arms off the roof of his car. The river was close; I could smell the oil and gas mix of boats. The top floor probably had a view. Though the streets were clean, the area was clearly depressed. But with a little attention—and a lot of money—I could see it as one of the city's newest residential hot spots.

David set his worn leather briefcase down and reached into the inner pocket of his suit coat. Pulling out a sheaf of papers, he flipped to the back, then glanced at the distant corner and the street sign. "Yes," he said, his soft voice tense but not worried.

Tugging my little red leather jacket down, I hiked my bag higher on my shoulder and headed to his side of the car, heels clunking. I'd like to say I was wearing my butt-kicking boots in deference to this being a run, but in reality I just liked them. They went well with the blue jeans and black T-shirt I had on; and with the matching cap, I looked and felt sassy.

David frowned at the chunking—or my choice of attire, maybe—steeling his features to bland acceptance when he saw me quietly laughing at him. He was in his respectable work clothes, somehow pulling off the mix of the three-piece suit and his shoulder-length, wavy black hair held back in a subdued clip. I'd seen him a couple of times in running tights that showed off his excellently maintained, mid-thirties physique—yum—and a full-length duster and cowboy hat—Van Helsing, eat your heart out—but his somewhat small stature lost none of its presence when he dressed like the insurance claims adjuster he was. David was kind of complex for a Were.

I hesitated when I came even with him, and together we eyed the building. Three streets over I could hear the shush of traffic, but here, nothing moved. "It's really quiet," I said, holding my elbows against the chill of the mid-May evening.

Brown eyes pinched, David ran a hand over his clean-shaven cheeks. "It's the right address, Rachel," he said, peering at the top floor. "I can call to check if you want."

"No, this is cool." I smiled with my lips closed, hefting my shoulder bag and feeling the extra weight of my splat gun. This was David's run, not mine, and about as benign as you could get—adjusting the claim of an earth witch whose wall had cracked. I wouldn't need the sleepy-time charms I loaded my modified paint ball gun with, but I just grabbed my bag when David asked me to come with him. It was still packed from my last run—storming the back room of an illegal spammer. God, plugging him had been satisfying.

David pushed into motion, gallantly gesturing me to go first. He was older than I by about ten years, but it was hard to tell unless you looked at his eyes. "She's probably living in one of those new flats they're making above old warehouses," he said, heading for the ornate stoop.

I snickered, and David looked at me.

"What?" he said, dark eyebrows rising.

I entered the building before him, shoving the door so he could follow tight on my heels. "I was thinking if you lived in one, it would still be a warehouse. Were house? Get it?"

He sighed, and I frowned. Jenks, my old backup, would have laughed. Guilt hit me, and my pace faltered. Jenks was currently AWOL, hiding out in some Were's basement after I'd majorly screwed up by not trusting him, but with spring here, I could step up my efforts to apologize and get him to return.

The front lobby was spacious, full of gray marble and little else. My heels sounded loud in the tall-ceilinged space. Creeped out, I stopped chunking and started walking to minimize the noise. A pair of black-edged elevators were across the lobby, and we headed for them. David pushed the up button and rocked back.

I eyed him, the corners of my lips quirking. Though he was trying to hide it, I could see he was getting excited about his run. Being a field insurance adjustor wasn't the desk job one might think it was. Most of his company's clients were Inderlanders—witches, Weres, and the occasional vampire—and as such, getting the truth as to why a client's car was totaled was harder than it sounded. Was it from the teenage son backing it into the garage wall, or did the witch down the street finally get tired of hearing him beep every time he left the drive? One was covered, the other wasn't, and sometimes it took, ah, creative interviewing techniques to get the truth.

David noticed I was smiling at him, and the rims of his ears went red under his dark complexion. "I appreciate you coming with me," he said, shifting forward as the elevator dinged and the doors opened. "I owe you dinner, okay?"

"No problem." I joined him in the murky, mirrored lift, and watched my reflection in the amber light as the doors closed. I'd had to move an interview for a possible client, but David had helped me in the past, and that was far more important.

The trim Were winced. "The last time I adjusted the claim of an earth witch, I later found she had scammed the company. My ignorance cost them hundreds of thousands. I appreciate you giving me your opinion as to whether she caused the damage with a misuse of magic."

I tucked a loosely curling lock of red hair that had escaped my French braid behind an ear, then adjusted my leather cap. The lift was old and slow. "Like I said, no problem."

David watched the numbers counting up. "I think my boss is trying to get me fired," he said softly. "This is the third claim this week to hit my desk that I'm not familiar with." His grip on his briefcase shifted. "He's waiting for me to make a mistake. Pushing for it."

I leaned against the back mirror and smiled weakly at him. "Sorry. I know how that feels." I had quit my old job at Inderland Security, the I.S., almost a year ago to go independent. Though it had been rough—and still was, occasionally—it was the best decision I'd ever made.

"Still," he persisted, the not unpleasant scent of musk growing as he turned to me in the confined space. "This isn't your job. I owe you."

"David, let it go," I said, exasperated. "I'm happy to come out here and make sure some witch isn't scamming you. It's no big deal. I do this stuff every day. In the dark. Usually alone. And if I'm lucky, it involves running, and screaming, and my foot in somebody's gut."

The Were smiled to show his flat, blocky teeth. "You like your job, don't you?"

I smiled right back. "You bet I do."

The floor lurched, and the doors opened. David waited for me to exit first, and I looked out onto the huge, building-sized room on the top floor. The setting sun streamed in the ceiling-to-floor windows, shining on the scattered construction materials. Past the windows, the Ohio River made a gray sheen. When finished, this would be an excellent apartment. My nose tickled at the scent of two-by-fours and sanded plaster, and I sneezed.

David's eyes went everywhere. "Hello? Mrs. Bryant?" he said, his deep voice echoing. "I'm David. David Hue from Were Insurance. I brought an assistant with me." He gave my tight jeans, T-shirt, and red leather jacket a disparaging look. "Mrs. Bryant?"

I followed him farther in, my nose wrinkling. "I think the crack in her wall might be from removing some of those supporting members," I said softly. "Like I said, no problem."

"Mrs. Bryant?" David called again.

My thoughts went to the empty street and how far we were from the casual observer. Behind me, the elevator doors slid shut and the lift descended. A small scuff from the far end of the room sent a stab of adrenaline through me, and I spun.

David was on edge too, and together we laughed at ourselves when a slight figure rose from the couch set adjacent to a modern kitchen at the end of the long room, the cupboards still wrapped in plastic.

"Mrs. Bryant? I'm David Hue."

"As prompt as your last yearly review claims," a masculine voice said, the soft resonances sifting through the darkening air. "And very thoughtful to bring a witch with you to check your customer's claim with. Tell me, do you take that off your end-of-the-year taxes, or do you claim it as a business expense?"

David's eyes were wide. "It's a business expense, sir."

I looked from David to the man. "Ah, David? I take it that's not Mrs. Bryant."

His grip on his briefcase shifting, David shook his head. "I think it's the president of the company."

"Oh." I thought about that. Then thought about that some more. I was getting a bad feeling about this. "David?"

He put a hand on my shoulder and leaned in. "I think you should leave," he said, the worry in his brown eyes running right to my core.

Recalling what he'd said in the elevator about his boss gunning for him, my pulse quickened. "David, if you're in trouble, I'm not leaving," I said, boots thumping as he hustled me to the lift.

His face was grim. "I can handle this."

I tried to twist from his grip. "Then I'll stay and help you to the car when it's over."

He glanced at me. "I don't think so, Rachel. But thanks."

The elevator opened. Still protesting, I was ill prepared when David jerked me back. My head came up and my face went cold. *Crap.* The lift was full of Weres in various levels of elegance, ranging from Armani suits and sophisticated skirt and top combos to jeans and blouses. Even worse, they all had the collected, confident pride of alpha wolves. And they were smiling.

Shit. David had a *big* problem.

"Please tell me it's your birthday," I said, "and this is a surprise party."

A young Were in a bright red dress was the last to step from the elevator. Tossing her thick length of black hair, she gave me a once-over. Though sure of herself, I could tell by her stance that at least, she wasn't an alpha bitch. This was getting weird. Alphas never got together. They just didn't. Especially without their respective packs behind them.

"It's not his birthday," the woman said cattily. "But I imagine he's surprised."

David's grip on my arm twitched. "Hello, Karen," he said caustically.

My skin crawled and my muscles tightened as the Weres ringed us. I thought of the splat gun in my bag, then felt for a ley line, but didn't tap it. David couldn't pay me to leave now. This looked like a lynching.

"Hi, David," the woman in red said, satisfaction clear in both her voice and in her stance behind the alpha males. "You can't imagine how overjoyed I was to find you had started a pack."

David's boss was now there too, and with quick and confident steps he moved between us and the elevator. The tension in the room ratcheted up a notch, and Karen slinked behind him.

I hadn't known David long, but I'd never seen this mix of

anger, pride, and annoyance on him before. There was no fear. David was a loner, and as such, the personal power of an alpha held little sway over him. But there were eight of them, and one was his boss.

"This doesn't involve her, sir," David said with a respectful anger. "Let her leave."

David's boss lifted an eyebrow. "Actually, this has nothing to do with you."

My breath caught. *Okay, maybe I was the one with the problem.*

"Thank you for coming, David. Your presence is no longer needed," the polished Were said. Turning to the others, he added, "Get him out of here."

I took a heaving lungful of air. With my second sight, I reached for a ley line, latching onto the one that ran under the university. My concentration shattered when two men grabbed my arms. "Hey!" I shouted as one ripped my shoulder bag off and sent it spinning to land against a stack of lumber. "Let go of me!" I demanded, unable to twist easily from their twin grips.

David grunted in pain, and when I stomped on someone's foot, they shoved me down. Plaster dust puffed up, choking me. My breath whooshed out as someone sat on me. My hands were pulled behind my back, and I went still. "Ow," I complained. Blowing a red curl from my face, I gave another squirm. Crap, David was being dragged into the elevator.

He was still fighting them. Red-faced and wrathful, his fists lashed out, making ugly sounding thumps when he scored. He could have Wered to fight more viciously, but there was a five-minute downtime when he would be helpless.

"Get him *out of here!*" David's boss shouted impatiently, and the doors shut. There was a clunk as something hit the inside of the elevator, and then the machinery started to lower the lift. I heard a shout and the sounds of a fight that slowly grew muffled.

Fear slid through me, and I gave another wiggle. David's boss turned his gaze to me. "Strap her," he said lightly.

My breath hissed in. Frantic, I reached for the ley line again, tapping it with a splinter of thought. Ever-after energy flowed through me, filling my chi and then the secondary spindle I could keep in my head. Pain struck through me when someone wrenched my right arm too far back. The cool plastic of a zip-strip was jammed over one wrist, snugged tight with a quick pull and a familiar ratcheting sound to leave the end dangling. My face went cold as every last erg of ever-after washed out of me. The bitter taste of dandelions was on my lips. *Stupid, stupid witch!*

"Son of a bitch!" I shouted, and the Weres sitting on me fell away.

I staggered to my feet and tried to wedge the flexible plastic-wrapped band off me, failing. Its core was charmed silver, like in my long-gone I.S. issue cuffs. I couldn't tap a line. I couldn't do anything. I seldom used my new ley line skills in defense, and I hadn't been thinking of how easy they could be nullified.

Utterly bereft of my magic, I stood in the last of the amber light coming in the tall windows. I was alone with a pack of alphas. My thoughts zinged to Mr. Ray's pack and the wishing fish I had accidentally stolen from him, and then me making the owners of the Howlers baseball team pay for my time doing it. *Oh . . . crap*. I had to get out of there.

David's boss shifted his weight to his other foot. The sun spilled over him to glint on the dust on his dress shoes. "Ms. Morgan, isn't it?" he asked companionably.

I nodded, wiping my palms off on my jeans. Plaster dust clung to me, and I only made things worse. I never took my eyes from him, knowing it was a blatant show of dominance. I had dealt a little with Weres, and none of them but David seemed to like me. I didn't know why.

"It's a pleasure to meet you," he said, coming closer and pulling a pair of metal-rimmed glasses from an inner pocket of his suit coat. "I'm David's boss. You can call me Mr. Finley."

Perching the glasses on his narrow nose, he took the stapled papers that Karen smugly handed him. "Forgive me if I'm a little slow," he said, peering at them. "My secretary usually does this." He looked over the papers at me, pen clicking open. "Your pack number is what?"

"Huh?" I said intelligently, then stiffened as the ring of Weres seemed to close in. Karen snickered, and my face warmed.

Mr. Finley's slight wrinkles bunched as he frowned. "You're David's alpha. Karen is challenging you for your place. There is paperwork. What is your pack number?"

My mouth dropped open. This wasn't about the Rays or the Howlers. I was the sole member of David's pack, yeah. But it was just a paper relationship, one designed so I could get my overly inflated insurance cheap, cheap, cheap, and David could keep his job and buck the system to continue working alone and without a partner. He didn't want a real pack, being a confirmed loner and good at it, but it was nearly impossible to fire an alpha, which was why he had asked me to start a pack with him.

My gaze darted to Karen, smiling like the queen of the Nile, as dark and exotic as an Egyptian whore. She wanted to challenge me for my position?

"Oh, hell no!" I said, and Karen snorted, thinking I was afraid. "I'm not fighting her! David doesn't want a real pack!"

"Obviously," Karen scorned. "I claim ascension. Before eight packs, I claim it."

There weren't eight alphas there anymore, but I thought the five that were left were more than enough to force the issue.

Mr. Finley let the hand holding the sheet of papers fall. "Does anyone have a catalog? She doesn't know her pack number."

"I do," sang out a woman, swinging her purse around and digging to bring out what looked like a small address book. "New edition," she added, and thumbed it open.

"This is nothing personal," Mr. Finley said. "Your alpha has become the topic of interest at the water cooler, and this is the simplest way to get David back on track and end the disturbing rumors that have been reaching me. I have invited the principal shareholders in the company as witnesses." He smiled without warmth. "This will be legally binding."

"This is crap!" I said nastily, and the surrounding Weres either chuckled or gasped at my temerity to swear at him. Lips pressed tight, I glanced at my bag and the splat gun halfway across the room. My hand touched the small of my back, looking for my nonexistent cuffs, long gone with my I.S. paycheck. God, I missed my cuffs.

"Here it is," the woman said, her head lowered. "Rachel Morgan. O-C(H) 93AF."

"You registered in Cincinnati?" David's boss asked idly, writing it down. Folding the pages over, he fixed on my eyes. "David isn't the first to start a pack with someone not of, ah, Were descent," he finally said. "But he is the first in this company to do so with the sole intent to save his job. This is not a good trend."

"Challenger's choice," Karen said, reaching for the tie to her dress. "I choose to Were first."

David's boss clicked the pen shut. "Then let's get started."

Someone grabbed my arms, and I froze for three heartbeats. Challenger's choice, my grandmother's ass. I had five minutes to subdue her while she Wered, or I was going to lose this.

I silently twisted, going down and rolling. There were several shouts when I knocked the feet out from whoever held me. Then my breath was crushed out of my lungs as someone else fell on me. Adrenaline surged painfully. Someone pinned my legs. Another pushed my head into the plaster-dust-covered plywood.

They won't kill me, I told myself as I spit the hair out of my mouth and tried to get a decent breath. *This is some asinine Were dominance thing, and they won't kill me.*

That's what I was telling myself, but it was hard to convince my trembling muscles.

A low snarl far deeper than it ought to have been rumbled thorough the empty top floor, and the three men holding me let me up.

What in hell? I thought as I scrambled to my feet, then stared. Karen had Wered. She had Wered in thirty seconds flat!

"How . . ." I stammered, not believing it.

Karen made one hell of a wolf. As a person she was petite, maybe 110 pounds. But turn that same 110 pounds into snarling animal, and you get a wolf the size of a pony. *Damn.*

A steady growl of discontent came from her, lips curling from her muzzle in a warning older than dirt. Silky fur reminiscent of her black hair covered her except for her ears, which were rimmed in white. Beyond the circle were her clothes, discarded into a pile on the plywood floor. The faces ringing me were solemn. It wasn't a street brawl but a serious affair that would be as binding as a legal document.

Around me, the Weres were backing up, enlarging the circle. *Double damn.*

Mr. Finley smiled knowingly at me, and my gaze darted from him to the surrounding alphas in their nice clothes and five-hundred-dollar shoes. My heart hammered, and I figured it out. I was in deep shit. They had bound themselves into a round.

Frightened, I eased into a fighting stance. When Weres bound themselves together outside their usual packs, weird stuff happened. I'd seen this once before at a Howlers' game when several alphas had united to support an injured player, taking on the player's pain so he could go on to win the game. Illegal, but wickedly hard to prove since picking out the alphas responsible in a huge stadium was next to impossible. The effect was temporary since Weres, especially alphas, couldn't seem to work under anyone's direction for long. But they would be able to hold it together long enough for Karen to hurt me really, really bad.

I settled my feet more firmly in their boots, feeling my fists begin to sweat. This wasn't fair, damn it! They took my magic away, so the only thing I could do would be to try to beat her off, but she wasn't going to feel a thing! I was toast. I was dog chow. I was going to be really sore in the morning. But I wasn't going to go down without a fight.

Karen's ears went back. It was the only warning I got.

Instinct overpowered training, and I backpedaled as she lunged. Teeth snapping where my face would have been, we went down, her paws on my chest. The floor slammed into me, and I grunted. Hot dog breath hit my face, and I kneed her, trying to knock her breath away. There was a startled yip, and dull claws raked my side as she scrambled up and back.

I stayed down, rolling to my knees so she couldn't push me over again. Not waiting, she jumped.

I cried out, stiff-arming her. Panic struck me when my fist went right square into her mouth. Her paws, the size of my hands, pushed at me as she frantically backed off, and I fell backward. I was lucky she hadn't twisted her head and taken a chunk out of my arm. As it was, I was bleeding from a nasty gash.

Karen's echoing, racking coughs turned into an aggressive growl. "What's the matter, grandma," I panted, flipping my braid out of the way. "Can't get Little Red Riding Hood down your throat?"

Ears pinned, hackles raised, and lips curled to show her teeth, she came at me.

Okay. Maybe that wasn't the best thing to say. Karen slammed into me like a flung door, rocking me back and sending me down. Her teeth went around my neck, choking. I grabbed the foot that was pinching me, digging my nails into it. She bit down, and I gasped.

I made a fist and punched her in the ribs twice. My knee came up and I got her somewhere. There was silky hair in my mouth, and I reached up and pulled an ear. Her teeth gripped harder, cutting off my air. My sight started to go black. Panicking, I went for her eyes.

With no thought but survival, I dug my nails into her eyelids. That, she felt, and yelping, she jerked off me. I took a ragged breath, levering myself up on an elbow. My other hand went to my neck. It came away wet with blood.

"This isn't fair!" I shouted, mad as hell as I scrambled up. My knuckles were bleeding, my side hurt, and I was shaking from adrenaline and fear. I could see Mr. Finley's excitement—smell the rising musk. They were all getting off on the chance to see one of their own "legally" maul a person.

"Nobody said it was supposed to be fair," the man said softly, then gestured to Karen.

But her impetus to attack hesitated at the ding of the elevator.

Despair crept over me. With three more alphas, she wasn't going to feel anything. Not even if I cut something off.

The doors slid open to show David leaning against the back of the lift. His face had a bruise that was likely going to turn his eye black, and his sport coat was torn and filthy. Slowly, he lifted his head, a murderous look in his brown eyes.

"Leave!" his boss said sharply.

"I forgot my briefcase," he said, limping forward. He took in the situation in a glance, still breathing heavily from escaping the three Weres who had dragged him off. "You challenge my alpha, I'm damn well going to be here to make sure it's a fair fight." Shambling to his briefcase, he picked it up, dusted it off, and turned to me. "Rachel, you doing okay?"

I felt a flush of gratitude. He wasn't coming to my rescue, he wanted to make sure they were playing fair. "I'm doing okay," I said, voice cracking. "But that bitch isn't feeling any pain, and they took away my magic." I was going to lose this. I was going to lose this so bad. *Sorry, David.*

The surrounding Weres glanced uneasily at each other now that they had a witness, and Mr. Finley's complexion darkened. "Finish it," he said roughly, and Karen came at me.

Her nails scraped on the plywood floor as they scrambled for purchase. Gasping, I fell to my back before she could push me down. Pulling my knees to my chest, I planted my feet against her as she landed on me and flung her over my head.

I heard a startled yip and thump and David shouting something. There were two fights going on.

I spun on my butt to face her. My eyes widened and I flung up an arm.

Karen smashed into me, pinning me to the floor. She covered me, and fear stabbed deep. I had to keep her from getting a grip on my throat again, and I cried out when she bit my arm.

I'd had enough.

Making a fist, I smashed it into her head. She jerked her muzzle up, raking my arm and sending a pulse of pain through me. Immediately she was back, snarling and more savage. But a ribbon of hope rose in me and I gritted my teeth. She had felt that.

I could hear thumps and cries in the background. David was interfering, breaking their concentration. The round was falling apart. I couldn't best Karen, but sure as hell she was going to walk away remembering me.

The anger and excessive adrenaline wouldn't be denied. "You stupid dog!" I shouted, slamming my fist into her ear again to make her yelp. "You're a foul-breathed, dung flop of a city-bred poodle! How do you like this? Huh!" I hit her again, unable to see from the tears blurring my vision. "Want some more? How about this?"

She latched onto my shoulder and picked me up, intending to shake me. A silky ear landed in my mouth, and after failing to spit it out, I bit down, hard.

Karen barked and was gone. Taking a clean breath, I rolled over onto all fours to see her.

"Rachel!" David cried, and my splat ball gun slid to within my grasp.

I picked the cherry-red gun up, and on my knees, aimed it at Karen. She sat back, her forelegs scrambling to halt her forward motion. Arms shaking, I spit out a tuft of white fur. "Game over, bitch," I said, then plugged her.

The puff of air from my gun was almost lost in someone's cry of frustration.

It hit her square in the nose, covering her face with a sleepy-time potion, the most aggressive thing a white witch would use. Karen went down as if strings were cut, sliding to land three feet from me.

I rose, shaking and so full of adrenaline I could hardly stand. Arms stiff, I aimed my gun at Mr. Finley. The sun had gone behind the surrounding hills across the river, and his face was shadowed. His posture was easy enough to read. "I win," I said, then smacked David when he put a hand on my shoulder.

"Easy, Rachel," David soothed.

"I'm fine!" I shouted, pulling my aim back to his boss before the man could move. "If you want to challenge my title, okay! But I do it as a *witch,* not with my strength washed out of me! This wasn't fair, and you know it!"

"Come on, Rachel. Let's go."

I was still aiming at his boss. I really, *really* wanted to plug him. But in what I thought was a huge show of class, I lowered the gun, snatching my bag from David as he handed it to me. Around me, I felt an easing of tension from the watching alphas.

Briefcase in hand, David escorted me to the elevator. I was still shaking, but I turned my back on them, knowing it would say more clearly than words that I wasn't afraid.

I was scared, though. If Karen had been trying to kill me, not just cow me into submission, it would have been over in the first thirty seconds.

David hit the down button, and together we turned. "This was not a fair contest," he said, then wiped his mouth to make his hand come away red with blood. "I had a right to be here."

Mr. Finley shook his head. "Either the female's alpha shall be present, or in the case of his absence, six alphas may serve as witness to prevent any . . ." He smiled. ". . . foul play."

"There weren't six alphas here at the time of the contest," David said. "I expect to see this recorded as a win for Rachel. That woman is *not* my alpha."

I followed his gaze to Karen lying forgotten on the floor, and I wondered if someone was going to douse her in saltwater to break the charm or just dump her on her pack's doorstep unconscious. I didn't care, and I wasn't going to ask.

"Wrong or not, it's the law," Mr. Finley said, the alphas moving to back him. "And it's there to allow a gentle correction when an alpha goes astray." He took a deep breath, clearly thinking. "This will be recorded as a win for your alpha," he said as if he didn't care, "provided you don't file a complaint. But David, she isn't a Were. If she can't best another with her physical skills, she doesn't deserve an alpha title and will be taken down."

I felt a stab of fear at the memory of Karen on top of me.

"A person can't stand against a wolf," Mr. Finley said. "She would have to Were to have even a chance, and witches can't Were."

The man's eyes went to mine, and though I didn't look away, the fear slid to my belly. The elevator dinged, and I backed up into it, not caring if they knew I was afraid. David joined me, and I gripped my bag and my gun as if I'd fall apart without them.

David's boss stepped forward, his presence threatening and his face utterly shadowed in the new night. "You are an alpha," he said as if correcting a child. "Stop playing with witches and start paying your dues."

The doors slid shut, and I slumped against the mirror. *Paying his dues? What was that supposed to mean?*

Slowly, the lift descended, my tension easing with every floor between us. It smelled like angry Were in there, and I glanced at

David. One of the mirrors was cracked, and my reflection looked awful: braid falling apart and caked with plaster dust, a bite mark on my neck where Karen's teeth had bruised and broken my skin, my knuckles scraped from being in her mouth. My back hurt, my foot was sore, and damn it, I was missing an earring. My favorite hoops, too.

I remembered the soft feel of Karen's ear in my mouth and the sudden give as I bit down. It had been awful, hurting someone that intimately. But I was okay. I wasn't dead. Nothing had changed. I'd never tried to use my ley line skills in a pitched fight like that, and now I knew to watch out for wristbands. Caught like a teenager shoplifting, God help me.

I licked my thumb and wiped a smear of plaster dust off my forehead. The wristband was ugly, but I'd need Ivy's bolt cutters to get it off. Removing my remaining earring, I dropped it in my bag. David was leaning into the corner and holding his ribs, but he didn't look like he was worried about running into the three Weres he had downed, so I put my gun away. Lone wolves were like alphas that didn't need the support of a pack to feel confident. Rather dangerous when one stopped to think about it.

David chuckled. Looking at him, I made a face, and he started to laugh, cutting it short as he winced in pain. His lightly wrinkled face still showing his amusement, he glanced at the numbers counting down, then pulled himself upright, trying to arrange his torn coat. "How about that dinner?" he asked, and I snorted.

"I'm getting the lobster," I said, then added, "Weres never work together outside their packs. I must have really pissed them off. God! What is their problem?"

"It's not you, it's me," he said, discomfited. "They don't like that I started a pack with you. No, that's not true. They don't like that I'm not contributing to the Were population."

The adrenaline was fading, making me hurt all over. I had a pain amulet in my bag, but I wasn't going to use it when David had nothing. And when in hell had Karen scored on my face? Tilting my head, I examined the red claw mark running close to my ear in the dim light, then turned to David when his last words penetrated. "Excuse me?" I asked, confused. "What do you mean, not contributing to the Were population?"

David dropped his gaze. "I started a pack with you."

I tried to straighten, but it hurt. "Yeah, I got the no-kids part there. Why do they care?"

"Because I don't have any, ah, informal relations with any other Were woman, either."

Because if he did, they would expect to be in his pack, eventually. "And . . ." I prompted.

He shifted from foot to foot. "The only way to get more Weres is by birth. Not like vampires who can turn humans if they work at it. With numbers come strength and power. . . ." His voice trailed off, and I got it.

"Oh, for crying out loud," I complained, holding my shoulder. "This was political?"

The elevator chimed and the doors opened. "'Fraid so," he said. "They let subordinate Weres do what they will, but as a loner, what I do matters."

I trooped out before him, looking for trouble, but it was quiet in the abandoned lobby, apart from the three Weres slumped in the corner. David had sounded bitter, and when he opened the main door for me, I touched his arm in a show of support. Clearly surprised, he glanced at me. "Uh, about dinner," he said, looking at his clothes. "You want to reschedule?"

My feet hit the pavement, the cadence of my boots telling me I was limping. It was quiet, but the stillness seemed to hold a new threat. Mr. Finley was right about one thing. This was going to happen again unless I asserted my claim in a way they would respect.

Breathing deeply of the chill air, I headed for David's car. "No way, man. You owe me dinner. How about some Skyline chili?" I said, and he hesitated in confusion. "Go through the drive-through. I have to do some research tonight."

"Rachel," he protested as his car gave a cheerful chirp and unlocked. "I think you deserve at least one night off." His eyes narrowed and he looked at me over the roof of his car. "I am really sorry about this. Maybe . . . we should get the pack contract annulled."

I looked up from opening my door. "Don't you dare!" I said loudly in case someone was listening from a top floor. Then my expression went sheepish. "I can't afford the rider everyone else makes me take out on my health insurance."

David chuckled, but I could tell he wasn't satisfied. We slipped into his car, both of us moving slowly when we found new pains and tried to find a comfortable way to sit. *Oh God, I hurt all over.*

"I mean it, Rachel," he said, his low voice filling the small car after our doors shut. "It's not fair to ask you to put up with this crap."

Smiling, I looked across the car at him. "Don't worry about it, David. I like being your alpha. All I have to do is find the right charm to Were with."

He sighed, his small frame moving in his exhalation, then he snorted.

"What?" I asked, buckling myself in as he started the car.

"The right charm to Were?" he said, putting the car into gear and pulling from the curb. "Get it? You want to be my alpha, but have nothing to Were?"

Putting a hand to my head, I leaned my elbow into the door for support. "That's not funny," I said, but he just laughed, even though it hurt him.

Two

Dappled patterns of afternoon light sifted over my gloved hands as I knelt on a green foam pad and strained to reach the back of the flower bed where grass had taken root despite the shade of the mature oak above it. From the street came the soft sound of cars. A blue jay called and was answered. Saturday in the Hollows was the pinnacle of casual.

Straightening, I stretched to crack my back, then slumped, wincing when my amulet lost contact with my skin and I felt a jolt of pain. I knew I shouldn't be working out there under the influence of a pain amulet, lest I hurt myself without realizing it, but after yesterday I needed some "dirt time" to reassure my subconscious that I was alive. And the garden needed attention. It was a mess without Jenks and his family keeping it up.

The smell of brewing coffee slipped out the kitchen window and into the peace of the cool spring afternoon, and I knew that Ivy was up. Standing, I gazed from the yellow clapboard add-on behind the rented church to the walled graveyard past the witch's garden. The entire grounds took up four city lots and stretched from one street to the other behind it. Though no one had been buried here for almost thirty years, the grass was mown by yours truly. I felt a tidy graveyard made a happy graveyard.

Wondering if Ivy would bring me coffee if I shouted, I nudged my knee pad into the sun near a patch of soft-stemmed black violets. Jenks had seeded the plot last fall, and I wanted to thin them before they got spindly from competition. I knelt before the small plants, moving my way around the bed, circling the rosebush and pulling a third of them.

I had been out there long enough to get warm from exertion, worry waking me before noon. Sleep hadn't come easily either. I'd sat up past sunrise in the kitchen with my spell books in search of a charm to Were into a wolf. It was a task whose success was slim at best; there were no spells to change into sentient beings—at least no legal ones. And it would have to be an earth charm since ley line magic was mostly illusion or physical bursts of energy. I had a small but unique library, yet for all my spells and charms, I had nothing that told me how to Were.

Inching my pad down the flower bed, I felt a band of worry tighten in me. As David had said, the only way you could be a Were was to be born that way. The bandage-covered tooth gashes on my knuckles and neck from Karen would soon be gone with no lingering effects but for what remained in my memory. There might be a charm in the black arts section of the library, but black earth magic used nasty ingredients—like indispensable people parts—and I wasn't going to go there.

The one time I had considered using black earth magic, I came away with a demon mark, then got another, then managed to find myself said demon's familiar. Lucky for me, I had kept my soul and the bargain was declared unenforceable. I was free and clear but for Big Al's original demon mark, which I'd wear along with Newt's mark until I found a way to pay both of them back. But at least with the familiar bond broken, Al wasn't showing up every time I tapped a ley line.

Eyes pinched from the sun, I smeared dirt over my wrist and Al's demon mark. The earth was cool, and it hid the upraised circle-and-line scar more reliably than any charm. It covered the red welt from the band the Weres had put on me, too. God, I had been stupid.

The breeze shifted a red curl to tickle my face, and I tucked it away, glancing past the rosebush to the back of the flower bed. My lips parted in dismay. It had been trampled.

An entire section of plants had been snapped at their bases and were now sprawled and wilting. Tiny footprints gave evidence of who had done it. Outraged, I gathered a handful of broken stems, feeling in the soft pliancy their unstoppable death. *Damn garden fairies.*

"Hey!" I shouted, lurching up to stare into the canopy of the nearby ash tree. Face warm, I stomped over and stood under it, the plants in my hand like an accusation. I'd been fighting them since they'd migrated up from Mexico last week, but it was a losing battle. Fairies ate insects, not nectar, like pixies did, and they didn't care if they killed a garden in their search for food. They were like humans that way, destroying what kept them alive in the long term in their search for short-term resources. There were only six of them, but they had no respect for anything.

"I said hey!" I called louder, craning my neck to the wad of leaves that looked like a squirrel's nest midway up the tree. "I told you to stay out of my garden if you couldn't keep from wrecking it! What are you going to do about this!"

As I fumed on the ground, there was a rustling, and a dead leaf fluttered down. A pale fairy poked his head out, the leader of the small bachelor clan orienting on me immediately. "It's not your garden," he said loudly. "It's my garden, and you can take a long walk in a short ley line for all I care."

My mouth dropped open. From behind me came the thump of a window closing; Ivy didn't want anything to do with what was to follow. I didn't blame her, but it was Jenks's garden, and if I didn't drive them out, it would be trashed by the time I convinced him to come back. I was a runner, damn it. If I couldn't keep Jenks's garden intact, I didn't deserve the title. But it was getting harder each time, and they only returned the moment I went inside.

"Don't ignore me!" I shouted as the fairy disappeared inside the communal nest. "You nasty little twit!" A cry of outrage slipped from me when a tiny bare ass took the place of the pale face and shook at me from the wad of leaves. They thought they were safe up there, out of my reach.

Disgusted, I dropped the broken stems and stalked to the shed. They wouldn't come to me, so I would go to them. I had a ladder.

The blue jays in the graveyard called, enjoying something new to gossip about while I struggled with the twelve-foot length of metal. It smacked into the lower branches as I maneuvered it against the trunk, and with a shrill protest, the nest emptied in an explosion of blue and orange butterfly wings. I put a foot on the first rail, puffing a red curl out of my eyes. I hated to do this, but if they ruined the garden, Jenks's kids would starve.

"Now!" came a loud demand, and I cried out when sharp pings pinched my back.

Cowering, I ducked my head and spun. The ladder slipped, crashing down into the very flower bed they had destroyed. Ticked, I looked up. They were lobbing last year's acorns at me, the sharp ends hard enough to hurt. "You little boogers!" I cried, glad I had on a pain amulet.

"Again!" the leader shouted.

My eyes widened at the handful of acorns coming at me. "*Rhombus,*" I said, the trigger word instigating a hard-learned series of mental exercises into an almost instinctive action. Quicker than thought, my awareness touched the small ley line in the graveyard. Energy filled me, the balance equalizing in the time between memory and action. I spun around, toe pointing, sketching a rough circle, and ley line force filled it, closing it. I could have done this last night and avoided a trouncing, but for the charmed silver they had put on me.

A shimmering band of ever-after flashed into existence, the molecule-thin sheet of alternate reality arching to a close over my head and six feet under my feet, making an oblong bubble that prevented anything more obnoxious than air to pass through. It was sloppy and wouldn't hold a demon, but the acorns pinged off it. It worked against bullets too.

"Knock it off!" I exclaimed, flustered. The usual red sheen of energy shifted to gold as it took on the main color of my aura.

Seeing me safe but trapped in my bubble, the largest fairy fluttered down on his mothlike wings, his hands on his narrow hips and his gossamer, spiderweb-draped hair making him look like a six-inch negative of the grim reaper. His lips were a stark red against his pale face, and his thin features were tight in determination. His harsh beauty made him look incredibly fragile, but he was tougher than sinew. He was a garden fairy, not one of the assassins that had almost killed me last spring, but he was still accustomed to fighting for his right to live. "Go inside and we won't hurt you," he said, leering.

I snickered. What were they going to do? Butterfly kiss me to death?

An excited whisper pulled my attention to the row of neighborhood kids watching from over the tall wall surrounding the graveyard. Their eyes were wide while I tried to best tiny little flying things, something every Inderlander knew was impossible. Crap, I was acting like an ignorant human. But it was Jenks's garden, and I'd hold them off as long as I could.

Resolute, I pushed out of my circle. I jerked as the energy of the circle raced back into me, overflowed my chi and returned to the ley line. A shrill cry came to ready the darts.

Darts? Oh swell. Pulse quickening, I ran to the far side of the kitchen for the hose.

"I tried to be nice. I tried to be reasonable," I muttered while I opened the valve and water started dripping from the spray nozzle. The blue jays in the graveyard called, and I struggled with the hose, jerking to a halt when it caught on the corner of the kitchen. Taking off my gloves, I snapped the hose into a sine wave. It came free, and I stumbled backward. From the ash tree came the high-pitched sounds of organization. I'd never hosed them off before. Maybe this would do it. Fairy wings didn't do well when wet.

"Get her!" came a shout, and I jerked my head up. The thorns they held looked as large as swords as they headed right for me.

Gasping, I aimed the hose and squeezed. They darted up and I followed them, my lips parting when the water turned into a pathetic trickle to arch to the ground and die. *What in hell?* I spun at the sound of gushing water. They had cut the hose!

"I spent twenty bucks on that hose!" I cried, then felt myself pale as the entire clan fronted me, tiny spears probably tipped with poison ivy. "Er, can we talk about this?" I stammered.

I dropped the hose, and the orange-winged fairy grinned like a vampire stripper at a bachelorette party. My heart pounded and I wondered if I should flee inside the church, and subject myself to Ivy's laughter, or tough it out and get a bad case of poison ivy.

The sound of pixy wings brought my heart into my throat. "Jenks!" I exclaimed, turning to follow the head fairy's worried gaze, fixed beyond my shoulder. But it wasn't Jenks, it was his wife, Matalina, and eldest daughter, Jih.

"Back off," Matalina threatened, hovering beside me at head height. The harsh clatter of her more maneuverable dragonfly-like wings set the stray strands of my damp hair to tickle my face. She looked thinner than last winter, her childlike features severe. Determination showed in her eyes, and she held a drawn bow with an arrow at the string. Her daughter looked even more ominous, with a wood-handled sword of silver in her grip. She had possession of a small garden across the street and needed silver to protect it and herself since she had yet to take a husband.

"It's mine!" the fairy screamed in frustration. "Two women can't hold a garden!"

"I need only hold the ground I fly over," Matalina said resolutely. "Get out. Now."

He hesitated, and Matalina pulled the bow back farther, making a tiny creak.

"We'll only take it when you leave!" he cried, motioning for his clan to retreat.

"Then take it," she said. "But while I am here, you won't be."

I watched, awed, while a four-inch pixy stood down an entire clan of fairies. Such was Jenks's reputation, and such was the capabilities of pixies. They could rule the world by assassinations and blackmail if they wanted. But all they desired was a small plot of ground and the peace to tend it. "Thanks, Matalina," I whispered.

She didn't take her steely gaze off them as they retreated to the knee-high wall that divided the garden from the graveyard. "Thank me when I've watered seedlings with their blood," she muttered, shocking me. The pretty, silk-clad pixy looked all of eighteen, her usual tan pale from living with Jenks and her children in that Were's basement all winter. Her billowy green, lightweight dress swirled in the draft from her wings. They were a harsh red with anger, as were her daughter's.

The faire of garden fairies fled to a corner of the graveyard, hovering and dancing in a belligerent display over the dandelions almost a street away. Matalina pulled her bow, loosing an arrow on an exhale. A bright spot of orange jerked up and then down.

"Did you get him?" her daughter asked, her ethereal voice frightening in its vehemence.

Matalina lowered her bow. "I pinned his wing to a stone. He tore it when he jerked away. Something to remember me by."

I swallowed and nervously wiped my hands on my jeans. The shot was clear across the property. Steadying myself, I went to the faucet and turned off the spraying water. "Matalina," I said as I straightened, bobbing my head at her daughter in greeting. "Thanks. They almost filled me with poison ivy. How are you? How's Jenks? Will he talk to me?" I blurted, but my brow furrowed and my hope fell when she dropped her eyes.

"I'm sorry, Rachel." She settled upon my offered hand, her wings shifting into motion, then stilling as they turned a dismal blue. "He . . . I . . . That's why I'm here."

"Oh God, is he all right?" I said, suddenly afraid when the pretty woman looked ready to burst into tears. Her ferocity had been washed away in misery, and I glanced at the distant fairies while Matalina struggled for her composure. *He was dead. Jenks was dead.*

"Rachel . . ." she warbled, looking all the more like an angel when she wiped a hand under her eye. "He needs me, and he forbade the children to return. Especially now."

My first wash of relief that he was alive spilled right back to worry, and I glanced at the butterfly wings. They were getting closer. "Let's go inside," I said. "I'll make you up some sugar water."

Matalina shook her head, bow hanging from her grip. Beside her, her daughter watched the graveyard. "Thank you," she said. "I'll make sure Jih's garden is safe, then I'll be back."

I looked to the front of the church as if I could see her garden on the opposite side of the street. Jih looked eight, but in pixy years she was old enough to be on her own and was actively searching for a husband, finding herself in the unique situation of being able to take her time as she developed her own garden, holding it with silver given to her by her father. And seeing that they had just evicted a clan of fairies, making sure there was no one waiting to jump Jih when she returned home sounded like a good idea.

"Okay," I said, and Matalina and Jih rose a few inches, sending the scent of green things to me. "I'll wait inside. Just come on in. I'll be in the kitchen."

In a soft clatter, they flitted up and over the tall steeple, and I watched, concerned. Things were probably tough for them while Jenks's pride kept them out of their garden and they struggled to make ends meet. What was it with small men and oversized pride?

Checking to see that my bandages hadn't come off my knuckles, I stomped up the wooden steps and wedged my gardening sneakers off. Leaving them there, I went in the back door and into the living room. The smell of coffee was almost a slap. A set of masculine boots clattered on the linoleum in the kitchen across the hall, and I hesitated. That wasn't Ivy. *Kisten?*

Curious, I padded to the kitchen. Hesitating in the open archway, I scanned the apparently empty room.

I liked my kitchen. No, let me rephrase. I loved my kitchen with the loyalty of a bulldog to his favorite bone. It took up more space than the living room and had two stoves—so I never had to stir spells and cook on the same flame. There were bright fluorescent lights, expansive counter and cupboard space, and sundry ceramic spelling utensils hanging over the center island counter. An oversized brandy snifter with my beta, Mr. Fish, rested on the sill of the single blue-curtained window over the sink. A shallow circle was etched in the linoleum for when I needed the extra protection for a sensitive spell, and herbs hung from a sweater rack in the corner.

A heavy, antique farm table took up the interior wall, my end holding a stack of books that hadn't been there earlier. The rest held Ivy's precisely arranged computer, printer, maps, colored markers, and whatever else she needed to plan her runs into boredom. My eyebrows rose at the pile of books, but I smiled because of the jeans-clad backside poking out from the open stainless-steel fridge door.

"Kist," I said, the pleased sound of my voice bringing the living vamp's head up. "I thought you were Ivy."

"Hi, love," he said, the British accent he usually faked almost nonexistent as he casually shut the door with a foot. "Hope you don't mind I let myself in. I didn't want to ring the bell and wake the dead."

I smiled, and he set the cream cheese on the counter and moved to me. Ivy wasn't dead yet, but she was as nasty as a homeless bridge troll if you woke her before she thought she should be up. "Mmmm, you can let yourself in anytime so long as you make me coffee," I said, curving my arms around his tapering waist as he gave me a hug hello.

His close-cut fingernails traced an inch above the new bruises and tooth marks on my neck. "Are you okay?" he breathed.

My eyes slid shut at the concern in his voice. He had wanted to come over last night, and I appreciated that he hadn't when I asked him not to. "I'm fine," I said, toying with the idea of telling him that they hadn't played fair, five alphas binding into a round to give their bitch the advantage in an already unfair fight. But it was so unusual an occurrence that I was afraid he would say I was making it up—and it sounded too much like whining to me.

Instead, I leaned my head against him and took in his scent: a mix of dark leather and silk. He was wearing a black cotton tee that pulled tight across his shoulders, but the aroma of silk and leather remained. With it was the dusky hint of incense that lingered around vampires. I hadn't identified that particular scent with vamps until I started living with Ivy, but now I could probably tell with my eyes closed whether it was Ivy or Kisten in the room.

Either scent was delicious, and I breathed deeply, willingly taking in the vampire pheromones he was unconsciously giving off to soothe and relax me. It was an adaptation to make finding a willing source of blood easier. Not that Kisten and I were sharing blood. Not me. Not this little witch. No how or ever. The risk of becoming a plaything—my will given to a vampire—was too real. But that didn't mean I couldn't enjoy the mild buzz.

I could hear his heartbeat, and I lingered while his fingers traced a yummy path to the small of my back. My forehead came to his shoulder, lower than usual, since he was in boots and I was in socks. His exhaled breath stirred my hair. The sensation brought my head up, and I met his blue eyes squarely from under his long bangs, reading in the normal-sized pupils that he had slaked his blood lust before coming over. He usually did.

"I like it when you smell like dirt," he said, his eyes half-lidded and sly.

Smiling, I ran a fingernail down his rough cheek. He had a small nose and chin, and he usually kept a day's worth of stubble to give himself a more rugged cast. His hair was dyed blond to match his almost-beard, though I had yet to catch him with darker roots or a charm to color it. "What's the real color of your hair?" I asked impulsively as I played with the wispy strands at the nape of his neck.

He pulled away, blinking in surprise. Two slices of toast popped up, and he shifted to the counter, bringing out a plate and setting the bread on it. "Ah, it's blond."

My eyes roved over his very nice backside, and I slumped against the counter, enjoying the view. The rims of his ears were a faint red, and I pushed into motion, leaning to run a finger along his torn ear where someone had ripped out one of the twin diamond studs. His right ear still held both studs, and I wondered who had the missing earring. I would have asked, but was afraid he'd tell me Ivy had it. "You dye your hair," I insisted. "What color is it, really?"

He wouldn't look at me while he opened the cream cheese and spread a thick layer on the toast. "It's sort of brown. Why? Is that a problem?"

Dropping my hands to his waist, I turned him around. Pinning him to the counter, I leaned until our hips touched. "God, no. I just wondered."

"Oh." His hands went about my waist, and clearly relieved, he inhaled slowly, seeming to take my very soul in with him. A spark of desire jumped from him to me, going right to my core to catch my breath. I knew he was scenting me, reading in the slight tension of my body pressing into him my willingness to turn our embrace into something more. I knew our natural scents mixing was a potent blood aphrodisiac. I also knew Ivy would kill him if he broke my skin even by accident. But this was all old news, and I'd be a fool if I didn't admit that part of Kisten's allure was the mix of deep intimacy he offered along with the potential danger of him losing control and biting me. Yeah, I was a stupid, trusting girl, but it made for great sex.

And Kisten is very careful, I thought, pulling coyly away at the low growl rumbling up through him. He wouldn't have come over if he wasn't sure of his control, and I knew he teased himself with my off-limits blood as much as I tested my will against the supposedly better-than-sex carnal ecstasy that a vampire bite could bring.

"I see you're making friends with your neighbors," he said, and I eased from him to reopen the window and wash my hands. If I didn't stop, Ivy would sense it and be out here glowering like a shunned lover. We were roommates and business partners—that was all—but she made no attempt to hide that she wanted more. She had asked me once to be her scion, which was sort of a number-one helper and wielder of vampire power when the vamp in question was limited by sunlight. She wasn't dead yet and didn't need a scion, but Ivy was a planner.

The position was an honor, but I didn't want it, even though, as a witch, I couldn't be turned vampire. It involved an exchange of blood to cement ties, which was why I had flatly refused her the first time she'd asked, but after meeting her old high school roommate, I thought she was after more than that. Kisten could separate the drive for blood from the desire for sex, but Ivy couldn't, and the sensations a blood-lusting vamp pulled from me were too much like sexual hunger for me to think otherwise. Ivy's offer that I become her scion was also an offer to be her lover, and as much as I cared for her, I wasn't wired that way.

I turned off the tap and dried my hands on the dish towel, frowning at the butterfly wings drifting closer to the garden. "You could have helped me out there," I said sourly.

"Me?" Blue eyes glinting in amusement, he set the orange juice on the counter and shut the fridge. "Rachel, honey, I love you and all, but what do you think I could have done?"

Tossing the dish towel to the counter, I turned my back on him, crossing my arms while I gazed out at the cautiously approaching wings. He was right, but that didn't mean I had to like it. I was lucky Matalina had shown up, and I wondered again what she wanted.

A warm breath touched my shoulder and I jerked, realizing Kisten had snuck up on me, unheard with his vamp-soft steps. "I would have come out if you needed it," he said, his rumbly voice going right into me. "But they were only garden fairies."

"Yeah," I said with a sigh. "I suppose." Turning, my eyes went over his shoulder to the three books on the table. "Are those for me?" I asked, wanting to change the subject.

Kisten reached past me to pluck an early daisy from the vase beside Mr. Fish. "Piscary had them behind glass. They look like spell books to me. I thought you might find something to Were in them. They're yours if you want them. I'm not going to tell him where they went."

His eyes were eager for the chance to help me, but I didn't move, standing beside the sink with my arms crossed, eyeing them. If the master vampire had them under glass, then they were probably older than the sun. Even worse, they had the look of demon magic, making them useless since only demons could work it. *Generally*.

Uncrossing my arms, I considered them again. Maybe there *was* something I could use. "Thanks," I said, moving to touch the top book and stifling a shudder when I felt a slight sponginess, as if my aura had gone from liquid to syrup. My torn skin tingled, and I wiped my hand on my jeans. "You won't get in trouble?"

The faint tightening of his jaw was the only sign of his nervousness. "You mean in more trouble than trying to kill him?" he said, flicking his long bangs from his eyes.

I gave him a sick smile. "I see your point." I went to get myself a cup of coffee while Kisten poured a small glass of orange juice and set it on a tray he pulled from behind the microwave. The plate of toast went on it, shortly followed by the daisy he'd taken from the windowsill. I watched, my curiosity growing when he gave me a sideways smile to show his sharp canines and hustled into the hallway with it all. Okay, so it wasn't for me.

Leaning against the counter, I sipped my coffee and listened to a door creak open. Kisten's voice called out cheerfully, "Good afternoon, Ivy. Wakey, wakey, eggs and bakey!"

"Shove it, Kist," came Ivy's slurred mumble. "Hey!" she cried louder. "Don't open those! What the hell are you doing?"

A smile curved over my face and I snickered, taking my coffee and sitting at the table.

"There's my girl," Kisten coaxed. "Sit up. Take the damn tray before I spill the coffee."

"It's Saturday," she snarled. "What are you doing here so early?"

As I listened to Kisten's soothing voice rise and fall in an unrecognizable patter, I wondered what was going on. From families of wealth, Kisten and Ivy had grown up together, tried the cohabitation thing, and parted as friends. Rumor had it Piscary planned for them to get together and have a passel of children to carry on his living-vamp line before one of them died. I was no expert in relationships, but even I could tell that wasn't going to happen. Kisten cared deeply for Ivy, and she for him, but seeing them together always gave me the feeling of a close brother/sister relationship. Even so, this breakfast in bed thing was unusual.

"Watch the coffee!" Kisten exclaimed, shortly followed by Ivy's yelp.

"You aren't helping. Get out of my room!" she snarled, her gray-silk voice harsh.

"Shall I lay out your clothes, love?" Kisten said, his fake British accent on full and laughter in his voice. "I adore that pink skirt you wore all last fall. Why don't you wear that anymore?"

"Get out!" she exclaimed, and I heard something hit the wall.

"Pancakes tomorrow?"

"Get the hell out of my room!"

The door clicked shut, and I met Kisten's grin with my own when he came in and went to the coffeemaker. "Lose a bet?" I guessed, and he nodded, his thin eyebrows high. I pushed out a chair kitty-corner from me with my foot and he settled in with his mug, his long legs going out to encircle mine under the corner of the table.

"I said you could go on a run with David and come home without turning it into a slugfest. She said you couldn't." He reached for the sugar bowl and dumped two spoonfuls in.

"Thanks," I said, glad he had bet against her.

"I lost on purpose," he said, crushing my vindication before it had taken its first breath.

"Thanks a lot," I amended, pulling my feet from between his.

Setting his mug down, he leaned forward and took my hands in his. "Stop it, Rachel. How else could I find an excuse to come over here every morning for a week?"

I couldn't be mad at him *now,* so I smiled, dropping my gaze to our twined hands, mine thin and pale beside his tan, masculine fingers. It was nice seeing them there together like that. The past four months he had not lavished attention on me, but rather was there and available whenever the mood struck either of us.

He was incredibly busy running Piscary's affairs now that the undead master vampire was in jail—thanks to me—and I was occupied with my end of Ivy's and my runner firm, Vampiric Charms. As a result, Kisten and I spent spontaneous snips of intense time together that I found both extremely satisfying and curiously freeing. Our brief, nearly daily conversations over coffee or dinner were more enjoyable and reassuring than a three-day weekend backpacking in the Adirondacks dodging weekend-warrior Weres and slapping mosquitoes.

He felt no jealousy about the time I spent pursuing my career, and I felt only relief that he slaked his blood lust elsewhere—it was a part of him I was ignoring until I found a way to deal with it. There were problems brewing in our future, as blood-chaste witches and living vampires were not known for making long-term commitments. But I was tired of being alone, and Kisten met every emotional need I had raised and I met all of his but one, allowing someone else to do that with no distrust on my part. Our relationship was too good to be true, and I wondered again how I could find comfort with a vampire when I'd never been able to hold onto it with a witch.

Or with Nick, I thought, feeling the expression leave my face.

"What?" Kisten said, more aware of my mood shift than if I had painted my face blue.

I took a breath, hating myself for where my thoughts had gone. "Nothing." I smiled thinly. "Just thinking how much I like being with you."

"Oh." His bristly face creased into a worried smile. "What are you doing today?"

I sat back, pulling my hand from his and putting my sock feet to either side of his lap so he wouldn't think I was drawing away. My eyes drifted to my shoulder bag and my checkbook. I wasn't desperate for money—wonder of wonders, since the calls for my services had dropped dramatically after the six o'clock news last winter had featured me being dragged down the street on my ass by a demon. And because I was heeding David's advice to take a few days off to mend, I knew I ought to spend the time in research, or balancing my bank account, or cleaning my bathroom, or doing something constructive.

But then I met Kisten's eyes, and the only idea that came to me was . . . ah, not the least bit constructive at all. His eyes were not calm. There was the faintest rising of black in them, the faintest thinning of blue. Gaze riveted to mine, he reached for one of my feet, bringing it onto his lap and starting to rub it. The intent behind his action strengthened when he sensed my pulse quickening, and his massage took on a rhythm that spoke of . . . possibilities.

My breath came and went. There was no blood lust in his eyes, only a desire that made my gut tighten and a tingle start at my demon scar.

"I need to . . . do my laundry?" I said, arching my eyebrows.

"Laundry." He never looked from me as his hands left my foot and started creeping upward. Moving, pressing, hinting. "That sounds like it involves water and soap. Mmmm. Could be slippery. And messy. I think I have a bar of soap somewhere. Want some help?"

Uh-huh, I thought, my mind pinging over the possible ways he could "help" me, and how I could get Ivy out of the church for a few hours.

Seeing my—well . . . willingness might be too weak a word—enthusiasm in my inviting smile, Kisten reached out and pulled my chair bumping and scraping around the corner of the table, snuggling it up to his with a living vampire's strength. My legs opened to put my knees to either side of him, and he leaned forward, the blue of his eyes vanishing to a thin ribbon.

Tension rising, I put my lips beside his torn ear. The scent of leather and silk crashed over me, and I closed my eyes in anticipation. "You have your caps?" I whispered.

I felt him nod, but I was more interested in where his lips were going. He cupped a hand along my jaw and tilted my face to his. "Always," he said. "Always and forever with you."

Oh God, I thought, just about melting. Kisten wore caps on his sharp canines to keep from breaking my skin in a moment of passion. They were generally worn by adolescent living vampires still lacking control, and Kisten risked a severe ribbing should anyone find out he wore them when we slept together. His decision was born from his respect for my desire to withhold my blood from him, and Ivy's threat to stake him twice if he took my blood. Kisten claimed it was possible to be bound and not become a vampire's shadow, but everything I had seen said otherwise. My fear remained. And so did his caps.

I inhaled, bringing the vamp pheromones deep into me, willing them to relax me, wanting the tingling promise that was humming in my demon scar to race through my body. But then Kisten stiffened and drew away.

"Ivy?" I whispered, feeling my eyes go worried as his gaze went distant.

"Pixy wings," he said, pushing my chair out.

"Matalina," I answered, sending my gaze to the open archway to the hall.

There was a distant thump. "Jenks?" came Ivy's muffled call from her room.

My lips parted in surprise. She had heard Matalina's wings through a closed door? Great. Just freaking great. Then she'd heard our conversation, too.

"It's Matalina!" I shouted, not wanting her to burst out thinking it was Jenks.

But it was too late, and I stood awkwardly when her door thumped open. Matalina zipped into the kitchen a heartbeat before Ivy staggered in, halting in an undignified slump with one hand supporting herself against the open archway.

She was still in her skimpy nightgown, her black silk robe doing next to nothing to hide her tall lanky build, trim and smooth-limbed from her martial arts practice. Her straight black hair, mussed from sleeping, framed her oval face in an untidy fashion. She'd had it cut not too long ago, and it still surprised me to see it bumping about just under her ears. It made her long neck look longer, the single scar on it a smooth line, now faint from cosmetic surgery. Wide-eyed from being jerked from her bed, her brown, somewhat almond-shaped eyes looked larger than usual, and her thin lips were open to show small teeth.

Head cocked, Kisten spun in his chair. Taking in her lack of clothes, his grin widened.

Grimacing at her less than suave entrance, Ivy pulled herself straight, trying to find her usual iron hold on her emotions. Her pale cheeks were flushed, and she wouldn't meet my eyes as she closed her robe with an abrupt motion. "Matalina," she said, her voice still rough from sleep. "Is Jenks okay? Will he talk to us?"

"God, I hope so," Kisten said dryly, turning his chair so he didn't have his back to Ivy.

The agitated pixy flitted to perch on the center island counter. A glittering trail of silver sparkles sifted from her, slowly falling to make a temporary sunbeam, clear evidence of her flustered state. I already knew her answer, but I couldn't help but slump when she shook her head, her wings stilling. Her pretty eyes went wide and she twisted the fabric of her silk dress. "Please," she said, her voice carrying a frightening amount of worry. "Jenks won't come to you. I'm so scared, Rachel. He can't go alone. He won't come back if he goes alone!"

Suddenly I was a whole lot more concerned. "Go where?" I said, crowding closer. Ivy moved in too, and we clustered before her, almost helpless as the tiny woman who could stand down six fairies started to cry. Forever the gentleman, Kisten carefully tore a tissue and handed her a piece the size of his thumbnail. She could have used it for a washcloth.

"It's Jax," Matalina said, holding her breath between sobs. Jax was her oldest son.

My fear quickened. "He's at Nick's apartment," I said. "I'll drive you over."

Matalina shook her head. "He's not there. He left with Nick on the winter solstice."

I jerked upright, feeling as if I'd been kicked in the stomach. "Nick was here?" I stammered. "At the solstice? He never even called!" I looked at Ivy, shocked. The freaking human bastard! He had come, cleared out his apartment, and left; just like Jenks said he would. And I thought he cared for me. I had been hurt and half dead from hypothermia, and he just left? As I fumed, the betrayal and confusion I thought long gone swelled to make my head hurt.

"We got a call this morning," Matalina was saying, oblivious to my state, though Kisten and Ivy exchanged knowing glances. "We think he's in Michigan."

"Michigan!" I blurted. "What the Turn is he doing in Michigan?"

Ivy nudged closer, almost coming between Matalina and me. "You said you think. You don't know for certain?"

The pixy turned her tear-streaked face to Ivy, looking as tragic and strong as a mourning angel. "Nick told Jax they were in Michigan, but they moved him. Jax doesn't know for sure."

They moved *him?*

"Who moved him?" I said, bending close. "Are they in trouble?"

The tiny woman's eyes were frightened. "I've never seen Jenks so angry. Nick took Jax to help him with his work, but something went wrong. Now Nick is hurt and Jax can't get home. It's cold up there, and I'm so worried."

I glanced at Ivy, her eyes dark with widening pupils, her lips pressed into a thin angry line. Work? Nick cleaned museum artifacts and restored old books. What kind of work would he need a pixy for? In Michigan? In the springtime when most pixies were still shaking off hibernation at that latitude?

My thoughts went to Nick's confidant casualness, his aversion to anything with a badge, his wickedly quick mind, and his uncanny tendency to be able to get ahold of just about anything, given time. I'd met him in Cincy's rat fights, where he had been turned into a rat after "borrowing" a tome from a vampire.

He had come back to Cincinnati and left with Jax, without telling me he was here. Why would he take Jax with him?

My face went hot and I felt my knees go quivery. Pixies had *other* skills than gardening. *Shit. Nick was a thief*.

Leaning hard against the counter, I looked from Kisten to Ivy, her expression telling me that she had known, but realized I'd only get mad at her until I figured it out for myself. God, I was so stupid! It had been there all the time, and I hadn't let myself see it.

I opened my mouth, jumping when Kisten jabbed me in the ribs. His eyes went to Matalina. The poor woman didn't know. I shut my mouth, feeling cold.

"Matalina," I said softly. "Is there any way to find out where they are? Maybe Jax could find a newspaper or something."

"Jax can't read," she whispered, dropping her head into her hands, her wings drooping. "None of us can," she said, crying, "except Jenks. He learned so he could work for the I.S."

I felt so helpless, unable to do anything. How do you give someone four inches high a hug? How do you tell her that her eldest son had been misled by a thief? A thief I had trusted?

"I'm so scared," the tiny pixy said, her voice muffled. "Jenks is going after him. He's going all the way up north. He won't come back. It's too far. He won't be able to find enough to eat, and it's too cold unless he has somewhere safe to stay at night." Her hands fell away, the misery and heartache on her tiny features striking fear in me.

"Where is he?" I asked, my growing anger pushing out the fear.

"I don't know." Matalina sniffed as she looked at the torn tissue in her grip. "Jax said it was cold and everyone was making candy. There's a big green bridge and lots of water."

I shook my head impatiently. "Not Jax. Jenks."

Matalina's hopeful expression made her look more beautiful than all of God's angels. "You'll talk to him?" she quavered.

Taking a slow breath, I glanced at Ivy. "He's sulked enough," I said. "I'm going to talk to the little twit, and he's going to listen. And then we'll both go."

Ivy straightened, her arms held tight at her sides as she took two steps back. Her eyes were wide and her face carefully blank.

"Rachel—" Kisten said, the warning in his voice jerking my attention to him.

Matalina rose three inches into the air, her face alight even as the tears continued. "He'll be angry if he finds out I came to you for help. D-Don't tell him I asked you."

Ignoring Kisten, I took a resolute breath. "Tell me where he's going to be and I'll find him. He isn't going to do this alone. I don't care if he talks to me or not, but I'm going with him."

Three

The coffee in my cup was cold, which I didn't remember until I had it to my lips. Sharp and bitter, the taste of it puckered my face an instant before I let it slip down my throat. Shuddering, I held another dollop on my tongue. A soft thrill lifted through me as I tapped the line in the graveyard and set my pencil down on the kitchen table.

"From candle's burn and planet's spin," I whispered awkwardly around the coffee, my fingers sketching out a complex figure. "Friction is how it ends and begins." Rolling my eyes, I brought my hands together to make a loud pop, simultaneously saying, *"Consimilis."* God help me, it was so hokey, but the rhyme did help me remember the finger motions and the two words that actually did the charm.

"Cold to hot, harness within," I finished, making the ley line gesture that would use the coffee in my mouth as a focal object so I wouldn't warm up . . . say . . . Mr. Fish's bowl. *"Calefacio,"* I said, smiling at the familiar drop of line energy through me. I tightened my awareness to let what I thought was the right amount of power run through me to excite the water molecules and warm the coffee. "Excellent," I breathed when the mug began to steam.

My fingers curled about the warm porcelain, and I dropped the line entirely. *Much better,* I thought when I went to take a sip, jerking back and touching my lip when I found it too hot. Ceri had said control would come with practice, but I was still waiting.

I set the mug down, pushing Ivy's maps farther out of my space and into hers. The robins were singing loudly, and I squinted, trying to read in the early dusk of the developing rain clouds as I leafed through Kisten's borrowed books. I'd have to leave in half an hour to accidentally run into Jenks on his run, and I was getting antsy.

Ivy was in one of her moods, and Kisten had hustled her out shortly after Matalina left so she wouldn't drive me crazy all afternoon. I'd find out soon enough what was bothering her, and maybe Kisten could take care of it for me instead.

My spine cracked when I straightened, arching my back and taking a deep breath. I pulled my fingers off the dusk-darkened print, feeling the tingle of disconnection strike through me like a reverse static shock. Kist's books were indeed demon texts. I'd quickly gotten used to the numb feeling of the pages, lured into exploring them when I realized every curse mixed earth and ley line magic, utilizing both to make more than the sum of the parts. It made for fascinating reading, even if my Latin sucked dishwater, and I was only now starting to remember I was supposed to be afraid of this stuff. It wasn't what I had expected.

Sure, there were the nasty spells that would turn your neighbor's barking dog inside out, strike your fourth-grade teacher with agony, or call down a flaming ball of hell to smack the guy tailgating you, but there were softer spells too. Ones I couldn't see harm in, spells that did the same things many of my eminently legal earth charms did. And that's what scared me the most.

Mood going introspective, I flipped the page and found a curse that would encase someone in a thick layer of air to slow their movements as if they were in molasses. I suppose one could use it to gain the advantage in a fight and kill them with a blow to the head or knife thrust, but would it tarnish one's soul if all you did was slow them down so you could slap a pair of cuffs on them? The more I looked, the harder it was to tell. I had assumed demon curses were black as a matter of course, but I truly couldn't see the harm here.

Even more worrisome was the potential power they all had. The curse detailed before me wasn't the illusion of molasses that black ley line witches used to give people bad dreams in which they were unable to escape something or to help a loved one. And it wasn't the earth charm that had to be laboriously cooked and targeted to a specific person, which resulted in slower reactions, not this almost complete immobility. The demon curse took the quick implementation and wide range of application of a ley line charm and harnessed it in a pair of "polarized" amulets, thereby giving it the reality and permanence of earth magic. It was a mix of both. It was the real thing. It was demon magic, and I was one of two people who could both walk under the sun and kindle it.

"Thanks, Trent," I muttered as I turned the page, my fingertips prickling. "Your dad was a peach."

But I wasn't complaining. I shouldn't have lived to puberty. The genetic aberration that I was afflicted with killed every witch born with it before they were two. I truly believed that Trent Kalamack's father hadn't known that the same thing that was killing me had made it possible for me to kindle demon magic, accidentally circumventing a genetic checks-and-balances. All he knew was his friend's daughter was dying of an ancient malady and he had the wisdom and technology—even if it was illegal—to save my life.

So he had. And it kinda worried me that the only other witch Trent's father had fixed was now suffering a living hell as the demon Algaliarept's familiar in the ever-after.

Guilt assailed me, quickly quashed. I had told Lee not to give me to Al. I'd warned him to get us the hell out of the ever-after when we had the chance. But no-o-o-o-o. The wicked witch from the West thought he knew everything, and now he was paying for his mistake with his life. It had been either him or me, and I liked where I lived.

A freshening gust of wind blew in, carrying the hint of rain and shifting the curtains. I glanced at the book before me and turned the page to find a curse to pull out someone's intelligence until they had the brain of a worm. Blinking, I closed the book. Okay, so it was easy to figure out that some of them were black, but was there such a thing as a white curse?

The thing was, I knew earth magic was powerful, but giving it the speed and versatility of ley line magic was frightening. And the mixing of the two branches of magic was in every curse. In the few hours I had been sitting here, I found curses that shifted mass to line energy or vice versa, so you could actually make big things little and little things big, not just project the illusion of a size change, as with ley line magic; and since it also involved an earth magic potion, the change was real—as in "having viable offspring" real.

Nervous, I pushed myself away from the table. My fingers tapped the old wood in a quick rhythm, and I glanced at the clock. Almost six. I couldn't sit here any longer. The weather was shifting, and I wanted to be in it.

Surging to my feet, I snatched the book up and knelt at the low shelf under the center island counter. I didn't want to shelve it with my usual library, but I certainly didn't want the three of them under my pillow, either. Brow creasing, I moved a mundane cookbook to serve as a buffer between my spell books and the demon tomes. So I was superstitious. So sue me.

The last two books slid into place, and I straightened, wiping my hands on my jeans while I looked at them sitting oh so nicely between the *Country Farm's Cookie Cookbook* I'd swiped from my mom and the copy of *Real Witches Eat Quiche* I had gotten from the I.S.'s secret Santa three years ago. You can guess which one I used the most.

Grabbing my bag, I headed out, boot heels clunking as I went down the hallway past Ivy's and my bedrooms and bathrooms and into the sanctuary. The pews were long gone, leaving only the faded reminder of a huge cross above where the altar once stood. Stained-glass windows stretched from knee height to the top of the twelve-foot walls. The open raftered ceiling was dusky with the early twilight from the clouds, and I would use my panties as a sun hat if I could hear the whispered giggles of pixies plotting mischief up there again.

The large room took up half the heated space in the church, and it was empty but for my plant-strewn desk on the ankle-high stage where the altar had stood and Ivy's baby grand piano just past the foyer. I'd only heard her play it once, her long fingers pulling a depth of emotion from the keys that I only rarely saw in her face.

I snatched my keys from my desk in passing, and they jingled happily as I continued into the dark foyer. Squinting, I plucked my red leather jacket and cap from the peg beside the four-inch-thick, twin oak doors. At the last moment, I grabbed Ivy's umbrella with the ebony handle before wedging the door open. There was no lock—only a bar to lower from the inside—but no one on this side of the ley lines would dare steal from a Tamwood vampire.

The door thumped shut behind me, and I flounced down the steps to the cracked sidewalk. The spring evening was balmy, the humidity of an approaching storm shifting the air pressure to make the robins sing and my blood quicken. I could smell rain and imagine the distant rumble of thunder. I loved spring storms, and I smiled at the fresh green leaves shifting in the rising breeze.

My steps quickened when I saw my car tucked in the tiny carport: a bright red convertible with two seats up front and two unusable seats in back. Across the street and a few houses down, our neighbor Keasley was standing at the edge of his front porch, his spine bent from arthritis and his head up as he tasted the changing wind. He raised a gnarly hand when I waved, telling me everything was fine with him. Unseen preschool-age kids were shouting, responding to the air pressure shift with less restraint than I was managing.

Up and down the street, people were coming out of their Americana middle-class homes, heads up and eyes on the sky. It was the season's first warm rain, and only three days out of a new moon. The I.S. would have a busy night trying to rein everyone in.

Not my problem anymore, I cheerfully thought as I settled in behind the wheel of my car and took the time to put the top down so I could feel the wind in my hair. Yeah, it was going to rain, but not for a few hours yet.

Saucy little red cap on my head, and wearing a snappy leather jacket to block the wind, I drove through the Hollows at a modest pace, waiting until I crossed the bridge and got on the interstate before I opened her up. The damp wind beating on my face brought every smell to me, sharper and more vivid than it had been for months, and the rumble of tires, engine, and wind muffling everything else was like freedom itself. I found myself inching past eighty when I saw the cruiser parked on an entrance ramp. It had the Federal Inderland Bureau emblem on it, and waving merrily, I tunked it down and got a headlight blink in return. Everyone in the human-run FIB knew my car—heck, they had given it to me. The FIB wouldn't stop me, but the Inderland run I.S. would, just out of spite for having quit their lame-ass, nationwide police force.

I tucked a strand of blowing hair behind my ear and warily checked behind me. I'd only had my car a couple of months, and already the entire fleet of I.S. flunkies doing street duty knew me by sight, taking every opportunity to help me rack up points on my license. And it wasn't fair! The red light I ran a month ago was for a darn good reason—and at five in the morning, no one had even been at the intersection but the cop. I still don't know where he had come from—my trunk maybe? And I'd been late for an appointment the time I got pulled over for speeding on 75. I hadn't been going *that* much faster than everyone else.

"Stupid car," I muttered fondly, though I wouldn't trade my little red ticket magnet for anything. It wasn't its fault the I.S. took every chance they could to make my life miserable.

But "Walkie Talkie Man" was cranked, Steriogram singing so fast only a vamp could keep up, and it wasn't long before the little white hand crept up to eighty again, pulling my mood along with it. I even found a cute-looking guy on a cycle to flirt with while I made my way to Edgemont where Jenks had his run.

The cessation of wind as I came off the interstate was almost an assault, and when a rumble of real thunder rolled over me, I pulled to the side of the road to put the top up. My head jerked up when the guy on the cycle whizzed past, his hand raised in salute. My faint smile lingered for a moment, then vanished.

If I couldn't get Jenks to talk to me, I was going to kill the little twit.

Taking a deep breath, I turned my phone to vibrate, snapped off the music, and pulled into traffic. I jostled over a railroad track, peering into the coming dusk and noting that the pace of the pedestrian and bike traffic had changed from casual to intense as the threat of rain increased. It was a business district, one of the old industrial areas that the city had thrown a lot of money at to turn it into a themed mall and parks to attract the usual outlying shops and apartments. It reminded me of "Mrs. Bryant's flat," and I frowned.

I drove past the address to evaluate the multistoried sprawling building. By the art deco and the mailbox drive-through, it looked like a manufacturing complex turned into a mix of light commercial and upscale apartments. I hadn't seen Jenks, but that wouldn't be unusual if he was tailing someone. Matalina said he was on a smut run to build up money to buy an airline ticket.

My brow was furrowed in worry when I turned the corner and got a lucky spot at the curb in front of a coffeehouse, jerking the parking break up and shifting the stick to neutral. Pixies couldn't fly commercially—the shifting air pressures wreaked havoc with them. Jenks wasn't thinking straight anymore. No wonder Matalina had come to me.

Snatching up my bag, I timed my move with traffic and got out. A quick look at the lowering clouds, and I reached for Ivy's umbrella. The smell of coffee almost pulled me inside, but I dutifully went the other way. A quick glance, and I slipped into the alley of the building in question, walking so my feet were silent in my vamp-made boots.

The scent of garbage and dog urine was strong, and I wrinkled my nose and pulled my jacket closer, looking for a spot where I could stay out of sight and watch the front door of the complex. I was early. If I could catch him before he went in, it would be all the better. But then I froze at the sound of a familiar wing clatter.

Face going still, I looked up the narrow passage to find a pixy dressed in a black body stocking rubbing a clean spot to see through on a dirt-grimed, bird-spotted, upper-story window.

Shame stilled my voice. God, I had been so stupid. I didn't blame him for leaving, for thinking I hadn't trusted him. The ugly truth was, I hadn't. Last solstice I had figured out that Trent Kalamack was an elf, and getting the wealthy son of a bitch to not kill me for knowing that the elves weren't extinct but had gone into hiding had taken a pretty piece of blackmail. Finding out what kind of Inderlander Trent was had become the holy grail of the pixy world, and I knew the temptation for Jenks to blab it would be too much. Even so, he deserved better than my lies of omission, and I was afraid he might not listen to me even now.

Jenks hovered, intent on whatever was inside. His dragonfly wings were invisible in his calm state, and not a hint of pixy dust sifted from him. He looked confident, and a red bandanna was tied about his forehead. It was protection against accidentally invading a rival pixy's or fairy's territory, a promise of a quick departure with no attempt at poaching.

I nervously gathered my resolve, glancing at the wall of the alley before I leaned against it and tried to look casual. "So, is she cheating on her husband?" I asked.

"Nah," Jenks said, his eyes focused through the glass. "She's taking an exercise class to surprise him on their twenty-fifth anniversary. He doesn't deserve her, the mistrusting bastard."

Then he jerked, slamming back six feet to nearly hit the adjacent building.

"You!" he cried, pixy dust sifting like sunbeams. "What the hell are you doing here?"

I pushed myself off the wall and stepped forward. "Jenks—"

He dropped like a stone to hover before me, finger pointing as the pixy dust he had let slip slowly fell over us. Anger creased his tiny features to make him grim and threatening. "She told you!" he shrilled, his jaw clenched and his face red under his short blond hair.

I took a step back, alarmed. "Jenks, she's only worried—"

"The hell with you both," he snarled. "I'm outta here."

He turned, wings a blur of red. Ticked, I tapped a line. Energy flowed, equalizing in the time it takes for a burst bubble to vanish. *"Rhombus,"* I snapped, imagining a circle. A sheet of gold hummed into existence, so thick it blurred the walls of the surrounding alley. I staggered, my balance questionable since I hadn't taken even the time to pretend to draw a circle in the air.

Jenks jerked to a stop a mere inch in front of the circle. "You sorry stupid witch!" he shrilled, seeming at a loss for something worse. "Let me out. I ought to kill your car. I ought to leave slug eggs in your slippers! I ought to, I ought to . . ."

Hands on my hips, I got in his face. "Yeah, you ought to, but first you're going to listen to me!" His eyes widened, and I leaned forward until he shifted back. "What is wrong with you, Jenks? This can't just be about me not telling you what Trent is!"

Jenks's face lost its surprise. His eyes touched upon the bandages and bruises on my neck, then dropped to my pain amulet. Seemingly by force of will, his eyes narrowed with an old anger. "That's right," he said, hovering an inch before my nose. "It's about you lying to me! It's about you not trusting me with information. It's about you pissing all over our partnership!"

Finally, I thought. *Finally.* I gritted my jaw, almost cross-eyed with him so close. "Good God! If I tell you what he is, will that make you happy?"

"Shut your mouth!" he shouted. "I don't care anymore, and I don't need your help. Break your circle so I can get the hell away from you, or I'll jam something where it shouldn't go, witch."

"You stupid ass," I exclaimed, warming. "Fine!" Furious, I shoved a foot into the circle. My breath hissed in when the circle's energy flowed into me. At the end of the alley the passing people gave us a few curious looks. "Run away!" I said, gesturing wildly, not caring what they thought. "Leave, you cowardly ball of spider snot. I've been trying to apologize for the last five months, but you're so preoccupied with your stinking little hurt feelings that you won't listen. I think you like being slighted. I think you feel secure in your downtrodden pixy mentality. I think you get off on the 'poor little pixy that no one takes seriously crap' that you wrap yourself in. And when I believed in you, you got scared and ran away at the first sign that you might have to live up to your ideas!"

Jenks's mouth was hanging open and he was slowly loosing altitude. Seeing him floundering, I surged ahead, thinking I might have finally shaken him loose.

"Go on and leave," I continued, my legs starting to shake. "Stay in your stinking little basement and hide. But Matalina and your kids are coming back to the garden. You can shove a cherry up your ass and make jam for all I care, but I need them. I can't keep those damn fairies out to save my dandelions, and I need my garden as much as I need backup on a night with a full moon. And your bitching and moaning don't mean crap anymore because I've been trying to apologize and all you've done is shit on me. Well, I'm not apologizing anymore!"

Still he hung in the air, his wings shifting to a lighter shade of red. He didn't seem to know what to do with his hands, and they tugged his bandanna and fell to his sword.

"I'm going to find Jax and Nick," I said, my anger lessening. I had said what I wanted, and all that was left was hearing what he thought. "Are you coming with me or not?"

Jenks rose. "My going north has nothing to do with you," he said tightly.

"Like hell it doesn't," I said, hearing the first heavy drop of rain hit the nearby Dumpster. "He may be your son, but it was my old boyfriend who got him in trouble. He lied to you. He lied to me. And I'm going up there so I can kick Nick's ass from here to the ever-after." Even I could hear my sullen tone, and Jenks gave me a nasty smile.

"Be careful," he goaded. "Someone might think you still like him."

"I do *not,*" I said, feeling a headache start. "But he's in trouble and I can't just let whoever it is kill him."

A bitter, saucy look returned to Jenks's face, and he flitted to the end of a two-by-four sticking out of a can. "Yuh-huh," he said snidely, hands on his hips. "Why are you really going?"

"I just told you why," I snapped, hiding my bitten hand when he looked at it.

His head bobbed up and down. "Yada yada yada," he said, making a get-on-with-it gesture with one hand. "I know why you're going, but I want to hear you say it."

I fumbled, not believing this. "Because I'm as mad as all hell!" I said, the rain falling steadily now. If we had to continue this conversation much longer, we were going to get soaked. "He said he was going to come back, and he did, just long enough to clear out his apartment and take off. No good-bye, not even an 'it was great, babe, but I gotta go now.' I need to tell him to his face that he crapped all over me and I don't love him anymore."

Jenks's tiny eyebrows rose, and I wished he was bigger so I could wipe the smirk off his face. "This is some female closure thing, isn't it?" he said, and I sneered.

"Look," I said. "I'm going to get Jax and pull Nick's sorry ass out from whatever mess he's in. Are you coming with me, or are you going to waste your time taking smut runs for a paycheck you will only waste on a plane ticket that will leave you hospitalized for three days?" I slowed, thinking I could chance appealing to his love for Matalina without him flying away. "Matalina is scared, Jenks. She's afraid you won't come back if you go alone."

His face emptied of emotion, and for a moment I thought I'd gone too far. "I can do this on my own," he said angrily. "I don't need your help."

My thoughts went to his iffy food supply and the cold northern nights. It could snow in May in Michigan. Jenks knew it. "Sure you don't," I said. I crossed my arms and eyed him. "Just like I could have survived those fairy assassins last year without your help."

His lips pursed. He took a breath to tell me something. His hand went up, finger pointing. I made my eyes wide and mocking. Slowly his hand fell. Still standing on the two-by-four, Jenks's wings drooped. "You're going?"

I fought to keep my surge of hope from showing. "Yes," I said. "But to even have a chance, I need a security bypass expert, reconnaissance, and someone I trust to watch my back. Ivy can't do it. She can't leave Cincinnati."

Jenks's wings hummed into motion, then stilled. "You hurt me bad, Rachel."

My chest clenched in guilt. "I know," I whispered. "And I'm sorry. I don't deserve your help, but I'm asking for it." I pulled my head up, pleading with him with my eyes. For the first time, his face showed the hurt I'd given him, and my heart broke again.

"I'll think about it," he muttered, taking to the air.

I took a faltering step after him. "I'm leaving tomorrow. Early noon."

Wings clattering, Jenks flew a swooping path back to me. I nearly raised my hand for him to land on, but it would hurt too much if he shunned it. "I suppose that's early for a witch," he said. The pitch of his wings rose until my eyeballs hurt. "Okay. I'll come with you, but I'm not coming back to the firm. This is a one-shot deal."

My throat closed and I swallowed down a lump. He'd come back. He knew it as much as I did. I wanted to shout an exuberant, "Yes!" I wanted to whoop to make the passing people stare, but what I did instead was smile shakily at him. "Okay," I said, so relieved I was almost crying.

Blinking profusely, I followed him to the head of the alley. Though Jenks would have snugged under my hat before, to get out of the rain, it was too much to ask just yet. "Can you meet me tonight at the church after midnight?" I asked. "I have a few charms to prep before we head out."

We left the alley together, the lighter gloom making me feel as if we had come out of a black hole. We were both walking on eggshells; the patterns were familiar, but the sensitivities were so very fragile.

"I can do that," Jenks said apprehensively, glancing up at the rain.

"Good. Good." I listened to my feet hit the sidewalk, the thumps jarring up my spine. "Do you still have your half of the phone set you gave me?" I could hear the hesitancy in my voice, and I wondered if Jenks could too. I had kept the phone he'd given me for the solstice. Hell, I had almost made it into a shrine.

I popped open Ivy's black umbrella, and Jenks flew under it. Five months ago he would have sat on my shoulder, but even this small show of trust caught at me.

"David brought it over," he said stiffly, keeping to the distant corner.

"Good," I said again, feeling stupid. "Can you bring it with you?"

"It's a little big for me to slip into my pocket, but I'll manage." It was sarcastic and biting, but he was sounding more like the Jenks I knew.

I glanced at him, seeing he was trailing the faintest wisp of silver sparkles. My car was just ahead, and I wondered whether he'd take offense if I offered him a ride home.

"Cowardly ball of spider snot?" Jenks said when I opened the door and he darted inside.

Swallowing hard, I stared across to the sidewalk and the people running for cover as the clouds opened and it began to pour. He was back. I had gotten him back. It wasn't perfect, but it was a start. Breath shaking, I folded the umbrella and ducked inside. "Give me a break," I said as I started the car and turned the heat on full to warm him up. "I was pressed for time."

Four

I held up the black lace top in consideration. Sighing, I decided against it, folding it up and jamming it back into the third drawer down. Sure, I looked good in it, but this was a rescue run, not spring break. Taking the short-sleeve peach-colored cotton shirt instead, I set it atop the jeans already packed in the suitcase my mom had given me for graduation. She insisted it hadn't been a hint, but I reserved my doubts to this day.

Moving to my top drawer, I grabbed enough socks and undies for a week. The church was empty since Ivy was out getting Jenks and his brood. The rain pattered pleasantly on my small stained-glass window propped open with a pencil, getting the sill wet but little else. From the dark garden came the trill of a toad. It mixed well with the soft jazz from the living room.

In the back of my closet I found the red turtleneck sweater I'd stored last week. I shook the hanger from it, carefully folded it, and set it with the rest. I added a pair of running shorts and my favorite black tee with staff on it that I'd gotten while working Takata's concert last winter. The temp could hit eighty as easily as thirty-five. I sighed, content. Midnight rain, toad song, jazz, and Jenks coming home. It didn't get much better.

My head rose at the creak of the front door. "Hey, it's me," came Kisten's voice.

And now it was better still. "Back here," I called, taking two steps to the hall, one hand on the doorframe as I leaned out. The lights were dim in the sanctuary, his tall silhouette mysterious and attractive as he shook the rain from his full-length slicker.

I ducked back inside and shut my underwear drawer just before Kisten came in, the soft and certain steps of his dress shoes distinct on the hardwood floor. The scent of pizza and someone else's perfume hung about him, and by his carefully styled hair, clean-shaven cheeks, expensive dress slacks and silk shirt, I knew he had come from work. I liked the respectable, financially successful club manager aspect of Kisten as much as his rougher, bad boy image. He could do both equally well.

"Hi, love," he said, hitting his fake British accent hard to make me smile. A rain-spotted paper grocery bag was in his hands, the top rolled down. I padded forward in my sneakers, having to reach to give him a hug. My fingers played with the damp tips of his hair as I drew away, and he smiled, enjoying the tease.

"Hi," I said, reaching for the bag. "Is that them?"

Nodding, he gave it to me, and I set it on the bed, opening it and peering inside. As I had asked, there was a pair of sweatpants and a soft flannel sweatshirt.

Kisten looked at the bag, clearly wanting to know why, but all he said was, "Ivy's out?"

"She went to get Jenks because of the rain." Pensive, I opened a lower drawer and packed another T-shirt. "She missed him as much as me," I finished softly.

Looking tired, Kisten sat at the head of my bed, his long fingers rolling the top of the bag down. I closed my suitcase but didn't zip it. It was unusual for him to leave Piscary's club mid-hours. Clearly something was bothering him. I straightened, arms crossed, and waited for it.

"I don't think you should go," he said, his voice serious.

My mouth fell open, surprise shifting to anger when I pieced it together. "Is this about Nick?" I said, turning to my dresser to pack the ungodly expensive bottle of perfume that kept my natural scent from mixing with a vampire's. "Kisten, I'm over him. Give me some credit."

"That's not why. Ivy—"

"Ivy!" I stiffened, glancing into the empty hall. "What about her? Is Piscary . . ."

His slowly moving head said no, and I relaxed a notch. "He's leaving her alone. But she relies on you more than you know. If you go, things might shift."

Flustered, I jammed the perfume into a zippy bag and dropped it into a pocket in my vanity case. "I'm only going to be gone for a week, maybe two. It's not as if I'm her scion."

"No. You're her friend. And that's more important than anything else to her right now."

Arms crossed, I leaned back against my dresser. "This isn't my responsibility—I have my own life," I protested. "Gods, we share rent. We aren't married!"

Kisten's eyes were dark in the dim light from my table lamp, his brow pinched with worry. "You have coffee with her every day when she wakes up. You're across the hall when she shuts the curtains before going to sleep. That might not mean much to you, but it's everything to her. You're her first real friend in . . . Damn, I think it's been over ten years."

"You're her friend," I said. "And what about Skimmer?"

"You're her only friend not after her blood," he amended, his eyes sad. "It's different."

"Well, just crap on that," I said, picking up my last favorite earring but not knowing what to do with it. Disgusted, I threw it away. "Ivy hasn't said anything to me about not leaving."

"Rachel . . ." He stood, coming to take my elbows in his grip. His fingers were warm, and I felt them tighten and relax. From the living room, jazz rose and fell. "She won't."

I dropped my head, frustrated. "Never once did I tell her I'd be anything but what we are now," I said. "We aren't sharing a bed or blood or anything! I don't belong to her, and keeping her together isn't my job. Why is this all on me, anyway? You've known her longer than I."

"I know her past. You don't. She leans on you more because of your ignorance of what she was." He took a hesitant breath before he continued. "It was ugly, Rachel. Piscary warped her into a viciously savage lover who couldn't separate blood from lust or love. She survived by becoming something she hated, accepting the pattern of self-abuse of trying to please everyone she thought she loved."

I didn't want to hear this, but when I tried to move, his grip tightened.

"She's better now," he said, his blue eyes pleading for me to listen. "It took her a long time to break the pattern, and even longer to start to feel good about herself. I've never seen her happier, and like it or not, it's because of you. She loves Skimmer, but that woman is a big part of what Ivy was and how she got there, and if you leave . . ."

My jaw tightened and I stiffened, not liking this at all. "I am *not* Ivy's keeper," I said, gut twisting. "I did not sign up for this, Kisten!"

But he only smiled, soft and full of understanding and regret. I liked Ivy—I liked her, respected her, and wished I had half her willpower—but I didn't want anyone relying on me that heavily. Hell, I could hardly take care of myself, much less a powerful, mentally abused vampire.

"She won't ask more than you can give," he said. "Especially if she needs it. But you did move in with her, and more telling, you stayed when your relationship began to evolve."

"Excuse me?" I said, trying to pull away. He wouldn't let go, and I jerked from him, falling two steps back.

Kisten's expression had a hint of accusation. "She asked you to be her scion," he said.

"And I said no!"

"But you forgave her for trying to force you, and you did it without a second thought."

This was crap. He had heard all of this. Why was he making such a big deal about it? "Only because I jumped on her back and breathed in her ear when we were sparring!" I said. "I pushed her too far, and it wasn't her fault. Besides, she was scared that if she didn't make me her scion, Piscary was going to kill me."

Kisten nodded, his calm state helping to dissipate my anger. "It was a no-win situation," he said softly. "And you both handled it the best you could, but the point is, you did jump on her knowing what it might trigger."

I took a breath to protest, then turned away, flustered. "It was a mistake, and I didn't think it was right to walk out because *I* made a mistake."

"Why not?" he insisted. "People leave all the time when someone makes a mistake."

Frightened, I went to push past him. I had to get out of there.

"Rachel," he said loudly, jerking me into him. "Why didn't you leave right then? No one would have thought any less of you."

I took a breath, then let it out. "Because she is my friend," I said, eyes down, and keeping my voice low so it wouldn't shake. "That's why. And it wouldn't be fair for me to leave because of my mistake, because she . . . relies on me."

My shoulders slumped, and Kisten's grip on me eased, pulling me closer.

"Damn it, Kist," I said, putting my cheek to his shirt and breathing in his scent. "I can hardly take care of myself. I can't save her too."

"No one said you had to," he said, his voice rumbling into

me. "And no one says it's going to stay this way. Helping to keep you alive and unbound with that scar of yours makes Ivy feel worthwhile—that she's making the world a better place. Do you know how hard that is for a vampire to find? She leans on you harder than me because she feels responsible for you and you owe her."

There is that, I thought, remembering how vulnerable my unclaimed vampire scar made me. But my debt to Ivy wasn't why I hadn't left. Nick had said I was making excuses to stay in an unsafe situation, that I had wanted her to bite me. I couldn't believe that. It was just friendship. Wasn't it?

Kisten's hand across my hair was soothing, and I put my arms around his waist, finding comfort in his touch. "If you leave," he said, "you take her strength."

"I never wanted this," I said. How had I become her lodestone? Her savior. All I wanted was to be her friend.

"I know." His breath moved my hair. "Will you stay?"

I swallowed, not wanting to move. "I can't," I said, and he gently pushed me back until he could see my face. "Jenks needs me. It's just a quick run. Five hundred miles. How much trouble could Nick and Jax be in? They probably just need bail money. I'll be back."

Kisten's face was creased, his elegant grace marred by sorrow. The caring he felt for me and for Ivy were mixed together and somehow beautiful. "I know you will. I just hope Ivy is here when you do."

Uncomfortable, I went to my closet and pretended to shuffle for something. "She's a big girl. She'll be fine. It's only a day's drive."

He took a breath to say something, then stopped, shifting from foot to foot as he changed his mind. Going back to the bed, he opened the crinkling bag of sweats and looked inside. "What do you want these for anyway? A disguise? Or is it to remember me by?"

Glad at the shift in topics, I turned with my butt-kicking boots in hand and set them by the bed. "Remember you by?"

A faint flush rimmed his ears. "Yeah. I thought you wanted them to put under your pillow or something. So it was like I was there with you?"

Taking the bag from him, I peered into it in speculation. "You wore them already?"

He rubbed a hand across his smooth chin, discomforted. "Ah, just once. I didn't sweat in them or anything. I dated a girl who liked wearing one of my shirts to bed. She said it was like I was holding her all night. I thought it was a, uh, girl thing."

My smile blossomed. "You mean, like this?" Feeling wicked, I pulled out the sweatshirt and slipped it on over my top. Holding my arms about myself, I shifted back and forth, my eyes closed and breathing deeply. I didn't care that the reason he smelled good was from a thousand years of evolution to make it easier for him to find prey.

"You wicked, wicked witch," Kisten whispered. The sudden heat in his voice pulled my eyes open. He took a slow breath, his entire body moving. "Oh God, you smell good."

"Yeah? What about now?" Grinning, I did jumping jacks, knowing the mixing of our scents would drive him slightly nuts.

As expected, his eyes dilated with a sudden blood lust, flashing to black. "Rachel," he said, his voice strained. "Don't."

Giggling, I evaded his reaching hand. "Wait! Wait!" I gasped. "I can make it worse."

"Stop," Kisten said, his voice low and controlled. There was a hint of threat in it, and when he reached for me again, I shrieked, darting around the end of the bed. With vampire quickness he followed, my back hitting the wall with a breath-stealing thump as he pinned me.

Eyes crinkled and smiling, I wiggled and twisted, enjoying pushing his buttons. After only a token show of resistance, I stopped, letting him find my mouth.

My breath left me in a slow sound as I eased against him, my arms crunched between us. His grip on my shoulders was firm and dominating. Possessive. But I knew he'd let go if I made one real motion to break free. Soft jazz completed my mood.

His fingers clenched and released, his lips moving lower until his mouth brushed my chin, following the line of my jaw to the hollow under my ear. My heart pounded and I tilted my head. In a surprised sound, my breath escaped when the tingling at my scar surged. With the quickness and sudden shock of a flag snapping in the wind, heat scoured me, following my veins and settling into an insistent pounding—demanding I follow it through to its natural end.

Kisten felt it, and as his breath quickened, I pulled my hands from between us, sending my fingers to the nape of his neck. My eyes closed as I felt his need, his desire, beat on mine to make it stronger. A sound escaped me as his lips gently worked my old scar. My body rebelled at the surge of passion, and my knees gave way.

He was ready for it, holding me firm to him. I wanted this. God, how I wanted it. I should have tried wearing something of his ages ago.

"Rachel," he whispered, his breathing harsh and heavy with desire.

"What?" I panted, my blood still humming though his lips weren't on my scar anymore.

"Don't ever—wear anything of mine—again. I can't . . ."

I froze, not understanding. I made a motion to break free, but he held me firm. Fear scoured painfully where passion once ran. My eyes flicked to his, seeing them lost and black, then to his mouth. He wasn't wearing his caps. *Shit, I had pushed him too far.*

"I can't let go of you," he said, his lips not moving.

Adrenaline surged, and a drop of sweat formed at his hairline. *Shit, shit, shit. I was in trouble.* My gaze flicked to the glint of fang at the corner of his mouth. From one breath to the next, the coin of desire had flipped from sex to blood. Damn, the next ten seconds were going to be really dicey.

"I think I can let go if you aren't afraid," he said, fear and blood lust mixed in his voice.

I couldn't look away from his black eyes. I could *not* look from his eyes. While Kisten unconsciously dumped pheromones into the air to make my vampire scar send wave after wave of passion through me in time with my hammering pulse, my gut twisted.

Mind racing, I forced my breathing to be slow and even. Fear would trip him over the edge. I'd pulled Ivy down once, and I knew if he was still talking, then the odds were highly in my favor. "Listen," I said, the ecstasy from my vampire scar mixing with my fear in an unreal slurry. It felt good. It was a rush, the thrill of sky-diving and sex all at the same time, and I knew that letting him bite me would triple the sensation. And I was going to let go of him and push him away. "I'm going to close my eyes because I trust you," I said.

"Rachel?"

It was soft and pleading. He truly wanted to let go. Damn it, this was my fault. Tension made my head hurt, and I closed my eyes on the black orbs his gaze had become. It made the fear ten times harder to surmount, but still, I trusted him. I could tap a line and send him flying into the wall—and if push came to shove, I would—but it would change our relationship utterly, and I loved him. It was a quiet, tentative love with the frightening promise that it would grow if I didn't screw it up. And I wanted a love based on trust, not who was stronger.

"Kisten," I said, forcing my jaw to unclench. "I'm going to let go of you, and you are going to let go of my shoulders and step back. Ready?" I could hear him breathe, harsh and insistent. It struck a chord inside me, and we both shuddered.

It would feel so damn good to let him bite me, his teeth sinking deep, pulling me to him, the pain twisted to pleasure, scouring through me like fire and stealing my breath, taking me to imagined heights of ecstasy. It would be incredible, the best thing I'd ever felt. It would change my life forever. *And it was not going to happen.* For all the promised pleasure, I knew it hid an equally ugly reality. And I was afraid.

"Now, Kisten," I said, eyes still closed, forcing my fingers to move.

My hands fell from him and he stepped away. My eyes flashed open. He had his back to me, a hand on the waist-high post at the foot of my bed. His free hand shook. I reached out, then hesitated. "Kisten, I'm sorry," I said, voice trembling, and he bobbed his head.

"Me too." His husky voice ran through me like water through sand, leaving me warm and tingly. "Do me a favor and don't do that again."

"You bet." Crossing my arms in front of me, I took off his sweatshirt and let it fall to the bed. The tingle at my neck faded, leaving me shaking and sick at heart. I had known mixing our scents was a blood aphrodisiac, but not how potent it was or that it could come on that fast. I was still making mistakes. Almost a year at this and I was *still* making mistakes.

Kisten's head came up, and I wasn't surprised to hear the front door open. In three seconds flat six streaks of silver and gold whizzed by my door at head height. Two more seconds and they raced back.

"Hi, Ms. Morgan!" came a high-pitched voice, and a pixy girl came to a short stop at the door, peering in with her dress fluttering about her ankles. Her face was flushed and her fair hair was swirling in the draft from her wings. There was a crash from the living room, and she darted off, shouting so high that my head hurt. The music blared, then cut out.

I took a step to the door, jerking to a stop when Matalina halted before me.

"I'm sorry, Rachel," the pretty pixy woman said, looking frazzled. "I'll take care of it. I'll get them out to the stump as soon as it stops raining."

Smoothing the rough edges of my bandaged knuckles, I tried

to wash away the last of my runaway passions and the fear from Kisten. He hadn't moved, clearly still trying to regain control. "Don't worry about it," I said. "I didn't have time to pixy-proof the church." There was another crash, this time from the kitchen. A handful of pixies flowed by, all talking at once, and Matalina followed, admonishing them to stay out of my cupboards.

My worry deepened when Ivy strode past. Jenks was on her shoulder, and he gave me an unsure look and a nod of recognition. Ivy caught sight of Kisten and she backpedaled, her shorter hair swinging. Her gaze went to his shirt on the bed, then took in my soft guilt and the tremor in my hands. Nostrils flaring, she scented the vamp pheromones and my fear, realizing in seconds what had transpired. I shrugged helplessly.

"We're back," she said dryly, then continued to the kitchen, the new loudness of her steps and the slight tension in her body the only sign that she knew I had pushed Kisten too far.

Kisten didn't meet my gaze, but my shoulders eased at the returning ring of blue in his eyes. "You okay?" I asked, and he gave me a closed-lipped smile.

"I shouldn't have given you a pair I already wore," he said, taking the shirt and stuffing it in the bag. "Maybe you should wash them."

I took the bag when he extended it, embarrassed. He followed me into the hallway, turning to the kitchen while I went the other way to get the washer going. The sharp scent of the soap ticked my nose, and I dumped in a full measure, then added a little more. I closed the lid and stood with my hands on the washer as it filled, my head bowed. My gaze fell on my bitten hand. Sometimes I thought I was the stupidest witch ever born. Straightening, I forced a pleasant expression onto my face and headed to the kitchen, anticipating Ivy's mocking look.

Unable to met anyone's eyes, I went straight to the coffeemaker to get a mug to hide behind. All the pixy kids were in the living room, and the sound of their play mixed with the soft hush of the rain past the open kitchen window. Ivy gave me one wry look before returning to her e-mails, having parked herself at her computer, out of the way in the corner. Jenks was on the sill, his back to me as he looked into the wet garden, and Kisten was sitting in my chair, his legs stretched to poke out past the corner of the table. No one was saying anything.

"Hey, uh, Kist," I stammered, and he pulled his head up. "I found a spell to Were with in one of the books you gave me."

He seemed to have found his calm, and though I was wire-tight, his eyes were weary. "No kidding," he said.

Encouraged, I brought out the book and thumped it open before him.

Jenks flitted over, nearly landing on my shoulder but choosing Kisten's at the last moment. He glanced down, his wings stilling before his head jerked up to mine. "Isn't that—"

"Yeah," I interrupted. "It's demon magic. But see? I don't have to kill anything."

Kisten blew out his breath, meeting Ivy's blank expression before easing away from the book. "You can do demon magic?" he asked.

I nodded and tucked a curl behind my ear. I didn't want to tell him why, and though Kisten was too much of a gentleman to ask when others could hear, Jenks was another story. Wings clattering, he put his hands on his hips and frowned at me in his best Peter Pan pose. "How come you can do demon magic and no one else can?" he asked.

"I'm not the only one," I said tightly, and then the metallic bong of the pull bell Ivy and I used for a doorbell vibrated through the damp air.

Ivy and Kisten both straightened, and I said, "It's probably Ceri. I asked her to come over to help me with my spells tonight."

"Your *demon* spells?" Jenks said bitingly, and I frowned, not wanting to argue.

"I'll let her in," Kisten said as he stood. "I've got to go. I—have an appointment."

His voice was strained, and I backed up, feeling like dirt when I saw his rising hunger. Crap, he was having a hard time staying balanced tonight. I was *never* going to do that again.

Kisten smoothly reached out, and I didn't move when he put his hands lightly on my shoulder and gave me a quick kiss. "I'll call you after we close. You going to be up?"

I nodded. "Kisten, I'm sorry," I whispered, and he gave me a smile before walking out with slow, measured steps. Riling him up without being able to satisfy his hunger wasn't fair.

Jenks landed on the table beside me, his wings clattering for my attention. "Rachel, that's demon magic," he said, his belligerent attitude not hiding his worry.

"That's why I asked Ceri to look at it," I said. "I've got this under control."

"But it's demon magic! Ivy, tell her she's being stupid."

"She knows she's being stupid." Ivy closed her computer down with a few clicks. "See what she did to Kist?"

I crossed my arms. "All right, it's demon magic. But that doesn't necessarily make it black. Can we hear what Ceri says before we decide anything?" *We. Yeah, we. It was we again, and it was going to stay that way, damn it.*

In a surge of motion, Ivy rose, stretching for the ceiling in her black jeans and a tight knit shirt. She grabbed her purse and shouted, "Wait up, Kist!"

Jenks and I stared at her. "You're going with him?" I asked for both of us.

Ivy's look, rife with disapproval, was aimed at me. "I want to make sure no one takes advantage of him and he ends up hating himself when the sun comes up." She shrugged into her jacket and put on her shades though it was dark out. "If you pulled that on me, I'd pin you to the wall and have at it. Kist is a gentleman. You don't deserve him."

My breath caught at the memory of my back to the wall and Kisten's lips on my neck. A spike of remembered need raced from my neck to my groin. Ivy sucked in her breath as if I'd slapped her, her heightened senses taking in my state as easily as I could see the sparkles sifting from Jenks. "I'm sorry," I said, though my skin was tingling. "I wasn't thinking."

"That's why I gave you the damn book," she said tightly. "So you wouldn't have to."

"What did she do?" Jenks asked, but Ivy had walked out, boot heels clunking. "What book? The one about dating vampires? Tink's panties, you still have that?" he added.

"I'll bring back a pizza," Ivy called, unseen from the hallway.

"What did you do, Rache?" Jenks said, the wind from his wings cooling my cheeks.

"I put on Kisten's shirt and did jumping jacks," I said, embarrassed.

The small pixy snorted, going to the windowsill to check on the rain. "You keep pulling stunts like that and people will think you want to be bitten."

"Yeah," I muttered, taking a sip of my cooling coffee and leaning against the center island counter. I was still making mistakes. Then I remembered what Quen had once told me. *If you do it once, it's a mistake. If you do it twice, it's not a mistake anymore.*

Five

I looked up when the soft conversation in the sanctuary gave way to clipped steps and Ceri peered hesitantly around the corner of the archway. Pulling the rain hood from her, she smiled, clearly pleased to see Jenks and me back on speaking terms. "Jenks, about Trent . . ." I said, seeing his wings turn an excited red. He knew that whatever Trent was, Ceri was the same.

"I can figure this out myself," he said, focusing on Ceri. "Shut your mouth."

I shut my mouth.

I stood and extended my hands to give Ceri a hug. I wasn't a touchy-feely person, but Ceri was. She had been Al's familiar until I stole her in the breath of time between her retirement and my attempted installment. Glancing briefly at my neck and bandaged knuckles, she pressed her lips disapprovingly, but thankfully said nothing. Her small, almost ethereal stature met mine, and the hand-tooled silver crucifix Ivy had given her made a cold spot through my shirt. The hug was brief but sincere, and she was smiling when she put me at arm's length. She had thin, fair hair that she wore free and flowing, a small chin, delicate nose, large pride, short temper, and a mild demeanor unless challenged.

She took off her rain cape and draped it over Ivy's chair, the self-proclaimed "throne" of the room. Al had dressed her commensurate to her earthly status while in his service—treating her as a favored slave/servant/bed warmer as well as an adornment—and though she now wore jeans and a sweater in her usual purple, gold, and black, instead of a skin-tight gown of shimmering silk and gold, the bearing was still there.

"Thanks for coming over," I said, genuinely glad to see her. "Do you want some tea?"

"No, thank you." She elegantly extended a narrow hand for Jenks to land on. "It's good to see you back where you can help the people who need you the most, master pixy," she said to him, and I would swear he turned three shades of red.

"Hi, Ceri," he said. "You look well-rested. Did you sleep well tonight?"

Her heart-shaped face went crafty, knowing he was trying to decipher what kind of Inderlander she was by her sleep patterns. "I have yet to take my evening rest," she said, shifting her fingers until he took to the air. Her gaze went to the open book on the table. "Is that it?"

A thrill of adrenaline went through me. "One of them. Is it demon?"

Tucking her long fair hair behind an ear, she leaned to take a closer look. "Oh yes."

Suddenly I was a whole lot more nervous, and I set my mug on the counter while my stomach churned. "There are a couple of charms I might want to try. Would you look at them for me and tell me what you think?"

Ceri's delicate features glowed with pleasure. "I'd love to."

I exhaled in a puff of relief. "Thanks." Wiping my hands on my jeans, I pointed to the curse to Were. "This one here. What about it? Do you think I can do it all right?"

The tips of her severely straight hair touched the stain-spotted, yellow text as she bent over the book. Frowning, she gathered the strands up and out of the way. Jenks flitted to the table as she squinted, alighting on the saltshaker. There was a crash from the living room followed by a chorus of pixy shrieks, and he sighed. "I'll be right back," he said, buzzing out.

"I've stirred this one before," she said, fingers hovering over the print.

"What does it do?" I asked, nervous all over again. "I mean, would it make me into a real wolf, or would I just look like one?"

Ceri straightened, her gaze darting to the hallway as Jenks's high-pitched harangue filtered in, making my eyeballs hurt. "It's a standard morphing curse, the same class that Al uses. You keep your intelligence and personality, same as when you shift with an earth charm. The difference is the blending of you and wolf goes to the cellular level. If there were two of you, you could have pups with a witch's IQ if you stayed a wolf through gestation."

My mouth dropped open. I reached out to touch the page, then drew back. "Oh."

With casual interest, she ran her finger down the list of ingredients, all in Latin. "This won't turn you into a Were, but this is how werewolves got started," she said conversationally. "There was a fad about six millennia ago where demons would torment a human woman in payment for a vanity wish by forcing a demon-wolf/human pairing. It always resulted in a human child that could Were."

My eyes darted to her, but she didn't notice my fear. God, how . . . disgusting. And tragic for both the woman and child. The shame of dealing with a demon would never fade, always tied as it was to the love of a child. I'd often wondered how the Weres had gotten started, since they weren't from the ever-after like witches and elves.

"Would you like me to make it for you?" Ceri asked, her green eyes placid.

I jerked, my focus sharpening. "It's okay to use?"

Nodding, she reached under the counter for my smallest copper spell pot. "I don't mind. I could do this one in my sleep. Making curses is what demon familiars do. It will take all of thirty minutes." Seemingly unaware of my bewilderment, she casually moved the curse book to the island counter. "Demons aren't any more powerful than witches," she said. "But they're prepared for anything, so it looks like they're stronger."

"But Al morphs so fast, and into so many things," I protested, leaning against the counter.

Tiny boots clicking, Ceri turned from one of my cupboards, a wad of wolf's bane in her hand. The stuff was toxic in large doses, and I felt a twinge of worry. "Al is a higher demon," she said. "You could probably best a lesser, surface demon with the earth magic you have in your charm cupboard, though with enough prep work a surface demon is as powerful as Al."

Was she saying I could best Al with my magic? I didn't believe that for a second.

With a preoccupied grace, Ceri lit the Sterno flame canister from a taper she started from the gas burner. The stove served as my "hearth fire," since the pilot light was always burning, and it made for a stable beginning to any spell. "Ceri," I protested. "I can do this."

"Sit," she said. "Or watch. I want to be useful." She smiled without showing her teeth, sadness clouding her clear eyes. "Where do you keep your blessed candles?"

"Um, in with the big silver serving spoons," I said, pointing. *Doesn't everyone?*

Jenks swooped in, gold sparkles sifting from him in agitation. "Sorry about the lamp," he muttered. "They will be washing the windows inside and out tomorrow."

"That's okay. It was Ivy's," I said, thinking they could break every light in the place if they wanted. It was more than nice having them back—it was right.

"Al is a walking pharmaceutical," Ceri said, flipping to an index to check something, and Jenks made a hiccup of surprised sound. "That's why demons want familiars experienced in the craft. Familiars make the curses they use, the demons kindling them to life, taking them internally, and holding them until invoking them with ley line magic."

With the first inklings of understanding, I pulled another demon book out and rifled through it, seeing the patterns in Al's magic. "So every time he morphs or does a charm . . ."

"Or travels the lines, he uses a curse or spell. Probably one that I made him," Ceri finished for me, squinting as she snatched one of Ivy's pens and changed something in the text, muttering a word of Latin to make it stick. "Traveling the lines puts a lot of blackness on your soul, which is why they're so angry when you call them. Al agreed to pay the price for pulling you through the first time, and he wants information to compensate for the smut."

I glanced at the circular scar on my wrist. There was a second one on the underside of my foot from Newt, the demon from whom I'd bought a trip home the last time I found myself stranded in the ever-after. Nervous, I hid that foot behind the other. I hadn't told Ceri because she was afraid of Newt. That she was terrified of the clearly insane demon and not Al made me feel all warm and cozy. I was never going to travel the lines again.

"May I have a lock of your hair?" Ceri asked, surprising me.

Taking the 99.8 percent silver snippers I'd spent a small fortune on that she was extending to me now, I cut a spaghetti-sized wad of hair from the nape of my neck.

"I'm simplifying things," she said when I handed it to her. "And you probably noticed he has a few shapes and spells that he enjoys more than others."

"The British nobleman in a green coat," I said, and a delicate rose color came over Ceri. I wondered what the story behind *that* was, but I wouldn't ask.

"I spent three years doing nothing but twisting that curse," she said, fingers going slow.

From the ladle came Jenks's attention-getting wing clatter. "Three years?"

"She's a thousand years old," I said, and his eyes widened.

Ceri laughed at his disconcertion. "That isn't my normal span," she said. "I'm aging now, as are you."

Jenks's wings blurred into motion, then stilled. "I can live twenty years," he said, and I heard the frustration in his voice. "How about you?"

Ceri turned her solemn green eyes to me for guidance. That elves were not entirely extinct was a secret I had told her to keep, and while knowing her expected life span wouldn't give it away, it could be used to piece the truth together. I nodded, and she closed her eyes in a slow blink of understanding. "About a hundred sixty years," she said softly. "Same as a witch."

I glanced uneasily between them while Jenks fought to hide an unknown emotion. I hadn't known how long elves lived, and while I watched Ceri weave my hair into an elaborate chain that looped back into itself, I wondered how old Trent's parents had been when they had him. A witch was fertile for about a hundred years, with a twenty-year lag on one end and forty at the tail end. I hadn't had a period in two years, since things pretty much shut down unless there was a suitable candidate to stir things up. And as much as I liked Kisten, he wasn't a witch to click the right hormones on. Seeing that elves had their origins in the ever-after, like witches, I was willing to bet their physiologies were closer to witch than human.

As if feeling Jenks's distress, Matalina flitted in trailing three of their daughters and an unsteady toddler. "Jenks, dear," she said, giving me an apologetic look. "The rain has slacked. I'm going to move everyone out so Rachel and Ivy can have some peace."

Jenks's hand dropped to his sword hilt. "I want to do a room-by-room check first."

"No." She flitted close and gave him a hovering kiss on the cheek. She looked happy and content, and I loved seeing her like that. "You stay here. The seals weren't tampered with."

My lower lip curled in to catch between my teeth. Jenks wasn't going to like my next move. "Actually, Matalina, I'd like you to stay, if you could."

Jenks jerked upward, a sudden wariness in him as he joined her, their wings somehow not tangling though they hovered side by side. "Why," he said flatly.

"Ah . . ." I glanced at Ceri, who was muttering Latin and making gestures over my ring of hair at the center of a plate-sized pentacle she had sifted onto the counter with salt. I stifled a feeling of worry; knotting your hair made an unbreakable link to the donor. The ring of twisted hair vanished with a pop, replaced with a pile of ash. Apparently this was okay, since she smiled and carefully brushed it and the salt into the shot-glass-sized spell pot.

"Rachel . . ." Jenks prompted, and I tore my gaze from Ceri; she had tapped a line, and her hair was drifting in an unfelt breeze.

"She might want a say in this next spell," I said. Nervous, I pulled the demon book closer and opened it to a page marked with the silk bookmark Ivy had gotten on sale last week.

Jenks hovered a good inch above the text, and Matalina gave a set of intent instructions to her daughters. With a whining toddler in tow, they darted out of the kitchen.

"Ceri," I prompted cautiously, not wanting to interrupt her. "Is this one okay to do?"

The elf blinked as if coming out of a trance. Nodding, she pushed her sleeves to her elbows and crossed the room to the ten-gallon vat of saltwater I used to dissolution used amulets. As I watched in surprise, she dunked her hands into it, arms coming up dripping wet. I tossed her a dish towel, wondering if I should start a similar practice. Fingers moving gracefully, she dried her hands while she came to peer at the spell book on the table. Her eyes widened at the charm I'd found to make little things big. "For . . ." she started, her gaze darting to Jenks.

I nodded. "Is it safe?"

She bit her lips, a pretty frown crossing her angular, delicate face. "You'd have to modify it with something to supplement bone mass. Maybe tweak the metabolism so it's not burning so fast. And then you'd have to take the wings into account."

"Whoa!" Jenks exclaimed, darting to the ceiling. "No freaking way. You aren't doing anything to this little pixy. No way. No how!"

Ignoring him, I watched Matalina take a slow, steady breath, her hands clasped before her. I turned to Ceri. "Can it be done?"

"Oh, yes," she said. "Much of it is ley line magic. And you have the earth charm ingredients in your stock. The hard part will be developing the supplemental curses to fine-tune it to limit his discomfort. But I can do it."

"No!" Jenks cried. "*Augmen.* I know that one. That means big. I'm not going to get big. You can forget it! I like who I am, and I can't do my job if I'm big."

He had retreated to where Matalina was standing on the counter, her wings unusually still, and I gestured helplessly. "Jenks," I coaxed. "Just listen."

"No." His voice was shrill as he pointed at me. "You are a freaky, misguided, crazy-ass witch! I'm not doing this!"

I straightened at the sound of the back door opening. The curtains fluttered, and I recognized Ivy's footsteps. The smell of pizza mixed with the rich scent of wet garden, and Ivy came in looking like a frat boy's fantasy in her rain-damp, sex-in-leather coat and a square box of pizza balanced on one hand. Short hair swinging, she noisily dropped the box on the table, taking in the room with a solemn, quiet face. She moved Ceri's rain cape to a different chair, and the tension ratcheted up a notch.

"If you're big," I said while Ivy got herself a plate, "you won't have to worry about the temperature fluctuations. It could snow up there, Jenks."

"No."

Ivy flipped the top open and took a slice, carefully putting it on a plate and retreating to her corner of the kitchen. "You want to make Jenks big?" she said. "Witches can do that?"

"Uh . . ." I stammered, not wanting to get into why my blood could kindle demon magic.

"*She* can," Ceri said, skirting the issue.

"And food won't be a problem," I blurted, to keep the subject to Jenks and off of me.

Jenks bristled despite the gentle hand Matalina put on his arm. "I've never had a problem keeping my family fed," he said.

"I never said you did." The smell of the pizza was making me feel ill as my stomach knotted, and I sat down. "But we're talking almost five hundred miles, if they are where I think they are, and I don't want to have to stop every hour for you to fight off roadside park fairies so you can eat. Sugar water and peanut butter won't do it, and you know that."

Jenks took a breath to protest. Ivy ate her pizza, scooting down in the chair and putting her heels on the table next to her keyboard, her gaze shifting between Jenks and me.

I tucked a red curl behind an ear, hoping I wasn't pushing our delicate working relationship too far. "And you can see how the other side lives," I said. "You won't have to wait for someone to open the door for you, or use the phone. Hell, you could drive. . . ."

His wings blurred into motion, and Matalina looked frightened.

"Look," I said, feeling uncomfortable. "Why don't you and Matalina talk it over."

"I don't need to talk it over," Jenks said tightly. "I'm not going to do it."

My shoulders slumped, but I was too afraid to push him further. "Fine," I said sourly. "Excuse me. I have to move my laundry."

Covering my worry with a false anger, I stomped out of the kitchen, sneakers squeaking on the linoleum and then the hardwood floors as I went to my bathroom. Slamming the white enameled doors harder than I needed to, I shifted Kisten's sweats to the dryer. Jenks didn't need them anymore, but I wasn't going to give them back wet.

I wrenched the dial to dry, punched the on button, and heard the drier start to turn. Arms shoulder width apart, I leaned over the dryer. Low temperatures would severely limit Jenks after sunset. Another month and it wouldn't matter, but May could be cold in Michigan.

I pushed myself up, resigned to dealing with it. It was his choice. Resolute, I padded toward the kitchen, forcing the frown from me.

"Please, Jenks," I heard Ivy plead just before I turned the corner, the unusual emotion in her voice jerking me to a stop. She never let her emotions show like that. "Rachel needs someone as a buffer between her and any vamp she runs into outside of Cincinnati," she whispered, unaware that I could hear. "Every vamp here knows I'll kill them twice if they touch her, but once she's out of my influence, her unclaimed scar is going to make her fair game. I can't go with her. Piscary—" She took a shaky breath. "He'd be really pissed if I left his influence. God, Jenks, this is just about killing me. I can't go with her. You have to. And you have to be big, otherwise no one will take you seriously."

My face went cold and I put a hand to my scar. *Crap. I forgot about that.*

"I don't need to be big to protect her," he said, and I nodded.

"I know that," Ivy said, "and she knows that, but a blood-hungry vamp won't care. And there might be more than one."

Insides shaking, I slowly backed up. My fingers felt for the knob of my bathroom door and I yanked it closed, slamming it, as if I'd just gotten out. Then I briskly entered the kitchen, not looking at anyone. Ceri was standing by my smallest spell pot with a finger stick in her hand; what she wanted was obvious. Ivy was pretending to read her e-mail, and Jenks was standing with a horrified look on his face, Matalina beside him. "So, I guess we're stopping every hour?" I said.

Jenks swallowed hard. "I'll do it."

"Really, Jenks," I said, trying to hide my guilt. "It's okay. You don't have to do this."

He flitted up, hands on hips while he got in my face. "I'm doing this, so shut the hell up and say thank-you!"

Feeling miserable and vulnerable, I whispered, "Thank you."

His wings clattered as he flitted shakily to Matalina with a little huff. She clutched at him, her beautiful angel face looking scared when she turned him so his back was to me and they started to talk, their words so high-pitched and fast I couldn't follow.

With the practiced silence of a slave, Ceri eased close to set the spell pot with the Were potion beside me. She placed the finger stick next to it with a small click and backed away. Still upset, I fumbled the sterile blade open and glanced at the brew. It looked like cherry Kool-Aid in the miniature copper pot.

"Thanks," I muttered. White or not, using demon magic wasn't what I wanted to be known for. The prick of the blade was a jolt, and I massaged my finger. Three drops of my blood went plopping into the vat, and the throat-catching scent of burnt amber rose as my blood kindled demon magic. *How nice is that?*

My stomach quivered, and I looked at it. "It won't invoke early?" I asked, and Ceri shook her head. Lifting the heavy tome, she moved it in front of me.

"Here," she said, pointing. "This is the word of invocation. It won't work unless you're connected to a line or you have enough ever-after spindled to effect a change. I've seen what you can hold, and it's enough. This one here"—she pointed farther down the page—"is the word to shift back. I suggest not using it unless you're connected to a line. You're adding to your mass on this second one, not removing it, and it's hard to know how much energy to withhold from your spindle to make up for the imbalance. It's easier to connect to a line and let it balance itself. Saltwater won't break demon magic, so don't forget the countercurse."

Nervous, I shifted my grip on the little copper pot. It would be enough potion for seven earth charms, but ley line magic was usually one spell per go. I looked again at the word of invocation. *Lupus*. Pretty straightforward.

"It won't work unless it's inside of you," Ceri said, sounding annoyed.

Jenks flitted close, hovering over the pages. His gaze moved from the print to me. "How is she going to say the word to shift back if she's a wolf?" he asked, and a flash of angst burned through me until I guessed it must be like any ley line charm that only required you to think it hard enough. Though shouting a word of invocation definitely added a measure of strength.

Ceri's green eyes narrowed. "Saying it in her mind will be enough," she said. "Do you want me to put it in a pentagram to keep it fresh, or are you going to take it now?"

I raised the spell pot, trying to smooth out my brow so I at least didn't look nervous. It was just an elaborate disguise potion, one that would make me furry and with big teeth. If I was lucky, I'd never have to invoke it. I felt Ivy's attention on me, and while everyone watched, I downed it.

I tried not to taste it, but the biting grit of ash and the bitter taste of tinfoil, chlorophyll, and salt puckered my lips. "Oh God," I said while Ivy grabbed a second slice of pizza. "That tastes like crap." I went to the dissolution vat and gave the empty spell pot a quick dunk before I set it in the sink. The potion burned through me, and I tried to stifle a shudder, failing.

"You okay?" Ivy asked as I shivered and the pot rattled against the sink before I let it go.

"Fine," I said, my voice rough. I'd just taken a demon spell. Voluntarily. Tonight I was peachy keen, and tomorrow I would be taking the bus tour of the nicest parts of hell.

Ceri hid a smile, and I frowned at her. "What!" I snapped, but she only smiled wider.

"That's what Al said whenever he took his potions."

"Swell," I snarled, going to sit at the table and pull the pizza closer. I knew it was anxiety that was making me irritable, and I tried to smooth my face out, pretending it didn't bother me.

"See, Matalina?" Jenks coaxed, and he flew to land beside her on the sill next to my beta. "It's fine. Rachel took a demon spell and she's okay. It will be easier this way, and I won't die of the cold. I'll be just as big as she is. It will be okay, Mattie. I promise."

Matalina rose in a column of silver sparkles. She wrung her hands and stared at everyone for a moment, her distress obvious and heartbreaking. In an instant she was gone, out into the rain through the pixy hole in the screen.

Standing on the sill, Jenks let his wings droop. I felt a flash of guilt, then stifled it. Jenks was going whether I was with him or not, and if he was big, he would have a better chance of coming back in one piece. But she was so upset, it was hard not to fccl likc it was my fault.

"Okay," I said, the bite of pizza tasteless. "What do we do first for Jenks?"

Ceri's slight shoulders eased and she gripped her crucifix with what was clearly an unknowing gesture of contentment. "His curse will have to be specially tailored. We should probably set a circle too. This is going to be difficult."

Six

The harsh smell of low-grade yarn dye didn't mix well with the luscious scent of leather and silk. Through it ran a dusky incense that soaked into me with each slow breath, keeping my muscles loose and slack. *Kisten.* My nose tickled, and I pushed the afghan from my face, snuggling deeper into the sound of his heartbeat. I felt him shift, and a sleepy part of me remembered we were in the living room on the couch, lying like spoons. My head was tucked under his chin, and his arm was over my middle, warm and secure.

"Rachel?" he whispered so softly that it barely stirred my hair.

"Mmmm?" I mumbled, not wanting to move. In the past eleven months I'd found that a vampire's blood lust varied like tempers, dependent upon stress, temperament, upbringing, and when they had slaked it last. I had gone into living with Ivy as a roommate as a complete idiot. Turns out she had been on the extreme end of the hairy-scary scale at the time, being stressed about Piscary wanting her to make me a toy or kill me, acerbated by her guilt at her desire for blood and trying to abstain from it. Three years of abstinence made for a very anxious vamp. I didn't want to know what Ivy had been before going cold turkey to try to remake herself. All I knew was she was much easier to live with now that she was "taking care of business," though it left her hating herself and feeling she was a failure every time she succumbed.

I'd found Kisten to be on the other end, with a laid-back temperament to begin with and no issues about satisfying his blood lust. And though I wouldn't feel comfortable napping in the same room with Ivy, I could snuggle up to Kisten, provided he took care of things beforehand. *And I didn't do jumping jacks in his sweatshirt,* I thought sourly.

"Rachel, love," he said again, louder, with a hint of pleading. I could feel his muscles tense and his breathing quicken. "I think Ceri is ready for you to kindle Jenks's spell, and as much as I'd love to pull blood from you, it might be better if you did it yourself."

My eyes flew open and I stared at the bank of Ivy's electronic equipment. "She finished it?" I said, and Kisten grunted when my elbow pushed off his gut when I sat up. My sock feet hit the rug, and my eyes shot to the clock on the TV. *It was past noon?*

"I fell asleep!" I said, seeing our pizza-crust-strewn plates on the coffee table. "Kist," I complained, "you weren't supposed to let me fall asleep!"

He remained reclining on Ivy's gray suede couch, his hair tousled and a content, sleepy look to his eyes. "Sorry," he said around a yawn, not looking sorry at all.

"Darn it. I was supposed to be helping Ceri." It was bad enough she was doing my spelling for me. To be sleeping when she did it was just rude.

He lifted one shoulder and let it fall. "She said to let you sleep."

Giving him an exasperated sigh, I tugged my jeans straight. I hated it when I fell asleep in my clothes. At least I had showered before dinner, thinking it only fair I get rid of the lingering scent of wearing his sweatshirt. "Ceri?" I said, shuffling into the kitchen. For crying out loud, I'd wanted to have Kisten's borrowed van packed and be on the road by now.

Ceri was sitting with her elbows on Ivy's antique table. Beside her was a pizza box, empty but for a single slice and an untouched container of garlic dipping sauce. Her long, wispy hair was the only movement, floating in the chill breeze from the window. The kitchen was cleaner than I ever managed when I did my spelling: copper bowls stacked neatly in the sink, the grit of salt under my feet from where she had made a circle, and a scattering of ley line magic paraphernalia and earth magic herbs. A demon book was open on the center counter, and the purple candle I burned last Halloween guttered even as I watched.

The early afternoon sun was a bright swath of light coming in the window. Past the drifting curtains, pixies shrieked and played, shredding the fairy nest in the ash tree with a savage enthusiasm. Jenks was sitting on the table, slumped against Ceri's half-empty cup of tea. "Ceri," I said, reaching to touch her shoulder.

Her head jerked up. "*O di immortals,* Gally," she said, clearly not awake. "My apologies! Your curse is ready. I'll have your tea directly."

Jenks took to the air in a clattering of wings, and my attention shot from him to her. "Ceri?" I repeated, frightened. *She called Algaliarept Gally?*

The young woman stiffened, then dropped her head into her hands again. "God help me, Rachel," she said, her words muffled. "For a moment . . ."

My hand slipped from her shoulder. She had thought she was back with Al. "I'm sorry," I said, feeling even more guilty. "I fell asleep and Kisten didn't wake me. Are you okay?"

She turned, a thin smile on her heart-shaped face. Her green eyes were tired and weary. I was sure she hadn't slept since yesterday afternoon, and she looked ready to drop. "I'm fine," she lisped faintly, clearly not.

Embarrassed, I sat before her. "Jeez, Ceri, I could have done something."

"I'm fine," she repeated, her eyes on the ribbon of smoke spiraling up from the candle. "Jenks helped me with the plants. He's very knowledgeable."

Eyebrows rising, I watched Jenks tug his green silk gardening jacket down. "You think I'm going to take a spell without knowing what's in it?" he said.

"Jenks helped you make it?" I asked.

She shrugged. "It doesn't matter who makes it, as long as you kindle it." Pale face smiling tiredly, she nodded to the potion and finger stick.

Moving slowly, I rose and went to Jenks's spell. The crack of the safety seal on the finger stick breaking was loud.

"Use your Jupiter finger," Ceri advised. "It will add the strength of your will to it."

It made a difference? I wondered, feeling ill from more than lack of sleep as I pricked my finger for three drops of blood. Kisten stirred in the living room when they went plopping into the spell pot and the scent of burnt amber rose. Jenks's wings blurred to motion, and I held my breath, waiting for something to happen. Nothing. But I had to say the "magic words" first.

"Done," Ceri said, slumping where she sat.

My eyes went to Kisten's lanky form when he strode into the kitchen, barefoot and rumpled. "Afternoon, ladies," he said, pulling the pizza box closer and dropping the last stiff slice on a plate. He wasn't the first guy to have a toothbrush at my sink, but he was the only one to have kept it there this long, and I felt good seeing him here in his disheveled, untucked-shirt state, content and comfortable.

"Coffee?" I asked, and he nodded, clearly not functioning on all levels yet as he dragged the plate from the table and headed into the hall, scratching the bristles on his jawline.

I jumped when Kisten pounded on Ivy's door and shouted, "Ivy! Get up! Here's your breakfast. Rachel is leaving, and you'd better hurry if you want to see Jenks change."

So much for coffee, toast, juice, and a flower, I thought, hearing Ivy's voice rise in disgust before Kisten shut her door and cut off her complaints. Ceri looked mystified, and I shook my head to tell her it wasn't worth explaining. I went to clean the coffeemaker, turning the water to a trickle when Kisten thunked my bathroom door shut and my shower started.

"So, we going to do this, Jenks?" I prompted while I swirled the water around.

His wings shading to blue, Jenks landed by the shot-glass-sized cup of brew. "I drink it?"

Ceri nodded. "Once it's in you, Rachel will invoke it. Nothing will happen until then."

"All of it?" I asked, eyes widening. "It's like, what, a gallon in pixy terms?"

Jenks shrugged. "I drink that much sugar water for breakfast," he said, and my brow furrowed. If he drank like that, we might be stopping every hour anyway.

My fingers fumbled to unroll the coffee bag, and the dark scent of grounds hit me, thick and comforting. I measured out what I needed into the new filter, then added a smidgen more while I surreptitiously watched Jenks procrastinate. Finally he scuffed his boots on the counter and spooned out a pixy-sized portion with a tiny glass. He downed the dripping cup in one go, making a face when he lowered the cup.

I flipped the coffeemaker on and leaned against the counter, arms crossed. "What does it taste like?" I asked, remembering the demon spell already in me. I was hoping he didn't say it tasted like my blood.

"Uh . . ." Jenks scooped out another cupful. "It tastes like the garden in the fall when people have been burning their leaves."

Dead ashes? I thought. *Gre-e-e-eat.*

Chin high, he swallowed it, then turned to me. "For the love of Tink, you aren't going to stand there and watch me, are you?"

Grimacing, I pushed myself from the counter. "Can I make you some tea?" I asked Ceri, not wanting to look like I was watching but not wanting to leave either. What if he had a reaction or something?

With a barely perceivable motion, Ceri regained her upright posture, my offer seeming to turn on an entirely new set of behaviors. "Yes, thank you," she said carefully.

I returned to the sink and filled the kettle, wincing at Jenks's tiny belch and groan. The sound of running water seemed to revive Ceri, and she rose, moving about the kitchen to put things away. "I can do that," I protested, and she watched my eyes go to the clock above the sink. *Crap, it was getting late.*

"So can I," she said. "You have a long way to drive, and all I have to do is—" She looked sourly about the kitchen. "I don't have anything to do but sleep. I should be thanking you. It was exhilarating to craft such a complex curse. It's one of my best efforts."

Her pride was obvious, and after the burner ignited under the kettle, I stood against the counter and watched Jenks belch and recite his ABCs at the same time. Would the man's talents never end? Curiosity finally prompted me to ask, "What was it like, being his familiar?"

Ceri seemed to grow drowsy as she stood in the sun at the sink and washed her teacup. "He is domineering and cruel," she said softly, head down as she watched her thin hands, "but my origins made me unique. He enjoyed showing me off and so kept me well. Once I became pliant, he often gave me favors and courtesies that most remained ignorant of."

My thoughts returned to her embarrassment when speaking of Al's favorite appearance of a British nobleman. They had been together for a thousand years, and there were countless cases of captives becoming enamored of their captors. *And that nickname . . .* I tried to meet her eyes, but she avoided it.

"I'll be back," Jenks said, patting his stomach. "This stuff makes you pee like a toad."

I cringed as he took to the air and flew heavily past Ceri and out the pixy hole in the screen. A glance at the spell pot brought my eyebrows up. It was half gone. *Damn, the man could slam it faster than a frat boy.*

"I made anywhere from thirty to fifty curses a day," Ceri said, taking a rag from the sink and wiping the island counter free of salt, "apart from warming his bed and putting food on his table. Every seventh day he would work in the lab with me, expanding my knowledge. This charm . . ." Eyes distant, she touched the counter beside the remaining brew. "This one we would have spent all day with, going slow so he could explain the complexities of mixing curses. Those days . . . I almost felt good about myself."

Clasping my hands about my middle, I felt cold at the hint of wistfulness to her voice. She nearly seemed to regret she wasn't working in a demon sweatshop anymore. Eyes distant, she took the boiling water from the stove and poured it into a small teapot.

Jenks returned without comment, settling before the brew with his little cup. The hair on the back of my neck pricked, and Ivy came in with a soft scuffing, hands busy tucking her shirt behind her jeans. Not meeting anyone's eyes, she shuffled to the coffeemaker and poured two mugs even as the last drips spilled onto the hot plate to sizzle. I looked up in surprise when she hesitantly set one beside me.

Kisten's words echoed through my thoughts as I watched her sit at her computer, reading the tension in her shoulders when she jabbed the on button and hit the shortcut to her mail. What he'd said about her leaning on me more than him because I didn't know her past tightened my gut. I looked at her as she sat at the far end of the kitchen, distant but a part of the group. Her perfect face was quiet and still, not a glimmer of her savage past showing. A chill went through me at what might lie beneath it, what might come out if I left her. Just how bad had it been?

Ivy looked from her monitor, her eyes fastening on me from under her short bangs. My gaze dropped. *Good Lord. It was only for a few days.*

"Thanks for the coffee," I said, uncurling my fingers and lacing them about the warm ceramic while I steeled my emotions. I had to go. Nick and Jax needed help. I'd be back.

She said nothing, her face showing no emotion. A screen of new e-mails came in one after the other, and she began winnowing through them.

Nervous, I turned to Ceri. "I really appreciate this," I said, thinking of the long drive ahead. "If it wasn't for your help, I wouldn't even try it. I'm just glad it's not a black charm," I added. White or not, using demon magic was not what I wanted to be known for.

In her spot in the sun, Ceri stiffened. “Um, Rachel?” she said, and my heart seemed to skip a beat. My head slowly lifted and my mouth went dry. Jenks stopped with his cup halfway to his mouth. He met my eyes, his wings going absolutely still.

“It’s a black charm?” I said, my voice squeaky at the end.

“Well, it’s demon magic. . . .” she said, sounding apologetic. “They’re all black.” She looked between Jenks and me, mystified. “I thought you knew that.”

Seven

I took a shaky breath and reached for the counter. *It was black? I had taken a black charm? This just keeps getting better and better. Why in hell hadn't she told me?*

"Hell no!" Jenks rose in a flurry of copper-colored sparkles. "Just forget it. Ivy, forget it! I'm not doing this!"

While Ivy snarled at Jenks that he would or she'd jam him through a keyhole backward, I wobbled to the table and slumped into my chair. Ceri was so odd, seemingly as innocent as Joan of Arc but as accepting of black magic as if she sat at Lucifer's feet and did his nails every other Wednesday. *They were all black, and she didn't see anything wrong with them?* Come to think of it, Joan of Arc had heard voices in her head telling her to kill people.

"Rachel . . ."

Ceri's hand on my shoulder pulled my head up and I stared. "I, uh," I muttered. "I kinda expected they were black, but you didn't seem to be having any problem making them, so . . ." I looked at the remainder of Jenks's potion, wondering if he quit now whether he'd be okay.

"He needs this curse." Ceri gracefully sat so I couldn't see Jenks and Ivy arguing at the far end of the table. "And the smut from one or two is trifling."

Matalina zipped in through the pixy hole in the screen at one of Jenks's sharp squeaks, bringing the smell of the spring noon with her. Her yellow dress swirled prettily about her ankles when she came to a short stop, her expression inquisitive as she tried to figure out what was going on. I couldn't seem to get enough air. *Trifling? Didn't she get it?*

"What if I only use them for good?" I tried. "Will they still stain my soul if I only do good with them?"

Matalina's wings stopped and she dropped three inches to the table, losing her balance and falling, to bend a wing backward. Ceri exhaled in obvious exasperation. "You're severely breaking the laws of nature with these curses," she lectured, her green eyes narrow, "far more than with earth or line magic on their own. It doesn't matter if they're used for good or bad, the smut on your soul is the same. If you mess with nature's books, you pay a price."

My eyes flicked past her to Matalina and Jenks. The small pixy woman had found her feet, and she had a hand on Jenks's shoulder as he hunched over his knees. He was hyperventilating by the look of it, pixy dust shading to red sifting from him to pool and spill onto the floor. It swirled in the draft from the window, and it would have been pretty if I hadn't known that it meant he was severely stressed.

Ivy's lips were a thin line. I didn't understand why she was arguing with him. I didn't expect him to go through with it if it was a black curse. *Damn it, Ceri had been calling them curses all along, and I hadn't been listening.*

"But I don't want my soul to go black," I almost whined. "I just got rid of Al's aura."

Ceri's delicate features went annoyed, and she stood. "Then get rid of it."

Jenks's head came up, his eyes looking frightened. "Rachel is *not* a black witch!" he shouted, and I wondered at his hot loyalty. "She's not going to foster it off on an innocent!"

"I never said she should," Ceri said, bristling.

"Ceri," I said hesitantly, listening to Matalina try to soothe her husband. "Isn't there another way to get rid of the reality imbalance than to pass it to someone else?"

Clearly aware of Jenks ready to fly at her, Ceri calmly went to her brewed tea. "No. Once you make it, the only way to get rid of it is to pass it to someone else. But I'm not suggesting you give it to an innocent. People will accept it voluntarily if you sweeten the deal."

I didn't like the sound of that. "Why would someone voluntarily take my blackness onto their soul?" I said, and the elf sighed, visibly biting back her annoyance. Tact wasn't in her repertoire, despite her kindness and overflowing goodwill.

"You attach it to something they want, Rachel," she said. "A spell or task. Information."

My eyes widened as I figured it out. "Like a demon," I said, and she nodded.

Oh God. My stomach hurt. The only way to get rid of it would be to trick people into taking it. Like a demon.

Ceri stood at my sink, the morning sun streaming about her making her look like a princess in jeans and a black and gold sweater. "It's a good option," she said, blowing at her tea to hasten its cooling. "I have too much imbalance to rid myself of it that way, but perhaps if I forayed into the ever-after and rescued people stolen and still in possession of their souls, they might take a hundred years of my imbalance in return for the chance to be free of the ever-after."

"Ceri," I protested, frightened, and she raised a soothing hand.

"I'm not going into the ever-after," she said. "But if the opportunity ever arose that I could help free someone, will you tell me?"

Ivy stirred, and Jenks interrupted her with a hot, "Rache is not going into the ever-after."

"He's right," I said, and I rose, my knees feeling weak. "I can't ask anyone to take the black I put on my soul. Just forget it." My fingers encircled the remainder of Jenks's potion and I headed for my dissolution vat. "I'm *not* a black witch."

Matalina heaved a sigh of relief, and even Jenks relaxed, his feet settling into a puddle of silver sparkles on the table, only to jerk upward when Ceri slammed her hand onto the counter. "You listen to me, and listen good!" she shouted, shocking me and making Ivy jerk. "I am not evil because I have a thousand years of demon smut on my soul!" she exclaimed, the tips of her hair trembling and her face flushed. "Every time you disturb reality, nature has to balance it out. The black on your soul isn't evil, it's a promise to make up for what you have done. It's a mark, not a death sentence. And you can get rid of it given time."

"Ceri, I'm sorry," I fumbled, but she wasn't listening.

"You're an ignorant, foolish, stupid witch," she berated, and I cringed, my grip tightening on the copper spell pot and feeling the anger from her like a whip. "Are you saying that because I carry the stink of demon magic, that I'm a bad person?"

"No . . ." I wedged in.

"That God will show no pity?" she said, green eyes flashing. "That because I made one mistake in fear that led to a thousand more, that I will burn in hell?"

"No. Ceri—" I took a step forward.

"My soul is black," she said, her fear showing in her suddenly pale cheeks. "I'll never be rid of it all before I die. I'll suffer for it, but it won't be because I'm a bad person but because I was a frightened one."

"That's why I don't want to do this," I pleaded.

She took a breath as if only now realizing she had been shouting. Closing her eyes, she seemed to steady herself. The anger had been reduced to a slow shimmer in the back of her green eyes when she opened them. Her usual mild countenance made it difficult to remember that she had once been royalty and accustomed to command.

Ivy took a wary sip of her coffee, her eyes never moving from Ceri. Kisten's shower went off, and the ensuing silence seemed loud.

"I'm sorry," Ceri said, head down, the sheet of her fair hair hiding her face. "I shouldn't have raised my voice."

I set the copper pot on the counter. "Don't worry about it," I said. "Like you said, I'm an ignorant witch."

Her smile was sour and showed a mild embarrassment. "No, you aren't. You can't know what you haven't been told." She ran her hands down her jeans, soothing herself. "Perhaps I'm more concerned than I want to admit about the payment I carry," she admitted. "Seeing you worry about one or two curses when I have several million on my soul made me—" She flushed delicately, and I wondered if her ears were a tiny bit pointed. "I was most unfair to you."

Her voice had acquired a noble cadence. Behind me, I heard Ivy cross her legs at her knees. "Forget it," I said, feeling cold.

"Rachel." Ceri hid her hands' trembling by clasping them. "The blackness these two curses carry is so small compared to the benefits that will come from it: Jenks safely journeying to help his son, you using a demon curse to Were so as to retain the title of David's alpha that you deserve. It would be more of a crime to let these things remain undone or slip away than to willingly accept the price to have them."

She touched the pot of remaining brew, and I eyed it with a sick feeling. I was not going to ask Jenks to finish it.

"Everything of value or strength has a price," she continued. "To let Jax and Nick continue to suffer because you were afraid makes you look . . . unconscionably timid."

Cowardly might be a better word, I thought, looking at Jenks and feeling ill, knowing that I had a curse inside me just waiting to be put into play—and I had done it to myself.

"I'll take the black for my curse," Jenks said abruptly, his face hard with determination.

From the table came Matalina's tiny hiccup, and I saw fear in her childlike features. She loved Jenks more than life itself. "No," I said. "You've only got a few years left to get rid of it. And it's my idea, my spell. My curse. I'll take it."

Jenks flew up in my face, his wings red and his face severe. "Shut up!" he shouted, and I jerked back so I could focus on him. "He's my son! I take the curse. I pay the price."

There was the sound of my bathroom door opening, and Kisten ambled into the kitchen, his shirt rumpled and with a sly smile. His hair was slicked back and his damp stubbled face caught the sun. He looked great, and he knew it. But his confidence faltered when he saw Ivy unhappy at her computer, Jenks and Matalina clearly distressed, me undoubtedly looking scared with my hands wrapped around my middle, and of course Ceri's exasperated expression as she once again found herself trying to convince the plebeians that she knew what was best for them.

"What did I miss?" he asked, going to the coffeemaker and pouring what was left into one of my oversized mugs.

Ivy pushed her chair out and looked sullen. "They're demon curses. It's going to leave a mark on Rachel's soul. Jenks is having second thoughts."

"I am not!" the small pixy shouted. "But I'll kiss a fairy's ass before I let Rachel pay the price for my curse."

Kisten slowly tucked his shirttails in and sipped his coffee. His eyes went everywhere, and he breathed deeply, absorbing the scents of the room and using them to read the situation.

"Jenks," I protested, then made a sound of defeat when he flew to the last of the potion and drank it, his throat moving as he gulped it down. Matalina dropped to the table, her wings unmoving. She was a small spot of brightness, looking more alone than I'd ever seen her while she watched her husband put his life in jeopardy for my safety and that of their son.

The kitchen was silent but for the sound of his kids in the garden when he belligerently dropped his pixy-sized cup into the spell pot with a dull clang.

"I guess that's it, then," I said, gathering myself and leaning so I could glimpse the clock above the sink. I didn't like this. Not at all.

Looking as if she was desperately trying not to cry, Matalina rubbed her wings together to make a piercing whistle, which gave us all of three seconds before what looked like Jenks's entire family flowed into the kitchen from the hallway. The sharp scent of ashes came in with them, and I realized they had come in down the chimney. "Out!" Jenks shouted. "I said you could watch from the door!"

In a swirl of Disney nightmare, his brood settled on the top of the door frame. Shrieks scraped the inside of my skull as they shoved each other, vying for the best vantage point. Ivy and Kisten cringed visibly, and Jenks made another whistle of admonishment. They obediently settled, whispering at my threshold of hearing. Ivy swore under her breath, her face taking on a dark cast. His tall stature graceful, Kisten crossed the kitchen to stand beside her, pouring half his coffee into her mug to try to pacify her. She wasn't at her best until at least sundown.

"Okay, Jenks," I said, thinking that willfully twisting a demon curse was spectacularly stupid and that I'd never hear the end of it if it killed me. What would my mother say? "Ready?"

The pixies lining the door frame squealed, and Matalina flitted to him, her pretty face pale. "Be careful, love," she whispered, and I looked away when they exchanged a last embrace, the two of them rising slowly in a cloud of gold sparkles before they parted. She went to the sill, wings moving fitfully to make glittering flashes of light. This was all but killing her, and I felt guilty even though it was probably the best way to ensure his safety.

Standing beside Matalina in the sun, Ceri nodded confidently. Kisten put a supportive hand atop Ivy's shoulder. Taking a breath, I went to the table, nervously settling myself at my usual spot and pulling the demon book of spells onto my lap. It was heavy, and my blood hummed in my legs, almost as if it was trying to reach the pages. *Oh, there's a nice thought.*

"What's going to happen?" Jenks asked, fidgeting as he landed on the center counter, and I turned sideways in the chair so I could see him.

I licked my lips and looked at the print. It was in Latin, but Ceri and I had gone over it while eating pizza before I fell asleep.

"The Demon Magic for Idiots version, please," he added, and a thin smile crossed me.

"I tap a line and say the words of invocation," I said. "To shift you back, I say it again. Same as with the Wereing charm."

"That's it?"

His eyes were wide, and Ceri sniffed. "You did want the short version," she said, moving everything off the island counter and to the sink. "I did a horrendous amount of prep work to make it that easy, Master Pixy."

His wings drooped. "Sorry."

Ivy held her arms close to her and frowned, her aggression clearly misplaced worry. "Can we get on with this?" she asked, and I dropped my head to the print again.

Exhaling, I stretched my awareness past the clapboard walls of the kitchen, past the flower beds already feeling the light presence of pixies, to the small underused ley line running through the graveyard. Touching it with a finger of thought, I stifled a tremor at the jolt of connection. It used to be that the flow of force into me had been slow and sedate. Not anymore.

The surge of energy coursed through me, backwashing through me in an uncomfortable sensation. It settled into my chi with the warmth and satisfaction of hot chocolate. I could pull out more and spindle it in my head to use later, but I didn't need it, so I let the heavy, resonating wash of energy find its way out of me and back into the line. I was a net through which the ley line ran, flowing free but for what I pulled out.

It all happened in the time between one heartbeat and the next, and I lifted my head, my eyes closed. My hair was moving in the wind that always seemed to be blowing in the ever-after, and I ran a hand over my loose curls to tame them. I thanked God that it was daylight and I couldn't see even a shadow of the ever-after unless I stood right in a line. Which I wasn't.

"I hate it when she taps a line," Ivy whispered to Kisten in the corner. "You ever see anything freakier than that?"

"You should see the face she makes when she—"

"Shut up, Kist!" I exclaimed, my eyes flashing open to find him grinning at me.

Standing with her teacup perched in her fingers and the sun streaming in around her, Ceri was trying to keep a scholarly air about her, but the snicker on her face ruined it.

"Is it going to hurt?" Jenks asked, gold pixy dust sifting from him in a steady stream.

I thought back to the gut-wrenching pain when I had turned into a mink and cringed. "Close your eyes and count down from ten," I said. "I'll hit you with it when you get to zero."

He took a breath, dark lashes fluttering against his cheeks. His wings slowly stilled until he came to a rest on top of the cleared island counter. "Ten . . . nine . . ." he said, his voice steady.

Setting the book on the table, I stood. Light and unreal from the line running through me, I reached out and put a hand over him. My knees were shaking, and I hoped that no one saw it. *Demon magic. God save me.* I took another breath. *"Non sum qualis eram,"* I said.

"Eight—"

Ivy gasped, and I staggered when Jenks was encased in the swirl of gold ever-after that had dropped from my hand to encompass him.

"Jenks!" Matalina cried, flying up into the utensils.

My breath was crushed out of me. Stumbling, I put a hand behind me, searching for support. I gasped when a torrent of line energy slammed into me, and I shoved the helping hands away. My head seemed to expand, and I cried out when the line exploded out of me and hit Jenks with a crack that had to be audible.

I fell, finding myself on the kitchen floor with Ivy's arms under my shoulders as she eased me down. I couldn't breathe. As I struggled to remember how to make my lungs work, I heard a crash in the hanging utensils, followed by a groan and a thump.

"Sweet mother of Tink," a new, lightly masculine voice said. "I'm dying. I'm dying. Matalina! My heart isn't beating!"

I took a clean breath, then another, propped up in Ivy's grip. I was hot, then cold. And I couldn't see clearly. Looking up past the edge of the counter, I found Kisten beside Ceri, frozen as if unable to decide what to do. I pushed Ivy's hand off me and sat up when I realized what had laid me out. It wasn't the force of the line I had channeled but the shitload of intent-to-pay-back that I had just laid on my soul. I had it, not Jenks, and it was going to stay that way.

Heart pounding, I got to my feet, my mouth dropping open when I saw Jenks on the counter. "Oh—my—God . . ." I whispered.

Jenks turned to me, his eyes wide and frightened. Angular face pinched, he looked at the ceiling, chest heaving as he hyperventilated. Ceri was at the sink, beaming. Beside me, Ivy stared, shocked. Kisten wasn't much better. Matalina was in tears, and pixy children were flying around. Someone got tangled in my hair, pulling me back to reality.

"Anyone younger than fifteen—out of the kitchen!" I shouted. "Someone get me a paper bag. Ivy, go get a towel for Jenks. You think you'd never seen a naked man before."

Ivy jerked into motion. "Not one sitting on my counter," she muttered, walking out.

Jenks's eyes were wide in panic as I snatched the bag Kisten handed me. Shaking it open, I puffed into it. "Here," I said. "Breath into this."

"Rache?" he gasped, his face pale and his shoulder cold when I touched him. He flinched, then let me hold the bag to his face. "My heart," he said, his words muffled around the bag. "Something's wrong! Rache, turn me back! I'm dying!"

Smiling, I held the bag to him as he sat on my counter, stark naked and hyperventilating. "That's how slow it beats," I said. "And you don't have to breathe so fast. Slow down," I soothed. "Close your eyes. Take a breath. Count to three. Let it out. Count to four."

"Shove it up your ass," he said, hunching into himself and starting to shake. "The last time you told me to close my eyes and count from ten, look what happened to me."

Ivy returned, draping the first towel over his lap and the second over his shoulders. He was calming down, his eyes roving over the kitchen, darting from the ceiling to the open archway. His breath caught when he saw the garden through the window. "Holy crap," he whispered, and I pulled the bag away. He might not look like Jenks, but he sounded like him.

"Better?" I said, taking a step back.

His head bobbed, and as he sat on the counter and concentrated on breathing, we stood with our mouths hanging open, taking in a six-foot pixy. In a word, he was . . . damn!

Jenks had said he was eighteen, and he looked it. A very athletic eighteen, with wide innocent eyes, a smooth young face, and a blond shock of curly hair all tousled and needing to be arranged. His wings were gone, leaving only wide shoulders and the lean muscles that had once supported them. He had a trim waist, and his feet dangling to the floor were long and narrow. They were perfectly shaped, and my eyebrows rose; I'd seen his feet before, and one had been terribly misshapen.

I silently cataloged the rest of him, realizing all his scars were gone, even the one he'd gotten from fairy steel. His incredibly defined abs were smooth and perfect, making him utterly lanky with the clean smoothness of late adolescence. Every part of him was lean with a long strength. There wasn't a fleck of hair on him anywhere but for his eyebrows and atop his head. I knew. I had looked.

His gaze met mine from under his mussed bangs, and I blinked, taken by them. Ceri had green eyes, but Jenks's were shockingly green, like new leaves. They were narrowed with anxiety, but even the fading fear couldn't hide his youth. Sure, he had a wife and fifty-four kids, but he looked like a college freshman. A yummy college freshman majoring in oh-my-God-I-gotta-get-me-some-of-that.

Jenks rubbed his head where he had hit the overhanging rack. "Matalina?" he said, the cadence of his voice familiar but the sound of it odd. "Oh, Matalina," he breathed when she dropped to land on his shaking hand, "you're beautiful. . . ."

"Jenks," she said, hiccuping. "I'm so proud of you. I—"

"Shhhh," he said, his face twisting in heartache when he found himself unable to touch her. "Please don't cry, Mattie. It's going to be okay. I promise."

My eyes warmed with unshed tears as she played with the folds of her dress. "I'm sorry. I promised myself I wasn't going to cry. I don't want you to see me cry!"

She darted up, zipping out into the hall. Jenks made a move to follow, probably forgetting he didn't have wings anymore. He leaned forward and fell to the floor, face first.

"Jenks!" I shouted when he hit with a dull smack and started swearing.

"Le'go! Let go of me!" he exclaimed, slapping at me as he wedged his legs under him, only to fall back down. His towel fell away, and he struggled to hold it in place and stand up all at the same time. "Damn it all to hell! Why can't I balance right?" His face went ashen and he quit struggling. "Crap, I gotta pee again."

I looked pleadingly at Kisten. The living vamp swung into motion, easily dodging Jenks's flailing arms and hoisting him up off the floor by his shoulders. Jenks was taller by four inches, but Kisten had done bouncer work at his club. "Come on, Jenks," he said, moving him into the hallway. "I've got some clothes you can put on. Falling down is a lot more comfortable when you have something between your ass and the carpet."

"Matalina?" Jenks called in panic from the hall, protesting as Kisten manhandled him to my bathroom. "Hey, I can walk. I just forgot I didn't have wings. Le'me go. I can do this."

I jumped at the sound of Kisten shutting the bathroom door.

"Nice ass, Jenks," Ivy said into the new silence. Shaking her head, she picked up the second towel Jenks had left behind, folding it as if needing to give herself something to do.

My breath came from me in a long exhalation. "That," I said to Ceri, "has got to be the most fantastic charm I've ever seen."

Ceri beamed, and I realized she'd been worried, waiting for

my approval. "Curse," she said, her eyes on her teacup as she blushed. "Thank you," she added modestly. "I wrote it down in the back with all the supplemental curses worked in on the chance you'd want to use it again. The countercurse is included, just as it's supposed to be. All you have to do is tap a line and say the words."

Countercurse, I thought morosely, wondering if that meant more black on my soul or if I had taken it all already. "Um, thanks, Ceri. You're incredible. I'll never be able to do a charm that complex. Thank you."

She stood in front of the window and sipped her tea, looking pleased. "You returned me my soul, Rachel Mariana Morgan. Making your life easier is a small thing."

Ivy made a rude sound and dropped the folded towel on the table. She didn't seem to know what to do next. *My soul. My poor, tarnished, blackening soul.*

My mouth went dry as the enormity of what I had done fell on me. Shit. I was playing with the black arts. No, not the black arts—which you could go to jail for—but demonic arts. They didn't even have laws for people practicing demonic arts. I felt cold, then hot. Not only had I just put a bunch of black on my soul, but I had called it a good thing, not bad.

Oh God, I was going to be sick.

"Rachel?"

I sank down into my chair feeling shaky. Ceri had her hand on my shoulder, but I hardly felt it. Ivy was shouting something, and Ceri was telling her to sit down and be still, that it was just the delayed shock of taking on so much reality imbalance and that I was going to be okay.

Okay? I thought, putting my head on the table before I fell over. *Maybe. "Rhombus,"* I whispered, feeling the eye-blink-fast connection to the line and the protective circle rise around me. Ceri leapt forward, joining me before it finished forming. I had practiced this ley line charm for three months, and it was white magic, damn it, not black.

"Rachel!" Ivy cried as the shimmering band of ever-after wavered into existence between us. I pulled my head up, determined not to spew. I wanted to see what I had done to my soul, and though I couldn't see my aura, I could see a reflection of the damage in the shimmering band of ever-after.

"God help me," I whispered, feeling my face go cold.

"Rachel, it's all right." Ceri was crouched before me, her hand gripping mine, trying to get me to look at her. "You're seeing an artificially inflated shade. It hasn't had a chance to soak in yet. It really isn't that bad."

"Soak in?" I said, my voice cracking. "I don't want it to soak in!" My aura had turned the usually red sheen of ever-after to black. Hidden in it was a shimmer of gold from my aura, looking like an aged patina. I swallowed hard. *I would not spew. I would not spew.*

"It will get better. I promise."

I met her eyes, the panic subsiding. It would get better. Ceri said so; I had to believe her.

"Rachel!" Ivy cried, standing helplessly outside the circle. "Take this down!"

My head hurt and I couldn't get enough air. "Sorry," I breathed, breaking my link with the line. The sheet of ever-after flickered and vanished, and I felt a surge through me when I emptied my chi. I didn't want anything extra in me right now. I was too full of blackness.

Looking embarrassed, Ivy forced the tension from her shoulders. She blinked several times, trying to recapture her usual placid calmness, when I knew what she wanted to do was give me a slap and tell me I was being stupid or give me a hug and tell me it was going to be okay. But she couldn't do either, so she just stood there, looking miserable.

"I gotta go," I said abruptly, surging to my feet.

Ceri gracefully stood and got out of my way, but Ivy reached for me. "Rachel, wait," she protested, and I hesitated, vision swimming as she gripped my elbow.

I couldn't stay there. I felt like a leper in a house of innocents, a pariah among nobles. I was covered in blackness, and this time it was all mine. "Jenks!" I shouted, yanking out of Ivy's grip and heading for my room. "Let's go!"

"Rachel, what are you doing?"

I went to my room, scuffed my shoes on, grabbed my bag, and pushed past her and into the hall. "Exactly what I had planned," I said, ignoring her, pacing far too close behind me.

"You haven't had anything to eat," she said. "You're still reeling from invoking that . . . spell. It won't kill you to sit down and have a cup of coffee."

There was a thump from my bathroom followed by Kisten's muffled exclamation. The door crashed open, and I stopped. Kisten was leaning against the washer, face contorted in pain as he tried to catch his breath. Jenks was holding the door frame, looking casual in Kisten's gray and black sweats, but his green eyes were stressed. "Sorry," he said, sounding as if he meant it. "I, uh, slipped." He ran his eyes up and down my haggard appearance. "Ready to go?"

I could feel Ivy behind me. "Here," I said, extending my suitcase. "Make yourself useful and get this in the van."

He blinked, then grinned to show even, very white teeth. "Yeah. I can carry that."

I handed it over, and Jenks stumbled at the weight. His head thunked into the wall of the narrow hallway. "Bloody hell!" he exclaimed, crashing into the opposite wall when he overcompensated. "I'm all right!" he said quickly, waving off any help. "I'm all right. Sweet mother of Tink, the damn walls are so close! It's like walking in a freaking anthill."

I watched to make sure he was going to be okay, reaching out when he started weaving once he lost the guidance of the walls and was in the open space of the sanctuary. His kids were with him, adding to the noise as they shouted encouragement and advice. Hoping he took the time to walk down the steps instead of trying to jump them, I headed for the kitchen. Ivy was hot on my heels, Kisten close behind, quiet and pensive.

"Rachel," Ivy said, and I stood in my kitchen and stared at Ceri, trying to remember why I had come in there. "I'm going with you."

"No, you aren't." *Oh yeah. My stuff.* I grabbed my shoulder bag, with its usual charms, then opened the pantry for one of the canvas carry bags Ivy used when she went shopping. "If you leave, Piscary will slip into your head."

"Kisten, then," she said, desperation creeping into her gray-silk voice. "You can't go alone."

"I'm not going alone. Jenks is with me."

I jammed the three demon books into the bag, then bent to get my splat gun from under the counter where I kept it at crawling height. I didn't know what I would need, but if I was going to use demon magic, I was going to use demon magic. My chest clenched and I held my breath to keep the tears from starting. *What in hell was wrong with me?*

"Jenks can hardly stand up!" Ivy said as I ran a hand through my charm cupboard and scooped them all into my shoulder bag.

Pain amulets, generic disguise charms . . . Yeah, those would be good. I pulled myself to a stop, heart pounding as I looked at her distress.

"You're not feeling right," Ivy said. "I'm not letting you walk out of here alone."

"I'm fine!" I said, trembling. "And I'm not alone. Jenks is with me!" My voice rose, and Kisten's eyes went round. "Jenks is all the backup I need. He is all the backup I *ever* needed. The only time I screw up royally is when he's not with me. And you have no right to question his competency!"

Ivy's mouth snapped shut. "That not what I meant," she said, and I pushed past her and into the hall. I almost ran Jenks down, and realized that he'd heard the whole thing.

"I can carry that," he said softly, and I handed the bag of demon texts to him. His balance bobbled, but his head didn't hit the wall like last time. He headed down the dark hall, limping.

Breath fast, I walked into Ivy's room, kneeling on the floor by her bed and pulling her sword out from where I'd seen her tuck it once. "Rachel," she protested from the hallway as I straightened up, gripping the wickedly sharp katana safe in its sheath.

"Can I take this?" I asked shortly, and she nodded. "Thanks." Jenks needed a sword. So he couldn't walk without running into things. He'd get better, and then he'd need a sword.

Kisten and Ivy trailed behind me as I slung the sword over my shoulder to hang with my bag and stomped down the hall. I had to be angry. If I wasn't angry, I was going to fall apart. My soul was black. I was doing demon magic. I was turning into everything I feared and hated, and I was doing it to save someone who had lied and left me to make my partner's son a thief.

Leaning into my bathroom in passing, I snapped my vanity case shut. Jenks was going to need a toothbrush. Hell, he was going to need a wardrobe, but I had to get out of there. If I didn't keep moving, I was going to realize just how deep into the shit I had fallen.

"Rachel, wait," Ivy said after I reached the foyer, snatched my leather jacket from its hook, and opened the door. "Rachel, *stop!*"

I halted on the stoop, the spring breeze lifting my hair and the birds chirping, my bag and Ivy's sword hanging from my shoulder, my vanity case in one hand and my coat over an arm. At the curb, Jenks was fiddling with the van's sliding door, opening and closing it like a new toy. The sun glistened in his hair, and his kids flitted about his head. Heart pounding, I turned.

Framed in the open door, Ivy looked haunted, her usually placid face severe, with panic in her dilated eyes. "I bought a laptop for you," she said, her eyes dropping as she extended it.

Oh God, she had given me a piece of her security. "Thank

you," I whispered, unable to breathe as I accepted it. It was in a leather case, and probably weighed all of three pounds.

"It's registered to you," she said, looking at it as I slung it over my free shoulder. "And I already added you onto my system, so all you have to do is plug in and click. I wrote down a list of local numbers for the cities you're going to be passing through to dial up with."

"Thank you," I whispered. *She had given me a piece of what made her life sane.* "Ivy, I'll be back." It was what Nick had said to me. But I'd come back. It wasn't a lie for me.

Impulsively I set my case on the stoop and leaned forward to give her a hug. She froze, and then hugged me back. The dusky scent of her filled my senses, and I stepped away.

Kisten waited quietly behind her. Only now, seeing Ivy standing there with one arm hanging down and the other clasped around her middle, did I understand what he'd been trying to tell me. She wasn't afraid for me, she was afraid for herself, that she might slip into old patterns without me there to remind her who she wanted to be. *Just how bad had it been?*

Ire flashed through me. Damn it, this wasn't fair. Yeah, I was her friend, but she could take care of herself! "Ivy," I said, "I don't want to go, but I have to."

"Then go!" she exploded, her perfect face creasing in anger and her eyes flashing to black. "I never asked you to stay!"

Motions stiff, she spun with a vamp quickness and yanked open the door to the church. It boomed shut behind her, and left me blinking. I looked at it, thinking that this wasn't good. No, she hadn't asked me, but Kisten had.

Kisten picked up my case, and together we went down the stairs, my laces flapping. Nearing the van, I awkwardly dug in my shoulder bag for the keys, then hesitated by the driver's side door when I remembered Kisten hadn't yet given them to me. They jingled as he held them out. From inside the van came the excited shrieks of pixies. "You'll keep an eye on her?" I asked him.

"Scout's honor." His blue eyes were pinched from more than the sun. "I'm taking some time off."

Jenks came from around the front of the van, silently taking my coat, vanity bag, and the sword—the last bringing a growl of anticipation from him. I waited until I heard the sliding door shut, then slumped at the sound of Jenks's passenger-side door closing.

"Kisten," I said, feeling a twinge of guilt. "She's a grown woman. Why are we treating her like an invalid?"

He reached out and took my shoulders. "Because she is. Because Piscary can drop into her mind and force her to do just about anything, and it kills a piece of her every time he does. Because he has filled her with his own blood lust, making her do things she doesn't want to do. Because she is trying to run his illegal businesses out of a sense of duty and maintain her share of your runner firm out of a sense of love."

"Yeah. That's what I thought." My lips pressed together and I straightened. "I never said I would stay in the church, much less Cincinnati. Keeping her together is not my job!"

"You're right," he said calmly, "but it happened."

"But it shouldn't have. Damn it, Kisten, all I wanted to do was help her!"

"You have," he said, kissing my forehead. "She'll be fine. But Ivy making you her lodestone wouldn't have evolved if you hadn't let it, and you know it."

My shoulders slumped. Swell, just what I needed: guilt. The breeze shifted his bangs, and I hesitated, looking at the oak door between Ivy and me. "How bad was it?" I whispered.

Kisten's face lost all emotion. "Piscary . . ." He exhaled. "Piscary worked her over so well those first few years that her parents sent her away for her last two years of high school, hoping he would lose interest. She came back even more confused, thanks to Skimmer." His eyes narrowed in an old anger, still potent. "That woman could have saved Ivy with her love, but she was so driven by the urge for better blood, hotter sex, that she sent Ivy deeper."

I felt cold, the breeze shifting my curls. I'd known this, but there was obviously more.

Seeing my unease, Kisten frowned. "When she returned, Piscary played on her new vulnerabilities, lapping up her misery when he rewarded her for behavior that went contrary to what she wanted to believe. Eventually she abandoned everything to keep from going insane, turning herself off and letting Piscary make her into whatever he wanted. She started hurting people she loved when they were at their most vulnerable, and when they abandoned her, she started enticing innocents."

Dropping his eyes, Kisten looked to his bare feet. I knew he was one of the people she had hurt, and I could tell he felt guilty for leaving her. "You couldn't do anything," I said, and his head jerked up, anger in his eyes.

"It was bad, Rachel," he said. "I should have done something. Instead, I turned my back on her and walked away. She won't tell me, but I think she killed people to satisfy her blood lust. God, I hope it was by accident."

I swallowed hard, but he wasn't done yet. "For years she ran rampant," he said, staring at the van but his eyes unfocused, as if looking into the past. "She was a living vampire functioning as an undead, walking under the sun as beautiful and seductive as death. Piscary made her that way, and her crimes were given amnesty. *The favored child.*"

He said the last with bitterness, and his gaze dropped to me. "I don't know what happened, but one day I found her on my kitchen floor, covered in blood and crying. I hadn't seen her in years, but I took her in. Piscary gave her some peace, and after a while she got better. I think it was so she wouldn't kill herself too soon for his liking. All I know is she found a way to deal with the blood lust, chaining it somehow by mixing it with love. And then she met you and found the strength to say no to it all."

Kisten looked at me, his hand touching my hair. "She likes herself now. You're right that she isn't going to throw it all away just because you aren't here. It's just . . ." He squinted, his gaze going distant again. "It was bad, Rachel. It got better. And when she met you, she found a core of strength that Piscary hadn't been able to warp. I just don't want to see it break."

I was shaking inside, and somehow my hands found his. "I'll be back."

He nodded, looking at my fingers within his. "I know."

I felt the need to move. I didn't care that it now came from the need to run from what I had just learned. My eyes dropped to the keys. "Thanks for letting me use your van."

"No biggie," he said, forcing a smile, but his eyes were worried, so terribly worried. "Just return it with a full tank of gas." He reached forward, and I leaned against him, breathing in his scent one last time. My head tilted and our lips met, but it was an empty kiss, my worry having pushed any passion out. *This was for Jenks, not Nick. I didn't owe Nick anything.*

"I slipped something in your suitcase for you," Kisten said, and I pulled away.

"What is it?" I asked, but he didn't answer, giving me a smile before he reluctantly stepped back. His hand trailed down my arm and slipped away.

"Good-bye, Kist," I whispered. "It's only for a few days."

He nodded. "'Bye, love. Take care of yourself."

"You too."

Bare feet soundless, he turned and went back into the church. The door creaked shut, and he was gone.

Feeling numb, I turned and yanked open my door. Jenks's kids flowed out of his open window, and I got in, slamming the door behind me. The laptop slipped under the seat with my bag, and I jammed the keys into the ignition. The big engine turned over and settled into a slow, even rumble. Only now did I look across to Jenks, surprised again at seeing him there, sitting beside me in Kisten's sweats and his shockingly yellow hair. *This was really weird.*

His seat belt was on, and his hands dropped from where he'd been fiddling with the visor. "You look small," he finally said, looking both innocent and wise.

A smile quirked the corner of my lips. Shifting into gear, I accelerated down the street.

Eight

"For the love of Tink," Jenks muttered, angling another one of the Cheetos into his mouth. He meticulously chewed and swallowed, adding, "Her hair looks like a dandelion. You think someone would have told her. There's enough there to make a quilt out of."

My gaze was fixed on the car ahead of us, going an aggravating fifty-six miles an hour on the two-lane, double-yellow-lined road. The woman in question had white hair frizzed out worse than mine. He was right. "Jenks," I said, "you're getting crumbs all over Kisten's van."

The crackle of cellophane was faint over the music—happy, happy music that didn't fit my mood at all. "Sorry," he said, rolling the bag down and shoving it in the back. Licking the orange from his fingers, he started messing with Kist's CDs. *Again.* Then he'd fiddle with the glove box, or spend five minutes getting his window at ju-u-u-ust the right height, or fuss with his seat belt, or any of the half a dozen things he'd been doing since getting in the van, all the while making a soft commentary that I think he didn't know I could hear. It had been a long day.

I sighed, adjusting my grip on the wheel. We had been off the interstate for the last 150 miles or so, taking a two-lane road instead of the interstate up to Mackinaw. The pine forest pressed close on either side, making the sun an occasional flash. It was nearing the horizon, and the wind coming in my window was chill, carrying the scent of earth and growing things. It soothed me where the music couldn't.

The National Forestry sign caught my eye, and I smoothly

braked. I had to get out from behind this woman. And if I heard that song one more time, I was going to jam Daddy's T-Bird down Jenks's throat. Not to mention "Mr. Bladder the size of a walnut" might need to use the can again, which was why we were on the back roads instead of the faster interstate. Jenks got frantic if he couldn't pee when he wanted to.

He looked up from rifling through the glove box as I slowed to bump over the wooden bridge spanning a drainage ditch. He'd been through it three times, but who knows? Maybe something had changed since the last time he had arranged the old napkins, registration, insurance, and the broken pencil. I had to remind myself that he was a pixy, not a human, despite what he looked like, and therefore had a pixy's curiosity.

"A rest stop?" he questioned, his green eyes innocently wide. "What for?"

I didn't look at him, pulling in between two faded white lines and shifting into park. Lake Huron lay before us, but I was too tired to enjoy it. "To rest." The music cut off with the engine. Reaching under the seat, my healing knuckles grazed my new laptop when I shifted the seat rearward. Closing my eyes, I took a slow breath and leaned back, my hands still on the wheel. *Please get out and take a walk, Jenks.*

Jenks was silent. There was the crackle of cellophane as he gathered up the trash. The man never stopped eating. I was going to introduce him to a mighty burger tonight. Maybe three-quarters of a pound of meat would slow him down.

"You want me to drive?" he asked, and I cracked an eyelid, looking askance at him.

Oh, there's a good idea. If we were stopped, it'd be me getting the points, not him. "Nah," I said, my hands falling from the wheel and into my lap. "We're almost there, I just need to move around a little."

With a wisdom far beyond his apparent age, Jenks ran his eyes over me. His shoulders slumped, and I wondered if he knew he was getting on my nerves. Maybe there was a reason pixies were only four inches tall. "Me too," he said meekly, opening his door to let in a gust of sunset-cooled wind smelling of pine and water. "Do you have any change for the machine?"

Relieved, I tugged my bag onto my lap and handed him a fiver. I'd have given him more, but he had nowhere to put it. He needed a wallet. And a pair of pants to put it in. I had hustled him out of the church so fast that all he had was his phone, clipped proudly to his elastic waistband, which had since been depressingly silent. We'd been hoping Jax would call again, but no such luck.

"Thanks," he said, getting out and tripping on the flip-flops I'd bought him at the first gas station we stopped at. The van shifted when he shut the door, and he made his way to a rusted trash can set about fifty feet from the parking lot, chained to a tree. His balance was markedly better, with only the usual trouble most people had walking with slabs of orange plastic attached to their feet.

He dumped the trash and headed for a tree, an alarming intentness to his pace. I took a breath to call out, and he jerked to a stop. Slumped, he scanned the park, making his way to a clapboard restroom instead. Such were the trials in a day of the life of a six-foot-four pixy.

I sighed, watching him slow at the bed of straggly daylilies to talk to the pixies. They buzzed about him in a swirl of gold and silver sparkles, coming from all over the park like fireflies on a mission. Within moments a cloud of glowing dust hovered over him in the darkening air.

I turned at the hush of a car pulling in a few slots down. Three boys like stair steps exploded out, arguing about who switched whose dead batteries in their handheld games. Mom said nothing, wearily popping the trunk and settling it all with a twelve-pack of double A's. Money was offered by Dad, and the three ran to the vending machines under a rustic shelter, shoving each other to get there first. Jenks caught the smallest before he fell into the flowers. I had a feeling Jenks was more worried about the plants than the boy. I smiled when the couple leaned against the car and watched them, exhaling loudly. I knew the feeling.

My smile slowly faded into melancholy. I had always planned on children, but with a hundred years of fertility facing me, I was in no hurry. My thoughts drifted to Kisten, and I pulled my eyes from the boys at the vending machines.

Witches married outside their species all the time, especially before the Turn. There were perfectly acceptable options: adoption, artificial insemination, borrowing your best friend's boyfriend for a night. Issues of what was morally right and wrong tended not to matter when you found yourself in love with a man you couldn't tell you weren't human. It sort of went with the whole hiding-among-humans-for-the-last-five-thousand-years thing. We weren't hiding now, but why limit oneself simply because there wasn't a safety issue anymore? It was way too soon for me to think about kids, but with Kisten, any children would have to be engendered by someone else.

Frustrated, I got out of the van, my body aching from my first day without a pain amulet since my beating. The couple drifted away, talking between themselves. *There wouldn't be any children with Nick either,* I reminded myself, *so it isn't like this is anything new.*

Painfully stretching to touch my toes, I froze, realizing I had put him in present tense. Damn. This was not a choice between them. *Oh God,* I thought. *Tell me I'm only doing this to help Jenks. That nothing is left in me to rekindle.* But the wedge of doubt wiggled itself between me and my logic, settling in to make me feel stupid.

Angry with myself, I did a few more stretches, and then, wondering if the black on my aura had soaked in, I tapped a line and set a circle. My lips curled in revulsion. The shimmering sheet of energy rose black and ugly, the reddish light of sunset coming in from around the trees adding an ominous cast to the black sheen. The gold tint of my aura was entirely lost. Disgusted, I dropped the line, and the circle vanished, leaving me depressed. Even better, Mom and Dad Cleaver called to their kids and, with an unusual hushed haste at their loud questions, jammed everyone into the car to drive away with a little squeak of tire on pavement.

"Yeah," I muttered, watching their brake lights flash red as they settled into traffic. "Run from the black witch." I felt like a leper, and leaned against the warm van and crossed my arms over my chest, remembering why my folks always took us to big cities or places like Disney World on vacation. Small towns generally didn't have much of an Inderland population, and those who did live in them usually played their differences down. Way down.

The *snick-slap-snick* of Jenks's flip-flops grew louder as he returned down the cracked sidewalk, the swirl of pixies dropping back one by one until he was alone. Behind him were the outlines of two islands, both so big they looked like the opposite shore. Far off to the left was the bridge that had clued me in that this was where Jax was. It was starting to glitter in the dimming light as night fell. The bridge was huge, even from this distance.

"They haven't seen Jax," Jenks said, handing me a candy bar. "But they promise to take him in if they do."

My eyes widened. "Really?" Pixies were very territorial, even among themselves, so the offer was somewhat of a shock.

He nodded, the half smile glimmering under his mop of hair turning him guileless. "I think I impressed them."

"Jenks, king of the pixies," I said, and he laughed. The wonderful sound struck through me, lifting my spirits. It slowly died to leave an unhappy silence. "We'll find him, Jenks," I said, touching his shoulder. He jumped, then flashed me a nervous smile. My hand fell away, and I remembered his anger at me for having lied to him. No wonder he didn't want me to touch him. "I'm sure they're in Mackinaw," I added, miserable.

His back to the water and his face empty of emotion, Jenks watched the sporadic traffic.

"Where else could they be?" I tore open my candy bar and took a bite of caramel and chocolate, more for something to do than hunger. The van was radiating heat, and it felt good to lean against the side of the engine. "Jax said they were in Michigan," I said, chewing. "Big green bridge held up by cables. Lots of fresh water. Fudge. Putt-putt golf. We'll find him."

Pain, hard and deep, crossed Jenks's face. "Jax was the first child Mattie and I were able to keep alive through the winter," he whispered, and the sweetness left the wad of sugar and nuts in my mouth. "He was so small, I held him in my hands to keep him warm for four months while I slept. I've got to find him, Rache."

Oh God, I thought as I swallowed, wondering if I had ever loved anyone that deeply. "We'll find him," I said. Feeling totally inadequate, I reached to touch him, pulling away at the last moment. He realized it, and the silence grew uncomfortable.

"Ready to go?" I said, folding the wrapper over the rest of the candy and reaching for the door handle. "We're almost there. We'll get a room, grab something to eat, and then I'm taking you shopping."

"Shopping?" His thin eyebrows rose, and he walked to the front of the van.

Our doors shut simultaneously, and I buckled myself in, refreshed, and my resolve strengthened. "You don't think I'm going to be seen with a six-foot piece of dessert dressed in a nasty pair of sweats, do you?"

Jenks brushed the hair from his eyes, his angular face showing a surprising amount of sly amusement. "Some underwear would be nice."

Snorting, I started the van and put it into reverse, snapping off the CD player before it started up again. "Sorry about that. I had to get out of there."

"Me too," he said, surprising me. "And I wasn't about to wear any of Kisten's. The guy is nice and all, but he stinks." He hesitated, plucking at his collar. "Hey, uh, thanks for what you said back there."

My brow furrowed. Checking both ways, I pulled onto the road. "At the rest stop?"

Sheepish, he shifted his shoulders in embarrassment. "No, in the kitchen about me being the only backup you ever needed."

"Oh." I warmed, keeping my eyes on the car ahead of us, a black, salt-rusted Corvette that reminded me of Kisten's other vehicle. "I meant it, Jenks. I missed you the past five months. And if you don't come back to the firm, I swear I'm going to leave you like this."

His panicked expression eased when he saw I was joking. "For the love of Tink, don't you dare," he muttered. "I can't even pix anyone. I sweat now instead of dusting, did you know that? I've got water coming off me instead of dust. What the hell can I do with sweat? Rub up against someone and make them puke in disgust? I've seen you sweat, and it's not pretty. I don't even want to think about sex, two sweaty bodies pressed against each other like that? Disgusting. Talk about birth control—it's no wonder you only have a handful of kids."

He shuddered and I smiled. *Same old Jenks.*

I couldn't keep myself from stiffening when he began rummaging in the music, and apparently sensing it, he stopped, putting his hands in his lap to stare out the front window at the darkening sky. We had come out of the woods and were starting to see homes and businesses strung out along the road in a thin strip. Behind them was the flat blue of the lake, gray in the fading light.

"Rachel," he said, his voice soft with regret. "I don't know if I can come back."

Alarmed, I looked at him, then the road, then at him again. "What do you mean you don't know. If it's about Trent—"

He held up a hand, his brow pinched. "It's not Trent. I figured out he's an elf after helping Ceri last night."

I jerked and the van crossed the yellow line. A horn blew, and I yanked the wheel back. "You figured it out?" I stammered, feeling my heart pound. "Jenks, I wanted to tell you. Really. But I was afraid you would blab, and—"

"I'm not going to tell anyone," he said, and I could see it was killing him. It would have brought him a huge amount of prestige in the pixy world. "If I do, then it means you were right in not telling me, and you weren't."

His voice was hard, and I felt a stab of guilt. "Then why?" I asked, wishing he had brought this up when we were parked, not when I was trying to navigate the outskirts of an unfamiliar town, bright with neon lights.

For a moment he was silent, his young face pensive as he put his thoughts in order. "I'm eighteen," he finally said. "Do you know how old that is for a pixy? I'm slowing down. You nicked me last fall. Ivy can snag me whenever she wants."

"Ivy's got Piscary's undead reactions," I said, scared. "And I was lucky. Jenks, you look great. You aren't old."

"Rachel . . ." he said around a sigh. "My kids are moving out to make their own lives. The garden is starting to go empty. I'm not complaining," he rushed on. "The wish for sterility I got from you is a blessing, since the last three years of children in a pixy's life have a very low life expectancy and it would kill Matalina knowing she was having children that wouldn't live a week past her. Little Josephina . . . she's flying now. She's going to make it."

His voice cut off, cracking, and my throat tightened.

"Between that wish and the garden," he continued, staring out the front window, "I'm not worried about any of my children surviving past Matalina and me, and I thank you for that."

"Jenks—" I started, wanting him to stop.

"Shut up," he said hotly, his smooth cheeks reddening. "I don't want your pity." Clearly angry, he put a hand on the open windowsill. "It's my own fault. It never bothered me until I got to know you and Ivy. I'm old. I don't care what I look like, and I'm mad as all hell that you two are going to have your damn runner business from now until forever and I'm not going to be a part of it. That's why I didn't come back. Not because you didn't tell me what Trent was."

I didn't say anything, gritting my jaw and miserable. I hadn't known he was that old. Signaling, I made a right turn to follow the strip along the water's edge. Ahead of us was the huge bridge connecting the upper peninsula of Michigan with the lower, all lit up and sparkling.

"You can't let that stop you from coming back," I said hesitantly. "I do demon magic and Ivy is Piscary's scion." Turning the wheel, I pulled into a two-story motel, an outside pool snuggled up in the el the rooms made. I stopped under the faded red and white striped canopy, watching the kids in swimsuits and plastic arm-cuffs run in front of the van, confident I wouldn't hit them. The mother trailing behind them gave me a grateful wave. I thought they must be either insane or Weres since it was only sixty out. "Any of us could die tomorrow," I finished.

He looked at me, the lines of anger smoothing out. "You won't die tomorrow," he said.

Putting the van into park, I turned to him. "How do you figure that?"

Jenks undid his belt and gave me a sideways smile that rivaled Kisten's for mischief. "Because I'm with you."

A groan slipped from me. I had walked right into that one.

Smiling, he got out, glancing up at the first stars, almost unseen behind the town's lights. Stiff from the long ride, I followed him into the tiny office. It was empty but for an astounding display of knickknacks and pamphlets. Hands out, Jenks headed for the shelves of miniatures like a starving man, his pixy curiosity and need to touch making the display irresistible. The door shut behind us, and seeing him lost in the throes of pixy bliss, I punched him in the arm.

"Ow!" he exclaimed, holding it and giving me an injured look. "What was that for?"

"You know why," I said dryly, finding a smile as I turned to the casually dressed woman who came in from a back room through an open archway. I could hear a TV in the background, and smell someone's lunch. Or dinner, rather, seeing as she was human.

She blinked as she took us in. "Can I help you?" she asked, becoming hesitant when she realized we were Inderlanders. Mackinaw was a tourist town, and probably not big enough to draw a huge resident Inderland crowd.

"Yes, a room for two, please," I said, reaching for the registration card and pen. A frown came over me at the form. *Well, we could go under my name,* I thought, writing Ms. Rachel Morgan in my big loopy script. The clicks of the ceramic and pewter figurines being picked up and set down were audible, and the woman behind the counter winced, watching him over my shoulder. "Jenks, could you get the plate number for me?" I asked, and he slipped out, the seashell door chime clunking roughly.

"That will be two twenty," she said stiffly.

Great, I thought. *Cheap, cheap, cheap. You gotta love small towns in the off-season.* "We're only staying the night, not the week," I said, putting down the church's address.

"That *is* the nightly rate," she said, her voice tartly smug.

My head came up. "Two hundred twenty dollars? It's the off-season," I said, and she shrugged. Shocked, I thought for a moment. "Can I get a discount for Were Insurance?"

Her eyes were mocking. "We only offer discounts for AAA."

My lips pressed together and I went warm. Slowly I curled my hand up and brought it below the level of the high partition, hiding my bandaged knuckles. *Crap, crap, crap. You gotta love those small-town mentalities.* She had upped the rates for us, hoping we'd go somewhere else.

"Cash," she added smugly. "We don't take plastic or personal checks."

The clipped sign behind her said they did, but I wasn't going to walk out of there. I had my pride, and money was nothing compared to that. "Do you have one with a kitchen?" I asked, shaking inside. *Two hundred and twenty dollars would really take a chunk out of my cash.*

"That will be thirty extra," she said.

"Of course it will," I muttered. Angry, I jerked my bag open and pulled out two hundreds and a fifty as Jenks came in. His eyes went from the money in my hand to the woman's satisfaction, and finally to my anger, figuring it out immediately. Hell, he had probably heard the entire conversation with his pixy hearing.

His gaze rose to the fake camera in the corner, then out the glass door to the parking lot. "Rache, I think we hit prime-time gold," he said, taking the pen chained to the desk and writing the plate number on the form. "Someone just peed *into* the pool, and I can smell shower mold from here. If we hurry, we can get a shot of the bridge at sunset for the opening credits."

The woman set a key on the counter, her motions suddenly hesitant.

Jenks flipped open his phone. "Do you still have the number for the county's health department from our last stop?"

I steeled my face into a bored countenance. "It's on my clipboard. But let's wait on the opening shot. We can do a sunrise frame. Tom had a cow the last time we burned film before he had a chance to canvas the local hot spots for the worst offenders."

The woman went ashen. I dropped the bills on the counter and took the worn key on its little plastic tag. My eyebrows rose; number thirteen, how apropos. "Thanks," I said.

Jenks jerked to get in front of me as I turned to leave. "Allow me, Ms. Morgan," he said, opening it gracefully, and I strode out the door, pride intact.

Somehow I managed to keep a straight face until the door clanked shut. Jenks snickered, and I lost it. "Thanks," I said between snorts. "God, I was ready to smack her a good one."

"No problem," Jenks said, scanning the rooms, his gaze settling on the last one tucked at the short end of the el. "Can I drive the van over there?"

I thought he more than deserved it, and I left him to work it out as I walked across the dark lot throwing up heat to the sounds of the kids splashing in the pool. The underwater lights had come on, and they reflected up against the open umbrellas to look inviting. If it hadn't been so cold, I'd have asked Jenks if pixies could swim. Finding out if my mental image of Jenks in a Speedo matched reality would be worth a few goose bumps.

The key stuck for a moment, but with a little wiggling it engaged and the door swung open. Out flowed the scent of citrus and clean linen.

Jenks pulled the van around to the empty spot before the door. The headlights fell into the room to show an ugly brown carpet and a yellow bedspread. Flicking on the light, I went in, heading for the pretend kitchen and the second door at the back. I set my bag on the bed, concerned when I realized the door led to the bathroom, not a second room.

Muttering about caves, Jenks came in with my suitcase, his eyes roving the low ceiling. He dropped my bag by the door, tossed me the keys to the van, and headed out, flicking the light switch several times because he could.

"Ah, Jenks," I called, fingers smarting from the keys. "We need a different room."

Jenks came in with my laptop and Ivy's sword, setting them on the round table under the front window. "How come? I was kidding about the shower mold." He took a deep breath, nose wrinkling. "That smells like . . . Well, it's not shower mold."

I didn't want to know what he was smelling, but when I silently pointed to the single bed, all he did was shrug, his lusciously green eyes innocent. Gesturing helplessly, I said, "One bed?"

"So?" Then he flushed, his eyes darting to the box of tissues on the bedside table. "Oh. Yeah. I won't fit in the Kleenex box anymore, will I?"

Not looking forward to talking to that lady, I headed for the door, snagging my shoulder bag in passing. "I'll get a new room. Do me a favor and don't use the bathroom. She'll probably charge us a cleaning fee."

"I'm coming with you," he said, falling into step with me.

The kids from the pool were making a quick, wet-footed dash to their room, shivering under skimpy white towels when we crossed the parking lot. Jenks opened the office door for me, and the sound of seashells clunking mixed with the sound of a tearful argument when we entered. "You charged them the Fourth of July weekend rate?" I heard a man say, and her blubbering answer. I looked at Jenks in a mute question, and he cleared his throat loudly. Silence.

After a hushed conversation, a short, follicle-challenged man in a plaid shirt emerged, brushing his balding plate. "Yes?" he said with an artificially interested look. "What can I get for you? Extra towels for the pool?" From somewhere out of sight the woman made a hiccup of a sob, and he reddened.

"Actually," I said, putting the room key on the chest-high partition between us, "I'd like to see about getting a different room. We need two beds, not one. My fault for not making that clear." I smiled as if I hadn't heard anything.

The man's gaze went to Jenks, and he flushed deeper. "Ah, yes. Number thirteen, right?" he said, snatching it and giving me a new one.

Jenks headed for the knickknacks, but at my heavy sigh, he went to the pamphlets instead. Setting my bag on the counter, I smugly asked, "What's the price difference for that?"

"None," was his quick reply. "Same rate. Anything else I can do for you? Make reservations for you and the rest of your party, maybe?" He blinked, looking ill. "Will they be staying with us as well?"

Jenks turned to look out the glassed door, his hand to his smooth chin while he tried not to laugh. "No," I said lightly. "They called to tell us they found a place on the other side of town that filled up their pool with lake water. That wins out over moldy bathrooms any day."

The man's mouth worked but nothing came out.

Jenks jerked into motion, and I glanced behind me to see him hunched and gripping one of the pamphlets close to his face.

"Thank you," I said, holding up the key and smiling. "We may be staying a second night. Do you have any two-day specials?"

"Yes, ma'am," he said, eyes going relieved. "Second night is half price during the off-season. I'll put you down for it if you like." He glanced at his unseen wife through the archway.

"That sounds great," I said. "And a late checkout for Tuesday?"

"Late checkout on Tuesday," he said, scribbling something in his registration book. "No problem. We appreciate your business."

I nodded and smiled, touching Jenks's arm and pulling him out the door since he wasn't moving, fixed to the pamphlet in his grip. "Thanks," I called cheerfully. "Have a good night."

The door chimes thunked dully, and I exhaled into the cooler night air. The parking lot was silent but for the nearby traffic. Satisfied, I glanced at the key in the dim light under the canopy. Room eleven this time.

"Rache." Jenks shoved the pamphlet at me. "Here. He's here. I know it! Get in the van. They close in ten minutes!"

"Jenks!" I exclaimed when he grabbed my arm and pulled me stumbling across the lot. "Jenks, wait up! Jax? He's where?"

"There," he said, shaking the pamphlet in front of my face. "That's where I would go."

Bewildered, I peered at the colorful trifolded paper in the dim light of the streetlamp. My lips parted and I reached to dig my keys out while Jenks threw our stuff back into the van and slammed the motel door shut, shaking in impatience.

The Butterfly Shack. Of course.

Nine

Humming nervously, Jenks put the jar of honey in the basket with my bandages and the rest of his groceries. He fidgeted, and my eyebrows rose. "Honey, Jenks?" I questioned.

"It's medicinal," he said, reddening and turning to stand before the array of baking supplies, feet spread wide in his Peter Pan pose. Reaching to a top shelf, he dropped a jar of yeast in with the rest. "Bee pollen," he grumbled under his breath. "Where in Tink's bordello do they keep the vitamin supplements? Can't find a bloody thing in this store. Who laid it out? Gilligan?" His head rose and he scanned the signs hanging over the aisles.

"The vitamins would be with the medicines," I said, and he jerked.

Clearly shocked, he stammered, "You heard that?" and I shrugged. "Damn," he muttered, walking away. "I didn't know you could hear that well. You never heard me before."

I trailed behind him, arms empty. Jenks insisted on carrying everything, insisted on opening every door for me, hell, he'd flush my toilet if I let him. It wasn't a macho thing, it was because he could. Automatic doors were his favorites, and though he hadn't played with one yet by getting on and off the sensor pad, I knew he wanted to.

His pace was quick, his steps silent in the new boots I had bought him all of an hour ago. He wasn't happy about me insisting we go shopping before seeing if Jax was at The Butterfly Shack, a butterfly exhibit and wildlife store, but he agreed that if Jax was there, he was hiding or he would have had the owner call us to come get him. We didn't know the situation, and if we knocked on the door and told the proprietor he had been harboring a pixy, one possibly wanted in connection with a theft, we might start a few tongues wagging.

So Jenks and I used the interim while the proprietor closed up shop and counted his money to do a little pre-break-in outfitting/shopping. I had been pleasantly surprised to find some upscale stores right beside the tourist-crap traps in an obviously new slab of light commercial buildings that had gone up in the last five years or so. The trees only had been in the ground that long. I was a witch; I could tell.

Since it was just before the tourist season, the selections were high and the prices were almost reasonable. That would change next week when school let out and the town tripled its population when the "fudgies"—tourists named after the candy Mackinaw was known for—descended on them.

Turns out, Jenks was a power shopper, which probably stemmed from his garden gathering background. In a very short time we had hit three clothes stores, a dance outlet, and a shoe mart. So now instead of a hunky young man in sweats and flip-flops, I was with a six-foot-four, athletic, angsty young man dressed in casual linen pants and matching fawn-colored shirt. Under it was a skintight two-piece suit of silk and spandex that had set us back a couple hundred dollars, but after seeing him in it, my head bobbed and my card came out. My treat.

I couldn't help but let my eyes ramble over him as he crouched before a display of vitamins and took off the shades I had bought him, not wanting a repeat of him grumbling over the sun all the way up there. Clearly bothered, he ran a hand under his cap in worry. The red leather should have clashed with what he had on, but on him? Yum.

Jenks looked really good, and I was wishing I had brought nicer clothes. And a camera. He was a hard man to keep up with once you got him out of sweats and flip-flops.

"Bee pollen," he said as he jiggled the sleeve of his new aviator jacket down and reached forward, blowing the dust from the lid of the glass jar. "This stuff tastes like it's already been through the bee," he said, rising to place it with the rest, "but seeing as the only flowers they have here are stale daisies and dehydrated roses, it will do."

His voice carried a hard derision, and I silently looked at the price. No wonder pixies spent more time in the garden than working a nine-to-five to buy their food like most people. The two bottles of maple syrup he wanted cost a whopping nine dollars. Each. And when I tried to substitute the fake stuff, he had added a third. "Let me carry something," I offered, feeling useless.

He shook his head, pace intent as he headed to the front. "If we don't go now, it will be too cold to find any pixies who might help. Besides, the owner has to be home and watching TV. It's almost nine."

I glanced at his phone clipped to his belt. "It's twenty past," I said. "Let's go."

"Past?" Jenks snickered, shifting the basket. "The sun's been down only an hour."

He skittered sideways when I snatched the phone from his belt and held it for him to see. "Nine-twenty," I said, not knowing if I should be smug or worried that his unerring time sense was off. I hoped Ceri hadn't ruined it.

For an instant Jenks looked horrified, then his mouth quirked. "We shifted latitude," he said. "I'm going to be . . ." He took the phone from me and peered at the clock. ". . . twenty minutes slow at sunset and twenty minutes fast at sunrise." Jenks chuckled. "Never thought I'd need a watch, but it would be easier than trying to switch over and then have to switch back."

I shrugged. I'd never felt the need for a watch unless I was working with Ivy and had to "synchronize" to keep her from having a fit, and then I just used Jenks. Feeling short next to his height, I steered him from the self-service line, or we would have been there all night. Jenks took charge of the basket, unloading it and leaving me to smile neutrally at the woman.

Her plucked eyebrows rose upon taking in the bee pollen, yeast, honey, maple syrup, beer, Band-Aids, and the ailing plant Jenks had rescued from the half-price rack in the tiny floral department. "Doing a little cooking?" she asked slyly, her grin thick with an amused conclusion as to what two people might be doing with a shopping list like ours. Her name tag said terri, and she was a comfortable twenty pounds overweight, with swollen fingers and too many rings.

Jenks's green eyes were innocently wide. "Jane, honey," he said to me. "Be a dear and run back for the instant pudding." His voice dropped, taking on a sultry depth. "Let's try butterscotch this time. I'm bored with chocolate."

Feeling wicked, I leaned against him, reaching to play with the curls about his ears. "You know Alexia is allergic to butterscotch," I said. "Besides, Tom will do *a-a-a-a-anything* for pistachio. And I have some of that in the fridge. Right beside the caramel drizzle and the whipped cream." I giggled, tossing my red hair. "God, I love caramel! It takes forever to lick off."

Jenks broke into a devilish grin, eyeing the woman from under his hat as he took a handful of toothbrushes from the grab rack and set them on the conveyer belt. "That's what I love so much about my Janie," he said, giving me a sideways hug that pulled me off balance and into him. "Always thinking of others. Isn't she the kindest soul you've ever met?"

The woman's face was red. Flustered, she kept trying to ring up the marked-down plant, finally giving up and putting it into a plastic bag. "Sixty-three twenty-seven," she stammered, not meeting Jenks's eyes.

Smug, Jenks pulled out the wallet he had bought all of fifteen minutes ago, shuffling to find the Vampiric Charms credit card. He carefully ran it through the machine, clearly enjoying himself as he punched the right buttons. Ivy had arranged for it ages ago, and Jenks's signature was on file as a matter of course. This was the first time he'd been able to use it, but he looked like he knew what he was doing.

The woman stared at the name of our firm when it popped up on her screen, her jaw falling to make a double chin.

Jenks signed the pad with a careful seriousness, smiling at the cashier as she extended the receipt and a strip of coupons. "Cheerio," he said, the plastic a soft rustle when he took all the bags and looped his arm through them. I glanced back when the glass doors swung apart and the night air, cold off the straits, set a few strands of hair to tickle my face. She was already gossiping with the manager, putting a hand to her mouth when she saw me look at her.

"Jeez, Jenks," I said, taking one of the bags so I could look at the receipt. *Over sixty dollars for two bags of groceries?* "Maybe we could have done something really disgusting, like lick her microphone." *And why had he bought so many toothbrushes?*

"You enjoyed it, and you know it, witch," he said, then snatched the ticker tape from me when I tried to throw it and the coupons away. "I want that," he said, tucking them in a pocket. "I might use them later."

"No one uses those," I said, head bowed while I dug in my bag for the keys. The lights flashed and the locks disengaged. Jiggling the bag on his arm, Jenks opened my door for me before going to the other side of the van and dropping his groceries beside his bags of slacks, shirts, silk boxers, socks, and a silk robe I would have protested over except that he was eventually going to get small again and I was going to claim it. The man couldn't have anything cheap, and I would've questioned his claim that oil-based fabrics would make him break out if I hadn't seen it for myself.

His door opened and he settled himself, carefully buckling in as if it was a religion. "Ready?" I said, feeling the ease of shopping start to shift into the anticipation of a run. An illegal run. Yes, we were rescuing Jenks's son, not robbing the place, but they would still throw our butts in jail if we were caught.

Jenks's head went up and down, and he zipped and unzipped the small waist pack he had put his few tools in. Taking a steadying breath, I started the van and headed to the shops and the theater. Bridge traffic was congested, and had been for the better part of the month, according to the disgruntled clerk in the shoe outlet. Apparently it was down to one lane either way while they scrambled to make maintenance repairs round-the-clock to finish before Memorial Day. Fortunately we didn't have to cross the huge suspension bridge, just weave past the confusion.

The van was blowing cold air even though I had the heater on, and I thanked the stars that Jenks was big. Tonight would have been iffy for him if he were four inches tall. I only hoped Jax had found somewhere warm. A butterfly exhibit would have enough food, but why heat it to a comfortable seventy-five degrees when fifty will do?

The theater was in a mazelike cluster of new shops catering to tourists on foot—sort of a mini-open-aired mall plopped beside the original downtown—but they had a special lot for the cinema, and I parked between a white truck and a rusting Toyota with a bumper sticker that said FOLLOW ME TO THE U.P., EH?

The engine cut out, and I looked across the van at Jenks in the new silence. The sound of slow crickets came in from the nearby empty field. He seemed nervous, his fingers quick as they fussed with the zipper on his pack. "You going to be okay?" I said, realizing this was the first time he had been on a run where he couldn't just fly out of danger.

He nodded, the deep concern on his face appearing out of place on someone so young. Rustling in a bag, he pulled a bottle of maple syrup out from behind the seat. His green eyes met mine in the uncertain light, looking black. "Hey, um, when we get out, will you pretend to fix your shoe or something? I want to take care of the cameras on the back of the building, and a distraction might help."

My gaze went to the bottle in his hand, then rose to his wary expression, not sure how a bottle of syrup was going to fix the cameras but willing to go along with it. "Sure."

Relieved, he got out. I followed suit, leaning against the van to take off my shoe and shake a nonexistent pebble out. I watched Jenks with half my attention, understanding when he let out a trill of a whistle, anxiously touching his red hat as a curious, aggressive pixy zipped up to him in the cooling dusk.

I missed what was said, but Jenks returned looking satisfied, the bottle of maple syrup gone. "What?" I said as he waited for me to fall into step with him.

"They'll put the cameras on loop for us when we leave the building," he said, not taking my arm as Kisten or Nick might, but walking beside me with an odd closeness. The shops lining the thoroughfare were closed, but the theater had a small crowd of what were clearly locals, to judge by the amount of noisy banter. The movie showing had been out for three weeks in Cincy, but there must not be a lot to do up here.

We neared the ticket booth and my pulse quickened. "They'll loop the cameras for a bottle of maple syrup?" I asked, voice hushed.

Jenks shrugged, glancing at the marquee. "Sure. That stuff is liquid gold."

I dug in my bag for a twenty as I took that in. Maybe I could make more pimping maple syrup to pixies than running? We bought two tickets to the SF film, and after getting Jenks a bag of popcorn, we headed into the theater, immediately going out the emergency exit.

My eyes went to the cameras atop the building, catching the faintest glint of streetlight on pixy wings. Maybe it was a little overkill, but being placed at the theater if The Butterfly Shack's alarms went off might be the difference between keeping my feet on the street and cooling them on a jail cot.

Together we made our way from the service entrances in back to the front, Jenks shedding clothes and handing them to me to stuff in my bag every few yards. It was terribly distracting, but I managed to avoid running into the Dumpsters and recycling bins. Upon reaching the shuttered tourist area, he was in his soft-soled boots and his skintight outfit. We had come out a few blocks from the theater, and it was creepy being on the street at night with everything closed, reminding me how far from home and out of my element I was. The Butterfly Shack was tucked into the end of a cul-de-sac, and we headed for it, feet silent on the cement.

"Watch my back," Jenks whispered, leaving me in a shadow while he twirled the long tool in his fingers into a blur, crouching to put his eyes even with the lock.

I gave him long glance, then turned to watch the empty foot street. *No prob, Jenks,* I thought. Sure, he was married, but I could look. "People," I breathed, but he had heard and was already behind the scrawny bushes beside the door. They were butterfly bushes, if I guessed right, and scraggly. Any other business would have torn them out.

Shrinking into my shadow, I held my breath until the couple passed, the woman's heels fast and the man griping they were going to miss the previews. Five seconds later Jenks was back at the door. A moment of tinkering, and he stood to carefully try the latch. It clicked open, a nice cheery green light blinking a welcome from the lock pad.

He grinned, jerking his head for me to join him. I slipped inside and moved to get out of his way. If there was more security, Jenks could tell better than I.

The door shut, leaving the wash of streetlight coming in the large windows. As smoothly as if on wings, Jenks glided past me. "Camera behind the mirror in the corner," he said. "Can't do anything about that one if I'm six feet tall. Let's get him, get out, and hope for the best."

My gut tightened. This was more loosey-goosey than even I liked. "The back?" I whispered, cataloging the silent shelves and displays of Amazon rain forest stuffed animals and expensive books on how to design a garden for wildlife. It smelled wonderful, rich with subtle perfumes of exotic flowers and vines filtering out from behind an obvious pair of glass doors. But it was cold. The tourist season wouldn't officially begin till next week, and I was sure they kept the temp low at night to extend the life of the insects.

Jenks slipped to the back, making me feel clumsy behind him. I wondered if he would even show up on the camera, he moved so stealthily. The soft sucking sound of the outer glass door of the casual airlock was loud, and Jenks held it for me, his eyes wide to take in what little light there was. Nervous, I ducked under his arm, breathing deeply of the scent of moist dirt. Jenks opened the second door, and the sound of running water joined it. My shoulders eased despite my tension, and I hastened to keep up as he entered the walk-through exhibit.

It was a two-story-tall room, glass-walled from ten feet up. The night was a black ceiling festooned with vines and hanging planters of musky smelling petunias and jewel-like begonias. Maybe forty feet long and fifteen feet wide, the room made a narrow slice of another continent. And it was cold. I clasped my shoulders and looked at Jenks, worried.

"Jax?" Jenks called, the hope in his voice heartrending. "Are you here? It's me, Dad."

Dad, I thought in envy. What I would have given to have heard that directed at me when I needed it. I shoved the ugly feeling aside, happy that Jax had a dad who was able to rescue his ass. Growing up was hard enough without having to pull yourself out of whatever mess you got yourself into when your decisions were faster than your brain. Or your feet.

There was a chirp from the incubators tucked out of the way. My brows rose, and Jenks stiffened. "There," I said breathlessly, pointing. "Under that cupboard, where the heat lamp is."

"Jax!" Jenks whispered, padding down the slate slabs edged with moss. "Are you okay?"

A grin heavy with relief came over me when, with a sprinkling of glowing dust, a pixy darted out from under the cupboard. It was Jax, and he zipped around us, wings clattering. He was okay. Hell, he was more than okay. He looked great.

"Ms. Morgan!" the young pixy cried, lighting the small space with his excitement and zipping around my head like an insane firefly. "You're alive? We thought you were dead! Where's my dad?" He rose to the ceiling, then dropped. "Dad?"

Jenks stared, transfixed at his son darting over the exhibit. He opened his mouth, then closed it, clearly struggling to find a way to touch his son without hurting him. "Jax . . ." he whispered, his eyes both young and old—pained and filled with joy.

Jax let out a startled chirp, slamming back a good two feet before he caught himself. "Dad!" he shouted, pixy dust slipping from him. "What happened? You're big!"

Jenks's hand shook as his son landed on it. "I got big to find you. It's too cold to be out without somewhere to go. And it's not safe for Ms. Morgan to be out of Cincinnati unescorted."

I made a face, chafing at the truth, though we hadn't even seen a vampire, much less a hungry one. They didn't like small towns. "Jax," I said impatiently, "where's Nick?"

The small pixy's eyes widened and the dust slipping from him turned thin. "They took him. I can show you were he is. Holy crap, he'll be glad to see you! We didn't know you were alive, Ms. Morgan. We thought you were dead!"

That was the second time he had said it, and I blinked in understanding. *Oh God.* Nick had called the night Al snapped the familiar bond between us. Al answered my phone and told Nick I belonged to him. Then the media thought I'd died on the boat Kisten blew up. Nick thought I was dead. That's why he had never called. That's why he didn't tell me he was back on the solstice. That's why he cleared out his apartment and left. He thought I was dead.

"God help me," I whispered, reaching out for the filthy incubator full of butterfly pupa. The budded rose left on my doorstep in the jelly jar with the pentagram of protection on it had been from him. *Nick hadn't left me. He thought I had died.*

"Rache?"

I straightened when Jenks tentatively touched my arm. "I'm okay," I whispered, though I was far from it. I'd deal with it later. "We have to go," I said, turning away.

"Wait," Jax exclaimed, dropping down to the floor and peering under the cupboard. "Here kitty, kitty, kitty . . ."

"Jax!" Jenks shouted in horror, scooping his son up.

"Dad!" Jax protested, easily slipping the loose prison of his father's fingers. "Let go!"

My eyes widened at the ball of orange fluff squeezing out from under the counter, blinking and stretching. I looked again, not believing. "It's a cat," I said, winning the Pulitzer prize for incredible intellect. Well, actually it was a kitten, so points off for that.

Jenks's mouth was moving but nothing came out. He backed up with what looked like terror in his wide eyes.

"It's a cat!" I said again. Then added a frantic, "Jax! No!" when the pixy dropped down. I reached for him, drawing away when the fluffy orange kitten arched its back and spit at me.

"Her name is Rex," Jax said proudly, his wings still as he stood on the dirty floor beside the incubator and scratched vigorously under her chin. The kitten relaxed, forgetting me and stretching its neck so Jax could get just the right spot.

I took a slow breath. *As in Tyrannosaurus rex? Great. Just freaking great.*

"I want to keep her," Jax said, and the kitten sank down and began to purr, tiny sharp claws kneading in and out and eyes closed.

It's a cat. Boy, you couldn't slip anything past me tonight. "Jax," I said persuasively, and the small pixy bristled.

"I'm not leaving her!" he said. "I would have frozen my first night if it wasn't for her. She's been keeping me warm, and if I leave, that mean old witch who owns the place will find her again and call the pound. I heard her say so!"

I glanced from the kitten to Jenks. He looked like he was hyperventilating, and I took his arm in case he was going to pass out. "Jax, you can't keep her."

"She's mine!" Jax protested. "I've been feeding her butterfly pupa, and she's been keeping me warm. She won't hurt me. Look!"

Jenks almost had a coronary when his son flitted back and forth before the kitten, enticing her to take a shot at him. The kitten's white tip of a tail twitched and her hindquarters quivered.

"Jax!" Jenks shouted, scooping him up out of danger as Rex's paw came out.

My heart jumped into my throat, and it was all I could do to not reach for him too.

"Dad, let me go!" Jax exclaimed, and he was free, flitting over our heads, the kitten watching with a nerve-racking intensity.

Jenks visably swallowed. "The cat saved my son's life," he said, shaking. "We aren't leaving it here to starve or die at the pound."

"Jenks . . ." I protested, watching Rex pace under Jax's flitting path, her head up and her steps light. "Someone will take her in. Look how sweet she is." I clasped my hands so I wouldn't pick her up. "Sure," I said, my resolve weakening when Rex fell over to look cute and harmless, her little white belly in the air. "She's all soft and sweet now, but she's going to get bigger. And then there will be yelling. And screaming. And soft kitty fur in my garden."

Jenks frowned. "I'm not going to keep her. I'll find a home for her. But she saved my son's life, and I won't let her starve here."

I shook my head, and while Jax cheered, his father gingerly scooped the kitten up. Rex gave a token wiggle before settling into the crook of his arm. Jenks had her both safe and secure—as if she was a child.

"Let me take her," I said, holding out my hands.

"I've got her okay." Jenks's angular face was pale, making him look as if he was going to pass out. "Jax, it's cold out. Get in Ms. Morgan's purse until we get to the motel."

"Hell no!" Jax said, shocking me as he lit on my shoulder. "I'm not going to ride in no purse. I'll be fine with Rex. Tink's diaphragm, Dad. Where do you think I've been sleeping for the last four days?"

"Tink's diaph—" Jenks sputtered. "Watch your mouth, young man."

This was not happening.

Jax dropped down to snuggle in the hollow of Rex's tummy, almost disappearing in the soft kitten fur. Jenks took several breaths, his shoulders so tense you could crack eggs on them.

"We have to go," I whispered. "We can talk about this later."

Jenks nodded, and with the wobbling pace of a drunk made his way to the front of the exhibit, Jenks holding the kitten and me opening doors. The scent of books and carpet made the air smell dead as we crept into the gift shop. I fearfully looked for flashing red and blue lights outside, relieved at finding only a comforting darkness and a quiet cobble street.

I said nothing when Jenks awkwardly got his wallet out from his back pocket with one hand and left every last dollar of cash I had given him on the counter. He nodded respectfully to the camera behind the mirror, and we left as we had come in.

We didn't see anyone on the way back to the parking lot, but I didn't take one good breath until the van door slammed shut behind me. Fingers shaking, I started the engine, carefully backing up and finding my way to the strip.

"Rache," Jenks said, eyes on the kitten in his arms as he broke his conspicuous silence. "Can we stop at that grocery store and pick up some cat food? I've got a coupon."

And so it begins, I thought, mentally adding a litter pan and litter. And a can opener. And a little saucer for water. And maybe a fuzzy mouse or ten.

I glanced at Jenks out of the corner of my eye, his smooth, long fingers gentling the fur between Rex's ears as the kitten purred loud enough to be heard over the van. Jax was cuddled between her paws, sleeping the sleep of the exhausted. A misty smile came over me and I felt myself relax. We'd get rid of her as soon as we found a good home.

Ri-i-i-ight.

Ten

"He's fine," I said into my cell phone, stomach tight as Rex stalked Jax across the bed. The pixy was sitting dejectedly on the lamp shade, his feet swinging while his dad lectured him.

"How did you find him so quick?" Kisten asked, his voice thin and tiny from too many towers between us.

I took a breath to tell Jenks about the cat, but he bent without slowing his harangue to scoop up the orange ball of warrior-in-training and hold her close, soothing her into forgetting what she was doing. My held breath escaped and I paused to remember what I had been saying.

"He was at a butterfly exhibit." I twisted in my seat by the curtained window, aiming the battered remote at the TV to click off the local ten o'clock news. There'd been no late-breaking story about intruders at the store, so it looked as if we'd be okay. I'd have been willing to bet that no one would even look at the camera records, despite the cash Jenks had left.

"He made friends with a kitten," I added, leaning for the last slice of pizza. The bracelet of black gold I had found in my suitcase glittered in the light, and I smiled at his gift, not caring right now that he probably gave the bit of finery to all his lovers as a not-so-subtle show of his conquests to those in the know. Ivy had one. So did Candice, the vamp who had tried to kill me last solstice. I especially liked the little skull charm he had on it, but maybe this wasn't such a good club after all.

"A kitten?" Kisten said. "No shit!"

Jingling the metallic skull and heart together, I chuckled.

"Yeah." I took a bite of my pizza. "Fed her butterfly pupa in return for her keeping him warm," I added around my full mouth.

"Her?" he asked, the disbelief clear in his voice.

"Her name is Rex," I said brightly, shaking my new charm bracelet down. *What else would a nine-year-old pixy name a predator a hundred times his size?* Eyeing Jenks holding the somnolent kitten, my eyebrows rose. "You want a cat?"

He laughed, the miles between us vanishing. "I'm living on my boat, Rachel."

"Cats can live on boats," I said, glad he had moved out of Piscary's quarters when Skimmer moved in. That he docked his two-story yacht at the restaurant's quay was close enough. "Hey, uh, how is Ivy?" I asked softly, shifting to drape the back of my knees over the arm of the green chair.

Kisten's sigh was worrisome. "Skimmer's been at the church since you left."

Tension stiffened my shoulders. He was fishing to find out if I was jealous; I could hear it. "Really," I said lightly, but my face went cold when I studied my feelings, wondering if the faint annoyance was from jealousy or the idea that someone was in my church, eating at my table, using my ceramic spelling spoons for making brownies. I threw the half-eaten slice of pizza back into the box.

"She's falling into old patterns," he said, making me feel even better. "I can see it. She knows it's happening, but she can't stop it. Rachel, Ivy needs you here so she doesn't forget what she wants."

My jaw stiffened when my thoughts swung to our conversation beside his van. After living with Ivy for almost a year, I had seen the marks Piscary's manipulations had left on her thoughts and reactions, though not knowing how they had gotten there. Hearing how bad it had been twisted my stomach. I couldn't believe she'd ever return to it voluntarily, even if Skimmer opened the door and tried to shove her through it. Kisten was overreacting. "Ivy is not going to fall apart because I'm not there. God, Kisten. Give the woman some credit."

"She's vulnerable."

Frowning, I swung my feet to kick repeatedly at the curtains. Jenks had put his ailing plant on the table, and it was looking better already. "She's the most powerful living vampire in Cincinnati," I said.

"Which is why she's vulnerable."

I said nothing, knowing he was right. "It's only a few days," I said, wishing I didn't have to do this over the stinking phone. "We're heading back as soon as we get Nick."

Jenks made a harsh grunt of sound, and I pulled my eyes from his plant. "Since when were we going to get Nick?" he said, his youthful face holding anger. "We came for Jax. We got him. Tomorrow we leave."

Surprised, my eyes widened. "Ah, Kist, can I call you back?"

He sighed, clearly having heard Jenks. "Sure," he said, sounding resigned that I wasn't coming home until Nick was safe. "Talk to you later. Love you."

My heart gave a pound, and I heard the words again in my thoughts. *Love you*. He did. I knew it to the core of my being.

"I love you too," I said softly. I could have breathed it and he would have heard.

The connection broke and I turned the phone off. It needed recharging, and as I gathered my thoughts for the coming argument with Jenks, I dug my adapter out of my bag and plugged it in. I turned, finding Jenks standing in his Peter Pan pose, hands on his hips and his feet spread wide. It had lost its effectiveness now that he was six-feet-four. But seeing as he was still in those black tights, he could stand anyway he wanted.

Rex was on the floor, blinking sleepily up at him with innocent kitten eyes. Jax took the opportunity to dart to the kitchen, alighting on one of the plastic cups in their little cellophane sleeves. Eyes wide, he watched us between bites of the nasty concoction of bee pollen and maple syrup his dad had made for him a moment after we walked in the door.

"I'm not leaving without Nick," I said, forcing my jaw to unclench. *He hadn't left me. He thought I had died. And he needed help.*

Jenks's face hardened. "He lured my son away. He taught him how to be a thief, and not even a good thief. He taught him to be a two-bit crappy thief who got caught!"

I hesitated, unsure if he was upset about the thief part or the bad thief part. Deciding it didn't matter, I took my own Peter Pan pose, pointing aggressively to the parking lot. "That van isn't turning south until we are *all* in it."

From the kitchen, Jax made an attention-getting clatter of wings. "They're going to kill him, Dad. He's all beat up. They want it, and they're going to keep beating on him until he tells them where it is or he dies."

Turning, Jenks scooped Rex up when the small predator realized where Jax was and began stalking him again. "Want what?" he said warily.

Jax froze in his reach for another cake of bee pollen and syrup. "Uh . . ." he stammered, wings moving in blurred spurts.

At that, I collapsed back into my chair and stared at the ceiling. "Look," I said, legs stretched out and tired. "Whatever happened, happened. Jenks, I'm sorry you're mad at Nick, and if you want to sit here and watch TV while I save Nick's ass, I won't think any less of you." His fingers caressing Rex froze, and I knew I'd hit a nerve. "But Nick saved my life," I said, crossing my knees as a feeling of guilt passed through me. *He saved my life, and I shack up with the first guy who shows an interest.* "I can't walk away."

Jenks shifted forward and back, his need to move obvious and odd now that he was full-sized and dressed in that far-too-distracting skintight outfit. Wishing he'd put something on over it, I pulled the map of the area I had bought in the motel office out from under the pizza box and opened it up. The crackle of map paper swung my thoughts to Ivy, and my worry tightened. *Skimmer was sleeping over?*

Skimmer was Piscary's lawyer, out from the West Coast and top of her class, eminently comfortable in using manipulation to get what she wanted. Ivy didn't want a vampiric lifestyle, but Skimmer didn't care. She just wanted Ivy, and if what Kisten had said was true, she didn't mind screwing Ivy's mental state up to get her. That alone was enough to make me hate the intelligent woman.

It hadn't surprised me to find that Skimmer was responsible for part of Ivy's problems. The two had undoubtedly run wild, gaining a reputation for savage bloodletting mixed liberally with aggressive sex. It was no wonder Ivy had twined the emotions of love and the ecstasy of bloodletting together so tightly that they were one in her mind. Back then, she was vulnerable and alone for the first time in her life, with Skimmer undoubtedly more than willing to help her explore the sophisticated vampiric bloodletting techniques Ivy had gained in the time Piscary had been at her. Piscary had probably planned it all, the bastard.

It wasn't a problem for a vampire that bloodletting was a way to show that they loved someone. But by the sounds of it, Piscary twisted that until the stronger Ivy's feelings of love were, the more savage she became. Piscary could take it—hell, he'd made her what she was—but Kisten had left her, and I wouldn't have been surprised if Ivy *had* killed someone she loved in a moment of passion. It would explain why she'd abstained from blood for three years, trying to separate her feelings of love from her blood lust. I wondered if she had, then wondered what kind of a hell Ivy lived in where the more she loved someone, the more likely she would hurt them.

Skimmer had no qualms about her deep affections toward Ivy, and though Ivy clearly loved her back, Skimmer represented everything that she was trying to escape. The more often Ivy shared blood with her past lover, the greater the chance that she would be lured into old patterns, savage bloodletting patterns that would rebound on her with a vengeance if she tried to love someone who wasn't as strong as she.

And I had just walked out, knowing Skimmer would probably step back in. God, I shouldn't have just left like that.

Just a few days, I reassured myself, moving the pizza box to the floor and clicking on the table lamp. "Jax," I said, arranging the map and pushing Jenks's recovering plant to the outskirts. "You said they had him on an island. Which one?"

He might still love me. Do I still love him? Did I ever love him, really? Or had it just been that I loved his acceptance of me?

My bracelet hissed against the map, and Jax flitted close, landing to bring the bitter scent of maple syrup to me. "This one, Ms. Morgan," he said, his voice high. Pollen crumbs fell, and I blew them away when Jax rose to sit on the table lamp's shade. From the corner of my sight I saw Jenks fidget. I couldn't do this with a half-trained pixy. I needed Jenks.

Fingertips brushing the large island in the straits, I felt like Ivy with her maps and markers, planning a run. My motions went still and my focus blurred. It wasn't her need to be organized, I suddenly realized. It was a front to disguise her feelings of inadequacy. "Damn," I whispered. This wasn't good. Ivy was a lot more fragile than she let on. She was a vampire, molded from birth to look to someone for guidance even if she could garner the attention in a room from simply walking in, and could snap my neck with half a thought.

Telling myself that Nick needed me more right now than Ivy needed me to keep her sane, I pushed my worry aside and looked at the island Jax had said Nick was on. According to the fishing pamphlet I took from the front office, Bois Blanc Island had been publicly owned before the Turn. A rather large Were pack had bought everyone else out shortly afterward, making the big island into a hunting/spa kind of thing. Trespassing wasn't a good idea.

Tension quickened my pulse when Jenks put Rex on the bed and edged closer, an odd mix of angsty teen and worried dad. Taking a breath, I said to the map, "I need your help, Jenks. I'll do it without backup if I have to. But every time I do, my ass hits the grass. You're the best operative outside of Ivy that I know. Please? I can't leave him there."

Jenks pulled a straight-backed chair from the kitchen, bumping it over the carpet, and sat down next to me so he could see the map right side up. He glanced at Jax on the lamp, pixy dust sifting upward from the heat of the bulb. I couldn't tell if he was going to help me or not. "What did you two get caught doing, Jax?" he said.

The pixy's wings blurred, and dust drifted from him. "You'll get mad." His tiny features were frightened. It didn't matter that he was an adult in pixy terms, he still looked eight to me.

"I'm already mad," Jenks said, sounding like my dad when I took a week's grounding instead of telling him why I'd been banned from the local roller rink. "Running off with a snapped-winged thief like that. Jax, if you wanted a more exciting life than a gardener, why didn't you tell me? I could have helped, given you the tools you need."

Eyebrows high, I leaned away from the table. I knew the I.S. hadn't taught Jenks the skills that landed him his job with them, but this was unexpected.

"I was never a thief," he said, shooting me a quick look. "But I know things. I found them out the hard way, and Jax doesn't need to."

Jax fidgeted, turning defensive. "I tried," he said, his voice small. "But you wanted me to be a gardener. I didn't want to disappoint you, and it was easier to just go."

Jenks slumped. "I'm sorry," he said, making me wish I was somewhere else. "I only wanted you to be safe. It's not an easy way to live. Look at me; I'm scarred and old, and if I didn't have a garden now, I'd be worthless. I don't want that for you."

Wings blurring, Jax dropped to land before his dad. "Half your scars are from the garden," he protested. "The ones you almost died from. The seasons make me think of death, not life, a slow circle that means nothing. And when Nick asked me to help him, I said yes. I didn't want to tend his stupid plants, I wanted to help him."

I glanced at Jenks in sympathy. He looked like he was dying

inside, seeing his son want what he had and knowing how hard it was going to be.

"Dad," Jax said, rising up until Jenks put up a hand for him to land on. "I know you and Mom want me to be safe, but a garden isn't safe, it's only a more convenient place to die. I want the thrill of the run. I want every day to be different. I don't expect you to understand."

"I understand more than you know," he said, his words shifting his son's wings.

Rex skulked to the pizza box on the floor and stole a crust, running to the kitchen. She hunkered down, gnawing on it as if it was a bone and watching us with big, black, evil eyes. Seeing her, Jenks took a deep breath, and tension brought me straight. He had decided to help me. "Tell me what you two got caught doing. I'll help get Nick out under two conditions."

My pulse quickened, and I found myself tapping my pencil on the table.

"What are they?" Jax asked, a healthy tone of caution mixing with hope.

"One, that you don't take another run until I give you the skills to keep your wings untattered. Nick is dangerous, and I don't want you taken advantage of. I may have raised a runner, but I did *not* raise a thief."

Pixy dust sifted from Jax as he looked from his dad to me and back again in wide-eyed amazement. "What's the other?"

Jenks winced, his ears reddening. "That you don't tell your mother."

I stopped my snicker just in time.

Jax's wings blurred into motion. "Okay," he said, and a zing of adrenaline brought me back to the map. "Nick and I were contracted by a Were pack. These guys."

He dropped from Jenks's hand to land on the island, and my thrill turned to unease. "They wanted a statue," Jax said. "Didn't even know where it was. Nick called up a demon, Dad." Dust sifted to make him look as if he was in a sunbeam. "He called up a demon and the demon told him where it was."

Okay. Now I'm officially worried. "Did the demon show up as a dog and turn into a guy wearing green velveteen and smoked glasses?" I asked, setting my pen down and holding my arms to myself. *Why, Nick? Why are you playing with your soul?*

Jax shook his head, green eyes wide and frightened. "It

showed up as you, Ms. Morgan. Nick was mad and yelled at it. We thought you were dead. It wasn't Big Al. Nick said so."

My first flush of relief turned to a deep worry. A second demon. Better and better. "Then what?" I whispered. Rex jumped into Jenks's lap, nearly giving me a heart attack since I thought she had been going for Jax. How Jenks knew she hadn't been eluded me.

The dust rose and fell from Jax. "The demon, uh, took what they agreed on and told Nick where the statue was. A vampire in Detroit had it. It's older than anything."

Why would a vampire have a Were artifact? I wondered. I glanced at Jenks, his hands keeping Rex from falling over while she inexpertly cleaned her ears.

Jenks puckered his brows, his smooth features trying to wrinkle but not managing it. "What does it do, Jax?" he said, shocking me again with how at odds his youthful face was to the tone of his voice. He looked eighteen; he sounded like he was forty with a bad mortgage.

Jax flushed. "I don't know. But we got it okay. The vampire had been staked in the 1900s, and it was just sitting there, forgotten in the slop."

"So you found it," I prompted. "What's the problem? Why are they hurting him?"

At that, Jax took to the air. Rex's eyes went black for the hunt, and Jenks soothed her, fingertips lost in her orange fur. "Uh," the pixy said, his voice high. "Nick said it wasn't what they said it was. Another pack found out he had it and made a better offer, enough to pay back what the first pack paid him to finance the snatch, plus a whole lot more."

Jenks looked disgusted. "Greedy bastard," he muttered, his jaw clenched.

I took an unhappy breath, leaning into my chair and crossing my arms over my chest. "So he sold it to the second group and the original pack wasn't happy about it?"

Jax shook his head solemnly, slowly drifting downward until his feet hit the map. "No. He said neither of them should have it. We were going to go to the West Coast. He had this guy who could give him a new identity. He was going to get us safe, then give the first pack their money back and walk away from the entire thing."

My face scrunched into a frown. *Right*. He was going to get himself safe, then sell it to the highest bidder online. "Where is it, Jax?" I asked, starting to get angry.

"He didn't tell me. One day it was there, the next it was gone."

In a sudden motion, Rex jumped up onto the table. Adrenaline surged, but Jax rubbed his wings together in a coaxing sound and the kitten padded over.

"It's not at our cabin, though," the small pixy said, standing under the kitten's jaw and stretching to rake his fingers under her chin. "They tore it apart." Stepping out from between Rex's paws, he met my eyes, looking scared. "I don't know where it is, and Nick won't tell. He doesn't want them to have it, Ms. Morgan."

Greedy S.O.B., I thought, wondering why I cared if he loved me or not. "So where's their money?" I asked. "Maybe all they want is that, and they'll let him go."

"They took it." Jax didn't look happy. "They took it the same time they took him. They want the statue. They don't care about the money."

I put my hand on the table to entice Rex to me but all she did was sniff my nails. Jenks curled a long hand under her belly to put her on the floor, where she stared up at him. "And they're here?" Jenks asked, my attention following his to the map.

Jax's head bobbed. "Yup. I can show you exactly where."

My eyes met Jenks's and we exchanged a silent look. This was going to take longer than a simple snatch and dash. "Okay," I said, wondering if there was a phone book in the room. "We're here at least another night, probably through the week. Jax, I want to know everything."

Jax shot almost to the ceiling. "All right!" he shouted, and Jenks glared at him.

"*You* are staying here," he said, his tone thick with parental control, though he looked like a kid himself. His arms were crossed, and the determination in his eyes would have rocked a bulldog back from a bone.

"Like hell I—" Jax made a startled yelp when Jenks snatched him out of the air. My eyes widened. I didn't know what Jenks was worried about. He hadn't slowed at all.

"You will stay *here,*" he barked. "I don't care how old you are, you're still my son. It's too cold for you to be effective, and if you want me to teach you anything, it starts now." He let go of Jax, and the pixy hovered right where Jenks had left him, looking scared. "You have to learn how to read before I can even take you out with me," Jenks muttered.

"Read!" Jax exclaimed. "I get along okay."

Uncomfortable, I rose and stretched, opening drawers until I found the yellow pages. I wanted to know my resources, seeing as we were out of Cincinnati. An island, for God's sake?

"I don't have to know how to read!" Jax sputtered.

"Like hell you don't," Jenks said. "You want this life? That's your choice. I'll teach you what I know, but you're going to earn it!"

I sat at the head of the bed, where I could see them while flipping through the thin pages. It was last year's book, but nothing changed fast in small towns. I slowed when I found a large number of charm shops. I knew there must be a resident population of witches taking advantage of the heavy-duty ley lines in the area.

Jenks's anger vanished as quickly as it had come, and more softly he said, "Jax, if you could read, you could have told us were you were. You could have hitched onto the first bus to Cincy and been home by sunset. You want to know how to pick the locks? Loop the cameras? Bypass security? Show me how bad you want it by learning what will help you the most first."

Jax scowled, slowly descending until his feet settled in a glowing puddle of pixy dust.

"Here." Jenks took the pencil I had left behind and leaned over the map. "This is how you write your name." A few more silent moments. "And that is the alphabet." I frowned at the sharp snap of the pencil being broken, and Jenks held the broken nub of graphite out to Jax. "Remember the song?" he prompted. "Sing it while you practice the letters. And L-M-N-O-P is not one letter, but five. It took me forever to figure that out."

"Dad . . ." Jax whined.

Jenks stood, tilting the lamp shade to better light the map. "There are fifteen makers of locks in the U.S. You want to know which one you're picking before you blow yourself and your runner into the ever-after?"

Making a sharp noise with his wings, Jax started writing.

"Make the letters as big as your feet," Jenks said as he came to see how I was progressing with the phone book. "No one can read your writing unless you do, and that's the entire point."

Guilt in his eyes, Jenks sat beside me, and I shifted so I wouldn't slip into him. From the table by the door came the alphabet song, sounding like a death dirge. "Don't worry about it, Jenks," I said, watching Rex follow him up onto the bed to make tiny jumps over the bedspread to him. "He'll be okay."

"I know he will," he said, the worry settling into his eyes. Rex plopped herself into his lap, and he dropped his gaze. "It's not him I'm worried about," he said softly. "It's you."

"Me?" I looked up from the turning pages.

Jenks wouldn't bring his gaze from the kitten, a puddle of orange in his lap. "I have only a year to get him up to snuff so you'll have backup when I'm gone."

Oh God. "Jenks, you aren't a carton of milk with an expiration date. You look great—"

"Don't," he said softly, eyes on his smooth fingers among Rex's fur. "I've got maybe one more tolerable year. When it goes, it goes fast. It's all right. I want to make sure you're okay, and if he's working for you, he won't be tempted to do anything stupid with Nick again."

I swallowed, forcing the lump out of my throat. I had not gotten him back just to lose him. "Damn it, Jenks," I said as Jax started the alphabet song again. "There's got to be a spell or a charm . . ."

"There isn't." Finally he met my eyes. They held a deep bitterness, touched with anger. "It's the way it is, Rache. I don't want to leave you helpless. Let me do this. He won't let you down, and I'll feel better knowing he won't be working for Nick or the likes of him."

Miserable, I sat beside him, wanting to give him a hug or cry on his shoulder, but apart from that time in front of Terri at the grocery store, he had always jumped when I touched him. "Thanks, Jenks," I said, turning to the pages before he could see my eyes swimming. There was nothing I could say that wouldn't make him and me feel worse.

His grip shifted in Rex's fur, clearly wanting to change the subject. "What do the boat rentals look like?"

Taking a breath, I focused on the time-smeared print. "Okay, but there's still the problem of noise." He looked blankly at me, and I added, "It would be stupid to think they don't watch the water, and it's not like we can just boat up to the beach and not expect to be seen. Even at night there's noise. It carries too well over water."

"We could paddle across," he suggested, and I gave him a telling look.

"Ah, Jenks? It's not a lake, it's a friggin' freshwater ocean. Did you see the size of the tanker going under the bridge when we came into town? The wake from it could tip us. I'm not canoeing it unless your name is Pocahontas. Besides, the ambient light will give us away, first-quarter moon or not. To expect fog is ridiculous."

He made a face, glancing at Jax and clearing his throat to get him to start singing again. "You want to fly it? I lost my wings."

"We're going to swim it." I flipped forward a few pages. "Underwater."

Jenks blinked. "Rache, you gotta stop using that sugar substitute. *Under* the water? Do you know how cold it is?"

"Just listen." I found the page, and after taking Rex off his lap, I dropped the book onto it. It was my turn to hold the cat. She wiggled and squirmed, settling as the warmth of my hands covered her. "Look," I said, charmed when Rex patted at my swinging bracelet. "They have scuba diving off the wrecks, charm enhanced so you don't freeze to death. The water's pretty clear here despite the current, and since they're privately owned, you can take whatever you want off the wrecks. It's a poor man's treasure-hunting excursion."

He snorted. "I've never been swimming, and unless you took a class I wasn't aware of, you don't know how to dive."

"Doesn't matter." I pointed to the half-page ad. "See? They're licensed to take you out regardless of experience. I've heard of these things. They teach you enough so that you don't kill yourself, then you go out with a guide. Once you sign that release form, they're off the hook except for gross negligence."

Eyebrows high, he looked at me. "Gross negligence? As in losing two divers? Won't someone notice when we don't get back on the boat?"

My fingers in Rex's fur moved faster, and she peered up at me with her sweet kitten face. "Well, I wasn't going to try and slip away from them. I, uh, was going to talk to the owner. Maybe arrange something."

Jenks glanced at his son literally hovering over his work, then back to me. "You'd trust a human to keep his mouth shut?"

"God, Jenks. You want me to knock them out and steal their stuff?"

"No," he said, the quickness of his reply telling me he thought I should do just that. Sighing, he frowned. "Let's just say you talk to the owner and they go along with your little stunt. How do you plan on getting back to the mainland with Nick?"

Yeah, there was that. "Maybe they'll give us an extra tank and stuff so we can all swim back. If we can't get to the mainland, we can get to Mackinac Island. Look, you could almost walk underwater to it. From there we can take the ferry to either side of the straits to help confuse our trail." Pleased, I tucked a curl out of my way.

Jenks rose, setting the book next to me on the bed. "It has a lot of ifs."

"It's one big if," I admitted. "But we don't have time for a week's worth of recon, and if we start asking around, they're going to know we're here. It's our best way to get on the island undetected. And I'd rather be out of sight underwater making my escape than on top of the water where they can follow us. We can come up anywhere on shore and disappear."

Jenks snorted. "How very James Bond of you. What if Nick's beat up so bad he can't swim?"

I felt a flush of worry. "Then we steal a boat. It's an island; they must have boats. That's not a bad idea in itself. We could boat all the way to Toledo if we have to. If you have a better idea, I'm listening."

Head down, he shook his head. "It's your run. Just tell me where to stand."

My first wash of relief that he would go along with it was short-lived as I started to make a mental list of what we'd have to do for the prep work. "New sleepy-time potions," I murmured, my fingers soothing Rex into sleep while Jenks went to check on Jax's progress. "A real map. And we need to do the tourist thing; talk to the local fishermen over coffee and find out what the boat patterns are coming off and going to Bois Blanc. You want to do that? You like to talk."

"Tink's panties, you're starting to sound like Ivy," Jenks complained lightly, leaning over the table and pointing out a mistake to Jax. I blinked, then turned from the sight of his eighteen-year-old butt in those black tights of his. *Married pixy—my new mantra.* "And that's not necessarily a bad thing," he added as he straightened.

I looked at the hotel phone, wanting to find out if they were open yet for the season or we would have to hang around a week, but I remained where I was with Rex. It was probably a human-run establishment and would be closed for the night. "No mistakes, Jenks," I said, feeling cold but for where Rex lay. "Nick's life might depend on it."

Eleven

The wind was bitter despite the bright morning sun, and I squinted at the horizon, holding onto the side of the boat as we jostled out to the wreck site. Jenks sat beside me in the lee of the cabin, both amazed and appalled that he could see his breath and wasn't freezing to death. It hadn't seemed this cold when we were on the dock, but it was frigid out here, with the water still holding the cold of ice, even through the rubber of the wet suit. *When in hell were they going to give us our warmth amulets?*

"You okay?" Jenks asked, his voice raised against the chortling engine.

I nodded, taking in his cold-reddened hands wrapped about his lidded coffee, trying to eek out some warmth from it as we bounced on the choppy waves the wind had whipped up. He looked nervous, though I didn't know why. He'd done well at the practice pool yesterday. I patted his knee, and he jumped. Cringing, I turned to watch the other passengers—high school students on a field trip.

We had lucked out yesterday. My call to Marshal's Mackinaw Wrecks got us an afternoon of practice at the high school pool and a place on today's boat. I still hadn't managed to talk to Captain Marshal, and it was down to the wire now. The man, whose day job was as thc high school's swim coach, had been very nice as he treaded water and painstakingly coaxed Jenks in past his knees, but everytime I tried to talk to him about why I wanted to go out on his boat, someone, usually his assistant, interrupted. Before I knew it class was over and Marshal was gone, without my having gotten more than a good look at him in his Speedo and a bad case of the flushing stammers as I tried to gain his attention and his help. The guy probably thought I was a flaky redhead. I knew his assistant, Debbie, did.

Today was the season's first run, traditionally taking out the high school dive team to find what the last winter's storm had unearthed before the currents could cover it again. Come Friday and the first of the fudgies, all the real stuff would be carefully cataloged, and the nails and buttons planted for the tourists would be in place. Ethical? I didn't know. It would be disappointing to spend this much money and have nothing to show for it, even if it was fake.

With his youthful physique, Jenks fit in, looking good in the rented wet suit and his red local-yokel knit hat down tight about his ears. Cheeks ruddy with cold, he sipped at his coffee, so thick with sugar it was syrupy. *God, he looked good enough to eat,* I thought, then flushed and crossed my legs at my knees despite making it harder to keep my balance.

"Want some coffee with your sugar, Jenks?" I asked, and he froze as a wave dropped us.

"You going to ask Captain Speedo before or after you get in the water?" Jenks shot back.

I gave him a soft thwack on his leg to burn off a burst of angst. He didn't jump this time and I felt better, not minding that he was quietly laughing at me.

While Jenks snickered, I turned to Marshal. The captain had been watching me from the corner of his eye since I boarded. Unlike the rest of us in wet suits, he was wearing only a black Speedo and a red windbreaker, his bare, comfortably muscled legs showing goose bumps. Clearly the man was cold but too much of a stud to admit it. Bracing myself against the bouncing waves, I opened my mouth to attract his attention, but Debbie called to him, drawing him away again.

Damn it. I slumped back down in my seat. What in hell was wrong with me?

Forcing my breathing to slow, I waited for his assistant to finish asking him whatever deathly important question she had. The sun glinted prettily on the water, and I found myself thinking this was an ungodly time to be out here, much less awake. Jenks was fine, seeing as he was usually up long before sunrise, and I could hear him muttering, "Nine forty-eight, nine forty-eight," as he tried to shift his internal clock. The thrum of the engine was lulling me into a drowsy state despite the caffeine and the nap Jenks had made me take yesterday.

Trying not to yawn, I straightened, my hand straying to my waist pack with my charms and splat gun safe in their zippy bags. A good deal of yesterday had been spent in the almost unusable kitchen. I'd purchased a disposable copper insert for spelling at a discount store, and Jenks traded maple syrup for everything else I needed to craft the sleepy-time charms and the scent disguise spells.

The paint ball gun shop had been the hardest to find, being "left where the old post office used to be, past the Baptist church that burned down in 'seventy-five, and right at the Higgan's farm turnaround. Can't miss it."

Between yesterday's predive class, grilling Jax for details, my six hours spelling, and the three hours we spent at the Mackinaw Fort doing the tourist thing, I was mentally and physically tired. But the oddest thing by far had been watching Jenks teach Jax how to read.

The little pixy was picking it up faster than I would have thought possible. While I stirred my spells, Jenks and Jax had watched *Sesame Street,* of all things, the music and puppets seemingly making a direct line to the pixy mentality. One song in particular seemed to have wedged itself into my head, the tune-worm settling firmly around my cerebral cortex like an alien from an SF movie.

Seeing my foot tapping to its catchy beat, I stilled it, wondering if I'd be stuck with the tune the rest of the day and what Elmo would find wrong with this situation. The splat gun in my fanny pack? The six-foot pixy beside me? Take your pick, Elmo, and try not to giggle.

Bois Blanc Island was taking on definition, the top of a lighthouse peeking over the trees making me glad I was going in underwater. We had already passed the no-automobile Mackinac Island, and the huge bridge was to the left and behind us, spanning the narrows between the two peninsulas. Yeah, narrows. It stretched over four freakin' miles. An oceangoing tanker was passing under the bridge, looking like a mouse under a chair.

The bridge was enormous, and according to the place mat under my burger last night, it came in only feet shorter in height than Carew Tower, the support towers being five hundred feet up and two hundred feet down to bedrock. It was the third longest suspension bridge in the world, the longest in the western hemisphere. It was a big sucker, claiming five men's lives in its construction, one never found; hitting water at that height was like hitting a cement parking lot. I'd expect to see something like it in a big city, not out in the boonies where moose and wolves crossed the ice in the winter.

I lurched when the thrum of the engine dropped in pitch and the boat slowed, rocking as our own wake rolled under us. The six guys clustered at the back of the boat jostled and pushed, showing off for Debbie, all done up in her rubber wet suit. Her chest looked like a Barbie doll's, whereas mine was more like her little sister Ellie's. I couldn't help but wonder if she was the reason most of the slobbering sacks of hormones had joined the diving club in the first place.

"God, I feel old, Jenks," I whispered, tucking a stray red curl behind an ear.

"Yeah, me too."

Damn it. I wondered if I could jam my foot any farther down my throat. The wind seemed to shift as the boat turned, and Debbie expertly hooked the buoy and tied us off. The diving flag went up the pole, the engine cut out, and the level of excitement grew.

"Divers, listen up!" Marshal said, standing to garner everyone's attention. "Look to your guides. They'll give you your warmth amulets and make sure they're working, though I'm sure you'll sing out once you hit the water if they aren't."

"You got it, Coach," one of the kids sang out in a high falsetto, gaining laughs.

"That's Captain when we're on the water, smartass," Marshal said, flicking a glance at Jenks and me. "Debbie, you take the boys," he said, unzipping his windbreaker. "I'll take Mr. Morgan and his sister."

Not feeling at all bad for the lie on the release form, I stood and the butterflies started.

"Any time, Rache," Jenks muttered, and I thwacked him with my foot.

Two of the boys gave each other high-fives, clustering around the woman in rubber as she comfortably fended off their exuberance. She knew them by name, and it looked like this was an old game. My pulse quickened when the line of tanks got shorter as they unlatched them from the side and spun them to the back of the boat. Everyone seemed to know what to do, even the guy who drove us out there, now settling himself in the bow in the sun with a handheld game.

"Miss?"

I jerked, bringing my attention back to find myself eye-to-chest with Captain Marshal. My God, he was tall. And really, really . . . hairless. Completely. Not a hint of hair on him marred the even honey tone of his skin. No beard. No mustache. No eyebrows, which had bothered me yesterday until I realized that like a lot of professional swimmers, he probably used a potion to remove it. Earth charms aren't very specific, taking off *everything,* which might sound like a good idea, but isn't unless you don't mind being bald. Everywhere.

He was smiling, his brown eyes expectant. The man was in his late twenties by the look of his lean muscled legs, bare to the wind, and the defined abs stacked above his tiny Speedo. Bald looked good on Marshal, I decided. Well-defined legs, wide shoulders, and in between was mmmm-mmmm good. And he was a witch with his own business. *My mother would love this one,* I mused, then grimaced, remembering the last time I'd thought that.

"I'll be your guide today," he said, glancing from me to Jenks, now standing behind me. "We're going to let the dive team get out of the way, and then we'll follow."

"Sounds good," I said, hearing a forced cheerfulness in my voice, but inside I was scrambling. There were too many people. I wanted to ask him privately, but I was running out of time.

"Here's your charms," Marshal continued, handing me a plastic bag with two redwood disks in them. His gaze landed on my neck, still bruised from Karen, and fell away. "They're already invoked. You can put them on now, though you'll be toasty until you get in the water."

"Uh, thanks," I stammered, fingering them through the insulating plastic. They were stickered with his name and license number on one side. All I needed to do was put one on so it touched my skin and even the slight chill from the morning would be gone.

I handed the bag to Jenks, who immediately shook one into his palm, sighing in relief at the warmth. Satisfied they worked, I gave serious consideration to shooting everyone with a sleepy-time charm and just stealing everything. "Um, Mr. Marshal . . ."

He ducked his head, smiling at me to show even white teeth. I could smell the heady scent of redwood coming from him like spice. He made his own charms; I could tell. "Captain Marshal," he said as if it was a joke. "Marshal is my first name."

"Captain Marshal," I amended. "Look, I've got to ask you something."

Debbie called, and he put up a long finger. "Just a sec," he said, and walked away.

"Damn it!" I exclaimed under my breath. "What in hell is wrong with that woman! Can't she do anything without asking him?"

Jenks shrugged, squinting at the morning sun as he took off his knit hat and messed with his gear. "She thinks you like him," he said, and I blinked.

"Miss?"

I jumped and spun when Marshal's hand landed on my shoulder.

He tightened his grip, and I looked into the depth of his brown eyes, surprised. "Ready to go?"

"Uh," I stammered, my gaze flicking behind him to Debbie. She was glaring, adjusting her fins with sharp motions before she fell over the back of the boat. It was just me, Marshal, Jenks, and the guy at the front of the boat hunched over his game in the sun. Yesterday's fiasco at the pool was making a whole lot more sense. "Ah, Marshal? About the dive . . ."

The witch's lips turned up into a smile. "It's okay, Ms. Morgan," he said solicitously. "We'll take it step by step. I know the straits look daunting, but you did well at the pool."

Pooal, I thought, liking his mild accent. "Uh, it's not that," I said as he selected a tank and beckoned me closer. But when I met his eyes, I was shocked to find him grinning at me, more than a hint of attraction in his dark gaze. "Captain Marshal, I'm very sorry," I said flatly. "I should have brought this up earlier. I didn't come out here to dive on the wreck."

"Sit," he said. "Right there so I can get your tank hooked up."

"Captain." He took my shoulders and sat me down, reaching to adjust my gear. "I meant to ask you before we got all the way out here . . ." I looked at Jenks for help, but he was laughing at me. "Damn it," I swore. "I'm sorry, Marshal. I'm out here on false pretenses."

"I'm flattered, Ms. Morgan," Marshal said, glancing up under his hairless eyebrows. "But you paid for a dive on my wreck, and I feel obligated to do my best to fulfill it. If you're going to be in town a few more days, maybe we can have dinner."

My jaw dropped, and I realized why he had been watching me. Oh God. Debbie wasn't the only one who thought I was interested in him. Suddenly I saw my stammering attempts at trying to talk to him in an entirely new way. Jenks snickered, and I felt myself blush.

"Captain Marshal," I said firmly. "I'm not looking for a date."

The man's face slowly lost its expression, his faint smile wrinkles easing to a smooth nothing as he straightened. "I, uh . . . You're not? I thought you two were brother and sister."

"He's my partner," I said, adding a quick, "business partner."

"You like women?" Marshal stammered, backing up a step and looking like he was going to die of embarrassment. "Shit, I hate it when I misread people. God, I'm sorry."

"No, it's not that either." I said, wincing as I pulled the hair out of my mouth, which the wind had tugged from my braid. "You're an attractive man, and any other time I would be salivating at the idea of a private lesson at your pool . . . *pooal* . . . but I need your help."

Marshal zipped his coat up, looking uneasy. I glanced at Jenks and took a breath. "My old boyfriend is on that island, and I need to rescue him without anyone knowing about it."

Smooth features blank, he stared at me, the sun glinting off the top of his head.

"I'm an independent runner," I said, shuffling in my waist pack and handing him one of my black business cards. "A pack of Weres kidnapped my old boyfriend and they're holding him. I need to get over there undetected, and you were in the book. Uh, if I could borrow a second set of gear and tanks for him to swim out with, that would be . . . great. I'm prepared to pay for it. You, uh, have my credit card on file, right?"

Brown eyes blinking, Marshal brought his gaze up from the business card. Squinting, he peered at Jenks, moving his head this way and that like an owl. An intent look came into his eyes, almost predatorial. Jenks backed up a step, and nervous, I watched. "What are you doing?" I finally asked.

"Looking for the camera."

My jaw clenched. "You don't believe me."

"Should I?"

Disgusted, I felt my anger rise. "Look," I said as the wake from a passing ship hit us and the bobbing boat added insult to my clenched stomach. "I could have come out here and shot you all with sleepy-time potions and took what I needed, but I'm asking for your help."

"And because you decided to not break the law means I

should?" he said, feet spread wide against the boat's movement. "Even if I wanted to, I couldn't let you swim off like that. Even if I *believed you,* I wouldn't let you swim off like that. Not only would I lose my license, but you'd probably kill yourself."

"I'm not asking you to break your license," I said belligerently. "I'm asking you to let me borrow a set of gear and tanks."

Marshal ran a hand over his bald head, nearly laughing in anger. "It took me three years to get my license," he said with a mixture of disbelief and frustration. "Three years. That was for the dive business. Add on another four to get my earth magic degree so I could make my own amulets and the boat could be cost effective. You're a selfish little white-bread brat if you think I'm going to jeopardize that because your boyfriend ran off and you want to catch him cheating on you. Everything was given to you, was it? You know nothing about hard work and sacrifice!"

"He did *not* run off with another girl!" I shouted, and the guy at the front of the boat sat up to look at us. Furious, I lowered my voice and stood so I could poke my finger at his chest—if I had the guts. "And don't you *dare* tell me I don't know anything about hard work and sacrifice. I worked for seven years as a peon in the I.S., busted my butt to break my contract with them, and put my life on the line every day trying to make rent! So you can shove your holier-than-thou crap right back up where it came from. My old boyfriend bit off more than he could handle and he needs my help. The Weres took him," I said, pointing to the island, "and you are my best shot at getting over there undetected!"

Seeming taken aback, he hesitated. "Why didn't you just go to the I.S.?"

My lips pressed together, thinking this could go south really fast if he called the I.S. out here with his radio. "Because they're incompetent boobs and rescuing people is what I do for a living," I said, and he eyed me suspiciously, his gaze going to my bruised neck again. "Look, I'm usually better at it then this," I added, refusing to explain the teeth marks. "I'm sort of out of my element up here. I tried to ask you earlier, but *Debbie* kept interfering."

At that, Marshal smirked and relaxed. "Okay. I'm listening."

I glanced at the bow of the boat and the man with his game. *Like he would even notice if a great white shark bit off the back of the boat?* "Thanks," I breathed, sitting down again. Marshal did the same, and Jenks dropped to sit cross-legged where he could see both of us. The sun glinted on his yellow hair, and it was obvious the warmth spell was working: his lips were red again and he was very relaxed, almost basking.

"See," I said, embarrassed, now that I seemed to have my hat in my hand. "My boyfriend, my old boyfriend," I reiterated, flushing, "turns out he's . . ." I couldn't tell him he was a thief. "He recovers things."

"He's a thief," Marshal said, and I blinked. Seeing my muddle, the man snorted. "Let me guess. He stole something from the Weres and got caught."

"No," I said, tucking a windblown strand away. "Actually, he was contracted by them to recover something, and when he found it, he decided to give them their money back and keep it. I need to get him off that island."

Marshal looked at Jenks, who shrugged.

"Fine," I said, feeling stupid. "I don't blame you if you want to take me back to the dock and tell me to get lost in a ley line. But one way or the other I'm going over the side of this boat. I'd rather it be in a wet suit with one of your charms." Eyes squinting, I peered at him. "Could I at least buy a spell from you? So he doesn't freeze on the way back?"

Marshal's smooth face scrunched up. "I'm not licensed to sell my charms, only use them in my work."

My head bobbed, and I felt a finger of relief wedge itself between my heart and the band wrapped about it. "Yeah, me too. How about a trade?"

He leaned toward me, and after meeting my eyes to ask for permission, took a deep sniff of me. I could smell a hint of chlorine on him over his redwood scent. Apparently I smelled witchy enough, since he settled back, satisfied. "What do you have?"

A exhalation of relief slipped from me. Pulling my waist pack around, I dug in it. "Ah, on me? Not much, but I can send you something once I get home. I've got some sleepy-time potions in splat balls and three scent amulets."

Jenks closed his eyes, seeming to soak in the sun. He was smiling.

"Scent amulets?" Marshal said, a hand tracing the line of muscle of his upper arm, hidden under his windbreaker. "When would I ever use one of those?"

Affronted, I froze. "I use them all the time."

"Well, I don't. I bathe every day."

Jenks snickered, and I warmed. "They aren't deodorant

charms," I said, offended. "They disguise your scent so Weres can't follow you."

Marshal glanced from me to the island. "You're serious. Damn, who are you, girl?"

Sitting straighter, I stuck my pasty white hand out, thinking it must be really clammy from the cold damp on the water. "Rachel Morgan, third partner of Vampiric Charms out of Cincinnati. That's Jenks, second partner of the same."

Marshal's hand was warm, and as we shook he gave Jenks a sideways glance, a smile quirking the corner of his lips. I didn't think he believed me yet. "You're the silent partner, eh?" Marshal said, and Jenks cracked an eyelid and let it shut. "You know," he went on, releasing my hand, "I was willing to go along with the joke because you're cute and we don't get many cute witch tourists. But this?" He gestured to the distant island. "Can't we just go to dinner?"

My eyes narrowed. I leaned forward until I was too close for my comfort. "Look, Mr. Captain of the good ship *Lollypop*. I don't *care* if you believe me or not. I *need* to get to the island. I'm *going* over the side of your boat. I want to trade for an extra charm from you so my boyfriend—" I gritted my teeth. "—my *ex*-boyfriend doesn't freeze on the way back. Actually, I want to trade for three, because I don't have any warmth amulets and I think they're pretty cool. The equipment, I'd like to arrange for an extended rental. If I lose them on the way, which is a distinct probability, you can take the price of them off my card. You got it on file."

He looked at me, and I felt queasy from the adrenaline. "Is it real?"

"Yes it's real! It ran through, didn't it?"

Hairless brow furrowed, he eyed me. "How do I know your magic is good? You smell good, but that doesn't mean fish guts."

I looked at Jenks, and he nodded. "He's a pixy," I said, tossing my head to him. "I made him big so he could handle the cold temps up here while we rescued his son." Okay, technically Ceri made the curse, but I could stir rings around this guy.

Marshal seemed impressed, but what he said was, "His son is your boyfriend?"

Exasperated, I felt my hands start to shake with my desire to scream. "No. But Jenks's son was with him. And he's not my boyfriend, he's my former boyfriend."

Exhaling long and slow, Marshal eyed first Jenks, then me. I waited, breath held.

"Bob!" the man shouted to the front of the boat, and I stiffened. "Come on back here and help me get my gear on. I'm going to take Mr. and Ms. Morgan on an extended tour." He looked at me, taking in my obvious relief. "Though I don't know why," he finished softly.

Twelve

I didn't like the cold. I didn't like the feeling of so much water pressing on me. I didn't like that in some way I was connected to the ocean, with nothing between me and it but water. And I really didn't like that I had watched *Jaws* last month on the Classic Channel. Twice.

We had been swimming for some time, caught between the gray of the water surface and the gray of the unseen bottom, deep enough that a passing boat wouldn't clip us but shallow enough that the light still penetrated well. Marshal was clearly on edge about leaving the security of the diving-boat flag, but he was young enough to like breaking the rules when it suited him. I think that was why he was helping me. Life up here couldn't be that exciting.

The claustrophobic feeling of breathing underwater had eased, but I still didn't like it. Marshal had taken a heading from the boat, and all we had to do was follow it using the compass in the air gauge. Jenks had taken point, I was second, and Marshal brought up the rear. It was cold despite the amulets, and the farther we went, the more grateful I was becoming.

Marshal wasn't getting anything out of this but a good story he couldn't tell anyone. He had only asked one thing of me, and I quickly agreed, adding my own request.

He would get us to the island undetected, but he was going to take his equipment back with him. It wasn't that he was worried about losing the investment in his gear, but that Jenks and I might try to swim back through the shipping channel and get ourselves chopped to bait by a tanker. Good enough reason, but I agreed to it not because of my safety, but Marshal's.

I wanted him out of there and safe. He lived here. If I got caught and the Weres suspected he had helped us, they might go after him. I made him promise he'd go back to his boat, finish his dive, and return to the dock as if nothing had happened.

I had asked him to forget me, but I selfishly hoped he wouldn't. It had been fun talking about spells with someone who stirred them for a living. I didn't find that very often.

Slowly the water around me brightened from light reflecting off the rising bottom, and my adrenaline spiked when I realized we'd reached the island. The current had kept the dropoff sharp, and about thirty feet from the shore we stopped, my fins resting on the smooth, fist-sized rocks the bottom was made of.

Step one—check, I thought when I broke the surface, my pulse pounding from the stress of the dive. Marshal had warned us, but it still came as a surprise. Swimming with the sedate pace of a fish sounded easier than it was. My legs felt like rubber and the rest of me like lead.

The return to wind and sound was a shock, and I squinted through my fogged-up mask at the empty shore. Relieved, I edged in until I could sit neck deep in slightly warmer water. Pulling off my mask and mouthpiece, I took in crisp air that didn't taste like plastic.

Jenks was up already, and red pressure lines marked his face. He looked as tired as I felt. Different muscles, I decided. Too cold, perhaps. Marshal came up beside me in an upwelling of bubbles, and I turned to the boat, glad to find its white smear some distance away. The farther it was, the less likely the Weres would think it was a threat.

"You okay?" I asked Jenks, and he nodded, clearly miserable with cold despite the amulet Marshal had given him. Satisfied to simply sit and catch my breath, I scanned the empty shore. It looked peaceful enough, with a few gulls stomping about on the narrow beach, screaming as they weighed the possibility of a snack coming their way.

"I could've flown that in three minutes," Jenks said, wiggling out of his harness.

"Yeah," I said, following suit. "And collapsed from cold halfway to become fish food."

"Jax made it," he said sourly. "And I might collapse from the cold anyway. How do you stand it, Rache? Tink's titties, I think parts of me fell off."

I snorted, removing my gloves to fumble numbly at my belt. With Jenks's help I got out of my own gear and felt a hundred times lighter. Somewhere along the way I'd scratched the healing gashes of my knuckles back open, but my hands were too cold to bleed. I looked at the white-rimmed wounds, thinking I'd never get them healed over at this rate.

Marshal stood, sleek in his custom-designed wet suit of gold and black, his mask resting atop his forehead. "Rachel," he said, his brown eyes worried. "I changed my mind. Leaving you here isn't a good idea."

Jenks glanced at me, and I stifled a sigh, having half expected this. "I appreciate that," I said, lurching to stand and almost falling down again, "but the best way you can help me is to get yourself back out to your boat and finish your day as if you'd never heard of me. If any Weres come sniffing around, tell them you took me out on your boat and I hit you on the head and stole your gear. You didn't go to the I.S. because you were embarrassed."

From beside me, Jenks looked at Marshal's muscular physique, clearly defined under the thick rubber, and chuckled. Marshal's smile widened, the water glinting on his face. "You're really something, Rachel. Maybe—"

Fins and gear in hand, I headed for the beach to get out of my wet suit. "No maybes," I said, not looking back. As my bare feet splashed in the sparkling surf, I dropped everything but my waist pack, reaching for a ley line and not finding one. I wasn't surprised. I had a spindle of ley line energy in my head, but I couldn't make a circle unless I tapped a line. It was limiting, but not debilitating.

"I've got your business card at the boat," Marshal insisted, following me. Jenks was right behind him, his pixy strength letting him carry his gear and our tanks both.

"Burn it?" I suggested. Stumbling on the smooth, fist-sized rocks, I sat down before I fell over. I didn't feel a bit like James Bond as I pulled a rock from under me and tossed it aside.

Jenks dropped everything where I had, then came to sit beside me with a weary sigh. With his help I peeled out of the wet suit, to feel cold and exposed.

Marshal stood awkwardly between me and the water, an obvious target should anyone come out of the nearby woods. "I should have known something was wrong when you wore running tights under your wet suit," he said as the suit came off.

The rocks were cold through the wet spandex, and setting my waist pack on my lap, I unzipped it. Everything was dry inside the zippy bags, and as Jenks got out of his suit, I put my lightweight running shoes on, fingers fumbling from the cold. Marshal's eyes widened at the splat gun peeking from around the rim. Letting him get an eyeful, I handed Jenks his scent disguise amulet, then dropped mine around my neck, tucking it behind the collar of my black two-piece running outfit. Reminded, I took Marshal's warmth charm and extended it to him. Marshal took a breath to protest, and I said, "It's got your name on it."

I nudged Jenks, and he reluctantly handed his over too. While he and I prepared to move, Marshal's expression slowly turned from puzzlement to alarm. It was a lot colder without the amulets, and I felt the wind keenly through the wet spandex. Tension had me stiff when I rolled up the wet suit as best I could and handed it to him.

"This isn't good," Marshal said as he took it and I sat on the rocks and looked up at him.

"No, it isn't," I said, cold, wet, and tired. "But here I am."

Feet shifting on the rocks, his glaze drifted to the splat gun, and while he fidgeted, I handed Jenks his share of the splat balls, which he dropped into a mesh bag hanging from his waist. I had offered to get him his own gun at the shop where I picked up the paint balls to fill with the sleepy-time potions, but he'd wanted the impressive-looking slingshot instead. It fastened to his arm and looked as effective as a crossbow. I was willing to bet he was as accurate with it too.

Ready to go, Jenks stood in a clatter of sliding stones, taking a stick of driftwood and swinging it as if it was a sword. He was gracefully controlled, and Marshal watched for a moment before he extended a hand to help me up. "You're a good witch, right?"

I took it, feeling the warmth and strength behind it. "Despite how it looks? Yes," I said, then tugged the cuff back down over my demon scar. My fingers slipped from his, and he dropped a step away. *I was a white witch, damn it.* Behind me, Jenks thrust and parried, silent but for his feet in the stones. We had to get going, but Marshal stood in front of me, looking sleek in his wet suit, warmth amulets dangling from his fingers.

He looked behind him at his boat and our gear piled on the

shore. Lips tight in decision, he bowed his head and peeled the sticker off an amulet. "Here," he said, handing me the charm.

I blinked, the cold vanishing as my fingers touched it again. "Marshal . . ."

But he was moving, lean muscles bunching as he gathered a handful of equipment and strode to the edge of the vegetation. "Keep them," he said as he dropped the gear in the scrub, then went back for another, second load. "I changed my mind. I thought you were joking about this rescue thing. I can't leave you here without a way off. Your boyfriend can use my gear. I'm going to tell my boys you panicked and made me radio the water taxi to get you back to land. If you have to swim for it, hug Round Island to get to Mackinac Island and take the ferry. You can leave everything in a locker at one of the docks and mail me the key. If you don't swim off, leave everything here, and I'll pick it up the next time we get a good fog."

My heart seemed to swell and my eyes warmed from gratitude. "What about your driver?"

Marshal shrugged, his rubber-clad shoulders looking good as the sun glinted on him. "He'll go along with it. We go way back." His eyes went narrow with worry. "Promise me you won't trying to cross the straits. It's too far."

I nodded, and he handed Jenks his amulet back. "Watch the ferries coming in to Mackinac Island. Especially the ones that hydroplane. They come in fast. There's a second warmth amulet in my gear for your boyfriend. I have it for emergencies." He winced, his hairless eyebrows rising. "This sounds like one."

I didn't know what to say. From beside me, Jenks peeled the sticker from his amulet and fed it to one of the gulls ringing us. It flew squawking away, three more in hot pursuit. "Marshal," I stammered. "You might lose your license." *Best-case scenario.*

"No, I won't. I trust you. You aren't a professional diver, but you're a professional something, and you need a little help. If you have any problem, just dump the gear and swim at the surface. I'd, uh, rather you didn't, though." His brown eyes seemed to flit among the trees. "Something weird has been going on over here, and I don't like it." He smiled, though he still looked worried. "I hope you get your boyfriend back okay."

Relief slipped into me. God, what a nice guy. "Thank you, Marshal," I said, leaning forward and pulling myself up to give him a kiss on the cheek. "Can you reach your boat okay?"

He nodded, discomfited. "I do a lot of free swimming. Piece of cake."

I remembered my stint of swimming in the frozen Ohio River, hoping he would be okay. "Soon as I can, I'll call you to let you know we made it okay and where your stuff is."

"Thanks," he said, head swinging back up to me. "I'd appreciate that. Someday I'm going to track you down, and you're going to tell me what this was all about."

I felt a sloppy smile come over me. "It's a date. But then I'll have to kill you."

Laughing, he turned to go, then hesitated, the sun glinting on his suit. "Burn your card?"

Brushing my wet hair back, I nodded.

"Okay." This time he didn't stop. As I watched, he waded into the surf, diving into a wave and starting for his boat with clean, smooth strokes.

"*Now* I feel like James Bond," I said, and Jenks laughed.

"Into the woods," Jenks said, and with a last backward look at Marshal, I headed for the scrub. The smooth rocks were hard to walk on, and I felt like an idiot wobbling after him. It was warmer without the wind, and after only a few steps the beach turned into a thick brush.

The first of the spring-green leaves closed over us, and as I picked my way through the vegetation, Jenks asked, "Do you like him?"

"No," I said immediately, feeling the tension of a lie. How could I not? He was risking his livelihood, and maybe his life.

"He's a witch," Jenks offered, as if that was all it took.

Toying with the idea of letting the stick I was holding fling back to slap him, I said, "Jenks, stop being my mother."

The brush thinned as we forced our way into the interior and the trees grew larger.

"I think you like him," Jenks persisted. "He's got a nice body."

My breath came quick. "Okay, I like him," I admitted. "But it takes more than a nice body, Jenks. Jeez, I do have a *little* depth. You've got a great body, and you don't see me trying to get into your Fruit of the Looms."

He reddened at that, and finally breaking through into a clearing, I stopped, trying to find my sense of direction. "Which way do you think the compound is, anyway?"

Jenks was better than a compass, and he pointed. "Want to run until we get close?"

I nodded. Jenks was wearing Marshal's warmth amulet and looked toasty, but it was too much for me. Without it I felt sluggish, and I hoped I didn't hurt myself until I warmed up. Between Jax and the old plot map in the local museum, we had a good layout of the island.

Jenks ran a finger between his heel and his shoe before taking a deep breath and breaking into a slow lope that wouldn't stress us too much and would give us time to dodge obstacles instead of running into them. Jax had said most of the buildings in use were by the island's lakes; that's where we were headed. I thought of Marshal swimming for his boat and hoped he was okay.

As usual, Jenks took point, leaping over decaying logs and dodging boulders the size of a small car, which had been dumped by the last glacier. He looked good running ahead of me, and I wondered if he would run a few laps with me at the zoo before I switched him back. I could use the morale boost of being seen with him. It was quiet, with only birds and animals disturbing the morning. A jay saw us, screaming as it followed until losing interest. A plane droned overhead, and the wind kept the tops of the trees moving. I could smell spring everywhere, and I felt as if we had slipped back in time with the clear air, the bright sun, and the spooked deer.

The island had been privately owned since forever, never developed from its original temperate-zone mix of softwood forest and meadow. Officially it was now a private hunters' retreat, patterned after Isle Royale farther north, but instead of real wolves tracking down moose, it was Weres sporting with white-tailed deer.

During a careful questioning, Jenks and I had found that the locals didn't think highly of either the year-round residents or the visitors who passed through their town on the way to the island, never taking the time for a meal or to fill up their gas tank. One man told Jenks they had to restock the deer every year since the animals could and did swim for the mainland—which made me all warm and fuzzy inside.

According to the records and what little Jax told us, a primitive road circled the island. I was breathing hard but moving well when we found it, and Jenks cut a hard right as soon as we crossed it. He slowed too, but we still ran right into the deer carcass.

Jenks jerked to a stop, and I plowed into him, pinwheeling to keep from falling into the hollowed-out body, its head flung over its back and its eyes cloudy.

"Holy crap," he swore, panting as he backed up, white-faced. "It's a deer, isn't it?"

I nodded, transfixed and breathing heavily. There was surprisingly little smell since the temperatures had been keeping the decomposition slow. But what worried me was that it had been gutted, the entrails eaten first and the rest remaining as a slow smorgasbord.

"Let's get out of here," I said, thinking that even though the Weres were on a private island, they were doing their entire species a great disservice. Remembering and honoring your heritage was one thing. Going wild was another.

We backed away, the low growl rumbling up from behind us pulling me to a heart-pounding halt. *Damn*. From the other side came a high yip. *Double damn*. Adrenaline pulsed through me, making my head hurt and my hand drop to the reassuring feel of my splat gun. Jenks turned, putting his back to mine. *Shit. Why couldn't anything be easy?*

"Where are they?" I whispered, bewildered. The clearing looked empty.

"Rache?" Jenks said. "My size recognition might be off, but I think it's a real wolf."

I followed his gaze, but I didn't see anything until it moved. My first flush of fear redoubled. A Were, I could reason with, shouting things like I.S. investigations, paperwork, and news crews, but what could you say to a wolf whose kill you ran into? And what in hell were they doing with real wolves? God, I didn't want to know.

"Get your ass up a tree," I said, fixed on the yellow orbs watching me. My gun was in my hand, arms extended and stiff.

"They're too thin," he whispered. "And I've got your back."

My gut clenched. Three more wolves came skulking out from the brush, snarling at each other as they closed the distance. It was a clear indication that we should leave, but there was nowhere to go. "How good are you with that slingshot?" I said loudly, hoping the sound of our voices would chase them off. *Ri-i-i-ight*.

I heard a low thrum of vibrating rubber, and the closest wolf yipped, shying before it snapped at its pack mate. "It didn't break against the fur," Jenks said. "Maybe if they're closer."

I licked my lips, my grip on my gun tightening. Crap, I didn't want to waste my spells on wolves, but I didn't want to end up like that deer either. They weren't afraid of people. And what that likely meant gave me an unsettled feeling. They'd been running with Weres.

My pulse jackhammered when the nearest wolf started an unnerving pace to me. The memory of Karen pinning me to the floor and choking me into unconsciousness raced through me. Oh God, these wolves wouldn't pull their punches. I couldn't make a protective circle.

"Use 'em, Rache!" Jenks exclaimed, his back to mine. "We've got three more coming from my side!"

Adrenaline burned, tripping me into an unreal high of the calm-of-battle. I exhaled and squeezed the trigger, aiming for the nose. The nearest wolf yelped, then dropped in its tracks. The rest charged. I gasped, praying the compressed air would hold out as I continued to shoot.

"Stop!" shouted a distant masculine voice. The sound of tearing bushes spun me.

"Rachel!" Jenks cried, falling away.

A black shadow crashed into me. I screamed, clenched into a ball as I hit the ground. Leaf mold hit my cheek. The musky scent of Were filled my senses. The memory of Karen's teeth on my neck paralyzed me. "They're alive!" I shouted, covering my face. "Damn it, don't hurt me, they're alive!" This wasn't an alpha contest, but an attack in the woods, and I could be as scared as I wanted.

"Randy, stand down!" the masculine voice shouted.

I still had my gun. I still had my gun. The thought of it slid through my panic. I could plug the son of a bitch if I needed to, but putting him down might not be the best way to go about this. Now that we were found, I'd rather talk my way out of it.

The Were standing over me grabbed my shoulder in his mouth, and I almost lost it. "I submit!" I shouted, knowing it would likely trigger a different set of reactions. My hand still gripped my gun, and if things didn't change really fast, I was going to drop him.

"Get off her," Jenks said, his voice low and controlled. "Now."

All I could see was werewolf hair, long, brown, and silky. The heat from him was a moist wave of musk. I shook from the adrenaline as the Were snarled, my shoulder still in its mouth. I heard three pairs of people feet come to a thumping halt around us.

"What is he?" I heard one whisper.

"He's going to be a chew toy if he doesn't put that slingshot down," another answered.

I took a breath, willing myself to stop trembling. "If this moldy wolf hide doesn't get off me, I'm going to *spell him!*" I shouted, hoping my voice wasn't shaking.

The Were growled, and I couldn't help but shriek, "I'll do it!" when his grip tightened.

"Randy, get your wormy ass off her!" the first voice exclaimed. "She's right. They aren't dead; they're knocked out. Stand down!"

The pressure on my shoulder increased, then vanished. Hand on my shoulder, I sat up, trying not to shake as I took in the clearing. It was full of downed wolves and Weres, all but one in their people shift.

Jenks was surrounded by three Weres in brown fatigues holding conventional weapons. I didn't know what they were, but they looked big enough to leave holes. He still hadn't lowered his arm with the slingshot on it, and it was pointed at a fourth Were standing a little apart from everyone else. *He* didn't have a drawn weapon, but it was clear he was in charge since he had a shiny little emblem on his cap instead of a patch like everyone else. He looked older too. There was a pistol in a holster on his belt, and brown face paint marked his skin. Swell, I'd fallen into a freaking survivalist group. Just peachy damn keen.

The Were that had pinned me was nosing the three downed wolves. In the nearby distance a wolf howled, and I shivered, pulling my legs straight. "Can I stand up?"

The Were with the emblem on his hat snorted. "I don't know, ma'am. Can you?"

Funny, funny man. Taking that as permission, I sullenly got to my feet, brushing the sticks and leaf mold off. He had a twang to his voice, as if having grown up in the South.

"Your weapon?" he said, eyes tracking my movements. "And the bag and any charms."

I debated for all of three seconds, then emptied the chamber and broke all the balls underfoot before tossing it. He caught it with an easy grace, an amused smile on him. His gaze lingered on my neck and the clearly Were bite marks, and I made a face of exasperation. God! Maybe I should have worn a turtleneck to storm the rebel fortress.

"Witch?" he said, and I nodded, throwing him my pack and two amulets. I could have given them to Marshal, for all the good they had done me.

"I came for Nick," I said, shivering in the new cold. "What do you want for him?"

The surrounding Weres seemed to relax. Jenks jerked when one reached for his slingshot, and I did nothing when they wrestled him to the ground and took it and his belt pack away, looking like bullies falling on a kid after school. Jaw gritted at the grunts and thumps of fists into flesh, I watched the leader instead, wanting to know whom we faced. He wasn't the alpha, I decided, while his men smacked Jenks into a temporary submission. But by his clean-shaven face and his bearing, he was high up in the pack.

Standing my height in heavy-looking military boots, he made a good-sized Were, well-proportioned and tidy in his fatigues, with narrow shoulders and a body that looked like it was used to running. Trim, not blocky in the least. Maybe late thirties, early forties—his hair was cut too close to his skull to know if it was gray or simply blond.

Jenks shoved the three Weres off him in disgust and got to his feet, a sullen, beaten pixy. He was bleeding from a scratch on his forehead, and his face went ashen when he saw the blood on his hands. With that, he lost all his will to fight, obediently wobbling into place behind me when we were encouraged to head back to the road.

Time to go meet the boss.

Thirteen

As we jostled down the shaded road, the wind from our passage dried my sweat and made my curls into lank tangles. Jenks and I were in the back of the open-aired Hummer—whoo-hoo, a convertible—the Were with the pin on his black cap sitting opposite us along with three other guys, weapons pointed. It was kind of sad, really, as it wouldn't take much to wrestle one away and fall out of the vehicle if I wanted to risk being shot. But Jenks was bleeding from a scalp wound, shaking as he sat beside me, his hand pressing the clean bandage they gave him against it. It hadn't looked bad when I first saw it, but by his reaction, he'd be dead in five minutes. I wanted to see how bad it was before we did anything spectacular.

The Were in wolf's clothing was up front with the driver, squinting against the wind, his tongue hanging out. It would have been funny if it hadn't been for the guns.

"Do they have to drive so fast?" I muttered to Jenks. "There're deer out here."

The guy in charge met my eyes. They were brown, pretty in the flickering light coming through the skimpy tree cover and reminding me of David's boss, being both everywhere and nowhere at the same time.

"They don't move much 'cept for dusk, ma'am," he said, and I bobbed my head. *Especially if they're dead and gutted,* I thought sourly.

Not really caring, I turned away. What I'd wanted to know had been answered; he wasn't adverse to Jenks and me talking. I didn't know if we were prisoners or guests. But there were those weapons . . .

Mr. I'm-in-charge adjusted his cap, then jiggled the driver's elbow, pointing to the radio. "Hey," he drawled into the mike after the driver passed it to him. "Somebody pick up."

After a moment a slurred, crackling "What?" came back.

The man's thin lips went thinner. "Three of Aretha's pack are down at Saturday's kill. I want a tank truck out there—now. Get a full data spread before you douse them."

"I don't have any saltwater made up," whoever it was complained. "No one told me we were collecting data this month."

"That's because we aren't," he answered, anger growing in his face, though it wasn't in his slow speech. "But they're down, and since Aretha has pups in her, I want an ultrasound. And be careful. They're riled up and likely to be unpredictable."

"An ultrasound?" came an indignant voice. "Who the hell is this?"

"This here is Brett," he drawled, shifting his cap farther back and squinting at the sun. We hit a bump, and I clutched at a support post. "Who the hell is this?"

There was no answer except static, and I snickered, glad I wasn't the only one in trouble. "So," I said when Brett gave the mike to the driver and settled back. "Are you a survivalist group or a wolf research station?"

"Both." He shifted his brown eyes between Jenks and me. The large pixy had his head bowed over his knees, ignoring everyone in his effort to keep his hand to his wound.

I pulled a strand of hair out of my mouth, wishing I had on more than my black tights. I looked like a thief, and the men surrounding me were getting their money's worth. They were in baggy camouflage, and from what I could see, each had a Celtic knot tattooed in the arch of their ears that matched the emblems on their hats. *Huh.*

Most packs had a tattoo that all members subscribed to, but they usually put them in a more traditional place. Weres loved body decoration, standing in stark contrast to vamps, who shunned getting ink even if a parlor would give them any. It seemed that pain was part of the mystique, and since vamps could turn pain into pleasure, it was a rare artist who would work on vamps, living or dead. But Weres indulged themselves freely, and the best artists could run on four feet as well as two. I was glad David hadn't brought up the idea of a pack tattoo.

Jenks was starting to hyperventilate, and I put a hand on his shoulder. "Take it easy, Jenks," I soothed, growing anxious when the light brightened and we slowed, easing into a pleasant-looking compound. There was a lake nearby, with a mishmash of small cabins and larger homes surrounding it, well-tended dirt paths everywhere. "I'll get you something as soon as we stop."

"You will?" he said, tilting his head to meet my eyes. "You'll fix it?"

I nearly laughed at his panicked expression until I remembered it was a pixy wife's ancestral duty to keep her mate alive and no one else's—and Matalina wasn't here.

"Matalina won't mind," I said, then wondered. "Will she?"

His eighteen-year-old features scrunched into relief. "No. I didn't want to assume—"

"Good Lord, Jenks," I said, weight shifting when we stopped. "It's no big deal."

Brett's eyes were bright in speculation at the exchange, and he made us remain seated until everyone else got out. The Were in wolf's clothing was last, and as soon as Jenks and my feet hit the parking lot, Brett directed us to head to the lake. The people who saw us were curious, but the only ones stopping to watch wore either bright flamboyant clothes or casual business attire, both of which looked out of place among the predominant fatigues. Clearly they were not military, and I wondered what they were doing there. Everyone was on two feet, which wasn't surprising since it seemed there were two or possibly three packs on the island—three *big* packs—and when packs mixed, fur flew if they didn't stay people.

It was highly unusual to have Were packs mixing like this. Indeed, I could see it in the thinly veiled disdain that the Weres in fatigues showed the street Weres, and the belligerent why-should-I-care-what-you-think attitude of the colorfully dressed pack in response.

Chickadees called in the chill spring air, and the sun was dappled through the pale green leaves of the saplings. It was a nice spot, but something smelled rank. Literally. And it wasn't the breath of the Were padding on four feet to my right.

My worried gaze followed Jenks's to the lake. Logs were arranged in a circle around a large defunct bonfire, and I could faintly smell the acidic odor of hurt and pain over the scent of old ash. All of a sudden I did *not* want to go over there.

Jenks stiffened, nostrils flaring. He dug in his heels with a defiant clench to his jaw. Tension slammed into me, and every man with a weapon tightened his grip as we came to a collective halt. The Were on four feet growled, ears flat and his lip curled to show white teeth.

"Now y'all just ease down," Brett said softly, cautiously evaluating Jenks's resolve and rocking back. "We aren't going to the pit. Mr. Vincent will want to see you." He cocked his head at the driver. "Put them in the living room, get them a med kit, and back off."

My eyebrows rose, and the men surrounding us with their matching fatigues and cute caps looked among themselves, their grips on their weapons shifting. "Sir?" the driver stammered, clearly not wanting to, and Brett's eyes narrowed.

"You got a problem?" he said, his slow drawl making twice as many syllables as was warranted. "Or is security for a witch and a—whatever he is—beyond you?"

"I can't leave them alone in Mr. Vincent's living room," the driver said, clearly worried.

A Jeep with a milky-white tank and coiled hose was leaving, and Brett smiled, squinting in the sun. "Deal with it," he said. "And next time, don't start to Were 'less I tell you. Besides, he looks smart," he added, indicating Jenks, "and right quiet. A gentleman. So I'm willing to wager he won't be doing anything rash." His amiable demeanor fell away to leave a hardened will. "Capiche?" he said to Jenks, every drop of casual country boy gone.

Jenks nodded, his face both serious and scared. I didn't care if this was their standard good cop/bad cop ploy as long as I didn't have to go to the lake. Relieved, I smiled at Brett, not having to fake my gratitude. In the brighter light at the outskirts of the parking lot, I could tell that his hair was silver with age, not sunlight, putting him closer to forty than thirty. Brett's answering smile made his face wrinkle, his eyes amused as he clearly realized I was playing the grateful captive and not as helpless as I let on.

"Randy?" he said, and the Were on four feet pricked his ears. "You're with me." Turning on a heel, he strode to the second largest building off the lot, the pony-sized Were trotting beside him. The driver watched them go, his lips moving in an unheard curse. With obvious anger he jerked his weapon, indicating we should take an alternate path. Jenks and I fell into step before they could touch us. *Time for a little bad cop?*

We were headed away from the pit, but I didn't feel much better. The walkway was made of flat slate, and Jenks's running shoes were silent beside mine. The Weres scuffed in their boots behind us. The building we were headed for looked like it had been built in the seventies, low-slung and made out of a salmon-colored stone, with high small windows that overlooked the lake. The middle section was taller, and I imagined it had vaulted ceilings since it wasn't quite high enough for a full second story. I slowed as I approached the entryway, thinking the massive wood and steel door looked like it belonged to a vault.

"You want me to just walk in?" I asked, hesitating.

He sneered, clearly not happy about his boss reprimanding him by giving him an awkward task that, if we ran, he would be punished for. Not to mention Brett had taken with him the only member of his team that might have a chance of catching us.

Taking that as a yes, Jenks reached in front of me to pull the door open, leaving his blood behind on it. It would be a good marker of where we were for someone looking if they forgot to clean it off. I don't think anyone even noticed, and we slipped inside.

"Down the hall and to the left," the driver said, gesturing with the butt of his weapon.

I was tired of his attitude; it wasn't my fault Brett was mad at him. I took Jenks's elbow—apparently the sight of his blood was making him woozy again—and led the way past sterile walls to a bright spot at the end of the hall. It was clearly a living room, and I evaluated it for possibilities while the driver had a hushed conversation with the armed sentry in the archway. More weapons, but no face paint or insignia on them this time apart from the tattoo.

The low ceilings of the hallway gave rise to that story and a half I had noticed from outside. To my right a bank of windows opened onto an enclosed courtyard landscaped with shrubs and a formal fountain. To my left was the exterior wall facing the lake, a catwalk tucked under the high windows. Defense was written all over the sunken room, and my mind pinged on my first idea—that this was a survivalist's group. I was willing to bet that when they left us alone, someone would still be watching, so it was no surprise when Jenks muttered, "There are six cameras in here. I can't place them all, but I can hear their different frequencies."

"No kidding," I said, eyes roving but seeing nothing in the plush sunken living room with two opposing couches, a coffee table, two chairs by the windows, and what I thought was a modest entertainment center until I realized it held two huge flat screen TV's, three satellite boxes, and a computer that would have made Ivy salivate.

I followed Jenks down the shallow step to sit at the couch, farthest in, barking out a derisive, "Hurry up with that first-aid kit," when the driver hustled everyone out.

He hefted his rifle in a show of aggression, and I gave him a simpering smile. "Right," I said, flopping on the couch and stretching my arms out along the top of it. "You're going to plug me in your boss's living room and get blood all over his carpet because I was snippy. Do you know how hard it is to get blood out of carpet? Be a good little pup and do what you're told."

Jenks fidgeted, and the man flashed red, his jaw muscles clenching. "You keep backing into your corner," he said as he lowered his weapon. "When it comes to it, I'll be there."

"Whatever." I looked at the ceiling, baring my already bruised throat to him though my gut twisted. With Weres, your rank determined how you were treated, and I wanted to be treated well. So I was going to be a bitch in more than one definition of the word.

I never heard him leave, but I let out my held breath when Jenks relaxed. "He's gone?" I whispered, and he made an exasperated face.

"Tink's panties, Rache," he said, sitting on the edge of the couch beside me and putting his elbow on his knee. "That was rash even for you."

I brought my head back down to look at him. Surrounded by carpet and walls, I could smell the lake on me, and I ran a hand through my tangled damp curls, getting my fingers stuck. I thought about pushing his elbow off his knee, but didn't since he was still bleeding. Instead I sat up and reached for the bandage pressed against his head.

"Don't," he said, sounding frantic as he drew back.

Lips pursed, I glared about the room at the unseen cameras. "Where's my damn first-aid kit!" I shouted. "Someone better bring me my kit, or I'm going to get pissed!"

"Rache," Jenks protested. "I don't want to see the pit. It smelled awful."

Seeing his worry, I tried to smile. "Believe me, I'm trying to stay out of it. But if we act like prey, they'll treat us like a wounded antelope. You've watched Animal Planet, right?"

We both looked up when a small girl dressed in jeans and a sweater came in from the room's only door. She had a tackle box in her hand, and she silently set it on the table before Jenks and me. Not meeting our eyes, she backed three steps away before turning around.

"Thank you," I said. Never stopping, she looked over her shoulder, clearly surprised.

"You're welcome," she said, stumbling on the step up out of the sunken area. Her ears went red, and I guessed she was no more than thirteen. Life was good in a traditional Were pack if you were on top, crap if you were on the bottom, and I wondered where she fit in.

Jenks made a rude sound, and I opened it up to find the usual stuff—minus anything sharp and pointy. "So why were you nice to her?" he asked.

I dug until I found a good sized bandage and a packet of antiseptic wipes. "Because she was nice to me." Pushing the tackle box aside to make room on the table, I sat sideways. "Now, are you going to be nice to me, or am I going to have to get bitchy?"

He took a deep breath, astonishing me when he went solemn and worried. "Okay," he said, slowly peeling the bandage away. Eyes fixed to the blood on it, he started to breathe fast. I almost smiled, seeing that it was little more than a scratch. Maybe if he was four inches tall and had a thimbleful of blood it might be a problem, but this was nothing. It was still bleeding, though, and I tore open the antiseptic wipes.

"Hold still," I said, pulling away when he fidgeted. "Darn it, Jenks. Hold still. It's not going to hurt that bad. It's just a scrape. The way you're acting, you'd think it was a knife wound that was going to need stitches."

His jerked his gaze from the bloodstained bandage to mine. The light coming in from the courtyard made his eyes very green. "It's not that," he said, reminding me that we were being watched. "No one but Matalina has ever tended me before. Except my mother."

I set my hands on my lap, remembering hearing somewhere that pixies bonded for life. A trickle of blood headed for his eyes, and I reached for it. "You miss Matalina?" I said softly.

Jenks nodded, his gaze going to the rag as I dabbed at his forehead, gently brushing aside his yellow curls. His hair was dry, like straw. "I've never been away from her this long before," he said. "Ten years, and we've never been apart for more than a day."

I couldn't help my twinge of envy. Here I was, tending an eighteen-year-old ready to die and missing his wife. "You're lucky, Jenks," I said softly. "I'd be ecstatic if I could manage a year with the same guy."

"It's hormonal," he said, and I drew away, affronted.

"I think I saw some alcohol in here," I muttered, flipping the tackle box back open.

"I meant between Matalina and me," he said, the rims of his ears reddening. "I feel bad for you, stumbling about searching for love. With Matalina, I just knew."

Making a sour face, I teased out another antiseptic wipe and carefully dabbed his scrape to pick out a leaf chip. "Yeah? Well witches aren't that lucky."

I threw the bloodied pad on the table, and Jenks slumped, going soft and misty-eyed. "I remember the first time I saw her," he said, and I made a *mmmm* of encouragement, seeing that he'd finally quit fidgeting. "I had just left home. I was a country boy. Did you know that?"

"Really?" The bandage I had pulled out was too big, and I rummaged for something smaller. Spotting a Handi Wipe, I gave it to him to clean his fingers with.

"Too much rain and not enough sun," he said as he set his rag aside and opened the package as if it held gossamer. Carefully, he unfolded the cloth. "The garden was bad. I could either fend for myself or take the food out of my sibling's mouth. So I left. Hitched a ride on a produce truck and ended in Cincinnati's farmers' market. I got beat up the first time I trespassed in the streets. I didn't know crap."

"Sorry," I said, deciding that Jenks might take offense at the Barbie Band-Aid and shuffled through until I found a He-Man one. *Just who were they giving first aid to? Kindergarteners?*

"It was just plain luck Matalina found me sleeping under that bluebell plant and not one of her brothers. Luckily she found me, woke me, and tried to kill me in that order. I was even luckier when she let me stay the night, breaking her family's first rule."

I looked up, my tension easing at the love in his eyes. It was shocking to see it there, honest and raw in so young a face.

He gave me a weak smile. "I left before sunup, but when I heard a new housing development was going in near Eden Park, I went to look over the plans. They were putting in lots of landscaping. I asked Matalina to help me, and when the trucks came, we were there. One person can't hold anything, but two can have the world, Rache."

I had a feeling he was trying to tell me more than his words were saying, but I didn't want to listen. "Hold still," I said, pushing his hair out of the way and putting the bandage on. I leaned back, and his bloodied hair fell to hide it. Turning to the table, I gathered my mess into a pile, not knowing what to do with it.

"Thank you," Jenks said softly, and I flicked a glance at him.

"No prob. Matalina stitched me up right nice, so I'm glad to return the favor."

There was a scuffing at the open archway and we turned. A small man in slacks and a red polo shirt had come in, his pace quick and confident—busy, was the impression I got. Two men in fatigues were right behind him. They had pistols in leg holsters, and I stood. Jenks was quick to follow, tossing his stained curls out of his way.

The man's hair was cut close to his head, military style, with a whiteness that stood out in sharp contrast to his deep tan and wind-roughened features. There was no beard or mustache, which didn't surprise me. Presence flowed from him like cologne as he stepped down into the living room, but it wasn't Trent Kalamack's confidence based on manipulation. No, it was a confidence born from knowing he could pin you to the floor and hurt you. He was in his early fifties, I guessed, and I'd dare call him squat and compact. None of it was flab.

"Boss man, I presume?" I whispered, and he came to a jerky halt four feet away, the table between us. His intelligence was obvious as he looked Jenks and me over, fingers fumbling at his shirt pocket for a pair of glasses while we stood there in our thief-black outfits.

The man took a breath and let it out. "Hell," he said to Jenks, his voice rough, as if he smoked a lot. "I've been watching you the last five minutes, and I don't know what you are."

Jenks looked at me and I shrugged, surprised to find him that open and honest. "I'm a pixy," Jenks said, tucking his hand behind his back so the man wouldn't try to shake it.

"By God, a pixy?" he blurted, brown eyes wide. Glancing at me, he put his glasses on, took a breath, and added, "Your work?"

"Yup," I said, reaching out to shake his hand.

My breath hissed and I jerked back when the two men that had come in with him cocked their weapons. I hadn't even seen them pull them.

"*Stand* down!" the man bellowed, and Jenks jumped. It was shockingly loud and deep, carrying the crack of a whip. I watched, heart pounding until the two men lowered their sights. They didn't put the guns away, though. I was starting to hate those little hats of theirs.

"Walter Vincent," the man said, hitting the *t*'s sharp and crisp.

I glanced at the men behind him, then extended my hand again. "Rachel Morgan," I said more confidently than I felt. "And this is Jenks, my partner." This was weird, civilized. *Yes, I've come to rob you, sir. / How delightful; won't you have some tea before you do?*

The Were before me pursed his lips, his white eyebrows going high. I could see his thoughts jumping and I found myself thinking he had a rugged attractiveness despite his age, and that he was likely going to have someone hurt me. I was a sucker for a smart man, especially when the brains came packaged in a body that was carefully maintained.

"Rachel Morgan," he said, his voice rising and falling in amazement. "I've heard of you, if you can believe it. Though Mr. Sparagmos is of the belief that you're dead."

My heart gave one hard beat. *Nick was here. He was alive.* I licked my lips, suddenly nervous. "It was only a bad hair day, but try telling that to the media." I exhaled, never looking away, knowing I was challenging him but feeling I had to. "I'm not leaving without him."

Head bobbing, Walter backed up two quick steps. The men behind him had a better shot at me, and my heart found a faster pace. Jenks didn't move, but I heard his breathing quicken.

"Truer words may never have been spoken," Walter said. It was a threat, and I didn't like the complete unconcern in his voice. Jenks moved to stand beside me, and the tension rose.

A small man in fatigues silently came in with a sheet of paper, distracting him. Walter's eyes slowly slid from me, and my pent-up shudder broke free. My lips pressed together in annoyance that he had gotten to me. Walter stood by the wide window, light spilling in over him and his paper as he squinted at it. While reading, he pointed to the first-aid kit, and silently the man collected it all and left.

"Rachel Morgan, independent runner and equal third holder in Vampiric Charms," Walter said. "Broke from the I.S. last June and survived?" His attention came back to me. Curiosity high in his rugged, tanned face, he sat in an overstuffed chair and let the paper fall to the floor. No one picked it up. I glanced at it, seeing a blurry shot of me with my hair all over the place and my lips parted like I was on Brimstone. I frowned, not remembering it being taken.

Walter put an ankle on one knee, and I pulled my gaze up, waiting.

"Only someone very smart or very wealthy survives an I.S. death threat," he said, thick powerful fingers steepled. "You aren't smart, seeing as we caught you, and you clearly work for your bread and butter. Being from Cincinnati, you're logically one of Kalamack's more attractive sacrificial sheep."

I took an angry breath, and Jenks caught my elbow, jerking me back. "I don't work for Trent," I said, feeling myself warm. "I broke my I.S. contract on my own. He had nothing to do with it, except that I paid for my freedom by almost nailing his ass for trafficking in biodrugs."

Walter smiled to show me small white teeth. "Says here you had breakfast with him last December after a night on the town."

My flush of anger turned to one of embarrassment. "I was suffering from hypothermia and he didn't want to drop me at the hospital or my office." One would have gotten the law involved, the other my roommate, both to be avoided if one's name was Kalamack.

"Exactly." Walter leaned forward, his eyes fixed on mine. "You saved his life."

Rubbing my fingers into my forehead, I said, "It was a one shot deal. Maybe if I had been thinking I would've let him drown, but then I would've had to give the ten thousand back."

Walter was smug as he leaned into his chair by the window, the sun glinting on his white hair. "The question you will answer is how did Kalamack find out about the artifact's existence, much less that someone knew where it was and where that person is?"

Slowly I sat on the edge of the couch, feeling sick. Jenks moved to the other side of the coffee table, sitting to watch my back, Walter, and the door all at the same time. Male Weres were known to cut females of any species a lot of slack since their hormones guided their thoughts, but eventually logic would kick in and things were going to get nasty. I glanced at the two men by the door, then the plate-glass window. Neither one was a good option. I had nowhere to go.

"I've nothing against you," Walter said, bringing my attention from the possibility of throwing one of them into the glass to break it, thus solving two problems at once. "And I'm willing to let you and your partner go."

Astonished, I stupidly did nothing when the small man pushed up from his chair in a smooth, very fast motion. The two men by the door were already moving. My breath caught and I stifled a gasp when the compact Were was suddenly on me.

"Rache!" Jenks shouted, and I heard the click of safeties. There was a scuffle that ended with his grunt of pain, but I couldn't see him. Walter's face was in the way, calm and calculating, his fingers lightly around my neck, just under my chin. Adrenaline pulsed to make my head hurt. Almost too fast to realize, the older Were had pinned me to the couch.

Heart pounding, I jerked back my first instinct to struggle, though it was hard, really hard. I met his placid brown eyes, and fear struck me. He was so calm, so sure of his dominance. I could smell his aftershave and the rising scent of musk under it as he hung over me, his small but powerful hand under my chin the only place we touched. His pulse was fast and his breathing quick. But his eyes were calm.

I didn't move, knowing it would trigger an entirely new set of ugliness. Jenks would suffer and then me. As long as I didn't do anything, neither would Walter. It was a Were mind game, and though it went against all my instincts, I could play it. My fingers, though, were stiff and my arm was tense, ready to jab his solar plexus even if it did get me shot.

"I'm willing to let you go," he repeated softly, his breath smelling of cinnamon toothpaste and his thick lips hardly moving. "You will return to Kalamack and tell him that it's mine. He won't have it. It belongs to me. Damn elf thinks he can rule the world," he whispered so only I could hear. "It's our turn. They had their chance."

My heart pounded and I felt my pulse lift against his fingers. "Looks to me like it belongs to Nick," I said boldly. *And how had he known Trent was an elf?*

I took a quick breath of air, jerking when he pushed himself away and was suddenly eight feet back. My gaze shot to Jenks. He had been dragged to the middle of the room, and he now held himself to favor his right leg. He gave me an apologetic look he didn't owe me, and the two men holding him let go at a small gesture from Walter. The dry blood in Jenks's his hair was turning a tacky-looking brown, and I forced my eyes from him and back to Walter.

Ruffled, I refused to touch my neck, instead draping my arms over the top of the couch. Inside I was shaking. I didn't like Weres. Either hit me or back off, but this posturing and threats was useless to me.

Exuding confidence and satisfaction, Walter sat, taking the couch opposite me and mirroring me almost exactly. Clearly the

Were wasn't going to break the silence, so I would. It would cost me points in this inane game, but I wanted to see the end of it before the sun went nova. "I don't give a damn about your artifact," I said, voice soft so it wouldn't shake like my hands were threatening to. "And as far as I know, Trent doesn't either. I don't work for him. *Intentionally.* I'm here for Nick. Now . . ." I took a slow breath. ". . . are you going to give him to me, or am I going to have to hurt a few people and take him?"

Instead of laughing, Walter's brow furrowed and he sucked on his teeth. "Kalamack doesn't know," he said flatly, making it a statement, not a question. "Why are you here? Why do you care what happens to Sparagmos?"

I pulled my arms from the couch, putting one hand on my hip and the other gesturing in exasperation. "You know, I asked myself that same question just this morning."

A smile came over the Were, and he glanced to a decorative mirror, presumably two-way. "A rescue of the heart?" he said, and I warmed at the mockery in his voice. "You love him, and he thinks you're dead. Oh, that's classic. But it's stupid enough to be the truth."

I said nothing, gritting my teeth. Jenks shifted closer, and the sentries adjusted the grip on their weapons.

"Pam?" Walter called, and I wasn't surprised when a diminutive woman entered, arms swinging confidently, an amulet dangling from her fingers. She was dressed in lightweight cotton capri pants and a matching blouse, her long black hair coming to her mid-back. Defined eyebrows, thick pouty lips, and a delicate facial bone structure gave me the impression of a china doll. *A very athletic china doll,* I amended when she pointedly dropped the amulet on the coffee table in accusation.

Truth charm, I guessed by the notches on the rim, and I pulled my gaze away from the clatter of it hitting the table. Weres used witch magic more than vamps, and I wondered if it was because they needed the boost of power more than the vamps, or if it was that vamps were so sure of their superiority they felt they didn't need witch magic to compete with the rest of Inderland.

"She's not lying," the woman said, giving me a quick smile that was neither warm nor welcoming. "About anything."

Walter sighed as if it was bad news. "I'm sorry to hear that," he said softly.

Damn. I looked at Jenks. His eyes were wide and he looked anxious. He had heard it too. Something had shifted. *Double damn.*

Six more men came in and Walter stood, curving his arm familiarly about Pam's waist and tugging her closer. "Pit them," he said, sounding regretful, and Jenks stiffened. "I want to know if anyone is coming after her." He smiled at Pam. "Try not to do anything that can't be undone? We may have to give them back to whoever backed her in this. She many not belong to Kalamack, but she belongs to someone."

"Whoa! Wait up," I said, standing. "You'd let me walk out of here if I worked for Trent and was after your stinking statue, but you're going to put me away if all I came for was Nick?"

Jenks groaned, and I froze when Walter and Pam looked to the truth amulet on the table. It shone a nice, friendly green. "And you knew it was a statue, how?" Walter said softly.

Crap on toast. Stupid, *stupid* witch. Now they wouldn't stop until they found out about Jax. I knew Jenks's thoughts were on a similar path when he jiggled on his feet, anxious.

"Find out what they know," Walter said, and a wild look came over Jenks.

I fought to not move as someone put his hands on me, exerting a steadily growing pressure to fall into motion. Brett's stocky figure eased into the archway, his expression clearly saying he thought they were making a mistake. "I'm not going to talk," I said, shaking inside. "There isn't a spell stirred that can make me saying anything, much less the truth."

Walter favored me with a smile that showed his small teeth. "I wasn't planning on using spells to make you talk. We have drugs for that," he said, and I went cold. "Sparagmos has quite a resistance to them and we've since turned to older methods. He's resisting those too, but maybe we can move him by hurting you. All he does is weep when we ask him where the statue is. Pam, will you supervise her interrogation? My ulcer acts up when I hurt a woman."

He started for Brett and the archway, leaving Jenks and me with a room full of weapons. Frantic, I looked from Jenks to Walter standing by the door, giving a quiet set of instructions to Brett. I scanned the room as if for options, finding none.

"If she knows, someone else does too. Find out who," Walter finished.

"Rache?" Jenks whispered, clearly tensed to move but waiting for me to give the word.

"I claim ascension," I said, frightened. *Oh God. Not again. Not on purpose.*

Walter jerked, but it was Pam who spun, her dark hair furling with the motion and her lips parted, a surprised doll with red cheeks.

"I claim the right for pack ascension," I said louder. I wasn't about to fight her, but I could stall for time. Kisten would know something was wrong if I didn't call him in three days. At that point I didn't care if I had to be rescued or not. "I want three days to prepare. You can't touch me," I added for good measure.

Anger pulled Walter's white eyebrows tight, and furrows lined his brow. "You can't," he said. "You aren't a Were, and even if you were, you'd be nothing but a two-bite whore."

Jenks didn't relax, but he was listening, as was everyone in the room. Poised. Waiting.

"I can," I said, shrugging out of the grip of whoever held me. "I do. My pack number is O-C(H) 93AF. And as an alpha, I can claim ascension over whomever in hell I want to. Look me up. I'm in the catalog." Shaking, I gave Pam a shrug I hope she understood meant it was nothing personal. She looked at the bruises on my neck, her eyebrows rising but her thoughts unknown.

"I don't want to front your lousy tick-infested pack," I said, making sure everyone knew where I was coming from. "But I want Nick. If I best your alpha, then I claim him and leave." I took a slow breath. "We all leave. Intact and unharassed."

"No!" Walter barked, and everyone but Pam and I jumped.

Jenks looked worried, his green eyes pinched. "Rache," he said, apparently not caring everyone could hear him. "Remember what happened the last time?"

I shot him a poisonous look. "I won last time," I said hotly.

"By a point of law," he said, jerking to a standstill when he tried to take a step and the men surrounding him threatened violence.

"Jenks," I said patiently, ignoring the pointed weapons. "We can try to fight our way out of some crazy survivalist's group, swim for shore, and hopefully elude them, or I can fight one stinking Were. One way, we end up hurt and with nothing. The other way, I'm the only one who gets hurt, and maybe we walk away from this with Nick. That's all I want."

Jenks's face fell into an unusual expression of hatred that looked wrong on him. "Why?" he whispered. "I don't know why you even care."

I dropped my eyes to the carpet, wondering that myself.

"This isn't a game," Walter said, his round face going red. "Get the medic up here with the drugs. I want to know who sent them and what they know."

The man grabbed me and I tensed.

"Ah, Walter, dear?" Pam said, and everyone in the room froze at the ice in her voice. "What, by Cerberus's balls, are you doing?"

In the silence, Walter turned. "She isn't a Were. I thought—"

His words cut off at Pam's low noise. Her eyes were squinting and her hands were on her hips. "I've been challenged." Her voice got louder. "How am I supposed to walk out of this room and not have every last whining dog think I'm a coward? I don't care if she's a leprechaun and has green tits, she just pissed in my food dish!"

Jenks snickered, making Walter's ears redden. "Sweetie . . ." he coaxed, but he was hunched and submissive. I cocked an eyebrow at Jenks. Maybe I'd been going about Weres all wrong. It was the women who held the balls of the alpha males that really had the power.

"Sugar Pup," he tried again when she pushed his hand off her. "She's stalling for time. I want to know who's coming to bail her out before they get here. She's not a Were, and I don't want to jeopardize gaining the artifact by adhering to old traditions that don't belong anymore."

"It's those traditions that put you where you are now," she said scathingly. "We don't have to give her three days." Pam turned to me, simpering. "We do it now. Think of it as me softening her up. It will be fun. And if she cheats with her magic, the pack can rip her to shreds."

My hope did the proverbial swirl down the crapper. Walter apparently didn't know what to do either as he stood in blank surprise while Pam kissed his cheek, smiling. "Give me twenty minutes to change," she said, then sashayed out.

I looked at Jenks. *Shit.* This was not what I had planned.

Fourteen

Little sun made it past the fragile spring leaves, and I shivered. *It is the cold,* I thought, not the rank smell of ash and emptied bowels or the people joining the noisy throng in twos and threes. And it wasn't that Jenks had his hands cuffed before him. And it couldn't be from the air of a festival growing as everyone gathered to see me get mauled. No, it had to be from the chill May afternoon.

"Yeah, right," I whispered, forcing my hands from my elbows and rocking to my toes to loosen my muscles. The scent of old smoke was strong from the nearby fire pit, almost hiding the rising odor of musk. I had a feeling they would've lit the bonfire to add to the travesty if it had been later. As it was, the people in fatigues and little caps were arranging themselves in small knots in one corner. Across the clearing, the street Weres in their baggy, colorful clothes were more cool as they portrayed an indifference that was fake but effective nonetheless. Between them was the third group, wearing slacks and dresses. They were quietly laughing at the guys in fatigues, but were clearly wary of the rougher, wild cannons the street Weres made with their show of jewelry and loud voices. The excited chatter was getting on my nerves.

Under it was the sensation of gathering power. It tickled through me, and my expression blanked as I slowly recognized the unfamiliar feeling. With thoughts of the fiasco at Mrs. Bryant's running through me, I opened my mind's eye to see the surrounding Weres' auras. My gut twisted as they swam into view.

Crap on toast, I thought, glancing worriedly at Jenks. All three packs had the same sheen of brown rimming their auras. Most

Weres had an outermost haze reflecting the predominant color of their male alphas, and the chance that all three alpha males on the island had brown auras was slim. They were bound into a round under one Were. Damn it, this wasn't fair!

And the bond was strong too, I realized as I scanned the compound for a way out of this. Strong enough to sense, as it hadn't been at David's intervention, which didn't bode well for the upcoming alpha contest. Listening to the jeers and chatter around me, I couldn't help but feel as if the extra strength came from the subordinate members joining it.

Walter wasn't an especially powerful alpha, and I wasn't vain enough to think that they had done this just to see me get torn apart. I was getting the sensation that they had been bound to a common goal for weeks, maybe. Days, at the least.

Disconcerted, I dropped my second sight and stretched where I stood, legs spread wide and bending at the waist to place the flat of my arms against the hard-packed dirt. I had to find a way to break the round or today would be a repeat of Karen without the happy ending.

My butt was in the air, with only my black tights between me and their imaginations, and at a rude laugh, I came up in a slow exhale. I turned to Jenks. They had let him wash the blood off his hair, and his blond mop was in loose ringlets, throwing his green eyes in stark relief. Youthful features pinched, he stood absolutely still for once, and I didn't think it was because of the armed guard. Actually, I was surprised they had him here, but he *was* providing a lot of entertainment and was a curiosity in himself. I could understand their confidence. Even if we got away, how could we escape survivalists, street-racer gangs, and Weres with credit cards?

About the only thing going for me was that my rudimentary ley line skills hadn't made it to Walter's report. I was a strict earth witch, according to it, and seeing as I hadn't made a circle or hit the wolves with anything other than an earth charm, they had no idea I could work the lines too. Just as well. They would have put one of those nasty black ratchet-wristbands on me for fear I'd tap a line through my familiar and make them all toads. That I didn't have a familiar was a mute point. The band would have still made me helpless, robbing me of the energy I had in my chi and spindled in my head. And I wanted to use it.

I looked at my feet and stifled a shiver of nervousness. I'd wanted to turn Jenks his proper size before this got started. Jax waited at the hotel, and as long as it was warm, Jenks could fly back and they could get out of here. This wasn't a rescue anymore; we were down to salvage.

Excitement rose through the surrounding Weres—sending the feeling of sandpaper over the skin of my aura now that I was aware of it—and I followed everyone's attention as Pam made her sedate way to us. Her red robe fluttered about her bare feet, and with her hair flowing about her, she looked exotic, walking under the trees as if belonging to the earth. My muscles tensed, and avoiding her eyes, I went to Jenks for a last word.

"Stop!" one of his guards barked before I had gone three feet, and I froze, hip cocked.

"Give me a break," I said loudly, as if I wasn't shaking inside. "What, by the Turn, do you think I'm going to do?"

Pam's voice rose high, carrying a derision I wasn't sure was aimed at me or the guys with guns. "Let her talk to him," she said. "It may be the last time she has her wits about her."

That's nice, I mused, the threat of their doctor with his needles keeping me quiet.

Pam swayed to a halt before two women. They didn't look enough alike to be friends. The tallest was wearing a well-worn leather halter and classically torn jeans, and the other had on an inappropriate dress suit and heels. Visiting alphas, I guessed.

The four men around Jenks had lowered their weapons a smidge, and I sidled past. I was finding it easier to ignore the barrels pointed at me, though stress had me wound tighter than Ivy's last blind date. "Jenks," I said. "I want to turn you small."

His worry melted into disbelief. "What the hell for?"

I grimaced, wishing the guards weren't hearing this. "You can fly back to the mainland while it's warm, get on a bus, go home, and forget I ever asked you to help me with this. I don't know if I have enough ever-after spindled to invoke both spells, and I can't let you risk being stuck like this if I—" I grimaced. "—if I get hurt," I finished. "I don't think Ceri can reverse the curse herself, so she'd have to twist a new one, and for that she'd need demon blood. . . ." I wanted him to tell me I was being an ass and that he was with me to the end, but I had to offer.

His brow furrowed. "Are you done?" he said softly. I said nothing, and he leaned forward, putting his lips beside my ear. "You're a dumbass witch," he whispered, his words soft but intent, and I smiled. "If I could, I'd pix you for a week for even suggesting I up and leave you here. You're going to unwind that ever-after in your head to Were. Then you're going to pin that woman. And then we will get the hell off this island with Nick.

"I'm your backup," he said, taking a flushed step backward. "Not a come-easy friend who flies away at the first sign of a problem. You need me, witch. You need me to carry Nick if he's unconscious, hotwire the jeep to drive back to the beach, and steal a boat if he can't swim. And Jax is fine," he added. "He's a grown pixy and can take care of himself. I made sure before we left that he knew the number to the church and could read Cincinnati off the bus schedule."

The lines in his face eased, and a crafty glint replaced the hard anger in his eyes. "I don't need to be small to get out of these cuffs." He sent one eyebrow up, turning into a scallywag. "Five seconds, easy."

The wash of relief flowing through me was distressingly short-lived. "But I'm not going to let her pin me," I said. "I'm going to fight until I can't anymore. If I die, you're stuck like this."

His smile widened. "Aw, you aren't going to die," he said mischievously.

"Why? Because you're with me?"

"Ooooh, she can be taught." Hiding his hands from the guards, he bent his thumb, moving it in a stomach-turning disjointedness so the cuffs could slide right off. "Now get out there and get a mouthful of bitch ass," he finished, jiggling his wrists so the metal links fell back in place.

I snorted. "Thanks, Coach," I said, feeling the first fingers of possibility ease my slight headache, but as I looked over the noisy throng, I grew depressed. I did *not* want to do this. It was a demon curse, for God's sake. *And the easiest way to get out of this,* I thought. Ceri had said the payment wouldn't be that bad. The smut would be worth escaping being drugged. I'd seen her make the curse. Nothing had died to make it. *I* was paying the price, not some poor animal or sacrificial person. Was it possible for a curse to be technically black but morally white? Did that make using it right, or was I just a chicken-ass taking the easy way out and rationalizing myself out of a lot of pain?

You can't do anything if you're dead, I told myself, deciding to worry about it later.

Nauseated, I looked over the heads of the growing conglomeration of Weres. The energy coming off them seemed to swirl around me like a fog, making my skin tingle. Okay . . . I was going to be a wolf. I wouldn't be helpless like before. Pam might not feel any pain, but if I got ahold of her neck, she was going down in a modified sleeper.

A quick glace at Pam, and I shook my hands to loosen them. As challenger, it was my place to assume the field first. Breath held, I took five steps into the clearing. The noise increased, and a swift memory of being a contestant in Cincy's illegal rat fights flitted through me and was gone. What was it with me and organized beatings, anyway?

Pam turned. Head high, she smiled at the women with her and touched the shoulder of the one with the most polish in parting. Light on her bare feet, she came forward, the crowd's noise turning softer, more intent. It was easy to see the predator in her despite her diminutive size, and she reminded me of Ivy, though the only similarity was their grace.

"Rache?" Jenks said loudly, the alarm in his voice bringing me around. He pointed with his chin to Walter approaching on the same path his wife had used. There were two men with him: one in a suit, and the youngest in head-to-toe red silk, his walk a jewelry-jangling swagger.

Walter halted at the edge of the circle, and on impulse I opened my second sight. Walter's aura wasn't rimmed in that hazy brown sheen—it was permeated with it. The entire three packs had begun to accept his dominance.

I quickly scanned the other two alpha males' auras. Theirs were clear of Walter's influence, as were their wives', but the visiting alphas had to know it was happening. That they were voluntarily letting him do this to their packs scared the crap out of me. Whatever Nick had stolen must be big for them to bind themselves for so long that Walter was starting to claim them all. It went against all Were tradition and instinct. It just wasn't done.

Walter looked utterly satisfied. He glanced at me, his eyebrows rising as if knowing I could visually see the mental connection he was fixing over another alpha's pack. Smirking, he looked to Pam and gestured.

Pam reached for the tie to her robe. "Wait!" I called, and a ripple of laughter went through them. They thought I was frightened. "I have a spell to Were with, and I don't want to get shot using it."

There was a collective hesitation, and most of the conversations were stilled, the street gang muttering the loudest. I shifted from foot to foot, waiting. Pam recovered smoothly, coming to a halt a good ten feet from me. "You can Were?" she said, a mocking smile on her. "Walter, honey, I didn't think earth witches could do that."

"They can't," he said. "She's lying so she can put a black spell on us."

"I can Were," I said, letting my second sight fade. "It's a ley line, ah, charm, and if I had wanted to put a spell on you, I would have done it already. I'm a white witch." My stomach hurt and I had to go to the bathroom. Oh God. I was a white witch, but it was a black curse. I had sworn I wouldn't, and here I was, jumping head first into the hole. It didn't matter that the black was negligible. It was going to be on my soul. What in *hell* was I doing here?

Walter looked at the crowd when a few called to get on with it. "Pam?" he asked, and the slight woman beamed, playing up to them.

"Challenger's choice," she said, and the assembled Weres cheered.

Walter nodded. "Your choice," he said to me. "Do you want to start on two feet, making part of the contest how fast you can Were, or do you want to Were and then begin?"

"I know what challenger's choice is," I said snottily. "I *have* done this before. And this isn't legal. My alpha isn't here, and there aren't six other alphas to adjudicate in his absence."

Walter's face showed shock for an instant, then he hid it. "We have six alphas," he said.

"*She* doesn't *count*!" I said, pointing, but all they did was laugh at me. *Like I really thought they would do this by the book?*

"We start from four legs," I said softly, knowing she was going to Were fast anyway, so I might as well have a chance to catch my breath before we got on with it.

The crowd liked that, and Pam nonchalantly undid the tie to her robe, letting it slip from her to pool at her feet and leave her stark naked. She looked like a goddess with her perfect tan, standing with one foot slightly before the other. Even her stretch marks added to her image of proud survivor. The noise of the crowd never changed or acknowledged her new, ah, look.

I flushed, dropping my gaze. God help me, I wasn't going to do the same. Jenks's clothes had vanished with even his scars when he turned. I expected it would be the same for me, and I wouldn't show up as a wolf in black tights and a lacy pair of underwear—as amusing as that would be. No way was I going to show them I was a nasty pasty color with freckles.

A shiver of adrenaline went through me. That, the crowd responded to, and I watched a visiting alpha bring her a sheaf of pungent wolf's bane. A murmur of approval rose when she curtly refused. No one offered me any. *Bitches.* Not that it would have helped.

Pam closed her eyes, and my lips parted as she started to change. I'd only seen Hollywood's version, and by God, they had it right. Her features molded, elongating in the face and thinning in the arms and legs in a gross caricature of human and wolf. I had no idea where she was getting the power to shift since Weres couldn't, and didn't, use ley lines to Were like werefoxes did, which was why they could control their size, a talent werewolves envied.

Pam collapsed to her—I guess they were almost haunches now—and propped herself up with her emancipated arms. Her entire skin flashed to black and silky fur appeared. A whine came from her, and her eyes flashed open, still human and grotesque. Her face was ugly, with a long muzzle still holding human teeth. She was neither wolf nor human, caught in the middle and completely helpless. *And damn, it was fast!*

"Rache!" Jenks shouted. "Do something!"

I looked across the cheering Weres to him as Pam fell over into a stiff-legged posture, shaking as her insides rearranged. *Oh yeah.* Heart pounding, I shut my eyes. Immediately the smell of rising musk and the stink of my own sweat struck me. Over it was the smell of maggot-infested flesh from the as yet unseen pit. I didn't think there was anyone still alive in it, but I couldn't tell for sure. The sound of the crowd beat on me, the waves of force coming off them distracting. I put my hands together over my chi and hoped it wasn't going to hurt too badly.

"Lupus," I breathed, my eyelashes fluttering.

I took a breath, eyes flashing open when the ever-after unrolled from my thoughts. Like a scab peeling away, it had a delicious painfulness, a feeling of returning to an earlier state. A sheet of black-stained ever-after filmed me, and I couldn't see clearly. My hearing was gone, wrapped in a muzzy blanket.

My balance shifted and my knees and hands hit the earth, almost seeming to sink. I threw my head back and gasped at the feeling of electricity stacking me differently. But it didn't hurt as the earth charm had when I turned into a mink. This wasn't a cobbling together of parts and pieces, but a pulse of growth from atoms to memories, natural and painless as breathing. I was alive, as if every nerve was feeling for the first time, as if the blood moved for the first time. I was alive. I was here. It was exhilarating.

Head up, I laughed, letting it spill from me, a chortling chuckle, that expanded into a howl. The black ever-after dropped from me and my hearing exploded into existence, filling my ears with the sound of me. I was alive, damn it, not just existing, and everyone would know.

My exuberant howl rose, silencing everyone. In the distance there was an answer. I recognized it. It was Aretha, the wolf we'd met when we first came on the island. She met my voice with her own, telling me she was alive too.

And then the price for me breaking the laws of nature hit me. My voice cut off in a strangled gurgle. Unable to breathe, I fell, clawing at my new muzzle with dull nails. Panicking, I felt the crushing weight of black soak in. I shuddered, and my eye stung as I forgot to close them and I rubbed my face into the earth. Tighter, the band of blackness clenched around my soul.

No! I thought, seeing the gray of unconsciousness tingle at the edge of my sight. I would survive. I wouldn't let it kill me. I could take this. Ceri had, and a thousand times worse. I could do this. But it hurt. It hurt like shame and despair made real.

My will rose, accepting what I had done. Panting, I forced my tongue into my mouth. There was dirt on it, and my teeth were gritty. Shaken, I lay and did nothing, content to feel my lungs work. Everything was in black and white except for the last few feet. I could see color if it was close enough. And as my eyes took in the world while I figured out how to get up, my mind started inventing colors until it seemed natural. The sounds, too, were alien. Piecing them together was beyond me, and what I couldn't decipher retreated into a background hiss.

"Rache!" Jenks shouted, and I winced when my ears flicked backward. Appalled, I felt my tail thump. *This is pathetic.* I held my breath to get up when I found I wasn't coordinated enough to do both at the same time, yet. Frustrated, I staggered to my feet, feeling the new way my muscles worked and nearly falling again.

Pam was still sprawled on the earth, panting as she finished changing. She had to be close; Karen had Wered in about thirty seconds. It was about that now. The scent of ash and decayed flesh was choking. Under it I could smell the packs about me like fingerprints, the scent of gunpowder on some, the stink of grease on others, mild, expensive fragrance on the rest. Pam was a weird mix, her alienness of being part human and part wolf like the taste of rotten eggs in my nose and on my tongue.

I sneezed, just about going over. The crowd gasped, and I suddenly realized they were silent, watching me in a mix of shock and awe. So I had Wered? So what? I had said I could.

"She's red!" someone whispered.

Surprised, I looked at what I could see of myself. *Holy crap, I was!* I was a freaking red wolf, with softly waving red fur that turned black about my feet. *Hey, I was pretty!*

On all fours, I swung my head up to Jenks. His eyes flicked to mine, then out again, telling me to pay attention to what was going on. "She's a red wolf," someone in baggy pants said, shaking his neighbor's arm. "She Wered perfectly." His voice grew in awe. "Look at her! She's a fucking red wolf!"

The murmur was lifted up and repeated, and if a wolf could flush, I did. What did it matter what color I was? All I had to do was pin Pam.

As if hearing my thoughts, Pam surged to her feet in a splurge of motion. She was huge, having retained all her human mass. Lips curling from her long muzzle, she let a soft growl slip from her, her brown eyes fixed on me. My pulse surged and my hind foot slipped back. The crowd cheered at that, hurting my ears. Pam's growl continued, promising me pain. Walter would probably try to stop her from killing me until I gave them the information they wanted, but I doubted he was going to be successful.

"Take your best shot," I barked, and she lunged, the packed dirt spurting out behind her.

Pam's rumble turned aggressive as she halved the distance between us. My thoughts lit on Karen, her jaws around my neck and my crippling fear. But then I saw the pride in her eyes, and something snapped. Under the fur and lean muscle, she was intelligent, and with that comes a knowledge of pain—even if she wouldn't feel it.

I forced my muscles to bunch and darted forward, silent and low to the ground.

We met in a confusion of snapping teeth and stumbling paws. She hadn't expected this, and her reach for my throat landed on my hindquarters. She twisted for my neck, forefeet almost on me. Belly on the ground, I ducked under her and found something to bite. It was a narrow leg of fur and bone. I bit down hard. *I would not die here because of another woman's pride.*

The ugly rasp of bone scraped my teeth like nails on a chalkboard. A yelp of pain burst from her, giving me a surge of hope. *She had felt it?*

Pam fell on me as I took her support away. She rolled and I

backed up on all fours. I was covered in dirt, and by the dull throb, I think she had bit my hip.

The Weres surrounding us screamed their approval, the well-dressed businessmen somehow looking uglier than the men in fatigues brandishing their weapons in salute of their alpha. Jenks looked ready to fly to my side, held back by increasingly lax solders. I wondered why they hadn't taken her pain other than when she Wered, then realized that's what they were after. David's boss had wanted a quick resolution to an office problem. But these Weres?

I scanned their faces as they cheered. They were savage, cocky, and looking for blood. This was not normal Were behavior, even if we were in the woods away from even the pretense of I.S. law. It wasn't just the military and street Weres either. The ones in business suits and dress shoes were in on it. And as Pam and I circled to access the damage, I had a sickening feeling the difference was from all of them binding together in a round. They *all* had the ego of an alpha flowing through them, but lacked the sophistication to deal with it. They were wallowing in the natural high, aggressive as an alpha but without the control.

I'd have been really worried about it if I didn't have Pam to deal with.

Across the clearing, Pam held a foot off the ground, her eyes determined. Crouched low, I snarled. I knew it was a submissive posture, but I wasn't a wolf inside.

"Rache!" Jenks shrilled an instant before Pam attacked. I backpedaled, but she found me. I went limp when her larger jaws gripped my neck and shook me. Pain flamed and my air was cut off. I all but panicked, sending my forefeet to find her eyes. They wouldn't reach.

She shook me again, her strength terrifying. My spine felt like it was on fire. Pain clouded my thoughts. The screams of the watchers beat at me, telling me to submit. Still in her grip, I swung my hind feet up, curling into a ball. I dug at her face, desperate. She yelped when I found her eyes, flinging me spinning to the feet of the watchers.

"Rachel!" Jenks cried, and I got to my feet, shaking.

"Get Nick!" I barked, hackles raised as I limped forward before I got kicked. I didn't know how this was going to end anymore. I wasn't going to submit. We didn't all have to die.

Pam was panting, the skin around one eye torn. Blood seeped from it, and she tracked my movement, accessing.

"Get Nick!" I shouted again, knowing he wouldn't understand. "I'll catch you up!"

I didn't know if it was the truth or a wish.

"This is hard, Rache," he said softly, but I could hear him. So could Pam. "I'll come back for you after I find him."

Pam's ears pricked as she realized we were still going to make a play for Nick. Head tilted to protect her eye, she sprang forward with a savage sound. She was headed for Jenks.

"Run!" I howled, leaping to intercept her. She skidded to a halt, with me between her and Jenks. I had bitten her twice, and she was learning that small meant faster. I couldn't look to see if he left, but by Pam's eyes tracking something behind me, I had to believe he had. No one was paying attention to him now. Determination swelled in me. He was my vanguard, and this time I had his back. I wouldn't let this she-wolf past me.

Pam shifted her feet in frustration. In what was probably an attempt to warn them, she lifted her muzzle to the sky and howled. The Weres surrounding us joined her, thinking she was trying to cow me. Their human voices almost matched hers.

"You won't get past me!" I barked, then in a bold show, I lifted my own head and howled, trying to drown out her voice. *I am alive. And I will stay that way!*

Pam's howl cut off in surprise, and my voice rose against the rest, its higher pitch sounding more authentic, ringing with defiance. From nearby came another howl. Aretha.

The surrounding Weres went absolutely silent, their faces wondering, fear in some of them. For a moment my voice twined with Aretha's alone, and then they died together.

Pam looked shocked that the wolf had answered me. She stood with her tail drooping, blood dripping from one eye and her rear foot held off the ground. I hurt everywhere: my back, my hip. And the smell of blood came from my pulsing ear. *When had she done that?*

But Jenks was waiting for me. Snarling, I gathered myself and lunged.

Pam fell back, jaws snapping at my neck as I tried for her front leg. I jerked out from under her, a sharp stab in my ear telling me she had scored again. I rolled, and she followed. Flipping to my feet, I met her yap with my own toothy, aggressive grin.

She came at me without pause, and I skittered away. The watchers were silent now. Breathless. Someone was going to die, and Jenks wasn't with me anymore.

I found her neck. My grip slipped when my teeth closed and she jerked back. She had my leg in her mouth, and a rush of adrenaline pulsed. I had half a second before she'd crush it.

I fell to the earth and pulled. Teeth closed on my footpad. I yipped, scrambling up and away. Panting, we hesitated. Behind us the circle of Weres had turned into knots of tense people. No one had noticed Jenks was gone. Pam gathered herself, and I felt a burn of anger.

I didn't have time for this.

But she hesitated, freezing as her attention went to the lake's edge behind me. My fur rose and my skin prickled. I didn't turn. I didn't need to, and alarm showed in Pam's eyes when she saw me track the second wolf skirting the edges of the parking lot behind her, visible past the knots of people. A frightened whisper rose, fingers pointing and hands going to mouths as they realized Aretha had braved the compound, desensitized to the smell of Weres and pulled by the sound of my fight with Pam. Aretha had come, and she didn't look happy.

Ears pricked, the wolf confidently padded across the lot and came under the shade of the surrounding trees. The first roundness of her belly gave witness to the pups she carried, and I felt afraid. Pam and I were fighting for dominance on her island. Her pack had surrounded us as we fought, blind to everything else. *Shit.*

Don't run, Pam, I thought when she went frightened. For all her Wereness, she was also human. She was hurt and surrounded by a wild alpha's pack. And she stank like Were, not wolf. "Pam!" I barked, seeing her start to turn. "Don't!"

But she did. Spinning, she ran, betting they would fall on me as she went for the safety of the buildings. As the joke goes, you don't have to be faster than the wolf chasing you, just faster than everyone else running away.

I jerked, digging my feet into the ground to keep from following when three gray shadows streaked past me after her. The crowd panicked, falling into chaos and scattering. Women screamed and men shouted. Someone shot their weapon off, and I skittered sideways, nails gouging the packed dirt. My pulse hammered.

But my eyes were riveted to the four wolves dodging trees and picnic tables. Terrified, Pam streaked past the security of walls and into the trees. In seconds they were gone. A yip of pain rose sharp over the noise of frightened people. Walter shouted for silence, and in the new stillness there were unseen savage snarls and barks. Then a terrifying silence.

White-faced, Walter gestured, and a cluster of men with unslung weapons raced into the trees after them. I felt sick. This wasn't my fault.

A feminine gasp pulled me spinning around. My heart pounded and I felt my knees go wobbly. Aretha had silently entered the clearing as if the surrounding people didn't exist. Ear flicking, she stopped a good fifteen feet from me, her fur the color of silver bark. I looked at her with my wolf eyes, seeing the grace and beauty—and her utter alienness. I might look like a wolf, but I wasn't one, and we both knew it.

I started, freezing again when she lifted her muzzle. An eerie, soft howl rose from her, picked up by three more voices along the ridge. She was checking to see who had won.

Adrenaline scoured through me. Aretha lowered her head, her yellow eyes fixing on me a last time before she turned and padded across the lot, satisfied.

The wind in the trees slipped down to ruffle the fur about my sore and battered body. *What in* hell *had just happened?*

A twig snapped, and I skittered like a shying horse, heart pounding when I came to an ungraceful halt. It was the street Weres' alpha, pale but determined with his pack around him. "It's not my fault!" I barked, knowing he wouldn't understand.

The Were's Brimstone-weathered face was one of awe as he flicked his eyes from me to where Aretha had vanished. His tattoos from multiple packs made him look rough and uncouth, but his face was as clean-shaven as Jenks's. Bending, he plucked a tuft of red hair that Pam had pulled from me, looking at it as if it meant something. "The she-wolf," he said to Walter, as his roving eyes told me he meant Aretha, "she chose Morgan to live and your alpha to die."

The surrounding Weres started to talk, their voices growing in anger as their shock wore off. I panted, my bruised paw held up off the ground while I waited, feeling the seconds slip away. A shudder rippled over me, making my fur rise. Something was happening.

The street Were tucked the red tuft behind his jacket as if he'd made a decision. "The oldest stories say the statue belonged to a red Were before it was lost," he said, and his wife joined him. "Morgan held her ground when your alpha ran," he said, gesturing. "She won. Give Sparagmos to her. Love will loosen that thief's memory when pain and humiliation won't. I don't care who holds the statue as long as I can have a part of it."

"You gave your allegiance to me!" Walter exclaimed.

"I said I'd follow you when you said you had it!" the young Were said, his hands making fists and his jewelry chiming. His wife was a head taller than he was, but it didn't make him look any less threatening. "You don't. Sparagmos does, and she's claimed him. Dissolve my blood oath. I'll follow a red wolf as soon as a white one. Either way, I'm not following you."

"You lowlife cur!" Walter snarled, red-faced, his white hair standing out starkly. "I have Sparagmos, and I'll have the statue, and I'll have your head as an ashtray!"

The crowd was splitting. I could see it. I could smell it. Old patterns were emerging, both comfortable and familiar. The hair on the back of my neck pricked, and with a small effort I pulled my second sight into focus. My heart quickened. A pearly white now rimmed the street Weres, and an earthy red covered the ones in suits. It had broken that fast.

The entire clearing had shifted. The street Weres were dropping back into the woods. I could smell the whiff of Brimstone. If they went wolf, nothing would contain them.

"Sir," a grief-stricken Were in fatigues interrupted, and I turned to the six men carrying Pam, their slow steps saying it was too late.

"Pam!" Walter exclaimed, grief raw in his voice. The Weres set her gently down, and the man fell to kneel beside her, savagely driving them away before his hands dove into her fur, pulling her up into him. "No," he said in disbelief, his wife's body close to him.

Aretha's pack had torn open Pam's throat, and her blood clotted her black fur and stained his chest. His head going back and forth, the powerful man struggled to find the pieces of his world, scattered like the dead leaves shifting between us.

"No!" Walter shouted, his head coming up and his eyes finding me. "I will *not* accept this. That witch wolf is *not my alpha,* and I will not give Sparagmos to her. Kill her!"

Gun safeties clicked off. *Holy shit!* Panicking, I leapt for the slice of parking lot I could see. An instant and I was through. A screamed curse spurred me on. Nails digging, I reached the woods. My feet slipped on leaves and weak-stemmed plants and I almost went down.

Struggling for balance, I kept driving forward. I listened for the sound of shots, but I was away—for the time being. They had Hummers and cell phones. Against that I had a six-foot pixy and a three-minute head start, tops. *Pam was dead.* This wasn't my fault!

Behind me came the distinctive calls of a mob organizing. They were all people right now, but that was going to change. I had known the peace wouldn't last. Weres were Weres. They never bonded together. They couldn't. It went against everything they were made of.

Thank God for that, I thought as I tracked the scent of snapped twigs, following Jenks. The pixy could find Nick by smell if nothing else. We could still get off this damned island. Maybe the breakup of the round would buy us a few minutes more.

Nick, I thought, my heart racing from more than my escape. So it wasn't the way we planned it. So sue me.

Fifteen

My pace wasn't smooth in any sense of the word, loping through the warming forest, stumbling every time my front foot came down too hard. There were booms in the distance that my wolf hearing couldn't identify, but nothing close. My back hurt in time with my steps, and my front paw was throbbing. The wind cut a sharp pain across my ear where it was laid open. I went as fast as I could, my nose a good four inches above the ground as I tracked the sapling-snapped scent of Jenks.

I was on borrowed time. The island was big, but not that big, and grief would likely make their feet faster, not slower. Eventually someone would catch up to me. If nothing else, Jenks would run into resistance when he found Nick. They had radios.

Faster, I thought, promptly tripping. Pain iced through me and I lunged to catch myself before my face plowed into the ground. My bruised foot gave way, and cursing myself, I held my head high and took the fall, biting my tongue as I came to a sliding halt in the dirt. I was tired of being a wolf. Nothing looked right, and if I couldn't run, there was little joy. But I couldn't say my trigger word and switch back until I reached the mainland and tapped a line.

Besides, I thought, getting up and shaking myself, *I'd be naked.*

I sneezed the dirt and leaf mold out of my nose, whining when my entire body spasmed in pain. The sharp crack of clean wood on metal rang out. My head came up and my breath heaved. A man shouted, "Just shoot him!" and there were three pops in quick succession.

Jenks! Forgetting my hurts, I jerked into a run.

The light brightened around me as the forest thinned. Shockingly fast, I came out into what looked like an old state park with logs bolted into the ground to show parking spots. A Jeep was parked in the shade of a cement-block building painted brown, and near the entrance I saw Jenks attacking two men with a length of wood still sporting leaves.

I bolted forward. Like a dancer, Jenks swung the stick in a wide arc, the wood hitting one man on the ear. Not watching him fall away in pain, Jenks spun, jamming the splintered butt into the solar plexus of the second man. With a silent ferocity, he spun to the first, bringing the stick down with both hands against the back of his neck. The man fell without protest.

Jenks shouted, an exuberant cry of success, as he spun the stick above his head in a wild spiral, slamming it first against the back of a knee, then the skull of the second man. I came to a four-posted halt, shocked. He had downed both of them in six seconds.

"Rache!" he cried cheerfully, tossing his blond curls out of his eyes to show his He-Man bandage. His cheeks were red and his eyes were glinting. "I take it we're going to plan B? He's inside. I can smell crap for brains from here."

Heart pounding, I vaulted over the downed Were in fatigues blocking the door, my nose taking in the stale coffee in the tiny kitchen, the forty-year-old mold in the bathroom, and the pine air freshener fighting the stale musk in the tiny living room festooned with weapons and a two-way radio frantically demanding that someone pick up. My muscles tensed at the scent of blood under the masking odor of chlorine. Nails clacking on white tile, I padded through the narrow hallway, searching.

There was a closed door at the end of a dark hallway, and I waited impatiently for Jenks. He reached over me, pushing it open with a squeak. It was dark, the dim light coming from a dust-caked high window of wire-embedded glass. The air stank of urine. There was a rickety table cluttered with metal and pans of liquid. Nick was gone, and my hope crashed to nothing.

"Oh my God," Jenks breathed, his breath catching.

I followed his eyes to a dark corner. "Nick," I whispered. It came out in a whine.

He had moved at the sound of Jenks's voice, his head lolling up, his eyes open but unseeing from under his long bangs. They had tied him against the wall in a crucifix position in a cruel mockery of suffering and grace. His clothes had burned patches, singed hair and red skin showing past them. Black crusts of blood marked him. His cracked and bleeding lips moved, but nothing came out. "I will not . . ." he whispered. "You can't . . . I will . . . keep it."

Jenks pushed past me, cautiously touching a knife to judge the silver content before picking it up. I was stuck in the threshold, not believing it. They had tortured him. They had hurt him for that damned statue. What in hell was it? Why didn't he just give it to them? It couldn't be money. Nick was a thief, but he loved life more. I think.

"You can't do anything here, Rache," Jenks said, his voice catching as he started to saw at Nick's bonds. "Go keep an eye on the front. I'll get him down."

I jerked when Nick began shouting, clearly thinking they were at him again, calling my name over and over.

"Knock it off, crap for brains!" Jenks yelled. "I'm trying to help you!"

"My fault," Nick moaned, collapsing to lean forward against his bonds. "He took her. He should have taken me. I killed her. Ray-ray, I'm sorry. I'm sorry . . ."

Shaken, I backed out of the room. They hadn't told him I was alive. Sickened, I turned tail and bolted, nails sliding on the tile. I tripped on the man at the door, rolling into the yard. The sun struck me, jolting my horror into the beginnings of anger. Nothing was worth this.

The blue jays were screaming in the distance, and the sound of an engine grew closer.

"Jenks!" I yipped.

"I hear them!" he shouted back at me.

Pulse racing, I looked at the men sprawled in the packed dirt. Grabbing the shoulder of the nearest, I dragged him into the building, not caring if I broke the skin or not. He might have been dead for all I cared. I jerked him halfway down the hallway in short splurges of motion, left him and went back for the second. Jenks was coming out the door as I got him past the sill and inside. I dropped him, my back hurting and my jaws aching.

"Good idea," Jenks said, Nick's arm draped over his neck and shoulder.

Nick hung against Jenks, clearly unable to support his own weight. His head was down and his feet moved sluggishly. His breath came in pained gasps. There were red pressure marks about his wrists, and it didn't look like he could move his legs yet. When he brought his head up, his eyes were cloudy with a smear of gel.

Arm moving slowly, he tried to wipe them, blinking profusely. A dry cough shook him. Clenching his arm about his lower chest, he held his breath to try to stop.

"Go," Jenks prompted, and I tore my eyes from Nick. I felt sick again, and as my paws hit the dirt outside, I wondered just where Jenks expected us to "go." There was only one road out of there, and someone was coming up it. And stumbling about with a sick man in the woods was a sure way to be caught.

"Just . . . go behind the building!" Jenks said, and I trotted an uneasy path beside him, feeling small. Nick tried to help as his muscles started to regain their movement. Jenks eased him to the ground, propping him up against the painted brick. It was chill back there, out of the sun, and he held his legs and groaned. I thought of Marshal's warmth amulets. We had only one left—if they hadn't found our gear. Maybe Nick and Jenks could share it somehow. My fur could keep me warm. *Could I swim that far as a wolf?*

"Stay here," Jenks said to me, standing to look tall. His brow was furrowed. "Keep him quiet. I can take care of them, and then we'll drive out of here."

I put a foot on his shoe for his attention, looking up at him pleadingly. I hadn't liked running apart. I didn't want to do it again. We did better together than alone.

"I'll be careful," Jenks said, turning toward the sound of an approaching vehicle. "If there're too many, I'll hoot like an owl." I raised my doggie eyebrows, and he chuckled. "I'll just shout for you."

At my head bob, he crept away, silent in his black tights and running shoes. I looked at Nick. He didn't have any shoes, and his pale feet looked ugly. *Nick,* I thought, nudging him.

He stirred, wiping the goo from his eyes and squinting. "You're too small for a Were. I thought you were a Were. Good dog. Good dog . . ." he murmured, sinking his fingers into my wavy red fur. He didn't know who I was. I didn't think he recognized even Jenks. "Good dog," he said. "What's your name, sweetheart? How did you get on this hellhole of an island?"

I took a heaving breath, hating this. He looked awful in the brighter light. Nick had never been a heavy man, but in the week Jaxs said he had been on the island, he had gone from trim to emaciated. His long hands were thin and his face was sallow. A beard hid his cheekbones, making him appear like a homeless man. He stank of sweat, filth, and a deep-seated infection.

Looking at him, one would never have guessed at his wickedly quick mind. Or know how easily he could make me laugh, or the love I felt for his complete acceptance of who I was without any need to apologize; a man whose danger was in calling demons and his willingness to risk everything to be smarter than everyone else.

Until I had accidentally made him my familiar and he seized when I pulled a line of ever-after through him. My eyes closed in a long blink as I recalled the three months of heartache when he avoided me, not wanting to admit that every time I pulled on a line, he relived the entire terrifying moment in his mind, until he couldn't even be in the same city.

I'm sorry, Nick, I thought, putting my muzzle on his shoulder and wishing I could give him a hug. The familiar bond was broken now. Maybe we could return to the way we were. But a wiser voice in me asked, *Do you want to?*

My head came up and my ears pricked at the sound of someone downshifting. I padded to the edge of the building, peeking around to see an open Jeep rocking to a stop. Nick moved to follow, and I growled at him. "Good girl," he said, thinking I was growling at them. "Stay."

My lip curled and I felt my annoyance rise. *Good girl? Stay?*

Two of the four men with weapons got out, calling out for Nick's captors. My pulse quickened as they entered the building. Jenks and I were running without even a sketch of a plan except for, "Stay here, I'll take care of them." What lame-ass kind of a plan was that?

Shifting my front feet, I was debating whether I should do something when Jenks fell out of the tree and into the Jeep. Two savagely powerful blows with his stick and the men in the vehicle silently slumped. Jenks jerked the cap off the last one's head even as he collapsed. Wedging it onto his head, he grinned and gestured for us to stay.

A shout came from inside the building, and Nick and I shrank back.

Heart pounding, I watched Jenks yank one of the men up. There were three quick pops from the building as the two men came out, and blood leaked out of the Were in front of Jenks, shot.

Jenks dropped the Were and jumped into the tree like a monkey. Branches shook and leaves drifted down. The two Weres with guns shouted at each other, stupidly running over and aiming into the canopy. And I say stupid because they completely forgot there might be someone else here.

"Sweetheart!" Nick shouted as I bolted out to help Jenks.

Thanks a hell of a lot, Nick, I thought as both Weres turned. I barreled into the first, my only goal being to knock him down. The man's eyes were wide. Snarling, I barked and yapped, trying to stay on top of him in the hopes that his buddy wouldn't shoot me lest he hit him instead.

There was the pop of a gun and the crack of wood. In my instant of distraction the Were shoved me off. "Crazy wolf!" he shouted, turning the barrel of his weapon at me. Behind him, Jenks stood frozen in panic. The first man was slumped at his feet, but Jenks was too far away to help me.

A boom of thunder echoed, and the man pointing his weapon at me jumped. My heart pounded and I frantically waited for the pain.

But the Were spun, leaving me to stare in surprise at the hole in his back. My attention flicked behind him to Nick, propped up against the building with a shotgun.

"Nick, no!" I barked, but he took aim again, and with his face white and his hands shaking, he shot him a second time. The Were's gun went off as the slug hit him, but it was a death pull. Nick's second shot had gone straight into his neck. I sprang away and the Were fell, choking as his lungs filled, drowning him in his own blood. He clawed at his throat, gasping.

God help me. Nick had killed him.

"You sons of bitches!" Nick cried from the dirt, having fallen from the recoil this time. "I'll kill you all, you fucking dog-face bastards! I'll kill you—" He took a shuddering breath. "I'll kill you all. . . ." He sobbed, crying now.

Frightened, I looked at Jenks. The pixy stood under the tree, white-faced and scared.

"I'll kill you. . . ." Nick said, hunched on all fours.

I slowly skulked over to him. I was a wolf, not a Were. He wouldn't shoot me. Right?

"Good girl," he said when I nudged him. He wiped his face and patted my head, a broken man. He even let me pull the shotgun from him, and my tongue worked at the bitter taste of gunpowder. "Good girl," he murmured, standing up and wobbling forward.

Though clearly not wanting to touch him, Jenks helped him into the back of the Jeep, where Nick collapsed. Jenks unceremoniously dumped the unconscious men in the front out of the vehicle, and I scrambled into the passenger side, trying to ignore that the man Nick shot had finally stopped making noises. Jenks started the Jeep, and after a few jerks while he learned the practical aspect of how to drive a stick, we started down the road. I touched the radio with my nose, and he turned it up so we could hear.

Jenks looked at me, the wind brushing his bangs back. "He can't swim," he whispered. "And we only have one warmth amulet."

"I can swim." Nick had his head in his hands, his elbows on his knees against the jostling of the rough road.

"They must have a dock somewhere," Jenks continued, not paying him any mind but for a nervous glance. "They probably already have people waiting for us, though."

"I'll kill myself before I let them take me back there," Nick said, thinking Jenks was talking to him. "Thank you. Thank you for getting me out of that hell."

Jenks's lips pressed together and his grip clenched the wheel as he shifted to a lower gear and took a tight turn. "I can smell an oil and gas mix to the south, almost exactly where we came in. It's probably the marina."

Nick pulled his head up, the wind shifting his lank hair from his eyes. "You're talking to the dog?"

Sparing him a glance from under his new cap, Jenks turned away. "She's a wolf. Get it right, crap for brains. Tink's knickers, you have got to be the stupidest lunker I've ever lit on."

Nick's eyes went wide and he clutched the side of the Jeep. "Jenks!" he stammered, going whiter. "What happened to you?"

Jenks's jaw clenched but he stayed silent.

Nick looked at me. "You're a person," he said, looking gaunt. "Jenks, who is she?"

I trembled, unable to say a thing. Jenks gripped the wheel tighter, and the engine nearly stalled when he slowed to go around a turn and didn't downshift. "No one cares little green turds about you," he said. "Who do you think she is?"

Nick took a gasping breath, leaning forward to slip to the floor of the Jeep. "Rachel?" he said, and I watched his pupils dilate just before he passed out and his head hit the seat.

Jenks took a quick look over his shoulder. "Great. Just freaking great. Now I'm going to have to carry him."

Sixteen

I had scrambled back to sit with Nick, worried at the stink of infection and that he hadn't regained consciousness yet. The wind from our passage as Jenks jostled us down the road to the supposed marina lifted the hair about my ears, giving me a fuzzy "view" of the sounds around me but an expanded picture of the smells. The chatter from the radio was loud and heavy, bringing Jenks up to speed on Pam's death and the breakup of the round. That we might have stolen a Jeep and were listening apparently hadn't crossed anyone's mind. The survivalists had divided their forces to maintain dominance of the island as well as search for us. It could only help.

Jenks adjusted his new Were cap, slowing when Brett's twang filtered out. I swiveled my ears forward, glad for the easier pace. "All teams keep a three-to-one ratio of fur to feet," the man was saying. "The cell is empty. They're armed, two dead, so watch your tail. No sign of their boat, so they're probably headed for the dock. I want a five-to-one-ratio there."

Jenks slowed to pull off into the short grass eking out a living by the packed dirt. I lifted my head in question, meeting his worried eyes with mine. *Why was he stopping?*

"They know we're coming," he said, awkwardly twisting to make a three-point turn and head back the way we'd come. "I can't fight that many Weres. We're going to have to swim."

My heart pounded and a whine slipped from me. Angular face tight, Jenks accelerated. "I won't let you drown," he said. "Or maybe we can find somewhere to hide until things settle," he added, knowing as well as I that the longer we remained, the more likely it was that we'd be caught. But Nick was unconscious, and the idea of me dog-paddling all the way was daunting even if I would have a break traversing Round Island in between. I couldn't swim it as a person. What would being a wolf do for me? The entire situation was crap, but we had to get off the island.

"Shut up! Everyone shut up!" came a frantic voice through the radio, and I leaned over Nick, my ears swiveling. "This is the lighthouse. We have a problem. Unknown incoming force! Six boats from the Mackinac ferry dock. Mixed Weres!" the high-pitched, young voice said. "Uniformed. They know she's in trouble, and they're coming for her!"

Really? Somehow I didn't think it was an unexpected rescue, but a second Were faction taking advantage of the chaos. *Damn it, that would make Mackinac Island tricky!*

Brett's voice crackled out, chilling me. "Radio silence. Search leaders check in by cell phone. The rest of you, find them! Fire on them if you have to, but they can't have Sparagmos!"

The radio turned to a grating hiss.

Jenks pulled the Jeep to the side of the road. "Wake him up," he said tightly, undoing his belt and getting out. "This is where we came in."

My nose wrinkled when I scented the faint taste of decay on the breeze as the heat of the sun hit that deer carcass. Muscles tense, I hesitated, then licked the side of Nick's nose, not knowing what else to do. Hell, it worked in the movies.

Feet spread wide, Jenks looked up and down the road, squinting from under his borrowed cap. My tongue had made a long wet mark on Nick, but otherwise there was no change. Leaning into the Jeep, Jenks jerked Nick's head up by the hair and slapped him.

Nick exploded into motion. Screaming obscenities, he lashed out, arms flung blindly. Frightened, I jumped from the Jeep. My nails dug into the dirt and I stared at him.

Wild-eyed, Nick took a shuddering breath upon realizing where he was. His haunted look turned into a glare, and he stared at Jenks standing belligerently with his hands on his hips and that pack hat on his head. The jays yelled back at him, and I wished they would shut up.

"We walk from here, crap for brains," Jenks said darkly. "Let's go. Ever scuba dive?"

Nick eased himself out of the Jeep, stumbling when his bare

feet hit the hard-packed road. "Once or twice," he rasped, hunched into himself and holding his ribs.

My ears pricked and I wondered if he was serious. If I wasn't so worried about Nick, I might be able to concentrate on keeping my own head above water. Jenks, too, seemed surprised, saying nothing more as he led the way into the scrub.

One foot raised, I hesitated. Jenks was going the wrong way, toward the interior, not the beach. A questioning whine brought him around, and he gestured for me to join him, kneeling just inside the scrub off the road. Nick wobbled into the brush, and I trotted to Jenks, worried.

The pixy peered into my eyes, and I was thankful he didn't try to pet me. "Nick stinks," he said, and Nick cleared his throat in protest. "They've got my scent, and yours," he added, "but they aren't as obvious as Nick's. If you still had your scent amulets, we might be able to slip their lines, but not the way we are. I'm betting both the island Weres and the ones coming from Mackinac will start their search from the beaches and move in."

So they catch us inland instead of on the beach, I thought, but Jenks shifted his weight, regaining my attention. "I want you to take crap for brains to that carcass and sit tight. Hide yourself in its stink. I'll drive the Jeep down the road to confuse the trail, then come back."

He wanted to separate? Again? My black paws fidgeted, and Jenks smiled.

"It'll be okay, Rache," he said. "I'll go tree to tree like a squirrel. They won't trail me to you. Once they pass us, we'll slip out clear and easy."

It wasn't him leading them back to us I was worried about, and I whined.

"You can do this," he said softly. "I know it goes against your nature to sit and hide, and if it was just us, I'd say charge ahead and kick anyone's ass between us and the water. . . ."

I made a doggie huff. Nick couldn't do it. We had to adapt to his condition. Agreeing, I sent my tail thumping. Yeah, it was degrading, but everyone knew dog-speak, and no one knew Rachel/wolf-speak but me.

Jenks smiled, standing to look tall above me. His pleased expression shifted to one of annoyance and he looked at Nick. "Got all that?" he asked, and Nick nodded, not looking up. "There's a deer carcass thirty feet from here. Go make nice with it."

With a numb weariness, Nick picked his way there, old leaves crunching under his bare feet.

"Stay down until I get back," Jenks said, carefully manipulating the keys so they wouldn't jingle.

I watched him retrace his steps, glancing both ways before breaking the camouflage of the surrounding brush and vaulting into the Jeep. Almost stalling it, he eased onto the road and drove away with the enthusiasm of an eighteen-year-old playing cops and robbers.

Not liking this at all, I turned and followed Nick. "A dead deer?" he said, squinting down at me as he lurched forward. "Is that what I smell?"

What could I say? Silent, I nudged my shoulder into him to force him to the right, trying to smell if Aretha was nearby. I didn't think so. It had gotten noisy, and though she wasn't afraid of Weres, it was likely she'd taken her pack to the thicker parts of the island.

Nick grimaced when we found the deer. I sat, wondering how we could make this work better. The clearing was covered with evidence of our earlier tussle. The smell of wolves, Jenks, me, and Weres were faint under the stench of decaying tissue and saltwater, but we couldn't just sit next to it and hope everyone avoided it because it stank.

Blue eyes pinched, Nick looked over the situation. "There," he said, his swollen hand shaking as he pointed to a deadfall where a downed tree had left a hole where its roots had been. "If I can get the deer over there . . ."

I watched him shake his sleeve down to use as insulation and grab the carcass by a hoof. Struggling, he started dragging it the necessary twenty feet. Nick went ashen when he unearthed a maggot farm under it, and gagging, I kicked leaves to cover them.

Nick, though, had a belly full of fear, which was apparently stronger than revulsion. Jenks was gone, and with that, I could almost see him starting to think again. With renewed strength he dragged the deer to the tree, its roots in the air. Getting the carcass before the hollow under the roots, he let the legs drop. He looked at me, and I bobbed my head. Though gross, if he wedged himself between the deer and the fallen snag, and maybe covered himself with leaves, he would be hidden from sight and smell.

Face twisted in disgust, Nick slowly found the ground between the deer and the exposed roots of the toppled tree, jerking when sticks hit his bare skin past the burn holes. Carefully raking the debris collected in the lee of the hollow, he covered himself, meticulously placing the dry leaves on top as he worked from his feet upward. "Good?" he asked when he finished, his head lightly covered. I nodded, and he closed his eyes, exhausted. His filth melted into the surrounding forest like camouflage; the scent of infection was hidden by the reek of decay.

Nervous, I eased closer, trying not to breathe as I crawled into the space behind him, settling myself so my head was on his shoulder, my ears brushing the top of the miniature cavelike shelter. It was a stretch, but I curled my tail over my nose as a filter. All that was left was waiting for Jenks. The sheltering roots made a roof against the open sky, and the scent of dirt was a pleasant alternative. It was all I could do to not jam my nose into it. A blue-eyed fly crawled over the deer, laying eggs I couldn't see. If it landed on me, I was outta there.

While the jays called and the wind brushed the treetops, I studied Nick's haggard face, so close beside mine. The warmth of our bodies touching was guiltily pleasant. His breathing was slow, and I realized he was asleep when his eyes jerked in REM sleep. I had no idea what he had endured, but I couldn't imagine whatever they wanted could be worth it.

The screaming of the jays grew closer, and with a wash of fear I realized their calls had meaning. Something small raced through the underbrush and was gone, fleeing. My ears pricked and I scanned what I could of the disturbed clearing. Softer, then growing louder, I heard a whisper of wind. I could hear leaves moving, then nothing. The scent of oil, gas, and nylon touched my nose, and a surge of adrenaline made me cold. They were around us. God save us, we had gone to ground none too soon.

Heart pounding, I looked into the silent green, afraid to shift my head. A leaf fluttered down, and I prayed Nick didn't wake. I couldn't see anyone, but I could hear them. It was as if ghosts were passing before me, silent and invisible but for their scent.

My eyes flicked to where the sun glinted on smooth skin. A trembling took my feet, and I forced myself to not move. There were two of them, one on two feet, one on four. I didn't think they were the island Weres, but rather, off the boats from Mackinac Island—their uniforms looked like government issue and their gear was more aggressive.

The taller Were grimaced at the stink, and I slitted my eyes to nothing when the one on four feet nudged his leg and silently pointed with his nose. With a whisper, the Were checked in using the radio clipped to his lapel. There was the pop of a channel opening thirty feet away, and I saw a distant shadow of brown and green come to a halt, waiting to see what they had found.

Shit. There was a line of them. If we were found, it wouldn't be two Weres I'd be fighting, but a platoon.

I caught the word Jeep, but there was no jubilation, so I figured Jenks was still at large. Only now did the two Weres enter the clearing, the one in fur finding the broken splat balls and the three damp spots where Aretha and her pack had been doused with salt-water to break the sleepy-time charm. The other touched the ground where the deer had lain. His head came up, his eyes going right to the deer. I panicked, thinking he had seen us, but with a click, he got the attention of the Were on four feet. Together they looked over the clearing where we had been attacked, discussing with body signals what might have happened. The deer, they avoided.

The screaming jays grew closer, calling from right overhead for an instant until they continued, following the unseen line. The Were in fur snapped his teeth, and the other rose. Taking a red flag from a pocket, he jammed it into the ground, marking the clearing. Silently they headed farther inland. There was the soft scritch of cloth rubbing, then nothing.

My blood pounded. To lay there and wait for them to pass us had been one of the most frightening things I'd ever done. The jays' noise went soft, and I exhaled, started to pant.

Waiting for Jenks, my thoughts returned to the soft sureness the invading Weres had shown. Their sly hesitancy made the stark brutality of the three packs I had just escaped stand out all the more. Weres weren't savage—they just weren't—and I felt a spike of worry remembering the ugly ferocity of them ringing me. It had been more than them wanting to see a fight. They had been like a different species, younger and more dangerous, lacking the control that the alphas gave them. The trouble a cocky Were pack in Cincy could get into was enough to give me the shivers. The only reason Inderlanders and humans could coexist was because everyone knew their place in the social order.

I was so intent on my thoughts that I all but barked in surprise when Jenks dropped out of the tree above me.

"Holy crap," he whispered, eyes dancing. "I was sure that one saw you. Damn, that deer stinks worse than a fairy's ass-wipe. Let's get out of here."

I couldn't agree more, and leaving my disturbing thoughts

about the strength Weres found in packing up, I crawled from my shelter, leaping over Nick in my haste. His eyes flashed open and he came up on an elbow after seeing Jenks, leaves falling to hide the deer's glassy eye. "I fell asleep," he said, sounding ashamed. "Sorry."

"We're behind their line." Jenks didn't offer to help him stand, and I waited while Nick slowly gained his feet using the snag as support. His hands were swollen and there was a soft sheen of moisture on some of the burns as they oozed, bits of leaf chips stuck to them. I whined at Jenks to be nicer, but he wouldn't look at me, moving to play vanguard to the road.

I tried to find evidence of the invading Weres' passage as we went, seeing nothing. Nick stumbled behind me, stinking of dead deer, and I tried to pick a way that would be easy for him. His breathing grew labored as the forest thinned and we came out onto the road. A quick dart across and the forest closed in again.

Jenks was nearly silent to my wolf hearing, and I was pretty quiet myself. Nick tried, but every misplaced step brought a stumbling snapping of twigs and leaves. Being barefoot didn't help, and I was wondering why we hadn't taken someone's boots. After a few moments I trotted to Jenks, giving the pixy a look I tried to make meaningful before I loped away to make sure no one was nearby. Sound didn't travel as well as one might think in the woods, and as long as no one was close, Nick could make all the noise he wanted.

"Rache," Jenks hissed as I trotted off. "You playing scout?" he guessed, and I bobbed my head in an unwolflike manner. Nick came even with him, panting. He leaned against a dead tree, which promptly snapped with the sound of a gunshot.

While Jenks cursed him in thinly veiled disgust, I slunk through the brush, starting a sweep to the left when I couldn't hear Nick stumbling about anymore. Somewhere ahead of us was our scuba gear. Maybe we could hide out on Round Island. Unless by some miracle Marshal was still there. I prayed he wasn't, not wanting to have to make that choice.

Jenks and Nick's forward progress was maybe a third of mine, and it wasn't long before I had made a complete circuit and found nothing. I started a back-and-forth pattern before them, one ear on their progress, one on the forest ahead. Sooner than expected the green light filtering through the leaves brightened and I heard the sound of what seemed surf. But my heart almost stopped. I realized that the hiss of what I had thought surf was radio static.

"Their radio silence is continued," a voice said, and I froze, one paw lifted as I slowly crouched, all of my muscles protesting. In the background were sporadic thumps echoing against water. I was sure this was where we came in and not the marina. And Brett had said they hadn't found our boat, which meant they hadn't found the scuba gear either. It must be the six boats we had heard about. *Great. Just great. Out of the frying pan and into government control.*

"They haven't regained him," a higher, masculine voice said through a radio. "The third air tank and gear says she's probably headed right for you. Move the boats behind the curve of the shore and keep watch. With any luck, they'll walk right in on you. If you retrieve him, don't wait. Move out and radio from the water."

"Aye, sir," the Were said, and the radio retreated to a hiss.

Damn it, I thought. They had seen the tanks from the water and landed right where we had to leave. They knew everything the island Weres did, having listened in to their efforts to regain us. Someone else wanted Nick too. *Just what the devil was this thing?*

I tried not to pant, my head weaving as I attempted to spot them. I caught a glimpse of a green outback hat and a clean-shaven face. The noise behind them became loud with decisions being made, and I got scared. Slowly I backed away, carefully putting my feet down until I couldn't hear voices anymore. Turning tail, I made a beeline to Jenks.

I found them together, Jenks looking marginally more accommodating as he held Nick's elbow and helped him over downed sticks. Nick moved like an eighty-year-old man, head down and struggling for balance. Jenks heard me and brought them to a stop. "Trouble?" he mouthed.

I nodded, and Nick groaned, looking desperate behind his beard.

"Shut up," Jenks whispered, and I shifted my sore front paw nervously.

"Show me," Jenks said, and leaving Nick to fend for himself, I led him to my spot. Jenks's motions grew slower, almost seductive, as the brush grew thicker at the edge of the island, until he eased into a crouch beside a tree at the edge of the brush.

I settled in beside the large pixy, panting as I relished the cooler air coming off the water. "Marshal is gone," Jenks said, his viewpoint higher than mine. "Good man. There're four Weres with semiautomatics. . . . That might be a Were in fur in the shadow of that tree. In any case, our gear is gone. Probably on one of the boats." His eyes squinted. "Tink's panties, if I was myself, I could just flit over and see, or get them to shoot themselves, or stab them in the eye with a thorn. How do you do this, Rache, being the same size as everyone?"

My teeth parted and I gave him a canine grin.

Jenks adjusted his weight, eyes fixed on the peaceful beach littered with boats drawn up onto the rocky shore. Two men were standing guard while two more prepared to move the first boat out. "I have an idea," he whispered. "You go over to that pile of breakwall rock, and when they're looking at you, I'll circle to come up behind them and whack them a good one."

His eyes were glinting, and while I wasn't keen on the looseness of the plan, I did like his confidence in it. And since we didn't have much of a choice, I flicked my ears.

"Good," Jenks whispered. "Get wet before they see you so you look black, not red."

Giving me a smile that made him look like he was plotting to steal the teacher's apple, not a boat from four Weres with semiautomatics, Jenks dropped back to tell Nick the plan. I headed out, skirting the brush line. My pulse quickened. I didn't like being a decoy, but since I could probably cross the beach in four seconds, coming to Jenks's aid wouldn't be hard.

My knees went wobbly at the expanse of stony beach between me and the surf line. The sun was sparkling on the water, and the waves looked formidable past the slight protection of the inlet. Two Weres with weapons were facing the forest, while two more readied to move the first boat, confident they would hear anyone coming from the water long before they were close enough to be a threat. They were right.

A last slow breath, and I trotted out, walking right into the cold water and rolling. Immediately I lost my need to pant, the water freezing without Marshal's amulet. My first feeling that having this second faction of Weres seeing our gear was bad luck shifted to possibly good luck. Nick couldn't survive water this cold, and now Jenks and I would only have to take out five people, not whatever they had at the marina waiting for us.

There was an attention-getting yap, and I swung my head up, going still as a startled wolf might. But I would have frozen anyway. Five people were watching me, four with weapons and one with teeth. I think it was this last one that scared me the most. Damn, he was big.

My pulse jackhammered. I had nowhere to go but the woods,

and if I was recognized as being more than a wolf, they would be on me in seconds. Fortunately, their expressions were curious, not suspicious.

A small movement behind them evolved into Jenks, and I fought with my instincts to watch him, instead pricking my ears and staring at them as if wondering if they were going to throw me the meat from their picnic lunch.

The men were talking softly, their hands loose on their weapons. Two wanted to lure me closer with food, and they told the one in fur to back off before he scared me.

Idiots, I thought, sparing them no pity when Jenks fell on them from behind. Screaming wildly, he swung his leaf-born stick and bludgeoned the first into unconsciousness before the rest even knew they were under attack. I sprang into movement, feeling like I was in molasses until I was free of the water. Jenks was a blur as he fought, but it was the Were in fur that I was worried about, and I ran across the rocky beach, flinging myself at his hindquarters.

Even now they didn't get it, and he turned with a yelp, surprised to find me on him.

Snarling, I fell away, hackles raised. Giving a short bark of realization, he sprang forward, ears back. Holy shit, he was huge, almost four times my current weight. Spine protesting, I skittered back, my only goal to remain out from between his teeth.

Immediately I knew I was in trouble. I couldn't put any distance between us. Pam had fought like a choreographed dancer. This guy was military, and I was way outclassed. Fear slipped into me, and I shifted directions erratically, zigzagging across the rocky beach, my bruised foot slipping on the smooth stones. A great paw hit me and I went sprawling.

Adrenaline pulsed, and I yipped as he fell on me. On my back, I clawed at his face, struggling to wiggle out. His breath was hot and his tongue was tattooed with a clover.

"Enough!" Jenks shouted, but neither of us paid any attention until a short burst of gunfire sent him jerking off me.

Panting, I flipped to my feet. Three men were unconscious, bleeding about their heads. A fourth looked sullen but beaten soundly. Jenks stood alone. The sun shone on his black tights and blond curls, and the semiautomatic in his hands gave his Peter Pan pose some threat.

"Nick!" he yelled, hefting the weapon. "Get out here. I need you to watch them for a sec. Think you can do that, crap for brains?"

The two Weres tensed when Nick wobbled out, but at Jenks's threat, they remained still. They shifted again when Jenks handed Nick his weapon, glancing among themselves as Nick held it with markedly less proficiency. Faces ugly, they settled back, clearly waiting.

With that gunfire, we had only minutes until all hell broke loose, and while Nick held them at a muscle-fatigued, shaking standstill, Jenks took the spark plugs from all but one boat, throwing them into the water with all the weapons he could find.

"Rache?" he said, gesturing from the boat he had chosen, and I willingly jumped onto it, nails skittering on the fiberglass deck. Slipping, I fell into the cockpit and the fake grass carpet. Our gear and wet suits were a pleasant surprise. I hadn't been looking forward to finding out what their loss would have done to my credit card balance. Marshal would be pleased.

Nick was next, wading out to the side and handing Jenks the weapon before lurching over the side. Cracked lip between his teeth, he cranked the engine as the requests for information coming from the radio on the beach grew intense.

Still in the water, Jenks pushed the boat out with one hand, keeping the weapon trained on them with the other. My mouth dropped when he flung himself up into a blackflip to land on the bow of the boat. The semiautomatic never lost its aim. The two Weres blinked but didn't move. "What, by Cerberus, are you?" one asked, clearly shocked.

"I'm Jenks!" he called back, clearly in an expansive mood, catching his balance when Nick revved the engine. Jenks turned the near fall into a graceful motion, slipping into the cockpit to stand beside me, weapon still pointed. Nick idled us around, then jammed the lever full throttle. Staggering, I caught my balance. Jenks doffed his hat to the watching Weres and laughed, throwing his weapon into our wake.

We sped away as the first of the returning Weres came boiling out of the forest, all snapping teeth and barking voices. Someone was already in the water looking for the spark plugs. We had done it—for the moment. All that was left was to make it across the straits without swamping ourselves in the heavy waves and get lost in the general populace. Then there was the matter of how to get Nick safe. And me, seeing that my cover was blown and every Were east of the Mississippi knew I had Nick—who knew where the statue was, whatever the statue was.

I squinted into the wind, my breath escaping in a doggy huff when I realized Nick's rescue was only starting. What could he have possibly stolen that was worth all this?

Jenks reach across and tunked the gas lever to slow us down. "How did you know how to use that weapon?" Nick asked him, his voice rough and his hands shaking on the wheel. He was squinting in the bright light as if he hadn't seen it for days. He probably hadn't.

Jenks grinned as we jostled over the waves, hitting every one wrong. His bandage was falling off, but his mood was both exhilarated and triumphant. "Ah-nold," he said, hitting an Austrian accent hard, and I barked in laughter.

I watched the island retreat behind us, relieved no one was following—yet. It would only take minutes to lose ourselves in the light boat traffic, maybe fifteen to reach the mainland. We would ditch the boat, keeping the gear to return to Marshal when we could. I didn't care if we had to take it to Cincy with us, he was going to get his stuff back.

Jenks tunked the speed down some more, and Nick tunked it back up. I couldn't blame him, but the waves were bouncing us around like a piece of popcorn. Jenks handled the jostling better than me despite my four feet against his two, and he started rummaging, opening every panel and lifting every seat. It was his pixy curiosity, and feeling ill, I wobbled to Nick, put my head into his lap and gave him the sad-puppy-dog-eyes look, hoping he'd slow our pace. Burn my britches if it didn't work, and smiling for the first time since I'd found him, he dropped a thin hand to my head before he decreased the speed.

"Sorry, Ray-ray," he murmured over the noise of the engine. "I can't . . . I can't go back." He swallowed hard and his breath quickened. "But you did it. Thank you. I owe you one. I owe you my life." Hands trembling, he met my eyes, his grip on the plastic-coated wheel clenching and releasing. "I thought you were dead. You have to believe me."

I did. He wouldn't have left that rose in the jelly-jar vase if he hadn't.

Jenks made a call of discovery. "Anyone hungry?" he shouted over the wind and engine. "I found their food stores."

Nick jerked. "I'm starved," he said, all but panicked as he looked over his shoulder.

Jenks's first ugly face emptied when he saw Nick's eyes.

"Yeah," he said softly, gesturing for Nick to move. "I guess you are. You eat. I'll drive."

I jumped up onto the copilot's chair to get out of the way, and Nick stood unsteadily, gripping the boat and shaking with the thumping of the waves. He wobbled to the back bench, taking a moment to arrange the wool blanket Jenks had found about his shoulders before settling himself and ripping open energy bars with his teeth since his nails were torn to the quick.

Jenks took his place behind the wheel. He turned the boat slightly to the bridge, and the ride smoothed out. I watched the play of emotions over his smooth face. I knew he was as mad as a jilted troll at the altar that Nick had led his son astray, but seeing Nick beaten, abused, and so weak he could hardly open that stupid wrapper, it was hard not to feel sorry for him.

Just wanting Jenks to lighten up a little, I put my head in his lap and peered up at him.

"Don't look at me like that, Rache," Jenks said, his eyes scanning the approaching shoreline for the run-down marina we had planned out earlier as a possible landfall. "I saw you pull it on Nick, and it doesn't work on me. I have fifty-four kids, and it won't work."

Sighing heavily, I arched my wolf eyebrows. Sure enough, he glanced down.

"Tink's panties," he muttered. "Okay. I'll be nicer. But as soon as he's better, I'm going to punch him."

Pleased, I pulled my head up and gave him a lick on his cheek.

"Don't do that," he muttered, wiping the moisture away. But his embarrassment was tinged with understanding.

I'd be content with that, but before I could teeter back and see if Nick would open one of those government-issue energy bars for me, Jenks stood, one hand on the wheel, the other holding his cap to his head. "Ah, Rache?" he said over the roar of the engine and the brush of wind. "Your eyes might be better than mine. Is that Ivy on the dock?"

Seventeen

Squinting into the wind, I sat on the copilot's chair watching the decades-old rusted gas pumps on the dock become clearer. Ivy was standing with the sun glinting on her short black hair, leaning casually against a piling. She was in jeans and a long sweater, but with the boots and shades, she managed to look svelte as well as ticked. A frumpy older man was next to her, and worry went through me at what had gone so wrong in Cincinnati that she had to come and get me. *Unless she's here because she thinks I can't handle this.*

The man beside her looked both nervous and excited in his faded overalls, holding himself a careful five feet away as the breeze shifted his plaid coat open to the wind. They probably didn't get many living vamps up here, and he was clearly more curious than wary.

Jenks decreased our speed, and I could hear the sounds from the shore. My emotions were swinging from one extreme to the other. If Ivy had come because she didn't think I could do this, I was going to be pissed—even if it wasn't going that well. If she was up here because there was a problem back home, I was going to be worried. I'd thought she couldn't even leave Cincinnati, so whatever it was, it must be bad.

My weight shifted as the boat slowed, and I fidgeted with worry. Jenks cut the gas to idle and we drifted closer. "Can we tie up here?" he shouted to the man, who was probably manager of the marina.

"You bet!" he called back, voice high and excited. "Take her right down to slip fifty-three. Your friend already paid for it." He pointed where he wanted us to go, looking flustered. "That's a big dog you got there. We have a leash law this side of the straits."

I watched Ivy for her reaction to seeing me as a wolf, but her expression behind the sunglasses was amused, as if it was all a big joke.

"Come on down when you get settled," the man said, hesitating when he saw Nick hunched under his blanket. "I need to register you."

Swell. Proof we were here.

Ivy was already walking down the empty dock to the slip the man had indicated. Behind me, Nick shuffled around, finding the docking ropes and flinging bumpers over the sides. "You ever dock a boat before?" he asked Jenks.

"No, but I'm doing okay so far."

I stayed where I was while the two men figured it out, easing our way into the slip in sudden bursts of engine and calls to go forward or reverse. Ivy stood on the dock and watched, as did a few people readying their boats for the water. Nervous, I slunk to the lowest part of the boat to hide. The island Weres and the Weres we stole the boat from would track us down, and a big red dog was memorable. We had to start putting distance between us and our borrowed boat.

Jenks cut the engine and levered himself out, landing lightly on the wooden dock to tie off the back end. Ivy rose from her crouch where she had tied the bow. "What in Tink's contractual hell are you doing here?" Jenks said, then glanced at the people nearby sanding the bottom of their boat. "Didn't think we could handle it?" he added, softer.

Ivy frowned. "Nice Band-Aid, Jenks," she said sarcastically, and he reached to touch it. "You're big enough to bite now, mosquito, so shut up."

"You'd have to catch me first," he said, flushing. "Give us some credit. It was only a snag and drag."

I would have told him to lighten up but my thoughts were spiraling around the same question. Clearly angry, Ivy nudged the rope over the edge so no one would trip on it. "Hello, Nick," she said, running her gaze over his blanket-draped, barefoot, hunched form. "Someone rocking your boat?"

Under her disapproving eye, Nick tried to pull to his full height, cutting the motion short with a grunt. He looked awful. His beard was nasty, his hair greasy, and his smell was pungent now that the wind wasn't pulling it away. "Hi, Ivy," he rasped. "Piscary send you out for some fudge?"

Stiffening, she turned. My pulse quickened at the reminder of the undead vamp. She shouldn't have been here. There was going to be a price to pay, which made me think it had to be more than her checking on Jenks and me. She could have called if that was all it was.

I made a little woof to get Jenks's attention, but it was obvious by his sudden concern that he'd come to the same conclusion. Hands on his hips, he took a breath as if to ask, glanced at Nick, then let it out. "Hey, uh, Ivy," he said, a whole lot nicer. "We need to get out of here."

Ivy followed his gaze to the smear the island made on the horizon. "Are you hot?" she asked, and when he nodded, she added, "Then let's get him in the van."

Finally, we were moving.

"You brought the van?" Jenks hopped back into the boat, the fiberglass under my feet barely trembling. "How did you know we were here?"

"I drove around until I found your motel," she said, eyes on me. "The town's not that big. I've got Kist's Corvette parked at the restaurant across the street from your room."

At least they were being nice to each other. I wanted some clothes and a moment to change, and if Ivy brought the van—which we'd packed in case we needed to bug out in a hurry—then all the better. Head weaving to gauge the distance, I jumped to the dock, my nails skittering. There was an *Ooooh* of appreciation from the people across the inlet sanding the bottom of their boat, and I flicked my ears back and then forward.

"I've got to go register," Jenks said, as if proud of it, then hesitated, his earlier annoyance gone. "I'm glad you're here," he said, surprising me. "*She* can't drive anymore, and I'm not getting in a car with crap for brains behind the wheel."

"That's enough!" I snapped, having it come out as aggressive barks. The entire marina took notice. Drooping, I sank to the damp planks like a good dog. It was Tuesday, but being the last Tuesday before Memorial Day, there were a few retirees working on their boats.

Jenks snickered. With a jaunty step, he headed to the bird-spotted dockmaster's office. I still didn't know why Ivy was there, and probably wouldn't as long as Nick was listening.

On the dock, Ivy dropped to one knee, peering at my eyes to make me uncomfortable. There was a new sparkle of gold in her earlobes. *When had she started wearing earrings?*

"Are you okay?" she asked, as if trying to see if it was really me. I shifted to snap at her, and she grabbed the ruff around my neck, holding me. "You're wet," she said, the warmth of her fingers finding my damp skin under the fur. That a mouthful of nasty teeth had just missed her arm seemed to have made no impression. "There's a blanket in the van. You want to change?"

Flustered, I pulled back gently, and this time she let go. I bobbed my head, turning to look at Nick. Seeing my attention on him, he drew the blanket tighter to hide his burned clothing, shivering. I wanted to talk to Ivy, but I wasn't about to turn witch where everyone could see. Having the surrounding locals watch her talk to a big dog was bad enough.

"Let's get out of here," she said, standing up and stepping into the boat. "Let me help you with your . . . scuba gear?" she finished after pulling off the tarp. Her eyes went to mine. "You can dive?" she asked, and I shrugged, in as much as a wolf could shrug.

With a rough motion, Ivy drew the cover back before the curious people still sanding that same three-foot section of boat could see. She eyed me, then the shack where Jenks was, wanting to talk to me alone. "Hey, Nick," she said, a ribbon of threat in her voice. "It's going to take some time to get this packed. They have facilities for people who have their boats here. You want to shower while we load the van?"

Nick's long face went longer as his lips parted. "Why do you care if I'm comfortable?"

True to form, Ivy sneered. "I don't. You reek, and I don't want you stinking up the van."

Brow furrowed, she looked to the shack on the dock. "Hey, old man!" she shouted, her voice echoing on the flat water in the harbor, and Jenks poked his head out of the dock office. "Buy him a shower, will you? We've got time."

We didn't, but Jenks nodded, vanishing back inside. My wolfen brow furrowed, and Nick didn't seem happy either, probably guessing we were getting rid of him for a moment. Lifting a cushion, he brought out a pair of gray flannel government-looking sweats and size-eleven sneakers that had been tucked away for a returning Were to slip into. They'd likely be too small, but it was better than what he was wearing. Hunched under his blanket, he tottered to the edge of the boat, halting before Ivy, since she was blocking his path.

"You're one lucky bastard," she said, hand on a hip. "I would have let you rot."

Hand clenching his blanket closed, he edged past her. "Ask me if I care."

Ivy gathered herself to come back with a remark, but then he reached for a piling to pull himself out and the blanket slipped to show the burn marks. Horrified, she met my gaze.

Unaware that she had seen, Nick clutched his things close and made his meticulous way to a nearby cinder-block building, following the blue-lettered sign that promised showers. The dockmaster ambled out of his office, plastic token in his hand. While the man gave Nick a bar of soap and a sympathetic touch on his shoulder, Jenks made his slow way to us.

Nick's gaunt, battered silhouette vanished around the corner, bare feet popping against the cement. Turning, I found Ivy beside the captain's chair. "My God, what did they do to him?" she whispered.

Like I could talk?

Jenks came to an awkward, scuffling halt on the dock above us, squinting as he looked at the island. "We don't have time for him to shower," he said, adjusting his clan cap, his Band-Aid gone. He had turned the cap inside out so the emblem was hidden, and it looked good on him. Probably start a new trend.

"He is not getting into Kisten's van smelling like that." Ivy's gaze went to the tarp hiding the gear. "What do you want to do with these?"

Jenks looked at me for direction, and I huffed. "Bring 'em," he said. "Marshal will want them back. Though I suggest we keep them until we're clear."

"Marshal?" Ivy questioned.

Grinning, Jenks resettled the tarp in the limited floor space and started moving the equipment onto it. "A local witch Rachel sweet-talked into letting us rent his equipment. Nice guy. He and Rachel have a date when this is over."

I whined, and Jenks laughed. Ivy wasn't amused, and she pushed off from the captain's chair, saying nothing and avoiding my gaze as she helped stack the gear into the sling of the tarp. Between her vampire strength and Jenks's pixy stamina, they lifted the tarp with all the equipment onto the dock, the watching people none the wiser for what was in it.

While I sat on the dock and watched, Jenks and Ivy wiped the boat free of fingerprints under the pretense of cleaning it. Snapping the weather tarps into place as they went, they worked their way from the bow to the stern, eliminating every shred of easily traced evidence that we had been in it. Jenks was the last to leave, vaulting to the dock to land beside me in a show of athletic grace that made Ivy's eyes widen in appreciation.

"Got your people legs, I see," she murmured, then grabbed one end of the tarp. Jenks grinned, and looking as if the rolled up tarp weighed no more than a cooler, the two of them headed for the van. I trailed behind, sullen and bad tempered. I had been up nearly twenty-four hours, and I was tired and hungry. If one of them tried to put a leash on me, I was going to take that someone down.

Jenks quickened his pace after they reached the gravel parking lot, in a good mood despite having missed his afternoon nap. "How did you know we might show up here?" he said as he dropped his end of the bundle and slid the side door to the van open with a harsh scraping sound.

"Dad!" Jax shrilled, exploding out to make circles about us. "How did it go? Where's Nick? Did you see him? Is he dead? Oh wow! Ms. Morgan is a wolf!"

"Ah," Jenks said, "we got him. He's in the shower. He stinks."

I went to jump into the van, stopping when Rex took one look at me, swelled into an orange puffball, and vanished in a streak of common sense under the front seat. *Poor kitty. Thinks I'm going to eat her.*

"Hey, Ms. Morgan!" the little pixy said, landing on my head until I flicked my ears at him. "Nick is going to be mad. Wait until you see what Ivy brought."

Jenks frowned. "That's Ms. Tamwood, son," he said, unloading the tarp into the van.

Jax flitted into the van, darting among the belongings we'd shoved in pell-mell earlier. The small pixy flitted to the floor and in a high voice tried to coax Rex out, using himself as bait. I sat in the sun and watched, mildly concerned that no one was stopping him. I wanted a pair of shorts and a shirt so I could change too, but I was in a hurry and figured I could change in the van behind the curtain. Jax had turned his efforts to get Rex out to obnoxious clicks and whistles, and it hurt my head.

Ivy yanked open the driver's side door and got in, leaving it ajar to let the cool afternoon breeze shift the tips of her hair. "You want to take Nick to Canada before you head home, or are you going to just cut him loose?"

I made a sick face, but seeing as I was a wolf, it probably looked like I was going to hawk up a bird. It wasn't that simple anymore, but I had to change before I could explain. The van smelled like witch, pixy, and Ivy, and I didn't want to get in until I had to. I could see my suitcase, but opening it was a different matter.

Jenks stepped into the van, lurching for Jax and missing. Mumbling almost aloud, he began arranging things so we'd all fit, all the while keeping a tight watch on his son.

"What is it, Rachel?" Ivy asked warily, watching me through the rearview mirror. "You don't look happy for someone who just finished a run, even if it was pro bono."

Jenks dropped my suitcase onto a box and opened it up. "It went great," he said, his youthful face eager as he sifted through my things. "By the seat of our pants, the way Rache works best."

"I hate it when you work like that," Ivy said, but I felt better that Jenks, at least, was thinking about me not having hands.

"They caught us, but Rachel worked out a deal to fight their alpha for Nick." Jenks held up a pair of my panties so everyone could see. "I've never seen a Were go wolf that fast. It was incredible, Ivy. Almost as fast as Rachel's magic."

I felt a spike of worry, remembering their savagery when they were bound under a common cause and one Were. It still had me on edge. Ivy went still, then turned in her seat to look at him. My tail swished in an apology, and a faint wrinkle showed in her brow. "Deal?"

Jenks nodded, hesitating between the long-sleeve T-shirt and the skimpier tank top. "If she pinned their alpha, we got Nick. I didn't see it all 'cause I was looking for crap for brains, but the sound of the fight brought in a real wolf pack. The alpha Rachel was fighting ran away. I say that means Rachel won." I breathed easier when he put the tank top back. "Wasn't her fault their alpha got chewed by real wolves."

Ivy took a breath in thought, holding it. I met her eyes, knowing she had figured out the real problem, and I winced. A quick shot of adrenaline shivered through me. "They know who you are?" Ivy said, her gaze following mine to the island behind us.

Hearing the concern in her voice, Jenks straightened until his head brushed the ceiling. "Aw, hell," he said. "We can't go home. They'll follow us, even if we don't have Nick. Damn it all to Disneyland! Where's crap for brains? Jax! What did you two steal, anyway? How are we going to convince four Were packs that we don't have it or that Nick told us where it is?"

Jax was gone. I'd seen him zip out of the van three pixy heartbeats after his dad had started using Disney's name in vain. Angry, Jenks jumped into the parking lot and headed for the showers, arms moving and face red. "Hey! Crap for brains!" he shouted.

I rose, stretching, before I loped after Jenks. He skidded to a halt when I stopped in front of him and leaned into his legs to try to tell him it was okay, that we'd find a way around this latest problem. Jenks peered down at me, his shoulders stiff. "I'll be nice," he said, his jaw tight. "But we're leaving, and we're leaving now. We've got to get under the leaves and hope spiders spin webs above us before they start looking."

I wasn't sure how spiders fitted into his equation, but I padded back to the van while he pounded on the shower door. Ivy got the engine going, and when I jumped into the front passenger seat, she leaned over to crack the window for me. The dusky scent of incense slipped over me, familiar and rich with undertones only my subconscious had been aware of before. Comforting.

The thump of a metal door closing pulled my attention to the lot. Jenks slipped into the van, clearly upset. Fifteen feet behind him I saw Nick, beard gone and hair dripping, spotting his gray sweats. He was moving better, head up and looking around. I had been right that the shoes were too small; he was still barefoot, the sneakers dangling from two fingers.

"You're too good to him, Rachel," Ivy said softly. "You should be spitting mad, and you aren't. He's a liar and a thief. And he hurt you. Please," she whispered. "Think about what you're doing?"

Don't worry about it, I thought, enduring the indignity of thumping my tail in an effort to convey I wasn't going to let Nick back into my life. But when the memory of his battered body and his will to remain silent against drugs and pain returned to me, I had a hard time staying angry with him.

Eighteen

"Good God," I whispered, sitting on the van's cot and looking at my legs, horrified. They were hairy—not wolf hairy, but an I-couldn't-find-my-razor-the-last-six-months hairy. Utterly grossed out, I took a peek at my armpit, jerking away. *Oh, that's just . . . nasty.*

"You okay, Rachel?" came Ivy's voice from the front of the moving van, and I snatched up my long-sleeve black shirt and covered myself, though a heavy curtain was between me and the rest of the world passing at an awkward start-and-stop thirty-five miles an hour.

"Fine," I said, hurriedly slipping into it and wondering why my nails were the right length, though they'd lost their polish. My red frizz was longer though, bumping about past my shoulders, where it had been before Al cut a chunk out of it last winter. I had a feeling my extra-hairy condition might be laid at the feet of Ceri. She had twisted the curse to switch me back, and apparently they hadn't shaved in the Dark Ages.

I was thankful as all hell that Jenks, Jax, and Rex were in Kisten's Corvette behind us. Getting dressed in the back of a van was bad enough. Doing it with pixies watching would have been intolerable. I'd done that before. I didn't want to do it again.

Shuddering at the long red hair on my legs, I shook out a pair of socks, wishing I had footies. My face scrunched up as I put them on. This was going to change as soon as I found ten minutes to myself in the bathroom with a bottle of Nair. Why Jenks had shown up smooth as a baby's butt was beyond me. Maybe pixies didn't have hair except atop their heads.

I jerked my jeans on, flustered when the distinctive sound of my zipper going up filled the silence. Grimacing, I drew the curtain aside and fluffed my hair. Before me rose the bridge, taking up much of the skyline. The traffic was still stop-and-go, even more so now that it was down to one lane in either direction due to construction. But Nick had his truck across the straits in St. Ignace, so that's where we were headed.

"Hi, guys," I said, finding a place to kneel where I could see out the front. "I'm back."

Ivy glanced at me through the rearview mirror, her gaze lingering on my frizzing red curls. Nick looked up from rummaging in the console for change for the bridge toll, smiling though a faint tremor showed in his pianist-long hands as he shuffled about. Finding the right amount, he sat back and pushed his damp hair from his forehead.

The shower had done him good. After a week of deprivation, his narrow physique was positively gaunt, making his clean-shaven cheeks hollow and his Adam's apple more prominent. Where his lean frame had made him look scholarly before, it now only left him skinny. The gray sweats hung loose on him, and I wondered when his last hot meal had been.

His blue eyes, though, had regained the sheen of intelligence as the shower, energy bars, and distance all helped him deal with what he'd endured. He was safe—for the moment.

My mind pinged back to him leaning against the brown cinder-block building, a broken man weeping as he pulled the trigger on the shotgun.

Ivy cleared her throat, and I met her gaze through the oblong glass, returning her accusing stare with a shrug. She knew what I was thinking.

"Watch the car!" I exclaimed, and she jerked her attention back to the road. I was already reaching for a handhold when she hit the brakes, narrowly missing the bumper of the Toyota before us. Swinging forward from the momentum, I glared at her.

Nick had braced himself against the dash, and though his look was full of disgust, he said nothing. Ivy smiled at the irate driver we had almost hit, showing her pointy canines so the guy would back off and be glad we weren't stopping to make sure everyone was okay.

As we waited for the light, I stretched for my bag and charms. Nick was hurting, and there was no need for it. Yeah, I was mad at him, but him being in pain wouldn't help anyone.

The smoothness of two pain amulets filled my hand, and I slowly dropped one. I didn't hurt at all since turning back into a person, my sore back and nipped hand completely pain free. Wondering, I dug deeper for a finger stick. The prick of the blade was easily dismissed, and I massaged the three drops out. The clean scent of redwood rose, and the blood soaked in.

"Ah, Rachel?" Ivy called intently, and I stuck my finger in my mouth.

"What?"

There was a short silence, then, "Never mind."

She cracked the window, and with the cool air off the water shifting my hair, I decided to hang back here for a while. Getting her home ASAP was an excellent idea. Vamps were homebodies—high-maintenance, party-till-you-die, don't-look-at-me-funny-or-I'll-kill-you homebodies, but homebodies nevertheless. And for obvious reasons. I still didn't know why she was here. How she was going to handle her hunger without the net of people she had left in Cincinnati worried me. Maybe it'd be easier out of Piscary's influence. God, I hoped so.

The van eased into motion, and I rifled through my bag for a complexion charm. It was too bumpy to put on makeup, but I could at least look rested and relaxed. *And it would get rid of the bags under my eyes,* I thought morosely, flipping open my little compact mirror. Squinting in the dim light, I looked closer.

"Hey, Ivy?" I bolted forward, hunched as I lurched up to the front. "Are my freckles gone?" Eyes wide, I leaned out between Ivy and Nick, tilting my head so they both could see.

Ivy glanced from the road to me, then back again. A slow smile spread across her face, telling me my answer before she said a word. "Open your mouth," she said.

Bewildered, I did, and she looked, making me nervous when she smoothly halted without watching the car that had stopped before us.

From my right came Nick's soft, "Are they gone?" and Ivy nodded.

"What's gone?" Shoving the pain amulet at Nick, I opened my mouth and tried to see what they were looking at. "My fillings are gone!" I exclaimed, shocked. Pulse hammering, I looked at my wrist. "That's still there," I said, looking at Al's demon mark and wanting to check the underside of my foot for Newt's, which I didn't because of all that hair. I looked at my elbow instead. "But the scar from when I fell off my bike isn't," I added.

Twisting, I tried to see the back of my shoulder where I'd cut myself falling into the lawn mower doing cartwheels. Ah, I had been doing the cartwheels, not the lawn mower.

"Your neck is unmarked," Ivy said softly, and I froze, meeting her eyes in the mirror. There was the faintest swelling of black. "Do you want me to see if it's really gone?" she asked.

I leaned back, suddenly aware of her. Nick cleared his throat in a subtle show against it, which halted my first impulse to say no. If it was gone, it would be worth all the blackness I had put on my soul. Despite my better judgment, I nodded.

Ivy exhaled long and slow, the sound setting my blood to thrum. Her eyes dilated to a full black, and I stiffened, fixed to them through the rearview mirror. Though her fingers were still on the wheel, I felt as if she was touching my neck with a shocking intimacy, pressing with a light but demanding insistence.

I inhaled, and like a sudden flame from a match, it sparked a tingling assault. Heat poured through me, following the line from my neck to my chi. A small sound escaped me, and if I'd been able to think, I would have been embarrassed.

Ivy broke our eye contact through the mirror, holding her breath as she struggled to pull her hunger back. "It's still there," she said, her voice both rough and smooth. Wavering where I sat, her eyes met mine and darted away. "Sorry," she added, fingers clenching the wheel.

Blood pounding, I retreated to the cot. To ask her to do that had been stupid. Slowly the tingling vanished. My scar wasn't puckering my skin, but obviously the vampire virus was still fixed there. I was terribly glad I was a witch and couldn't be Turned. Ever. I had a feeling that was one of the reasons Ivy put up with so much of my crap.

The van was uncomfortably silent, windy now that Ivy had rolled the window completely down. It was cold, but I wasn't going to say anything. My perfume, which blocked my scent from mixing with Ivy's, was in here somewhere. Maybe I ought to find it.

The tension slowly eased as we moved to the bridge. I looked at my hands in the dusk of the van, seeing them smooth and perfect, every flaw that marked my passage through time gone. It seemed like the curse had reset everything: no freckles, no childhood scars, no fillings . . .

Panic slid through me. Frightened, I lurched to the front, kneeling between them. "Nick," I whispered. "What if I lost what Trent's dad—"

Nick smiled, smelling like hotel soap as he took my hand. "You're fine, Ray-ray. If the vamp virus is still fixed in your cells, then whatever Trent's father changed will be there too."

I felt unreal as I pulled my hand from his. "Are you sure?"

"Your freckles are gone but you still have your sensitivity to vampires. That would suggest the charm resets your form by your DNA. And if your DNA was changed, by a virus or . . ." His eyes flicked to Ivy staring out the window, her grip deceptively loose on the wheel. ". . . something else, the change is carried over." Smiling, he leaned closer. I froze, then jerked back when I realized he was going to kiss me.

Face emptying of emotion, Nick settled in his seat. Flushing, I moved away. I didn't want him to kiss me. *What in hell is wrong with him?*

"It wasn't a charm, it was a demon curse," Ivy said darkly, jerking the car into motion. Though the traffic was stop-and-go, the roughness had been on purpose. "She put a hell of a lot of black on her soul while saving your ass, crap for brains."

Nick's eyes widened and he turned in his seat. His expression grew haunted. "A demon curse? Ray-ray, please tell me you didn't buy a demon curse to help me."

"I'm a white witch, Nick," I said tartly, my words harsher at the reminder of what I'd done to myself. "I didn't make a deal with anyone. I twisted the curse myself." Well, Ceri twisted it, actually, but pointing *that* out didn't seem prudent.

"But you can't!" he protested. "It's demon magic."

Ivy tunked the brakes, and I caught my balance when the van stopped quick at a new yellow light. Behind us, Jenks blew the car's horn, which Ivy ignored. "Are you calling her a liar?" she said, turning in her seat to look at Nick squarely.

His long face reddened, his newly shaved cheeks a shade paler. "I'm not calling her anything, but the only place you can get a working demon charm is from a demon."

Ivy laughed. It was ugly, and I didn't like it. "You don't know shit, Nick."

"Stop it, both of you!" I exclaimed. "God, you're like two kids fighting over a frog."

Angry, I retreated to sit on the cot, leaving two silent, sullen people in the front. The soft clinks of the toll money slipping through Nick's fingers were loud. As we crept forward in the slow line, I forced myself to be calm. Most likely Nick was right that I wouldn't suddenly find myself dying from a childhood disease again, but it was still a worry.

"Look there," he said suddenly, his voice thick with warning. "Ray-ray, stay down."

Immediately I crowded to the front to earn Ivy's huff of impatience. Before us spread the bridge, its glory marred by construction crews. We were nearly on it, and the guy holding the Slow sign was watching everyone far too intently. I could tell from three cars away that he was a Were, a Celtic knot tattoo encompassing his entire right shoulder.

"Damn it," Ivy muttered, her jaw clenching. "I see him. Rachel, hold on."

I braced myself when Ivy flicked the turn signal and pulled a right to get out of the bridge traffic at the last moment. Peering out the dirty square of a window in the back, I saw Jenks following. Jax and Rex were scampering about on the dash, and I don't know how Jenks managed to keep the car on the road.

The van rocked as it found its new momentum, and I felt ill. "Now what?" I said, finding Jenks's old flip-flops and putting them on.

Ivy sighed. Her grip on the wheel tightened and relaxed. Glancing into the rearview mirror, her eyes met mine. Nick's truck would have to wait. I listened to the traffic and Nick's frightened breathing. I could almost hear his heart, see it pulse in his neck as he fought the fear of his entire week of torture.

"I'm hungry," Ivy abruptly said. "Anyone want a pizza?"

Nineteen

Eyes on the rearview mirror, Ivy eased the van to a halt in the restaurant lot in the shade between two semis. The sound of traffic was loud through her window, and I couldn't help but be impressed at being so well hidden this close to the main road. Shifting the gearshift into park, she undid her seat belt and turned. "Rachel, there's a box under the floorboard. Will you get it for me?"

"Sure." While Ivy got out, I scuffed back the throw rug and pried up the metal plate to find, instead of a spare tire, a dusty cardboard box. Trying to keep it from touching me, I set it on the driver's seat. Ivy looked out from between the two trucks when Jenks parked across the lot. She whistled, and Jax darted up before his dad could even get out of the car.

"What's up, Ms. Tamwood?" the small pixy said, stopping before her. "Why did we stop? Are we in trouble? Do you need gas? My dad has to pee. Can you wait for him?"

I was pleased to see that Jax was wearing a scrap of red tucked into his belt. It was a symbol of good intentions and a quick departure should he stray into another pixy's territory. Seeing him learning the ropes made me feel good, even if the reason behind it was depressing.

"The Weres have the bridge," Ivy said, gesturing for Jenks to stay where he was beside Kisten's car. He was fumbling with his inside-out cap, and with the jeans he now had on over his running tights and his aviator jacket, he looked good. "Tell your dad to get a table if it looks okay," Ivy added, squinting from behind her sunglasses. "I'll be there in a sec."

"Sure thing, Ms. Tamwood."

He was gone in a clattering of wings. A light breeze shifted Ivy's hair, and standing beside the open door, she pried the dusty flaps up to pull out a roll of heavy ribbon. A faint smile quirked the corner of her mouth, and Nick and I waited for an explanation.

"I haven't done this in years," she said, looking to the narrow slice of visible parking lot. "I don't think they saw us," she said, "but by tonight they will have tracked you and Jenks to your motel, and that lady will tell them you were driving a white van. If we're going to be in town longer than that, we need to change a few things."

I recognized the thick tape in her hands as magnetic striping, and my eyebrows went up. *Cool. A vehicle disguise.*

"There's a license plate somewhere in there," she said, and I nodded, going back for it. "And the screwdriver?"

Nick cleared his throat, sounding impressed. "What is that? Magnetic pinstripe?"

Ivy didn't look at him. "Kisten has black lightning and flaming crosses too," she said.

And illegal flash paint, I mentally added when she shook a can of specially designed spray paint.

She moved the box to the running board of the nearby semi. The door thumped shut, sealing Nick and me inside. "By the time I get done with her, she could win the goth division in a car show," she said.

Smirking, I handed her the Ohio plate and screwdriver through the window. Even the tags were up to date.

"Sit tight," she said, taking them. "Nobody moves until I get Jenks's take on the restaurant."

"I'm sure it's fine," I said, moving to the front seat. "I'm so hungry, I could eat a seat cushion."

Ivy's brown eyes met mine from over her sunglasses, and her motion of shaking the spray can slowed. "It's not the food I'm worried about. I want to be sure it's mostly human." Her face went worried. "If there are any Weres, we're leaving."

Oh, yeah. Worried, I slumped behind the wheel, but Ivy looked unconcerned, taking a rag from the box and starting to wipe the road dust off the van. I was glad she was there. Sure, I was a classically trained runner, and while subterfuge was a part of that, hiding from large numbers of people out to get you wasn't. This stuff was what she had cut her teeth on. I guessed.

Nick undid his belt when Ivy edged out of sight. I could hear her work, the sporadic hisses of paint followed by squeaks as she wiped down the bumpers before the illegal paint took. The smell of fixative tickled my nose. I glanced at Nick, and he opened his mouth.

"Hey, a disguise sounds like a good idea," I blurted, twisting to reach my bag. "I've got a good half dozen in here. They're for smell, not looks, since Weres track by smell and will find us that way long before they see us. They took the ones I had on the island, but I made extra."

I was babbling, and Nick knew it. He puffed his breath out and settled back while I rummaged for them. "A disguise sounds good," he said. "Thanks."

"No prob," I answered, bringing out a new finger stick along with a handful of amulets. I broke the safety seal and arranged four amulets on my knees. I didn't know how to treat Nick anymore. We had done well together until it fell apart, but it had been a long, lonely three months until he finally left. I was mad at him, but it was hard to stay that way. I knew it was my need to help the downtrodden, but there it was.

The silence was uncomfortable, and I pricked my finger anew. I invoked them all to make the scent of redwood blossom, then handed him the first. "Thank you," he said as he took it, lacing it over his head, where it fell to clink against his pain amulet. "For everything, Ray-ray. I really owe you. What you did . . . I can never repay you for that."

It was the first time we'd been alone since pulling him out of that back room, and I wasn't surprised at his words. I flashed him a blank smile then looked away, draping my amulet over my head and tucking it behind my shirt to touch my skin. "It's okay," I said, not wanting to talk about it. "You saved my life; I saved yours."

"So we're even, huh?" he said lightly.

"That's not . . . what I meant." I watched Ivy spray an elaborate symbol on the hood, her hidden artistic talents making something both beautiful and surprising as she blurred the gray paint into the white of the van to look very professional. Glancing at me in question, she tossed the can to the box and went to the back to change the plate.

Nick was silent, then, "You can Were, now?" he asked, stress wrinkles crinkling the corners of his eyes. The blue of them seemed faded somehow. "You make a beautiful wolf."

"Thank you." I couldn't leave it at that, and I turned to see him miserable and alone. *Damn it, why did I always fall for the underdog?* "It was a one-shot deal. I have to twist a new curse if I want to do it again. It's . . . not going to happen again." I had so much black on my soul, I'd never be rid of it. I wanted to blame Nick, but *I* was the one who took the curse. I could have submitted to the drugs and stuck it out until someone came to rescue my ass. But no-o-o-o. I took the easy way by using a demon curse, and I was going to pay for it dearly.

His head went up and down, not knowing my thoughts but clearly glad I was talking. "So it isn't like you're a Were now in addition to being a witch."

I shook my head, startled when my longer hair brushed my shoulders. He knew the only way to become a Were was to be born one; he was trying to keep the conversation going.

Ivy came to the door, smelling of the fixative and wiping the gray from her fingers with a rag. "Here," she said, handing the old plate through. "If you look in the console, there should be an altered registration taped to the top. Can you switch them out?"

"You bet." *Swell. Let's add falsifying legal documents to the list,* I thought, but I took the Kentucky plate and screwdriver, giving her two amulets in their place. "These are for you and Jenks. Make sure he puts it on. I don't care what he says it makes him smell like."

Ivy's long fingers curved around them, shifting so they dangled from the cord and wouldn't effect her. "Scent disguise? Good thinking—for you." Showing the faintest blush of nervousness, she handed one of them back. "I'm not wearing one."

"Ivy," I protested, having no clue why she'd never accept any of my spells or charms.

"They don't know what I smell like, and I'm not wearing it!" she said, and I put up a hand in surrender. Immediately her brow smoothed, and she dug in a pocket for the keys to the van, handing them to me through the window. "I'll be right back," she said. "If I'm not out in four minutes, go." I took a breath to protest, and she added, "I mean it. Come rescue me by all means, but plan it out, don't burst in with your hair flying and in flip-flops."

A half smile came over me. "Four minutes," I said, and she walked away. I watched her in the side mirror. Her shoulders were hunched and her head was down—and then she was gone.

"I've got a bad feeling about this," I said.

"What?" Nick said softly. "That she's walking into a trap?"

I turned to him. "No. That she's not going to leave until it's over."

Worry filled his eyes; he was going to say something I didn't want to hear. "Rachel—"

"By the Turn, I'm hungry. I hope she hurries up," I babbled.

"Rachel, please. Just listen?"

I closed the console and eased into the seat. This conversation would happen whether I wanted it to or not. Breath slipping from me, I looked at him, to find his haggard face determined.

"I didn't know you were alive," he said, panic in his eyes. "Al said he had you."

"He did."

"And you never answered your phone. I called. God knows I did."

"It's at the bottom of the Ohio River," I said flatly, thinking he was a wimp for not calling the church. Then I wondered if he had and Ivy simply hung up on him.

"The paper said you died in a boat explosion saving Kalamack's life."

"I almost did," I said, remembering waking up in Trent's limo, having passed out after I pulled the man's freaking elf-ass out of the freezing water.

Nick stretched a swollen hand across the consol between us, and I jerked out of his reach. Making a frustrated sound, he put an elbow on his closed window and looked at the nearby semi. "Damn it, Ray-ray, I thought you were dead. I couldn't stay in Cincinnati. And now that I find you're alive, you won't even let me touch you. Do you have any idea how I mourned?"

I swallowed, the memory of the budded red rose in the jelly jar vase with the pentagram of protection on it lifting through me. My throat tightened. *Why did it have to be so confusing?*

"I missed you," he said, brown eyes thick with pain. "This isn't what I had planned."

"Me neither," I said, miserable. "But you left me long before you left Cincinnati. It took me a long time to get over you lying to me about where you had been, and I'm not going back to the way things were. I don't care that it wasn't about another woman. Maybe that I could understand, but it was money. You're a thief, and you let me believe you were something else."

Nick slumped into a defeated stillness. "I've changed."

I didn't want to hear this. They never changed, they simply hid it better. "I'm seeing someone," I said, my voice low so it wouldn't shake. "He's there when I need him, and I'm there for him. He makes me feel good. I don't want to return to how things were, so don't ask me to. You were gone, and he—" I wiped a hand under my eye, embarrassed that they were wet. "He was there," I said. *He helped me forget you, you bastard.*

"You love him?"

"Whether I love him or not isn't relevant," I said, hands in my lap.

"He's a vampire?" Nick asked, not moving one inch, and I nodded.

"You can't trust that," he protested, long hands gesturing weakly. "He's just trying to bind you to him. You know that. God, you can't be that naive! Didn't you just see what happened with your scar? With Ivy?"

I stared at him, my feelings of betrayal rising anew, both angry and frightened. "You told me once that if I wanted to be Ivy's scion, that you would drive me back to the church and walk away. That you loved me enough to leave if it meant I would be happy." My heart was pounding and I forced my clenched hands apart. "Well, what's the difference, Nick?"

He bowed his head. When he looked up, his face was tight with emotion. "I hadn't lost you then. I didn't know what you meant to me. I do now. Ray-ray, please. It's not you making decisions anymore, but vampire pheromones. You've got to get out before you make a mistake you can't walk away from!"

A movement in the mirror caught my eye. *Ivy. Thank God.* I reached for the door handle. "Don't talk to me about making mistakes," I said, grabbing my bag and getting out.

I slammed the door, glad to see Ivy for the distraction if nothing else. The van was now gray at the bottom, shading to white at the top and plastered with professional-looking decals. The cloying scent of fixative was a fading hint. Ivy was watching the nearby road as she approached, her subtle finger motions telling me to stay between the shelter of the dirty trucks.

Rocking to a halt, I crossed my arms and waited by the back bumper, lips pressed while Nick shut his door and shuffled forward. "All clear inside?" I said brightly when Ivy joined us. "Good. I'm starved."

"Just a minute, I want my stuff." Slipping past me, she yanked the driver's side door open and retrieved a rolled-down paper bag from under the front seat. She shut the door hard before pushing past Nick and pulling me into her wake. A pause at the head of the shelter the two semis made, and we started for the restaurant, my flip-flops noisy next to her vamp-soft steps. Behind us, I could hear Nick. By all rights, as the most vulnerable member of the group, he should have been between us, but I didn't feel like protecting him, and the danger was minimal.

"Your hair is longer," Ivy said as we crossed the paved lot to the low wood-slatted building snuggled in among the pines. *Squirrel's End? How . . . redneck.*

"You aren't kidding," I said, wincing at the memory of my legs. "You didn't happen to bring a razor with you, did you?"

Her eyes widened. "A razor?"

"Never mind." *Like I was going to tell her I looked like an orangutan?*

"Are you okay?" she asked again, her voice heavy with concern.

I didn't look at her. I didn't need to. She could read my emotions on the wind easier than I could read a billboard at sixty miles an hour. "Yeah," I said, knowing she wasn't asking about the run, but about Nick.

"What did he do?" she said, her arms moving stiffly. "Did he make a pass at you?"

I glanced askance at her, then back to the nearing door. "Not yet."

She snorted, sounding angry. "He will. And then I'll kill him."

Annoyance sifted through me, the jolts from my steps going all the way up my spine. "I can take care of myself," I said, not caring that Nick was listening.

"I can take care of myself too," she said. "But if I'm making an ass out of myself, I'd hope you'd stop me."

"I am *handling* this," I said, forcing my voice to be pleasant. "How about you?" I asked, turning the tables. "I didn't think you could leave Cincinnati."

Her expression went guarded. "It's only for a day. Piscary will get over it." I was silent, and she added, "What, like the city will fall apart because I'm not there? Get real, Rachel."

My head nodded, but I was still worried. I needed her help planning how to get out of my latest fix, but she could do it by e-mail or phone if she had to.

"We should be safe enough here for a while," she said, her eyes canvassing the building as we slowed at the door and Nick came even with us. "It's all humans."

"Good," I replied faintly, feeling out of place and vulnerable. Paper sack crinkling, Ivy opened the door for me with her free hand, leaving Nick to handle the swinging, blurred-glass door by himself. I had shifted back to witch with absolutely nothing in my stomach at all, and starved, I breathed deeply of the smell of grilled meat. It was nice in there: not too bright, not too dim, no smoky smell to ruin it. There were animal parts on the walls and few people, seeing as it was Tuesday afternoon. Maybe a tad too cold, but not bad.

The menu was on the wall, and it looked like basic bar food. There were no windows but for the door, and everyone seemed willing to mind their own business after their first long look. The short bar had three fat men and one skinny one, each sitting on green vinyl stools torn to show the white padding. They were shoving food in their mouths as they watched a recap of last week's game, talking to a matronly woman with big hair behind the bar.

It was only three in the afternoon—according to the clock above the dance floor whose hands were fishing poles and numbers were fly lures. A dark jukebox filled a distant corner, and a long light with colored glass hung over a red-felted pool table.

The bar had Northern Redneck all over it, which made me all warm and fuzzy. I didn't like being the only Inderlanders in the place, but it was unlikely anyone would turn ugly. Someone might get stupid after midnight with seven shots of Jäger and a room of humans to back him, but not at three in the afternoon and only five people in the place counting the cook.

Jenks and Jax were at a table in the rear, a bank of empty booths between them and the wall. The large pixy waved for us to join them, and I felt a moment of worry that he had his shirt open to show his scent amulet. I was guessing he was proud he was big enough to have one and wanted to show it off, but I didn't like flaunting my Inderland status. They had an MPL—a Mixed Public License—posted, but it was obvious that this was a local human hangout.

"I'm going to the restroom," Nick muttered.

He made a beeline for the archway beside the bar, and I watched him, the idea flitting through me that he might not come back. I looked at Jenks, and after I nodded, the big pixy sent Jax to follow him. Yeah, I was stupid when it came to matters of the heart, but I wasn't *stupid.*

Ivy's presence hung a shade too close for comfort as we wove through the empty tables, past the pool table and the gray-tiled dance floor. Jenks had his coat off and his back to the wall, and Ivy took the chair beside his before I could. Peeved, I put my fingers on the worn wood of the chair across from her, twisting it sideways so I could see the door. The guys at the bar were watching us, and one moved down a stool to talk to his neighbor.

Seeing that, Ivy frowned. "Stand up, pixy," she said, her low voice carrying an obvious threat. "I don't want Rachel sitting next to crap for brains."

In a heartbeat Jenks's amusement turned to defiance. "No," he said, crossing his arms. "I don't want to, and you can't make me. I'm bigger than you."

Ivy's pupils swelled. "I would have thought you'd be the last person equating greater size with greater threat."

His foot under the table jiggled, squeaking. "Right." With an abrupt motion he pushed his chair out, snatching up his coat and edging from behind the table to take the seat next to mine. "I don't like sitting with my back to the door either," he grumbled.

Ivy remained silent, the brown returning to her eyes quickly. I knew she was carrying herself carefully, very aware that the clientele wasn't used to vampires and voluntarily putting herself on her best behavior. That Jenks had moved to suit her hadn't gone unnoticed, and I fixed a cheerful smile to my face when the woman approached, setting down four glasses of water with moisture beading up on them. No one said anything, and she fell away a full four feet, pulling a pad of paper from her waistband. What she wanted was obvious. Why she hadn't said anything in greeting was obvious too; we had her on edge.

Ivy smiled, then toned it down when Becky, by her name tag, paled. Putting the flat of my arms on the table, I leaned forward to look brainless. "Hi," I said. "What's the special?"

The woman darted a glance at Ivy, then back to me. "Ah, no special—ma'am," she said, reaching nervously to touch her white hair, which had been dyed blond. "But Mike in the back makes a damn, uh, he makes a good hamburger. And we've got pie today."

Nick silently joined us, with Jax on his shoulder, looking uncomfortable as he took the last seat next to Ivy and across from Jenks. The woman relaxed a notch, apparently realizing he was human and deciding the rest of us were probably half tamed. I didn't know how they did it since they couldn't smell Inderlander on us, as we could on ourselves. Must be some secret human finger motion or something.

"Hamburger sounds good," Ivy said, her eyes down to look meek, but with her stiff posture it only made her look pissed.

"Four hamburgers all around," I said, wanting to be done with it and eating. "And a pitcher of Coke."

Nick scooted his chair closer to the table, Jax leaving him for the warmer light hanging over the table. "I'd like two hamburgers, please," the gaunt man said, a hint of defiance in his voice, as if he expected someone to protest.

"Me too," Jenks chimed up, bright eyes wickedly innocent. "I'm starved."

Nick leaned to see the menu on the wall. "Does that come with fries?"

"Fries!" Jenks exclaimed, and Jax sneezed from the lamp hanging over the table. Pixy dust sifted down along with the mundane type. "Tink-knocks-your-knickers, I want fries too."

The woman wrote it down, her plucked and penciled-in eyebrows rising. "Two half-pound burgers with fries for each of the gentleman. Anything else?"

Nick nodded. "A milk shake. Cherry if you have it."

She blew out her breath, taking in his gaunt frame. "How about you, hon?"

Becky was looking at Jenks, but he was eyeing the jukebox. "Coke is fine. Does that thing work?"

The woman turned, following his gaze to the machine. "It's busted, but for five bucks you can use the karaoke machine all you want."

Jenks's eyes widened. "Most excellent," he said in a surfer-boy accent. From above us came Jax's exuberant shout that all the bugs in the lamp shade had been dried out by the heat and he was going to eat their wings like chips if she didn't mind.

Oh God. And it had been going so well.

Ivy cleared her throat, clearly appalled when Jax flitted from lamp to lamp, growing more excited by the amount of pixy dust he was letting slip. "Ah, I think that will do it," I said, and the woman turned away, bumping into a table as she watched Jax on her way to the kitchen. The hair on the back of my neck had pricked; everyone in the bar was looking at us. Even the cook.

Jenks followed my gaze, his blond eyebrows high. "Let me take care of this," he said, standing up. "Rache, do you have any money? I spent mine at The Butterfly Shack."

Ivy's eyes darkened. "I can handle this."

A small noise came from Jenks. "Like at the FIB?" he scoffed. "Sit down, weenie vamp. I'm too big to get shoved into a water cooler."

Feeling the tension rise, I shuffled in my bag and handed Jenks my wallet. I didn't know what he had in mind, but it was probably a lot less scary than what Ivy had planned, and it wouldn't land us in the local jail either. "Leave some in there, okay?"

He gave me a lopsided, charming smile, his perfect teeth catching the light. "Hey, it's me." Making a click to tell Jax to join him, he ambled to the bar, his pace more provocative than it ought to have been. The man couldn't have any idea how good he looked.

"No honey toddies!" I shot after him, and he raised a backward hand. Ivy wasn't happy when I met her gaze. "What?" I protested. "You've seen him on honey."

Nick snickered and set his glass of water down. Jax flew a glittering path to the karaoke machine ahead of his dad, Jenks's pace intent as he followed. Becky had her eyes glued to the small pixy as she talked on the phone, and I had a feeling he was intentionally dusting heavy. I wondered how this would get everyone's eyes off us. A distraction, maybe?

The father and son clustered at the screen, a reading lesson ensuing while they looked at the song menu. Ivy glanced at them, then Nick. "Go help them," she muttered.

Nick pulled his gaunt face up to hers. "Why?"

Ivy's jaw clenched. "Because I want to talk to Rachel."

Frowning, Nick rose, his chair scraping on the wooden floor. Our drinks arrived, and the woman set his cherry shake, three glasses of Coke, and a condensation-wet pitcher on the table. Milk shake in hand, Nick shuffled to Jenks and Jax, looking tired in his gray sweats.

I sipped my Coke, feeling the bubbles burn all the way down. My stomach was empty and the smell of the cooking meat was giving me a headache. Setting the glass aside so I didn't slam it, I slumped, relying on Ivy to keep an eye on my back. I watched her relax muscle by muscle until she was calm.

"I'm glad you're here," I said. "I really made a crap pit of everything. He was in the middle of a survivalist group, for God's sake. I never expected that." *I should have done more recon,* I thought, but I didn't need to say it. It was obvious.

Ivy shrugged, glancing at Nick, Jenks, and Jax. "You got him out. I wasn't planning on staying," she added, "but since I'm here, I'll stick around."

I blew my breath out, relieved. "Thanks. But is that . . . prudent?" I hesitated, then ventured, "Piscary's going to be royally ticked if you aren't there by sundown."

Her gaze tracked Jax flitting madly from Nick to Jenks. "So

what?" she said, fingers fidgeting with her new earrings. "He knows I'll be back. It's only a six-hour drive."

"Yes, but you're out of his influence, and he doesn't—" My words cut off when she rolled her fingertips across the table in a soft threat. "He doesn't like that," I boldly finished, pulse quickening. Here, surrounded by humans, was probably the only place I'd dare push her like this. She was on her best behavior, and I was going to use it for all it was worth.

Ivy bowed her head, the black sheet of her shorter hair not hiding her face. The dusky scent of incense became obvious, and a soft tickle shivered through me. "It will be okay," she said, but I wasn't convinced. She lifted her head, and a faint blush of worry, or perhaps fear, colored her. "Kisten is there," she said. "If I leave, no one cares but the higher-ups—who aren't going to do anything anyway. Kisten is the one who can't leave. If he does, it will be noticed, talked about, and acted upon by idiots who haven't had their fangs for a month. We're fine."

This really wasn't what I had been worried about. Part of me wanted to take her explanation at face value and drop it, but the other part, the wiser, stupider half of me, wanted her to be honest so there would be no surprises. I turned when the front door opened and a woman came in, talking loudly to Becky as she shrugged out of her coat and headed for the back.

"Ivy," I said softly, "what about your hunger? You don't have your usual . . ." I stopped, not sure what to call the people she tapped for blood. *Donors? Special friends? Significant others?* I settled on, "Support net?"

Ivy froze, sending a jolt of adrenaline through me. *Crap. Maybe I should keep my mouth shut.* "Sorry," I said, meaning it. "It's not my business."

"Your timing sucks," she said, and the tension eased. I hadn't overstepped the friendship boundaries.

"Well . . ." I said, wincing. "I don't know what you do."

"I can't go out and knock up a streetwalker," she said bitterly. Her eyes were hard, and I could tell she wasn't responding to me but to a deeper guilt. "If I let it be a savage act that I can satisfy with anyone, I'll be a monster. What kind of a person do you think I am?"

"That's not what I said," I protested. "Cut me some slack, will you? I don't know how you take care of yourself, and I was too afraid to ask until now. All I know is you go out anxious and jittery and come home calm and hating yourself."

My admission of fear seemed to penetrate, and the creases in her forehead smoothed. She uncrossed her legs, then crossed them under the table. "Sorry. It surprised me you asked. I should be good for a few days more, but the stress—" Ivy cut her thought short and took a breath. "I have a few people. We help each other and go our separate ways. I don't ask anything from them, and they don't ask anything from me. They're vamps, in case you're interested. I don't make ties with anyone else . . . anymore."

Single, bi vamp looking for same for blood tryst, not relationship, I thought, hearing her unspoken desire in her last sentence, but I wasn't ready to deal with it.

"I don't like living like this," Ivy said, her words unaccusing and her eyes a deep, honest brown. "But it's where I am right now. Don't worry about it. I'll be okay. And as far as Piscary is concerned, he can burn in hell—if his soul hadn't already evaporated."

Her face was expressionless again, but I knew it was a front. "So you're going to stay?" I asked, both embarrassed and proud that I had learned I could ask for help when I needed it, and boy did I need it.

She nodded, and I exhaled, reaching for my drink. "Thank you," I said softly.

The idea of leaving everything to play dead the rest of my life scared the crap out of me the way a death threat couldn't. I liked my life, and I didn't want to have to leave it and start over. It had taken me too long to find friends who would stick with me when I did something stupid. Like turning a simple snag and drag into an interspecies power struggle.

Shifting one shoulder up and down in a half shrug, Ivy reached under her chair for that paper bag. "Do you want your mail," she asked, "seeing as I brought it all this way?"

She was changing the subject, but that was fine by me. "I thought you were kidding," I said as Ivy set the sack on the table and I dragged it closer. Jenks and Jax were excited about something they had found on the list, and people had given up watching them in glances and were blatantly staring. At least they weren't looking at us.

"It's the package I'm curious about," Ivy said, glancing at Nick and Jenks while they pointed at the screen.

I dumped everything out, putting the obvious thank-you-for-saving-my-ass note from a previous run back in the bag along with the insurance bill from David's company and a late season seed catalog. What was left was a paper-wrapped parcel the size of my two fists. I looked closer at the handwriting, my eyes jerking to Nick in the corner. "It's from Nick," I said, reaching for a table knife. "What is he sending me when he thinks I'm dead?"

Ivy's face held a silent distain clearly directed at Nick. "I'd be willing to bet it's whatever the Weres are after. I thought it was his handwriting, but I wasn't sure."

Very conscious of Nick slurping his shake and reading track titles over Jenks's shoulder, I pulled the package off the table and put it in my lap. My pulse quickened and I made short work of the outer wrapping. Fingers cold, I opened the box and pulled out the heavy drawstring bag. "It's got lead in it," I said, feeling the supple weight of the fabric. "It's wrapped in lead, Ivy. I don't like this."

She casually leaned forward to block Nick's view. "Well, what is it?"

Licking my lips, I tugged the opening wider and peered down, deciding it was a figurine. I gingerly touched it, finding it cold. More confident, I drew it out and set it on the table between us. Staring at it, I wiped my hands off on my jeans.

"That is . . . really ugly," Ivy said. "I think it's ugly." Her brown eyes flicked to me. "Is it ugly, or just weird?"

Goose bumps rose, and I stifled a shiver. "I don't know."

The statue was a yellowish color with stained striations running through it. Bone, I guessed. Very old bone; it had left the cold feeling on my hands that bone does. It stood about four inches high and was about as deep. And it felt alive, like a tree or a plate of moldy cheese.

I furrowed my brow as I tried to figure out what it was a statue of. Touching only the base, I turned it with two fingers. A noise of disgust slipped from me; the other side had a long muzzle twisted as if in pain. "Is it a head?" I guessed.

Ivy put her elbow on the table. "I think so. But the teeth . . . Those are teeth, right?"

I shivered, feeling like someone had walked over my grave. "Oh," I whispered, realizing what it reminded me of. "It looks like Pam when she was in the middle of Wereing."

Ivy flicked her eyes to mine and back to the statue. As I watched, her face went paler and her eyes went frightened. "Damn," she muttered. "I think I know what it is. Cover it up. We are in deep shit."

Twenty

I jerked when Nick suddenly appeared at the table. His long face was flushed, angry and frightened all at the same time—a dangerous mix. "What are you doing?" he hissed at Ivy, snatching the statue up and holding it close. "You brought it here? I sent it to her so no one would find it. I thought she was dead. They couldn't make me tell who had it if I sent it to a dead woman, and you brought it here? You damned fool vampire!"

"Sit," Ivy said, her jaw clenched and her eyes shifting to black. "Give it to me."

"No." Nick's grip tensed to a white-knuckled strength. "Save the aura shit for someone it works on. I'm not afraid of you."

He was, and Ivy's hand trembled. "Nicholas. I'm hungry. I'm tired. I don't give a crap about your stupid ass. My partner is in deep shit because of you. *Give it to me.*"

Adrenaline pulsed, hurting my head. Nick was near panic. The karaoke machine started up with something sad and melancholy. Jenks was watching us, but the rest of the bar hadn't a clue that Ivy was about ready to lose it, pushed to the edge from stress and being far from home.

"Nick," I soothed. "It'll be okay. Give it to me. I'll put it away."

Nick shifted and Ivy jerked, almost reaching for him. Licking his cracked lips, Nick said, "You'll hold it for me?"

"I'll keep it," I assured him, fumbling for the lead-lined bag and extending it. "Here."

Hollow-cheeked face frightened, he carefully placed it into

the pouch. His swollen fingers started curving around it, and I pulled it to me, tightening the drawstrings. It wasn't any magical hold it had on him; it was greed.

Hand shaking, Ivy grabbed her drink and downed it to ice. I kept an eye on her while I put the statue in my bag, then put the bag on my lap. It felt heavy, like a dead thing. From the corner came Jenks singing "Ballad of the Edmund Fitzgerald." The skinny guy at the bar was watching him, having turned completely from the game recap. *Jenks could sing?*

"Sit," Ivy breathed, and this time Nick did, taking Jenks's spot beside me and putting Jenks's coat on the chair beside Ivy. "Where did you find that?" she muttered.

"It's mine."

I shifted in my chair, smelling our food coming. The woman didn't look at anyone as she placed the food down and left. The tension was so thick, even she could sense it. I stared at my plate. There was my fabulous burger, oozing juice, with lettuce, onions, mushrooms, cheese, and, oh God, there was bacon on it too. And I couldn't eat it because we had to argue about Nick's ugly statue first. *Well, to hell with that,* I thought, removing the top bun and picking the onions off.

Ivy refilled her glass from the pitcher, a growing rim of brown around her pupils. "I didn't say whose is it. I said, where did you find it?"

Nick pulled his plate closer, clearly wanting to ignore her but making the healthy decision not to. "I can't believe you brought it here," he said again, motions jerky as he rearranged his pickles. "I sent it to Rachel so it would be safe."

Ivy glared at him. "If you use smart people in your takes without telling them, don't complain when they do the unexpected and ruin your plans."

"I thought she was dead," Nick protested. "I never expected anyone to come *help* me."

I ate one of Jenks's fries. There wasn't any ketchup on the table, but asking for some would get us thrown out. Humans blamed the Turn on tomatoes, but they were the ones who had done the genetic tinkering. "And why are they willing to pack up to get ahold of it?" I asked.

Nick looked ill. "I don't have to tell you anything."

My lips parted in disbelief, and I turned to Ivy. "He's still running his scam."

"I'm not." His eyes were wide in an innocence that couldn't reach me anymore. "But the Weres can't have it. Don't you know what it is?"

His last words were a hushed whisper, and Ivy glanced past me to the door as three underdressed, giggling women pranced in. Immediately Becky started in with a high-pitched chatter, her eyes tracking to Jenks. I think she had called them about fresh meat.

"I know what it is," Ivy said, dismissing the women. "*Where did you find it?*"

One of the guys at the bar was humming. While we sat hunched over our food and argued, Jenks had some guy at the bar singing about a tanker that had sunk forty-some years ago. Shaking my head in wonder, I returned my attention to Nick. "We're waiting," I said, then wrangled my burger to my mouth. My eyes closed as I bit into it. Sweet bliss, it was good.

His eyes stressed, Nick picked up one of his burgers, leaning his elbows on the table. "Rachel, you saw how there were three packs on that island, didn't you? All working together?"

I scrambled for a napkin. "It was freaking weird," I said around my full mouth. "You should have seen how fast their alpha Wered. And they were nasty too. Like alphas without the restraint. Cocky little bastards . . ." My words trailed off as I took another bite.

"That's what it does," Nick said, and Ivy swore under her breath. "I found it in Detroit."

"Then it's the focus?" she whispered, and I waved a hand for their attention, fry weaving between the two of them, but they weren't listening to me. "That thing can't be the focus," Ivy added. "It was destroyed five millennia ago. We don't even know if it even really existed. And if it did, it sure as hell wouldn't be in Detroit."

"That's where I found it," Nick said, then took a bite. A small moan came from him. "You can't destroy something that powerful," he mumbled. "Not with rocks and sticks. And not with magic." He swallowed. "Maybe with a car crusher, but they didn't have them back then."

"What is it?" I insisted, only marginally aware of the flirting going on across the room between the stanzas of men dying on the waves. *Get a clue, Jenks.*

Ivy pushed her untouched plate with her burger away. "It's trouble," she said. "I was going to make him give it to the Weres, but now—"

"Damn it!" I shouted, and the three women ogling Jenks giggled and jiggled—in that order. I lowered my voice. "Someone tell me what I have sitting on my lap before I explode."

"You're the professor," Ivy said bitingly to Nick, taking a fry from Jenks's plate. "You tell her."

Nick washed a bite of his first burger down and hesitated. "Vamps can either be born or bitten, but the only way to become a Were is to be born one."

"Duh," I said. "Witches are like that too, along with most of Inderland."

"Well . . ." Nick paused, his eyes flicking everywhere. ". . . the Were holding that thing can make a Were by a bite."

I chewed and swallowed. "And they want to kill you for that?"

Ivy brought her head up. "Think about it, Rachel," she cajoled. "Right now, vampires are at the top of the food chain."

I made a telling face at her as I took another bite, wrangling a piece of bacon.

"What I mean is we have more political power than any other Inderlander species," she amended. "Because of how we're structured, everyone looks to someone else, the top vampires owing so many favors that they're as effective as a political house member. It's a tight web, but we generally get what we want. Humans would get itchy with their trigger finger except that our numbers are held static by only the undead being able to infect a human with enough virus to make it even possible to Turn them."

I stole another of Jenks's fries, wishing I had ketchup.

"Weres, though," Nick said, "don't have political power as a group because they won't look to any but their pack leader. And their numbers can't increase any faster than their birthrate." Leaning forward, Nick tapped the table with a swollen finger, his entire mien changing as he became the instructor.

"The focus makes it possible for the number of Weres to increase very quickly. And the multiple packing you saw on the island is nothing to what will happen when it gets out that the focus is intact. Everyone will want a part of it, merging their pack into the one that holds it. You saw what they were like. Can you imagine what would happen if a vampire ran into a pack of Weres acting like that?"

Jenks's half-eaten fry dangled from my fingers, forgotten. Slowly it was starting to sink in, and it didn't look good. The problem wasn't that the focus would allow Weres to pack up. The problem was that the focus would *keep* them packed up. Worried, I glanced at Ivy. Seeing me understand, she nodded.

The island Weres had been together for days, maybe weeks, and that had been with only the promise of the focus. If they had it, the round would be permanent. I thought back to the ring of Weres surrounding me on the island, the three packs united under one Were holding the strength of six alphas. Their cocky, savage attitude had been shocking. Walter had not only drawn his dominance from them, but also channeled it back into every member without the tempering calm and moral strength that all alphas had. That wasn't even bringing up how fast they could Were if they muted each other's pain. Add to that their new aggressiveness and a resistance to pain?

I set Jenks's fry down, no longer hungry. Weres were fairly submissive in Inderland society, the alphas the only ones having enough personal power to challenge the vampires' political structure. Remove that submissive posture, and the two species were going to start clashing. A lot. That's probably why the vamps had hidden the focus in the first place.

Crap, if the vampires knew about it, they would be after me too. "This isn't good," I said, feeling ill.

Making a puff, Ivy leaned back. "You think?"

From across the bar, Jenks finished his song, immediately falling into a sleazy version of "American Woman," gyrating his hips and making the three women and one of the truck drivers cheer and whistle. Jax was above him, making sparkles. I wondered if anyone had any inkling the world was changing, starting right here in this little bar.

Wiping my fingers clean, I reached for the bag on my lap. "It can shift the balance of Inderland power," I said, and Ivy nodded, the tips of her hair swinging.

"With the explosive destruction of dropping a tiger into a dog show," she said dryly. "It's believed that Weres used to have a political structure very similar to that of the vampires. Better, since Weres never betrayed another as vampires are known to do for blood. Their hierarchy revolved around who held the focus, and eliminating it shattered the Weres' social structure, politically castrating them and leaving them squabbling in small packs."

Nick started on his second burger. "They were going to forcibly convert humanity, according to the demon texts," he said, taking off the top bun to eat it like an open-faced sandwich. "Those who wouldn't voluntarily become a Were were killed. Entire families whelped or murdered in the name of Were conquest over vampires. They would have had a good chance of succeeding but the witches crossed from the ever-after about that time and sided with the humans and vampires. Using witch magic, we beat them back."

Nervous, I slipped my flip-flop off and on to make a popping sound. I wondered what he had given a demon for learning this. I'd never heard it before, but Ivy had, so maybe I just hadn't taken the right class. I couldn't help thinking that perhaps witches were really at the top of the food chain, our independent ways and lack of political structure aside. Every earth spell on the market, whether used by human, vampire, or Were, was made by a witch. Without us, their little political wars would be fought with sticks, stones, and nasty words.

"The focus was destroyed," Ivy said, her voice low and her eyes thick with worry.

Nick shook his head. Gulping down a swig of soda, he said, "It's demon made, and only a demon can destroy it. It has been passed from vampire to ranking vampire for generations."

"Until you sold a piece of your soul for it," I whispered, and Nick went white. *Stupid-ass human,* I thought, then hid my own wrist.

Jenks finished his song amid cheers and friendly shouts. He bowed and blew kisses, stepping off the stage and making his light-footed way to us. A camera flashed, and I wished I had remembered mine. Jax flitted over the ladies at the bar, charming them thoroughly and helping his dad avoid them. The mood of the bar had shifted dramatically thanks to Jenks; now even the looks our way from the truckers had a touch of daring voyeurism.

"Food's here?" Jenks said, handing me my wallet before dropping down and grappling with the first of his burgers with the enthusiasm of a starving adolescent. Jax stayed with the women, distracting everyone and staying safely out of the adult conversation. "What'd I miss?" Jenks added, taking a bite.

I sucked at my teeth and gave Ivy a wry look. "Nick swiped a Were artifact that can tip the balance of Inderland power and start a vampire-Were war," I said, putting my wallet away next to the Were statue. *I needed to call David and get his take on this. On second thought, maybe I shouldn't.*

Jenks froze, his cheeks bulging with food. He met everyone's eyes to figure out if we were joking, but it wasn't until Nick nodded that he remembered to swallow. "Holy crap," he said.

"That's about it." I sighed. "What are we going to do with it? We can't give it to them."

Nick picked at his fries. "I'm the one who started this. I'll take it and disappear."

In a smooth motion of grace, Ivy reclined in her chair. She looked calm and possessed, but I could tell by her fingers searching for her missing crucifix that she wasn't. "It's not that simple now, professor. They know who Rachel is. Jenks they might give up on, but by saving your ass, Rachel put her own on the line. She can't go back to Cincinnati as if it never happened. They will follow her through hell for that thing." Putting the flat of one arm on the table, she leaned forward, her face threatening. "They will hurt her just like they hurt you to get it, and I'm not going to let that happen, you dumb little shit."

"Stop it," I said as Nick reddened. "We can't give it back. What else do we have?"

Ivy picked a sesame seed off her burger, looking sullen. Nick, too, had a chip the size of Montana on his shoulder. Jenks was the only one whose face was creased in thought, not anger. "Can you make everyone forget about it?" he asked as he chewed. "Or at least forget about us?"

I pushed my plate away. "Too many people. I'd miss someone. Not to mention it would be a black earth charm. I'm not doing it." *But I'd twist demon curses?* No accounting for tastes, I guess. But Ceri's curse hadn't involved hurting people other than me.

Jenks chewed slowly. "How about putting it into hiding again?"

"I'm not putting it back," Nick protested. "I spent a year's income getting it."

Ignoring him, I frowned. *Was he still running his take?*

"They'd still come after Rachel," Ivy said. "If you can't make everyone forget," she said to me, "I can only think of one thing to get your life back after crap for brains screwed it up."

Nick took an angry breath. "You call me that again and I'm going to—"

Ivy moved. I jumped, managing to keep my reaction to a small hop when she sent her arm forward and grabbed Nick under his chin. Nick's eyes widened but he didn't move. He had grown up in the Hollows and knew that moving would only make things worse.

Ivy's eyes were almost entirely black. "You'll what, crap for brains?"

"Ivy . . ." I said tiredly. "Stop it."

Jenks looked from me to Ivy, his eyes bright and his face worried. "Lighten up, Ivy," he said softly. "You know she always sides with the underdog."

Jenks's words penetrated where mine hadn't, and in a flash of brown Ivy's pupils returned to normal. Smiling beatifically, she let go, catching Nick by the collar of his sweatshirt before he could rock back, pretending to adjust it for him. "Sorry, Nickie," she said, her pale fingers patting his hollow cheek a smidgen too hard.

As I tried to purge the adrenaline from me, Nick scooted his chair away, cautiously rubbing his throat. Moving a shade too fast, Ivy refilled her glass from the pitcher. "There's only one solution," she said, bending her straw exactly upright. "Professor here has to die."

"Whoa, whoa, whoa!" I exclaimed, and Nick stiffened, his face red in anger. "Ivy, that's enough."

Jenks pulled his plate of fries closer. "Hey, I'm right there with you," he said, his eyes roving the bar, probably for the nonexistent ketchup. "It would solve everything." He hesitated, wiping his fingers on a napkin. "You grab him, and I'll get your sword from the van."

"Hey!" I shouted, angry. I knew they weren't serious, but they were starting to tick me off. I lowered my voice when the giggling women at the bar looked at us. "Nick, relax. They aren't going to kill you."

Snickering, Jenks started on his fries, and Ivy took on a confident, almost seductive stance, slouching in her chair and smiling with one side of her mouth. "All right," she said. "If you're going to get bent out of shape about it, we won't kill him. We'll stage his spectacular, public death along with the destruction of that thing."

Nick stared at Ivy's confident figure. "I will *not* let you destroy it," he said vehemently.

She arched her eyebrows. "You can't stop me. It's the only option we have to get those Weres off Rachel's tail, so unless you have a suggestion, I suggest you shut up."

Nick went still. I eyed his brow furrowed in thought, then slid my gaze to Jenks. Jenks was watching him too, his mouth full but his jaws not moving. We exchanged a knowing look. Someone who endured a week of torture wouldn't give up that easy. Ivy didn't seem to notice, but Ivy didn't know Nick like I was starting to know Nick. *God, why was I even trying to help him?* I thought, jiggling my foot to make my flip-flops pop. Depressed, I reached for my soda.

"So you stage my death and the destruction of the focus," the apparently subdued human said, and Jenks returned to eating, pretending ignorance. "I think they're going to notice when the ambulance takes me to the hospital instead of the morgue."

Ivy's eyes tracked someone headed our way. Glass in hand, I turned to find Becky with three drinks holding umbrellas and cherries on sticks. My eyes went to the flirting women, and I cringed. Oh . . . how nice. They were trying to pick him up.

"I can get us a body," Ivy said into the silence.

I choked on my drink, coughing at the string of thoughts that remark engendered, but Becky had come forward and I couldn't say a word—even if I could catch my breath.

"Here you go, hon," she said, smiling as she set the drinks squarely before Jenks. "From the ladies at the bar."

"Oh, wow," Jenks said, apparently forgetting what accepting drinks from strangers meant when one was over four inches tall. "Look, pixy swords!"

He reached for the cherry picks, eyes glinting, and I interrupted with a quick, "Jenks!"

Ivy exhaled, sounding tired, and Jenks glanced from one of us to the other. "What?" he said, then reddened. Wincing, he looked up at Becky. "Hey, um, I'm married," he said, and I heard someone swear from the bar. It wasn't the trucker, thank God. "Maybe," he said, pushing them reluctantly to her, "you should return them to the ladies with my, uh, regrets."

"Well, shoot," Becky said, smiling. "You just keep them. I told them a hunk like you would be already hooked, landed, filleted, and cooked." Her smile widened. "And eaten."

Ivy exhaled, and Nick didn't seem to know whether to be proud or embarrassed for his species. Jenks shook his head, probably thinking of Matalina as he pushed them away.

"Did you say you had pie?" Ivy asked.

"Yes, ma'am." Becky smoothly took up the drinks, pixy swords and all. "I have butterscotch or apple. I'll bring out a wedge of apple, seeing as you're allergic to butterscotch."

Ivy blinked but her smile never faltered. "Thank you." She pushed her untouched hamburger at her, and the woman obligingly took both it and my plate. "Put a scoop of ice cream on it?" she asked. "And coffee. Everyone want coffee?" She looked inquiringly at us, smiling in a way that made me decidedly nervous, especially after that "I can get us a body" remark, and I nodded. *Coffee? Why not?*

"Sugar and cream," Jenks added faintly, and Becky sashayed

away, loudly proclaiming to the three women at the bar that she had known it all along.

Ivy watched her go, then looked at me with a questioning scrutiny. I suddenly realized Becky must have talked to Terri from the grocery store. Feeling another one of my stellar, embarrassing moments coming on, I hunched forward and took another sip, hiding behind the glass. No wonder the entire bar was being nice to us. They thought I was a nympho who liked doing it with three people and pudding.

"Why am I allergic to butterscotch?" Ivy asked slowly.

My face flamed, and Jenks stammered, "Ah, Rachel and I are lovers with a thing for foursomes and pudding. Apparently she thinks you and Nick are Alexia and Tom. You're allergic to butterscotch, and crap for brains likes pistachio."

"Stop calling me that," Nick muttered.

Ivy let her breath out. Her eyebrows were arched, and she looked bemused. "Okay . . ."

I set my drink down. "Can we get back to how we're going to kill Nick? And what's this about a dead body? You'd better start talking quick, Ivy, 'cause I'm not going to play hide-and-seek with a dead guy in my trunk. I did that in college, and I'm not going to do it again."

A smile quirked Ivy's mouth. "Really?" she asked, and I flushed.

"Well, he wasn't dead," I muttered. "But they told me he was. Scared the crap out of me when he kissed my ear when I tried to lug him into—" I stopped when I felt Becky at my elbow, a tray of coffee and pie in her hand.

Smirking, Becky gave everyone their coffee and set a piece of pie à la mode in front of Ivy. Humming "American Woman," she took Jenks's and Nick's empty plates and left.

I eyed the ice cream and then my fork. "You going to eat all that?" I asked, knowing from experience Ivy rarely finished anything.

Glancing at me for permission, Ivy took my coffee cup off its saucer and put the ice cream in its place. I pulled it closer, feeling the tension start to ease. I didn't have a spoon, but my fork worked, and I wasn't going to ask Becky for one.

Ivy carefully cut the point from her pie and pushed it away to eat last. "I propose we pull a Kevorkian," she said, and I went cold from more than the ice cream.

"That's illegal," Jenks said quickly.

"Only if you get caught," Ivy said, eyes on her pie. "I have a friend of a friend—"

"No." I set my fork down. "I'm not going to help a vampire cross over. I won't. Ivy, you're asking me to kill someone!"

My voice had risen, and Ivy tossed her hair from her eyes. "He's twenty, and he's in so much pain he can't use the can without someone helping him."

"No!" I said louder, not caring people were starting to look. "Absolutely not." I turned to Jenks and Nick for support, appalled to see their acceptance of this. "You guys are sick!" I said. "I'm not going to do that!"

"Rachel," Ivy said persuasively, brown eyes showing an unusual amount of emotion. "People do it all the time."

"This people right here doesn't." Flustered, I pushed the ice cream away, wondering if it had been part of her plan to get me to accept. She knew I was a sucker for ice cream. I scowled at the laughter from the bar, turning to see Becky gossiping to the truck drivers, bent over with her rear in the air. It occurred to me they probably thought I had just been propositioned for something even a redheaded nympho would say no to. Crossing my arms in front of me, I glared at Ivy.

"He'd do it himself," Ivy said softly. "God knows he has enough courage. But he needs his life insurance check to set himself up, and if he kills himself, he loses it. He's been waiting a long time."

"No."

Ivy's lips pressed together. Then her brow smoothed. "I'll call him," she said softly. "You talk to him, and if you still feel the same way, we'll call it off. It will be up to you."

My head hurt. If I didn't say yes now, I would look meaner than Satan's baby-sitter. "Alexia," I said loud enough for the bar to hear. "You are one sick bitch."

Her smile widened. "That's my girl." Clearly pleased, she picked up her fork and ate another bite of pie. "Can you make a charm to make someone look like little professor here?"

Nick stiffened, and Jenks chuckled, "Little professor . . ." as he dumped a fourth packet of sugar into his coffee. I felt like I was in my high school lunchroom, plotting a prank.

"Yeah, I can do that," I said. Sullen, I pushed the melting ice cream around on my plate. Doppelganger charms were illegal, but not black. Why not? I was going to freaking kill someone.

"Good." Ivy speared the last of her pie, going still in thought before she ate the point, and I knew she was making a wish. *And people thought I was superstitious?* "Now all we have to do is find a way to destroy that thing," she finished.

At that, Nick stirred. "You're not going to destroy it. It's over five thousand years old."

I sent my flip-flops popping. "I agree," I said, and Nick shot me a grateful glance. "If we can substitute a fake Nick, then we can substitute a fake statue."

Ivy leaned back in her chair with her coffee. "I don't care," she said. "But you . . ." She pointed a finger at Nick. ". . . aren't going to get it. Rachel is going to put it into hiding, and you—get—nothing."

Nick looked sullen, and I exchanged that same knowing look with Jenks. This was going to be a problem. Jenks stirred his coffee. "So . . ." he said, "how are we going to knack Nick?"

I thought his verbiage left something to be desired, but I let it pass, ignoring my melting bribe. "I don't know. I'm usually on the saving-your-butt end of things."

Blowing across his mug, Jenks shrugged. "I'm partial to crushing their chest until their ribs crack and their blood splatters like Jell-O in a blender without a top." He took a sip, wincing. "That's what I do to fairies."

I frowned, appalled when he added two more packets of sugar.

"We could push him off a roof," Ivy suggested. "Drown him, maybe? We've got lots of water around here."

Jenks leaned conspiratorially toward Ivy, his green eyes darting merrily between mine and hers. "I'd suggest jamming a stick of dynamite up his ass and running away, but that might really hurt whoever is taking his place."

Ivy laughed, and I frowned at both of them. The karaoke machine had started up again, and I felt ill when "Love Shack" began bouncing out. *Oh my God.* The skinny trucker was up on the stage with the three bimbos as backup.

I looked, then looked again. Finally I tore my eyes away. "Hey," I said, feeling the weight of the last twenty-four hours fall on me. "I've been up since yesterday noon. Can we just find somewhere to crash for the day?"

Immediately Ivy grabbed her purse from under her chair. "Yeah, let's go. I have to call Peter. It will take him, his scion, and his mentor a day to get up here. You sleep, Jenks and I will come up with a few plans, and you can pick the one that your magic will work the best with." She glanced at Jenks, and he nodded. Both of them turned to me. "Sound okay?"

"Sure," I said, taking a slow breath to steady myself. Inside I was shaking. I wasn't too keen on picking *any* plan that involved killing someone. But the Weres wouldn't give up on Nick unless he was dead; and unless there was a body, they would know it was a scam.

And I wanted to go home. I wanted to go home to my church and my life. They would hound me to the ends of the earth if they knew the focus was found and in my possession.

I stood, feeling as if I was slipping into places that I had once vowed I would never go. If we were caught, we would be tried for murder.

But what choice did I have?

Twenty-one

The scent of cinnamon and cloves was thick in the motel room, making it smell like the solstice. Nick was making ginger drops, and the warmth of the tiny efficiency oven was pleasant at my back. It wasn't unusual for him to bake, but I thought it more likely he was trying to bribe me into talking to him than a desire for homemade cookies. And since Jenks had the TV on a kids' show for Jax, and Ivy wouldn't let Nick plan his own demise, the human had little to do.

The Weres knew Jenks, so Ivy had gone shopping while I slept, laden down with a grocery list and my shoe size. All of us going out for food three times a day—or in Jenks's case, six—didn't seem prudent. We had found a suite five minutes from the bar, and after giving the low-ceilinged rooms done in brown and gold the once-over, I stated clearly that *I* had the van. Ivy took the bed in the tiny room off the main room, Nick got the bed in the main room, and Jenks wanted the sofa sleeper, happily opening it up and putting it away twice before Ivy and I finished unloading the van; she didn't want Nick touching anything. The van was tight and cold, but it was quiet, and with the circle I'd put up while I slept, safer than the motel.

I had woken cranky and stiff that morning at an ungodly nine o'clock, unable to go back to sleep after my twelve-hour nap. And since Jenks and Jax were both up, and Nick, of course, was awake, I thought I'd take the opportunity to get a jump on the magic prep. *Yeah. Right.*

"Want to lick the spoon, Ray-ray?" Nick said, his gaunt face looking more relaxed than I'd seen it since . . . last fall.

I smiled, trying to keep it noncommittal. "No thanks." I bent my attention back to the laptop screen. With Kisten's help, Ceri had e-mailed me the earth charm I needed to make the disguise amulets, with her additions to turn it into an illegal doppelganger spell. It was still white, but I wasn't familiar enough with the additional ingredients to sensitize it to mimic a particular person.

Stretching, I pulled my scratch pad closer and added pumpkin seeds to my list. The bulb over the oven glinted on my no-spell charm bracelet, and I jiggled the black gold, making an audible show of my break with Nick. Ignoring it, he continued to wedge blobs of cookie dough onto a nasty-looking pan. Then he hesitated, clearly wanting to say something but deciding against it. The first batch of cookies had come out of the oven not long ago, and the smell was heaven.

I was avoiding the cookies on some vague principle, but Jenks had a plateful as he leaned over Jax's work on the table by the curtained window. Though the TV was on, neither was paying attention to it, absorbed in their practice. Rex sat in the warmth of Jenks's lap, her pretty white paws tucked sweetly under her as she stared at me from across the room. That Jax was strutting atop the table didn't seem to be important to her right now.

Ever the vigilant father, Jenks had a gentling hand about her fur in case she remembered Jax and took a swipe at him. But the kitten was fixed on me, giving me a mild case of the creeps. I think she knew I had been that wolf, and was waiting for me to turn back.

Her ears swiveled to the back room, and a sudden thump sent her skittering. Jenks yelped when her claws dug into him, but she was already under the bed. Jax was after her in a sprinkling of gold pixy dust, coaxing in a high-pitched voice that grated on my eyeballs. From Ivy's room came a torrent of muffled curses. *Great. Now what?*

The door to Ivy's room was flung open. She wore her usual silk nightie, and her short black hair was tousled from her pillow. Lean and sleek, she stomped across the nasty carpet, looking intent on mayhem.

The Electric Company theme song bounced as she strode into the kitchen. Eyes wide, I turned to keep her in view. Nick stood in the corner, satisfaction gleaming in his eyes, the bowl of dough in his long hands. Lips pressed tight, Ivy grabbed an oven mitt, pulled open the oven, and yanked out the tin of baking cookies. It made a muffled clatter when she dropped it onto the tin with its blobs of uncooked dough waiting to go in the oven.

Her brown eyes fixed on Nick's for an instant, then she grabbed the two tins with the oven mitt and strode to the door. Still silent, she opened it, dropping everything on the walk outside. Her speed was edging into a vamp quickness when she returned, jerking the bowl out of Nick's unresisting grip and swiping the cookies cooling on the counter into it.

"Ivy?" I questioned.

"'Morning, Rachel," she said tightly. Ignoring Jenks, she opened the door and dropped the metal mixing bowl onto the walk with the rest. Plucking the cookie out of Jenks's hand, she flicked it over the threshold, slammed the door, and vanished into her room.

Bewildered, I glanced at Jenks. The pixy shrugged, then turned the volume down on the TV. I followed his gaze to Nick. His expression was positively vindictive. My eyes narrowed and I leaned back, crossing my arms. "What was that all about?" I asked.

"Ooooh, I forgot," he said, lightly snapping his healing fingers. "Vampires are sensitive to the scent of cloves. Golly, the smell must have woken her up."

My jaw tightened. I hadn't known that. Apparently neither had Jenks, since he was the one who had gone shopping. Nick turned to the sink a little too slowly to hide his smile.

I took a breath, deciding he was lucky Ivy hadn't smacked him hard enough to knock him out. In the shape he was in, it wouldn't take much. My eyes fell on the pain amulet he was wearing, thinking the entire situation was stupid. Jenks told me earlier that Ivy had been on the Internet all last night as Nick tried to sleep. Payback?

My fingers tapped the laminated table. Standing, I closed the lid on my laptop, then slid my demon curse book off the table and into my arms. "I'll be in the van," I said blandly.

"Rachel—" Nick started, but I snatched up my list and pencil and walked out of the kitchen, the heavy book making me awkward and unbalanced. It kind of went with my mood.

"Whatever, Nick . . ." I said tiredly, not turning around.

Jenks was a mix of wary alertness. The paper on the table before him was strewn with Jax's work. He was getting better.

"I'll be in the van, if you need me," I said in passing.

"Sure." His eyes went from me to Jax trying to coax Rex out from under the bed. The sight of a pixy holding up a bedspread calling "Kitty, kitty, kitty" looked risky even to me.

"Rachel," Nick protested when I opened the door, but I didn't turn. Reversing my steps, I snatched up my bag with the focus in it. No need to leave *that* sitting around.

"You stupid lunker," Jenks said as I left. "Don't you know she always sides with—"

The door clicked closed, cutting off his words. "The underdog," I finished. Depressed, I leaned against the door, the focus tucked between me and my demon book, my head bowed. Not this time. I wouldn't side with Nick, and despite the cookie incident, Nick was the underdog.

Birdsong and the chill of morning pulled my head up. It was quiet and damp, the rush-hour traffic nonexistent. The sun was trying to break through the light fog, giving everything a golden sheen. The nearby straits were probably beautiful, not that I could see them from where I stood.

Gathering my resolve, I shifted the weight of the demon book and dug in my pocket for the van's keys. We'd parked in the shade of a huge white pine between the road and the motel so I could set a circle without people running into it. The new hundred-dollar running shoes that Ivy had bought me were silent on the pavement, and it felt odd being up this early. Creepy. Habit made me shift through the keys so they didn't clink, and only the muffled thunk of the van unlocking broke the stillness until I lugged the side door open in a sound of sliding metal and rolling rubber. Still peeved, I stepped up and in, and slammed the door shut in frustration.

I dropped the demon book on the cot and sat next to it. Elbows on my knees, I kicked my bag under me. I didn't want to be there, but I wanted to be in the motel room less. The silence grew, and I reluctantly slid the curse book onto my lap. I was here, I might as well do something. Wedging off my shoes, I sat cross-legged with my back to the drape drawn between me and the front seat. It was dim, and I tugged the little side curtain open to let in the light.

My lightning charm rasped on the yellowing pages as I leafed through the tome looking for anything familiar. There wasn't a table of contents, making it difficult to satisfy my curiosity. Big Al used demon magic to look like people he had never seen, plucking their description and voice from memories like I picked flowers from my garden. I wasn't going to twist a demon curse for a disguise when I could use an illegal, white earth charm, but comparing the two might give me insight into how the three branches of magic pulled on each other's strengths.

The Latin word for copy caught my attention, and I leaned closer, feeling my legs protest. I needed to get out and run; I was stiffening. Slowly I pieced it out, deciding the word actually translated into transpose. There was a difference. The curse didn't make someone look like someone else, it moved the abilities of one person into another. My lips parted. That's how Al not only turned himself into Ivy, but took the abilities of a vampire as well.

My eyebrows rose, and I wondered whom Al got his vampiric abilities from. Piscary, in return for a favor? A lesser vampire he had in the ever-after? Ceri would know.

Gaze dropping to my bag, my pulse quickened at the thoughts sliding through me. I couldn't duplicate the focus without commissioning an artist—who would take forever and then have to be charmed into forgetfulness—but maybe if I moved its power to a new thing . . .

"Demon curse, Rachel," I whispered. "You're a bad girl to even think it."

The sound of a motel door opening and closing pulled a thread of caution through me. I didn't hear footsteps. Berating myself for not having done it sooner, I tapped a line. *"Rhombus,"* I whispered, instigating a series of hard-practiced lessons that flicked a five-minute setup and invocation of a circle into a heartbeat. The zing of ever-after tingled through me, making it feel as if my body was humming. It was fascinating that the line here "tasted" different, more electrical almost. I think it was all the ground water.

"Yikes," came Jenks's soft voice. "When she wants to be alone, she doesn't leave any bones about it, does she?"

There was a high-pitched answer, and I pushed the book off my lap and lurched past the curtain and into the front. "Jenks," I called, tapping the glass before I stuck the key in the ignition and rolled the window down. "What's up?"

The tall pixy turned from unlocking Kisten's Corvette. Smiling, he squinted in the haze and crossed the parking lot, two amulets about his neck and a red baseball cap on his head. One was for scent, the other, an over-the-counter charm, turned his hair black. It wasn't much, but it would do. His feet edged the black haze of ever-after between us, and I dropped the circle, my pulse temporally quickening at the surge of power before I disconnected from the line.

"I need some more toothbrushes," he said, coming closer. "And maybe some fudge."

Knealing on the seat, I put my crossed arms on the windowsill. Toothbrushes? He had six open on the bathroom counter. "You know, you can reuse those," I said, and he shuddered.

"No thanks. Besides, I want to take Jax on a lesson on low-temperature runs so Ivy can smack crap for brains a good one if he wants to keep antagonizing her."

"Hi, Ms. Morgan," Jax chimed out, Jenks's hat lifting to show Jax peeping from under it.

A smile curved over me. "Hi, Jax. Keep your dad's back, okay?"

"You bet."

Pride crinkled Jenks's eyes. "Jax, do a quick reconnaissance of the area. Watch your temps. And be careful. I heard blue jays earlier."

"Okay." Jax wiggled out from under his dad's hat and zipped off in a clatter of wings.

I exhaled, a mix of melancholy and pride over Jax learning a new skill. "Will you stop calling Nick crap for brains?" I asked, tired of playing referee. "You used to like him."

Jenks made a face. "He turned my son into a thief and broke my partner's heart. Why should I give him a draft of consideration?"

Surprised, my eyebrows rose. I hadn't known my falling out with Nick bothered him.

"Don't get all girly on me," Jenks said gruffly. "I may only be eighteen, but I've been married for ten years. You turned into a slobbering blob, and I don't want to see it again. It's pathetic, and it makes me want to pix you." His face grew worried. "I've seen how you get around dangerous men, and you always fall for the underdog. Nick is both. I mean, he's dangerous and he's been hurt, and hurt bad," Jenks rushed on, mistaking my sick look for fear. *Crap, was I that transparent?* "He's going to hurt you again if you let him—even if he doesn't mean to."

Disconcerted, I brushed the dampness of fog from my arm. "Don't worry about it. Why would I go back? I love Kisten."

Jenks smiled, but his brow was furrowed. "Then why did we come out here?"

I fixed my gaze on the curtained windows of the motel. "He saved my life. I might have loved him. And I can't pretend my past didn't happen. Can you?"

There wasn't much Jenks could say to that. "You need anything while I'm out?" he said, clearly changing the subject.

My lips curved upward. "Yeah. Can you get one of those disposable cameras?"

Jenks blinked, then smiled. "Sure. I'd love a shot of you and me together in front of the bridge." Still smiling, he whistled for Jenks and turned away.

The reminder of why we were there intruded, and my stomach clenched. "Uh, Jenks. I could use something else too." His eyes went expectant, and I licked my lips nervously. *You're a bad girl, Rachel.* "I need something made from bone," I said.

Jenks's eyebrows rose. "Bone?"

I nodded. "About fist-sized? Don't spend a lot of money on it. I'm thinking I might be able to move the curse from the statue to something else. It needs to have been alive at some point, and I don't think wood is animate enough."

Feet scuffing, Jenks nodded. "You got it," he said, turning to the dry, desperate-sounding clatter of pixy wings. It was Jax, and the exhausted pixy almost fell into his dad's hand.

"Tink's dia—uh, diapers," Jax exclaimed, changing his oath mid-phrase. "It's cold out here. My wings don't even work. Jeez, Dad, are you sure it's okay for me to be out here?"

"You're fine." Taking off his hat, Jenks raised his hand and Jax made the jump to his head. Jenks carefully replaced his cap. "It takes practice to know how long your wings will work in low temps and get yourself to a heat source in time. That's what we're doing this for."

"Yeah, but it's cold!" Jax complained, his voice muffled.

Jenks was smiling when he met my gaze. "This is fun," he said, sounding surprised. "Maybe I should go into business training pixy backups."

I chuckled, then turned solemn. It would make his last months more enjoyable if he could teach what he could no longer do. I knew Jenks's thoughts were near mine when the emotion left his face. "Jenks's school for pixy pirates," I quipped, and he smiled, but it faded fast.

"Thanks, Jenks," I said as he made motions to return to the car. "I really appreciate this."

"No prob, Rache." He touched his hat. "Finding stuff is what pixies do fourth best."

I snorted, pulling myself in and already knowing what Jenks thought pixies did first best. And it wasn't saving my ass like he told everyone.

Rolling up the window against the chill, I returned to my cot, wondering if Kisten had a second blanket in there somewhere. The rumble of the Corvette rose, fading to the ambient sound of passing traffic when Jenks drove off. "Bone," I mumbled, writing the word beside the Latin. My breath caught, then slipped from me in chagrin when the pencil faded. *That's right.* Ceri had used a charm to fix the print to the page. Next time I talked to her, I'd ask.

"Why?" I mumbled, feeling my mood sour. It wasn't as if I was going to make a practice of using these curses. Right? Eyes closing, I let a sound slip from me as I pushed my fingers into my forehead. *I am a white witch. This is a one-shot deal.* Too much ability leads to confusion over what's right and wrong, and obviously I was confused enough already. Was I a coward or a fool? God help me, I was going to give myself a headache.

The squeak of the motel door opening brought my head up. There wasn't an accompanying sound of a car starting, and my face blanked when a tap came on the back door of the van. A shadow moved past the dirt-smeared window. "Ray-ray?"

I should have reset my circle, I thought sourly, forcing my shoulders down and trying to decide what to do for an entire five seconds: an eternity for me.

"Rachel, I'm sorry. I brought you some hot chocolate."

His voice was apologetic, and I exhaled. Closing my "big book of demon curses," I went to the back door, thinking I was making a mistake when I opened it.

Nick stood there in his borrowed gray sweats, looking like he was ready for a run in the park: tall, lean, and battered. A survivor. He had a foam cup of instant hot chocolate in his hands and a pleading expression in his eyes. His hair was swept back and his cheeks were clean-shaven. I could smell the shampoo from his shower, and I lowered my eyes at the memory of how silky his hair was when it was toweled dry and still damp, a whisper over my fingertips.

Jenks's warning resounded in me, and I stifled my first feeling of sympathy. *Yes, he had been hurt. Yes, he had the potential to be dangerous. But damn it, I didn't have to let it get to me.*

"Can I come in?" he asked after I'd silently stared at him for a good while. "I don't want to sit alone in that motel room knowing a vamp is sleeping behind a flimsy door."

My pulse quickened. "You're the one who woke her up," I said, hand on my hip.

He smiled, to turn himself charmingly helpless. He wasn't. He knew I knew he wasn't. "I got tired of being called crap for brains. I didn't know everyone would leave."

"So you pushed her buttons, relying on Jenks and me to buffer the retaliation?" I asked.

"I did say I was sorry. And I never claimed it was smart." He raised the hot chocolate. "Do you want this or should I go?"

Logic railed against emotion. I thought of Ivy, knowing I

wouldn't want to be alone in the same motel room with an angry vampire either. And there wasn't much sense in saving someone if you were going to let your partner take him apart the first chance she got.

"Come on in," I said, sounding like it was a concession.

"Thanks." It was a grateful whisper, his relief obvious. He handed me the hot chocolate and, using the side of the van to steady himself, stepped up and in. His pain amulet swung, and he tucked it behind his shirt as he straightened in the low height. I could tell by his stiff motions and his grimace that the amulet wasn't working to cover all the pain. I had only the one pain amulet left until I made more, and he'd have to ask for it.

Clearly cold, Nick shut the door, sealing us in the same darkness that I had been in before, but now it was uncomfortable. My hands on the hot chocolate, I sat dead center on the cot, forcing him to sit on the pile of boxes across from me. There was more room than before, because Ivy had dumped off Marshal's stuff at the high school pool, but it was still too close. Gingerly settling himself, Nick tugged his sleeves down to hide his shackle marks and set his clasped hands in his lap. For a moment the silence was broken only by the hush of traffic.

"I don't want to bother you," he said, watching me from under his fallen bangs.

Too late. "It's okay," I lied, crossing my legs at my knees, very conscious of the demon text beside me on the bed. I took a sip of hot chocolate, then set it on the floor. It was too early for me to be hungry. The silence stretched. "How is the amulet holding up?"

A relieved smile came over him. "Great, good," he rushed to say. "Some of the hair on my arms is starting to grow back. By this time next month I might look . . . normal."

"That's good. Great." *If we managed to evade the Weres and live that long.*

His eyes were worried as he glanced at the book beside me, taking up the space so he wouldn't. "Do you need any help with the Latin? I don't mind interpreting it for you." His long face scrunched up. "I'd like to do something."

"Maybe later," I said guardedly. My shoulders eased at his admission of uselessness. Ivy and Jenks were making a point to keep him out of everything, and it would have bothered me too. "I think I have a curse I can use. I want to talk to Ceri about it first."

"Rachel . . ."

Oh God. I've heard that tone before, usually coming out of me. He wants to talk about us. "If she says the imbalance won't be too bad," I rushed to say, "I'm going to move the magic from the focus to something else, so we can destroy the old statue. It shouldn't be too hard."

"Rachel, I—"

Pulse quickening, I tugged the demon book closer. "Hey, why don't I show you the curse. You could—" He moved, and my eyes jerked up. He didn't look dangerous, he didn't look helpless, he looked frustrated, as if he was screwing his courage up.

"I don't want to talk about the plan," he said, leaning over the space between us. "I don't want to talk about Latin or magic. I want to talk about you and me."

"Nick," I said, my heart pounding. "Stop." He reached for my shoulder, and I jumped, lashing out to block his hand before he could touch me.

Startled, he jerked away. "Damn it, Rachel!" he exclaimed. "I thought you were dead! Will you just . . . Will you just let me give you a hug? You're back from the dead, and you won't let me even touch you! I'm not asking to move in with you. All I want is to touch you—to prove to me you're alive!"

I let out my held breath, then caught it again. My head hurt. I did nothing as he shifted to sit beside me, moving the book out of the way. Our body weight slid us closer, and I shifted to face him, my knees forcing us apart.

"I missed you," he said softly, his eyes scrunched with old pain, and this time I did nothing as his arms went around me. The scent of cinnamon and flour filled my senses, instead of musty books and the snap of ozone. His hands were light, almost not there. I felt his body relax, and he exhaled as if he'd found a piece of himself. *Don't,* I thought, tensing. *Please don't say it.*

"Things would have been different if I had known you were alive," he whispered, his breath shifting the hair about my face. "I never would have left. I never would have asked Jax to help me. I never would have started this fool snatch. God, Rachel, I missed you. You're the only woman I've met who understands me, who I never needed to explain why. Hell, you didn't even leave when you found out I called up demons. I . . . I really missed you."

His hands clenched for an instant and his voice cracked. He had missed me. He wasn't lying. And I knew what it was like to be alone and the rarity of finding a kindred soul, even if he was screwed up. "Nick," I said, my heart pounding.

My eyes closed as his hands moved, pulling through my hair. I reached up, stilling them, bringing them back down to my lap. The memory of him tracing the lines of my face filled me. I remembered the touch of his sensitive fingers, following my jawline, running down my neck to follow the curves of my body. I remembered his warmth, his laughter, and his eyes sparkling when I twisted a phrase to mean something entirely new and naughty. I remembered the way he made me feel needed, appreciated for *who and what I was,* never having to apologize for it, and the contentment I found in sharing ourselves. We'd been happy together. It had been great.

And I made a good decision.

"Nick." I pulled away, my eyes opening when his hand brushed my cheek. "You left. I got myself together. I won't go back to where we were."

His eyes went wide in the low light. "I never left you. Not really. Not in my heart."

I took a breath and let it go. "You weren't there when I needed you," I said. "You were somewhere else. Stealing something." His expression went empty, and a flash of anger pressed my lips together, daring him to deny it. "You lied to me about where you were going and what you were doing. And you took Jenks's son with you. You turned him into a thief with your promises of wealth and excitement. How could you do that to Jenks?"

Nick's eyes were emotionless. "I told him it was a dangerous job and it didn't pay well."

"To a pixy, you live like a king," I snapped, feeling my heartbeat quicken.

"The familiar bond is broken. We can start over—"

"No." I shifted from him, feeling the betrayal again. *Damn him.* "You can't be part of my life anymore. You're a thief and a liar, and I can't love you."

"I can change," he said, and I groaned with disbelief. "I *have* changed," he said, so earnestly that I thought he might believe he had. "When this is over, I'll go back to Cincinnati. I'll get a noon to midnight job. I'll buy a dog. Get cable TV. I'll stop it all for you, Rachel."

His hands went out and took mine, and I looked at my fingers cradled between his long pianist hands, damaged and raw, but sensitive, enfolding mine as his arms had once protected me, kept me alive when I was bleeding my life out.

"I love you that much," he whispered. My head pounded, and

he brought my fingers to his lips and kissed them. "Let me try. Don't throw this second chance away."

I couldn't seem to get enough air. "No," I said, voice low so it wouldn't tremble. "I can't do this. You won't change. You might believe you can, and maybe you will, but in a month, a year, you'll find something, and then it will be, 'Just one more, Ray-ray. Then I'll stop forever.' I can't live like that." My throat was tight and I couldn't swallow.

I pulled my eyes to his, reading in his shocked expression that he had been about to say that right now, that he still wanted to walk away from this with money in his pocket. That he may have meant everything he'd said, but also wanted to convince me to put my, Ivy's, and Jenks's life on the line for money. He was still running his damn snatch, even while knowing that if the statue wasn't destroyed, it would put my life in jeopardy.

Betrayal bubbled up, making my stomach clench. "I have a good life," I said, feeling his grip on my fingers loosen. "It doesn't include you anymore."

Nick's jaw clenched and he drew back. "But it includes Ivy," he said bitterly. "She's hunting you. She's going to make you her toy. It's always the thrill of the hunt for vampires. That's all. And once she gets you, she'll drop you and move on to someone new."

"That's enough," I said, my voice harsh. It was my greatest fear, and he knew it.

He smiled bitterly. "She's a vampire. She can't be trusted. I know she's killed people. She uses them and abandons them. *That's what they do!*"

I was shaking in anger. Kisten's bracelet hung heavy on me like a sign of ownership. "She only takes blood from people who freely give it. And she *doesn't* abandon them!" I shouted, unable to keep my voice down. "She *never* left me!"

Nick's face went hard at the accusation. "I may be a thief," he insisted, "but I never hurt anyone who didn't deserve it. Even by accident."

My breath was fast and I stood. He looked up at me, his face rigid with frustration. "You hurt me," I said.

A hopeless look flashed across him. He reached for my hands, and I stepped back. "So she's a vampire," I said loudly. "I'm *a witch!* What makes you any safer? What about you, Nick? You call up demons! What did you give that demon for the location of that . . . thing!"

Shock flashed over him for my having turned this on him.

Clearly uncomfortable, he glanced at my bag on the floor and eased away. "Nothing important."

He wouldn't look at me, and my predatory instincts stirred. "What did you give the demon?" I prompted. "Jax said you gave him something."

Nick took a quick breath. His eyes met mine. "Rachel, I thought you were dead."

A cold feeling of worry slid through me. Jax had said the demon showed up as me. Had the demon known about me, or just plucked my image out of Nick's head? "What demon was it?" I asked, thinking of Newt, the insane demon who shoved me back into reality last solstice. "Was it Al?" I said softly, seething inside.

"No, it was someone else," he said, looking sullen. "Al didn't know where it was."

Someone else? Okay, Nick knew more than one demon. "What did you give it for the location of the focus?" I asked, trying to at least look calm.

Nick's eyes lit up and he scooted forward on the cot. "That's just it, Rachel. Al always wanted useless stuff like what your favorite color was, or if you used lip gloss, but all this one wanted was a kiss."

The air slipped out of me, and I couldn't seem to make my lungs move to pull more in. *Nick gave Al information about me in return for favors?* "All it wanted was a kiss?" I managed, still trying to grasp what Nick had done. I'd feel betrayed later. Right now I only felt sick. Hand on my stomach, I turned sideways. Had the demon looked like me when Nick kissed it? *Oh God. I didn't want to know.*

"What . . ." Somehow I took a breath. "What demon was it?" I asked, knowing he wouldn't be able to tell me without risking his soul.

Sure enough, Nick stood up, his hands spread placatingly. "I don't know. I went through Al for that one. He took his own cut for brokering my question. But it was worth it."

I turned, and Nick blinked at the fury creasing my brow. "You son of a bitch," I whispered. "You've been selling me out to demons? You've been buying demon favors with information about me? What did you tell them!"

Eyes wide, Nick backed up. "Rachel . . ."

My breath hissed out. In a quick motion, I leapt at him, pinning him against the door with my arm under his neck. "What did you tell Al about me!"

"It's not that big of a deal!" His eyes were bright, and what looked like a laugh was quirking his lips. *He thought it was funny?* He thought I was overreacting, and it was all I could do to not crush his windpipe right there and then.

"Just stupid stuff," he was saying, his voice high but light. "Your favorite ice cream, what color your eyes are after a shower, how old you were when you lost your virginity. God, Rachel. I didn't tell him anything that could hurt you."

Outraged, I pushed into his neck, then rebounded to stand two steps away. "How could you do that to me?" I whispered.

Nick rubbed his throat and moved from the door, trying to hide that I'd hurt him. "I don't know why you're so upset," he said sullenly. "You wouldn't believe the information I got in return. I didn't tell him anything important until I thought you were dead."

My eyes widened and I reached for the wall before I fell over. "You were doing this before we broke up?"

His hand still on his throat, Nick looked at me, his own anger growing. "I'm not stupid. I didn't tell him anything important. Ever. What is the big deal?"

With an effort, I unclenched my teeth. "Tell me this, Nick," I said. "Did the demon look like me when you kissed it? Was that part of the deal? That you pretended it was me?"

He said nothing.

My finger trembled as I pointed to the door. "Get out. The only reason I'm not handing you back to the Weres is because they have to see you die, and right now I'm thinking of taking the pretend part out. If you *ever* tell another demon anything about me, I'll . . . I'll do something bad to you, Nick. So help me God, I'll do something very bad."

Furious, I yanked the heavy side door open. The sound of the metal scraping shocked through me. God! He had been buying demon magic and favors with information about me. For months. *Even while we were together.*

"Rachel—"

"Get. Out."

My voice was low in threat, and I didn't like the sound of it. At the scuff of his feet hitting the pavement, I shoved the door shut. Breath held, I clasped my arms about myself and just stood there. My head hurt and the tears welled up, but I wasn't going to cry.

Damn him. Damn him to hell.

Twenty-two

Miserable, I wouldn't leave the van, afraid if I saw Ivy or Jenks I would blurt out what Nick had done. Some of my reticence was because I needed him to finish this run, and if they leaned on him hard, he might leave. Some of it was shame for having trusted him. Hell, most of it was. Nick had betrayed me on so many levels, and he didn't even get why I was upset. I hadn't been prepared for this. God! What an ass.

"I ought to give him back to the Weres," I whispered, but they had to see him die with the focus. There was no guarantee that he'd stop telling Al where I was ticklish, or that I sometimes hid the remote from Ivy just to get a rise out of her, or any of the hundreds of things I had shared with him when I thought I loved him. I shouldn't have trusted him. But I wanted to trust. Damn it, I *deserved* to be able to trust someone.

"Bastard," I muttered, wiping my eyes. "You son of a bitch bastard."

The chatter of the maids and the thumps of their cart as they wheeled it down the cracked sidewalk were soothing. It was past noon, and the motel was empty but for us. Being Wednesday, it would likely stay that way.

I lay curled up on the cot, my head on the clean smell of the borrowed hotel pillow, and my shoulders covered by the thin car blanket. I wasn't crying. I was *not* crying. Tears were leaking out as I waited for the ugly feelings to fade, but I wasn't crying, damn it!

Sniffing loudly, I reassured myself that I wasn't. My head hurt and my chest hurt, and I knew if I cared to unclench my hands from the blanket clutched under my chin that they would be trembling. So I lay there and wallowed, falling into a light doze as the heat of the day warmed the van. I barely heard the sound of Jenks and Jax returning to the room. But the shout filtering through the open door jerked me awake.

"I thought he was with you!" Ivy shouted. "Where is he?"

Jenks's response was unheard, and I jumped at the hammering on the van door. Sitting up, I put my sock feet on the floor, drained of emotion.

"Nick!" Ivy shouted. "Get your ass out here!"

Numb, I stood, grabbed the sliding door, and pulled it back with a crunch of metal to look at Ivy with bleary, empty eyes.

Ivy's anger froze, her eyes almost black as she scanned the van and saw me hunched under my blanket. The fog had lifted, and a cold breeze shifted the tips of her sin-black hair, shimmering in the light. Behind her, Jenks lingered in the doorway to the motel room, Jax on his shoulder, six bags with colorful logos in his grip and a question high in his eyes. "He's not here," I said, keeping my voice low so it wouldn't rasp.

"Oh God," Ivy whispered. "You've been crying. Where is he? What did he do to you?"

The protective tone in her voice hit me hard. Miserable, I turned away, my arms about my middle. She followed me in, the van unmoving when her weight hit it. "I'm fine," I said, feeling stupid. "He . . ." I took a deep breath and looked at my hands, perfect and unmarked. My soul was black, but my body was perfect. "He's been telling Al stuff about me in return for favors."

"He what!"

Jenks was suddenly beside her. "Jax, did you know about this?" he said tightly, the depth of his anger looking wrong on his youthful features.

"No, Dad," the small pixy said. "I only watched the one time."

Ivy's face was pale. "I'll kill him. Where is he? I'm killing him right now."

I took a breath, more grateful than I probably should have been that they would defend me like this. Maybe I was just trusting the wrong people. "No you aren't," I said, and Jenks jiggled on his feet, clearly wanting to protest. "He didn't tell Al anything too bad—"

"Rache!" Jenks yelped. "You can't defend him! He sold you out!"

My head jerked up. "I'm not defending him!" I exclaimed.

"But we need him alive and cooperative. The Weres have to see him die along with that . . . thing," I said, nudging my bag with a foot. "I'll think about beating him to a pulp later." I looked up at Ivy's blank expression. "I'm going to use him, then cut him lose. And if he ever does anything like that to me again . . ."

I didn't need to finish the thought. Jenks shifted from foot to foot, clearly wanting to take things into his own hands. "Where is he?" the pixy asked, grim-faced.

My breath came and went. "I don't know. I told him to go away."

"Go!" Ivy exclaimed, and I made a wry face.

"Out of the van. He'll be back. I still have the statue." Depressed, I stared at the floor.

Jenks hopped out of the van, and the light coming in brightened. "I'll find him. Bring his punk-ass back here. It's been a while since we . . . talked."

My head came up. "Jenks . . ." I warned, and he held up a hand.

"I'll behave," he said, gaze darting over the parking lot and to the nearby bar, his face frighteningly hard. "I won't even let him know you told us what he did to you. I'll pick out a movie from the front office on the way back, and we can watch it, all nice and friendly like."

"Thanks," I whispered.

My head was down and I didn't hear him leave, but I looked up when Jax's wings clattered and found them gone. Ivy was watching me, and when I shrugged she shut the door to seal out the cold air. The sound of the metal on metal struck through me, and I gathered myself into some semblance of order. Ivy hesitated, looking torn between wanting to comfort me and afraid I'd take it the wrong way. And there was the blood thing too. It had only been a day since she had sated it, but it had been a very stressful day. Today wasn't looking any easier.

I looked at the matted throw rug, wondering what kind of person I was, afraid to hug my friends, and sleeping with people who used me. "I'll be okay," I said to the floor.

"Rachel, I'm sorry."

My throat hurt. I put my elbows on my knees, set my head into my cupped hand and closed my eyes. "I don't know. Maybe it was my fault for trusting him. I never dreamed he would do something like this." I sniffed loudly. "What's *wrong* with me, Ivy?"

I was disgusted with myself, the emotion edging into self-pity, and I met her gaze in surprise when Ivy whispered, "There's nothing wrong with you."

"Yeah?" I shot back, and she went to the van's tiny sink and plugged in the electric kettle. "Let's take a look at my track record. I live in a church with a vampire who is the scion of a master vampire who would just as soon see me dead."

Saying nothing, Ivy got out an envelope of cocoa so old it was stiff with moisture.

"I date her old boyfriend," I continued bitterly, "who used to be said master vampire's scion, and *my* ex-boyfriend is a professional thief who calls demons and trades information about me for tips to steal artifacts that can start an Inderland power struggle. There's something *wrong* when you trust people who can hurt you so badly."

"It's not that bad." Ivy turned with the chipped mug in her hand, head down as she broke chunks of cocoa against the side of the mug with an old spoon.

"Not that bad?" I said with a bark of laughter. "It's been hidden for five thousand years. Piscary is going to be majorly pissed, along with every master vampire in every city on the entire freaking planet! If we don't do this right, they're all going to be rapping on my door."

"I wasn't talking about that. I meant about you trusting people who can hurt you."

I flushed, suddenly wary of her, standing over there at the end of the van in the dark. "Oh."

The water from the kettle started to steam, blurring her features as it rose. "You need the thrill, Rachel."

Oh God. I stiffened, glancing at the closed door.

Ivy's posture shifted irritably, and she flowed into motion. "Get off it," she said, setting the mug on the tiny counter space and unplugging the kettle. "There's nothing wrong with that. I've watched you ever since we partnered in the I.S. Every guy who tried to date you, you drove away when you found out the danger was only in your imagination."

"What has that got to do with Nick selling me out to a demon?" I said, my voice a shade too loud for prudence.

"You trusted him when you shouldn't have so you could find a sense of danger," she said, her expression angry. "And yes, it hurts that he betrayed that trust, but that's not going to stop you from looking for it again. You'd better start picking where you find your thrills a little better, or it's going to get you killed."

Flustered, I put my back to the wall of the van. "What in hell are you talking about?"

Ivy turned to face me. "*Being* alive isn't enough for you," she said. "You need to *feel* alive, and you use the thrill of danger to get it. You knew Nick dealt in demons. Yes, he overstepped his bounds when he traded information about you to them, but you were willing to risk it because the danger turned you on. And once you get over the pain, you're going to trust the wrong person again—just so you can find a jolt in that it might all go bad."

I was afraid to speak. The scent of cocoa rose as she poured hot water into the mug. Afraid she might be right, I considered it, looking over my past. It would explain a lot. All the way back to high school. *No. No freaking way.* "I do not need a feeling of danger to get turned on," I protested hotly.

"I'm not saying that's bad," she said neutrally. "You're a threat, and you need the same. I know, because I live it. All vampires do. That's why we keep to our own but for cheap thrills and one-night stands. Anyone less a risk than ourselves isn't enough to keep up, keep around, keep alive, or understand. Only those born to it are capable of understanding. And you."

I didn't like this. I didn't like it at all. "I have to go," I said, shifting my weight to stand.

The palm of her hand flashed out, hitting the side of the van to bar my way and stop me cold. "Face it, Rachel," she said when I looked up, frightened. "You've never been the safe, nice girl next door, despite everything you do to be that person. That's why you joined the I.S., and even there you didn't fit in, because, knowing it or not, you were a possible threat to everyone around you. People sense it on some level. I see it all the time. The dangerous are attracted by the lure of an equal, and the weak are afraid. Then they avoid you, or go out of their way to make your life miserable so you'll leave and they can continue deluding themselves that they're safe. You trusted Nick knowing he might betray you. You got off on the risk."

I swallowed a surge of denial, remembering the misery of high school and my history with bad boyfriends. Not to mention my idiotic decision to join the I.S., and then my even more idiotic attempt to quit when Denon started giving me crap runs and the thrill was taken away. I knew I liked dangerous men, but saying it was because I was equally dangerous was ludicrous . . . or would have been if I hadn't just spent yesterday as a wolf/witch hybrid courtesy of a demon curse that *my* blood kindled, and I now sat in a brand-new Rachel skin with no freckles or wrinkles.

"So you're a threat," Ivy said, the scent of cocoa rising between us as she sat on the boxes across from me. "So you need the rush of possible death to keep your soul awake and turn you on. That's not bad. It just says you're one powerful bitch, whether you know it or not." Tilting forward, she handed me the chipped mug. "Dangerous doesn't always equal untrustworthy. Drink your cocoa and get over it. Then find someone to trust who's worth trusting you back."

Jaw clenched, I looked at the mug in my grip. *It was for me?* I had made her cocoa the night Piscary had raped her: mind, body, and soul. I pulled my eyes up her tight jeans and her long shapeless black sweater that hung mid-thigh.

"That's why I wait," she whispered when our eyes met.

I took a hasty breath when I realized the unseen scar beneath my new skin was tingling.

Ivy must have sensed it, for she stood. "I'm sorry," she said, reaching for the door.

"Ivy, wait." What she'd told me scared me, and I didn't want to be alone. I had to figure this out. Maybe she was right. *Oh God, was I really that screwed up?*

Her long fingers gripped the handle, ready to pull the door open. "The van stinks of us both," she said, not looking at me. "I should be good for a few days more, but the stress . . . I've got to get out of here. I'm sorry—damn it." She took a deep breath. "I'm sorry, but I can't comfort you without my blood lust getting in the way." She looked up at me, her smile faint and carrying old pain. "Not much of a friend, am I?"

Without getting up, I fumbled my fingers past the curtain of the window above me and pushed the bottom out to open it. My heart pounded, and I took in the pine-scented air and hush of the passing traffic. "You're a good friend. Does that help?" I asked in a small voice.

Ivy shook her head. "Come back to the room. Jenks will drag Nick in soon. We can all watch a movie and pretend nothing happened. It should be tremendously awkward. Tons of fun. I'll be fine as long as I don't sit next to you."

Her expression was calm, but she sounded bitter. My face scrunched up and I curved my fingers around the warmth of the cocoa. I didn't know what to think, but I was very sure I didn't want Nick to know he had made me cry. "You go. I'll come in when my eyes aren't so red."

I felt a sense of loss when Ivy stepped out of the van and then turned with her arms about her in the chill. It was obvious she knew the longer I stayed out here, the harder it was going to be for me to find the courage to come in. "Don't you have a complexion charm?" she asked.

"They don't work on bloodshot eyes," I hedged. *Damn it, what was wrong with me?*

Ivy squinted in the glare and sharp breeze, then her face brightened. "I know . . ." she said, coming back in and slamming the door shut behind her to seal out the cold. I watched her push aside the front curtain and rummage in the console. Her eyes had returned to normal, the fresh air doing as much as the shift in topics. "Kisten probably has one in here," she muttered, then turned with a tube of what looked like lipstick. "Ta-da!"

Ta-da, huh? I pulled myself straighter as she maneuvered around the clutter and sat on the cot beside me. "Lipstick?" I said, not used to having her that close.

"No. You put it under your eyes and the vapors keep the pupil constricted. It'll take the red out too. Kist uses it for hangovers—among other things."

"Oh!" I abruptly felt twice as unsure, not having known there was such a thing. I had always trusted a vampire's pupils to give away their mood.

Legs crossed at the knees, she uncapped it and twisted until a column of opaque gel rose. "Close your eyes and look up."

My lips parted. "I can put it on."

A puff of annoyance came from her. "If you put on too much or get it too close to your eye, you can damage your vision before it wears off."

I told myself I was being stupid. She looked okay; she wouldn't have come back in if she wasn't. Ivy wanted to do something for me, and if she couldn't give me a hug without her blood lust tainting it, then by God I would let her put that gunk under my eye. "Okay," I said, resettling myself and looking up. *You need the thrill of danger* flitted through my mind, and I quashed it.

Ivy shifted closer, and I felt a light touch under my right eye. "Close your eyes," she said softly, her breath stirring a curl.

My pulse quickened, but I did, and my other senses kicked in stronger. The gel smelled like clean laundry, and I stifled a shudder when a cold sensation moved under my eye. "You, ah, don't use this a lot, do you?" I asked, starting when her finger touched my nose.

"Kisten uses it when he works," she said shortly. She sounded fine—distracted and calm. "I don't. I think it's cheating."

"Oh." I seemed to be saying that a lot today. The cot shifted when she moved back and away from me. I lowered my head and blinked several times, the vapors leaving a stinging sensation that I couldn't imagine was making my eyes any less red.

"It's working," she said with a small, contented smile, answering my question before I asked it. "I thought it would on witches, but I wasn't sure." She motioned me to look at the ceiling again so she could finish, and I lifted my chin and closed my eyes.

"Thank you," I said softly, my thoughts becoming more conflicted and confused. Ivy had said vampires only bothered to get to know people as powerful as themselves. It sounded lonely. And dangerous. And it made perfect sense. She was looking for that mix of danger and trustworthiness. *Was that why she put up with my crap? She was looking to find that in me?*

A ribbon of angst pulled through me, and I held my breath so Ivy wouldn't sense it in my exhalation. That I needed danger to feel passion was ridiculous. It wasn't true. *But what if she was right?*

Ivy had once said that sharing blood was a way to show deep affection, loyalty, and friendship. I felt that way about her, but what she wanted from me was so far from what I understood that I was afraid. She wanted to share with me something so complex and intangible that the shallow emotional vocabulary of human and witch didn't have the words or cultural background to define it. She was waiting for me to figure it out. And I lumped it all with sex because I didn't understand.

A tear slipped from under my eyelid at Ivy's loneliness, her need for emotional reassurance, and her frustrations that though I could understand what she wanted, I was afraid to find out if I had the capacity to meet her halfway, to trust her. And my breath caught when she wiped the moisture away with a careful finger, unaware that it was for her.

My heart pounded. The underside of my other eye grew cold, and she leaned away. Breath shallow with the thoughts pinging through me, I looked down, blinking profusely. There was the click of Ivy putting the top on the tube, and she gave me a guarded smile. I felt poised on the chance to make tomorrow vastly different from today, and a pulse of emotion struck through me, unexpected and heady. *Maybe I should listen to those who were my closest kin in terms of my soul,* I thought. *Maybe I should trust those willing to trust me back.*

"There you go," Ivy said, not knowing that lightning was falling through my thoughts, realigning them to make space for something new.

I looked at her beside me, her legs crossed at her knees while she lifted the front curtain to toss the tube to the front seat. In a thoughtless motion, she reached out and smeared a pinky under my eye to even it out. The scent of clean laundry wafted up. "My God," she whispered, her brown eyes on her work. "Your skin is absolutely perfect. It's really beautiful, Rachel."

Her hand dropped and my gut tightened. She gathered herself and stood, and I heard myself say, "Don't go."

Ivy jerked to a stop. She turned with an exaggerated slowness, her posture wire-tight as she stared. "I'm sorry," she said, her voice as numb as her face. "I shouldn't have said that."

I turned my lips in to moisten them, heart pounding. "I don't want to be afraid anymore."

Her eyes flashed to black. A spike of adrenaline pulled through me to set my heart racing. Ivy fumbled behind her, her face paling when she found herself on unfamiliar territory. "I need to leave," she said as if trying to convince herself.

Feeling unreal, I reached out and shut the window, drawing the curtain. "I don't want you to." I couldn't believe I was doing this, but I wanted to know. I had lived my life not knowing why I never fit in, and with her simple explanation, I had both found an answer and a cure. I was lost, and Ivy wanted to kick the rocks from my path. I couldn't read the words, but Ivy would set my fingers to trace the letters to redefine my world. If she was right, my hidden threat had made me a pariah among those I would love, but I could find understanding among my strength-crippled kin. If that meant I needed to find another way to show someone that I cared, maybe I should hide my fears until Ivy could silence them. She trusted me. Maybe it was time I trusted her.

Ivy saw my decision, her face stilling when her instincts hit her hard. "This isn't right," she said. "Don't make me be the one to say no. I can't do it."

"So don't." A thread of fear slid through me, turning into a sliver of delicious tension to settle deep in my groin and tingle my skin. *God, what was I doing?*

I felt her will battle her desires, and I watched her eyes, finding no fear in their absolute blackness. I was covered in her scent. Mine was laced about the van like silk scarves, mixing with hers, teasing, luring, promising. Piscary was too far away to interfere. The chance might never come again. "You're confused," she said, holding herself carefully, unmoving and still.

My lips tingled when I licked them. "I am confused. I'm not afraid."

"I am," she breathed, and her dark lashes drooped to rest atop her pale cheeks. "I know how this ends. I've seen it too many times. Rachel, you've been hurt and aren't thinking clearly. When it's done, you'll say it was a mistake." Her eyes opened. "I like how everything is. I've spent the better part of a year convincing myself that I'd rather have you as a friend who won't let me touch her than someone I touched only to frighten away. Please, tell me to leave."

Adrenaline coursed to settle deep. I stood, out of breath. My thoughts lit upon the dating guide she had given me and the sensations, both exquisitely alluring and darkly terrifying, that she had pulled from me before I learned what not to do. The idea flitted through me that I was manipulating her even now, knowing that she couldn't best her drives when someone was willing. I could manipulate Ivy to any end, and it sent a surge of anticipatory terror through me.

Standing before her, I shook my head.

"Tell me why. . . ." she whispered, her face creased in a deep pain, as if feeling herself starting to slip into a place she had been both fearing and wanting to go.

"Because you're my friend," I said, voice trembling. "Because you need this," I added.

Relief showed in the depths of her eyes, black in the dim light. "Not enough. I want to show you so badly that it aches," she said, her voice a gray ribbon. "But I won't do this if you can't admit it's for you as much as me. If you can't, then it's not worth having."

I stared in a near panic for what she was asking me to come to grips with. I didn't even know what to call the emotions that were making my eyes warm with unshed tears and my body long for something I didn't understand.

Seeing my frightened silence, she turned away. Her long fingers gripped the handle to open the door, and I stiffened, seeing everything dissolve to become an embarrassing incident that would forever widen the chasm between us. Panicked, I said, "Because I want to trust you. Because I do trust you. Because *I want this.*"

Her hand fell from the door. As my pulse thundered, I saw her fingers tremble, knowing she heard the truth in my voice even as I accepted it. She felt it. She smelled it in the air with her incredible senses and her even more incredible brain that could decipher it. "Why are you doing this to me?" she said to the door. "Why now?"

She turned, her haunted eyes shocking me. Breath shallow, I stepped closer, reaching out but hesitating. "I don't know what to do," I said. "I hate feeling stupid. Please do something."

She didn't move. A tear had slipped from her, and I reached to wipe it away. Ivy jerked, catching me about the wrist. Her fingers were stark next to the black gold of Kisten's bracelet, their long whiteness covering my demon mark. I stifled my instinctive jerk, going pliant when she pulled me close, leading my hand to the small of her back.

"This isn't right," she whispered, our bodies not touching but for her hair mingling with mine and my arm around her waist and her grip on my wrist.

"So make it work," I said, and the brown ring about her eye shrank.

She took the air deep into her, closing her eyes and scenting the possibilities of what I would and wouldn't do. Her eyes were black when they opened, the last sliver of brown gone. "You're afraid."

"I'm not afraid of you. I'm afraid I won't be able to forget. I'm afraid it will change me."

Ivy's lips parted. "It will," she breathed, inches away.

I shivered and closed my eyes. "Then help me not be afraid until I understand."

Her fingers lightly touched my shoulder, and I jumped, eyes flashing open. Something shifted. I took a breath, then gasped when she slid into motion. I staggered backward—her one hand gripping my shoulder, the other still holding my wrist behind her—and she followed until my back hit the wall. Eyes wide and fixed to hers, I held my breath, unwilling to object. I'd seen this before. God, I'd lived it.

Expression intent, Ivy's unchecked blood lust struck a chord and made my blood pound. Her fingers pressing into me grew firmer and her breath quickened. I told myself this was what I wanted. Believing it. Accepting it. "Don't be afraid," she breathed as she held herself poised.

"I'm not," I lied, a tremble shaking me. *Oh God, it was going to happen.*

"If you are, you'll trigger paralysis. It's not under my conscious control, and it's triggered from your fear." Her gaze broke from mine, and I felt a delicious dropping sensation plink through me when she looked at my neck. I closed my eyes as a slurry of bliss and fear rose inside me. I took in the feeling of her being so close, accepting it. *Did I need danger to remember I was alive? Was it wrong? Did it matter if no one but me cared?*

Head bowed, Ivy leaned close. "Please don't be afraid," she said, her words a tingle against my skin, to pulse deeper. "I want you to be able to touch me back . . . if you want to."

Her last words sounded lost and alone, afraid to risk the hurt again. My eyes flashed open. "Ivy," I pleaded. "I told you. This is all I can give—"

She moved, and my words froze when she put a finger to my lips. "It's enough."

Ivy's feather-light touch sent a spark of adrenaline through me. I took a clean breath when the weight of her finger fell away. I exhaled, and her free hand slipped into the narrow space between the wall of the van and the small of my back. My eyes shut as her fingers pressed into me, pulling me forward. Breath shaking, I locked my knees, wise to the sudden rush that would send me tumbling down. I felt emotion rise, knowing she was experiencing it too. "Ivy?"

I sounded frightened, and she pushed my hair aside, whispering, "How I've wanted this," her lips brushing the smooth skin under my ear. The warm dampness of her breath made me shiver at the mix of the familiar and the unknown. With a soft exhalation, she shifted her head and her lips found my collarbone, teasingly shy of my old scar. Tendrils pulsed in time with my heart, building on the ones before to an unseen height. *Oh God. Save me from myself.*

Tension pulled my eyes open when her fingers traced a trail down my neck. Sensation blossomed, and I threw my head back and sucked in the air. Her arm slipped around my waist, catching me before I fell.

"Rachel, I . . . God you smell good," she said, and a torrent of heat flowed through me as her lips brushed against me with her words. The smoothness of her teeth across my skin sent my pulse pounding as I fought for breath. "You won't leave?" she asked. "Promise you won't."

She wasn't asking me to be her scion; she was only asking me not to leave. "I won't leave."

"You give this to me?"

Shaking inside, I whispered, "Yes."

Ivy exhaled, sounding as if she had been freed. My blood rose, mixing with my lingering fear of the unknown to drive her to a fever pitch. Her lips touched my lower neck and vertigo spun the room, burning tracings of desire to settle deep and low in me. I exhaled into the promise of more to come, calling it to me. I breathed it in like smoke, the rising passion starting a feeling of abandonment inside. I didn't care anymore if it was right or wrong. It just was.

Her grip on my shoulder tightened, and slowly there was a gentle pressure upon my skin, and her teeth slid into me without preamble.

I groaned at the rush of fear and desire. My knees gave way, and Ivy shifted her hold. Her touch was light—keeping me upright while I went flaccid, my body struck into overload—but her mouth on my neck was savage with a fierce need. And then she pulled on me.

My air came in a rush. Gasping, I stiffened, my hands springing up to clutch at her, clenching when she threatened to pull away in fear that she had hurt me. "No," I moaned, fire running through me. "Don't stop. Oh . . . God . . ."

My words hit her, and she dug her teeth into me, harder. My breath exploded. For an instant I hung, unable to think. It felt that good. My entire body was alive and aching. A sexual high flowed through me, a torrent of promise.

Somehow I took a breath, then another. They were fast, stumbling over each other. I clutched at her, wanting her to continue but unable to say it. Her lips pulled away from me, and in a rush of sensation, the world spun back into something I could recognize.

We had moved from the wall of the van and stood against the closed door. Ivy was holding me upright against her with the fierce demand of possession. Though she had taken her lips from me, her breath came and went on my broken skin, almost an exquisite torture. There was no fear. "Ivy," I said, hearing it come from me as almost a sob.

And with that small encouragement that everything was okay,

she bowed her head to me again, her mouth finding me to draw from me both my blood and my volition.

I tried to breathe, failing. I clutched her to me, tears slipping from under my closed eyes. It was as if her soul was liquid fire and I could feel her aura, swirling about mine. She wasn't just taking my blood, she was taking my aura. But I wouldn't miss what she could steal, and I wanted to give it to her, to coat her in a small part of me and protect her. Her needs made her so fragile.

The vampire pheromones rose like a drug, making her teeth into spikes of arousal. My fingers spasmed and my rough touch sparked through her. She lunged into me again, her teeth bringing me to a gasping stiffness. I couldn't think, and I held her to me, frantic she'd leave.

Through our auras mixing, I could sense her desperate need, her want for security, her desire for satisfaction, her unearthly hunger for my blood, knowing that even if I gave it freely, she would be haunted by shame and guilt.

Compassion swirled from nowhere in the high I was lost in. She needed me. She needed me to accept her for what she was. And when I realized that I had it within myself to give her at least this small part of me, the last of my fear melted away. My eyes opened, unseeing on the wall of the van. *I trusted her,* I thought, as the edges of our auras blurred into one and the last of my barriers began to fall.

And Ivy knew the instant they did.

A soft sound came from her, delight and wonder. As she held my head unmoving and her lips worried my neck, her hand slipped lower until it found my waist. Her long fingers hesitated, and while she pulled harder to make a silver spike dive through me, her cool palm slipped under my shirt to brush my middle, fingertips searching. I jerked, and she followed me.

"Ivy," I heaved, a new fear slicing through the ecstasy. "Wait . . ."

"But I thought . . ." she whispered, her voice a dark heat, and her hand went unmoving.

"You said the blood was enough," I continued, hovering near panic, trying to focus but finding it hard to open my eyes. My heart was pounding. I couldn't get enough air, and I couldn't find the desire to push her away. I blinked, wavering when I realized she was entirely supporting my weight. "I . . . can't. . . ."

"I misunderstood," she said, cradling my head against the hollow between her shoulder and her neck. The touch of her hand upon my neck grew firmer, losing its gentle feeling, to become dominating. "I'm sorry. Do you want me to stop entirely?"

A hundred thoughts dropped through me, of how stupid I was, of how vulnerable I had made myself, of the risk I was taking, of the future I was mapping for myself, of the glorious adrenaline rush she was taking me on. "No," I breathed, lost in the thought of what it would feel like to bury my face in the hollow between her ear and neck and return the favor.

A low sigh of pleasure rose soft and almost unheard, and her hand slid from my shoulder to find my back. Pressing me closer, she pulled on me again. I gasped, my hands clutching at her as I imagined the warmth of my blood filling her, knowing how it would taste, knowing how it filled the terrible hollow her future as an undead bestowed upon her.

I jerked wire-tight as teeth drove into me again. The desire to respond in kind and the need to hold back touched every part of me alight. Oh God, the twin emotions of denial and desire were going to kill me, so intense I couldn't tell if they were pain or pleasure.

Ivy's breath on my skin grew ragged, and my muscles loosened when the last of my fear slipped from me, and like the ting of a bell faded to nothing. She held me upright, her grip now devoid of any tenderness while her teeth dug deeper and the hunger pooled into her, filling old chasms, pulling on me to take the blood I willingly gave her.

I took a shuddering breath, feeling the vamp pheromones soak into me, soothing, luring, promising a high like no other. It was addictive, but I was beyond caring. I could give Ivy this. I could accept what she gave in return. And as she held me upright and filled her body with my blood and her soul with my aura, tears slipped from me. "Ivy?" I whispered breathlessly as the room spun with vertigo. "I'm sorry I took so long to listen."

She didn't answer, and I groaned when she jerked me against her, her mouth becoming deliciously savage, sending jolts through me as she searched for more, both of us lost in a haze of fulfillment. But faint in the back of my thoughts a warning stirred. Something had changed. Her touch wasn't careful. It had become . . . harsh.

My eyes opened and I stared unseeing at the dark wall of the van as my pulse went thready. It was getting hard to think around the swirl of intoxicating elation. My breath was ragged from a heavy lethargy, not passion. She was taking too much, and I moved my hand from where it was holding her shoulder to gently push her away and see her eyes.

It wasn't much of a push, but Ivy felt it.

Her grip on me tightened, turning painful even through the vamp pheromones. My thoughts pinged back to her tenderness before I reaffirmed it would only be blood we shared—and terror struck through me.

God help me. I had asked her to take the softer emotions of love away. I had asked her to divorce herself from the caring and love Kisten said she shackled her blood lust with—which only left hunger. She wasn't going to stop. She had lost herself.

Fear scoured through me. She tasted it on the air, and without a sound she jerked me off balance. Crying out, I fell. Ivy followed, and we landed together against the tiny counter.

"Ivy! Let go!" I exclaimed, then moaned when she bit deeper until it hurt.

Adrenaline surged. I fought to get free, and Ivy's grip broke. She fell away, and breathing heavily, I held my hand to my bleeding, throbbing neck and stared at her.

Her look was knowing, like that of a predator, and as ecstasy pounded through me in time with my heartbeat, my legs gave out and I slid helplessly to the floor.

Ivy stood above me, my blood red within her mouth. She looked like a goddess—above all law both of the mind and soul. Her eyes were black and she smiled without memory, knowing that I was hers to do with what she wanted with no concept of right or wrong. Ivy was gone, controlled by the hunger I forced her to feel without the buffer of love. *Oh God. I had killed myself.*

I saw her thought to finish this an instant before she moved.

"Ivy, no!" I exclaimed, putting up an arm to fend her off.

It did no good.

I shrieked when she fell on me. It was every nightmare come true. I was helpless as she pinned my shoulders to the floor of the van. I took a breath to scream, but it turned into a moan of passion when she found my neck. A feeling of silver ice cracked through me. Ecstasy brought me to a heaving, arched-back pose for an instant before I fell, gasping for air.

We settled against the floor again as one, her hair falling soft about my throat in a silken brush as she buried her teeth deep and pulled once more. Moaning, I hung in a haze of pain, fear, and elation, her teeth inside me both fire and ice. I stared at the ceiling, focus gone while the heavy lethargy of paralysis filled my veins and exquisite rapture struck me alight even as I lost the will to move.

Ivy had done as I asked. She had abandoned her feelings of love, and was out of control. And as she let go of my arms to pull my neck to her mouth, I floated in realization that had come too late. I had asked her to change for me, and I was going to die for my temerity and stupidity.

A seeping numbness filled me. My pulse went faint and my limbs went cold. I was going to die. I was going to die because I was afraid to admit I might love Ivy.

I felt the distant thump as my hand fell from Ivy to hit the dirt-caked rug. It echoed through me, coming again and again, growing in strength as if it was my failing heartbeat. Someone was shouting distantly, but it paled in importance next to the glimmers of light that rimmed the edge of my sight, mimicking the exquisite sparkles in my mind and body. I exhaled as Ivy took everything, shivering as my aura slipped from me along with my blood. Ivy was the only warm thing in the world, and I wished she would press closer so I wouldn't die cold.

The thumping of my heart seemed to hesitate at the frightening sound of metal tearing. Cold and light spilled over us, and I moaned when Ivy pulled away from me.

"Ivy!" Jenks shouted, and I realized that the thumping hadn't been my heart but Jenks pounding at the back door. "What are you doing!"

"She's *mine*!" Ivy snarled, unreal and savage.

I couldn't move. There was a thundering bump, and the van rocked. The air flashed cold, and I whimpered. I hunched into myself, pulling my knees to my chest. My fingers went warm at the blood coming from me as I found my neck, then cold. I was alone. Ivy was gone. Someone was shouting.

"You stupid, stupid vampire bitch!" he exclaimed. "You promised! You promised me!"

I clutched in upon myself, squinting in the cold, shivering violently as I looked out the back of the van. Something had happened. I was cold. It was bright. Ivy was gone.

There was the snap of dragonfly wings. "Jenks . . ." I breathed, eyes slipping shut.

"It's me, Ms. Morgan," Jax's higher voice said, and I felt the warm wash of pixy dust over my fingers clamped to my neck. "Tink's knickers, you're bleeding yourself out!"

But Ivy was crying, forcing my thoughts out of the dark van and into the sun.

"Rachel!" Ivy shouted, panic in her voice. "Oh God. Rachel!"

There was the ting of metal scraping, and a scuffle of feet.

"Get *back*!" Jenks demanded, and I heard Ivy cry out in pain. "You can't have her. I told you I'd kill you if you hurt her!"

"She's bleeding!" Ivy begged. "Let me help!"

I managed to crack my eyes. I was on the floor of the van, the scent of the matted green rug pressing into me musty and sharp. I could smell blood and cocoa. Shivering, I tried to see past the bright glare of the sun.

"Don't move, Ms. Morgan," Jax said intently, and I struggled to comprehend. My fingers were both warm and cold from my blood. There was another scrape of metal on stone, and I pulled my eyes to it, trying to focus.

The back of the van was open. Jenks was standing between Ivy and me, her long sword in his hand. Ivy was hunched and holding her bleeding arm, tears dampening her cheeks with desperate sorrow. My eyes met her panicked ones, and she lunged for me.

Jenks blurred into motion, Ivy's katana slashing. She fell away, sprawling to roll on the pavement as she scrambled to remain out of his reach. My pulse leapt in fear when he followed, the sword clanging into the pavement three times, always an instant after she moved. My God, he was fast—and I think it was only his desire to stay between her and me that kept him from following to give a killing stroke.

"Jenks! Get out of my way!" she cried as she rolled to her feet with her hands raised placatingly. "She needs me!"

"She doesn't need you," he snarled. "You almost killed her. You *stupid* vampire! You couldn't wait to get out from Piscary's influence, could you? You seduced her, and then almost killed her. *You could have killed her!*"

"It wasn't like that!" Ivy pleaded, crying now. "Let me get to her. I can help!"

"Why the hell do you care?" There was another clang of stone and metal, and I forced myself to breathe when my vision started to go black.

"Rachel!" Ivy cried, drawing my gaze to her. "I'm sorry. I didn't know this would happen! I thought I was better! I really did. I'm sorry. I'm sorry!"

Jenks made a fierce cry, lunging. Ivy sprang back, arms pinwheeling. He followed her down, and the two froze when she landed against the pavement. Blood leaked from between her fingers clenched about her upper arm, and my heart seemed to hesitate when Jenks ended his last sword swing inches from her throat. Fighting my numb daze, I dragged myself to the door. He was going to kill her. He had killed before to save my life. He was going to kill Ivy.

Jenks stood with his feet widespread and his stance terrible. "You stupid, selfish whore of a vampire," he intoned. "You said you wouldn't. You promised. Now you've ruined everything. You couldn't accept what she could give, so you took it all!"

"I didn't." Ivy sprawled in the sun with her sword at her throat, the sun glinting on it and her tears. "I told her no. I told her to stop," she wept. "She asked me to."

"She wouldn't ask for this," he spat, jerking the sword so it touched her white skin to leave a line of red. "You ruin everything you love. *Everything,* you screwed-up bitch. But I'll be damned before I let you ruin Rachel."

Ivy's eyes darted to mine, her face tear-streaked and terrified. Her mouth moved but no words came out. My gut twisted when I saw her accept his words as truth. Jenks held the sword to her throat; he was going to use it and Ivy would do nothing to stop him.

Jenks shifted his grip. He pulled the sword back. Ivy looked at me, too lost in guilt to do anything.

"No," I whispered, panicking. My grasping fingers reached the edge of the van and, feet scrabbling weakly, I pushed myself forward. Jax was in my way, shrilling something and his dragonfly wings sparkling in my darkening vision.

"Jenks, stop!" I cried out, falling out of the van. Ice hard and cold, the pavement hit my shoulder and hip, scraping my cheek. I took a breath that was more like a cry, focusing on the gray pavement as if it was my coming death. *Oh God. Ivy was going to let Jenks kill her.*

"Rachel!" There was the clatter of the sword falling, and suddenly Jenks was there, his arms picking me up and cushioning me against the hard ground. Struggling, I focused on him, shocked he was so close. He didn't like anyone touching him.

"It wasn't her fault," I breathed, focusing on his eyes. They were so green, I forgot what I wanted to say. My breath sounded harsh and my throat hurt. "It wasn't her fault."

"Shhhh," he whispered, his brow creasing when I moaned as he hoisted me into his arms and lurched to his feet. "It's going to be all right. You're going to be all right. She's going to leave. You don't have to worry about her again. I won't let any vampire hurt you. I can do this. I'll stay big, and make sure no one hurts you again. It'll be okay. I'll make sure you're safe."

The vampire saliva was wearing off fast. As he carried me, I could feel a heavy pain starting to take hold and unconsciousness gather. I was cold, and shivers shook me.

Jenks's motion stopped, and he cradled me close as he stood over Ivy. His arms filled with a hard tension. "Leave," Jenks said. "Get your things and go. I want you out of the church by the time we get back. If you stay, you're going to kill her, just like everyone else stupid enough to love you."

A sound broke from her, and he walked away, pace fast as he headed for the warm darkness of the motel room.

I couldn't find the air to speak. Ivy's heavy sobs came one after the other. I didn't want her to leave. Oh, God. I had only wanted to show I trusted her. I only wanted to understand her—and myself.

Jenks's shadow fell over me, and I trembled. Tears spilled from me as I saw everything crash down to ruin. I could hear her crying, alone and lost. She was going to leave. She was going to leave because of what I had asked her to do. And as I listened to Ivy crying, alone and guilt-strewn on the pavement, something broke inside. I couldn't lie to myself anymore. It was going to kill me.

"I asked her to bite me," I whispered. "Jenks, don't leave her there. She needs me. I asked her." A sob rose in me, hurting as it broke free. "I only wanted to know. I didn't think she'd lose control like that."

Jenks jerked to a stop under the motel overhang. "Rachel?" he said, bewildered. There was the snap of dragonfly wings, and I wondered how he could carry me if he was a pixy.

I couldn't see Ivy, but her sobs had stopped and I wondered if she had heard me. I choked on my harsh breath. Jenks's shocked eyes were inches from mine. I had promised I wouldn't leave, and I refused to let her run away in guilt. I needed them both. I needed Ivy.

"I had to know," I whispered, and Jenks's face went panicked. "Please," I breathed, my vision starting to mercifully darken. "Please get her. Don't leave her alone." My eyes closed. "I hurt her so badly. Don't let her be alone," I said, but I didn't know if it made it into words before I passed out.

Twenty-three

I was moving, and it was confusing the hell out of me. I didn't think I was unconscious, and I certainly didn't know what was going on, but someone had their arms around me and I could smell the sharp scent of chlorophyll. Piecing together if I was outside with my eyes shut or inside with my eyes open was beyond me. I was cold, but I'd been cold for forever.

I did recognize the dropping sensation followed by a bed pressing into me. I tried to speak but failed. A wide hand cradled my head, and the pillow under it was pulled away. I sank deeper into the comforter as someone propped up my knees and tucked the pillow under it.

"Stay with me, Rache," came a voice, accompanied by the smell of fudge, and I tried to remember how to open my eyes. Hands were on me, light and warm. "Don't pass out. Let me get some water in you first, then you can rest."

My head lolled, accompanied by a pulsing pain in my neck. The voice had been soft, but there was panic under it. The thought of water gave me a name to the feeling I couldn't figure out. *I'm thirsty. Yes, that's what I'm feeling.*

I felt sick, and my lids fluttered as I hung in a state too fatigued to move. I remembered this. I had done this before. "Where's Keasley?" I whispered, hearing it come from me in a soft breath of air. No one heard me over the sound of running water.

"Jax, get a straw," the intent voice said. "In the trash by the TV."

There was the sound of cellophane crackling, and someone moved my legs to wedge another pillow under them. It was as if a veil dropped away, and suddenly everything had meaning. My eyes opened and reality realigned itself. I was in the motel room. I was on the bed with my feet propped higher than my head. I was cold. Jenks had carried me in, and that winged spot of sunshine hovering by the TV was Jax.

Oh God. I had asked Ivy to bite me.

Taking a deep breath, I tried to sit up.

Jenks abruptly had his hands on me, pressing my shoulder down. *He's got big hands,* I thought, trying to focus. *And warm.*

"Not so fast," he said. "Can you swallow?"

My eyes flicked to the plastic cup in his hand. I licked my lips. I wanted it, but my neck hurt. It hurt bad. "Where's Ivy?" I slurred.

Jenks's expression closed. I focused on his green eyes while the edges of my sight grayed. Nausea tightened my gut. Kisten said she had forgotten control while under Piscary's ungentle touch, possibly killing people in the throes of blood passion. I'd thought she was better. Kisten said she was better. She looked better. Apparently by asking her to divorce her feelings of love from her hunger, I'd taken away what she had used to shackle it. In three minutes I threw her back into the pit of depravity she had struggled so long to escape. I had done it to her. Me.

"I'm sorry," I said, starting to cry, and he took both my hands in one of his to stop them from moving upward to my neck. "I only wanted to understand. I didn't mean to tip her over the edge. Jenks, don't be mad at her."

His fingertips brushed the hair from my forehead, but he wouldn't meet my gaze, not yet ready to believe. Though his smooth features looked too young for someone who had adult kids, the deep-set pain born in understanding said he had endured a lifetime of joy and sorrow.

"Let me get some water in you before you pass out," he said, turning away. "Jax!" he snapped, sounding very unlike himself. "Where's that straw? I don't want her lifting her head."

"Which one is hers, Dad?" the adolescent pixy said, his voice high in worry.

"It doesn't matter. Just get one!"

The reflected light on the ceiling darkened, and from the open door came a hesitant, "She had the Sprite. And her cup is the one with all the buttons punched in."

Jax rose three feet in a glittering column of sparkles.

How about that? Those plastic dents are of some use after all.

"Get the hell out of here," Jenks said, seething. The warmth of his fingers slipped from me as he rose to stand above me.

Guilt hit hard, and I wanted to curl up and die. *What had I done? I couldn't fix this.* All I'd wanted was to understand Ivy, and now I was lying in a motel room with holes in my neck and my two best friends fighting. My life was a pile of shit. "Jenks," I whispered, "stop."

"She wants me here," Ivy came back with immediately. I could tell she was still in the threshold, and she sounded desperate. "It was an accident. I'll never touch her again. I can help. I know what to do."

"I bet you do," he said snidely, putting his hands on his hips. Now that he was six-foot-four, it didn't look as aggressive, somehow. "We don't need you! Get out!"

I wished they would figure this out so someone would give me some water. Jax hovered above me, a red straw taller than he was in his grip. Feeling distant and unreal, I made my eyes wide so I could focus on him. "Dad?" the small pixy called, worried, but they weren't listening.

"You little twit," Ivy snapped. "It was an accident! Didn't you hear her?"

"I heard her." He left me, his feet silent on the carpet. "She'll say anything you want now, won't she? You bound her to you! Damn it, Ivy! You weak-willed, jealous sack of vampire spit. You said you could handle this! You promised me you wouldn't bite her!"

His shouting was furious, and I went even colder. What if she *had* bound me to her? Would I be able to tell?

I desperately wanted to turn my head, but Jax was standing on my nose, his bare feet warm, the scent of sugar and wax coming from the drop hanging on the end of the straw. I wanted it, then felt guilty for wanting water when my friends were going to kill each other.

"I'm not going to tell you again, Jenks. Get out of my way."

There was an intake of breath, and Jax let out a yelp and darted to the ceiling. I heard a grunt followed by a rolling thump. Adrenaline surged, and I pushed myself up, then slumped against the headboard, neck protesting.

They were grappling on the floor, moving too fast for my blood-starved brain to follow. The small end table had been knocked over, and they were a confusing tangle of legs and arms.

"You're a lying, manipulative, vamp-bitch whore!" Jenks shouted, twisting violently out of her grip. She leapt at him from a crouch, and the two crashed to the wall. Jenks moved blindingly fast, flowing out from under her, grabbing her arm and landing atop her back, pinning her to the carpet. My God, he was quick.

"Ow," Ivy said to the wall, abruptly still with Jenks atop her, her arm held at an awkward angle. His other hand held a dagger to her kidneys. *When had he gotten a dagger?* "Damn it, Jenks," she said, making a little wiggle. "Get off."

"Tell me you're going to leave and not come back," he said, breath fast and blond hair in disarray, "or I'll break your arm. And you're going to stay away from Rachel. Got it? And if I see her trying to get to you because you bound her to you, I'll find you and kill you twice. I'll do it, Ivy. Don't think I can't!"

My mouth went dry and I started to shake. I was going into shock. My hand pressed to my neck was sticky. I wanted to tell them to stop, but it was all I could do to stay upright.

Ivy wiggled, stiffening when Jenks poked her. "Listen to me, pixy man," she said, her face turned to the wall. "You're quick, you're fast, and if you stick that into me, I'm going to smack you into the ever-after. I didn't bind her to me. I tried to leave, and she asked me to stay. She wanted to know. Damn it, Jenks, she wanted to know!"

Focus blurring, I tried to pull the bedspread over me, my fingers as strong as string, accomplishing nothing. Jenks started at the movement, realizing I was upright and watching. His angular, beautifully savage face lost its emotion. "You seduced her," he said, and I dropped my eyes, shamed. All I had wanted was to understand. How could so much go wrong from wanting to understand?

Her cheek pressed against the carpet, Ivy made a helpless bark of laughter. "She seduced me," she said, and I wavered from the pain and blood loss, knowing it was the truth. "I left, but she called me back. I would have left even then, but she said she wanted this for her. Not for me, but for her. I told you if she ever admitted that, I wouldn't walk away. I didn't lie to you!"

My breathing had quickened, giving me a feeling of disjoined airiness. I was hyperventilating. Jax was flitting over me, trying to dust my bite but only making me squint to see through the sparkles. At least I think the sparkles were from him. God I hurt. I was going to either die or throw up.

Jenks pricked Ivy's sweater with his knife and she jerked. "If you're lying to me—"

Ivy's shoulders lost all their tension, and she surrendered visibly. "I thought I was better," she said, guilt slamming into me at the pain in her voice. "I worked *so hard,* Jenks. I thought I'd finally— She didn't want . . . she couldn't handle the sex, so I tried to separate it from the blood. I wanted *something* of her. And she was able to give me the blood. I—I lost control of the hunger again. Damn it, I almost killed her."

His eyes on me, Jenks let go of her arm. It hit the floor with a thump. Ivy slowly pulled it into a more comfortable position. "You didn't separate the sex from the blood, you took the love from it," Jenks said, and I wavered, my pulse hammering. *What had I asked her to do?* "You take that away, and all that's left *is* the hunger."

My breath came in short splurges as I fought to remain upright. Did everyone know more about vampires than me? Jenks was a pixy, and he knew more about vampires than I did.

"I tried," Ivy whispered. "She doesn't want me to touch her that way." She took a shuddering breath, broken.

Jenks flicked a glance at me, seeing my cold face and realizing that she was telling the truth. Slowly he slid off her, and Ivy pulled herself upright, knees to her forehead, arms wrapped about her shins. She took a gasping breath and held it.

"Rachel didn't think it was wrong, did she?" Jenks pressed.

"She said she was sorry for waiting so long," Ivy whispered as if she didn't believe it. "But she saw the hunger, Jenks. She saw it raw, and I hurt her with it. She's not going to want anything to do with me—knowing that."

It was a very small voice, vulnerable and afraid, and Jenks watched me, not her. "Why are you trying to hide what you are?" he said softly, his words for both of us. "Do you think seeing your hunger shocked her? Do you think she's so shallow that she'd condemn you for it? That she didn't know it was in you and loved you anyway?"

Ivy shook with her head on her knees, and tears slipped from me. My head hurt and my neck throbbed, but it was nothing compared to my heartache.

"She loves you, Ivy. God knows why. She made a mistake in asking you to separate the love from the hunger, and you made a mistake thinking you could."

"I wanted what she could give me," Ivy said, curled up into herself. "Just that much would have been enough. Never again," she said. "Never, never, Jenks. She's safe. You're right. I destroy everything I touch."

I struggled to keep from passing out. She wasn't a monster. "Ivy?"

Her head jerked up. Her face was white and tracked with tears. "I thought you were unconscious," she said, scrambling to her feet and wiping her face.

Blinking, I wavered where I sat. Guilt lay thick on me, and Jenks sat cross-legged by the open door in a patch of sun, a faint, sad smile on him.

She stood in a frozen quandary. "Are you okay?" she asked, clearly wanting to rush over but afraid to. Between the blood loss and the absurdity of the question, I almost laughed.

"Uh-huh," I said, giving up on trying to have this make sense. "Can I have some water?" I whispered, then tipped over.

My neck sent a stab of pain to shock me and I couldn't breathe; my face was buried in the covers. I tried to cry out but was helpless. Damn it, even my arms wouldn't work.

"Oh God," Ivy said, her hands cold as she pulled me up. I took a grateful breath, trying to focus through the hurt. Jenks was at my feet, and he tugged them down until I was flat on my back and looking up at them with wide eyes, teetering on unconsciousness again now that the adrenaline had played itself out. The asinine relief that I had shaved my legs lifted through me and was gone.

"Here, Dad," Jax offered, that red straw in his two-fisted grip.

Jenks grabbed that absurdly small cup of water, never sloshing it as he retrieved it from the nightstand. "She's bleeding again," he said, his voice and face grim. "Dust her."

"Don't give her the water yet." Ivy was a confusing blur as I tried to focus. "I've got something to put in it."

Struggling to keep from passing out, I watched her snatch up her purse and rummage through it. My stomach clenched when she brought out a small vial. "Brimstone?" I whimpered, waiting for Jenks's protest.

But all I heard was his soft, "Not so much this time."

Ivy's oval face scrunched in anger as she unscrewed the top. "I know what I'm doing."

Jenks glared at her. "She's too weak for what you usually give her. She can't eat enough to support that high a metabolism with all the blood you took out of her."

"And you know all about that, don't you, pixy?" she said sarcastically.

So much for playing nice. Tired, I let my eyes shut while they argued, hoping I didn't die in the interim and make the problem moot. I wasn't ever going to get my water. Ever.

"Rachel?"

It was close and direct. Startled, I opened my eyes. Jenks was kneeling beside the bed with that cup and straw in his hand. Ivy was behind him, her arms crossed over her chest, cheeks spotted with red. Anger and worry warred in her expression. I'd missed something. "No Brimstone," I slurred, my hands rising to push it away. My throat tightened as my emotions swung from one extreme to the next. They were so worried about me.

Jenks furrowed his brow, looking too severe for someone so young. "Don't be stupid, Rache," he said, catching my arms and easily forcing them down. "You either take it with Brimstone or you'll be flat on your ass for four weeks."

He was swearing. I knew I must be doing better. I could smell the water. I couldn't move my arms under his soft restraint, and I felt sick. *Why were they making me do this?*

I looked at the straw, and taking that as a yes, Jenks slipped it between my lips. Breath held, I sucked it down, thinking the rusty water tasted better than the last cold beer I'd had. Tears started leaking out, my emotions thoroughly out of control. I thought of Ivy doing the same to me, bleeding me dry with that same metallic taste of me in her mouth.

I started to cry, choking on the water. *Damn it, what in hell was wrong with me?*

"That's enough," Ivy said softly. Through my watering eyes, I saw her reach out in concern, her hand touching Jenks's shoulder. He jumped, and Ivy pulled away, her face full of an inner pain.

She thought she was a monster. She thought she couldn't touch anyone without ruining them, and I had proved her right.

The enormity of her life's misery fell on me, and I started to shake.

"She's going into shock," Ivy said, oblivious to the real reason. I'd hurt her. I thought I had been strong enough to survive her, and by failing, I'd hurt her.

Jenks set the cup aside and rose. "I'll get a blanket."

"I've got it," she said, already gone.

My hands fluttered, and I realized I was getting sticky blood all over the bed. They were trying to help, but I didn't deserve it. I wished it had never happened. I had made a mistake, and they were both being so nice about it.

Another tremor shook me. I tried to scrunch up into myself for warmth. His green eyes pinched, Jenks pulled me upright, slipping in behind me. Curving his arms around me, he kept me from shaking apart.

Ivy wasn't pleased. "What are you doing?" she asked from across the room, her lips pressed tight as she shook out a brown motel blanket.

"I'm keeping her warm."

Jenks smelled like green things. His arms wrapped around me, and his front pressed into my back. My head was spinning and my neck was a hurting ache. I knew I shouldn't be sitting up like that, but I couldn't remember how to say "Down." I think I was still crying, since my face was wet and those noises in the background sort of sounded like me.

Ivy sighed, then came forward. "She's going to pass out if you keep her head up like that," she muttered as she draped the blanket over us.

"Pixy dust will hold her together for only so long," Jenks said softly. "And I don't want Jax to be fighting the gravity blood flow when he stitches her up."

My eyes flashed open. *Stitches? Crap, not again. I'd just gotten rid of my scars.* "Wait," I said, panic bringing me stiff at the thought of what it was going to feel like now that the vampire saliva was dormant. "No stitches. I want my pain amulet."

They didn't seem to understand me. Ivy bent close, looking at my eyes, not me. "We could take her to Emergency."

From behind me, Jenks shook his head. "The Weres would track us from there. I'm surprised they haven't found us already. I can't believe you bit her. We have four Were packs scenting for our blood, and you think *now* is a good time to change your relationship?"

"Shut the hell up, Jenks."

My stomach turned. I wanted my pain amulet. I wasn't a brave person. I'd seen the movie where they stitched up the guy with no anesthetic and bailing wire. It hurt. "Where's my amulet?" I pleaded, heart pounding. "Where's Keasley? I want Keasley."

Ivy pulled away. "She's going incoherent." Her brow furrowed, wrinkling her usually placid face. "Rachel?" she said loudly and with exaggerated slowness. "Listen to me. You should be stitched. Just four tiny stitches. I didn't rip you. It will be okay."

“No!” I exclaimed, my vision darkening. “I don’t have my pain amulet!”

Ivy gripped my shoulder through the blanket. Her eyes were full of compassion. “Don’t worry. With your head up like this, you’re going to pass out in about three seconds.”

She was right.

Twenty-four

"Jenks, stop picking everything up before you break something," I said, then drew my hand back from one of the ceramic knickknacks neatly arranged on the store shelves. It was a pumpkin with a little cat beside it, and it reminded me of Rex.

"What?" Grinning, Jenks tossed three ceramic bells into the air and juggled them.

I pointed at the handwritten sign with YOU BREAK IT, YOU BUY IT on it. I was tired, hungry, and my new stitches hidden under my red turtleneck ached 'cause I was stupid and I deserved to hurt. Even so, the last thing I needed was to pay for broken merchandise.

Jenks watched my mood, his roguish smile fading. Tossing all three up high into the open second story, he seriously caught them one by one and set them back where they belonged. "Sorry," he said meekly.

I puffed my air out and touched his shoulder to tell him it was okay. Between the blood loss and Ivy's force-fed Brimstone, I was damn tired. Hands behind his back, Jenks continued perusing the shelves looking for a chunk of bone. He hadn't found any yesterday, and I needed it to finish this run and get the hell home.

Under the disguise amulet, Jenks looked very different with black hair and a darker complexion. He had his new aviator jacket on over the T-shirt he had bought in the previous store, making him a sexy, leggy, hunk o' pixy ass in jeans. No wonder he had fifty-four kids and Matalina smiled like Mona Lisa.

Married pixy, I told myself, forcing my eyes back to the shelf of ceramic animals. *Fifty-four kids. Beautiful wife, sweet as sugar, who would kill me in my sleep while apologizing for it.*

Jenks wasn't happy about me being out here, but when I had woken up at a late three P.M. and found Ivy and Nick had taken the bus across the straits to get his truck, I had to get out. As usual, the Brimstone had made me hungry and nauseous, filling me with a brash stupidity that I was sure came from the upper that made Brimstone so popular on the streets. Seems if you took enough medicinal grade, you still got a buzz. *Thanks a hell of a lot, Ivy.*

It was her fault I was restless; moving seemed to help. Though I knew Ivy would disagree, I thought it unlikely that the Weres would look for us here when it was more likely we had hightailed it to Cincinnati. But I wasn't going home until this was done. I wouldn't take a war back to my streets, my neighbors.

"Oh, wow," Jenks breathed. "Rachel, look at this!"

I turned, finding him standing proudly before me with a red and black striped hat on his head. The thing must have been a foot tall, like a weird top hat. "That's nice, Jenks," I said.

"I'm going to get it," he said, beaming.

I took a breath to protest, then let it out. It was on sale. Five bucks. Why not?

My fingers trembled as I sifted through a display of beads, trying to decide if they were made of bone. I'd been out here with Jenks for an hour, and though he was loaded down with fudge, T-shirts, and useless bric-a-brac only a twelve-year-old or a pixy could love, I hadn't found anything suitable yet. I knew it wasn't smart to be out there, but I was a runner, damn it, and I could take care of myself—as long as I had Jenks to back me up, anyway. That and my splat gun tucked in my shoulder bag, loaded with sleepy-time charms.

A smile quirked the corners of my mouth as I watched Jenks ogle a rack of plastic dinosaurs. He still had that hat on, but with his physique, the man could wear anything. Feeling my attention on him, he glanced up and away. Sure, he was oohing and ahhing over the trashiest stuff, but his eyes were constantly shifting, scanning the area more closely than a candy shop owner with a store full of elementary kids.

I knew he wished Jax was with us to play scout, but the pixy had gone with Ivy and Nick. Ivy wasn't letting Nick out of her sight since Jenks had found him in Squirrel's End trying to leave his sorrow in an empty glass. If she hadn't hated him before, she did now, seeing that he had put everything in jeopardy to slam down a few in the comfort of humans.

"Rache." Jenks was suddenly at my elbow. "Come and look at

what I found. It's made of bone. I think it's perfect. Let's get it and get out of here."

His brow was creased in concern, because of my increasing fatigue, and deciding I had pushed my luck far enough, I shuffled after him. I was tired, the blood loss starting to win out over Ivy's Brimstone cocktails. Hiking my bag higher, I stopped beside a case full of American Indian stuff: tomahawks, little drums, carved totem poles, strings of beads and feathers. There was some turquoise in there, and realizing by the price tags that it wasn't tourist crap but real artwork, I leaned forward. Didn't Indians carve stuff out of bone?

"Look at that necklace," Jenks said proudly, pointing through the glass. "It's got a hunk of bone for the pendant. You could get that. Put the demon curse in it, and bang! Not only do you have a new focus, but you've got yourself some kick-ass Native American bling."

Hunched over the display case, I glanced wearily up at him.

"Oh!" he exclaimed, and I followed his gaze to an ugly totem shoved into the corner of the case as if in apology. "Look at that! That would look great in my living room!"

I exhaled slowly, dubiously eyeing it. The thing stood about four inches high, and the animals portrayed were so stylized, I couldn't tell if they were beaver, deer, wolves, or bear. Blocky teeth and big eyes. It was ugly, but a right kind of ugly.

"I'm getting it for Matalina," he said proudly, and my eyes widened as I tried not to imagine what to a pixy would be akin to a six-foot totem pole in the middle of Matalina's living room. I had no idea how pixies decorated, but I couldn't imagine the woman would be pleased.

"Ma'am?" he called out, his posture upright and eager. "How much is this?"

I leaned heavily on the counter as the woman finished up at the register and hustled over. Tuning her and Jenks out as they haggled over the price, I looked at the necklace. It was out of my easy price range, but there was a statue of a wolf next to it. It was expensive too, but if it didn't work, I could bring it back.

Reaching a decision, I straightened. "Can I see that wolf statue?" I asked, interrupting Jenks trying to sweet-talk the woman into giving him a senior citizen discount. She wasn't buying that he had kids and a mortgage. I couldn't blame her. He looked like he should be in high school with that funky hat on.

Her eyebrows high and her expression cagy, the woman unlocked the case and set the statue in my hand. "It's bone, right?" I asked, turning it over to see the MADE IN CHINA sticker. *Not so authentic, then, but I wasn't going to complain.*

"Ox bone," the woman said warily. "No regulations on importing ox bone."

I nodded, setting it on the counter. It was pricey, but I wanted to go home. Or at least back to my motel room. "Would you give us a price break if we bought two pieces?" I asked, and a satisfied smile spread over the woman's face.

Delighted, Jenks took over, overseeing her wrap both pieces up and boxing them individually. My pulse slow and lethargic, I dug in my bag for my wallet.

"My treat," Jenks said, his young features looking innocent and flustered. "Go stand by the door or something."

His treat? It was all coming out of the same pot. Eyebrows high, I tried to look past him, but he got in my way, pulling off his hat and using it to hide something he had slipped onto the counter. I caught a glimpse of a bottle of Sun-Fun color-changing nail polish, then smiled and turned away. Next year's solstice gift, maybe?

"I'll be outside," I said, seeing an empty bench in the middle of the open-air mall. Jenks mumbled something, and I leaned into the glass door, glad it moved easily. The air smelled like fudge and water, and with slow steps I made a beeline for the bench before the young family with ice cream cones could reach it.

I exhaled as I settled myself on the wooden bench. The wind was light in the protected area, and the sun was warm. I breathed deeply, pulling in the scent of the marigolds behind me. It was right on the cusp of being able to plant annuals up there, but they would be sheltered from frost, being surrounded by so much stone.

Though the tourist season hadn't officially started, it was busy. People with colorful sacks drifted aimlessly in a contented pattern of idle amusement that was comforting to see, humans mostly, with the odd witch making a statement with his or her dress. It was hard to tell who was who otherwise—unless you got close enough to smell them.

The sound of unseen pixy wings was a soft, almost subliminal hum. My hands drifted up to my scent amulet, making sure it was touching my skin. I knew I shouldn't have been out there alone, but I was under two disguises. What were the chances the Weres would even be looking for me here? And if they were, they would never recognize me.

I glanced up when the shop door opened and Jenks came out, squinting in the brighter light until he put his shades on. The top of that hat poked out from the bag he carried, and I smiled. His head turned to the end of the mall where we had parked Kisten's Corvette. It was obvious he wanted to hustle me over there and get me home, but upon seeing me slumped in fatigue, he came to a silent standstill above me. Slowly I drew my head up.

"Are you—" Jenks started.

"I'm fine," I lied, wanting to pluck my turtleneck off my stitches. Jax had used dental floss, but they still pulled on the fabric. "The couch left me tight, is all."

He grinned, sitting down cross-legged on the bench as if it was a toadstool. Jenks had slept in the van last night so neither Ivy nor I had to. Hell, I didn't even want to ride in it again—which was probably why Ivy had taken a cab across the straits to get Nick's truck.

"I was going to ask you if you were hungry and wanted a hamburger," he said, squinting, "but I like your idea better. I could go for a little scuffle. Loosen up. Get the blood flowing."

I hated feeling weak. Taking a weary breath, I straightened. "Jenks, sit like a man. That was cute when you were four inches tall, but now you look prissy."

Immediately he put his feet on the ground, knees together and a worried look on him. Puffing the hair from my eyes, I gave up and rolled my turtleneck down. So I had been bitten by a vamp. Lots of people were. "That doesn't look much better," I said.

"Well, how the hell am I supposed to sit!" he exclaimed.

Lacing my fingers over my head, I stretched carefully, feeling the stitches pull. Kisten's bracelet shifted to my elbow to make a cold spot of metal against my skin. "Have you seen Kisten slouch in the kitchen?"

With a hesitant slowness that could have been provocative, Jenks extended his legs. Lean in his tight jeans, he slumped until his neck rested atop the back of the bench. His arms went out to run along the length of the worn wood and his feet spread suggestively.

Oh—my—God. Flushing, I sat up straight. "Yeah," I said faintly. "That's better." *Fifty-four kids. Fifty-four kids. And where was that camera he was going to buy for me?*

"Give me a minute to catch my breath," I said, sneaking glances at him. "Then we can head to the car. I need a few more things to make the demon spell, but I'm too tired to do it now." It grated on me to admit it, but it was kinda obvious.

Jenks sat up with a little grunt, rummaging in a pocket of his coat to bring out a folded napkin. "Here," he said, handing it to me. "Ivy said you might be stupid enough to leave the motel, and if you did to give you this."

Irritation filled me, and I unfolded it to find one of her Brimstone cookies. "Damn it, Jenks!" I hissed, folding it up and glancing at the passing people. "You want to see me in jail?"

He smirked. "Then eat it and get rid of the evidence. Tink's a Disney whore, Rache, you're worse than my kids. You need it. It's medicinal. Just eat the damned cookie."

I felt it light in my hand, thinking it wasn't as simple as he made it out to be. The only reason I was out here was because the dose I'd taken before bed had woken me with the jitters. 'Least, I was blaming it on that. I felt like crap, though, so I opened it up and nibbled a corner.

Immediately Jenks's posture relaxed. I followed his gaze across the busy plaza to the hanging planters, finally spotting the pixies. They were chasing a hummingbird off, their ferocity surprising me. It was too early for fairies to be back from Mexico, and with a little practice, the pixies might be able to hold the plaza when they migrated up.

The silence grew as I broke off a second corner off Ivy's cookie and guiltily ate it. I hated being on Brimstone, but I hated being flat on my back more. *There had to be another way,* I thought. But it would shorten my fatigued state from three weeks to three days. It wasn't magic, but it was close. I could actually feel the drug taking hold, making my pulse quicken and the slight trembling of my fingers disappear. No wonder this stuff was illegal.

Jenks was quiet, watching the passing people with interest while he waited for my strength to return. I didn't have a dad to talk stuff over with, and my mom was too far away. Jenks was a heavy third of our firm; what he thought mattered. I took a breath, worried about what he might say after I told him what really had me out there, running from my thoughts.

I'd done some thinking that morning, hunched over the sink and squinting into the shower-fogged mirror to inspect my new stitches and scraped face. The tears were small and harmless looking, nothing like the savage rips Al had given me—but they forced me to question how long I had been pushing Ivy into biting me—'cause this hadn't come out of nowhere. So while the shower ran from hot to cold, I sat on the edge of the tub with a towel wrapped around myself, shaking and almost physically ill with the thought that Ivy had been right about at least part of it. All it had taken was a brush with death for me to admit it.

So maybe I *had* wanted her to bite me even before I moved in with her. That did mean I needed a subliminal feeling of danger to become passionate. Nobody was that screwed up.

"Thanks for helping me," I said, trying to work up to what I wanted to say. "With Ivy."

Jenks shrugged. Shifting position, he pulled himself together and watched the pixies with a professional interest. "What was I supposed to do? Walk away?"

I looked at my half-eaten cookie. Nick might have. Nick almost did the first time I had goaded Ivy into trying to bite me. Until I said no to her and she insisted. Then he stepped in to help. Looking back on the incident, it seemed obvious I had been jonesing for a bite.

"Sorry," I said, thinking of how tenuous I'd made everything. "I wasn't thinking."

Making a rude snort, he crossed his legs. "Do tell, Miss witch princess," he said. "Ivy was handling it, and you go and get curious, tipping her into all but killing you. Bloody hell! When are you going to stop being afraid of yourself?"

I ate a bite of cookie, a big one this time. "I'm scared," I said after I forced it down, dry.

"We're fine," Jenks said loudly, his eyes on the hanging flowers and clearly not knowing where my thoughts were. "We're all fine. Ivy said she isn't going to bite you again. We'll go out for pizza at Piscary's when we get home, and everything will return to normal. You're safer now than your first night spent under the same roof."

I put the last of the cookie in my mouth, nervously folding the crumbs up into the napkin. Jenks was probably right about Ivy never again initiating a bite between us. But she hadn't initiated the first one either. The thing was, I didn't want everything to return to normal.

Jenks swiveled to face me. "Ah, you are too scared to let her bite you again, right?"

A slow breath slipped past my lips and adrenaline zinged through me, pushed by fear. It was a feeling I was beginning to understand. *I didn't need fear to feel passion. I didn't.*

"Crap on my daisies," Jenks breathed. "You aren't. Rache . . ."

Frightened, I shifted to put my elbows on my knees, wadding the napkin up and squishing it as if it was my shame. "I'm in trouble," I whispered. "She didn't bind me, but she may as well have."

"Rache . . ." It was soft and pensive, and it ticked me off.

"Just listen, will you?" I snapped, then slumped back, squinting into the sun as I looked at nothing. My throat was tight, and I shoved the napkin in a pocket. "I . . . I learned something about myself. And I'm scared it's going to kill me if I ignore it. It's just . . . God! How could I be that blind about myself?"

"It might be the vamp pheromones," Jenks coaxed. "You aren't necessarily attracted to women just because you want to sleep with Ivy."

My eyes widened and I turned to him, shocking myself that he was still wearing that disguise and only his eyes looked like him. "I don't want to sleep with Ivy!" I said, flustered. "I'm straight. I . . ." I took a deep breath, afraid to admit it aloud. "I want to try to find a blood balance with her."

"You what?" Jenks blurted, and I sent my gaze to the people around us to remind him we weren't alone. "She would have killed you!" he said, hushed now, but no less intense.

"Only because I asked her to ignore her feelings for me." Flustered, I tucked a wayward strand of hair behind an ear. "Only because I let her bite me without the buffer of emotion that she uses to control her hunger."

Jenks leaned closer, his curls flashing blond in the sun for an instant as his disguise charm bobbled. "But you're straight," he said. "You just said you were."

Blushing, I pulled the bag that had the fudge in it closer. Hunger gnawed at my middle—thanks to the Brimstone—and I dug for the little white box. "Yeah," I said, uncomfortable as I remembered her gentle touch on me growing intimate when she misunderstood. "But after yesterday, it's pretty obvious she *can* share blood without the sex." I darted a look at him, even as a shiver rose through me, unstoppable, at the reminder of how good it had felt.

"And she almost killed you trying," Jenks protested. "Rache, she is still messed up, and this is too much, even for you. She can't do it. You're not physically or mentally strong enough to keep her under control if she loses it again."

I hunched in worry, hiding my concern in trying to get the taped box open. "So we go slow," I said, wrenching the thin white cardboard to no avail. "Work up to it, maybe."

"Why?" Jenks exclaimed softly, his brow pinched in worry. "Why risk it?"

At that, I closed my eyes in a slow rueful blink. Crap. Maybe

Ivy was right. Maybe this was just another way to fill my life with excitement and passion. But then I remembered our auras mixing, the desperation her soul was drowning in, and how I had eased her pain—if only for an instant.

"It felt good, Jenks," I whispered, shocked to find my vision blurring with unshed tears. "I'm not talking about the blood ecstasy. I'm talking about my being able to fill that emotional void she has. You know her as well as I do, maybe better. She aches with it. She needs to be accepted for who she is so badly. And I was able to do that. Do you know how good that felt? To be able to show someone that, yes, you are someone worth sacrificing for? That you like them for their faults and that you respect them for their ability to rise above them?"

Jenks was staring at me, and I sniffed back the tears. "Damn," I whispered, terrified all of a sudden. "Maybe it is love."

Reaching slowly, Jenks took the box of fudge from me. Twisting to a pocket, he flipped open a knife and cut the tape. Still silent, he handed me the open box and tucked the knife away. "Are you sure about this?" he asked worriedly.

I nodded, cutting a slab of fudge off with that stupid little plastic knife they put in with it. "God help me if I'm wrong, but I trust her. I trust her to find a way to make it work and not kill me in the process. I want it to work."

He fidgeted. "Have you considered this might be a knee-jerk reaction to Nick?" he said. "Are you trusting Ivy now because Nick hurt you and you simply want to trust somebody?"

I exhaled slowly. I'd already mulled that around in my head, trying it on and dismissing it. "I don't think so," I said softly.

Jenks reclined against the bench, pensive. Thoughtful myself, I put the bite of fudge in my mouth and let it dissolve. It was butterscotch in salute to Ivy's new "allergy," but I hardly tasted it. Silent, I handed him the box of candy.

"Well," Jenks said, ignoring the knife and just breaking off a piece. "At least you aren't doing this because of your oh-so-endearing need to mix danger with passion. At least it better not be, or I'll pix you from here to the day you die for using Ivy like that."

Endearing need . . . My neck throbbed when I jerked upright, choking as I swallowed. "I beg your pardon?"

He looked at me, eyebrows high and the sun glinting on his disguise-black hair. "You do the damnedest things in order to rile yourself up. Most people settle for doing it in an elevator, but not you. No, you have to make sure it's a vampire you're playing kissy-face with."

Heat washed through me, pulled by anger and embarrassment. Ivy had said the same thing. "I do not!"

"Rache," he cajoled, sitting up to match my posture. "Look at yourself. You're an adrenaline junkie. You not only need danger to make good in the bedroom, you need it to get through your normal day."

"Shut up!" I shouted, giving him a backhanded thwack on his shoulder. "I like adventure, that's all."

But he laughed at me, eyes dancing in delight as he broke off another chunk of fudge. "Adventure?" he said around his full mouth. "You keep making stupid decisions that will get you into just enough trouble that there might be the chance you can't get yourself out of. Being your safety net has been more fun than all my years at the I.S."

"I do not!" I protested again.

"Look at yourself," he said, head bowed over the fudge box again. "Look at yourself right now. You're half dead from blood loss, and you're out shopping. These disguises look great, but that's all they are: thin sheets of maybe standing between you and trouble."

"It's the Brimstone," I protested, taking the box of fudge out of his hands and closing it up. "It makes you feel indestructible. Makes you do stupid things."

He glanced from the white box to me. "Brimstone doesn't have you out here," he said. "It's your recurring lame-decision patterns that have you out here. Living in a church with a vampire, Rache? Dating a guy who summons demons? Bumping uglies with a vampire? Those caps Kisten wears won't mean crap if he loses control, and you know it. You've been flirting with being bitten for the last year, putting yourself in situation after situation where it might happen, and the first time you get Ivy out of Piscary's influence, what do you do? Manipulate her into it. You're an adrenaline addict, but at least you're making money off it."

"Hey!" I exclaimed, then lowered my voice when two passing women glanced at us. "Ivy had something to do with yesterday."

Jenks shrugged, extending his legs and clasping his hands behind his head. "Yeah. She did come up here after you. 'Course, I think part of that was her knowing you might take the opportunity after you did jumping jacks in Kisten's sweats. It didn't take much convincing on her part to bite you, did it? Nah, you were primed and ready to go, and she knew it."

Damn it, he was laughing at me. My brow furrowed, and I shoved the fudge back in a bag and out of his reach. I was not that stupid. I did *not* live my life trying to get into trouble just so I could have a good time in bed.

"I always have a good reason for the things I do," I said, peeved. "And my decisions don't hinge on what might put excitement in my life. But since I quit the I.S., I've never had the chance to make good decisions—I'm always scrambling just to stay alive. Do you think I don't want the little charm shop? The husband and two-point-two kids? A normal house with the fence and the dog that digs up my neighbor's yard and chases their cat into a tree?"

Jenks's gaze was even and calm, wise and even a bit sad. The wind ruffled his hair, and the sound of the pixies grew obvious. "No," he said. "I don't think you do." I glared, and he added, "I think it would kill you quicker than going to see Piscary wearing gothic lace. I think managing to find a blood balance with Ivy is going to be the only way you're going to survive. Besides . . ." He grinned impishly. ". . . no one but Ivy will put up with the things you need or the crap you dish out."

"Thanks a hell of a lot," I muttered, slumping with my arms crossed over my chest. Depressed, I stared at the pixies, then did a double take when I realized they'd killed the hummingbird and were gathering the feathers. *Crap, pixies were wicked when threatened.* "I am not that hard to live with."

Jenks laughed loudly, and I glanced at him, drawn by the different sound. "What about your upcoming demand to be free to sleep with whoever you damn well please while sharing blood with her, knowing she'd rather have you sleep with her?" he asked.

"Shut up," I said, embarrassed because that was one of the things I had on my list to talk to Ivy about. "She knows I'm never going to sleep with her."

The man passing us turned, then whispered something to his girlfriend, who promptly eyed me as well. I grimaced at them, glad I was wearing a disguise.

"It takes an incredibly strong person to walk away from someone they love," Jenks said, holding up two fingers as if making a list. "Especially knowing they will do something asinine, like shopping when their blood count is so low they ought to be in the hospital. You should give her credit for respecting you like that."

"Hey," I exclaimed, annoyed. "You said she wouldn't mind."

Grinning, he slid down a few feet. "Actually I said what she doesn't know won't hurt you." He put up a third finger. "You leave windows open when the heat is on."

A family of three walked past, the kids like stairsteps and noisy with life. I watched them pass, thinking they were the future I had been working for, just walking away and leaving me behind. *Was that a problem?* "I like fresh air," I protested, gathering up my things. It was time to leave.

"You're a whiner too," Jenks said. "I've never *seen* anyone so pathetic when you're sick. 'Where's my pain amulet? Where's my coffee?' God almighty, I thought I was bad."

I stood, feeling renewed from the Brimstone boost. It was a false strength, but it was there nevertheless. "Put down your fingers, Jenks, or I'm going to break them off and shove them somewhere."

Jenks stood as well, tugging his aviator jacket straight. "You bring home demon familiars. 'Oh isn't she sweet?'" he said in a high falsetto. "'Can we keep her?'"

I hiked my shoulder bag up higher, feeling the comfortable weight of my splat gun inside. "Are you saying I should have let Al kill Ceri?" I said dryly.

Laughing, he gathered up his sundry bags, consolidating them into two. "No. I'm saying that it takes a very strong person to let *you* be *you*. I can't think of anyone better than Ivy."

My breath escaped me in a huff. "Well I'm glad we have your blessing."

Jenks snorted, his gaze going over the heads of the tourists to the archway and the parking lot where the car was. "Yeah, you got my blessing, and you've got my warning too."

I looked at him, but he wasn't paying me any attention, scanning the area now that we were ready to move again.

"If you think living with Ivy and trying to avoid getting bitten was difficult, wait until you try living with her while trying to find a blood balance. This isn't an easier road, Rache," he said, gaze distant and unaware of the worry he was starting in me. "It's a harder one. And you're going to be hurting all the way along it."

Twenty-five

The wind was whipping the decorative flags at the archway to the parking lot, and I blinked at them, fascinated. I had the remains of a burger in one hand, and a fizzy drink in the other. Jenks had insisted I get some iron-rich protein in me to chase down the Brimstone, but I suspected it had only been an excuse to get the drink, which he then spiked with even more Brimstone. Why else would I be feeling this great when my life was in the crapper? And I was feeling pretty damn good, like a weight had lifted and the sun was starting to shine.

Ivy would return soon, and though I had been all tough-girl by coming out here, it seemed prudent to get back before she found out I was gone. If Jenks and she were to be believed, I structured my life to be as horrific as possible to have fun in bed, but having Ivy mad at me might be too much for even me right now.

"What time is it?" I asked, squinting in the stiffer breeze and looking for the car. People bothered at our slow pace hustled past us, but I was enjoying the wind and the view of the straits.

Jenks snickered, clearly guessing where my thoughts were. He had slammed his twenty-ounce Dew and shook for a good thirty seconds, jittery and bright eyed, making me wonder which one of us was the better bet to drive home. Juggling his bags, he checked his wrist, beaming. "Four forty-six," he said. "Only a minute off that time."

"By the time you get acclimated, we'll be heading home," I said, then pushed into motion. "When did you get a watch?"

"Yesterday with Jax," he said, stretching to see the parking lot over the heads of the surrounding people. "I got you a camera too, and my knife. I don't like being this big."

I wasn't going to tell him it was illegal to carry a concealed knife. Besides, he was a pixy. The law didn't apply to him. I smiled at the way the sunlight glittered on his hair, even if it was black. "Big bad wolfs," I said, then sucked down another swig of pop, stumbling on the curb as we found the street. "We're going to blow their damned house down."

His motions seamless, Jenks took my drink away and dropped it into the nearest trash container. "You okay?"

"Oh yeah," I said enthusiastically. I handed him the last of my burger, which he threw away for me too. "You ought to know. You're the one who keeps spiking my food."

Giving me a wry look, Jenks gallantly took my arm. A giggle slipped from me at the show of support, appalling me. Damn it, this wasn't fair. If they got me hooked on Brimstone, I was going to be majorly pissed—if I could remember why I was mad at them, that is.

Still laughing, I pulled my head up, going cold with a pulse of fear. Leaning against Kisten's Corvette were Brett and Walter Vincent, the first one scanning the faces of the people leaving the mall, the second doing the same but with a murderous intensity. Immediately I realized what had happened, and I thanked God we weren't at the motel, trapped in a little box of a room. Jenks and I were under a disguise, and though they hadn't known about Kisten's car, it probably smelled like the pixy, seeing as he drove it yesterday. They had found us.

"Oh, fudge," I whispered, leaning heavily on Jenks's arm. Just that fast, I had gone from exuberant to panic, the Brimstone taking over my moods. "You got anything more lethal than that knife on you?" I asked.

"No. Why?" His forward momentum barely hesitated as he looked up from watching my feet. "Oh," he said softly, his fingers tightening on my arm for an instant. "Okay."

I wasn't surprised when he did an abrupt turn-about and wheeled us back into the mall. Bending close, Jenks sent the aroma of dry meadow over me. "Your disguises are working," he whispered. "Pretend we just forgot something and have to go pick it up."

I found myself nodding, scanning the contented faces around me, searching for anger in the vacationing people. My pulse was fast and my skin tingling. Pam was dead; they would be after me for that if nothing else. Weres were timid, apart from the alpha and the first few down, and since the round was broken, they would stay in the background and keep our squabble private. We'd be okay unless we got ourselves in a blind alley. And there weren't many of those in Mackinaw City.

"I'm going to call Ivy," I said, pulling my bag around and opening it.

Body tense, Jenks drew me to a stop to put my back to a brick wall and stand partially in front of me. It was a candy shop—big surprise there—and my stomach growled as I hit speed dial. "Come on, come on," I crabbed, waiting for it to go through.

The circuit clicked open and Ivy's voice filtered out. "Rachel?"

"Yeah, it's me," I said, shoulders easing in relief. "Where are you?"

"On the bridge back. Why?" She hesitated, and I could hear the distinctive sound of Nick's truck. "Why do I hear people?" she added suspiciously.

Jenks winced, and I squinted in the sun, backing up until the overhang put me in the shade. "Uh, Jenks and I went on a procurement run."

"Shopping?" she yelped. "Rachel! Damn it, can't you just sit still for a couple of hours?"

I thought of the Brimstone running rampant through me, deciding that no, I couldn't.

Jenks tossed his head, and I followed his grim gaze to a pair of elegantly dressed tourists. They had shopping bags, but they were a little too attentive. Turning his back to them, Jenks angled to block their view of me. *Damn it, this was getting dicey.* My pulse quickened and I hunched into the phone. "Look, I did some thinking, and you're right." I peeked around Jenks, then rocked back. "How long will it take for you to get to that open-air mall?"

"You did some thinking?" Ivy said softly, sounding vulnerable.

Jenks scanned the plaza. "Tick-tock, Rache."

Anxious, I turned to the phone. "Yeah. I need to start making smarter decisions. But we're at that mall and Brett and Walter are sitting on the car." The good feeling the Brimstone had instilled in me had sifted to fear, and I clamped down on my rising panic. At its heart, Brimstone was an intensifier. If you were happy, you were really happy. If you were sad, you were suicidal. Right now I was scared out of my mind. Until it wore off, I was going to be a roller coaster of emotions. *Damn it, I didn't have time for this!*

Ivy snarled something at Nick, and I heard a horn blast. "How many?" she asked tightly.

I looked past Jenks, seeing sunlit flowers and cheerful storefronts. "Four so far, but they have phones. We're wearing disguises, so they probably don't know it's us." *Calm down, Rachel,* I told myself, trying to use the drug to my advantage. *Think.*

"I knew this was going to happen. I knew it!" Ivy shouted.

"Well, I'd rather meet them here than the motel," I said, doggedly trying to pull my emotions from fear back to invincibility. It wasn't working. I was still scared.

"The bridge is still one lane either way," Ivy snarled. "I can't get around this guy. Give the phone to Jenks. I want to talk to him."

Jenks paled and shook his head.

"Jenks!" she exclaimed, "I know you can hear me. I can't believe you let her talk you into this. I told you she needed at least another course of Brimstone before she could work in the kitchen, much less go out!"

"I'm not that weak," I said indignantly, but Jenks was way ahead of me, and he took the phone, holding it so we could both hear.

"She ate that last cookie, Ivy," he said, clearly offended. "And I just gave her another dose of the stuff. She's running on full. I'm not stupid."

"I knew it!" I said, glancing past Jenks at the drifting people. "You slipped me some!"

There was a short silence, and Ivy said softly, "You picked up more Brimstone?"

Jenks met my eyes. "Yeah. And don't worry. I paid cash. It's not on the card."

"Where did you get the money, Jenks?" Ivy asked, the threat clear in her voice.

"It wasn't that expensive," he said, but I could tell he thought he'd done something wrong by his suddenly worried look.

"You ass!" Ivy said. "Get her the hell out of there! You bought street-grade, you stupid pixy! She's higher than a kite!"

Jenks's mouth worked but nothing was coming out.

"Uh, Ivy?" he squeaked. "We gotta go."

"Don't hang up!" Ivy yelled. "Give me to Rachel. Jenks, give the phone to Rachel!"

Jenks went to end the call, and I snatched the phone. I was on street-grade Brimstone? Swell. Just swell. I thought it was hitting me a little hard. I could hear Ivy telling Nick what had happened, catching the word "invincible" and "get herself killed." Jenks turned to scan the area, his posture tense and guilty looking.

"Hey, Ivy," I said, my mood having done a quick shift to anger. "The next time you and Jenks want to play doctor, just shove the Brimstone up your ass, okay? Both of you. I'm not your freaking play-doll."

"I'm on my way," Ivy said, ignoring me. "Rachel, just . . . sit somewhere. Can you do that? I'll get you out."

I leaned against the brick wall, feeling every little projection dig into me through my shirt. "Take your time," I said flippantly, ticked and nerved-up all at the same time. The adrenaline was flowing, and Brimstone had my skin tingling. "Jenks and I are going to plan B."

"Plan B?" Ivy said. "What is plan B?"

Jenks reddened. "Grab the fish and run like hell," he muttered, and I almost giggled.

"I'm going to walk out of here," I said, deciding I'd rather be invincible than scared, "and catch the trolley back to the motel. And if anyone stops me, I'm going to kick—their—ass."

"Rachel," Ivy said slowly, "it's the Brimstone. You aren't thinking. Just sit tight!"

My eyes narrowed. "I can take care of myself," I said, starting to feel really good. It wasn't the Brimstone. No, I lived for excitement! I made decisions based on what would screw my life up the most! I was a messed-up, screwed-up stupid witch who had to mix danger with her sex life in order to get turned on, and I was going to live a very short, exciting life. I went to end the call, then hesitated. "Hey, you want me to keep the phone line open?"

"Yes," she said softly. "No. Yes."

I sobered at the worry in her voice. "Okay."

My blood tingled through me, and I tucked the phone into my waistband, upside down so the mike was exposed and not muffled by my jeans. Ivy would be able to hear everything that happened. I looked at Jenks, seeing his worry and tension. "Well?" I said, pushing myself off the wall. "What do you think?"

"I think Ivy's going to kill me," he whispered. "Rachel. I'm sorry. I didn't know."

I took a breath, exhaling long and slow. It was done. If anything, I ought to thank him; I was up and walking, able to run even if I was going to pay for it later. "Don't worry about it," I said, touching his shoulder. "Just stop making my decisions for me, okay?"

My roving eyes fell upon the bench he and I had been sitting on. My mouth went dry and I tried to swallow. Brett was standing by it, his arms crossed and his eyes fixed on me. He was smiling. At me. "Shit," I breathed. "Jenks, they know it's us."

He nodded, his youthful face going serious. "He showed up a few minutes ago. We have six at the exit behind us and four at the bend the other way."

"And you just let me keep talking to Ivy?" I said, not believing it.

A shrug lifted his shoulders. "They're Weres. They aren't going to make a scene."

Normally I would have agreed with him. Heart pounding, I snuck a look at the six Weres at the exit. They had scads of jewelry and were in bright colors, making them from the street pack. Bringing up my second sight, I felt the last of my bravado wash out of me. Their auras were rimmed in brown again. How had Walter managed to pull them back together like that?

"Ah, Jenks?" I said, knowing Ivy was listening. "They're in a round. They aren't going to just sit there. We have to leave before the rest arrive."

Jenks looked at me, looked at the Weres, then looked at me again. His gaze went to the roof, and he was probably wishing he could fly. "There's only one layer of shops," he said suddenly. "Let's go."

Grabbing my arm, he pulled me into the fudge store. Feet stumbling, I followed him in, breathing deeply of the rich scent of chocolate. There was a small line at the counter, but Jenks plowed to the front of it amid a chorus of indignant protest. "Pardon, me. 'Scuse us," he said, flipping the barrier up between the front and the back.

"Hey!" a large woman called out, her apron tied with the smartness of a uniform. "You can't come back here!"

"Just passing through!" Jenks called cheerfully. The bags he held rattled, and letting go of my arm for a moment, he dipped a finger into the puddle of fudge cooling on a marble table. "Needs more almond," he said, tasting it. "And you're cooking it half a degree too long."

The woman's mouth opened in surprise, and he pushed past her and into the kitchen.

"There," I said, and Jenks's eyes shot to the back door, outlined by the boxes stacked around it. The security door was open to let the hot air of the kitchen escape through a normal-looking screen door. Beyond that were the employees' cars in a nasty-looking alley, and beyond that, the main road. In the distance, the straits sparkled, looking as big as a lake.

"Ready?" Jenks asked.

I jerked my splat ball gun out of my bag. "Yup. Let's go."

"What the hell are you doing back here?" a masculine voice called.

I turned, and the man's eyes went wide at my cherry-red gun, then he got nasty. "This is my place of business!" he shouted. "Not a paint ball stadium! Get out! Get out!"

"Sorry," I mumbled, then bolted for the door when he shambled forward, hands reaching. Jenks and I dove through it, skittering into the alley in a surge of adrenaline. The bang of the heavy door slamming shut shot through me.

"Oh look, Jenks," I said, as we slowed to get our bearings. "A dead-end alley."

The wind was brisk, blowing up and against the back of the store, and with my blood humming and my steps quick, I started for the street and the cracked sidewalk beside it. It would take the Weres some time to work their way out and around to the back of the store unless they trashed the fudge shop. But I didn't think they would. Like their supposedly distant wild brethren, Weres weren't aggressive unless defending their own. But they were in a round, so who knew what they would do.

"Ivy," I said breathlessly as we jogged to the road, knowing she could hear. "We're outside between the mall and the— Shit!" I exploded, skittering to a halt when, in a sliding sound of gravel on pavement, a trio of Weres skidded around the corner.

They were wearing khaki pants and matching polo shirts to make them look like they were in uniform. Even worse, one of them dropped a duffel bag, and after unzipping it, started tossing nasty looking weapons to his buddies. I stood there, frozen. Were they nuts? This went way beyond a public show of strength. Hell, even vamps never did this! Not in broad daylight and on the street where any passing human could see, anyway.

Someone cocked their weapon, and Jenks jerked me back. My mouth was still hanging open when we landed against a salt-rusted four-door, the front full of crumpled fast food sacks.

Brett came around the corner, his pace fast and his eyes darting everywhere. Seeing me, he smiled. "We have them, sir," he said into the phone at his ear, slowing to a stop behind the three Weres with aggressive stances. "Behind the fudge shop. It's all over but the howling."

Heart pounding, I looked at the road and the sporadic traffic. The memory of finding Nick tied to the wall swam up from my subconscious. A chill purged everything from me but a fierce determination. I wasn't strong enough to survive that. I couldn't let them take me.

"You want me to make a circle and wait for Ivy, or you want to fight our way out, Jenks?" I said, my grip on my splat gun going sweaty.

In a sliding sound of metal, Jenks pulled a dull metal bar from the nearby recycling bin, swinging it a couple of times. The three Weres with guns took a more aggressive stance. "You think we need Ivy?" he asked.

"Just checking," I answered, then turned to the Weres, my arms shaking. "Right. Like you're going to shoot us?" I taunted. "If we're dead, you can't beat Nick's location out of us."

Brett's jaw clenched. From the other side, three more Weres loped into view, to make seven men. I had fourteen sleepy-time potions. I had to act, and act now.

"Subdue them," Brett said, squinting from the sun. Annoyed, he snatched the weapon from the nearest man. "Use your fists. You outnumber them, and I don't want the I.S. out here because of weapon discharges."

Adrenaline surged, making me feel weak, not strong. From beside me, Jenks shouted, then leapt forward. Half the Weres came to meet him, their speed and ferocity shocking.

Panic struck. Taking aim, I downed one with a charm. Then another. I wanted to help Jenks, but they were coming too fast. One slipped past him, and I gasped, falling to one knee.

"Not today, you son of a bitch!" I exclaimed, plugging him. He slid to within three feet of me. I leveled my gun for the next one. He got three steps closer than the first.

"Jenks! Fall back!" I shouted, retreating with my gun going *puff-puff-puff*.

Three more went down. Frantic, I tossed the hair from my face. There were a lot more then seven Weres. I had downed at least that many. Where in hell was Ivy?

"Rache!" Jenks shouted in warning. "Behind you!"

I spun. A Were in leather was running for me. Behind him, the door to the kitchen was wide-open and full of rough-looking Weres in street clothes.

I stumbled backward. They had come through the shop? Damn it! I had been afraid they would. They were not acting normal!

"Rachel!" Jenks shouted again as the Were smiled to show his beautiful, beautiful teeth and closed his grease-stained fingers about my wrist. Big mistake.

Grunting, I twisted my arm to grip his own thick wrist. My right foot came up and my sneaker smacked him in the kidneys. Wrenching around, I used his own weight to yank him down, falling to kneel so his elbow hit my upraised knee, bending it backward and snapping. He grunted as his elbow shattered.

Puffing in satisfaction, I let him go and got to my feet. *Where in hell was my splat gun?*

Spotting it alone on the pavement, I darted for it.

"Hey!" I shouted, my foot pulled out from under me. Arms flailing to get between my face and the uprushing pavement, I hit the cement. Shocked, I twisted to find the Were I had downed wasn't withering in pain and holding his broken arm, but using it!

"You bloody bastard!" I shouted, kicking at his face. "Let me go!"

But he didn't, grimily holding on. Panic slid through me as I realized they were using the full potential of the round and someone was muting his pain. He utterly ignored the broken nose I gave him with my heel, and I smacked him again. Blood gushed and he finally let go, but not before he fastened one of those damned zip-strips on my foot.

"You freaking bastard!" I shouted, scrabbling for my gun and plugging him right in the face. Furious, I turned to the two Weres following him and shot them too.

The three collapsed, and shuddering, I got to my feet, holding three more at bay, my arms shaking as I shifted the aim from one to the other.

"Jenks!" I shouted, and he was suddenly at my back. Stupid, *stupid* witch. Until I got the thing off, I wouldn't be able to make a circle. All I had were the four charms in my gun and Jenks, his back now pressing lightly against mine.

I could smell the sweat on him, reminding me of a meadow somehow. He had lost his disguise amulet at some point and his blond curls were tousled. The cut on his forehead was bleeding again, and red streaked his hands. My face went ashen when I realized it wasn't his but from the five Weres he had beaten into unconsciousness with that pipe.

Brett stood with Walter behind two military Weres, their weapons cocked and ready to gun us down if they couldn't subdue us any other way. Past them, traffic passed, and curious onlookers were being soothed by professional-looking Weres in suits and ties, probably explaining this away as being a movie shoot or something. Behind us, the street Weres waited, hanging back but ready to descend when someone gave the order.

I swallowed hard. With the strength of four alphas at his fingertips, Walter had driven them into a higher pitch of aggression, and with the lack of pain, there was nothing to stop them. Just the thought of gaining the focus had been enough to get them back together.

Incredible, I mused, grip shifting on my splat gun as I tried to figure out how four charms would be of much help. What would happen if they actually got the focus was a nightmare in waiting. Every single Were would want a piece of it. The alphas would come flocking, and soon the major cities would be fighting their own little turf wars as vampires started taking them out, having decided they didn't like aggressive Weres who felt no pain and could Were as fast as witch magic. And with the focus binding them, the round wouldn't break apart. No wonder the vampires had hidden the ugly thing.

"Jenks," I panted, knowing Ivy could hear. "They tagged me with one of those zip-strips. I can't make a circle to hold them off anymore. We can't let them get the focus. And I'm not strong enough to keep my mouth shut if they capture me."

Jenks glanced at me and away. His grip tightened on the bloody pipe. "Any ideas?"

"Nope." I panted, shifting my feet. "Unless you can hold them off long enough for me to get this damned strip off my foot."

He jiggled out his knife, handing it to me. It was smeared with blood, and I felt sick. "I'll keep them off you," he said, his face going grim.

I handed it back, knowing he was more effective with it than I was. "They're designed to be tamper resistant. It's going to take a pair of bolt cutters."

Jenks shifted his balance to his toes. "Then we fight until Ivy gets here."

"Yep," I agreed, fear settling firmly in me. This was bad. This was really bad.

My gaze darted to Brett as he scuffed his feet. Walter had joined him, the savage glint in his eyes born from his grief. From behind me came the sound of the street Weres pulling chains from around their waist and the snick of knives being opened.

Damn it all and shit on it. I did not want to die like this.

"Ma'am?" Brett drawled, drawing my attention to him. "It would save everyone a good deal of trouble if you would surrender your weapon and come with us."

"Trouble?" I shouted back, releasing some pent-up frustration. "For who?" My gaze traveled over the Weres. They kept filing in, surrounding us. There were five alphas now. The street Weres at our backs, military Weres at the front, and the credit card Weres at the outskirts, keeping everything nice and quiet and the pedestrian traffic moving.

My stomach clenched when I realized three of the street Weres behind the Dumpster weren't injured, but shifting. They were shifting in broad daylight. In a public street. With the intent to tear me to pieces. And they were doing it really fast.

"Ma'am," Brett tried again, playing the good cop or simply buying time for the turning Weres. "Put down your weapon and kick it to me."

"Go to hell, Brett," I said darkly. "I've seen how you treat your guests. I know what it is now, and you aren't getting it. And this isn't a weapon, it's a *gun*!"

Angry and frightened, I took aim and shot him.

A blur dove between us. One of his men took it instead. The Were hit the ground and skidded to a stop, out cold before his face ground into the pavement. Brett seemed shocked I'd actually shot at him, and I shrugged. At the outskirts, stupid people clapped in appreciation. I could not believe this. I was going to be hacked to shreds to the accompaniment of applause.

Brett glanced at them, then frowned. "Shoot her," he said softly. "Just shoot her in the leg."

"Good going, Rache," Jenks muttered.

Safeties clicked off. I spun. I had three charms left, and I wanted those four-legged bastards asleep before they finished putting on their wolf's clothing. Ignoring the chaos, I calmly plugged them both.

The street Weres surrounding them exploded in anger. I backpedaled as they rushed me.

"No!" Brett shouted, red-faced as he gestured. "Get out of the way!"

Jenks was a blur of motion, the thuds of the bar meeting flesh sickening. The occasional chime of metal on metal rang out as someone threw a chain into the mix. My first thought, that we were going to die, turned into an ironic relief. As long as the street Weres were surrounding us, the military faction couldn't shoot.

One of the Weres broke through Jenks's defenses, and I sprang forward. Grabbing the hairy arm someone conveniently gave me, I twisted and shoved. The Were stumbled away, howling in pain as I dislocated his shoulder. A nasty grin came over me. He had felt that. The bond was breaking. They were acting independently, and the round was falling apart!

A sharp crack shocked through me and I jumped. They were shooting anyway!

A closer burst of gunfire brought me spinning around. The Weres fell back, their aggression flaking to nothing as the packs divided. Heart in my throat, I found Jenks, weapon aimed at the sky and a savage expression on his face. The more disciplined military faction held their ground, but the street Weres panicked. In an instant they were gone, streaking past Jenks and me and dragging their downed companions, whether in fur, leather, or polyester.

"Hold together!" Walter shouted from behind a row of men, but it was too late. "Damn you!" he swore. "Hold together! He's not going to shoot you!"

Faint on the cool spring air was the sound of sirens.

"Tink's diaphragm, it's about time," Jenks swore. The Weres who were left heard it too, and they began to exchange looks as they panted. The crowd watching started to break up, their steps fast and their faces pale as they realized that was real blood on the pavement.

"You know who I am?" Jenks shouted, bloody but unbowed. "I'm Jenks!" He took a breath, grinning. "Boo!"

Several of the well-dressed Weres jumped, and a few of the military Weres touched their tattoos as if for luck or strength.

Walter shoved himself to the front. "Hold together!" he shouted as his control over the second pack slipped away. "You swore an oath to me. You swore, damn it!"

The alpha male in a suit gave him an ugly look. Saying nothing more, he turned and walked away. His wife slipped an arm in his, seamlessly snagging a store bag and heading for the top of the wide alley. There were no more bystanders watching now, and they melted seamlessly into the tourist traffic.

Hunched and panting, I watched unbelieving as the ring of business Weres dispersed. I smiled sweetly at Walter, hefting my splat gun. It was empty, but he didn't know that. The sirens grew closer. If they had held together for five minutes more, they would have had us. It hadn't been the sirens, it had been their inability to stay together. Without the focus, they couldn't hold together when things got sticky.

Choleric, Walter gestured to Brett.

"Rache!" Jenks shouted.

At least a dozen weapons turned to us. There was only one thing to do, and I did it.

Grunting, I leapt at Brett. It surprised him, and though he was by far the better military person, I got him down, attacking not like a professional, but like a sissy girl with my arms around his knees. We hit the pavement together and I scrambled for a better hold.

My arm went around his neck and I wrenched an arm painfully. And while he would have felt no pain had they still been in a round, he certainly felt it now. "Tell them to back off!" I shouted.

Brett started to laugh, the sound choking off when I pulled.

"Ow," he said, as if I was simply bending back a finger, not ready to dislocate his shoulder. "Ms. Morgan. What the hell do you think you're doing, ma'am?"

I could hear Nick's truck. "Getting the hell out of here," I said, stumbling as Jenks helped me stand upright without losing my grip. It was as awkward as all get-out, but we managed. A ring of weapons pointed at us. Jenks took my place, his face ugly as he bent his arm and pressed a knife to Brett's throat.

"You ever see a pixy battlefield?" he whispered in the Were's ear, and Brett lost the vestiges of humor. White-faced, he went passive. Which was really scary in itself.

The flash of a blue truck sped past.

"Too far, Ivy!" Jenks shouted, and there was the squeal of brakes quickly followed by the horns and the gunning of an engine.

I looked at my waistband and the phone. An insane need to giggle rose through me. I sure hoped we weren't roaming.

Another squeal of tires, and Nick's blue truck rocked to a stop at the end of the alley.

"Mom's here to pick us up, Jenks," I quipped, limping to the curb. "I'll get the bags."

I scooped up one of our bags, seeing as it was on the way and it sort of added to the travesty. My empty splat gun never shifted from Walter, though he was behind two rows of men. Coward.

"Hi, Ivy," I said tiredly, tossing the bag into the truck bed and lurching in after it. Yeah, it was illegal to ride in the back, but seeing that we had just somehow beaten up three Were packs, I wasn't going to worry about it. "Thanks for the ride."

Nick was in the front seat, and pale. He handed a pair of bolt cutters through the window.

"Hey, thanks!" I said, then started when Brett came thumping in beside me like a sack of potatoes. The Were was unconscious, and I looked at Jenks in question when he followed him in, admittedly a hell of a lot more gracefully. "I don't want a hostage," I said. Then wondered when Jenks had knocked him out. He wasn't dead, was he?

Grim-faced, Jenks shouted, "What are you waiting for, Ivy? God to say go?"

The truck lurched, and I steadied myself against the long silver locker Nick had bolted to the truck bed. My sweat went cold in the new breeze, and thinking we had done it, I pulled the hair from my eyes and smiled at Jenks. My smile faded.

As we jostled into traffic, he was using a plastic cord to truss Brett up with a painful savagery. I thought back to seeing his kids tearing apart the fairy nest in his garden. This was a side to him I'd never truly seen before, since the difference of our sizes had insulated me from it.

From inside the truck came Nick's petrified voice, "Go faster, Ivy! They're behind us!"

Wedging myself into the corner, I held my hair out of the way and blinked. I had expected to see Jeeps or Hummers. What I found were three Weres in wolf skin, tearing down the street after us. And they were fast. Really fast. And they didn't stop for red lights either.

"Son of a Disney whore," Jenks swore. "Rache, you got any more charms in that gun?"

I shook my head, scrambling for a way out of this. My eyes darted to my ankle. "Jenks, get this thing off me."

Brett was coming around, and when he tried to get upright, Jenks lashed out, savagely connecting with his head right behind his ear. Brett's eyes rolled back and he passed out.

"Hold on!" Nick shouted. "Right turn!"

Tossing my splat gun into the front, I gripped the side of the truck. The wheels skittered and hopped, but Ivy kept it on the road. Nick yelled an obscenity, and a motor home flashed by, tires squealing. I didn't want to know how close we had come to becoming a hood ornament.

My heart pounded and my gaze shot to my foot at the feel of cold steel against my skin. Jenks's shoulder muscles bunched, and as we hit a pothole, the charmed silver band snapped.

Frantic, I sent my gaze behind us. Holy crap, they were right there!

"Ivy!" I shouted, stomach clenching. "When I say, hit the breaks."

"Are you crazy!" she shouted, glancing back at me, her short black hair framing her face and getting into her eyes.

"Just do it!" I demanded, tapping a line. Line energy filled me, warm and golden. I didn't care that it was tainted black, it was mine. I took a breath. This was going to hurt if I didn't do it right. *Big circle. Big circle.* "Now!" I shouted.

The breaks screamed. I lurched, shocked to find Jenks's arm between my head and the metal cabinet. Brett slid forward and groaned.

"Rhombus!" I shouted, the word raging from me hard enough to hurt my throat.

Heady and strong, the line energy flashed through me, expanding upward from the circle I had imagined painted on the pavement. It wasn't strong enough to hold a demon, but it would hold together long enough for what I wanted. I hoped.

I tossed my hair from my eyes even before the truck stopped rocking. Elation filled me as the pursing Weres slammed right into my circle.

"Yes!" I shouted, then spun at the sound of crunching metal and screams. It wasn't us. We were stopped! I sucked in my breath when I realized an oncoming car had smacked into the other side of my circle, amber and black in the sun. Aw, shit. I'd forgotten about the other lane.

Horns blew, and the car that had hit my circle was rear-ended.

"Oh, that was just beautiful!" Jenks said in admiration. His eyes were on the Weres making painful splurges of motion on the pavement. Apparently running into a wall hurt if you didn't have a round of alphas taking away your pain.

People were starting to get out of their cars, dazed and excited. "Sorry!" I called out, wincing. Breaking my connection with the line, I took down the circle.

In the distance were sirens, and I could see flashing lights.

Jenks tapped the window, and Ivy slowly accelerated, taking the first left she could and doubling back a street over, trying to put as much distance between us and the sirens as she could. I exhaled, falling to slump against the tool locker. I put a hand through the window, finding Ivy's shoulder. She jumped, and I whispered, "Thanks," before I pulled my hand out. We had made it. We were alive and together. And we had a hostage.

"Damn it all back to the Turn!" Jenks swore.

Nick turned to look at us, and I nudged Jenks's foot. He was messing about in his bag and he looked ticked. "What is it, Jenks?" I breathed as we jostled along, tired, so tired.

"I lost my fudge!" he swore. "That woman took my fudge!"

Twenty-six

The hamburger place was busy with kids, moms, and teenagers cutting loose after school, telling me more clearly than a page of demographics that the resident population was decidedly slanted to human. I slumped deeper into the molded plastic, my lips curling when I found the table sticky from someone's pop. Brett snickered, and I made a face at him. The defiant Were was sitting across from me, handcuffed with his own steel to the table support bolted to the floor. Pride had him hiding the fact, and no one was paying us any mind. Just two people having coffee. 'Least we would be when Jenks got back with the drinks.

The Brimstone had worn off somewhere between shaking the Weres and Ivy and Nick dropping us off here, and fatigue was seeping into me like water through mud. Ivy was sure that they knew how to track Brett's location from an active phone, and the two of them were leading the Weres on a wild goose chase until we figured out what to do with him.

That we had a hostage had really put a crimp in my already stellar day. Jenks, Ivy, and I had already gone round about it. Nick listened wide-eyed as Jenks adamantly protested that we should keep him to kill in cold blood as a warning if the Weres so much as sniffed too close to us. The scary thing was, Jenks was ready to carry it out.

This was the shocking, ruthless side to Jenks that was seldom seen and easy to miss behind his lighthearted mien—the part of him that kept his family fed and their heads underground when the snow flew. Taking Brett hostage had been as natural as breathing to him, and I truly believed he'd kill the Were with just as much thought. Though carefree and one of the best friends I'd ever had, Jenks was a cell phone, computer-savvy savage, living without law and holding to his own morals alone. I thanked God I fit in there as being important to him.

It was the first time Jenks and I had disagreed on how to handle a run. Hell, it was the first time he'd had an opinion. I think taking Brett hostage had triggered something in his pixy makeup. I was sure the argument wasn't over yet, but I did *not* want a hostage.

But I hadn't wanted Ivy to drop us off at a burger joint either, I thought sourly, hunching deeper into Jenks's aviator jacket, which he was letting me wear. I had wanted to go to Squirrel's End, where I could have a beer and quietly shake in the corner. The patrons there would have only snickered and poked each other at seeing the handcuffs. Ivy nixed it, though, pulling Nick's truck into Burger-rama saying that Squirrel's End smelled like us, and only the sanitation practices of a fast food place would hide that we'd been there and stop the trail cold.

Whatever. I was bone-tired, aching from our street brawl, and thirsty enough to down a two-liter bottle of Coke by myself. And why in hell hadn't I at least *brought* my pain amulet? It had been stupid going out like this. God help me, but if the Weres didn't kill me, I could probably do it myself.

Brett and I both jumped at the high-pitched shriek from the kid at the top of the slide behind him, and our eyes met briefly. The primary-colored play equipment was literally crawling with screaming, runny-nosed kids in open winter coats, throwing the tops that came with the mini-meals this week at each other.

My pulse slowed, and as Jenks charmed the ladies behind the counter into flustered goo, I tried to look cool and professional among the plastic toys and paper hats. It wasn't going to happen, so I tried for dangerous. I think I managed cranky when several children went wide-eyed and silent after passing my table. My hand lifted to hide the scrape on my face I got hitting the pavement, and I tried again to brush my jeans free of the dirt from the alley. Maybe I looked worse than I thought.

Brett looked great, having sat most of the scuffle out. The clean smell of woodsy aftershave came from him, and the light glinted on the silver of his short hair. Though small, he looked like he could lope from there to the state line without stopping—apart from the cuffs.

I smelled the hot meadowy scent of Jenks before I saw him,

and I straightened, sliding down to make room. Jenks set the cardboard tray with two large coffees and a weenie-sized cup of steaming water that was an odd shade of pink onto the table. *Herbal tea?* I thought, claiming a coffee. Since when did Jenks like herbal tea?

I looked up from trying to pry the lid off my cup when Jenks pulled it out from my fingers. "Hey!" I said, and he put the lame cup of pink water in front of me. "I don't want tea," I said indignantly. "I want coffee."

"Diuretic." Jenks sat beside Brett. "It will do more harm than good. Drink your decaf tea."

Remembering our argument and thinking this was his way of getting back at me, my eyes narrowed. "I almost died back there," I said irately. "If I want a damn coffee, I'm going to have a damn coffee." Daring him to protest, I took my coffee with a huff.

Brett watched the exchange with interest. Eyebrows high, he reached for the second coffee, and Jenks intercepted his reach. The Were hesitated, then settled into his plastic seat with nothing. "What are you going to do with me, ma'am?" he said, the light twang in his voice obvious among the midwestern accents around us.

How in hell should I know? "Oh, I've got big plans for you," I lied, surprised at the ma'am. "Jenks wants to string you up as an object lesson. I'm halfway to letting him have his wish." I leaned back, tired. "It works great when he murders garden fairies."

Brett glanced warily at Jenks—who was nodding zealously—and I felt a weary lassitude slip over me. Crap. Why did the Brimstone pick now to wear off? A chill ran through me, tight on the heels of the idle thought that taking it to get through this week might not be a bad idea.

The Were's eyes traveled over me, hesitating at my torn turtleneck before rising to my face. From there, they never moved, but his focus kept shifting as he monitored the room by the sounds behind him. It gave me the creeps.

I sent my eyebrows up—wishing yet again that I could do the one eyebrow thing—casually tearing three packets of sugar open at once and dumping them in not because I liked it but because the coffee smelled that old. "I know where it is," I said lightly.

Just the fact that Brett didn't move said volumes. Jenks scowled, clearly not liking what I was doing, but I didn't want a hostage. I wanted to send Brett back with a message that would buy me some time and space. Now that the island Weres knew we were still in Mackinaw, they would keep looking until they found us. That we had Brett for a hostage wouldn't stop them—he had screwed up royally, and unlike the fairies that Jenks was used to dealing with, I think the Weres would just as soon see him dead—but maybe a show of goodwill and a big fat lie would buy us time enough to get my con in place.

I hoped.

"Sparagmos told you where it is," Brett said, his disbelief obvious.

"Of course he did," Jenks said, breaking his silence. "We've got it, and you don't."

Na, na, na, na-a-a-a, na. "I can put my hands on it," I amended, nudging Jenks's foot. *Shut up, Jenks.* I liked him better quiet. This was the last time we took a hostage.

Brett looked relaxed even though his one hand was cuffed under the table. Behind him, kids were fighting, hurting my ears. "Give it to me," he said. "I'll take it to Mr. Vincent and convince him to leave you alone."

Jenks jerked into motion, reaching for Brett. The Were blocked it. Someone hit a coffee and it spilled. Gasping, I stood when it threatened to run into my lap. "Damn it, Jenks!" I swore, pulling every eye to us. "What in hell are you doing?"

The restaurant was abruptly silent. A unified, "Ooooh," rose from the ball pit, and I flushed. Clear in the silence, the person coming over the loudspeaker wanted to know if he could substitute bottled water for the pop. I winced apologetically to the offended mothers speaking in hushed voices to their soccer-mom friends. "Sorry," I muttered. I sat down, and the level of noise resumed. *Crap. That had been my coffee.*

"You are in no position to be making deals or demands," Jenks said nastily as people turned away. "And if you or your mange-ridden curs touch her, you'll find everyone you care about dead one morning."

Brett's face went red.

"Just stop it," I griped, thinking this wasn't the way to arrange a cease-fire. But it told me I was right that Brett had to placate Walter with something to ease his return into the pack. Brett was in trouble; it wasn't only Jenks who wanted to kill him.

The small man's expression went sour and he settled back, clearly a lot more cautious now that he knew how fast Jenks could move. Heck, it impressed me.

"Look," I said, wedging a wad of napkins out of the dispenser and mopping up my coffee. I couldn't help but wonder if Jenks had done it intentionally. "All I want is Nick free from your reprisals. You can take Walter the stinking statue as far as I'm concerned."

Brett's dark eyes went suspicious. "You still expect me to believe you aren't working for someone and that you risked your life for . . . for him?"

My lips curled into a sour smile. "Don't call me stupid," I warned him. Jenks pushed the tea at me, and I ignored it. "I need a day to get the statue here," I lied. "A day to get it here and tie a pretty ribbon around it for you."

The tiny clink of his cuffs made Brett's eyes twitch. "You're going to give it to me," he said flatly.

I wrapped my fingers around my foam cup to hide their trembling. "Yup. And it was your idea too."

Jenks looked at me in bewilderment, and I smiled. "I want you to back off. All of you," I added, squeezing the tea bag to make a thin rivulet of red drain into the cup. I was thirsty, and if I made for that second coffee, Jenks would probably spill it too. "I don't need to leave town to get it. I can have it here by sunset tomorrow. Watch us if you want, but one sniff I think is too close and the exchange is off and we are gone." I leaned over my tea. "Jenks and I cleaned your clocks with a pipe and some stupid sleepy-time charms. You want to risk finding out what we're really capable of when all you have to do is wait a lousy thirty-six hours?"

"An exchange?" Brett mocked, and Jenks made an odd rumble, leaving me wondering if pixies could growl. "Seems to me like it's more of a payment for getting us to leave you alone."

In a smooth, unhurried motion, Jenks reached out and slapped him. "Seems to me you should pull the brains out of your ass."

"Jenks!" I exclaimed, glancing over the fishbowl of a restaurant to see if anyone saw him.

"He's a dead wolf!" Jenks protested, gesturing sharply. "I could slice him open and leave him for the maggots, and *he* thinks he has some leverage."

My eyes narrowed. "But we aren't going to do that. Stop hitting him."

"It's what they did to Nick," he offered, starting our argument anew. "Why are you giving him any consideration beyond the chunk of meat that he turned himself into by letting us take him hostage?"

Under the table my knees were shaking. "Because that's how

we work when we're five feet tall, unless we're ignorant animals playing in the woods."

Jenks slumped back with his coffee to look sullen.

Brett's teeth were clenched at my unflattering comparison to his pack. Remembering what they had done to Nick, it was hard not to let Jenks have his way. Frustrated, I tried to hide my shaking fingers by taking a sip of my tart tea while Jenks continued to dump every last sugar packet into his coffee. I could scent his anger over the odor of french fries and bad coffee, like burnt acorns.

"I am going to give Walter the statue you couldn't retrieve through a week of torture," I said. "In return, you are going to convince Walter to give me Nick's life and not hold me responsible for Pam's death. You will leave *all* of us alone and not seek any retaliation. Ever." My eyebrows rose. "You do, and I'll come right back up here and take it back."

Brett's faint wrinkles bunched. "Why should I do that?" he asked.

"Because it was your idea," I said lightly. "And it's the only thing that's going to keep you alive. As soon as my ride gets here, I'm outta here." I took a slow breath, praying I wasn't making a mistake. "I'm going to call Walter and tell him where you are and congratulate him on having such a wonderful second in command who convinced me to give you the statue. There will be someone watching you. If Walter accepts my terms, he takes you and walks away. If not, he can leave you cuffed to the table, and you become Jenks's responsibility."

Jenks straightened and started to grin.

"The way I figure it," I said, looking through the huge plate-glass windows at nothing, "your alpha is one pissed puppy at you for having not only letting us slip through your fingers, but then being careless enough to get taken and putting him in this awkward position."

I leaned close enough that my words were a palpable sensation of my will against his face. "If you can't convince him that we're enough of a threat that he should accept my terms and back off for thirty-six hours *and* that because of your stellar negotiating skills that I will give it to *you and you alone,* he will have no reason to keep your hide attached to your soul. He's going to kill you unless you can redeem yourself. Not right away, but he'll do it. A slow slide in the hierarchy, giving everyone a shot at you on your way down. So I think a thank-you to me is in order for giving you a surefire way back into his good graces."

Brett's brown eyes were empty, again telling me he was in big trouble. "I suggest," I said, seeing Ivy and Nick pull up in the van, "that you work really hard to get Walter to see things my way. Unless you give him the focus, you'll be an ongoing reminder of *his* mistake of sending you against a superior foe without the proper understanding of what you were facing. We might look like incompetent flakes, but we've survived demons." Shaking inside, I leaned away. "I'm giving you a chance to save your skin. Take it."

The Were's eyes followed mine to the van. "Ma'am," he said slowly. "You are one hell of a negotiator."

I smiled, and Jenks and I both rose before Ivy could come in. "Thirty-six hours," I said, picking up my tea. I tried to look confident and in control, but I doubted I managed it.

Brett cocked his head. "You're not going to give it to me. You're stalling for time."

Jenks took my elbow before I fell over, and I forced myself not to show my angst. "Maybe, but he's going to kill you all the same." I arched my eyebrows and tried to look tough. "What do you owe Walter, anyway?"

The Were dropped his eyes. I turned aside, shaking; he had acknowledged me as his superior. Damn. "God help me, Jenks," I whispered as I tottered to the door. "I hope he does it."

"He will." Jenks glanced over his shoulder at Brett. "Walter will tear him apart slowly." His green eyes met mine. "That was slick. Where did you learn so much about Weres?"

"If you're beaten up by them twice in one week, you start to pick things up," I said, leaning heavily on him.

Jenks was quiet, then, "You want me to have Ivy call her vampire friend?"

Nodding, I dropped my cup in the trash on the way out. I felt as if a noose was closing even tighter, but I didn't see any other options. Already my mind was making a list: call Ceri for the recipes I wanted that I didn't already have, check the yellow pages for a spell shop that carried raw materials. Somewhere I'd have to sleep and come up with a plan.

Maybe, I thought as Jenks opened the door for me and I stepped out into the late afternoon sun, *I'd get lucky and dream of one*.

Twenty-seven

It was one of the oddest charm outlets I had ever been in, nothing like the richly scented earth magic shops I usually frequented, being brightly lit against the dark and spacious, and having a small spot up front to sit in cushy chairs and sip the marvelous coffee the owner made. The shelves were glass, and ley line paraphernalia was arranged like knickknacks. Jenks would have had an orgasm of delight.

There were only a small section of earth magic charms, and the traditional redwood scent was largely overpowered by the aroma of ginger coming from the proprietor's coffeemaker. I felt strangely out of place, thinking the banners with dragons and white-bearded wizards next to the crucibles made everything look silly. An earth witch would have sneered at most of the ritual stuff in there, but maybe that's what ley line magic used. Something was off with the merchandise, though. It didn't smell right. Literally.

Ivy was halfway across the store with my basket of goodies after I snarled at her that I was fine and to stop hovering. Now I was sorry, but she had been acting weird since picking Jenks and me up at the mall—depressed almost, avoiding me but always near—and it was getting on my nerves. It didn't help that I was feeling vulnerable, my knees shaky from blood loss again now that Jenks's street-grade Brimstone had worked itself out.

I had found the shop in the yellow pages, and after I showered and stuffed myself on an entire box of macaroni and cheese, Ivy drove me over. She'd insisted, saying the Weres would know the moment I put my toe on the street. They had, and we'd been followed by two street racers glowing blue and green neon from underneath. It was worrisome, but between the thirty-six hour truce, my magic, and Ivy's presence, they'd probably leave us alone.

As I hoped, Walter had backed off. Jax had said the trio of Weres in fatigues who picked Brett up was rough, but the lie that Brett convinced me to release the statue to him alone had kept him alive. I don't know why I cared. I really didn't.

I think Walter was using the time as I was: fortifying defenses and getting everyone in place for a last attack if I reneged on our arrangement. I was, but if I did it right, he'd never guess it had been my intent from moment one. The packs could not have the focus. The thing was demon crafted, and any power gained from it was artificial and would ultimately lead to their damnation, dragging most of Inderland along with them, probably.

My phone was to my ear while I shopped with Ceri, five hundred miles away and standing in my kitchen with Kisten. Ivy had asked him to watch the church and field the calls, and I didn't want to know what my kitchen looked like with nothing between it and pixy chaos but a vampire. Ceri was off checking some point of charm, and I could hear Kisten talking to Jenks's kids. The muted familiar sounds of home were both comforting and depressing.

I picked up a large smoked bottle of generic fixative I could use for the demon transference curse, blanching when I saw the price. *Holy crap.* Maybe I could get away with the smaller bottle. I turned the smoked bottle over in my hand and squinted at the liquid. It was supposed to have camphor in it, but all I smelled was lavender. I didn't like buying premade stuff, but I was pressed for time.

Seeing me holding the bottle, Ivy started my way to put it in the basket, halting when I returned it to the shelf and frowned. God help her, but I wasn't that weak. I could hold a stinking bottle of fixative without a Brimstone boost.

I had fixed my own lunch today, after the sandwich Ivy gave me made my fingertips tingle. I don't know how she managed to slip Brimstone into it without me realizing, but I was still mad from the two of them dosing me up without my knowledge, even if the high from Jenks's street-grade Brimstone had made the difference in where I was sleeping tonight.

Picking up the smaller bottle of fixative, I sighed, feeling my knees shake. Maybe I should just accept the Brimstone Ivy kept pushing on me and let it go. I was tired from simply walking around. Ivy wouldn't tell me how much blood she'd taken, and

Jenks was no help, seeing as he thought a bleeding hangnail was reason for panic.

Shades of gray, I thought, knowing I was slipping into places I had vowed I'd never go. Damn it, I used to be able to see black and white, but things got fuzzy right about the time I found my last I.S. paycheck cursed.

My gaze drifted to the window, black with night and acting like a mirror. Seeing my reflection, I adjusted the collar of my little red jacket. It went great with the black staff shirt from Takata's last concert. Thanks to my last pain amulet, nothing hurt, but looking at my slumped stance, I decided I didn't look tired, I looked sick. My gut clenched when I realized I looked like a vampire's shadow, well-dressed, thin, sophisticated—and ill.

Pulse hammering, I turned away. *No more Brimstone,* I thought. *Ever. There is black. There is white. Gray is a cowardly excuse to mix our wants with our needs.* But I wasn't sure I could believe it anymore as I stood in a charm shop buying materials to twist a black curse. *Just this once,* I thought. *Just this once, and never again.*

Phone still tucked to my ear, I set the fixative down. I would have hung up and called her back later, but I was enjoying hearing the sounds of normalcy, soft and distant, five hundred miles away. It seemed farther. Relaxing, I reached for an elaborately inlaid wooden box. It was beautiful, and curiosity and a love for fine workmanship prompted me to open it to find it held magnetic chalk. It was ungodly expensive, and its presence solidified that there was a population of practicing ley line witches nearby.

I abruptly realized the proprietor was watching me over her coffee mug, and I intentionally kept fiddling with the chalk, inspecting the seals as if I was considering buying it. I hated it when they watched me as though I might steal something. Like the illegal hex above the door that would give you zits wasn't enough of a deterrent?

Technically a black spell, I mused. So why didn't I turn her in?

"Magnetic chalk?" Ivy said from my elbow, and I jumped, almost dropping the phone between my ear and my shoulder.

"I don't need it," I said, trying to cover my surprise. "Especially in a box like that. Salt works just as well, and you only have to vacuum when you're done."

Reluctantly I let my fingers slip from the beautifully crafted container. It was dovetailed, the only metal on it the hinges, latch, and reinforced corners of black gold. Once the chalk was gone, it would make an excellent place to store anything that needed extra precautions. It was the nicest thing in the shop, in my opinion.

My eyebrows rose at the package of herbs in the basket that I hadn't put there. "Is that catnip?" I asked, seeing the cellophane printed with little black footprints.

"I thought Rex might leave Jax alone if she had something else to do." Brown eyes showing embarrassment, she dropped a step away. "You okay? Do you want to sit down?"

It was the third time she'd asked since leaving the motel, and I stiffened. "I'm fine," I said. *Liar,* I thought. I was tired, weary in heart and body.

The soft clatter of the phone being picked up rustled in my ear. "Ceri," I said, before she could say anything. "Just how much fixative do I need for the transference curse?"

The sound of the pixies shrieking diminished, and I guessed Ceri had moved into the living room. "A thumb drop," she said, and I gratefully took up the smaller bottle.

"My thumb?" I complained. "What is that, about a teaspoon? Why can't they use normal measurements?"

"It's a very old curse," Ceri snapped. "They didn't have teaspoons back then."

"Sorry," I apologized, my eyes meeting Ivy's as I placed the fixative into the basket. Ceri was one of the nicest, most giving people I knew, but she had a temper.

"Do you have a pencil?" the elf in hiding said politely, but I could hear her annoyance at my impertinence. "I want you to write this down. I know you have the inertia dampening curse in one of the books with you, but I don't want you to translate the Latin wrong."

I glanced at the proprietor—who was starting to eye Ivy skulking about—and turned my back on her. "Maybe you could give me just the ingredients right now." The clutter in my basket was odd enough already. If the proprietor was worth her salt, she'd be able to tell I was making a disguise charm. The only difference between my legal disguise charms and the illegal doppelganger spells was a point of law, a few extra steps, and a cellular sample of the person to copy. I didn't think she'd be able to tell I was also going to twist a demon curse to move the power from the statue to something else. What she would make of the ingredients for the inertia damping demon curse was anyone's guess. Ceri said it was a joke curse, but it would work.

Joke curse, I thought sourly. It was still black. If I was caught,

I'd be labeled a black witch and magically castrated. I wasn't fooling myself that this was anything other than wrong. No "saving the world" crap. It was wrong.

Just this once, echoed in my thoughts, and I frowned, thinking of Nick. Telling Al about me had probably started with just one harmless piece of information.

Ceri sighed. "All you need for the joke curse is dust from inside a clock and black candles made from the fat of the unborn. The rest is incantation and ritual."

"The unborn?" I said in a horrified, hushed whisper. "Ceri, you said it wasn't that bad."

"The fat of an unborn pig," she reiterated, sounding angry. "Honestly, Rachel."

My brow furrowed. Okay, it was a fetal pig, the same thing biology students dissect, but it sounded close to the slaughtering-goats-in-your-basement kind of magic. The transference curse looked harmless apart from the black it would put on my soul, and the disguise charm was white—illegal, but white. The inertia-dampening curse was the worst of the lot—and it was the one that would keep Jenks alive—a joke curse. *Just this once.*

I was so stupid.

Stomach roiling, my thoughts flicked to Trent and his illegal labs, which saved people so he could blackmail them into seeing things his way. He, at least, didn't pretend to be anything other than what he was. Things had been a lot easier when I didn't have to think. But what was I supposed to do? Walk away and let the world fall apart? Telling the I.S. would make matters worse, and giving the statue to the FIB was a joke.

Angry and sick inside, I sidestepped Ivy to get to the candles. I'd already been there to pick out my colored candles for the transference curse. Behind the carved castles and colorful "dragon eggs" were the real goods, arranged by color and size, branded at the bottom with either what the fat had been rendered from or where they had first been lit. The woman's selection was surprisingly good, but why they were hidden behind such crap was beyond me.

"Taper or barrel?" I asked Ceri, crouching to reach one with pig scratched on it. You can't light a candle in a pig, so it was a good bet that's where the fat had come from. I'd never been in a ley line charm shop other than the university's, and that didn't count since they only carried what the classes needed. Maybe there was a spell that used "dragon eggs," but I thought they looked lame.

"Doesn't matter," Ceri answered, and with the smallest taper in hand, I turned and rose, almost running into Ivy. She winced and backed up.

"I'm fine," I muttered, setting the candle in the basket. "Did you see any packaged dust?"

Ivy shook her head, the tips of her black hair shifting about the bottom of her ears. There was a rack of "pixy dust" by the register that was just glitter. Jenks would laugh his ass off. Maybe the real stuff was behind it, like the candles.

"You sound tired, Rachel," Ceri said, question high in her voice as I moved to the rack.

"I'm fine." Ceri said nothing, and I added, "It's stress." *Just this once.*

"I want you to talk to Kisten," she said firmly, as if she was doing me a favor.

Oh God. Kisten. What would he say if he knew Ivy had bitten me? "I told you so," or maybe "My turn"? "Ceri," I protested, but it was too late, and as Ivy fingered a display of amber bottles that were good to store oil-based potions in, Kisten's masculine voice came to me.

"Rachel . . . How's my girl?"

I blinked rapidly, the threatened tears shocking me. *Where had they come from?* "Ah, I'm fine," I said, missing him terribly. Bad things had happened, and I'd been carrying the pain since. I needed to talk to him, but not standing in a charm shop with Ivy listening.

Ivy had stiffened at the sudden emotion in my voice, and I turned my back on her, wondering if I should tell her that the glass container shaped like a full moon in her grip was generally used to store aphrodisiac potions.

"Good," he said, his voice going right through me. "Can I talk to Ivy?"

Surprised, I turned to her, but she had heard him and shook her head. "Uh . . ." I stammered, wondering if she was afraid of what he'd say to her if he knew what had happened. We were both chickenshit, but we would be chickenshit together.

"Ivy, I know you can hear me," Kisten said loudly. "You have a big problem waiting for you when you get back from your *vacation.* Everyone knows you're out of the city. You're his scion, not me. I can't go up against even the youngest undead. The only thing keeping a lid on this is that most of them are my patrons and they know if they act up, I'll ban them."

Ivy walked off, her boots loud against the hardwood floor. Her passive response surprised me. Something was really bothering her.

"She walked away," I said, feeling guilty Ivy had come up there to help me.

Kisten's sigh was heavy. "Will you tell her that there was a riot in the mall downtown last night? It was at four in the morning so it was mostly living vampires, thank God, and some Weres. The I.S. handled it, but it's going to get worse. I don't want a new master vampire in the city, and neither does anyone else."

I stood before the rack of pixy dust and rifled through the hanging vials, reading the tiny cards attached to each. If Piscary lost control of Cincinnati, Trent would have free rein. But I didn't think it was a power play by the undead vampires *or* Trent. It was more likely that the riot had been the Mackinaw Weres looking for me. No wonder Walter had agreed to a thirty-six-hour truce. He had to get his pack together.

Tired, I let the vials slip through my fingers. "I'm sorry, Kisten. We have a couple of days before we can call this done. It depends on how fast I can do the prep work."

He silently took that in, and I could hear Ceri singing with the pixies in the background. "Can I help?" he asked, and my throat tightened at the concern in his voice, even as I heard his reluctance to leave Cincinnati. But there wasn't anything he could do. It would be over one way or the other by tomorrow night.

"No," I said softly. "But if we don't call you by tomorrow midnight, we're in trouble."

"And I'll fly up there in two hours," he assured me. "Are you sure there's nothing I can do? Call someone? Anything?"

Shaking my head, I fingered a book on how to knot love charms from hair. These things were illegal. Small towns have very little in the way of policing witches, but then I saw that it was a fake, a novelty item. "We have it okay," I said. "Will you feed Mr. Fish for me?"

"Sure. Ivy told me."

"He only needs four grains," I rushed. "Any more and you'll kill him."

"Don't worry about it. I've had fish before."

"And stay out of my room," I added.

He started making a fake radio hiss, whistling and popping. "Rachel? The connection is going bad," he said, laughing. "I think I'm losing you."

A smile, the first in days, touched me. "I love you too," I said, and he stopped.

There was a suspicious hesitation. "Are you okay?" he asked.

Worry slid through me. He was starting to pay attention. "Why?" I said, realizing my hand had gone up to cover my neck. "Um, yeah," I reiterated, thinking it had sounded guilty. "I'm just stressed. Nick . . ." I hesitated. I couldn't tell him Nick had been playing kiss-and-tell. It was embarrassing to have been that stupid. "I told Nick to kiss off, and it bothered me," I said. *Not really a lie. Not really.*

He was silent, then, "Okay. Can I talk to Ivy?"

Relieved, I exhaled into the mike. "Sure."

I handed the phone to Ivy—who had come up behind me to listen, presumably—but she closed the top and handed it back. "He can handle it a few days more," she said, then turned to the counter. "Do you have everything? It's getting late."

Tension edged her voice. She was trying to hide her mood, but not doing very well. Concerned, I took the basket from her. "Everything but the dust. Maybe she has some behind the counter. God, I'm tired," I finished without thinking. Ivy didn't say anything, and I put the basket on the counter, eyeing the aphrodisiac bottle Ivy set by her catnip.

"What?" Ivy said, seeing me look at it.

"Nothing. Why don't you put your stuff in with mine?"

She shook her head. "I'm going to get something else too, but thanks."

The woman behind the counter set her coffee on her stained hot plate, her fingers reaching to take my things out of the basket. "Will that be all then, ladies?" she asked, hiding her wariness of Ivy behind her professionalism.

"You don't happen to have clock dust?" I asked, feeling it was a lost cause.

Immediately she lost her tinge of her nervousness. "From stopped clocks? Sure enough I do. How much do you need?"

"Thank the Turn," I said, leaning against the counter as my muscles started to feel the weight of standing too long. "I didn't want to have to go to Art Van and dust their floor samples. I just need a, uh, pinch."

Pinch, dash, smidgen. Yeah, real exact measurements. Ley line magic sucked.

The woman glanced at the front door. "Be but a sec," she said, then, with the fixative in her hand, she went into a back room. I stared at Ivy.

"She took my stuff," I said, bewildered.

Ivy shrugged. "Maybe she thinks you're going to run out the door with it."

It seemed like forever, but the woman came back, her loud steps warning us. "Here you go," she said, carefully setting a tiny black envelope down with the fixative. The bottle now had a string tag around it with an expiration date. I picked it up, feeling a different weight to it.

"This isn't the same bottle," I said suspiciously, and the woman smiled.

"That's the real product," she explained. "There aren't enough witches up here to support a charm shop, so I mix tourist trinkets with the real stuff. Why sell real fixative to a fudgie when they're just going to put it on a shelf and pretend they know what to do with it?"

I nodded, now realizing what had been bothering me. "It's all fake? None of it is real?"

"Most of it's real," she said, her ringed fingers punching the register with a stiff firmness. "But not the rare items." She looked at my pile. "Let me see, you're making an earth magic disguise charm, a ley line inertia joke spell, and . . ." She hesitated. "What on earth are you going to use the fixative for? I don't sell much of that."

"I'm fixing something," I said guardedly. Crap, what if the Weres found out? They might realize I was going to move the power of the artifact before we blew it up. If I asked her to keep quiet about it, she would likely blab it all over the place. "It's for a joke," I added.

Her eyes flicked to Ivy and she grinned. "Mum's the word," she said. "Is it for that gorgeous hunk of man with you? Saints preserve us, he's beautiful. I'd love to trick him."

She laughed, and I managed a weak smile. Did the entire city know Jenks? Ivy rocked back a step in irritation, and the woman finished wrapping my black candle in matching tissue paper and bundled everything into a paper sack. Still smiling, she totaled it up.

"It'll be $85.33 with tax," she said, clearly satisfied.

I stifled my sigh and swung my shoulder bag forward to get my wallet. This was why I had a witch's garden—and a clan of pixies to maintain it. Not only was ley line magic stupid, but it was expensive if you didn't render your own fetal pigs for making candles. *Just this once.*

Ivy pushed her two things forward, and looking the proprietor in the eye, said clearly, "Just put it on my bill. I need three ounces of Special K. Medicinal grade, please."

My lips parted and I flushed. Special K? That was Cincy slang for Brimstone, K of course said to stand for Kalamack.

But the woman hesitated only briefly. "Not from the I.S., are you?" she asked warily.

"Not anymore," Ivy muttered, and flustered, I turned my back on them. Ivy saw nothing wrong with an illegal drug that had kept vampire society healthy and intact for untold years, but buying in front of me made me feel all warm and fuzzy.

"Ivy," I protested when the woman disappeared into the back room again. "Trent's?"

Ivy gave me a sidelong glance, eyebrows high. "It's the only brand I'll buy. And I need to restock my cache. You used it all."

"I'm not taking any more," I hissed, then straightened when the woman returned, holding a palm-sized package wrapped in masking tape.

"Medicinal?" she said, glancing at the aphrodisiac bottle. "You store it in that, lucky duck, and you'll be the one that's going to need medical attention."

Ivy's face blanked in surprise, and I dragged my bag from the counter, ready to flee. "It's an aphrodisiac bottle," I said. "Don't pick things up unless you know what they are—Alexia."

Ivy looked as guiltless as a puppy as she dropped the package into her open purse.

The woman smiled at us, and Ivy counted out thirteen hundred-dollar bills and coolly handed them over.

I blinked. Holy shit. Kalamack's medicinal stuff was five times as expensive as the street variety.

"Keep the change," Ivy said, taking my elbow and moving me to the door.

Twelve hundred dollars? I had sucked down Twelve hundred dollars of drugs in less than twenty-four hours? And that wasn't counting Jenks's contribution. "I don't feel well," I said, putting a hand to my stomach.

"You just need some air."

Ivy guided me across the store and took my bag from me. There was the jingle of the door, and a flush of cool air. It was dark and cold on the street, matching my mood. Behind us came the sliding sound of an oiled lock, and the CLOSED sign flickered on. The store's posted hours were from noon to midnight, but after a sale like that, you deserved to go home early.

Fumbling, I put a hand on the bench under a blue and white trolley-stop sign and sat down. I didn't want to chance spewing in Kisten's Corvette. It was the only thing we could drive around town in now that the truck had been seen fleeing a crash and neither Ivy nor I wanted to get in the van.

Shit. My roommates were turning me into a Brimstone addict.

Ivy gracefully folded herself to sit beside me, all the while scanning the street. "Medicinal grade is processed six times," she said, "to pull out the endorphin stimulants, hallucinogenic compounds, and most of the neuron stimulators, to leave only the metabolism upper. Technically speaking, the chemical structure is so different, it's not Brimstone."

"That's not helping," I said, putting my head between my knees. There was gum stuck to the sidewalk, and I nudged it with my toe, finding it hardened to an immovable lump from the cold. *Breathe: one, two, three. Exhale: one, two, three, four.*

"Then how about if you hadn't taken it, you'd be laying in bed needing Jenks's help to use the bathroom?"

I pulled my head up and took a breath. "That helps. But I'm still not taking any more."

She gave me a short-lived close-lipped smile, and I watched her face go as empty as the dark street. I didn't want to get up yet. I was tired, and it was the first time we had been together alone since—since the bite. Returning to the motel room with Jenks, Jax, the kitten, and Nick to make my peachy-keen illegal charms and black curses had all the appeal of eating cold lima beans.

A station wagon passed us, the muffler spewing a blue smoke that would have earned the driver a ticket in Cincinnati. I was cold, and I hunched into my coat. It was only eleven-thirty, but it looked like four in the morning. "You okay?" Ivy said, obviously having seen me shiver.

"Cold," I said, feeling like a hypochondriac.

Ivy crossed her legs at her knees. "Sorry," she whispered.

I lifted my gaze, finding her expression lost in the shadow from the streetlight behind her. "It's not your fault I didn't bring my winter coat."

"For biting you," she said, her voice low. Her attention touched upon my stitches, then dropped to the pavement.

Surprised, I scrambled to put my thoughts in order. I'd thought

I was going to be the one to bring this up. Our pattern had always been: Ivy does something to scare me, Ivy tells me what I did wrong, I promise Ivy not to do it, we never bring it up again. Now she wanted to talk?

"Well, I'm not," I finally said.

Ivy's head came up. Shock shone from her dark eyes, raw and unhidden. "You said on the phone that you'd done some thinking," she stammered. "That you were going to make smarter decisions. You're leaving the firm, aren't you? As soon as this run is over?"

Suddenly I saw her depression in an entirely new light, and I almost laughed in relief for my misunderstanding. "I'm not leaving the firm!" I said. "I meant smarter decisions on who I trusted. I don't want to leave. I want to try to find a blood balance with you."

Ivy's lips parted. Turned as she was to me, the streetlight glinted on her perfect teeth, and then she snapped her mouth shut.

"Surprise," I said weakly, my pulse fast. This was the scariest thing I'd done in a while—including standing down three Were packs.

For six heartbeats Ivy stared at me. Then she shook her head. "No," she said firmly, resettling herself to face forward and put herself in shadow. "You don't understand. I lost control. If Jenks hadn't interfered, I would have killed you. Jenks is right. I'm a danger to everyone I care about. You have no idea how hard it is to find and maintain a blood relationship. Especially if I leave you unbound." Her voice was calm but I could hear panic in it. "And I'm by *God* not going to bind you to me to make it easier. If I do, everything would be what *I* want, not what *we* want."

I thought of Jenks's warning and had a doubt, then remembered Kisten telling me of her past and felt a stab of fear. But the memory of her heavy sobs as she lay crumpled on the pavement filled me, the despair in her eyes when Jenks said she ruined everything she cared about. No, he had said she ruined everything she loved. And seeing that same despair hiding in her fierce words, determination filled me. I couldn't let her believe that.

"You said I needed to trust the right people," I said softly. Heart pounding, I hesitated. "I trust you."

Ivy threw her hands in the air in exasperation and turned to face me. "God, Rachel, I could have killed you! As in dead! You know what that means? Dead? I do!"

My own ire flared, and I sat up. "Yeah? Well . . . I can be a little more savvy," I said belligerently. "I can take some responsibility for keeping things under control, be a little more aware of what's going on and not let you lose yourself . . . like that. We'll do better next time."

"There isn't going to *be* a next time." Stoic and unmoving, Ivy sat deathly still. The streetlight glinted on her short hair, and she stared at the shadowy pavement, intermittently lit from yellow bulbs. Abruptly she turned to look at me. "You say you want to find a blood balance, but you just refused to take more Brimstone. You can't have your cake and eat it too, witch. You want the blood ecstasy? You need the Brimstone to stay alive."

She thought this was about the ecstasy? Insulted she thought me that shallow, my lips pressed together. "This isn't about you being Ms. Good Feeling and filling me with that . . . that euphoria," I said angrily. "I can get that from any vamp on the riverfront. This is about me being your friend!"

Emotion poured over her face. "You made it very clear you don't want to be that kind of a friend!" she said loudly. "And if you aren't, then there's no way I can do this! I tried to fix myself, but I can't. The only way I can keep from killing people now is if I shackle the hunger with love, damn it! And you don't want me to touch you that way!"

I'd never seen her show her feelings like this, but I wasn't going to back down—even though she was starting to scare me. "Oh, get off it, Ivy," I said, sliding a few inches from her. "It's obvious from yesterday that you can share blood without sleeping with someone." She gaped at me, and I flushed. "Okay, I admit it—it didn't turn out all that well, but God! It kind of surprised both of us. We just need to go slow. You don't have to have sex to find a feeling of closeness and understanding. Lord knows I feel that way about you. Use that to shackle your hunger." My face flushed hot in the cool night air. "Isn't that what love is?"

She continued to look at me, hiding her emotions again behind her black eyes.

"So you almost killed me," I said. "I let you do it! The point is, I saw you. For one instant you were the person you want to be, strong and comfortable with who she is and what she needs, with no guilt and at peace with herself!"

Ivy went pale in the streetlight. Terrified. Embarrassed, I looked away to give her time to cover her raw emotions.

"I liked being able to put you there," I said softly. "It's a hell of a good feeling. Better than the euphoria. I want to put you there again. I . . . liked seeing you like that."

Ivy stared at me, her hope so fragile, it hurt to see it. There was a sheen of moisture to her eyes, and she didn't say anything, just sat with a stiff, frightened posture.

"I don't know if I can do this," I admitted, talking because she wasn't. "But I don't want to pretend it didn't happen. Can we just agree that it did and play it day by day?"

Taking a breath, Ivy broke out of her stance. "It happened," she said, voice shaking. "It's not going to happen again." I leaned forward to protest, but she interrupted me with a quick, "Why didn't you use your magic to stop me?"

Surprised, I sat back. "I—I didn't want to hurt you."

She blinked fast, and I knew she was trying not to cry. "You trusted that I wouldn't kill you, even by accident?" she asked. Her perfect face was again blank of emotion, but I knew it was the only way she had to protect herself.

Remembering what Kisten had once said about living vampires craving trust nearly as much as they craved blood, I nodded. But the memory was followed by fear. He also said Piscary had warped her into something capable of mindlessly killing what she loved so he could lap up her despair when she came to him, shamed and broken. But she was not that same person. Not anymore. "I trusted you," I whispered. "I still do."

A truck was approaching, the headlights shining on her face to show a shiny track of moisture. "That's why we can't do this, Rachel," she said, and I was afraid that Piscary might own her still.

The approaching panel truck drove past too slowly. A sliver of warning brought me still, and I watched it without appearing to, taking the cold night air smelling of diesel fuel deep into me. The truck braked too long and was hesitant when it made the turn.

"Yes, I saw it," Ivy said when my shoes scraped the cement. "We should get back to the room. Peter will be here by sunup."

She was ending the conversation, but I wasn't going to let her go that easy. "Ivy," I said as I rose, gathering my bag from beside hers, wanting to try again. "I—"

She jerked to her feet, shocking me to silence. "Don't," she said, eyes black in the streetlight. "Just don't. I made a mistake. I just want everything to be the way it was."

But I didn't.

Twenty-eight

There was an unfamiliar car next to Nick's dented pickup when we pulled into the motel's lot. Ivy was driving, and I watched her eyes go everywhere before she turned the wheel and stopped in an open spot. It was a black BMW with a rental sticker. At least it appeared black; it was hard to tell in the streetlight. Engine still running, Ivy looked at it, her gaze giving nothing away. Thinking Walter had changed his mind, I went to get out.

"Wait," Ivy said, and I tensed.

From our room, a shaft of light spilled from a curtain being pulled aside. Nick's long face peered out, and upon seeing us, he let the fabric fall. Ivy cut the engine, the low rumble dying to leave only the memory of it echoing. "Okay," she said. "Now you can get out."

I would have gotten out even if it had been Water, but relieved, I yanked the door open and eased from the leather seats. Our cut-short conversation at the trolley stop had left me unsettled. I'd let her think all she had to do was say no and everything was settled, but she would be replaying the conversation in her head for days. And when the time was right, I was going to bring it up again. Maybe over a carton of red curry takeout.

I got our bags from the back, their soft rattle mixing with the aggressive rumble of the street-racer escort we had to the motel. "I hate plastic," Ivy said, taking the bags from me and rolling them so they quit rattling.

The door to our room opened and I squinted at the light. *So that's why Ivy always used canvas bags*. It wasn't because she was especially ecominded. They were quiet.

The light cut off as Nick slipped out and eased the door shut behind him. The street Weres in the lot across the road revved their cars, and I waved sarcastically to them. They didn't wave back, but I saw the flicker of a lighter when they lit up and settled in.

Nick looked more than a little concerned as he came to meet us, his eyes fixed on the Weres. His tall, gaunt stature still leaned slightly, and he favored his left foot. "Your vampire friends are here," he said, pulling his attention from the Weres to touch on the black BMW. "They flew in from Chicago on a puddle jumper soon as the sun was down."

My attention jerked to the motel room door and I stopped moving. *Great. I looked like warmed-up crap.* "What are they doing here already?" I asked no one in particular. "They aren't supposed to be here until almost dawn. I don't have any of my spells made up yet."

Ivy looked bothered too. "Apparently they wanted some time to settle in before sunrise," she said, running her hands down her leather pants and tugging her coat straight.

Rudely knocking Nick's shoulder, she pushed past him. I fell into place behind her, ignoring Nick trying to get my attention. Jenks had been running interference for me, telling Nick I was tired from too much spelling and the scuffle with the Weres. He didn't know Ivy and I had had a blood tryst, and though I didn't give a fig leaf what the bastard thought, I was guiltily glad that the collar of my jacket made it hard to see my tiny stitches.

Ivy walked in without preamble, dropping the bags just inside the door and moving to the three people at the table by the curtained window. They looked terribly out of place in the low-ceilinged room full of beds and our suitcases, and it would have been obvious who was in charge even if Ivy hadn't stopped before the oldest, gracefully executing a soft bow that was reminiscent of a martial arts student to her instructor. He smiled to show a slip of teeth and no warmth.

I took a slow breath. This might be a little hairy.

DeLavine was one of Chicago's higher master vampires, and he looked it, dressed in dark slacks and a linen shirt. He had trimmed and styled sand-colored hair, a youthful face, and a sparse frame that gave him an ageless look. It was probably a charm that kept him looking a late thirty-something. Most likely he was wrinkled and twisted. Vampires usually spent every last penny of their first life, using a yearly witch potion to look as young as they wanted.

His eyes were dark, showing only the slightest widening of

pupils. A twinge came from my neck when his gaze traveled lightly over me in dismissal. His attention returned to Ivy, making me both relieved and ticked; he thought I was her shadow. How nice was that?

DeLavine sat like a king surrounded by his court, a glass of water on the scratched table beside him and his legs confidently crossed. Atop the back of an empty chair was a carefully folded, long cashmere coat; everyone else was still wearing theirs. He had the air of someone who had taken time out of his busy schedule to personally take his child to the doctor's office and was waiting to see how they were going to help his little boy get over the chicken pox.

Though concerned, he wasn't worried. He reminded me of Trent, but where Trent moved on logic, DeLavine clearly moved out of hunger or a forgotten sense of responsibility. Rex sat in the middle of the floor before him, head cocked as if trying to figure out what he was.

I'm right there with you, cat.

Standing behind DeLavine was a living vampire. The woman was nervous, an unusual emotion for a high-blood vampire. She was thin and graceful, which was a trick since she was kind of big on top and hippy. Her straight, unstyled long hair was graying, though she looked no older than me. If not for her worry, she would have been beautiful. Haunted-looking, her eyes constantly moved, landing on me more often than not. Clearly she wasn't comfortable with this. Her hands were on the shoulders of a second, seated vampire. *Peter?*

He was obviously ailing, sitting as if trying to pull himself straight but not quite able to manage it. His vivid blue eyes were surprising against his black hair and dark complexion. Pain showed in the tension his pleasant expression carried, and I could smell an herb that should have been prescription only but wasn't because humans didn't know it was a massive painkiller when mixed with baking powder.

His slacks and casual shirt were as expensive looking as his mentor's, but they and his coat hung on him as if he had lost a lot of weight. He seemed in full control of his faculties despite the painkiller, his gaze meeting mine with the look of someone seeing their savior.

I didn't like that. If things went as planned, I was going to kill him. *Shades of gray. Just this once. Gotta save the world and all that.*

Nick edged in behind me, moving furtively to the kitchen, where he leaned against the sink with his arms crossed, the bulb over the stove making him even more gaunt. I imagined he was trying to stay unnoticed, but no one wanted to acknowledge his existence anyway.

Between Nick and the vampires, Jenks sat cross-legged on the couch beside the artifact. I had put the ugly thing in his keeping, and he took the task seriously. He looked odd sitting like that, but the hard slant to his eyes balanced out his prissy-boy image. Ivy's sword across his knees helped too. The vampires were ignoring him. If I was lucky, they'd ignore me.

"DeLavine," Ivy said respectfully, dropping her coat on the bed and inclining her head. She had the air of a favored messenger that was to be treated well. The undead vampire lifted a hand in acknowledgment, and she turned to Peter. "Peter," she said more casually, gesturing for him to remain seated as she shook his hand.

"Ivy Tamwood," the ailing vampire said pleasantly, his voice resonant for his narrow, disease-thin body. "I've heard much about your good works. Thank you for seeing me."

Good works? I thought, then remembered the missing-person runs that had populated her schedule during the first three months of our firm's existence.

"It's a pleasure to meet you," he continued, releasing her hand. "You can imagine the uproar you put my house in when you called." He smiled, but I saw a tinge of fear.

"Shhhh," the undead vampire admonished, sensing it and patting his knee. "It's a moment of pain. Nothing you haven't lived your entire life with." It was the first time he had spoken, and his voice carried an accent so faint it showed only in a soft lengthening of vowels.

Peter dropped his eyes, head bobbing. I thought I was going to be sick. This was wrong. I didn't want to do it. I hadn't wanted to from the first. We could find another way.

"DeLavine, Peter," Ivy said, motioning for me to come forward. "This is my partner, Rachel Morgan. It will be her spells that will make this work."

I couldn't help but notice that the woman behind them was being disregarded and didn't seem to have a problem with that. Feeling like a prize mule, I took off my cap and shambled forward, conscious of my hat-flattened hair, my faded jeans, and my STAFF T-shirt. At least it was clean.

"Pleasure to meet you, sir," I said, not offering my hand to DeLavine. No freaking way. "Peter," I added, shaking his.

He smiled to show me his teeth, his hand cold as it slipped into mine. There was a strength to his grip, but I could see the fear in his eyes. *I couldn't do this.*

"Rachel Morgan," the ailing vampire said, his gaze touching upon my neck and politely rising back to my eyes. "I'd like to talk to you about why I—"

"Rachel," DeLavine interrupted softly, and I started. "I want to see you. Come here."

My gaze jerked to Ivy and my pulse leapt. Her face was blank of emotion, and with that comfortable thought, I turned to him. When dealing with an unfamiliar vampire, it was always better to acknowledge their existence, then talk to their subordinates unless they showed an interest. *Oh God, I didn't want to be interesting.*

"So you will free my Peter of his mortal pain," he said, his voice going right to the bottom of my lungs and making it hard for me to breathe.

"Yes, sir." I looked him in the eye and fought the familiar rising pull of tingles.

He gazed back, more than a hint of testing seduction in his widening pupils. Behind me, I felt Ivy step forward, and from the corner of my sight, Jenks slowly uncrossed his legs to put his feet on the floor. Tension pulled through me, and though DeLavine's focus never moved from me, I knew he was becoming aware that I wasn't for casual use and discard, despite what I looked like.

The refined man stood in a soft rustle, and I retreated a step, common sense overpowering my desire to appear cavalier. Rex, too, got to her feet, stretching before going to twine about the vampire's feet. I forced myself to breathe, and Ivy's presence behind me imparted a feeling of security I knew was false. My legs felt questionable, and his pupils widened when he sensed it. *I'm not afraid,* I thought, lying to myself. Well, not any more than would help keep me alive.

"I know you," DeLavine said, and I steeled myself against the pheromones he was kicking out. He reached forward, and I stifled my jerk when he arranged a strand of wild hair. "Your youth distracted me. I almost didn't see since you're all but ignorant of yourself. You're Kalamack's witch."

"I'm not his. I don't work for him. Much," I protested, putting little weight behind it, then stiffened when he distinctly pushed Ivy out of the way and circled behind me. I heard her fall back, catching herself but not protesting. In the kitchen, Nick paled. Jenks stood, his sword gripped tightly. Peter looked distressed, and the woman tensed. DeLavine was aware of everyone, but focused entirely on me.

"You are a remarkable woman," the undead vampire said from behind my shoulder. There were no tingles, no hint of passion, but it was coming, I could feel it simmering under his silky voice. "And your skin . . . so perfect, not a mark from the sun. But, bless my soul," he said with a mocking slowness. "Someone . . . has bitten you."

He exhaled, and my eyes closed when a wash of bliss rose from my new wound, melting my fear like spun sugar. He was bespelling me. I knew it. I couldn't fight it. And God help me, I wanted to. All I could manage was a small sound in protest when his fingers moved the collar of my leather jacket aside.

"No," Ivy whispered, fear in her voice. My eyes opened, only to be caught by DeLavine's. He was before me now, a hand raised against Ivy behind me. Rex twined about my feet, purring. *This wasn't supposed to happen. This is* not *what was supposed to* happen!

Jenks's face was drawn tight. He had been told not to interfere, knew it would make matters worse. Beyond him, Nick was stiff with horror. I didn't think it stemmed from DeLavine. I think it was from the new stitches on my neck and what they meant. Ivy had bitten me, and my face warmed at his unvoiced accusation. He thought I had failed, that I had let my passions rule me and let Ivy take advantage of it.

My jaw clenched and my chin rose. It was none of Nick's business what I did with whom. And I hadn't given in because of passion; I had tried to understand her, or maybe myself.

But DeLavine took it as defiance and gently caressed the sore edges of my bite.

Adrenaline jerked through me. My weakened pulse tried to absorb it, and failed. I gasped when feeling raced from his soft brush against the healing wound, streaming through me, both familiar and alien since it came from an unfamiliar vampire. The difference struck a chord in me I hadn't known was there, and my vision darkened when my blood loss couldn't cope with the new demand.

Jenks moved. From the edge of my sight I saw Ivy crash into him. "Sorry," she grunted, making a mallet of her hands by covering her fist with another and slamming it into his head.

Mouth open, Nick stood in the kitchen, watching the pixy's

eyes roll up and him drop like a stone, unconscious. The human backed up until he could back up no more. He thought Ivy had given me to DeLavine. What she had done was save Jenks's life, and probably everyone else's, since a pitched fight would set DeLavine off. This way, only I would die.

"Let me . . ." DeLavine whispered for me alone, and he circled with Rex trailing happily behind him, the vampire scenting everything, weighing, calculating.

My breath came in a heave, and I held it. My knees were locked to keep me upright. Ivy couldn't do a thing, and I could hear her frustration in her breathing as she forced herself to not interfere. She couldn't best DeLavine. Not without leaning on Piscary's strength, and she was out of his influence. DeLavine knew it. That we had invited him here to help Peter meant little.

"Bitten and unbound," the undead vampire said, and a shudder rippled through me. "Free for the taking. I sense two demon marks on you. I feel two bites, but only one reached your soul, and so carefully—so careful she was, a kiss so soft, but a whisper. And someone . . . someone has put their mark in your very . . . cells. Claimed by many, belonging to none. Who would look to me to get you back?"

"No one," I rasped, and his eyes fixed on mine, stilling my next word. I stood upright under his control and would have fallen if his will wasn't propping me up.

"Please," Ivy whispered, standing beside Jenks slumped on the floor. "I beg favor."

With a light interest, DeLavine touched the unscared side of my neck. "What?" he said.

"Leave her as mine." Ivy's pale face made her eyes look even blacker. "I ask this as a thank-you for helping Peter." She licked her lips and held her arms down. "Please."

DeLavine lifted his eyes from me, and I blinked, finding a thread of will returned to me. "This," the vampire said, lifting my chin with a finger, "should belong to a master, not you. Piscary has indulged you beyond reason. You're a spoiled child, Ivy, and you should be punished for stepping out of your master's influence. Taking her as mine will bother Kalamack and put me in good with Piscary."

Ivy's eyes flicked to me and away. I could almost feel her thoughts realign themselves, and my pulse hammered when her posture melted from tense to seductive.

God save us. She was going to give him what he wanted so he would leave me alone. I couldn't let her do this. I couldn't let her turn herself into filth for me. But as tingles raced through me to set my mind confused, I could only watch.

"Such a sweet sip," DeLavine said, his back to Ivy. A new glint was in his eyes, making me unsure if he was talking about Ivy or me. "A wolf in sheep's clothing, stinking of Brimstone, but still very weak," he said. "I might kill you by mistake, witch. But you'd enjoy it." He inhaled, taking my volition. Exhaling, his breath under my ear sent a jolt of desire right to my core. "Do you want this?" he breathed.

"No," I whispered. It was easy. Ivy had given me the fear to find the strength to say it.

But DeLavine was delighted. "No!" he exclaimed, his pupils wide and dilated, his lust-reddened lips curling upward. "Curiouser and curiouser." His fingers traced the line along my shoulder that I knew he wanted to send his nails, digging to cause pain and a delicious path of blood to my neck that his mouth could follow.

Eyes on mine, he smiled to show his long canines. The thought of them sinking into me pulled a shiver from the depths of my soul. I knew how it would feel, and the fear of my blood being raped from me mixed with the memory of how good it could be. I closed my eyes, starting to hyperventilate, fighting him, losing to him. DeLavine eased closer, almost touching. I could sense his need to crush my will rise higher. He didn't care about Peter. Not anymore. I was too damn interesting.

"So strong a will," he said. "I could flake your consciousness from your soul like stone."

He moved, and behind him I saw Ivy gather her resolve. *No,* I pleaded silently, but her fear for me was stronger than her fear for herself. Guilt, shame, and relief kept me silent when, shifting forward with a sigh to tell him where she was, she touched DeLavine's shoulder.

I watched in horror and fascination as Ivy's long leg slipped between his from behind. She curved a sinuous arm around his chest so that her fingertips played with the base of his neck. Tilting her head, she sent her lips to mouth his ear. And while DeLavine looked at me with Ivy bringing his hunger fully awake, she whispered, "Please?"

My blood pounded as she put her teeth on his ear and tugged. "I'm fond of her. . . ." she added. "I want to keep her the way she is."

DeLavine took his eyes from me, and I felt the tears start, even as the vampire pheromones and watching them play whipped my libido high. *This was so wrong.*

Ivy flowed around him to get between us. Standing with her legs wide, she ran her hands over him between his suit coat and shirt. She threw her head back, and a laugh of delight came from her, shocking me. "I can feel your scars!" she giggled, turning it into a soft, desire-filled sound of deviltry at the end. She was Ivy, but she wasn't. Playful, sensual, and domineering, this was a side of her she hadn't wanted to show me. This was Ivy doing what she did best.

Both captivated and repulsed, I couldn't look away as she bent her lips to his neck and his eyes closed. He exhaled, his hands trembling as he grasped her wrists and held them down.

"Tonight?" Ivy whispered, loud enough for me to hear. And DeLavine opened his eyes, smiling wickedly as he met my gaze.

"Bring her."

"Alone," she countered, pulling her hands from his grip to explore his inner thigh. "What I want to do would kill her." She laughed, ending with an eager moan. The playful sound of desire turned my stomach. This was probably what she had been in those years she wouldn't talk about, and she was returning to it to keep me safe.

God, how did I get to this place where my friends sell themselves to keep me alive?

Ivy shifted, doing something I couldn't see to make DeLavine's eyes widen. Peter hissed, and I wasn't surprised to find a jealous, sullen expression on his face. The woman behind him was running her fingers over him in distraction, but it didn't appear to be helping.

"Innocence can be exhilarating," Ivy murmured. "But experience? There's a reason Piscary indulges me," she said, the syllables as certain and warm as summer rain to make my pulse quicken. "Would you like to know . . . why? Not many do."

DeLavine smiled. "Piscary will not be pleased."

"Piscary is in prison," she said, pouting. "And I'm lonely."

The pheromones they were kicking out had tingles of passion pulsing through me. I was either going to climax where I stood or vomit. Ivy had left Skimmer and followed me here to escape her past, and now she was returning to it to save my life. I was going to unwittingly kill her. I made her bite me, and now she was whoring herself to keep me safe. She thought I was going to save her, but I was going to kill her.

All but forgotten, Peter stirred. “Please, DeLavine,” he said sullenly, and I despaired at the filth I was wallowing in, the system that Ivy had worked within her entire life. “She knows the spells,” Peter continued. “I hurt so badly.”

DeLavine let go of my will. My pulse beat wildly, and with his support ripped away, my muscles gave a massive spasm and went limp. Barely conscious, I crumpled.

“For you, Peter,” I heard from above me as I worked my arms under me so I could push my face off the floor. Dizzy, I wedged myself into a seated position. The undead vampire was ignoring me, his gaze tracking the perimeter of the room. Ivy had unwrapped herself from him and was standing at the curtained window, her head bowed as she tried to bring herself down. Guilt hit me, and I took a breath that was almost a cry.

“There are a few things I want from this,” DeLavine was saying, having apparently forgotten me lying on the floor. “Peter wants his last sight to be of the setting sun.”

“That can be accommodated,” Ivy said softly. Her voice was still husky, and I ignored the memory of hearing it whisper in my ear. Head down, I crawled to Jenks, checking his pulse and pulling back his eyelids to see if his eyes dilated. He was okay, and I slumped against the front of the couch, content to stay on the floor. Ivy wouldn’t look at me, and quite frankly, I didn’t want her to. How could . . . How could I ever repay her for this?

“Accommodated?” DeLavine scooped up Rex and looked into her green eyes. The cat looked away first. “There is no accommodate. Do it.”

“Yes, DeLavine.” Ivy turned, and I stifled a shudder at the thinnest brown rim to her eyes. They were almost fully dilated, and just standing there breathing, she looked like she wanted to pin someone to the floor and have at it.

Peter looked ticked that Ivy was taking something from his mentor that he wanted, and Peter’s future scion was frightened as she saw her future, turned into nothing more than a source of blood and memory. When Peter died, she would have a shell of the man she fell in love with. She knew it, but she wanted it all the same.

“I’m concerned about possible damage to his facial structure,” DeLavine said, gently setting Rex down and going to Peter. Not a hint of his blood lust showed, but I could feel it, shimmering under his voice. “Auto crashes can be extremely disfiguring, and Peter has suffered so many indignities already.”

From the floor, I watched DeLavine run a finger down Peter’s jawline, the touch both possessive and distant. It was nauseating. Peter's temper eased, his manner softening.

"Yes, DeLavine," Ivy said. "The charms will minimize that."

Oh, yeah. That's why they had come to the motel. "I, uh—" I jerked when everyone's eyes fell on me. "I need a swab of Peter's mouth so I can sensitize the disguise charm to him."

Ivy's hunger was chilling. Recognizing my fear, she pushed herself into motion, going into the kitchen and my spelling supplies strewn all over creation. Nick backpedaled out of her way. Head down, she shuffled about, striding back to Peter with a cellophane-wrapped cotton swab. I would have at least watched to be sure Peter gave a gloppy enough sample, but DeLavine was moving again.

I pulled myself into a ball as he headed for me. Fingers grasping, I fumbled for Ivy's sword, pulling it awkwardly out from where Jenks had let it fall. *This was wrong, so wrong.*

DeLavine gave me a raised eyebrow glance, then dismissed me as he picked up the artifact, sitting alone and vulnerable on the bedside table. He had looked at me, but it had been different. He had seen me, calculated the risk, and dismissed me, but this time he'd looked at me as a possible threat and not just a walking sack of blood. I wondered what had changed.

"This is it?" he murmured, casually moving out of the sword's easy reach.

My fingers tightened on the hilt, but I didn't think it was the blade that had him watching me while seeming not to.

Ivy came closer, the open cellophane-wrapped swab in her grip. She seemed to have regained control, only a remnant of her runaway hunger perceptible in her subtlest movements. "It will be destroyed with Peter," she said, but DeLavine wasn't listening, focused entirely on the ugly statue perched on the tips of his fingers.

"Such a wonder," he mused aloud. "So many lives ended forever because of it. It should have been destroyed when it was unearthed, but someone got greedy—and now they're dead. I am . . . wiser than that. If I can't have it, no one will." DeLavine took the thumb of his free hand and pierced the tip of his index finger. "Peter?"

"Yes, DeLavine?"

I held my breath as a drop of blood welled. With a careful attention, the undead vampire smeared it onto the statue. A shudder passed over me as it soaked in to leave a dark stain.

"Make sure," DeLavine said softly, "that this gets destroyed." He looked at me and smiled to show his long canines.

"Yes, DeLavine."

With a confident satisfaction, DeLavine set the marked statue down. My lips curled as it seemed to me that the pain etched in the figure's face was deeper. Turning with an exaggerated slowness, the undead vampire sent his gaze across the room, landing on Nick scrunched in the corner of the kitchen. "This is repulsive," he said, and suddenly the room was. "A dirty little hole stinking of emotion. We'll stay somewhere else. Peter, we are leaving. Audrey will make the arrangements to get you where you need to be come sunset."

Audrey, I thought, glancing at the woman. So she had a name. I shifted my feet so he wouldn't step on them, and he made his casual way to the door, snagging his coat on the way. Peter slowly rose, Audrey helping him with a professional grip that wouldn't hurt her back. The ailing vampire met my eyes, clearly wanting to talk to me, but DeLavine took his other arm in a show of concern born from memory, not love, and escorted him to the door.

Ivy opened it for them, and DeLavine hesitated while Peter and Audrey continued out.

My grip tightened on the hilt, but I could do nothing when the vampire bent to whisper in Ivy's ear, his hand curving about her waist possessively. My pulse pounded as she looked at the floor. Damn it, this wasn't right. She nodded, and I felt as if I had sold her to him.

The door shut behind him, and her shoulders slumped.

Twenty-nine

"Ivy—"

"Shut up."

I dropped the sword and pulled my knees to my chin to make room when she knelt beside Jenks. With her vampire strength, she yanked him upright to lean against the couch, giving him a shake. "Jenks!" she demanded. "Open your eyes. I didn't hit you that hard."

He didn't respond, his head lolling and blond hair falling about his angular features.

"Ivy, I'm sorry," I said, my pulse quickening in guilt. "You . . . Oh God, tell him you changed your mind. We'll figure something out."

Close beside me, Ivy gave me an unreadable look, her hands on Jenks's shoulders, her oval face empty of emotion. "I wouldn't have offered if I wasn't prepared to follow through."

"Ivy—"

"Shut up!" she shouted, startling me. "I want to do it, okay? I can't touch *anything* without killing it, so I'm going to go back to things that are *already dead!* I'm doing this for me, not you! I'm going to enjoy myself, so just *shut the hell up, Rachel!"*

Face hot, my mouth fell open. It had never occurred to me she might want to. "I . . . I thought you only shared blood with people you—"

"Yeah, I tried that, didn't I. It didn't work. If I can't have you, I may as well go back to the way I was. Shut. Up."

I shut up. I didn't know what to think. Was she saying that to make me feel less guilty, or was she serious? She had damn well looked like she knew what she was doing, wrapped around DeLavine like that. I couldn't believe she really meant it. Not after her confession only an hour old. Apparently we were both going places we didn't want to—me forward and her back. "Ivy?" I said, but she wouldn't look at me.

"Jenks," she said, spots of color showing on her cheeks. "Wake up."

His breathing quickened, and it was no surprise when his smooth features scrunched in hurt. Eyes still closed, he reached for his head. Nick had come out of the kitchen, standing to look like a fifth wheel beside the TV, arms crossed over his faded T-shirt. Rex was having a field day, purring and rubbing on everyone, clearly happy we were on her level.

"Ow," Jenks said when his fingertips found the bump, and his eyes flew open. "You hit me!" he shouted, and Ivy let go. He fell against the couch, anger in his green eyes until he saw me beside him, probably looking as bad as I felt. His gaze shot to the empty table, then searched until he found the statue. "Holy crap, what did I miss?" he said.

"Sorry." Ivy stood and offered him a hand up. "He would have killed you."

So she hit him and risked giving him a concussion? Yeah, that made sense.

His gaze went to me, and my breath caught at the fear in it. "Are you all right? Did he touch you?"

"Of course he touched me," I said, getting to my feet and wavering until I found my balance. "He's an undead vampire. They can't look without touching. They can't not touch. I'm a freaking vampire candy cane and they all want a lick."

"Damn it all to hell!" Jenks rose, touching the back of his head when it probably protested at the quick motion. "Stupid pixy. Stupid green-assed, moss-wipe, thumb up my ass pixy! You knocked me out cold, Ivy!"

"Jenks," I protested, "leave her alone." But he wasn't mad at her, he was mad at himself.

"Tagged by a whiny little vamp," he said, gesturing. "Rache, take this sword and stick it in me. Just go and stick it in me. I'm a back-drafted, crumpled-winged, dust-caked, dew-assed excuse of a backup. Worthless as a pixy condom. Taken down by my own partner. Just tape my ass shut and let me fart out my mouth."

I blinked, impressed. Rex was twining about my feet, and

needing some comfort, I picked her up. Immediately she jumped to the couch and bounced to Jenks, stretching against his leg. The pixy yelped when she flexed her claws into him, and the kitten skittered under the bed.

"Look! She drew blood. Rache! Your damn orange cat scratched me. I'm bleeding!"

"Rex!" Jax shouted, coming out from behind the top of the curtain. "Dad, you scared her! Rex, are you okay?" He darted under the bed after her.

"That is so unsafe," I muttered. Tired, I hobbled to the kitchen to get away from Jenks, who had collapsed onto the bed and was holding his leg as if Rex had hit a femoral vein. I jerked to a stop before I ran into Nick. "Hi, Nick," I muttered, hitting the *k* with an excess amount of force. "Get out of my way. I have a lot to do before I kill Peter and Ivy goes on her *big date.*"

His long face worried, he took a breath to say something. I wasn't going to listen. I owed him nothing. Feeling like I was eighty years old, I shambled around him.

"I can help," he said, and I dropped into one of those nasty kitchen chairs, put my elbows on the table and slumped forward. I was tired, hungry, and ticked. I had completely lost control of my life. It wasn't a simple snag and drag anymore. No, now I had to save the world from my former boyfriend and my roommate from herself. *What the hell. Why not?*

Ivy had gotten my bags from where she dropped them by the front door. Silent and clearly embarrassed, she set them on the table, making a show of putting Peter's swab before me. Jenks had apparently decided he wasn't bleeding to death, and with his very lack of movement, pulled my attention to him.

Standing, he first looked at the artifact, then flicked his gaze at Nick. I nodded, understanding. With a casual slowness, Jenks picked up the artifact and limped forward. My eyes were on Nick from around the curtain my fallen curls made.

My stomach caved in when Nick watched Jenks without appearing to. He wanted it. He still wanted to snatch it from us and sell it to the highest bidder, even if it would mean I'd have to go into hiding to keep the Weres from tracking me down and killing me for it. Whether he would or not was still unanswered, but he was considering it. *Son of a bitch.*

The vamp-bloodied artifact was set thumping down in front of me, and Jenks pulled the bags closer to indulge his pixy curiosity. "Catnip?" he said, pulling it out and opening it.

"It's for Rex," Ivy volunteered, suddenly sounding shy, of all things.

A grin flashed over Jenks, and he made a soft trill of a whistle. Immediately Jax buzzed out from under the bed. "Catnip!" the small pixy shouted, grabbing a handful and darting away.

"Oh, hey! Fudge!" Jenks exclaimed, finding the half-pound box I had bought to replace what he'd lost. "Is this mine?" he asked, green eyes alight.

I nodded, trying to stifle my anger at Nick. Jenks enthusiastically leaned against the counter and opened the box. Bypassing the plastic knife, he broke off about a third of it and took a huge bite. Ivy watched, appalled, and I shrugged. His mouth moving as he hummed, Jenks finished unpacking the sacks. I was half dead, Ivy was whoring herself to keep me safe, but Jenks was okay as long as he had chocolate.

It was getting tight in the tiny kitchen, but I didn't want either of them to leave. I felt cold and vulnerable, and the closeness was helping me distance myself from the play DeLavine had made for me. Inside I was shaking for what Ivy was doing for me—what she was falling back into—and if they left, it would start to show in my fingers.

"Rachel?" Nick said from the outskirts. "Can I help?"

Ivy bristled, but I stretched across the table and handed him a swab. "I need a sample," I said. "It's an illegal charm, but I didn't think you'd mind."

Face tight with frustration, he took it, turning away when he ran the cotton around the inside of his mouth. I remembered what DeLavine had said about so many people having marked me and squelched a feeling of shame. I didn't belong to anyone. But seeing Nick unable to enter the comfort I had found among my friends, I felt my Inderlander roots hard and strong.

Nick didn't understand. He never would. I'd been stupid thinking I could find anything lasting with him, and he had proved it by having no problem selling slivers of me to Al.

I wouldn't look at him when Nick handed me the swab, safely back in its cellophane wrapper. He moved as if to speak and I blurted to Ivy, "Piscary won't mind you helping Peter, will he?" Eyes down, I wrote Nick's name on the packet with a squeaky, big black marker.

"No." The sound of water trickling into the coffeemaker blurred her voice. "Piscary doesn't care one way or the other. Peter isn't important to him. To anyone. To anyone but his scion, anyway. It's likely that he'll simply fade from DeLavine's awareness when he's distracted by more exciting things."

Like you? I thought, but I didn't say it aloud.

Ivy turned, her black hair swinging to show her earrings. "I'm making coffee," she said. "Do you want some?"

Not if it was laced with Brimstone. Crap on toast, I was tired. "Please," I said, feeling Nick's gaze heavy on me.

"Jenks?" she offered, getting a tiny hotel mug down from the bare cupboard.

Jenks looked appraisingly into the box of fudge, hesitating before he closed it and set it aside. "No thanks," he said, starting to mess with my spelling supplies.

"Rachel," Nick tried again. "Can I sketch a pentagram for you or something?"

Ivy's head came up, and I moved my fingers to tell her I could handle it. "No," I said shortly, pulling my demon book closer and opening it up. My eyes lifted to the artifact, wondering if Nick had had the opportunity to switch it out with a fake, but I didn't think so. And there couldn't be two such ugly things.

"Ray-ray—" Nick tried again, and Ivy slammed the cupboard.

"What the hell do you want?" she said virulently, brown eyes fixed on him.

"I want to help Rachel," he shot back, stiff and a little afraid.

Jenks snorted, crumpling up the empty bag and throwing it away. "You can help Rachel by dropping dead."

"That's still an option," said Ivy.

I didn't have time or the energy to deal with this. "I need quiet," I said, feeling my blood pressure rise. "That's all I need. That's it. Just quiet."

Nick stepped back, his arms crossing over his faded shirt to make him look alone. "Okay. I'll . . ." He hesitated, gaze flicking to Ivy and Jenks beside me, taking up all the room so he couldn't come in. His held breath slowly escaped him, and not having finished his thought, he walked away, his movements full of frustration. Slumping into the chair Peter had been sitting in, he stretched his long legs out and ran his hand through his hair, staring at nothing.

I would not feel bad for him. He had sold me out. The only reason I hadn't walked off from this was because the Weres would hound me forever if they didn't see the thing destroyed, and for that I needed Nick. And I needed him cooperative.

Jenks pulled a chair from under the kitchen table and sat beside me. I blinked in surprise when I realized he had correctly put everything into three piles. "Do you need any help?" he asked, and Ivy snickered.

"Help from a pixy?" she scoffed, and Jenks bristled.

"Actually," I said before he could start swearing at her, "could you get Nick out of here?" I didn't want him to see the transference curse. God knows who he would sell it to. He couldn't invoke it without my or demon blood, but he could probably get some from Al in exchange for my underwear size.

A nasty smile curved over Jenks, but it was Ivy who put her palm aggressively on the table and said, "I'm doing it. I want to talk to him."

I looked up, wondering, but she had turned away. "Come on, crap for brains," she said, grabbing her purse in passing and heading for the door. "Rachel forgot something, and since I don't know anything about ley line magic, you're coming with me to make sure I get the right thing. Anyone else want anything while I'm out?"

Nick's face went defiant, and I simpered, knowing it was petty but unable to stop myself. "Watch out for the Weres," I said. Maybe that had been mean, but I was mean. Just ask the kids I kept chasing out of my graveyard. They could play hide-and-seek somewhere else.

"I'm out of toothbrushes," Jenks said, going to putter with the coffeemaker.

Ivy waited for Nick to shrug into the fabric coat that had been stashed in his truck. "You can use those more than once," she said, as I'd already told him, and Jenks shuddered.

Clearly aware he was being gotten rid of, Nick yanked the door open and walked out. Ivy gave me a wicked, closed-lipped smile and followed him. "I'm not afraid of you," Nick said as the door shut and my stress level dropped about six points.

"Here's your coffee," Jenks said, setting it down in front of me.

He poured me coffee? I looked at it, then up at him. "Is there Brimstone in it?"

Jenks plopped into the chair beside mine. "Ivy told me to put some in, but I thought you were well enough to decide."

My blood pressure went right back up, and remembering my reflection in the store window, I hesitated, wondering if I was being wise or stupid. Brimstone would keep me alert for hours while I made whatever charms I needed, simultaneously increasing my blood count to pretty near normal. When I fell asleep, I'd wake refreshed, hungry, and feeling almost as well as before I was bitten. Without it, I'd be spelling while fatigued. My legs would shake every time I stood, and my sleep would end with me waking up feeling like crap.

But using black magic or illegal drugs to simply to make my life easier was a lie of convenience—one that would delude me into believing I had the right to flaunt the rules, that I lived above them. *I will not turn into Trent.*

I exhaled in a long puff. "I'm not going to do it," I said, and he nodded, his green eyes creased with worry. Though he clearly disagreed, he accepted my decision, which made me feel better immediately. I was in charge of my life. Me. *Ri-i-i-ight.*

"Which spell first?" Jenks asked, extending a hand for Jax when the pixy flitted to us. His wing was bent and he was leaking dust from it, but neither Jenks nor I said anything. It was nice seeing the little pixy taking an interest in what his dad thought was important—even if he was out here only because Rex had scored on him.

I tapped the pages, nervous. "You didn't lose the bone statue with your fudge, did you?"

A smile curved over Jenks. "Nope." Jax rose to the overhanging light as his dad went to his growing pile of bags beside the TV. I'd never seen a man who could outshop me, but Jenks was a master. I tried not to watch when he bent to shuffle about, striding quickly back to the kitchen with the twin boxes. He set them on the table, and pixy dust sifted over us while he opened them up. The first one was that god-awful carved totem, and leaving it to stare at me, he opened the second. "Not a scratch," he said, green eyes giving away his satisfaction.

I picked up the wolf statue, feeling the weight and coldness of bone. It wasn't a bad choice for moving the Were curse to. Focus going distant, I remembered Nick's greed, and my eyes went to Jenks's totem. "Hey, uh, has Nick seen this?" I said, indicating the wolf statue.

Jenks sniffed in disgust, leaning to balance his chair on two legs. "I haven't shown it to him, but he's probably pawed through my stuff."

An idea was sifting through my mind, but I refused to feel guilty for not trusting Nick. "Hey, this is a really neat statue," I said, setting down the wolf and picking up the totem. "Matalina is going to love it. I should have gotten one. It'd look great in Mr. Fish's bowl."

Jenks let the chair fall to four legs. "Mr. Fish's bowl?" he said quizzically, and I darted a glance at the motel room door. Jenks's expression went knowing, then angry; he might be interior-decorating challenged, but he was not a stupid man. "You're worried about . . ."

I made a small noise, not wanting him to say aloud I was worried about Nick stealing the little wolf statue, so clearly the better choice for a demon curse. But they were both made out of bone, so . . .

"Yeah," Jenks said suddenly, taking the totem from me and setting it in the middle of the table. "I'll pick one up for you the next time I go out."

There had only been the one in the case, but seeing his understanding, I took a slow breath and reached for my recipe. Pencil in hand, I bowed my head over it and tucked a curl behind an ear. Fool me once, shame on you. Fool me twice, and you can kiss your ass good-bye.

Thirty

Motions steady, I massaged my stuck index finger for the blood needed to invoke the last inertia-dampening spell. My finger was starting to hurt after all the charms I'd invoked. It wasn't as if I could draw a vial of my blood and dole it out by eye-dropper. If the blood didn't come right from the body, the enzymes that quickened the spell would break down and the spell wouldn't invoke. There were a lot of charms on the table, this second pair of inertia-dampening spells being a quick, guilty addition.

The blood wasn't coming, so I painfully squeezed until a beaded drop of red formed. It plopped onto the first half of the charm, then I squeezed again until the next plop hit the second amulet. The blood soaked in with an eerie swiftness, sending the scent of burnt amber to stain the stale motel room air. What I would have given for a window that opened.

Burnt amber, not redwood, proof it was demon magic. God, what was I doing?

I glanced over the quiet, dusky room, the light leaking in around the closed curtains telling me it was nearing noon. Apart from a nap around midnight, I'd been up all morning. Someone had obviously slipped me some Brimstone. *Damn roommates, anyway.*

Rubbing my thumb and finger together, I smeared the remnants of blood into nothing, then stretched to put the matched, invoked charms with the rest, beside Jenks. He was sitting across from me, his head slumped onto the table while he slept. Doppelganger charm for Peter, doppelganger charm for Nick, regular disguise charm for Jenks. *And two sets of inertia-dampening amulets,* I thought, gentling the newest in with the rest. After meeting Peter, I was changing the plan. No one knew it but me.

The clatter of the amulets didn't wake Jenks, and I sat back, exhaling long and slow. I was weary from fatigue, but I wasn't done yet. I still had a curse to twist.

Pulling myself upright, I reached for my bag, moving carefully so I wouldn't disturb Jenks. He'd sat watch over me while I slept, forgoing his usual midnight nap, and was exhausted. Rex was purring on his lap under the table, and Jenks's smooth, outstretched hand nearly touched the cup-sized minitank of saltwater containing the sea monkeys he'd bought somewhere along the way. "They're the perfect pets, Rache," he had said, eyes bright with anticipation with what his kids would say, and I hoped we all lived long enough to worry about how we were going to get them home.

I smiled at his youthful face looking roguishly innocent while he slept. He was such an odd mix, young, but a tried-and-true father, provider, protector—and almost at the end of his life.

My throat tightened and I blinked rapidly. I was going to miss him. Jax could never take his place. If there was a charm or spell to lengthen his life, I'd use it and damn the cost. My hand reached to push his hair back from his eyes, then dropped before it touched him. Everyone dies. The living find a way to assuage the loss and go on.

Depressed, I cleared a spot on the table. With the extra sea salt Jenks had gotten with his new pets, I carefully traced three plate-sized circles, interlacing them to make seven distinct spaces formed by three arcs from each circle. I glanced over the dusky room before retrieving the focus from my bag, which had been at my feet all night, safe from Nick.

Jenks was sleeping at the table, Ivy was sleeping in the back room, having returned from her "date" shortly after sunrise, and Nick and Jax were outside making sure the air bag wouldn't engage when Jenks ran the Mack truck into it tonight. And the NOS. Mustn't forget the NOS that Nick had in his nasty truck, which would be rigged to explode on impact. I'd have no better time than now to do this. I'd like to say that I had waited this long so it would be quiet and I'd be undisturbed. The reality was, I was scared. The statue's power came from a demon curse, and it would take a demonic curse to move it. A demon curse. *What would my dad say?*

"What the hell," I whispered, grimacing. I was going to kill Peter. What was a little demonic-curse imbalance compared to that?

Stomach knotting, I placed the statue into the first circle, stifling a shudder and wiping my fingers free of the slimy feel of the ancient bone. Jenks had watched me do this earlier, so I knew what came next, but unbeknownst to everyone but him, it had been a dry run using the wolf statue. I'd lit the candles but hadn't invoked the curse. The little wolf with its fake curse had been sitting on the table all night, Nick carefully avoiding looking at it.

Another glance at the light leaking around the curtains, and I rose, going to Jenks's things piled carelessly by the TV. I plucked the totem from his belongings, feeling guilty though I had already asked to use it. Nervous, I placed his carved totem with the stylized wolf on top in the second circle. In the third, I placed a lock of my hair, twisted and knotted.

My stomach clenched. How many times had my father told me never to knot my hair even in fun? It was bad. Tying hair into knots made a very strong bond to a person, especially when you knotted your own hair. What happened to the bit of hair I placed in the third circle would happen to me. Conversely, what I said or did would be reflected in the circle. It wasn't a symbol of my will, it *was* my will. That it was sitting in a circle to twist a curse made me ill.

Though that might be from the Brimstone, I thought, not putting it past Jenks, even though he'd agreed with my decision to stop taking it. At least it had been medicinal grade this time, and I wasn't dealing with the roller-coaster moods.

"Okay," I whispered, hiking my chair closer to the table. I glanced at Jenks, then got my colored candles from my bag, the soft crackle of the matching colored tissue paper they were wrapped in soothing. I had used white candles the first time, picked up by Ivy out "shopping" with Nick, a bitter touch of honesty to the lie our lives had become.

I set them down and wiped my palms on my jeans, nervous. I'd lit candles from my will only once before—mere hours ago, actually—but since my hearth—the pilot light on my kitchen stove—was five hundred miles south of there, I'd have to use my will.

My thoughts drifted to Big Al standing in my kitchen, lecturing me on how to set candles with their place names. He had used a red taper lit from his hearth, and it would probably please him that I'd learned how to light candles with ley line energy. I had Ceri to thank for that, since it was mostly a modified ley line charm she used to heat water. Lighting them from my will wasn't nearly as power-retentive as using hearth fire, but it was close.

"Ley line," I whispered, focus blurring as I reached for the line I'd found halfway across the town. It felt different from the line in my backyard, wilder, and with the steady, slow pulselike change and characteristic fluidity of water.

The influx of energy poured through me, and I closed my eyes, my trembling foot the only indication of the torrent of energy filling my chi. It took all of a heartbeat, feeling like forever, and when the force balanced, I felt overly full, uncomfortable.

Jaw clenched, I tossed my red frizz out of my eyes and scraped a bit of wax off the bottom of the white candle, holding it to the back of my teeth with my tongue. *"In fidem recipere,"* I said, to fix the candle in the narrow space where the circle holding the totem and the circle holding the knot of my hair bisected. My thumb and first finger pinched the wick, and I slowly separated them, willing a spot of heat to grow between them as I thought the words *consimilis calefacio,* setting into motion a complex, white ley line charm to heat water.

Okay, so it heated the moisture between my fingers until the wick burst into flame, but it worked. And the wax I'd scraped off on my teeth was the focal object, so I didn't set the kitchen on fire. My attention flicked to the small burn mark on the table. Yeah, I was learning.

I gazed, fascinated, when the wick first glowed, then caught as the wax melted from the virgin wick and the flame took. *One down, two to go.*

The black candle was next, and after I scratched the white wax off my teeth, I replaced it with a bit of the black candle before I set it in the space connecting the totem and the statue circles. *"Traiectio,"* I breathed, lighting this one as well.

The third candle was gold, to match my aura, and I placed it in the space between the statue and my knot of hair. *"Obsignare,"* I said, lighting the candle with a studied thought.

My pulse increased. This was as far as I'd gone earlier that morning under Jenks's eye. I brought my head up, seeing his breathing shifting the hair about his small nose. God, he had a small nose, and his ears were cute.

Stop it, Rachel, I berated myself. I wanted to finish this before I set the smoke alarm off. I pulled a gray taper from my bag, setting it in the very center of the three circles, where they all bisected. This was the one that scared me. The first candle had been set with protection, the second with the word for transference, and the third with the word that would seal the curse so it couldn't unravel. If the gray candle lit itself at the end, then I had successfully twisted the curse and I was officially an intentional practitioner of the dark arts.

God, please forgive me. It's for a good reason.

In the glow of my three candles, I massaged my finger, forcing out a welling of blood. My bleeding finger scribed a symbol I didn't know the meaning of, then I wiped the remainder on the candle. I felt as if my will left me with that simple drop of blood, smeared on the faded laminate before the gray pillar of wax given meaning from my intent.

Shaking, I pulled my hand out of the three circles. I scooted my chair back and stood so that when the circles formed, I wouldn't accidentally break them by having my legs in the lower halves. I gave a final look at the three lit candles and the one marked with my blood. The table glowed in candlelight, and I wiped my hands on my jeans.

"Rhombus," I whispered, then touched the nearest circle with my finger to close all three.

I jerked when the ever-after flowed out of me and a haze of black aura rose to envelop the candles, totem, statue, and my knot of hair. I'd never set bisecting circles before, and where they existed together, the gold of my aura was clearer, making glittering arcs among the black smut. Though small, the circles were impenetrable by everything but me since I was the one who had set them. But sticking my finger into the circle to influence what was inside would break the circle, and if I had made them large enough for me to fit in, my soul would be in danger of being transferred along with the original curse.

It was my knot of hair that made this possible. It was my bridge inside. The black candle would go out when the power was moved from the statue to the totem; the white candle would go out to protect and prevent any part of me from being sucked into the new artifact along with the old artifact's power that I would be channeling; and the gold candle would go out when the transfer was complete, sealing it so it couldn't unravel by itself.

My body resonated with the power of the unfamiliar line. It wasn't unpleasant at all, and I wished it was. Grimacing, I reached out my will. *"Animum recipere."*

I held my breath against the rising strength and the taste of ash flowing into me from the focus, overwhelming my sense of self until I was everything it was. My vision blurred and I wavered on my feet. I couldn't see, though my eyes were open.

It sang to me, it lured me, filling me as if twisting my bones and muscles. It would make me everything I wanted, everything that was promised but that I continually denied myself. I felt the wind in my face and the earth under my paws. The sound of the spinning earth filled my ears, and the scintillating scent of time was in my nose. It coursed in a torrent too fast to be realized. It was what made a Were—and it hurt. It hurt my soul that I couldn't be this free.

Hunched, I struggled to keep my breathing even so I wouldn't wake Jenks. I could be everything if I accepted it fully, took it entirely into me. And it made promises, making me long for it. If I'd had any doubt that Nick had done a switch, they were set to rest now.

But I wasn't a Were. I could understand the lure since I had run with as wolf, fought as a wolf, and existed for a short time with the wind bringing me messages. But I wasn't a wolf. I was a witch, and the lure wasn't enough for me to break my circle and take it as mine forever, destroying me in the process.

"Negare," I whispered, shocked when the word came from me. I had meant to say no. I had meant to say no! But it had come out of me in Latin. *Damn it, what was happening to me?*

Pulse pounding and feeling out of control, I saw the white candle go out. I stiffened as I felt everything in me being poured into the cheap carved bit of bone. I clutched at myself, holding myself together as the demon curse left me, taking with it the ache and lure. The extinguished white candle of protection kept me intact, holding me so that only the curse left, and absolutely nothing more or less went with it.

The black candle went out, and I jerked. Not breathing, I watched the three circles, knowing the transfer was complete and the curse almost set anew. I could feel the energy in the totem, swirling, looking for a lessening of my will so it could pour out and be free. I fixed my eyes on the gold candle, praying.

It went out as the gray candle lit, and I slumped in relief. It was done.

Eyes closing, I reached for the back of the chair. I had done it. For better or worse, I was the first demon magic practitioner this side of the ley lines. Well, there was Ceri, but she couldn't invoke them.

Fingers shaking, I smeared the salt circle to break it. My aura touched it, and the line energy flowed out of the circle and into me. I let go of the line, and my head bowed. I had all of three seconds before reality balanced itself, reaching out to bitch-slap me a good one.

I gritted my teeth so I wouldn't gasp. Stumbling backward, I reached for the wall, hitting the cupboards and sliding to the floor when I didn't find it fast enough. Panic jerked through me. I knew this was going to happen—had been expecting it. I would survive.

I couldn't breathe, and I hung my head and pretended it was all right as the black soaked in, coating me in another layer, molding to my sense of self and changing it. My demon marks throbbed, and I scrunched my eyes shut and listened to my pulse thunder. *I accept this,* I thought, and the band about my chest loosened. I took a gasping breath that sounded like a sob.

Tears were leaking out, and I realized someone had a hold on my shoulder as I sat with my back against the cupboards. "Jenks?" I burbled. I felt a moment of despair as I decided it didn't hurt as much this time. I was becoming used to it. Damn it, I didn't want this to become easy. It should hurt. It should scare me so badly that I never wanted to do it again.

"You okay?" he said, and I nodded, not looking up from his knees so he crunched before me. He had nice knees. "Are you sure?" he asked again, and I shook my head no.

His breath came and went, and I didn't move, trying to realign my thinking. I was a demon curse practitioner. I was a dealer in the black arts. I didn't want to be. I didn't want this.

I brought my head up. Relief tricked through me as I saw only concern, not disgust, in his worried face. I pulled my knees to my chest and held them, breathing slowly. His hand was still on my shoulder, and I wiped my eyes. "Thanks," I said, gathering myself to get up. "I think I'm all right now. It hit me hard is all."

His green eyes were narrowed in concern. "The imbalance?"

I stared at him, then decided he must have been listening the night Ceri explained it to me. "Yeah."

He stood and extended a hand to help me rise. "I never felt anything when I got big."

My heart clenched, and I pulled my hand from his warm one after I found my feet. "Maybe you'll get hit with it when I untwist the curse and you get small again," I lied.

Jenks's lips were tight with anger. "You hurt like that when you turned into a wolf too. I told you I'd take the black for becoming big. It's mine."

"I don't know how to give it to you," I said, depressed. "And even if I did, I wouldn't."

"Rachel, that's not fair," he said, his voice rising.

"Just shut up and say thank you," I said, remembering him saying the same thing to me when he agreed to become big so nasty-wasty vampires wouldn't bite me.

"Thank you," he said, knowing exactly what I was saying. We helped each other out. Keeping track of who was saving whom's ass was a waste of time.

Depressed, I shuffled to the table, thinking the circles and extinguished candles—all but the gray one—looked like something you'd see on a teenage witch's dresser. Pulse slowing, I plucked the extinguished candles from where they sat, rolling them up in their white, black, and gold tissue paper before snapping a rubber band around them and dropping them in my bag. That little box with the magnetic chalk would have been a nice place to keep them.

While Jenks pretended interest in his sea monkeys, I put my knotted hair on a saucer and set the burning gray candle to it. The ring of hair flared up, curled in on itself, and died. Feeling safer, I blew the candle out, then maneuvered around Jenks to wash the ash down the sink. I wanted all evidence of this gone as fast as possible.

"Sorry for waking you up," I said. Reaching for the salt, I rubbed the blood symbol off the table with a paste of it.

Jenks straightened from where he'd been leaning over his pets. His eyes were worried. "Did you know you look really scary when you do ley line magic?"

A sliver of fear took me. "How?" I asked, conscious of my two demon marks, weighing heavily on my wrist and the underside of my foot.

Dropping his eyes, Jenks shrugged. "You look tired, older. Like you've done it so many times that you don't care anymore. It's almost as if you have a second aura, and when you do ley line magic, it becomes dominant."

My lips curved down and I went to wash my fingers. "A second aura?" *That sounded absolutely fabulous. Maybe it was because I was my own familiar?*

He nodded. "Pixies are sensitive to auras. You really damaged yours with that last curse." Jenks took a breath. "I hate Nick. You're hurting yourself to help him, and he doesn't even care. He sold you out. Rache, if he ever hurts you again—"

"Jenks, I . . ." I fumbled. I put a hand on his shoulder, and this time he didn't flinch. "If I'm going to be able to walk away from this, I have to do it. This is for me, not him."

Jenks pulled back, looking over the empty room. "Yeah, I know."

I felt odd as he went to the table and looked at the remnants of the demon curse. "That's the real one?" he said, not touching it.

Pushing myself into motion, I picked up the totem. It felt heavier, though I knew it was an illusion. "Matalina is going to love it," I said, handing it to him. "Thanks for letting me borrow it. I don't need it anymore."

Jenks's eyes widened as it settled into his grip. "You want me to hold the real one?"

"He's going to try to steal it," I said, thinking I'd been stupid to trust Nick in the first place. "If you have it, he'll get the wrong one."

Depressed, I hefted the old statue. It felt dead inside, like a chunk of plastic. "I'll keep this one with me along with the wolf statue," I said, dropping the statue into my bag.

The front door opened, spilling light over the unmade beds. Jenks turned smoothly to the door, but I jumped when Nick came in, dirty and smelling of grease. Jax was on his shoulders, immediately abandoning him to see how his new pets were doing.

My hand slid across the table, brushing the salt circle into my hand and dropping it into the sink. I wondered how bad it smelled of extinguished candle, burned hair, and burnt amber.

There was a thump from the back bedroom, and Ivy came out in her bathrobe, hair in disarray, and hunched like a bridge troll. Snarling at Nick about the noise, and with a hand over her face, she limped past Jenks and me to vanish into the bathroom. Immediately the shower went on. The clean scent of oranges slipped under the door with the steam. I didn't want to know what she'd done last night to be limping today. I didn't.

Guilt-strewn and weary, I sat at the table. Jax found the ounce-sized container of sea monkey food, and Jenks stopped him, explaining he couldn't feed them since they hadn't hatched yet. Jax belligerently pointed out two bouncers, naming them Jin and Jen. The small pixy started to glow, which attracted the brine shrimp, and Jax had a fit of delight when they bounced closer. I couldn't help but smile. It was still on me when I turned, finding Nick awkwardly waiting for me. My smile faded, and he clenched his jaw.

"The truck is set, Ray-ray," he said with a false cheerfulness. "It will look like a defect when the air bag doesn't work." He winced. "I, uh, couldn't let a truck run into me—even if I knew I was going to wake up alive."

"Trust is the difference between you and us Inderlanders,"

Jenks said loudly, popping the lid to the sea monkey food. Jax grabbed a handful the size of a pinhead and dropped it in with encouraging words, enticing Jin and Jen to the surface with a bright glow. This was a hell of a lot safer pet for a pixy than the kitten, and I wondered if that was why Jenks had bought them.

I stifled a sigh, turning it into a yawn. I knew Nick wasn't keen on his truck being the sacrificial vehicle, but it wasn't as if he would be able to drive it again. He was going to be playing dead for the rest of his life. *Coward.*

"Thanks, Nick," I said, leaning away with crossed arms and preparing for a fight. "Now would you go out there and hook it back up? I'm riding with Peter. If I'm going to kill him, I'm not going to let that poor boy die alone."

Thirty-one

Ivy stood just outside the bathroom, wrapped in a white motel towel, short black hair dripping from thin spikes. "You aren't going to be riding with Peter, Rachel. No fucking way!"

I pressed my lips together and fought to not back up. *Okay, so she does swear, but only when extremely pissed.*

Jenks had retreated to the living room, looking like he wished he had never barged in on Ivy in the shower, terrified into playing the tattletale when I told him he was going to be running into me right along with Peter. Nick stood beside him in his grease-stained overalls, and they gave the impression of two boys who had jumped in the creek wearing their good go-to-church clothes five minutes before Pa hitched up the horse.

"Nick," I said, and he started. "We have four hours before we meet Audrey and Peter." *Four hours. Maybe I could get some sleep.* "Can you have the air bag fixed by then? I'd feel better if I had it to supplement the inertia-dampening curse."

"Ivy's right," he said, and I frowned. "There's no reason for you to risk your life."

Ivy laughed bitterly. "She isn't. Rachel, you are *not* getting in Nick's truck."

I turned to my spells on the table, pulse quickening. Her pupils were dilating, but it was in anger, not hunger. I knew this game of arguing with a vampire. "Everything is set," I said. "I made a second pair of inertia-dampening amulets for me, so there's no problem."

Ivy pointed, unaware I could see the new long scratch on the soft part of her arm running from her wrist to her elbow. “It’s *not* going to *happen,* Rachel!”

“It will work,” I said. “It’s only a joke spell.” *Curse, actually, but why bring* that *up?*

Jenks sat on the edge of the bed, white-faced. “Don’t ask me to do this.”

Nick shuffled nervously, looking like a garage repair guy in his blue overalls. Frustrated, I rubbed my temples. “The Weres won’t believe I let Nick run off with it and we’re trying to catch him,” I said. “Especially if there happens to be an accident. I’m not stupid enough to let Nick swipe the artifact, and they know it.”

There had been a spike of pleasure saying that. He would look back on the incident when it was over and know I had been thumbing my nose at him. But nervousness returned when I caught sight of Ivy. Scooping up Rex, I sat in a kitchen chair. “It’s no big deal,” I said, fingers moving to lull her into staying. “The charms will keep me safe. You can follow in the van, and we’ll say we’re on the way to the drop site in two vehicles. Telling them Nick ran off with it will only get them going after him themselves. They might catch him.” *Not that I really cared.*

Ivy shook her head. “This is asinine. I’ve already got it worked out. Peter and crap for brains trade places. We tell the Weres Nick ran off with it and that Jenks went pixy-native to try and catch him. Jax takes his place on your shoulder, and while under a disguise, Jenks runs the Mack truck over Peter by ‘accident’ while we try to catch him. Truck explodes. Fake statue is destroyed. Peter gets carted to the morgue or the hospital, where we can pull his plug if we need to. Weres go away—we go for a beer. I spent hours coming up with this. Why are you screwing it up, Rachel?”

Rex jumped off my lap, back nails gouging as she skittered to hide behind Jenks’s ankles. I stood, angry. “I’m not screwing it up! And I’m going to ride with Peter! I’m not going to let him die alone,” I said, coming out with what was really bothering me.

Ivy huffed, clutching the towel higher about her. “You’re alone when you die, even if you’re surrounded by hundreds.”

Her arm was oozing to stain the white towel, and only now realizing it, she flushed. Angry, I rounded on her. “Have you *ever* been there when someone dies?” I asked, shaking. “Have you ever held their hand while their strength left them? Have you ever felt the gratitude in their touch that you were there when they stopped breathing? Have you!”

Ivy's face went white.

"I'm *killing him,* Ivy! It is my decision. And I'm going to be there so I understand what it means." I caught my breath, hating myself when my eyes filled. "I have to be there so I know if it was a good thing when it's all done."

Ivy went still as a pity born in understanding reached her eyes. "Rachel, I'm sorry. . . ."

Clutching my arms around myself, I bowed my head so I couldn't see anyone. Ivy stood in her towel and made a wet spot on the floor as she dripped. The scent of the citrus shampoo she used became pronounced, and the silence grew awkward.

From across the room, Nick shifted his weight and took a breath.

"Shut up," Ivy snarled, hitching her towel higher. "This doesn't concern you." Her gaze went to my stitches, and I lifted my chin. I wasn't bound to her. I could do anything I damn well pleased.

Jenks was pale. "I can't do it," he said from the bed. "I can't hit you with a truck."

"See?" Ivy said, catching her towel when she gestured. "He's not going to do it. I don't want you to do it. You aren't doing it!" She started for her room, Nick moving out of her way.

"This is a better plan!" I exclaimed, heading after her. "I'll be fine!"

"Fine?" She lurched to a stop, spinning. "That Mack truck is going to roll over Nick's little blue Ford like it's a cupcake! And you're not going to be in it. The run is off."

"It's not off! This is how we're going to do it!"

Ivy turned. Her eyes were full black. A shiver of fear took me, rocking me to a halt. But I wasn't going to let Peter die alone. I gathered my nerve, and Nick stepped forward.

"I'll do it," he said, his eyes flicking from Ivy to me. "I'll drive the Mack truck."

Ivy's anger hesitated, and I ran my eyes over him in surprise. "No," she said flatly. "Absolutely not. You're going with Audrey and staying out of it. I don't trust you."

Nick clasped his hands, then let them go. "Rachel's right. This is a better plan. They won't be watching Audrey's motel room. After Peter switches places with me, I can leave under a regular disguise charm, cross the bridge, get the truck. Hell, it's DeLavine's truck. Audrey can give me the key."

"No!" Ivy shouted. "I won't let shit for brains run over you. It isn't going to happen!"

I rubbed my temples, thinking that actually this was a lot easier than what we'd originally planned. "Ivy—"

"No!"

Nick made a frustrated noise, gesturing at nothing. "I'm not going to kill Rachel!" he exclaimed. "I love her, but if the only way to make her safe is to run her over with a Mack truck, then I, by God, am going to be the one to do it!"

Ivy looked at him as if she had eaten a pile of crap—or maybe she was looking at him as if he was a pile of crap. "You don't know the meaning of love—Nick."

I was shaking inside. Having Nick run into me instead of Jenks wasn't what I had planned, but it would work. Swallowing, I turned to the kitchen. He could use the regular disguise charm already made up. *Oh God. What was I doing?*

Ivy took a deep breath. "Rachel. I don't trust him."

"When did you ever?" I sat at the table before everyone saw me shake. "I'll be fine. Putting me with Peter will ensure they believe the statue burned with the truck. This is the best plan we have. I don't want to have to do this again if they realize that the statue wasn't destroyed."

Nick shifted from foot to foot and ran a hand over his stubble. "I'll fix the air bag," he said, apparently deciding I was going to get my way. "And the NOS," he added.

Suddenly I was a lot more nervous. "Are they watching?" I asked, meaning the Weres across the street.

Jenks made a soft chirp of a whistle, and Jax came out of hiding to land on his shoulder.

"Yeah," Nick said, head down. "But from the conversation Jax has been catching, they think I'm modifying the NOS tanks in case I need to leave in a hurry." He swallowed to make his Adam's apple move. "I rigged it to explode on impact, but I'll disengage that too. I'll set up a button for you to push after you get out."

Jenks looked at Ivy, then stood up, heading for the door. "We've got four hours. I'll make sure it's not going to explode until you want it to," he said.

Nick's expression clouded. "I know what I'm doing."

"Jax?" Shoulders hunched, Jenks never slowed down on his way to the door. "Come on. You should know how to rig a radio signal."

I felt better knowing Jenks was good with explosives too. Nick jiggled on his feet, looking as if he wanted to give me a hug but knew better, then followed Jenks out. The door opened, and I saw three street Weres across the way, yawning as they leaned against their little tricked-out car with wax paper cups of coffee in their grips. It had been cold this morning, but they looked warm enough now that the sun was high, and sun glinted on their bare shoulders and multiple tattoos.

Ivy scowled at them before looking at Nick's retreating back. "If Rachel gets hurt, you won't have to worry about Weres killing you because I'll find you first, little thief."

My gut clenched. She would go along with it. It was done. I was going to be with Peter when Jenks plowed into us. "I'll be fine," I said, feeling my pulse quicken. "Between the air bag and the charm, it will be like I'm riding in God's arms."

The door closed behind Nick, Jenks, and Jax, the slice of afternoon sun vanishing as if it had never existed. Ivy turned, bare feet silent as she limped to her room. "What if God wants you home early?"

Thirty-two

A witch, a vampire, and a pixy walk into a bar, I thought as I led the way into the Squirrel's End. It was early, and the sun had yet to set when the door swung shut behind Jenks, sealing us in the warm air smelling faintly of smoke. Immediately Nick yanked it open to come in behind us. *And there's the punch line.*

Ivy's lips were pressed tight as she took in the low-ceilinged room, scanning it for Audrey and Peter. It was Friday night, and already busy. From across the room, Becky, our waitress from before, recognized us and waved. Ivy responded with an empty look, making the woman go uncertain. "There," Ivy said, nodding to an empty table in the darkest corner.

I unzipped my coat and shook my new bracelet from Kisten down. "You're an Inderland ambassador," I said. "Make an effort."

Ivy turned to me, her sharply defined eyebrows high. Jenks snickered as she forced the edges of her lips to curl upward. She had put on some makeup, seeing as we were out here for a last supper kind a thing, and she looked more predatorial than usual in her leather pants, clingy shirt, and boots. She and Jenks had ridden over in Kisten's Corvette since she would *not* get in the van with me, and she smoothed a hand over her short hair to make sure every strand was in place. Drops of gold glittered from her lobes, and I wondered why she was wearing them.

It was obvious she wasn't happy about Nick driving the truck into me, but her logic told her my emotionally charged modifications wouldn't only make it more believable, but logistically easier. Relying on Nick had us both worried, but sometimes intuition had to take a backseat. That was when I usually got in trouble.

"They aren't here yet," she said, showing how worried she was by stating the obvious.

Jenks adjusted the collar of his jacket to hide his tension with a smooth casualness. "We're early," he said. Unlike Ivy, he was handling the stress well. He smiled at the women turning to look at him, and there were quite a few jostling their tablemates' elbows and pointing him out. Running my eyes over Jenks, I could see why.

He was still an eyeful at six-foot-four, especially now that he was acting his size. He had on his aviator jacket, and with his sunglasses and one of the Were's caps turned inside out, he looked good—damn good in an individualistic, innocent sort of way.

"Ah, why don't we go sit?" I suggested, becoming uncomfortable at the giggles. *Whoo-hoo! The Inderland nymphos are here! Who brought the pistachio pudding?*

We pushed into motion, and Ivy snagged Nick's elbow. "Get some water for Rachel and an orange juice for me," she said, her white fingers gripping him tighter than was polite or necessary. "Just orange juice. I don't want anything in it. Understand?"

Nick jerked out of her hold. He never would have managed it if she hadn't let him. Frowning, he shook his cloth coat out and went to the bar. He knew he was being gotten rid of.

Nick fit in well here, and it wasn't just the human/Inderland thing. The bar was replete with skinny women in skimpy outfits, chunky women in skimpy outfits, women who never let their glass hit the table and looked old before they should in skimpy outfits, and men in fleece shirts and jeans who looked desperate. Facial hair optional. *Oh yeah, this was a great place to eat before I bit the big one.*

Maybe I was a little depressed.

A woman in a red dress cut too low for her hips waved to Jenks. She was standing by the karaoke machine, and I rolled my eyes when it started playing "American Woman." Jenks grinned, heading off in that direction until Ivy dragged him backward to the table.

The woman at the machine pouted. Ivy fixed a look on her, whereupon the woman went ashen. Her girlfriend got scared and pulled her to the bar as if Ivy was going to drain the both of them. Irritated at their ignorance, I hiked my bag higher and plodded after Ivy and Jenks.

My fingers were starting to sweat, but I couldn't let go of my shoulder bag. Inside it was the defunct focus and the wolf statue. The real focus was sandwiched between Jenks's silk boxers at the motel, though only Jenks and I knew it. I'd have told Ivy, but leaving it unattended didn't fit in with her plan, and I wasn't up to arguing with her. Nick wanted the focus. I had to believe he'd steal anything I was protecting. *God, please prove me wrong?*

In my bag with the two fakes was half of my inertia-dampening curse. Nick had the other half and would be putting it on the grille of the Mack truck. When they got close, they would take effect and muffle my motions. Nick had his own inertia-dampening curse along with a normal disguise charm and the two illegal charms to make him into Peter's doppelganger and vice versa. I wouldn't dare use them in Cincinnati, where bouncers wore spell-check amulets as a matter of course, but I could get away with it here. Small-town life clearly had advantages, but having to educate the locals would get tedious.

Ivy was the first to the table, predictably taking the chair with her back to the wall. Jenks took the one next to her, and I reluctantly sat with my back to the room, scooting my chair in with a thump that was unheard over the music. Depressed, I gazed at the wall behind Ivy. *Swell. I was going to have to look at a stuffed mink nailed to the wall all night.*

The hair on the back of my neck prickled, and I turned when Ivy's eyes jerked to the door. Our Were escort had arrived, looking more out of place than we did. I wondered how long Walter would be able to hold all three packs together once the "focus" was destroyed. Seconds, maybe? Brett was with them, bruised and moving slow. Walter must have farmed him out to the street pack as punishment. Clearly he was at the bottom of their social ladder and taking a lot of abuse. *Not my fault,* I thought. At least he was alive.

They settled at the bar, and I gave Brett a sarcastic "kiss-kiss" bunny ear gesture before I turned to sit properly. Watching the humans around them stiffen and mutter, I was glad my little party of freethinking sexual gamers had already been accepted.

Jenks's casual tracking of someone behind me gave me warning, and I leaned away when Becky bustled forward. She stood a step farther back than usual, but after Ivy's stellar welcome, I didn't blame her. It was noisy, and I wished they'd turn the music down. I couldn't hear a thing over the electronic pop music. Must have been retros night at the old Squirrel's End.

"Welcome back," she said, looking sincere though nervous.

"What can I get you? Twenty-five bucks gets you a wristband and all the beer on tap you can drink."

Damn. Either it was really good beer or the locals could slam it.

Ivy wasn't listening and Jenks was making eyes at one of the women playing pool. She looked like Matalina with the cue in her hand and her little filmy skirt that barely covered her butt when she leaned over to take a shot. Disgusted, I tapped his shin. *What was it with men?*

Jenks jumped, and I smiled sweetly at him. "Could we have a plate of fries?" I asked, thinking that to ask them to put chili on it would get us thrown out.

"You betcha. Anything else?"

Eyeing her over his sunglasses, Jenks became sex incarnate. "What's on the desert menu, Becky? I need something . . . sweet."

Ivy raised one eyebrow and slowly turned her attention to him. We exchanged looks as the matronly woman grew flustered, not at what he said, but at how he'd said it.

"Peach cobbler?" Becky encouraged. "Made it yesterday, so the top is still crunchy."

Jenks carefully slid an arm behind Ivy. Without a show of emotion, she grabbed his wrist and set it on the table. "Put some ice cream and caramel on that, and you've got a deal," he offered, and Ivy gave him an irritated look. "What?" he said with a shit-eating grin. "I'm going to need all the sugar I can get to keep up with you two ladies tonight."

Becky's plucked eyebrows rose higher. "Anything else?"

"How about one of those drinks with the cherries on little swords?" Jenks asked. "I like those swords. Can you put a cherry on a sword for each of us?" His smile grew seductive, and he bent toward Becky, hiding his wrist. I think Ivy had bruised it. "I like to share," he said. "And if these two aren't happy when the sun comes up, I'm going to be a dead man."

The woman's eyes darted between Ivy and me. Ivy's lip quirked once, then steeled her features to a severe emptiness. Playing up to them, I cracked my knuckles in warning.

"Ooooh, hit me baby," Jenks said, moving suggestively where he sat.

"That's my job, sweetie," Ivy purred, pulling him close and tucking her head into the hollow between his shoulder and ear. Her hand was a stiff claw upon his pristine neck, and I saw a flicker of concern in Jenks before he realized she was playing and was nowhere close to losing it. "I'm the bad vamp this time," she purred. "She's the good witch."

Ivy drew her hand back to give him a tart slap on the face, but Jenks was faster, catching her wrist. Eyes sultry, he kissed her fingertips.

"Mmmm," Ivy said, her dark eyelashes fluttering against her pale cheeks and her lips parting. "You know what I like, pixy dust."

Becky's face reddened. "Just the cobbler?" she stammered. "And the drink?"

Ivy nodded, her free hand wrapping around Jenks's and her tongue coming out to lick his fingertips. Jenks froze, truly surprised. The woman took a breath and walked away, her steps unheard over the noise. Great. Now I probably wouldn't get my fries.

Jenks reclaimed his hand, a faint flush on his face. "Four spoons!" he shouted after her.

My breath escaped me in a hiss. "You two are awful!" I said, frowning at Ivy as she shifted away from Jenks, a satisfied-cat smile on her face.

"Maybe," Ivy agreed, "but the Weres were watching us, not Audrey and Peter."

I stiffened, seeing Ivy mentally tick item number two off her list. We had moved that much closer to the end of this, and the first of the butterflies rose in me.

"Jenks tastes like oak leaves smell," Ivy said, ignoring his fluster as he tapped the table in rhythm with the karaoke machine.

Jenks squirmed, looking all of eighteen. "Don't tell Matalina about that, okay?"

Ivy said nothing, and I forced myself to the back of my chair. What was keeping Nick? Maybe he'd seen the nice display of low-class Inderlander at our table and decided to stay at the bar. Or perhaps he didn't want to cross the room and draw the Weres' attention to himself. Regardless, I could use that water.

Slowly Ivy's tension started to filter back, unusual for her. For all my nervousness, Jenks and I were handling this better than she was, and I could understand why. Every run was personal to me. Ivy, though, wasn't used to having the outcome of a run mean this much to her. She didn't have the patterns of behavior to cope, and it showed around her eyes.

"It'll be okay," I said, stifling the urge to reach across the table and pat her hand. The memory of her fingers gripping my waist, the rush of her teeth in me, lifted through my thoughts, and I stifled a shiver of adrenaline.

"What?" Ivy said belligerently, her eyes flashing black.

"It'll work," I said, putting my hand under the table so I wouldn't touch my stitches.

She frowned, the rim of brown growing about her eyes. "A Mack truck driven by your ex-boyfriend is going to run over you, and you say everything is going to be okay?"

Well, when she put it like that . . .

Jenks snorted, shifting his chair a little farther from Ivy. "Crap for brains is back."

I turned in my seat, almost glad to see Nick. He had a glass of water with a slice of lemon and two drinks of differing shades of orange. One had a carrot stick in it, and he put the other before Ivy as he eased into the chair beside me. I resettled my bag on my lap and tried to make it look like I wasn't concerned about it.

Ivy curved her fingers about her drink. "That had better not have alcohol in it," she said, looking at Nick's drink. Jenks reached to take it, and Nick jerked it away, all but spilling it.

"You aren't drinking anything if you're aiming a truck at Rachel," the large pixy said.

Bothered, I grabbed the glass and brought it to my nose. Before Nick could protest, I took a sip, almost spitting it out. "What in hell is that?" I exclaimed, running my tongue around the inside of my mouth. It was mealy, but sweet.

"It's a Virgin Bloody Rabbit." Sullen, Nick pulled it closer. "There's no alcohol in it."

Bloody Rabbit? It was a Virgin Bloody Mary made with carrot juice. "These are better made from tomato juice," I said, and Nick blanched.

Jenks tapped his fingers on the table, smiling when Becky stopped at our table and set down a plate of ice cream and pastry along with his four-cherry drink and the requested number of spoons. No fries. Big surprise. "Thanks, Becky," Jenks called after her over the music, and her neck went red.

Ivy took one of the spoons and delicately scooped a dollop of ice cream, placing it succinctly into her mouth. She pushed it away as if done, saying, "Peter is in the bathroom."

My heart gave a thump. *Check.*

Nick took a shaky breath. I wouldn't look at him, pretending interest in plucking the cherry with the longest stem out of Jenks's drink. Nick stood, and Ivy reached across the table to grab his wrist. He froze, and my eyes went from his still swollen masculine fingers to Ivy's face. Her eyes were black, a severe anger shining from behind them.

"If you don't show up on that bridge," she said, lips hardly moving. "I swear I'll find you. And if you hurt her, I'll make you a shadow, begging me to bleed you every night for the rest of your pathetic life." Looking like a wraith, she inhaled, taking away the warmth of the room. "Believe it."

I sent my eyes up the faded flannel of his shirt to find him ashen and afraid. For the first time, he was afraid. I was too. Hell, even Jenks had drawn away from her.

He jerked from her. Clearly shaken, he stepped out of her easy reach. "Rachel—"

"Good-bye, Nick," I said flatly, feeling my blood pressure rise. I still didn't understand how he could think that selling Al information about me, even harmless information, wasn't a betrayal of everything we had shared.

I didn't watch him leave. Eyes lowered, I took a sword-pierced cherry. The sweet mush was bland in my mouth. Swallowing, I set the red plastic sword beside Jenks for him to take home to his kids. "I'm tired of this," I whispered, but I don't think anyone heard me.

Jenks took a scoop of the cobbler, watching me with his intent green eyes. "You going to be okay?" he asked around his full mouth.

Picking up a spoon, I held the plate so I could wrangle an even bigger bite of ice cream. "Just dandy." *Why was I eating? I wasn't hungry.*

The music finally died, and in the renewed sound of chatter, Ivy held a napkin to her mouth and muttered, "I don't like this. I don't like it at all. I don't like Nick. I don't trust Nick. And if he doesn't show up with that truck to do his part, I'm going to kill him."

"I'll help," Jenks offered, carefully cutting the remaining ice cream in two and claiming the largest half.

"Okay, I made a mistake in trusting him. Can we move on to something else?" I said, scraping the lion's share of caramel to my side of the plate. *God help me, but I had been stupid. Stay with your own kind, Rachel. Not that your track record there is much better.* "But I do trust his greed," I added, and Jenks's eyebrows rose.

Shifting my shoulder, I touched my bag on my lap. "He wants the statue. He's going to show, if only to try and steal it back after all is said and done."

Ivy crossed her arms in front of her and seethed.

Jenks cocked his head in thought and ate another bite of cobbler. "You want me to have Jax shadow him?" he asked, and I shook my head.

"It might be too cold," I said. "He can sit this one out."

"He's doing well with low-temp excursions," Jenks said around his full mouth, then swallowed. "I'm proud of him." A satisfied smile hovered in his eyes. "He can read now," he added softly. "He's been working hard at it. He's serious about taking after his old man."

My smile faltered at the reasons for the lessons. Jenks didn't have many more battles left to fight. Ivy steadied herself, visibly forcing herself to be cheerful.

"That's great," she said, but I could hear her stress. "What grade level is he at?"

Jenks pushed his plate away. "Tink's titties, I don't know. Enough to get by."

I sent my attention to the bathroom door when Nick came out, his head down, clearly worried. I exhaled in a slow puff, leaning back into my chair. "Oh that's just swell," I said sourly. "Something's wrong with the charms."

Triangular face worried, Jenks followed my gaze, saying nothing. Ivy didn't look at all, and waited for it as Nick sat down before his Virgin Bloody Rabbit and took a gulp.

"My shoes are too tight," he whispered, fingers shaking.

Mouth open, I stared. It hadn't been Nick's voice. "Peter?" I breathed, shocked. My eyes jerked from him to Ivy and Jenks. "My God. Can I cook, or can I cook!"

Ivy's breath slipped from her in a slow sound. *Check* I thought, seeing her mentally cross off the next item on her list.

Grinning, Jenks started to eat again, this time working on my half of the ice cream.

I tried not to look at Peter, but it was hard not to. The vampire sat beside me, his arms resting on the table as if tired, the barest tremble in his fingers, which were a shade shorter than Nick's, and thin, not swollen. The two men had exchanged clothes along with identities, and it was eerie how complete the change was. Only in the eyes could I see a clear difference. Peter had a haze from the painkiller he had taken so he could walk upright. Just as well I'd be driving.

"No wonder those things are illegal," Ivy said, hiding her words behind her glass of juice.

My worry deepened when Jenks added, "His aura is the same."

"Shit," I whispered, my stomach knotting. "I forgot about that."

Jenks finished the ice cream and pushed the plate away with a little sigh. "I wouldn't worry about it," he said. "Weres can't use the ever-after. They can't see auras."

Embarrassed, I hunched over my drink. "You can. And you can't use the ever-after."

He grinned. "That's because pixies *are* ever-after. We're magic, baby. Just ask Matalina."

Ivy snickered. She took a cherry, and Jenks put her sword with mine when she casually handed it to him.

"You know," I said, "you can buy a box of those for a buck fifty in any grocery store."

Jenks shrugged. "Where's the fun in that?"

Watching the banter, Peter smiled, making my heart ache when I remembered Nick looking at me like that. "I wish I had the chance to know you before all this," he said softly. "You fit well together. Like a vampire camarilla, but without the jealousy and politics. A real family."

My good mood died. Jenks played with his fork to get it to balance on its tines, and Ivy became very interested in the Weres at the bar.

Peter blinked rapidly, a nervous reaction I'd never seen in Nick. "I'm sorry," he said. "Did I say something—"

Ivy interrupted him. "Peter, we've got about an hour until Nick gets into place with that bridge traffic. Do you want something to eat?"

I gathered myself to look for Becky, yelping when Jenks kicked me under the table. I glared at him until he said, "You don't like Nick. Nick can get his own food."

Feeling stupid, I slumped in my chair. "Right." So I tried not to fidget as Peter took the next five minutes to get Becky's attention. From the corner of my sight I watched Nick leave the bathroom, looking like the ailing vampire who was sitting beside me, trying to attract anyone in an apron. Hell, Nick even walked like Peter, slow and pained. It was creepy. He was good at this.

Professional thief, I reminded myself as I gripped my bag to assure myself it was still in my possession. How I could have been so blind? But I knew my ignorance had been born out of my need for that damned acceptance I hungered after almost as badly as Ivy lusted after blood. We weren't as unalike as it seemed when you got right down to it.

The jitters started when Nick passed out of my sight. I turned my attention to Ivy, reading his progress across the bar by where her eyes went. "He's good," Ivy said, sipping her juice. "Audrey didn't recognize him until he opened his mouth and said hi."

"Did the Weres smell him?" I asked, and she shook her head.

Beside me, Peter gritted his teeth, and I was glad he'd had the opportunity to say good-bye to Audrey properly. He was a good person. It wasn't fair. Maybe he could bring the memory of suffering and compassion into his undead existence, but I doubted it. They never did.

Ivy tapped her fingers on the table, and Jenks heaved a sigh. "They're gone," Ivy said.

I put the flat of my arm on the table, forcing my foot to not jiggle. All that was left was waiting for Nick's phone call that he was in place.

Check.

Thirty-three

So this is what it feels like to be a murderer, I thought, taking a tighter grip of the wheel of Nick's truck, squinting from the low sun. I was nervous, sweaty, shaky, and I wanted to throw up. *Oh yeah. I can see why people get off on this.*

Beside me in Nick's jeans and cloth coat, Peter watched the passing view as we drove to the bridge, half of Nick's inertia-dampening curse fixed to the bumper. Peter's left hand cradled the defunct statue with DeLavine's blood smear on it. His right hand, looking slightly smaller than Nick's, was holding the handle of the door. I was pretty sure it was nerves since he didn't know the door had a tendency to fly open when you went over a bump.

Nick's truck was old. It rattled when it shook. The shocks were bad but the brakes were excellent. And with the NOS, it could be startlingly fast. Just what every successful thief needs.

Silent, we endured the stop-and-go traffic to get onto the bridge, my attention on Ivy and Jenks behind us as much as on the cars ahead of me jockeying to get on the bridge. It had been Ivy's idea to do this on the bridge. The stiff wind would hamper the Weres' sense of smell, and the bridge itself would prevent a helicopter ambulance and slow things down. But most of all, we needed a stretch of several miles without a shoulder to minimize Were interference after the crash. The five-mile bridge gave us that along with a nice margin to actually run into each other. The goal was the bridge apex, but a mile either way would work.

My eyes flicked to the rearview mirror, but I didn't feel any better seeing Ivy and Jenks in Kisten's Corvette running as a buffer between us and the Weres from the bar. "Put your seat belt on," I said. I thought it was stupid, like dragging the saddle behind you when you went looking for your horse fleeing the burning barn, but I didn't want to get pulled over for failure to wear a belt and have it all come crashing down when the cop realized Nick's newly flash-painted truck was the same one that had fled the scene of a crash yesterday.

The click was loud when Peter fastened his belt. We were going to be run over by a Mack truck. I didn't think it would make a difference if he had on his seat belt or not.

Oh God. What was I doing?

The traffic light finally turned green, and I pulled onto the bridge, headed for St. Ignace on the other side of the straits. I gripped the wheel tighter, stomach knotting. The bridge was a mess. The two northbound lanes were closed off, making traffic two-way on the southbound. Midway down the span there were big machines and powerful lights to turn the coming night to day as the workers tried to meet their pretourist-season deadline. They had missed it. Red cones separated the two lanes, allowing traffic to easily switch to the other side when needed. The bridge was an incredible five miles long, and every foot of it had needed repair.

Peter exhaled as we accelerated to a steady forty miles an hour, the opposing traffic doing the same an unnerving three feet away. Past the vacant northbound lane and thick girders, I could see the islands, gray and smudged from the distance. We were really high up, and I felt a moment of quickly stifled fear. Despite the stories, witches couldn't fly. 'Least not without a staff of charmed redwood that cost more than the Concord.

"Peter?" I said, not liking the silence.

"I'm fine," he said, his grip tensing on the statue. His voice was cross, sounding nothing like Nick. I couldn't help my awkward smile of understanding, remembering Ivy bothering me with the same question. My stomach gave a lurch.

"I wasn't going to ask how you were doing," I said, fiddling with the two charms about my neck. One was for pain that wouldn't cover the hurt caused by being hit, the other was to keep my head from meeting the dash. Peter had refused both.

My eyes lifted to the rearview mirror to see that Ivy and Jenks were still behind us. "Do you want me to turn the lights on?" I asked. It was our agreed upon signal to abort the plan. I wanted him to say yes. I didn't want to do this. The statue didn't matter right now. Peter did. We could find another way.

"No."

The sun was setting past him, and I squinted at him. "Peter . . ."

"I've heard it all," he said, his voice rough as he kept his stiff position. "Please don't. It comes down to one thing. I'm dying. I've been doing it for a long time, and it hurts. I stopped living three years ago when the medicine and charms quit working and the pain took everything away. There's nothing left of me *but* hurting. I fought for two years with the thought that I was a coward for wanting to end the pain, but there is nothing left."

I snuck a glance at him, shocking myself when I saw Nick sitting there, his jaw clenched and his brown eyes hard. It sounded like it was a story he had told too many times. As I watched, his shoulders slumped and he let go of the door. "This lingering isn't fair to Audrey," he said. "She deserves someone strong, able to stand beside her and meet her bite for bite in the passion she's aching to show me."

I couldn't let that go without saying something. "And becoming an undead is fair to her?" I said, making his jaw clench again. "Peter, I've seen the undead. That won't be you!"

"I know!" he exclaimed, then softer, "I know, but it's all I've got left to give her."

The whirl of air under the tires rose above the sound of the engine as we went over the first of the grates designed to lighten the bridge's load.

"She knows it won't be me," Peter said, his voice calm. He seemed to want to talk, and I would listen. I owed him that.

He met my gaze and smiled a scared little-boy smile. "She promised me she'll be happy. I used to be able to dance with such passion that it could drive her wild. I want to dance again with her. I will remember her. I will remember the love."

"But you won't feel it," I whispered.

"She'll feel love for the both of us," Peter said firmly, his eyes on the passing bridgework. "And in time, I'll be able to fake it for her."

This was not happening. "Peter—" I reached forward to turn on the lights, and he stopped me with a shaking hand on my wrist.

"Don't," he said. "I'm already dead. You're only helping me move forward."

I could not believe this. I didn't *want* to believe it. "Peter, there's so much you haven't done. That you might do. There are new medicines every day. I know someone who can help you." *Trent could help him,* I thought, then cursed myself. *What in hell was I thinking?*

"I've had all the medicines," Peter said softly. "Legal and otherwise. I've heard the lies, I've believed the promises, but there's nothing left to believe in but death. I'm moved around like a table lamp, Rachel." His voice faltered. "You don't understand because you aren't done living yet. But I'm done, and when you're done . . . you just know."

The car ahead of me flashed its brake lights and I took my foot off the accelerator. "But a lamp can light a room," I protested, my will weakening.

"Not when the bulb is broken." His elbow was on the windowsill and his head was in his cupped hand. The setting sun became flashes on him as the girders holding the bridge arched up. "Maybe by dying I can be fixed," he said over the rumble of a passing truck. "Maybe I can do some good when I'm dead. I'm not good for anything alive."

I swallowed hard. He wouldn't do anything after he died, unless it met his needs.

"It's going to be okay," Peter said. "I'm not scared of death. I'm scared of dying. Not dying, but how I'm going to die." He laughed, but it was tinged with bitterness. "DeLavine told me that being born and dying are the only two things we do perfectly. There's a hundred percent success rate. I can't do it wrong."

"That sounds funny coming from a dead man," I said, my breath catching when a big truck went past, shaking the grate we were on. *This was wrong. This was so wrong.*

Peter pulled his elbow from the window and looked at me. "He said how I feel when I die is the one thing I have control over. I can be afraid, or I can go boldly. I want to do it bravely—even if it hurts. I'm tired of hurting, but I can take a little more."

I was starting to shake, though the air from the setting sun coming in was warm and my window was down. His soul would be gone forever. The spark of creativity and compassion—gone.

"Can . . . can I ask you something?" I ventured. The oncoming traffic had grown thin, and I prayed that they hadn't shut down the southbound lane for some reason. It was probably just Nick driving slow so we would meet somewhere in the middle as planned.

"What?"

His voice was tired and weary, and the sound of lost hope in it knotted my stomach tighter. "When Ivy bit me," I said, darting a glance at him, "some of my aura went to her. She was taking my aura along with my blood. Not my soul, just my aura. The virus needs blood to stay active, but is it more than that?"

His expression was unreadable, and I rushed forward with the rest of it while I still had time. "Maybe the mind needs an aura to protect it," I said. "Maybe the still-living mind needs the illusion of a soul about it, or it will try to get the body to kill itself so that the soul, the mind, and the body will be back in balance."

Peter looked at me from Nick's face, and I saw him for what he was: a frightened man who was stepping into a new world with no safety net, both extremely powerful and tragically fragile, reliant upon someone else to keep his mind and body together after his soul was gone.

He didn't say anything, telling me I was right. My breath quickened and I licked my lips. Vampires take auras as their own to fool their mind that a soul still bathed it. It would explain why Ivy's father risked his own death to provide her mother with his blood and his alone. He bathed her mind in his aura, his soul, in the hopes that she would remember what love was. And perhaps, in the instant of the act, she did.

I finally understood. Exhilarated, I stared at the road ahead, not seeing it. My heart was pounding and I felt light-headed.

"That's why Audrey insists on being my scion," he said softly, "even though it's going to be very hard on her."

I wanted to stop. I wanted to stop right there in the middle of the freaking bridge and figure this out. Peter looked miserable, and I wondered how long he had agonized over remaining as he was and causing her pain, or becoming an undead and causing her a pain of another kind. "Does Ivy know?" I asked. "About the auras?"

He nodded, his eyes lighting briefly upon my stitches. "Of course."

"Peter, this is . . . is—" I said, bewildered. "Why are you hiding this from everyone?"

He ran a hand over his face, the angry gesture so reminiscent of Nick that it shocked me. "Would you have let Ivy take your blood if you knew she was taking your aura, the light from your soul?" he asked suddenly, his eyes fixing on mine vehemently.

I glanced from the road, blurting, "Yes. Yes, I would have. Peter, it's beautiful. It brings something right to it."

His expression went from anger to surprise, and he said, "Ivy is a very lucky woman."

Feeling my chest clench, I blinked rapidly. I wouldn't cry. I was frustrated and confused. I was going to kill Peter in less than three miles. I was on a train I couldn't stop. I didn't need to cry, I needed to understand.

"Not everyone sees it like that," he said, the shadows of the passing girders falling on him. "You're truly odd, Rachel Morgan. I don't understand you at all. I wish I had time to. Maybe after I'm dead. I'll take you dancing and we can talk. I promise I won't bite you."

I can't do this. "I'm turning the lights on." Jaw clenched, I leaned to reach the knob. He wasn't done yet. There was more for him to learn. More he could tell me before he dropped his thread of consciousness forever.

Peter didn't move as I pulled the knob. I leaned into the seat, my face going cold when the dash remained dark. I pushed the knob in and pulled it back out. "They aren't working," I said as a car passed us. I pushed it in and tried again. "Why aren't they working, damn it!"

"I asked Jenks to disengage them."

"Son of a bitch!" I shouted, hitting the dash and hurting my hand through the pain amulet. "That damn son of a bitch!" Tears started leaking out, and I twisted in the seat, desperate to stop this.

Peter took my shoulder, pinching me. "Rachel!" he exclaimed, his guilt-ridden expression looking at me from Nick's face tearing at me. "Please," he begged. "I wanted to end it this way because it would help someone. I'm hoping that because I'm helping you, God will take me even without my soul. Please—don't stop."

I was crying now. I couldn't help it. I kept my foot on the accelerator, maintaining that same fifteen feet between me and the next car. He wanted to die, and I was going to help him whether I agreed with it or not. "It doesn't work that way, Peter," I said, my voice high. "They did a study on it. Without the mind to chaperone it, the soul has nothing to hold it together and it falls apart. Peter, there will be nothing left. It will be as if you never existed—"

He looked down the road. His face paled in the amber glow. "Oh God. There he is."

I took a breath, holding it. "Peter," I said, desperate. I couldn't turn back. I couldn't slow down. I had to do this. The shadows from the girders seemed to flash faster. "Peter!"

"I'm scared."

I looked over the cars to the white truck heading for us. I could see Nick, Peter's doppelganger disguise gone and the legal one in place. Hand fumbling, I found Peter's. It was damp with sweat, and he clutched it with the strength of a frightened child. "I'll be here," I said, breathless and unable to look from the looming truck. *What was I doing?*

"Please don't let me burn when the tanks explode? Please, Rachel?"

My head hurt. I couldn't breathe. "I won't let you burn," I said, tears making my face cold. "I'll stay with you, Peter. I promise. I'll hold your hand. I'll stay until you go, I'll be there when you leave so you won't be forgotten." I was babbling. I didn't care. "I won't forget you, Peter. I'll remember you."

"Tell Audrey that I love her, even if I don't remember why."

The last car between us was gone. I took a breath and held it. My eyes were fixed on the truck's tires. They shifted. "Peter!"

It happened fast.

The truck veered across the temporary line. My feet slammed into the breaks, self-preservation taking control. I stiffened my arm, clenching the wheel and Peter's hand both.

Nick's truck swerved. It loomed before us, the flat panel of the side taking up the entire world. He was trying to get entirely across the lane and miss me. I spun the wheel, teeth gritted and terrified. He was trying to miss me. He was trying to hit the passenger side only.

The truck smashed into us like a wrecking ball. My head jerked forward, and I gasped before the inertia-dampening curse took hold. I couldn't breathe as the air bag hit my face like a wet pillow, hurting. Relief filled me, then guilt that I was safe while Peter. *Oh God, Peter . . .*

Heart pounding, I felt as if I was wrapped in muzzy cotton. I couldn't move. I couldn't see. But I could hear. The sound of squealing tires was swallowed by the terrifying shriek of twisting metal. I managed a breath, a ragged gasp in my throat. My stomach lurched, and the world spun as the momentum swung us around.

Pushing at the oil-scented plastic, I forced it away. We were still spinning, and terror shocked through me as the Mack truck plowed into the temporary guardrail and into the empty northbound lanes. Our vehicle shook as we hit something and came to a spine-wrenching halt.

I pushed the bag down, fighting it, shaking, blinking in the sound of nothing. It was smeared with red, and I looked at my hands. They were red. I was bleeding. Blood slicked them where my nails had cut through my palms. *Yes,* I thought numbly, seeing the gray sky and dark water. *That's what the hands of a murderer should look like.*

Heat from the engine washed over me, pulled from the breeze on the bridge. Safety glass covered the seat and me. Blinking, I peered out the shattered front window. Peter's side of the truck was smashed into a pylon. There would be no getting him out that way. We had been knocked clean into the empty northbound lane. I could see the islands past Peter and the guardrail they were repairing. Something . . . something had ripped the hood off Nick's blue truck. I could see the engine, steaming and twisted. Shit, it was almost in the front seat with me along with the front window.

A man was shouting. I could hear people and car doors shutting. I turned to Peter. *Oh, hell.*

I tried to move, shocked when my foot caught, panicking until I decided it wasn't moving because it was stuck, not because it was broken. It was wedged between the console and the front of the seat. My jeans were turning a wet black from the calf down. I think I had a cut somewhere. My eyes traveled numbly down my leg. It was my calf. I think I'd cut my calf.

"Lady!" a man said as he rushed up to my window, gripping the empty frame with a thick hand, a wedding ring on his finger. "Lady, are you okay?"

Peachy, I thought, blinking at him. I tried to say something but my mouth wasn't working. An ugly sound came out of me, chilling.

"Don't move. I called the ambulance. I don't think you're supposed to move." His eyes went to Peter beside me, and he turned away. I heard the sound of retching.

"Peter," I whispered, my chest hurting. I couldn't breathe deeply, so keeping my breaths shallow, I struggled with my seat belt. It came undone, and while people shouted and gathered like ants on a caterpillar, I pulled my foot free. Nothing hurt yet. I was sure that would change.

"Peter," I said again, touching his face. His eyes were closed but he was breathing. Blood seeped from a ragged cut over his eye. I undid his seat belt, and his eyelids fluttered.

"Rachel?" he said, his face scrunching up in hurt. "Am I dead yet?"

"No, sweetheart," I said, touching his face. Sometimes the transition from living to dead goes in a heartbeat, but not with this much damage, and not with the sun still up. He was going to take a long nap to wake hungry and whole. I managed a smile for him, taking my pain amulet off and draping it over him. My chest hurt, but I didn't feel anything, numb inside and out.

Peter looked so white, his blood pooling in his lap. "Listen," I said, adjusting his coat with my red fingers so I couldn't see the wreckage of his chest. "Your legs look okay, and your arms. You have a cut above your eye. I think your chest is crushed. In about a week you can take me dancing."

"Out," he whispered. "Get out and blow up the truck. Damn it, I can't even die right. I didn't want to burn." He started crying, the tears making a clear track down his bloodied face. "I didn't want to have to burn. . . ."

I didn't think he was going to survive this even if the ambulance got to him in time. "I'm not going to burn you. I promise." *I'm going to be sick. That's all there is to it.*

"I'm scared," he whimpered, his breath gurgling from his lungs filling with blood. I prayed he wouldn't start coughing.

Broken chips of safety glass sliding, I pulled myself closer, gently holding his shattered body to me. "The sun is shining," I said, eyes clenching shut as memories of my dad flooded back. "Just like you wanted. Can you feel it? It won't be long. I'll be here."

"Thank you," he said, the words terrifyingly liquid. "Thank you for trying to turn the lights on. That makes me feel as if I was worth saving."

My throat closed. "You are worth saving," I said, tears spilling over as I rocked him gently. He tried to breathe, the sound ugly. It was pain given a voice, and it struck through me. His body shuddered, and I held him closer though I was sure it hurt him. Tears fell, hot as they landed on my arm. There was noise all around us, but no one could touch us. We were forever set apart.

His body suddenly realized it was dying, and with an adrenaline-induced strength, it struggled to remain alive. Clutching his head to my chest, I held him firmly against the massive tremor I knew was coming. I sobbed when it shook him as if he were trying to dislodge his body from his soul. *I hated this. I hated it. I had lived it before. Why did I have to live it again?*

Peter stopped moving and went still.

Rocking him now for me, not him, I shook with sobs that hurt my ribs. *Please, please let this have been the right thing to do.*

But it didn't feel right.

Thirty-four

"Rachel!" Jenks cried, and I realized he was with me. His hands were warm and clean, not sticky like mine—and after struggling with the door to the truck, he reached inside the window to unlatch it. I let my grip on Peter loosen as it opened. My leg, twisted behind me, felt kind of cold, and I looked at, going woozy. There was a dark, wet stain on my jeans, and my brand-new running shoe now had a red stripe. *Maybe my leg was hurt more than I thought?*

"Get Peter out," I whispered. "Ow. Ow, hey!" I exclaimed when Jenks dragged me across the seat and away from Peter. His arms went around me in a cradle, and with me getting Peter's blood all over him, he carried me to a clear space on the cold pavement.

"Up," I whispered, cold and light-headed. "Don't lay me down. Don't hit the button before you get him out. You hear me, Jenks. Get him out!"

He nodded, and I asked, "Where's the truck driver?" remembering not to call him Nick.

"Some lady in a lab coat is looking at him."

Fumbling, I pulled my half of the inertia-dampening charm from around my neck. I slipped it to Jenks, and he replaced it with the remote to ignite the NOS. Palming it, I watched him nudge the amulet through the nearby road grate, destroying half the evidence that we were committing insurance fraud. *David would have kittens.*

"Wait until I get back before hitting that, will you?" he muttered, his eyes darting to my closed grip. Not waiting for an answer, he loped to the truck shouting for two men in the crowd to help him, and a woman descended upon me.

"Get off!" I exclaimed, pushing, and the narrow-faced woman in a purple lab coat fell away. *How had she gotten there so fast? The coming ambulance wasn't even a noise yet.*

"I'm Dr. Lynch," she said tightly, frowning at the blood I'd left on her lab coat. "Just what I need. You look like you're a worse PITA patient than me."

"PITA?" I asked, slapping at her when she took my shoulders and tried to lay me down.

She pulled back, frowning. "Pain in the ass," she explained. "I need to take your blood pressure and pulse supine, but after that you can sit up until you pass out, for all I care."

I tried to see around her to Jenks, but he was inside the truck with Peter. "Deal," I said.

Her eyes went to my leg, wet from the calf down. "Think you can put pressure on that?"

I nodded, starting to feel sick. This was going to hurt. Holding my breath against the wash of pain, I let her take my shoulders and ease me down. Knee bent, I clamped my hand to the part of my leg that hurt the most, making it hurt more. While she took her God-given sweet time, I listened to the sounds of panic and stared at the darkening sky framed by the bridge's cables, holding my ribs and trying not to look like they hurt lest she wanted to poke them too. I thought of my pain amulet, praying it had eased Peter when nothing else had. I deserved to hurt.

She muttered at me to hold still when I turned my head to look at the passing traffic. A black convertible was parked just inside the closed northbound lane. *Hers?*

I jerked at the ugly ripping sound and the sudden draft on my leg. "Hey!" I shouted, putting my hurt palms against the pavement and levering myself up. I held my breath as my sight grayed at the pain, then got mad when I realized she had cut my jeans up the seam to my knee. "Damn it, those were fifty bucks!" I exclaimed, and she gave me a cold look.

"I thought that would get you up," she said, moving my bloody hand back to my leg and taking my blood pressure and pulse a second time.

I could tell she was a high-blood living vampire despite her trying to hide it in the old way, and I felt safe with her. Her blood lust would be carefully in check while she worked on me. That's the way living vamps were. Children and the injured were sacred.

Still mad about my jeans, I took a shallow breath, staring at the chaos lit by the orangey yellow glare of the setting sun. "Let's see it," she said, and I released my hold on my leg.

Worried, I peered down. It didn't look bad from a bleeding-to-death standpoint—just a slight oozing and what looked like a huge bruise in the making—but it hurt like hell. Saying nothing, Dr. Lynch opened her tackle box and broke the seal on a small bottle. "Relax, it's water," she said when I stiffened as she went to pour it on me.

She had to hold my leg still with an iron grip as she poked and prodded, cleaning it while muttering about torn arterioles and them being a bitch to stop bleeding but that I'd survive. My three-year-old tetanus shot seemed to satisfy her, but my stomach was in knots when she finally decided I had been tortured enough and slipped a stretchy white pressure bandage over it.

Someone was directing traffic to keep the rubberneckers moving and the bridge open. Two cars of Weres had stopped to "help," worrying me. I wanted them to see the statue rolling around on the floor of the front seat, but having them this close was a double-edged sword.

Slowly I tucked the remote to blow the NOS under my good leg and out of sight. The wind through the straits pushed my hair out of my eyes, and as I looked at the faces pressed against the windows as they passed, I started to laugh, hurting my ribs. "I'm okay," I said when the woman gave me a sharp look. "I'm not going into shock. I'm alive."

"And it looks like you're going to stay that way," she said, taking both my hands and setting them so they hung past the shelf of my lap. "Aren't you the lucky one?"

She poured more water on my hands to get the grit off, then set them palm up on my lap to make a wet spot. Disgusted, I watched her pluck a second packet from her tackle box and rip it open. The scent of antiseptic rose, whipped away from the wind. Again I jumped and ow'ed as she brushed the grit and glass from my hands, earning another "wimp" look from her.

More people had stopped, and Nick's truck's paint job was showing where the metal had crumpled. Jenks was inside with Peter. They were trying to get him out. Weres had gathered at the outskirts, some in jeeps, some in high-end cars, and some in little street racers. I felt the remote under my leg, wanting to use it and finish this run. I wanted to go home.

Nick. "Where's the guy who hit us?" I said, scanning the faces and not seeing him.

"He's fine apart from a damaged knee," she said as she finished and I pulled my hands close to inspect the little crescent moons from my nails cutting my palms. "It might need surgery at some point, but he'll live." Her deeply brown eyes flicked to my dental-floss stitches. "Your gnomon is with him," she finished, and I blinked. *Gnomon? What in hell was that?*

"She's keeping him occupied until the I.S. gets here to take his statement," she added, and my eyes widened. The woman meant Ivy. She thought I was Ivy's scion, and gnomon was the flipside of the relationship. It made sense—a gnomon was the thingy on a sundial that casts a shadow. I was about to tell her Ivy wasn't my gnomon, then didn't. I didn't care what she thought.

"The I.S.?" I said with a sigh, starting to worry now that it looked like I was going to survive. Motions quick, she fixed a big bandage over each palm. I hadn't forgotten about the I.S., but if Nick's truck wasn't burning before they arrived, it was going to be a lot harder to get rid of that defunct statue.

Her attention followed mine to the truck, her shoulders stiffening when Jenks and two men pulled Peter's broken body out. I expected her to get angry they were moving him, surprised that she was messing with the living and not him, obviously the worse off—until she leaned close with her little penlight and flashed it in my eyes, saying, "You cried for Peter. No one ever cries for us."

I pulled out of her grip, shocked. "You know . . ."

She moved, and I panicked. With vampire quickness she was atop me, knees to either side of my thighs, pinning me against the barrier. Her one hand was behind my neck holding me unmoving, the other held that light as if it was a dagger pointed at my eye. She was inches away, her closeness going unnoticed or considered okay by way of her official-looking lab coat.

"I'm here because DeLavine told me to come. He wanted to make sure you survived."

I took a breath, then another. She was so close, I could see the soft imperfections in her cheek and neck where she had been professionally stitched. I didn't move, wishing I wasn't so damn interesting to the undead. What in hell was their problem?

"I'd tell him to leave you alone," she said, her breath lost in the wind, "because I think you'd kill him if he tried to hunt you, but it would make him interested, not simply—concerned."

"Thanks," I said, heart pounding. *God help me, I would never understand vampires.*

Slowly she lowered the penlight and got off. "Good reflexes. No head trauma. Your lungs sound clear. Don't let them cart you off to Emergency. You don't need it, and it will only jack up your insurance," she said, switching from scary-ass vampire to professional health provider in seconds. "I'm done here. You want a pain amulet?"

I shook my head, guilt for being alive cascading through me when Jenks and two men set Peter gently on the ground apart from everyone. Jenks crouched to close his eyes and the other two men backed away, frightened and respectful. The woman's face blanked. "I wasn't here, okay?" she said. "You bandaged your own damn leg. I don't want to be subpoenaed. I wasn't here."

"You got it."

And she was gone, the purple lab coat flapping about her calves as she lost herself in the crush of growing turmoil surrounding the single spot of stillness that was Peter, alone on the pavement, broken and bloody.

Feeling the adrenaline crash, I met Jenks's gaze. He sank to the pavement beside me so he could see Peter from the corner of his eye. Respect for the dead. He handed me my shoulder bag and I put it on my lap, hiding the remote to blow the NOS. "Push it," he said.

There were sirens in the distance. They weren't approaching quickly, but that would change when they reached the bridge and the closed northbound lanes. Behind Jenks was Nick's truck, a twisted chunk of metal with wheels and no hood. It was hard to believe I had survived it.

The Weres were starting to edge in, clearly wanting to swipe the statue. No one was within that golden circle of twenty feet or between the truck and the questionable safety of the temporary railing and a possible fall. Jenks leaned closer, and with him protecting my face with his body, I clenched my eyes shut and pushed the button.

Nothing happened.

I opened one eye and looked at Jenks. His expression was horrified, and I pushed the button again.

"Let me try," he said, snatching it away and pushing it himself. The little bit of plastic made a happy clickity-click sound, but there was no big ba-da-boom after it.

"Jenks!" I exclaimed barely above a whisper. "Did you *fix* this too?"

"It's not my fault!" he said, green eyes wide. "I rigged it myself. The NOS should have blown. Damn friggen moss-wipe remote. I should have had Jax do it. I can't solder with that stupid-ass iron Nick had. I must have fused the fairy fucking thing."

"Jenks!" I admonished, thinking that was the worst thing I'd ever heard him say. Starting to get one of those "Oh crap" feelings, I looked at the Weres. As soon as official people started poking around in there, that statue would be gone and my life with it when they realized it was a fake. "Can you fix it?" I asked, my stomach knotting.

"Five minutes with an iron I don't have in a private space that doesn't exist on a bridge six hundred feet above the water surrounded by two hundred good Samaritans who don't know crap. Sure. You bet. Hell, maybe it's just the battery."

This wasn't good. I sat and stewed while Jenks took out the battery and shocked himself on his tongue. While he swore and danced from the mild zing, I pulled my knees to my chest to get up, wincing at the dull throb in my leg. Ivy and Nick were still beside the flat panel of the Mack truck, Nick looking nothing like himself under his legal disguise charm. The wind coming up through the grating they stood on sent her hair flying. She gestured with a small movement, and I gave her a lost look. Her lips pressed together and she rounded on Nick.

Nick's head was down, and it stayed that way as she put her hands on her hips and shot unheard questions at him. Blood soaked one of his pant legs and he looked pale. That he was hurt would make it easier to get him to the hospital where the vampire doctor waited, ready to pronounce him dead of a complication, mix up the paperwork, and shuffle him both out the back door and out of my life forever. Peter would be moved to the vamp wing underground until his body repaired itself. Everything was perfect. But the damn truck wasn't exploding.

"What are our options?" I asked Jenks, taking the remote and dropping it into my bag.

"It might be the switch on the tanks," he said. "If Jax was here—"

"He's not."

Jenks took my elbow when I swayed. "Can you blow it with your ley line magic?"

"You mean like with me lighting candles?" Hiking up my shoulder bag, I shook my head. "Can't tap a line over water. And I don't have a familiar to connect through to a land line." My mind jumpcd to Rcx. *Maybe I ought to remedy that. This is getting old.*

"Nick might."

A shiver went through me, remembering when I channeled Trent's ability to tap a line last year to make a protection circle. I had hurt him. I didn't care if I hurt Nick right now—I just wanted to finish this run—but the question might be academic; I didn't know if Nick *had* a familiar. "Let's go ask," I said, lurching into motion.

My chest hurt, and as I gripped it with my arms, I forced a slow breath into me and tried to pull myself upright. It wasn't worth the effort to look unhurt, so I gave up, hunching over and breathing shallowly. The wind sluicing through the straits had a chill in it, and the setting sun was lost behind the clouds. It was going to get cold very quickly. Relegating Jax to cat-sitting duties at the motel had been a good idea.

Ivy heard my footsteps on the grating and turned with a frown she reserved only for me, a mix of anger and worry. She was ticked. Big surprise there.

"Rachel," Nick breathed, holding out his hands as if I would take them. I stopped, and his hands fell.

"I wouldn't touch a strange man like that," I said, reminding him that he was still under a disguise. "Especially one that just hit me."

His eyes flicked to my dental-floss stitches, and my face warmed. He saw me stiffen, then forced his face smooth. Though he looked nothing like himself, I could tell it was him. Not only was there his voice, but I could see Nick in little mannerisms that only an ex-lover might notice: the twitch of a muscle, the curve of a finger—the glint of annoyance in his eye.

"My God," he said again, softer. "That was the hardest thing I've ever done. Are you okay? Are you sure you're not hurt?"

Hardest thing he'd ever done? I thought bitterly, the entire right side of my body sticky with Peter's blood. All he had done was hit me with a truck. I had held Peter while he died, knowing it was wrong but the only thing that would be right.

"The remote doesn't work, Nick," I said shortly, watching for his tells. "You know anything about that?"

Eyes wide in an emotion I couldn't read, he looked at my bag, telling me he'd seen me put the remote in it. "What do you mean, it doesn't work? It's got to work!"

He reached for it, and I grunted when Jenks yanked me back. My sneakers fumbled for purchase on the metal mesh. In a blink Ivy was between us. The nearby people were getting nervous—thinking we were going to take justice into our own hands—and the Weres watched, evaluating whether this was a scam or a real accident. Peter's body was lying on the pavement, looking like Nick. Someone had covered him with a coat, and a part of me hunched into itself and cried.

"Don't touch me," I all but hissed, hurting but ready to slug Nick. "You did this, didn't you? You think you're going to get that empty artifact and sell it to them. You'll be in hiding, so they'll come after me when they find out it's not real. It's not going to happen. I won't let you. This is *my* life you're screwing over, not just yours."

Nick shook his head. "That's not it. You've got to believe me, Ray-ray."

Shaking from adrenaline, I turned sideways. I didn't like having my back to the truck with the empty focus in it. Ivy had been watching it—along with Nick—but there were too many Weres lurking as accident witnesses for my liking. "Have a good life, Nick," I said. "Don't include me in it." Ivy and Jenks flanked me, and we walked away. *What was I going to do?*

"I hope you're happy as Ivy's shadow," he said loudly, his voice full of a vitriolic hatred that he'd probably been denying since Ivy first asked me to be her scion.

I turned, my bandaged hand atop my neck hiding my stitches. "We aren't . . . I'm not—" *He had just blown our cover. Son of a bitch . . .*

Three official-looking cars pulled up using the unopened northbound lane, their rear-window lights flashing amber and blue: two FIB, one I.S. The truck wasn't burning yet. *Shit on crap, could it get any worse?*

Looking like himself even with the disguise, Nick slumped against the panel of the white Mack truck and held his bleeding knee. His mocking gaze flicked to the cars behind us, their doors slamming shut and loud orders being given to secure the vehicle and get the rubberneckers moving. Three officers headed for us.

"You're rat piss," Jenks said suddenly to Nick. "No, you're the guy who puts rat piss on his breakfast cereal. We save your worthless human ass, and this is how you thank her? If you come back, I'll kill you myself. You're a foul pile of fairy crap that won't grow stones."

Nick's face went ugly. "I stole a statue," he said. "She killed someone and twisted a demon curse to hide that she still has it. I'd say I'm better than a foul, demon-marked witch."

I sputtered, pulse pounding as I felt myself go light-headed. *Damn him!*

Ivy leapt at Nick. Jenks yanked her back, using her shifting momentum to swing himself into Nick. Hands made into fists, Jenks punched him solidly on his jaw.

I took a gasping breath, and the I.S. guys turned their walk into a run. Angry, but with a modicum of restraint compared to Jenks, I got in Nick's face. "You sorry-assed bastard!" I shouted, spitting hair out of my mouth. "*You* ran into *us*!"

I wanted to say more, but Nick pushed himself at me. Jenks was still holding him, and all three of us went down. Instinct kept my hands before my face, and the bandages on my palms were the only thing that saved my skin. Pain shot through my ribs and hands as I hit the grating. The cold metal pressed into my leg where my jeans were torn.

"Get off her!" Ivy snarled. She yanked Nick up and away, and suddenly I could breathe again I looked up in time to see him spin into Jenks. Like a choreographed dance, Jenks cocked his fist and this time connected right under his jaw. Nick's eyes rolled up and he crumpled.

"Damn, that felt good," the pixy said, shaking his hand as a thick I.S. officer grabbed his shoulders. "You know how long I've wanted to do that?" he said, letting the men drag him off. "Being big is good."

Shaking so hard I felt I might fall apart, I got up, bobbing my head at the FIB officer's unheard questions and obediently going where he directed me, but I lost it when a hand closed on my arm.

"Rachel, no!" Ivy shouted, and I turned my spin-and-kick into a spin-and-hair-toss. Adrenaline cleared my thoughts, and I took a painfully deep breath. The man released me, knowing I had almost landed one on him. His mustache bunched and his eyebrows were high, questioning, as he looked at me with new eyes.

"He killed him!" I shouted for the benefit of the watching Weres and starting to cry like a distraught girlfriend. "He killed him! He's dead!"

The sad reality was the tears leaking from me weren't that hard to dredge up. How could Nick say that to me even in anger? A foul, demon-marked witch. He had called me a foul demon-marked witch. My sense of betrayal rose higher, cementing my anger.

Jenks wiggled out of the grip of the two men holding him, and as they shouted and tried to catch him, he darted for my bag on the pavement. Grinning, he tucked my phone and my wallet inside before shaking everything down. I wasn't sure, but I think the remote went through the grating, and I breathed easier.

An I.S. officer grabbed him, cuffing him before shoving him back into our little group. The man shuffled through my bag before returning it to me. I thought it better to let the stone-faced guy have his way than bring up my rights.

"Thanks," I muttered to Jenks, feeling my ribs ache as I looped the strap over my shoulder. I looked at Nick's wrecked truck as we passed. The artifact was still there, thanks to an excited FIB guy in a brown suit keeping everyone back.

"My pleasure," he said, limping.

"I meant for hitting him."

"So did I."

The I.S. officer at my elbow frowned, but when he saw the covered body, he seemed to ease. Jenks had punched Nick, not done anything permanent. *Like killing him.* "Ma'am," the officer said. "I'd ask you to stay away from the other party until we get this sorted out."

Party. Yeah, this was one big joke. "Yes, sir," I said, then stiffened when he slipped one of those plastic-coated charmed-silver wraps on my wrist and tightened it with a slick motion.

Damn it all to hell. "Hey!" I protested, feeling abused as Jenks and Ivy exchanged tired looks. "I'm fine! I'm not going to hurt anyone. I can't even do ley line magic." *Not on this bridge anyway.* The officer shook his head, and I felt trapped, the weight of Kisten's bracelet caught between my skin and the restraint. "Can I sit with . . . with my boyfriend?" I managed a warble in my voice, and the beefy man put a comforting hand on my shoulder.

"Yes, ma'am," he said, his voice softening. "They're taking him to the hospital to pronounce him. You can ride with him if you want. I'm sorry. He looked like a nice guy."

Plan A for getting the wacko witch off the accident scene. Right out of the handbook. "Thank you," I said, wiping my eyes.

"You were the driver, ma'am?" he asked as we walked, and when I nodded, he added, "May I see your license?"

Aw, shit. "Yes, sir," I said, fumbling in my bag for it. In five minutes the Cincinnati branch of the I.S. would be telling him all about me. We halted at the back of a black I.S. blazer, the tailgate down to show an open kennel. *There was a dog out here?* Behind me, I heard Ivy and Jenks telling the officers with them that they were my roommates. *Oh God. Ivy's Brimstone. I probably smelled like an addict. Accident. Points. What if they took my license?*

The officer before me squinted to see my license in the fading light, smiling when he looked up. "I'll have this right back to you, Ms. Morgan. Then you can go with your boyfriend and get yourself looked at." Eyebrows high, he glanced at my bandaged hands and ripped jeans before nodding to Jenks and Ivy and trotting away to leave us with two officers.

"Thank you," I said to no one. Exhausted, I leaned against the truck. Jenks had been cuffed to the truck, and the two FIB guys moved a short distance, close enough to intervene if necessary but clearly waiting for more I.S. personnel to handle our interrogation. Holding my elbows with my scraped hands, I watched my life swirl down the crapper.

Rubberneckers passed with an infuriating slowness, faces pressed against the windows as they struggled to see in the deepening dusk. My new jeans were ripped almost to the knee. The truck refused to burn. A fourth Were pack wearing military dress uniforms had joined the three already here, all of them edging the limits of the FIB and I.S. officers keeping them back. Had I forgotten anything? Oh yeah. I had helped kill someone, and it was going to turn around and bite me on the ass. I didn't want to go to jail. Unlike Takata, I looked awful in orange.

"Damn it," Ivy said, licking a thumb and trying to rub out the new scrape on her leather pants. "These were my favorite pair."

My gaze went to the truck. The knot in my stomach grew tighter. Leaning, I reclined against the Blazer's tailgate and silently fumed as I categorized the arriving Inderlanders into their jobs, pulled in from their scattered locations.

The willowy blond witch was probably their extraction specialist, not only comforting information from distraught victims but from testosterone-laden bucks who wouldn't talk to anyone unless it might get her into bed with them. Then there was the guy too fat to do real street work but who had a mustache, so he *had* to be important. He'd be good at keeping angry people apart and would tell me he could get me a deal if I was willing to spill. The dog team was at the Mack truck since he was the one who had crossed the yellow line, but I was sure he'd get to the pickup soon, then probably make a little visit over here.

I looked for, and finally found, the officer who was slightly off and took his job too seriously to be safe. This was the guy that no one trusted and even fewer liked, usually a witch or Were, too young to be a fat man with a mustache but too gun-happy to be a data guy. He was walking around the broken pickup, hiking up his belt with his weapon and looking at the girders as if they might hold a sniper ready to take us all out. *And don't forget the I.S. detective,* I thought. I didn't see him or her, but since someone had died, one would show up soon.

FIB officers were everywhere, taking their measurements and pictures. Seeing them in control of the site kind of threw me, but remembering the intensive data the Cincinnati FIB had shared with me during a murder investigation, I probably shouldn't have been surprised.

Ivy slumped against the side of the I.S. vehicle, arms crossed and thoroughly ticked. She stared at the ambulance Nick was in as if she could kill him by her gaze alone. Me? I was more worried about how we were going to get that truck burning. I was getting the feeling it wasn't going to happen. A heavy wrecker was inching its way into place, rollers moving with a sedate laziness. Apparently they wanted to get it off the bridge before the news crews showed up.

Slipping out of his cuffs, Jenks levered himself to sit beside me on the tailgate, a pained grunt coming from him. "You okay?" I asked, though clearly he wasn't.

"Bruise," he said, eyes fixed to Nick's blue truck. With an obnoxious beeping, the wrecker backed up to it.

"Here," I said, pulling my bag around and starting to rummage. "I've got an amulet. Ivy never takes any of my amulets, and I'm not used to you being big enough to use them."

"Why aren't you using it?" he said, stretching his shoulder with a pained look.

"I have no right to," I said, my throat closing when I glanced at Peter. I was glad he wasn't trying to convince me otherwise, and I hardly felt the prick of the finger stick for the blood to invoke it. Ivy shifted, telling me she had noticed the fresh blood despite the wind, but she was the last vamp I had anything to be worried about. Usually.

"Thanks," he said as he draped it over his head in obvious relief. "I wonder if there's any way you can make tiny amulets? I'm going to miss these."

"It's worth a try," I said, thinking that unless that truck spontaneously combusted from Ivy's glare, I'd have about a week to find out. Once the Weres realized the artifact was fake, they'd be knocking on my door. Assuming I didn't land in jail. I felt as if we were three kids standing outside the principal's office. Not that I had any experience in that area. Much.

Nick's truck went atop the wrecker in a horrendous noise of whining winches and complaining hydraulic machinery. The garage guy moved slowly, his dirty blue overalls and cap pulled down low, pressing levers and buttons seemingly at random. The overzealous I.S. guy was telling him to hustle and get his vehicle out of the way before the first news van arrived.

The driver walked with a limp, almost unnoticed amid the FIB and I.S. uniforms, and I thought it rude they made the old man move faster than he comfortably could.

Someone had moved one of the massive construction lights to illuminate the area, and as the distant generators rumbled to life a quarter mile away, a soft glow swelled into a harsh glare, washing out the gray of the fading sunset. Slowly the background rumble became unnoticed. Mind whirling for an idea, I dropped the spent finger stick in my shoulder bag and sighed.

I froze, fingers brushing the familiar objects in my bag. Something was missing besides the remote. Shocked, I stared into the dark fabric bag, tilting it so the growing light would illuminate what it could. The sight of my things scattered on the grating when Nick knocked me down passed through my mind. "It's gone," I said, feeling unreal. I looked up, meeting first Jenks's and then Ivy's wondering gaze as she pulled herself away from the vehicle.

"The wolf statue is gone!" I said, trying to decide if I should laugh or curse that I had been right in not trusting Nick. "The bastard took it. He knocked me down and took it!" I had been right to leave the totem shoved between Jenks's silk underwear and his dozen toothbrushes. Damn it, I'd have been happy to have been wrong this one time.

"Piss on my daises . . ." Jenks said. "That's why he picked a fight."

Ivy's bewildered face cleared in understanding. At least she thought she understood. "Excuse me," she said, pushing herself away from the I.S. vehicle.

"Ivy, wait," I said, wishing I'd told her what I had done, though it wasn't as if I could shout that Nick had a fake. I pushed from the tailgate. Pain shot through me, reminding me I had just been hit by a truck. "Ivy!" I shouted, and an I.S. guy headed after her.

"Won't take but a moment!" she called over her shoulder. She stormed across the closed lanes, uniforms coming from all over to head her off. I moved to follow, immediately finding my elbow in the grip of one of the mustache guys. Images of court dates and jail cells kept me still as the first man to touch Ivy went down when she stiff-armed him in the jaw.

A call went up, and I watched with a sinking sensation, remembering when she and Jenks had taken out an entire floor of FIB officers. But it was I.S. runners this time. "Maybe we should have told her," I said, and Jenks smirked, rubbing his wrist where his cuffs had been.

"She needs to blow off some steam," he said, then whispered, "Holy crap. Look."

His green eyes were brilliant in the mercury light hammering down on us, and my jaw dropped when I followed his gaze to the wrecker. The brighter light made obvious what the shadows had hid before. The garage guy's hands were spotlessly clean, and the dark stain on the knee of his blue overalls was too wet to be oil.

"Nick," I breathed, not knowing how he got his hair that dirty white so fast. He was still wearing my disguise amulet, but with the overalls and cap, he was unrecognizable.

Jenks stood beside me, whispering, "What in Tink's garden of sin is he doing?"

I shook my head, seeing the Weres watching him too. *Double damn, I think they knew it was him.* "He thinks he has the focus," I said. "He's trying to get the original too."

"Leaving us holding the bag?" Jenks finished in disgust. "What a slug's ass. If he doesn't go to the hospital and die on paper, then we have a dead vamp to explain and will be brought up on insurance fraud. Rache, I'm too pretty to go to jail!"

Face cold, I turned to Jenks, my stomach in knots. "We have to stop him."

He nodded, and I cupped my hands to my mouth. "Ivy!" I shouted. "The wrecker!"

It wasn't the smartest thing to do, but it got results. Ivy took one look and realized it was Nick. Crying out, she slugged the last

I.S. agent and took off running, only to be brought down by a lucky snag by a previously felled officer. She sprawled, cuffs on her in two seconds flat.

Jenks flowed into motion, distracting the surrounding FIB officers. Thinking this was going to look great on my résumé, I sidestepped them and ran for the wrecker. People were shouting, and someone had probably pulled a weapon as I heard, "Stop, or I'll use force!"

Force my ass, I thought. If they shot me, I'd sue their bright little badges from here to the Turn. I didn't have anything stronger than a pain amulet. I'd been searched, and they knew it.

It was right about then that Nick realized I was coming for him. Clearly frightened, he jerked the door open. A cry went up when his engine revved, loud over the generators. There was a piercing whistle, and the leader of the unknown military faction waved his hand above his head as if in direction. Horns started to blow when three street racers stopped in traffic and Weres got out. Grim-faced, they closed in. They weren't happy. Neither was I.

"Stop him!" came a bark of a demand, and I picked up my pace. I was going to get to Nick first, or whoever beat me to him was going to get my foot in their gut. He had hurt and betrayed me, leaving me to clean up his mess and take his fall. Twice. Not this time.

My gaze was fixed fervently on the truck as it lurched, almost stalling, but a flash of pixy dust jerked me to a stop. "Jax?" I exclaimed, shocked.

"Ms. Morgan," the adolescent pixy said, hovering before my nose with an amulet as big as he was, his eyes bright and his wings red in excitement. "Nick wanted me to tell you he's sorry and he loves you. He really does."

"Jax!" I said, blinking as even the sparkles from his dust faded. My eyes went to the truck. The wheels were smoking as Nick tried to get the heavy vehicle moving. With a lurch, the wheels caught. My face went cold as I realized it was headed right for me. I watched him fight the huge wheel, arms stiff and fear in his eyes, struggling to turn it.

"Rachel, get out of the way!" Ivy screamed over the rumble of the engine.

I froze as the wheels turned, missing me, the tires taking the weight compressing dangerously. Jenks crashed into me, knocking me farther out of the way. Stifling a gasp, I hit the pavement for the *third* time in the last hour. The truck roared past in a frightening noise and a breeze of diesel fumes. A crack followed by a boom shook my insides, the sound rolling over my back like a wave. Jenks held my head down and a second boom followed the first.

What in hell was that? Heart pounding, I pushed Jenks off me and lifted my head. The wrecker was careening out of control, the tires blown out. Someone had shot out his tires?

I scrambled up when the wrecker with Nick's truck swerved wildly to avoid the scattering news crews. Tires squealing and gears grinding, the brakes burned as he locked them. Momentum kept the vehicle moving—careening into the temporary railing.

"Nick!" I screamed when the wrecker crashed through it like toast. With a shocking silence, it was gone.

Heart in my throat, I hobbled to the edge, too hurt to stand upright. Jenks was behind me, and he yanked me back when I reached the crumbling edge. The wind gusted up from the distant water, blowing my hair out of my eyes. I looked down, dizzy.

Hand to my stomach, I started to hyperventilate. My sight grew gray, and I pushed Jenks's hand off me. "I'm okay," I mumbled, but there wasn't anything to see. Six hundred feet makes even a wrecker small.

Nick had been in it. *God help me.*

"Easy, Rache," Jenks said, easing me back and making me sit.

"Nick," I mumbled, forcing my eyes wide as the cold pavement met my rear. I wasn't going to pass out. Damn it, I wasn't! I looked at the edge, the roadway cracked to show the metal embedded in it, threatening to give way where the truck's weight had hit it hard. Shiny shoes clustered around me, belonging to the officers peering down. At the edges of the excited crowd were the Weres. They were dressed in suits, leather, and military uniforms, but the look on their faces was the same. Disbelief and shock. It was gone.

The crackle of a radio intruded, coming from the I.S. officer swearing softly as he peered over the edge. "This is Ralph," he said, thumbing the button. "We have two trucks off the bridge and a body in the water. Smile everyone. We're going to make the evening news."

I missed what was said back, lost in the hiss of bad reception and the thundering of my heart as I tried to fit it into my head. *He had gone over the bridge. Nick had gone off the bridge.*

"Yup," the man said. "Confirm a commercial vehicle towing a pickup truck off the bridge and a body in the water. Better get the boat out here. Anybody got Marshal's number?"

He listened to the response, then clipped it to his belt. Hands on his hips, he stared down. Soft swear words dropped from him like the gray smoke from his cigarette, mixing with the faint scent of incense. Ralph was a living vamp, the first local I'd seen apart from the one who had bandaged my leg. I wondered whose neck he didn't bite to get stuck with a job up here, so far from the bustle of the city they thrived on.

I pulled my head up. "Will he be all right?" I asked, and Ralph glanced at me, surprised.

"Lady," he said, noticing me, "he died of a heart attack before he hit the water. And if that didn't get him, he died on impact. At this height, it's like hitting a brick wall."

I blinked, trying to take that in. *A brick wall.* It would be the second brick wall Nick hit today. My focus blurred, the sight of Jax and that amulet filling my memory. What if . . .

"The body?" I insisted, and he turned, impatient. "When can they retrieve the body?"

"They'll never find it," he said. "The current will take it, moving it out into Lake Huron faster than green corn through a tourist. He's gone. The only way he would have survived was if he was dead already. Damn, I'm glad I'm not the one who has to talk to the next of kin. I bet he's got three kids and a wife."

I hunched over, the reality of what had happened sinking in. God bless it, I was twice the fool. Nick hadn't died going over the edge. This had been a scam right from when I told him he couldn't have the statue—and I had walked right into it.

"His name was Nick," I whispered, and the I.S. officer spun from the drop, surprise on his age-lined face. Ivy and Jenks stiffened. I was blowing our cover, but we were going to be questioned before too long, and I wanted our stories to be the same. "Nick Sparagmos," I added, thinking fast. "He was helping us with a piece of art I was contracted to recover. I'm an independent runner out of Cincinnati and this was a run." *The truth is good.*

"He wasn't supposed to be here," I continued as Ivy's tension pulled her shoulders tight. "But when that guy hit us and killed Peter . . ." I took a breath, the heartache real. "Peter was only supposed to make sure it got to the right people okay. He wasn't supposed to get hurt. The people we recovered it from . . . I think the accident was their attempt to get it back before we handed it over. Nick came out with the wrecker to make sure they didn't get it. The artifact was still on the truck. He was going to get it out of here, but someone shot the tires out. Oh God, he went right over the edge." *And a little lie mixed in with the truth keeps me showering alone.*

Jenks put a hand on my shoulder and gave it a squeeze to tell me he understood. Peter had been killed in the pickup truck in an accident to satisfy the insurance company. Nick had died when he went over the edge to satisfy the Weres. That Nick was the driver of the Mack truck as well wouldn't even be considered, the driver's absence explained as a hit and run. If anyone got curious and found out the truck belonged to DeLavine, he'd be the one slapped with the illegal early termination lawsuit from the insurance company, not me.

It sounded good to me. I was going to stick with it.

I could almost feel the worry ease out of Jenks, but Ivy was still a knot of tension, not knowing that Nick had gotten away with absolutely nothing.

The I.S. officer who had taken my license ambled up to the man before me. "Hi, Ralph. You got out here quick." He turned to me, camaraderie in the witch's eyes as he handed me my license back. "Ms. Morgan, what are you doing this far out of the Hollows?"

"Cincinnati?" Ralph looked at me in surprise. "You mean Rachel Morgan?" His gaze went to Ivy. "You're Piscary's girl. What are you doing this far north?"

"Getting my partner's boyfriend killed," she said, and the man took her ugly look as dark humor. Officer Ralph already had his cuff key out and was getting them off her, frowning when he realized Jenks wasn't in his. I held up my wrist with my little black strap, and he snipped it off with a special pair of clippers on his key chain. I wanted one of those.

"Where are you staying?" Ralph asked as Ivy rubbed her freed wrists. "I'm going to want to talk to you before you go home."

Ivy explained while I stared at the water. Nick wasn't dead, and the shock of seeing him go over the edge was evolving into a nasty feeling of satisfaction. I had beat him. I had beat Nick at his own game. Knees shaking, I stumbled away. Ivy hurriedly finished up with Ralph, and with her on one side and Jenks on the other, I started to chuckle. I didn't know how we were going to get to the room. Three of us wouldn't fit in Kisten's Corvette very well.

"Tink's daisies," Jenks whispered to Ivy behind my back. "She's lost it."

"I'm fine," I said, cursing myself and laughing. "He's fine. The crazy bastard is fine."

Jenks exchanged a sorrowful glance at Ivy. "Rache," he said softly. "You heard the man. I read the place mat about how many people they lost building the bridge. He wouldn't survive hitting the water. And even if he did, he'd be unconscious and drown. Nick is gone."

We passed the news crews, and I took a shallow breath, finding comfort in that my ribs hurt. I was alive, and I was going to stay that way. "Nick knew that too," I admitted in the dimmer light. "And yeah, he's gone, but he's not dead."

Jenks took a breath to protest, and I interrupted.

"Jax was here," I said, and Jenks pulled us all to a stop in the middle of the closed northbound lane. People swirled around us, but we were forgotten.

"Jax!" Jenks exclaimed, yanked into silence by Ivy.

"Shut up," she snarled.

"He had an inertia-dampening amulet," I said, and Jenks's face went from hope to a heartbreaking look of understanding. "Jax was here to fly it down to the water before the tow truck hit."

"And the NOS," I continued as Jenks paled. "It never exploded. He used the charges to blow the tires, knowing the truck was heavy enough to go through the temporary railing."

Ivy's face was empty, but her eyes were starting to go black with anger.

Shaking my head, I looked away before she scared me. "I'll give Marshal a call, but I bet he's missing some equipment. I never looked to see what Nick had in that truck locker he's got. He's swimming out of here, and I bet Jax is with him."

A pained sound came from Jenks, and I wished I could have said it wasn't true. Feeling his pain, I met his eyes. They showed a deep betrayal he would never talk about. Jenks had taught Jax all he could in the last few days with the idea that the pixy would take his place. And Jax had taken that and used it to burn us. With Nick.

"I'm sorry, Jenks," I said, but he turned away, shoulders hunched and looking old.

Ivy tried to tuck a strand of too-short hair behind her ear. "I'm sorry too, Jenks, but we have a big problem. As soon as Nick gets himself safely settled as a nonentity, he's going to sell that thing and all hell is going to break loose between the vamps and the Weres."

Something in me hardened, and the last of my feelings for

Nick died. I smiled at Ivy without showing my teeth, hiking my bag farther up my bruised shoulder. "He won't sell it."

"And why not?" she asked, snarky.

"Because he doesn't have the real one." I looked for Kisten's Corvette, finding it standing by a pylon. Maybe we could splurge and move to the Holiday Inn tonight. I could use a hot tub. "I didn't move the curse to the wolf statue," I added, remembering I was in the middle of a thought. "I moved it to the totem Jenks was going to give Matalina."

Ivy stared at us, reading in Jenks's lack of response that she was the only one who hadn't known. He was staring at nothing, pain still etched in his posture that his son had just buried in the dirt everything he cared about. "When were you going to tell me?" she accused, blush coloring her cheeks. She looked good when she was mad, and I smiled. A real one this time.

"What," I said, "and risk spending the next two days trying to convince you to change your plan?" She huffed, and I touched her arm. "I tried to tell you," I said. "But you stormed off like you were an avenging angel."

Ivy eyed my fingers on her arm, and I pulled them away, hesitating a bare instant.

"Nick's an ass," I said. "But he's smart. If I had told you, you would have acted differently and he would have known."

"But you told Jenks," she said.

"It's hiding in his jockey shorts!" I said in exasperation, not wanting to talk about it anymore. "God, Ivy. I'm not going to mess with Jenks's underwear unless he knows about it."

Ivy pouted. The six-foot sexy vampire in scraped black leather crossed her arms before her and pouted. "I'm probably going to have to do more community service for hitting all those I.S. officers," she grumbled. "Thanks a hell of a lot."

I slumped, hearing forgiveness in her words. "At least he didn't get it," I offered, and Ivy threw a hand in the air and tried to look disgusted, but I could tell she was relieved.

Jenks found a thin smile, his gaze going to Kisten's Corvette. "Can I drive?" he asked.

Lips pressed, Ivy frowned. "We're not going to all fit in that. Maybe we can bum a ride from Ralph. Give me a moment, okay?"

"We can fit," Jenks said. "I'll move the seat back and Rachel can sit on my lap."

Ivy went one way and Jenks went the other. My protest froze when I found a point of stillness in the swirling mess of reporters, officers, and watchers. My lips parted. It was Brett, standing on a cement barrier so he could look over the crowd. He was watching me, and when our eyes met, he touched the brim of his cap in salute. There was a rip in it where the emblem had been removed, and with a significant motion he took it off and let it fall. Turning away, he started to walk for the Mackinaw City end of the bridge. And he was gone.

I realized he thought I had done it, and went cold. He thought I'd blown out the tires of the wrecker and killed Nick for trying to do a double run on me. Damn. I didn't know if that kind of reputation would save my life or get me killed.

"Rache?" Jenks returned from pushing the passenger's seat back as far as it would go. "What is it?"

I put a hand to my cold face and met his worried eyes. "Nothing." Determined to figure it out later, I sent my thoughts instead to the bath I was going to take. I had beaten Nick at his own game. The question was, would I survive it?

Thirty-five

My boot heel slipped on the uneven sidewalk, and the sound of me catching my step was dull in the air heavy from the evening's rain. The faint twinge in my leg reminded me that it wasn't quite right yet. The sun was long gone, and clouds made the night darker than it ought to be, close and warm. I splashed through a puddle, in too good a mood to care if my ankles got wet. Pizza dough was rising in my kitchen, and I had a grocery sack of toppings.

Lunch was going to be early tonight; Ivy had a run, and Kisten was taking me to a movie and I didn't want to fill up on popcorn. Passing under a lamp-lit, pollution-stunted maple, I reached to touch its leaves in passing, smiling at the green softness brushing my skin. They were damp, and I let my hand stay wet and cool in the night air. The street was quiet. The only human family living there was inside watching TV, and everyone else was at work or school. The hum of Cincinnati was far away and distant, the rumble of sleeping lions.

I adjusted the strap of my new canvas grocery bag, thinking that in the time we'd been gone, spring had shifted into high gear. It was almost a year since I'd quit the I.S. "And I'm alive," I whispered to the world. I was alive and doing well. No, I was doing great.

A soft clearing of a throat zinged through me, but I managed not to jerk or alter my pace. It had come from across the street, and I searched the shadows until I found a well-muscled Were in jeans and a dress shirt. He had been shadowing me all week. It was Brett.

I forced my jaw to unclench and gave him a respectful nod, receiving a snappy salute in return. Free arm swinging, I continued down the street, hitting the puddles that were in my way. Brett wouldn't bother me. That he was looking for the focus had occurred to me—either wanting to confirm that it was truly gone, or use it to buy his way back into Walter's good graces if it wasn't—but I didn't think so. It looked like he was going loner when he dropped his cap on the Mackinac Bridge and walked away. But he was just watching now. David had done the same for months before he finally made his presence known. When unsure of their rank, Weres were patient and wary. He'd come to me when he was ready.

And I was in far too good a mood to worry about it. I was so glad to be home. My stitches were out and the scars were thin lines easily hidden. My limp was fading, and thanks to that curse I used to Were, I had absolutely no freckles. The soft air slipped easily in and out of my lungs as I walked, and I felt sassy. Sassy and badass in my vamp-made boots and Jenks's aviator jacket. I was wearing the cap Jenks had stolen from the island Weres, and it added a nice bit of bad girl. The guy behind the counter at the corner store had thought I was cute.

I passed my covered car in the open garage and my mood faltered. The I.S. had suspended my license. It just wasn't fair. I had saved them a dump truck of political hassle, and did I get even a thank-you? No. They took my license.

Not wanting to lose my good mood, I forced my brow smooth. The I.S. had publicly announced on the back page of the Community Section of the paper that I was cleared of all suspicion of any wrongdoing in the accidental deaths that had taken place on the bridge. But behind closed doors some undead vamp had given me a hard time for trying to handle such a powerful artifact instead of bringing it to them. He didn't back off until Jenks threatened to cut off his balls and give them to me to make a magic bola. You gotta love friends like that.

The undead vampire didn't get me to confess that I'd meant to kill Peter, and that cheesed him off to no end. He had been beautifully dangerous, with snow-white hair and sharp features, and even though he whipped me up to the point where I would have had his baby, he couldn't scare me into forgetting I had rights. Not after I'd survived Piscary—who didn't care about them. The entire nationwide I.S. was pissed at me, believing the focus had gone over the edge with Nick instead of being turned over to them.

There was a continuous twenty-four-hour search going on for the artifact on the bottom of the straits. The locals thought they were stupid since the current had put it in Lake Huron shortly after the truck hit the water, and I thought they were stupid because the real artifact was hidden in Jenks's living room. With their official stand being what it was, the I.S. couldn't lock me up, but with the added points after the accident with Peter, they *could* suspend my license. My choices were riding the bus for six months or gritting my teeth and taking driver's ed. God no. I'd be the oldest one in the class.

My mood tarnishing, I took the church's stairs two at a time, and felt my leg protest. I pulled the heavy wooden door open, slipped inside and breathed deeply, relishing the scent of tomato paste and bacon. The pizza dough was probably ready, and Kisten's sauce had been simmering for the better part of the day. He had kept me company in the kitchen all afternoon while I finished restocking my charm cupboard. Even helped me clean my mess.

I shut the door with hardly a thump. All the windows in the church were open to let in the moist night. I couldn't wait to get into the garden tomorrow, and even had a few seeds I wanted to try out. Ivy was laughing at me and the stack of seed catalogs that somehow found me despite my address change, but I'd caught her looking at one.

Tucking a stray curl behind my ear, I wondered if I might splurge for the ten-dollar-a-seed packet of black orchids she'd been eyeing. They were wickedly hard to get and even more difficult to grow, but with Jenks's help, who knew?

Slipping off my wet boots and coat, I left them by the door and padded in my socks through the peaceful sanctuary. The hush of a passing car came in through the high transom windows above the stained-glass windows. The pixies had worked for hours chiseling the old paint off and oiling the hinges so I could open them with the long pole I'd found in the belfry stairway. There were no screens, which was why the lights were off. There were no pixies either. My desk was again my desk. *Thank all that was holy.*

My wandering attention touched on the potted plants Jenks had left behind on my desk, and I jerked to a halt, seeing a pair of green eyes under the chair, catching the light. Slowly my breath slipped from me. "Darn cat," I whispered, thinking Rex was going to scare the life out of me if she didn't break my heart first. I crouched to try to coax her to me, but Rex didn't move, didn't blink, didn't even twitch her beautiful tail.

Rex didn't like me much. She liked Ivy just fine. She loved the garden, the graveyard, and the pixies that lived in it, but not me. The little ball of orange fluff would sleep on Ivy's bed, purr under her chair during breakfast for tidbits, and sit on her lap, but she only stared at me with large, unblinking eyes. I couldn't help but feel hurt. I think she was still waiting for me to turn back into a wolf. The sound of Kisten and Ivy's voices intruded over the slow jazz. Hiking the canvas bag higher, I awkwardly inched closer to Rex, hand held out.

Ivy and I had been home a week, and we were all still in emotional limbo. Three seconds after Ivy and I walked in the door, Kisten looked at my dental floss stitches, breathed deeply, and knew what had happened. In an instant, Ivy had gone from happy-to-be-home to depressed. Her face full of an aching emptiness, she'd dropped her bags and took off on her bike to get it "checked over."

Just as well. Kisten and I had a long, painful discussion where he both sorrowed after and admired my new scars. It felt good to confess to someone that Ivy had scared the crap out of me, and even better when he agreed that in time she might forget her own fear and try to find a blood balance with me.

Since then he'd been his usual self. Almost. There was a sly hesitancy in his touch now, as if he was holding himself to a limit of action to see if I would change it. The unhappy result was the mix of danger and security that I loved in him was gone. Not wanting to interfere in anything Ivy and I might find, he had put me in charge of moving our relationship forward.

I didn't like being in charge. I liked the heart pounding rush of being lured into making decisions that might turn bad on me. Realizing as much was depressing. It seemed that Ivy and Jenks were right that not only was I an adrenaline junkie, but I needed a sensation of danger to get turned on.

Thinking about it now, my mood thoroughly soured, I crouched beside my desk, arm extended to try to get the stupid cat to like me. Her neck stretched out and she sniffed my fingers, but wouldn't bump her head under my hand as she would Ivy's. Giving up, I stood and headed for the back of the church, following the sound of Kisten's masculine rumble. I took a breath to call out and tell them I was there, but my feet stilled when I realized they were talking about me.

"Well, you did bite her," Kisten said, his voice both lightly accusing and coaxing.

"I bit her," Ivy admitted, her voice a whisper.

"And you didn't bind her," he prompted.

"No." I heard the creak of her chair as she repositioned herself, guilt making her shift.

"She wants to know what comes next," Kisten said with a rude laugh. "Hell, I want to know myself."

"Nothing," Ivy said shortly. "It's not going to happen again."

I licked my lips, thinking I should back out of the hallway and come in making more noise, but I couldn't move, staring at the worn wood by the archway to the living room.

Kisten sighed. "That's not fair. You strung her along until she called your bluff, and now you won't go forward, and she can't go back. Look at her," he said, and I imagined him gesturing at nothing. "She wants to find a blood balance. God, Ivy, isn't that what you wanted?"

Ivy's breath came harsh. "I could have killed her!" she exclaimed, and I jumped. "I lost control just like always and almost killed her. She let me do it because she trusted me." Her words were now muffled. "She understood everything and she didn't stop me."

"You're scared," Kisten accused, and my eyes widened at his gall.

But Ivy took it in stride as she laughed sarcastically. "You think?"

"No," he insisted, "I mean you're scared. You're afraid to try to find a balance you can both live with, because if you try and can't, she leaves and you've got nothing."

"That's not it," she said flatly, and I nodded. That was part of it, but not all.

Kisten leaned forward; I could hear the chair creak. "You think you don't deserve anything good," he said, and my face went cold, wondering if there was more to this than I had thought. "Afraid you're going to ruin every decent thing you get, so you're going to stick with this shitty half relationship instead of seeing where it might go."

"It's not a half relationship," Ivy protested.

He touched the truth, I thought. *But that's not what keeps her silent.*

"Compared to what you might have, it is," he said, and I heard someone get up and move. "She's straight, and you're not," Kisten added, and my pulse quickened. His voice was now coming from where Ivy sat. "She sees a deep platonic relationship, and you *know* that even if you start one, you'll eventually delude yourself into believing it's deeper. She'll be your friend when what you want is a lover. And one night in a moment of blood passion, you're going to make a mistake in a very concrete way and she'll be gone."

"Shut up!" she shouted, and I heard a slap, perhaps of a hand meeting someone's grip.

Kisten laughed gently, ending it with a sigh of understanding. "I got it right that time."

His liquid voice, gray with truth, sent a shiver through me. *Back up,* I told myself. *Back up and go play with the cat.* I could hear my heartbeat in the silence. From the disc player, the song ended.

"Are you going to share blood with her again?"

It was a gentle, hesitant inquiry, and Ivy took a noisy breath. "I can't."

"Mind if I do?"

Oh God. This time I did move, pulling the canvas bag tight to me. Kisten already had my body. If we shared blood, it would be too much for Ivy's pride. Something would break.

"Bastard," Ivy said, pulling my retreat to a halt.

"You know how I feel about her," he said. "I'm not going to walk away because of your asinine hang-ups about blood."

My lips parted at his bitter accusation, and Ivy's breath hissed. "Hang-ups?" she said vehemently. "Mixing sex with bloodletting is the only way I can keep from losing control with someone I love, Kisten! I thought I was better, but *obviously* I'm not!"

It had been bitter and accusing, but Kisten's voice was harsh with his own frustration. "I don't understand, Ivy," he said, and I heard him move away from her. "I never did. Blood is blood. Love is love. You aren't a whore if you take someone's blood when you don't like them, and you aren't a whore for wanting someone you don't like to take your blood."

"This is where I am, Kisten," she said. "I'm not touching her, and neither are you."

My pulse pounded, and I heard in his heavy exhalation the sound of an old argument that had no answer. "Rachel's worth fighting for," he said softly. "If she asks me, I won't say no."

I closed my eyes, seeing where this was heading.

"And because you're a man," Ivy said bitterly, "she won't have a problem when the blood turns to sex, will she."

"Probably not." It was confident, and my eyes opened.

"Damn you," she whispered, sounding broken. "I hate you."

Kisten was silent, and then I heard the soft sound of a kiss. "You love me."

Mouth dry, I stood in the hallway, afraid to move in the silence the last sound track had left.

"Ivy?" Kisten coaxed. "I won't lure her from you, but I won't sit by and pretend I'm a stone either. Just talk to her. She knows where your feelings are, and she still has the room next to yours, not an apartment across the city. Maybe . . ."

My eyes closed in the swirl of conflicting feelings. The image of me sharing a room with Ivy flitted through my mind, shocking me. Of me slipping between those silken sheets and sliding up to her back, smelling her hair, feeling her turn over and seeing her easy smile four inches from mine. I knew how her eyes would be lidded and heavy with sleep, the soft sound of welcome she would make. *What in hell was I doing?*

"She's rash," Kisten said, "impulsive, and the most caring person I have ever met. She told me what happened, but she doesn't think anything less of you, or herself, even when it went wrong."

"Shut up," Ivy whispered, pain and self-reproach in her voice.

"You opened the door," he accused, making her come to grips with what we had done. "And if you don't walk her through it, she'll find someone who will. I don't have to ask your permission. And unless you tell me right now that someday you're going to try to find a blood balance with her, I will if she asks me."

I shivered, jerking when a soft brush on my leg made me jump. It was Rex, but I was little more to her than something to brush up against as she headed to the living room, following the sound of Ivy's distress.

"I can't!" Ivy exclaimed, and I jumped. "Piscary . . ." She took a gasping breath. "Piscary will step in and he'll make me hurt her, maybe kill her."

"*That's* an excuse," he hammered on her. "The truth is that you're scared."

I stood in the hallway and trembled, feeling the tension rise in the unseen room. But Kisten's voice was gentle now that he'd gotten her to admit her feelings. "You should tell her that," he continued softly.

Ivy sniffed, half in sorrow, half in bitter amusement. "I just did. She's in the hall."

I sucked in my breath and jerked upright.

"Shit," Kisten said, his voice panicked. "Rachel?"

Pulling up my shoulders, I raised my chin and went into the

kitchen. Kisten scuffed to a halt in the hall, and tension slammed into me. His lanky build, wide shoulders, and my favorite red silk shirt took up the archway. He had on boots, and they looked good peeping from under his jeans. His bracelet felt heavy on me, and I twisted it, wondering if I should take it off.

"Rachel, I didn't know you were there," he said, his face creased. "I'm sorry. You aren't a toy that I have to ask Ivy's permission to play with."

I kept my back to him, shoulders stiff while I opened the canvas sack and took things out. Leaving the cheese, mushrooms, and the pineapple where they were, I strode to the pantry, hanging my grocery bag up on the hook I'd nailed in yesterday. Images of Ivy's comfortable room, of Kisten's face, his body, the way he felt under my fingers, the way he made me feel, all flashed through me. Pace stilted, I went to the stove and took the lid off the sauce. Steam billowed up, the rising scent of tomato making the wisps of my hair drift. I stirred without seeing as he came up behind me. "Rachel?"

My breath came out, and I held the next one. I was so confused.

Softly—almost not there—Kisten put a hand on my shoulder. Tension slipped from me, and sensing it, he leaned until his body pressed against my back. His arms went around me, imprisoning me, and my motions to stir the pot stilled. "She knew the moment I came in," I said.

"Probably," he whispered into my ear.

I wondered where Ivy was—if she had stayed in the living room or fled the church entirely, shamed that she had needs and fears like the rest of us. Kisten took the spoon from me, setting it between the burners before turning me around. I pulled my eyes to his, not surprised to see them narrow with concern. The glow from the overhead light shimmered on his day-old stubble, and I touched it because I could. His arms were about my waist, and he gave a tug, settling me closer into him. "What she can't say to your face, she'll say when she knows you're listening," he said. "It's a bad habit she picked up in therapy."

I had already figured that one out, and bobbed my head. "This is a mess," I said, miserable as I looked over his shoulder to the dark hallway. "I never should have—"

My words cut off when Kisten pulled me closer. Arms about his waist and my head against his chest, I breathed deeply the scent of leather and silk, relaxing into him. "Yes," he whispered. "You should have." He pushed me back until I could see his eyes.

"I won't ask," he said earnestly. "If it happens, it happens. I like things the way they are." His expression grew sly. "I'd like it better if things changed, but when change is too quick, the strong break."

My eyes on the archway, I stood and held him, not wanting to let go. I could hear Ivy in the living room, trying to find a way to make a graceful entrance. The warmth of his body was soothing, and I held my breath against the thought of his teeth sinking into me. I knew exactly how good it would feel. *What was I going to do about that?*

Kisten's head came up an instant before the peal of the front doorbell echoed through the church. "I got it!" Ivy shouted, and Kisten and I pulled apart before her boots made a soft brush down the hall. The light flicked on in the hallway, and I heard the beginnings of a low conversation. The mushrooms needed cutting, and Kisten joined me as I washed my hands. We jostled for space at the sink, bumping hips as he pushed me into a better mood.

"Cut them at an angle," he admonished when I reached for the cutting board. He had his hands in the flour bag, then clapped them once over the sink before putting himself at the center island counter and the ball of dough he had set to rise under a piece of linen.

"It makes a difference?" Still melancholy, I moved my stuff to the opposite side of the counter so I could watch him. "David?" I shouted, eating the first mushroom slice. It was probably him, seeing as I'd asked him to come over.

A low noise escaped Kisten, and I smiled. He looked good over there. A brush of flour made a domestic smear on his shirt, and he had rolled up his sleeves to show his lightly tanned arms. Seeing him gently handling the dough and watching me at the same time, I realized the thrill was back—the delicious danger of what-if. He had told Ivy he wasn't going to walk away from me; I was on dangerous ground. Again.

God save me. I thought in disgust. *Could I* be *any more stupid?* My life was so messed up. How could I just stand here and cut mushrooms as if everything was normal? But compared to last week, maybe this *was* normal.

My attention came up when David walked in ahead of Ivy, his slight build looking blocky before her sleek grace. "Hi, David," I said, trying to clear my mind. "Full moon tonight."

He nodded, saying nothing as he took in Kisten casually pulling the dough into a circle. "I can't stay," he said, realizing we were making lunch. "I have a few appointments, but you said it was urgent?" He smiled at Kisten. "Hi, Kisten. How's the boat?"

"Still afloat," he said, eyebrows rising as he took in David's expensive suit. He was working, and he looked the part despite the heavy stubble the full moon made worse.

"It won't take long," I said, slicing the last mushroom. "I've got something I want you to take a look at. Picked it up on vacation, and I want your opinion."

His eyes went wondering, but he unbuttoned his long leather duster. "Now?"

"Full moon," I said cryptically, sliding the sliced mushrooms into my smallest spell pot and quashing the faint worry that I was breaking rule number two by mixing food prep and spell prep, but they were just the right size to hold toppings. Ivy quietly went to the fridge, getting out the cheese, cooked hamburger, and the bacon left over from breakfast. I tried to meet her eyes to tell her we were okay, but she wouldn't look at me.

Angry, I slammed the knife down, careful to keep my fingers out of the way. *Silly little vamp, afraid of her feelings.*

Kisten sighed, his eyes on the disk of dough he had tossed professionally into the air, "Someday, I'm going to get you two ladies together."

"I don't do threesomes," I said snidely.

David jerked, but Kisten's eyes went sultry and pensive, even as he caught the dough. "That's not what I was talking about, but okay."

Ivy's cheeks were red, and David froze as he took in the sudden tension. "Uh," the Were said, half out of his coat. "Maybe this isn't a good time."

I dredged up a smile. "No," I said. "It's just everyday normal crap. We're used to it."

David finished taking off his coat, frowning. "I'm not," he muttered.

I went to the sink and leaned toward the window, thinking David was a bit of a prude. "Jenks!" I shouted into the dusky garden, alight with pixy children tormenting moths. It was beautiful, and I almost lost myself in the sifting bands of falling color.

A clatter of wings was my only warning, and I jerked away when Jenks vaulted through the pixy hole in the screen. "David!" he called out, looking great in his casual gardening clothes of green and black. Hovering at eye level, he brought the scent of damp earth into the kitchen. "Thank Tink's little red shoes you're here," he said, pulling up two feet when Rex appeared in the doorway, her eyes big and her ears pricked. "Matalina is about ready to dewing me. You gotta get this thing out of my living room. My kids keep touching it. Making it move."

I felt myself blanch. "It's moving now?"

Ivy and Kisten exchanged worried looks, and David sighed, putting his hands into his pockets as if trying to divorce himself from what was coming. He wasn't that much older than me, but at that moment he looked like the only adult in a room full of adolescents. "What is it, Rachel?" he said, sounding tired.

Suddenly nervous, I took a breath to tell him, then changed my mind. "Could you . . . could you just take a look at it?" I said, wincing.

Jenks landed on the windowsill and leaned casually against the frame. He looked like Brad Pitt gone sexy farmer, and I smiled. Two weeks ago he would have stood with his hands on his hips. This was better, and might explain Matalina's blissful state lately.

"I'll have the boys bring it up," Jenks said, tossing his hair out of his eyes. "We've got a sling for it. Won't take but a tick, David."

He zipped back out the window, and while David looked at his watch and moved from foot to foot, I pushed the window all the way up, struggling with the rain-swollen frame. The screen popped out, and the air suddenly seemed a lot fresher.

"This doesn't have anything to do with the Were sentry at the end of the block, does it?" David asked wryly.

Whoops. I turned, my eyes going immediately to Ivy, sitting before her computer. I hadn't told her Brett was shadowing me, knowing she'd throw a hissy. *Like I couldn't handle one Were who was scared of me?* Sure enough, she was frowning. "You saw him, huh?" I said, putting my back to her and moving the sauce to Kisten.

David shifted his weight and glanced at Kisten as he nonchalantly spread it thinly on the dough. "I saw him," David said. "Smelled him, and nearly dropped my cell phone down the sewer calling you to ask if you wanted me to, ah, ask him to go away until he . . . mmmm."

I waited in the new silence broken by shrill pixy whistles coming from the garden. David's face was red when he swung his head back up and rubbed a hand across his stubble.

"What?" I said warily.

David looked discomfited. "He, ah . . ." A quick glance at Ivy, and he blurted, "He gave me a bunny kiss from across the street."

Ivy's lips parted. Eyes wide, her gaze touched on Kisten, then me. "Excuse me?"

"You know." He made a peace sign and bent his fingers twice in quick succession. "Kiss, kiss? Isn't that a vampire . . . thing?"

Kisten laughed, the warm sound making me feel good. "Rachel," he said, sifting the cheese over the red sauce. "What did you do to make him leave his pack and follow you all the way down here? By the looks of it, I'd say he's trying to insinuate himself into your pack."

"Brett didn't leave. I think they kicked him out," I said, then hesitated. "You knew he was there, too?" I asked, and he shrugged, eating a piece of bacon. I ate one too, considering for the first time that perhaps Brett was looking for a new pack. I had saved his life. Sort of.

Jenks came in the open window, making circles around Rex until the cat chittered in distress. Laughing, Jenks led her into the hall as five of his kids wafted over the sill, toting what looked like a pair of black lace panties cradling the statue.

"Those are mine!" Ivy shrieked, standing up and darting to the sink. "Jenks!"

The pixies scattered. The statue wrapped in the black silk fell into her hand.

"These are mine!" she said again, red with anger and embarrassment as she pulled them off the statue and shoved them in her pocket. "Damn it, Jenks! Stay out of my room!"

Jenks flew in just under the ceiling. Rex padded in under him, her steps light and her eyes bright. "Holy crap!" he exclaimed, making circles around Ivy, wreathing her in a glittering band of gold. "How did your panties end up in my living room?"

Matalina zipped in, her green silk dress furling and her eyes apologetic. Immediately, Jenks joined her. I don't know if it was his joy of reuniting with Matalina or his stint at being human-sized, but he was a lot faster. With her was Jhan, a solemn, serious-minded pixy who had recently been excused from sentry duties in order to learn how to read. I didn't want to think about why.

Ivy dropped the new focus onto the counter beside the pizza, clearly in a huff as she backed away and sat sullenly in her chair, her boots on the table and her ankles crossed. David came closer, and this time I couldn't stop my shudder. Jenks was right. It had shifted again.

"Good God," David said, hunched to put it at eye level. "What is it?"

I bent my knees, crouching to come even with him, the focus between us. It didn't look like the same totem that I had put in Jenks's suitcase. The closer we had gotten to the full moon, the more it looked like the original statue, until now it was identical except for a quicksilver sheen hovering just above the surface like an aura.

Ivy was wiping her fingers off on her pants, and she quit when she saw my attention on them. I couldn't blame her. The thing gave me the willies.

Kisten added the last of the meat, pushing the pizza aside and putting his elbows on the counter, an odd look on him as he saw it for the first time. "That has got to be the ugliest thing in creation," he said, touching his torn earlobe in an unconscious show of unease.

Matalina nodded, a pensive look on her beautiful features. "It's not coming back in my house," she said, her clear voice determined. "It's not. Jenks, I love you, but if it comes back in my house, I'm moving into the desk and you can sleep with your dragonfly!"

Jenks hunched and made noises of placation, and I met the small woman's eyes with a smile. If all went well, David would be taking it off our hands.

"David," I said, pulling myself straight.

"Uh-huh . . ." he murmured, still staring at it.

"Have you ever heard of the focus?"

At that, a fearful expression flashed across his rugged features, worrying me. Taking a step forward, I slid the pizza stone off the counter. "I couldn't just give it to them," I said, opening the oven door and squinting in the heat that made my hair drift up. "The vampires would slaughter them. What kind of a runner would I be if I let them get wiped out like that?"

"So you brought it here?" he stammered. "The focus? To Cincinnati?"

I slid the stone into the oven and closed it, leaning back to take advantage of the heat slipping past the shut door. David's breath was shallow and the scent of musk rose.

"Rachel," he said, eyes riveted to it. "You know what this is, right? I mean . . . Oh my God, it's real." Tension pulling his small frame tight, he straightened. His attention went to Kisten, solemn behind the counter, to Jenks standing beside Matalina, to Ivy, snapping a fingernail on the rivet on her boot. "You hold it?" he said, looking panicked. "It's yours?"

Running my fingers through the hair at the back of my head, I nodded. "I, uh, guess."

Kisten jerked into motion. "Whoops," he said, reaching. "He's going down!"

"David!" I exclaimed, shocked when the small man's knees buckled.

I stretched for him, but Kisten had already slipped an arm under his shoulders. While Ivy fiddled with the rivet on her boot with a nail in feigned unconcern, Kisten lowered him into a chair. I edged the vampire out of the way, kneeling. "David?" I said, patting his cheeks. "David!"

Immediately his eyes fluttered. "I'm okay," he said, pushing me away before he was fully conscious. "I'm all right!" Taking a breath, he opened his eyes. His lips were pressed tightly together and he was clearly disgusted at himself. "Where . . . did you get it?" he said, his head down. "The stories say it's cursed. If it wasn't a gift, you're cursed."

"I don't believe in curses . . . like that," Ivy said.

Fear slid through me. I believed in curses; Nick had stolen it—Nick had fallen off the Mackinac Bridge. *No, he had jumped.* "Someone sent it to me," I said. "Everyone who knew I had it thinks it went over the bridge. No one knows I've got it."

At that, he pulled himself upright. "Just that loner out there," he said, shifting his feet but staying seated. He glanced at Kisten, who was at the sink, washing the topping bowls as if this was all normal.

"He doesn't know," I said, wincing when Ivy went to set the timer on the stove. *Crap, I'd forgotten to again.* "I think Kisten's right that he might be trying to get into our pack, seeing as I trounced him." I frowned, not believing that he was digging for information and would go back to Walter after the insult of being given to the street pack.

Nodding, David's gaze returned to the focus. "I got notification that you won another alpha contest," he said, clearly distracted. "Are you okay?"

Jenks lifted off the table, making glittering sparkles around me and bringing Rex to my feet when he landed on my shoulder. "She did great!" he said, ignoring the small cat. "You should have seen her. Rachel used the Were charm. She came out the size of a real wolf but had hair like a red setter." He flitted up, moving to Ivy. "Such a *pretty puppy* she was," he crooned, safely on Ivy's shoulder. "Soft fuzzy ears . . . little black paws."

"Shut up, Jenks."

"And the *cutest* little tail you've ever seen on a witch!"

"Put a cork in it!" I said, lunging for him. Fighting Pam hadn't been a fair contest, and I wondered who had credited me with the win at the Were registery. Brett maybe?

Laughing, Jenks zipped up and out of my reach. Ivy smiled softly, never moving except for putting her feet on the floor where they belonged. She looked proud of me, I think.

"Red wolf," David murmured, as if it was curious but not important. He had scooted his chair to the table and was reaching to the statue. Breath held, he touched it, and the carved bone gave way under his pressure like a balloon. He pulled back, an odd sound slipping from him.

Nervous, I sat down kitty-corner to him, the statue between us. "When I moved the curse to it, it looked like a totem pole, but every day it looked more like it did when we first got it, until now it looks like this. Again."

David licked his lips, dragging his attention from it for a brief second to meet my eyes, then back to the statue. Something had shifted in him. The fear was gone. It wasn't avarice in his gaze, but wonder. His fingers curled under, a mere inch from touching it, and he shuddered.

That was enough for me. I glanced at Ivy, and when she nodded, I turned to Jenks. He stood beside Mr. Fish and his tank of sea monkeys on the windowsill, his ankles crossed and his arms over his chest, but I still saw him as six-foot-four. Feeling my gaze on him, he nodded.

"Will you hold it for me?" I asked.

David jerked his hand away and spun in his chair. "Me? Why me?"

Jenks lifted smoothly into the air in a clatter of wings and landed next to it. "Because if I don't get that freaky thing out of my living room, Matalina is going to leave me."

My eyebrows rose, and Ivy snickered. Matalina had almost pinned Jenks to the flour canister when we had walked in, crying and laughing to have him home again. It had been hard on her, so hard. I'd never ask him to leave again.

"You're the only Were I trust to hold it," I said. "For crying out loud, David, I'm your alpha. Who else am I going to give it to?"

He looked at it, then back to me. "Rachel, I can't. This is too much."

Flustered, I moved my chair beside him. "It's not a gift. It's a burden." Steeling myself, I pulled the statue closer. "Something this powerful can't go back into hiding once it's in the open," I said, looking at its ugly curves. I thought I saw a tear in its eye—I wasn't sure. "Even if accepting it might cause everything I care about to go down the crapper. If we ignore it, it's going to bite us on our asses, but if we meet it head on, maybe we can come out better than when we went in."

Kisten laughed, and in front of her computer, Ivy froze. By her suddenly closed expression, I realized that what I had said could also be applied to her and myself. I tried to catch her gaze, but she wouldn't look up, fiddling with the same rivet on her boot. From the corner of my sight Jenks's wings drooped as he watched us.

Oblivious, David stared at the statue. "Okay," he said, not reaching for it. "I'll . . . I'll take it, but it's yours." His brown eyes were wide and his shoulders were tense. "It's not mine."

"Deal." Pleased to have gotten rid of it, I took a happy breath. Jenks, too, puffed out his air. Matalina hadn't been happy with it being in their living room. It was sort of like bringing a marlin home from vacation. Or maybe a moose head.

The pizza had a bubble starting to rise, and Kisten opened the oven to stick a toothpick through the dough to release the hot air under it. The odor of tomato sauce and pepperoni billowed out, the scent of security and contentment. My tension eased, and David picked the focus up.

"I, ah, I think I'll take this home before I finish my appointments," he said, hefting it. "It feels . . . Damn, I could do anything with it."

Ivy put her feet on the floor and stood. "Just don't go starting a war," she grumbled, heading out to the hall. "I've got a box you can put that in."

David set it back on the table. "Thanks." Face creasing in worry, he edged it closer in a show of possession—not greed, but of protection. A smile came over Kisten as he saw it too.

"You, ah, sure the vampires won't be after it?" the small man said, and Kisten pulled out a chair and sat in it backward.

"No one knows you have it, and as long as you don't start rallying the Weres to you, they won't," he said, draping his arms over the top of his chair. "The only one that might know about it would be Piscary." He glanced at the empty hallway. "By way of Ivy," he said softly. "But she's very closed with her thoughts. He would have to dig for it." Kisten's look went worried. "He doesn't have any reason to think it's surfaced, but word gets around."

David put his hands into his pockets. "Maybe I should hide it in my cat box."

"You have a cat?" I asked. "I'd put you as a dog person."

His gaze darted over the kitchen when Ivy came in and put a small cardboard box on the table. Jenks landed on it and started tugging at the tape holding it. "It belonged to an old girlfriend," David said. "You want it?"

Ivy went to flick Jenks away to open the box herself, then changed her mind. "No," she said as she sat and forced her hands into her lap. "Do you want ours?"

"Hey!" Jenks shouted as the tape gave way and he flew back from the momentum. "Rex is *my* cat. Stop trying to give her away."

"Yours?" David said, surprised. "I thought she was Rachel's."

Embarrassed, I shrugged with one shoulder. "She doesn't like me," I said, pretending to check on the pizza.

Jenks landed on my shoulder in a soft show of support. "I think she's waiting for you to turn back into a wolf, Rache," he teased.

I went to brush him off, then stopped. A ribbon of memory pulled through me—of how he had treated me when he was big—and I made a soft "Mmmm" instead. "Have you seen her stare at me?" I turned, seeing her doing it now. "See?" I said, pointing at her in the middle of the threshold, her ears pricked and a curious, unafraid look on her sweet, kitten face.

David pulled the scarf from the collar of his duster and wrapped the focus up. "You should make her your familiar," he said. "She'd like you then."

"No fairy crap way!" Jenks shouted, wings a blur as he went to hold the box open for David. "Rachel isn't going to draw any ever-after through Rex. She'll fry her little kitty brain."

Might be an improvement, I thought sourly. "It doesn't work that way. She has to choose me. And he's right. I'd probably fry her little kitty brain. I fried Nick's."

A shudder rippled over David. The entire kitchen seemed to go still, and I looked worriedly at Ivy and Kisten. "You okay?" I said when they met my blank stare with my own.

"Moon just rose," David said, wiping a hand across his dark stubble. "It's full. Sorry. Sometimes it hits hard. I'm cool."

I gave him a once-over, thinking he looked different. There was a smoother grace, a new tension to him—like he could hear the clock before it ticked. I yanked open the drawer for the pizza cutter, shuffling around. "You sure you can't stay for some lunch?" I asked.

There was the skitter of cat claws on the linoleum, then David gasped. "Oh my God," he breathed on the exhale. "Look at it."

"Holy crap!" Jenks exclaimed, and Ivy took an audible breath.

I turned, pizza cutter in hand. My eyebrows rose and I blinked. "Whoa."

The cursed thing had turned completely silver, malleable like liquid. It looked entirely like a wolf now too, lips pulled from her muzzle and silver saliva dripping down to melt into the fur at the base. And it was her. Somehow I knew it. A shudder went through me as I thought I might hear something but wasn't sure. "You know what?" I said, my voice shaky as I looked at it in its box, cushioned by David's scarf. "You can have it. I don't want it back. Really."

David swallowed. "Rachel, we're friends and everything, but no. There is no way in hell I'm taking that thing into my apartment."

"It's not going back into my house!" Jenks said. "No freakin' way! Listen to it! It's making my teeth hurt. I already get misery once a month from twenty-three females, and I'm not putting up with it from some weird-ass Were statue on the full moon. Rachel, cover it up or something. Tink's tampons, can't you all hear that?"

I picked the box up, and the hair on my arms rose. Stifling a shudder, I opened the freezer and shoved it between the cold-burned waffles and the banana bread that tasted like asparagus that my mom had brought over. The fridge was stainless steel. It might help.

The phone rang and Ivy jumped up, heading for the living room as Jenks hovered over the sink and shed golden sparkles. "Better?" I said when I closed the freezer, and he sneezed, nodding as the last glitters fell.

Ivy appeared in the archway with the phone, her eyes black, and clearly ticked, to judge by her wire-tight stance. "What do you want, crap for brains?"

Nick.

Jenks jerked three feet into the air. I was sure my eyes were full of pity, but Jenks shook his head, not wanting to talk to his son. That Nick had romanced his son from him for a life of crime was far worse than anything Nick had ever done to me.

Not knowing what I was feeling, I held my hand out. Ivy hesitated, and my eyes narrowed. Grimacing, she slapped the phone into my palm. "If he comes here, I'll kill him," she muttered. "I mean it. I'll drive him up to Mackinaw and throw him over for real."

"Take a number," I said when she sat in her spot before her computer. Clearing my throat, I put the receiver to my ear. "Hello-o-o-o-o, Nick," I said, hitting the *k* hard. "You're the world's biggest jerk for what you did to Jax. You ever show your scrawny face in Cincinnati again, and I'm going to shove a broomstick up your ass and set it on fire. You got that?"

"Rachel," he said, sounding frantic. "It's not real!"

I glanced at the fridge, putting my hand over the receiver. "He says he's got the fake one," I said, simpering. Kisten snorted, and suddenly smug, I turned back to Nick. "What?" I said, my voice light and flowery. "Didn't your statue go silvery, Nickie da-a-a-a-arling?"

"You know damn well it didn't," he said, voice harsh. "Don't mess with me, Rachel. I need it. I *earned* it. I promised—"

"Nick," I soothed, but he was still talking. "Nick!" I said louder. "Listen to me."

Finally there was silence but for the hiss and buzz of the line. I looked over the kitchen, warm with the scent of pizza and the companionship of my friends. The new picture of Jenks and me that I'd stuck to the fridge caught my eye. His arm was over my shoulder, and we were both squinting from the sun. Ivy wasn't in it, but she had taken it, and her presence was as strong as the bridge behind us. The picture seemed to say it all.

So I lived in a church with pixies and a vampire who wanted to bite me but was afraid to. So I dated her old boyfriend who was likely going to spend his free time convincing me he was a better choice, when he wasn't angling for a threesome. And yeah, I was alpha of a pack and the only curse I could Were with was black, but that didn't mean I was going to. No one *knew* I had a Were artifact in my freezer that could set off a vamp/Were power struggle. My soul was coated with darkness from saving the world, but I had a hundred years to get rid of it. And so what if Nick might be smarter than me? I had friends. Good ones.

"Tag, darling," I said into the receiver. "You lose."

I hit the off button mid-protest. Tossing the phone to Ivy, I smiled.